The Tome of Horrors 4

Credits

Lead Designer

Scott Greene

Designers/Contributors

Erica Balsley, Casey Christofferson, Jim Collura, Lance Hawvermale, Patrick Lawringer, Phillip Larwood, Bill Webb

Cover Artists

Charles A. Wright & MKUltra Studios

Interior Artist

Chris McFann

Development

Bill Webb, Scott Greene, Skeeter Green

Playtesters/Feedback

Kristi Arenas, Erica Balsley, Rebecca Charles, Chris Gann, Danielle Gordon, Scott Greene, Meghan Greene, Shane Griffin, Claire Hatch, Matt Hicks, Justin Heaton, Aaron Holloway, Shelly Isaacson, John Lloyd, David Lomas, Hannah Parks, Randy Polston, Brandon Reed, Russ Shuler, Keith Tallent, Michael Tallent, Eileen Wick.

Special Thanks To

Amy, Mark, Peyton, Tracey, Meghan, Erica, Dave, Sammy, Elijah, Abby, Kevin "Boz" Baase the Creature Catalog guru, Erik Mona and the Paizo gang for keeping the game going, the "One Step at a Time" crew on the Necromancer Games forums, all the Necromancer Games, Frog God Games, and Paizo fans around the world, Mike Chaney, Ryan Dancey, and of course E. Gary Gygax, Dave Arneson, Clark Peterson, and Bill Webb.

Dedication

This book is dedicated to Eric "Shade" Jansing (1971–2012). Thanks for keeping the Creature Catalog flame burning at ENWorld. You will be missed my friend.

Dedication

This book is dedicated to Ransom Jones (1958–2012); one of the best people I've ever known. Always missed; never forgotten.

INTRODUCTION

One can simply never have enough monsters. The greatest trick a GM can play is to show up with something new that the players have never heard of before. Anyone who has been doing this for very long knows the drill, "Goblins, ok, fighters to the front so they get multiple attacks", or "a troll! Get fire and acid ready!".

Imagine what happened to the first group of players that encountered a nilbog—and watched it grow in size as the fighters each hit it 5 times. What about a pyrohydra—fire had no way to stop it from growing new heads… "Oh my, what do we do now?" may have been the next battlecry.

Its not always necessary to make every monster a death-dealing enigma, however fear of the unknown is one of the strongest tools in the GM's arsenal. It keeps players on their toes and makes the game more fun. Certainly the old mundane standby's need a place at the table (and the miniature case). After all, what is a dungeon without a troll or ten?

One of the things I have been most proud of about my career in the game industry has been my company's ability to bring new and interesting denizens to light. Starting with our collaboration with White Wolf on the Creature Collection in 1999, and continuing with our award winning Tome of Horrors series and Monstronomicon, Necromancer Games, and its spawn Frog God Games have always been at the leading edge of the new monster game.

Thus we are proud to bring you Tome of Horrors IV, fresh from the mind of that evil genius Scott Greene and his henchwoman Erica Balsley (otherwise known as D&D Chick). This book will be our first foray into the world of color monster books. All of these critters are never seen before and new to the table, and I am told, are anxious to get off the page and onto what they do best…eat adventurers.

Much in the same way I like my monsters to use the unexpected tactics my dungeons are so famous for, Scott and his crew have come up with a vast array of new beasts and demons to frighten and challenge your players. I personally cannot wait for this book to ship, as there are several creatures I cannot wait to add to my bi-monthly Rappan Athuk updates!

Enjoy this new trove of monsters, and feedback is, as always, welcome!

— Bill Webb
CEO Frog God Games

Table of Contents

Table of Contents

Addath

This creature appears to be a giant twenty-legged spider with no head. Its underside holds a large ravenous maw from which four long foul tentacles emerge.

ADDATH	CR 16

XP 76,800
CE Huge aberration
Init +6; **Senses** blindsight 60 ft., darkvision 60 ft., tremorsense 60 ft.; **Perception** +26

AC 28, touch 10, flat-footed 26 (+2 Dex, +18 natural, –2 size)
hp 220 (21d8+126)
Fort +15; **Ref** +11; **Will** +14
Defensive Abilities bristles, spider poison immunity; **DR** 15/ cold iron; **Resist** cold 20, fire 20; **SR** 27

Speed 40 ft., climb 40 ft.
Melee 4 tentacles +24 (2d6+10 plus grab), bite +24 (4d6+10 plus poison)
Space 15 ft.; **Reach** 10 ft.
Special Attacks bristles, constrict (2d6+10), poison, swallow whole (4d6+15 acid damage, AC 19, 22 hp)

Str 31, **Dex** 15, **Con** 23, **Int** 12, **Wis** 14, **Cha** 14
Base Atk +15; **CMB** +27 (+31 grapple); **CMD** 39 (51 vs. trip)
Feats Bleeding Critical, Cleave, Critical Focus, Great Fortitude, Improved Critical (tentacle), Improved Initiative, Lightning Reflexes, Power Attack, Vital Strike, Weapon Focus (bite, tentacle)
Skills Acrobatics +15, Climb +42, Escape Artist +26, Perception +26, Stealth +18, Survival +16
Languages Common, Undercommon

Environment any underground
Organization solitary
Treasure standard

Bristles (Ex) Long bristles cover the addath's spidery legs. With the addath's erratic movements in combat, any creature adjacent to and attacking the addath has a chance of being hit by the bristles. Each time a creature attacks an addath with a melee attack it must make a DC 22 Reflex save to avoid being punctured by several bristles. Each time a creature is punctured by these bristles, it takes 1d6 points of piercing damage and is exposed to the addath's poison. A creature that grapples an addath is automatically hurt by these bristles. The save DC to avoid the bristles is Dexterity-based.
Poison (Ex) Bristles or bite—injury; *save* DC 26 Fort; *frequency* 1/round for 6 rounds; *effect* 1d6 Strength damage; *cure* 2 consecutive saves. The save DC is Constitution-based.
Spider Poison Immunity (Ex) An addath is immune to the venom of ordinary spiders, giant spiders, and phase spiders.

Tentacles (Ex) The addath's tentacles are always a primary attack for the creature. It can transfer a grabbed creature from a tentacle to its mouth as a move action.

The addath is a fearsome subterranean hunter that makes its home in caves, caverns, and ruins. It is a highly aggressive predator that paralyzes its victim, carries it back to its nest, and devours it at its leisure.

Addaths do not spin webs, but live in large tunnels and chambers or within ruined structures that can accommodate their massive size. Addath lairs are typically littered with the bones and carcasses of uneaten meals and so emanate the stench of death that is easily detectable (and functions as a warning to others not to intrude).

An addath stands almost 20 feet tall. Its body is dark in color and covered with dark (usually black) hairs. Its legs are long and sleek and covered in deadly black bristles. The creature's mouth is located on its underside and is surrounded by four long tentacles. The tentacles are slick and hairless and either dark brown or black in color. The creature's eyes, tiny and almost undetectable are spaced evenly around its central form.

Addaths, when hunting, attack from ambush, usually clinging to an overhang or ceiling and waiting for prey to pass beneath. Some prefer hiding in shadows and springing out when prey is detected, and still others prefer hiding in huge pits and holes, rushing forth whenever their tremorsense detects movement in the area. Addaths attack by grabbing their prey with their tentacles biting it repeatedly. Addaths try to stay in melee range at all times, knowing eventually a creature can't help but contact its poisonous bristles.

Algidarch

This monstrous humanoid is dressed in furs and carries a massive sword slung across its back. Its flesh is bluish-white, and its hair the color of snow.

ALGIDARCH	CR 5

XP 1,600
CE Large humanoid (cold, giant)
Init +0; **Senses** low-light vision; **Perception** +7
Aura cold (10 ft., 1d6 cold)

AC 16, touch 9, flat-footed 16 (+7 natural, –1 size)
hp 66 (7d8+28 plus 7)
Fort +9; **Ref** +2; **Will** +4
Immune cold
Weaknesses vulnerability to fire

Speed 40 ft.
Melee greatsword +10 (3d6+9) or 2 slams +10 (1d6+6 plus 1d6 cold)
Space 10 ft.; **Reach** 10 ft.
Special Attacks avalanche, freezing wind

Str 22, **Dex** 10, **Con** 18, **Int** 10, **Wis** 11, **Cha** 12
Base Atk +5; **CMB** +12; **CMD** 22
Feats Intimidating Prowess, Iron Will, Power Attack, Toughness
Skills Climb +6, Intimidate +7, Perception +7, Stealth +1 (+5 in snow), Survival +5; **Racial Modifiers** +4 Stealth in snow
Languages Giant

Environment cold hills and moutains
Organization solitary, pair, gang (3–4), hunting band (3–4 plus 5–8 frost men, 1–2 winter wolves), or tribe (5–16 plus 50% noncombatants, 4–8 frost men, 4–6 winter wolves, plus 1 adept, cleric, or sorcerer of 3rd–5th level; 1 barbarian of 4th–6th level)
Treasure standard (greatsword, other treasure)

Avalanche (Su) Once per day, as a standard action, an algidarch can cause a deluge of snow and ice to rains down in a 60-foot radius. This ability has a range of 100 feet. Creatures caught in the area take 5d6 points of cold damage and the avalanche affects a creature as if hit with a bull rush (CMB +17). A DC 17 Reflex save reduces the damage by half. The save DC is Constitution-based.
Freezing Wind (Su) Once per day, as a standard action, an algidarch can create a freezing wind that functions as a *wind wall* spell (CL 7th) and that deals 5d6 points of cold damage (DC 17 Fortitude save for half) to creatures affected by the wind. The save DC is Constitution-based.

Algidarchs are an offshoot of giants (possibly jotuns or frost giants) and dwell in crude structures built atop hills and rocky outcroppings. Entire villages are sometimes found jutting from the side of a cliff or hill. Villages are normally ruled by a chieftain (a fighter of 6th–8th level) and some contain witch doctors or shamans (both being witches, sorcerers, or clerics of 4th–6th level).

Algidarchs are a selfish, malevolent race that takes great pride in both of those facts. They frequently waylay travelers on nearby roads, stealing goods, treasure, women, and whatever else they desire at the time. Captured humanoids are kept as slaves or sold to other giant races as slaves. Algidarchs rarely eat humanoids they capture. In tough times when food is scarce they might, but the meat portion of their diet is generally deer, elk, moose, and even mastodon.

Algidarch adults stand around 9 feet tall and weigh roughly 1,000 pounds.

Skin color among algidarchs is always pale with a slight hint of blue. Algidarchs' hair is always worn long and though color can vary slightly, it is almost always white or some shade of white. Most males have long beards they wear braided or tied. Females are slightly smaller in stature than males, but no less effective in combat. Algidarchs can live to be 225 years old.

An algidarch announces its presence by flooding the area with freezing winds and a sudden avalanche. This avalanche can take the form of their special ability or can be a true avalanche caused by several algidarchs perched atop a snow-covered hillside or mountaintop. Survivors are attacked in melee with the intent of capturing or killing them. Slain opponents are left to scavengers after their bodies are looted.

Amalgamation

A large collection of items rises up, forming into a swirling chaos that is the body of this being. The items move about throughout its bulk, somehow not touching one another in their mad dance.

AMALGAMATION	CR 20

XP 307,200
N Gargantuan construct
Init +9; **Senses** blindsight 100 ft., darkvision 60 ft., low-light vision; **Perception** +5

AC 25, touch 25, flat-footed 16 (+10 deflection, +9 Dex, –4 size)
hp 225 (30d10+60)
Fort +10; **Ref** +19; **Will** +15
DR 10/—; **Immune** construct traits (+60 hp), magic

Speed 10 ft., fly 50 ft. (perfect)
Melee varies +33 (damage by weapon)
Ranged varies +35 (damage by weapon)
Space 20 ft.; **Reach** 15 ft.
Special Attacks multiple attacks, swarm attack (10d6)

Str 24, **Dex** 28, **Con** —, **Int** —, **Wis** 20, **Cha** 1
Base Atk +30; **CMB** +41; **CMD** 60
SQ item use

Environment underground
Organization solitary
Treasure standard (varies with individual Amalgamation)

Item Use (Su) The amalgamation can use any of the items contained within its bulk. When activating magic items, it is considered to be using them as if a person of the required class, with a 20 in any relevant ability scores (or its natural scores, whichever are better). Furthermore, because of its innate magical nature, the save DC against any effects produced by magic items is 2 greater than normal. Finally, it can wield weapons and items as if it were of the appropriate size class for their type, so it suffers no hit penalties for being a Gargantuan construct with such items. Unless instructed otherwise, the amalgamation uses items at random from its bulk. However, it does not target them randomly—it uses them with care and precision, as if it had 18 Intelligence. Items with limited uses, such as scrolls and wands, are expended normally.

Multiple Attacks (Ex) The amalgamation can activate and use up to five items per round. It can therefore attack with weapons, activate magic items, hurl alchemical items like thunderstones, or slam random objects against opponents.

Swarm Attack (Ex) The amalgamation can move over enemies and damage them with the flying weapons and objects composing its bulk. It does this simply by moving over its victims, who are allowed either a DC 34 Reflex save or an attack of opportunity against the amalgamation, at their option. Anyone who begins their turn engulfed by the amalgamation takes 10d6 points of damage per round, with a DC 34 Reflex save allowed for half. This is not considered an area effect for the purposes of evasion and similar abilities. The damage inflicted by the amalgamation overcomes all forms of damage reduction except epic. The save DC for both Reflex saves is Dexterity-based. Further, this damage is considered continuous for the purposes of determining if it disrupts spellcasting, concentration and the like.

Immunity to Magic (Ex) The amalgamation is immune to any spell or spell-like ability that allows spell resistance. In addition, certain spells and effects function differently against the creature, as noted: *Dispel magic* and *greater dispel magic* can be used to deactivate magic items, as per a targeted item dispel. *Mage's disjunction* causes it to subside into quiescence for 1d4+1 rounds, during which time it is considered helpless.

The amalgamation is a special creation used by certain ancient spellcasters to defend their hordes and treasure vaults—for even should the guardian fall, most of the items being guarded would be destroyed, and hence not fall into enemy hands. The creature is composed of a large number of magical and mundane items, and it can use any of them to attack. Because of its magical nature, the amalgamation can even wield magic items such as wands without penalty. The amalgamation resembles a vortex or cloud of items 20 ft. in diameter, swirling within a shimmering field of energy. The precise appearance of the construct depends on the items that comprise its bulk.

Credit

Originally appearing in *Rappan Athuk Reloaded* (© Necromancer Games, 2006)

Amber Skeleton

This amber-colored skeleton shambles forward wielding a spear encased in crackling fire.

AMBER SKELETON	CR 6

XP 2,400
N Medium construct
Init −1; **Senses** darkvision 60 ft., low-light vision; **Perception** +0

AC 21, touch 9, flat-footed 21 (−1 Dex, +12 natural)
hp 69 (9d10+20)
Fort +3; **Ref** +2; **Will** +3
DR 10/—; **Immune** construct traits (+20 hp), magic
Weaknesses vulnerability to water

Speed 30 ft.
Melee spear +14/+9 (1d8+7 plus 2d6 fire) or 2 slams +14 (1d8+5 plus 2d6 fire)
Special Attacks fire bolt, heated body

Str 21, **Dex** 9, **Con** —, **Int** —, **Wis** 11, **Cha** 1
Base Atk +9; **CMB** +14; **CMD** 23

Environment any
Organization solitary or gang (2–5)
Treasure none

Fire Bolt (Su) Once per round, as a standard action, an amber skeleton can discharge a line of fire from its spear. The bolt has a range of 40 feet and deals 6d6 points of fire damage against a single target (Reflex save DC 14 for half). This is a function of the amber skeleton and not the spear itself. The save DC is Constitution-based.

Heated Body (Ex) Any creature striking an amber skeleton unarmed or with natural weapons takes 2d6 points of fire damage (no save). Weapons striking an amber skeleton take this same fire damage unless the attacker succeeds on a DC 14 Fortitude save. Damage caused to weapons in this manner is not halved, but hardness does prevent some of the damage dealt. The save DC is Constitution-based.

Immunity to Magic (Ex) An amber skeleton is immune to spells or spell-like abilities that allow spell resistance. Certain spells and effects function differently against it, as noted:
A magical attack that deals fire damage heals 1 point of damage for each 3 points of damage the attack would otherwise deal. If the amount of healing would cause the amber skeleton to exceed its full normal hit points, it gains any excess as temporary hit points. An amber skeleton gets no saving throw against fire effects.

Vulnerability to Water (Ex) A significant amount of water, such as that created by a *create water* spell, the contents of a large bucket, or a blow from a water elemental, that strikes an amber skeleton forces the creature to make a DC 20 Fortitude save to avoid being staggered for 2d4 rounds. An amber skeleton that is immersed in water must make a DC 20 Fortitude save each round (the DC increases by +1 each subsequent round) or take 1d6 points of damage each round until the water is gone.

Amber skeletons are constructed and used by high level spellcasters, often acting as guardians to keep secret some unknown or lost knowledge.

An amber skeleton appears as an amber-colored skeleton, about 7 feet tall, with two large gemstones that function as eyes. It is often mistaken for an undead creature. The gemstones can be pried out of a destroyed amber skeleton with a DC 20 Strength check. Each gemstone is worth 1,000 gp if fully intact and not damaged when it is removed.

Construction

An amber skeleton's body is made from 3,000 pounds of amber worth a total of 5,000 gp.

AMBER SKELETON
CL 12th; **Price** 69,000 gp

CONSTRUCTION
Requirements Craft Construct, *animate objects, flame strike, geas/quest, spell turning*, creator must be caster level 12th; **Skill** Craft (sculptures) or Craft (stonemasonry) DC 16; **Cost** 64,000 gp

Animal, Elemental

At various places in the planes, rifts of special tears appear and allow the mundane creatures of one plane to intermix with the creatures of other planes. On these occasions, it is most often not the terrible beasts such as demons or angels that pour through, but much less powerful (but not harmless) creatures mirroring the beasts of the natural realm.

FIRE CRAB, SMALL   CR 1/2

XP 200
N Tiny vermin (fire)
Init +2; **Senses** darkvision 60 ft.; **Perception** +4

AC 18, touch 14, flat-footed 16 (+2 Dex, +4 natural, +2 size)
hp 5 (1d8+1)
Fort +3; **Ref** +2; **Will** +0
Immune fire, vermin traits
Weaknesses cold vulnerability

Speed 30 ft., swim 20 ft.
Melee 2 claws +0 (1d2–2 plus grab and heat)
Space 2–1/2 ft.; **Reach** 0 ft.
Special Attacks constrict (1d2–2), heat (1d4 fire damage)

Str 7, **Dex** 15, **Con** 12, **Int** —, **Wis** 10, **Cha** 2
Base Atk +0; **CMB** +0 (+4 grapple); **CMD** 8 (20 vs. trip)
Skills Perception +4, Swim +10; **Racial Modifiers** +4 Perception, uses Dex to modify Swim

Environment any warm or hot
Organization solitary or clutch (2–20)
Treasure none

These small crabs are about the size of a man's fist. They are a deep reddish color, tapering to yellow on the underbelly.

The fire crab's heat extends roughly 3 to 5 ft.

Fire crabs are omnivorous; they feed on other animals and any plant life that survives the fire crabs native environment. The fire crabs may survive temperatures lower than 100 degrees for 1 hour per point of Constitution, or run the risk of freezing.

FIRE CRAB, MEDIUM   CR 2

XP 600
N Medium vermin (fire)
Init +1; **Senses** darkvision 60 ft.; **Perception** +4

AC 16, touch 11, flat-footed 15 (+1 Dex, +5 natural)
hp 19 (3d8+6)
Fort +5; **Ref** +2; **Will** +1
Immune fire, vermin traits
Weaknesses cold vulnerability

Speed 30 ft., swim 20 ft.
Melee 2 claws +4 (1d4+2 plus grab and heat)
Special Attacks constrict (claw) 1d4+2, heat (+1d6 fire damage)

Str 14, **Dex** 12, **Con** 14, **Int** –, **Wis** 10, **Cha** 2
Base Atk +2; **CMB** +4 (+8 to grapple); **CMD** 15
Skills Perception +4, Swim +10; **Racial Modifiers** +4 Perception, uses Dex to modify Swim

Environment any warm or hot
Organization solitary or clutch (2–20)
Treasure none

Significantly larger than their cousins, the medium fire crab is a

monstrosity slightly larger than a dog. The pincers, if they could extend fully (the joints of a fire crab almost turn in on themselves), would reach some 10 ft. or more.

The coloration of a medium fire crab varies from a bright red to nearly maroon in older specimens.

Fire crabs are omnivorous; they feed on other animals and any plant life that survives the fire crabs native environment. The fire crabs may survive temperatures lower than 100 degrees for 1 hour per point of Constitution, or run the risk of freezing.

FIRE FISH   CR 1

XP 400
N Small animal (aquatic*, fire)
Init +6; **Senses** low-light vision, tremorsense 10 ft.; **Perception** +7
Aura heat (5 ft. radius)

AC 14, touch 12, flat-footed 13 (+1 Dex, +2 natural, +1 size)
hp 13 (3d8)
Fort +3; **Ref** +5; **Will** +2
Immune fire
Weaknesses vulnerability to cold

Speed swim 40 ft.
Melee slam –1 (1d4–4 plus heat)
Special Attacks heat (1d4 fire damage)

Str 3, **Dex** 14, **Con** 10, **Int** 1, **Wis** 12, **Cha** 5
Base Atk +2; **CMB** +0; **CMD** 12
Feats Alertness, Improved Initiative
Skills Perception +7, Sense Motive +3, Swim +16; **Racial Modifiers** uses Dex to modify Swim

Environment Plane of Fire
Organization solitary or school (4–80)
Treasure none

Aquatic Firefish can swim and breathe in molten lava as easily as a regular fish in water. They are 'aquatic' only in the sense that their natural environment is lava instead of water.

Light orange to bright red in color, the fire fish is approximately the size of a common salmon. Firefish frequently stay in their schools; a solitary fish is easy prey for many predators.

Firefish spawn yearly, and attempt to return to their place of origin to do so. If unable, a firefish locates a warm, rocky area to deposit their eggs. The females perish within a day after depositing the eggs. The males, after fertilizing the eggs, swim off, living perhaps another week before perishing.

These are just a few of the possible creatures available, but they should be a good starting point to create other elemental animals.

Credit
Originally appearing in *Rappan Athuk Reloaded*
(© Necromancer Games, 2006)

Argos

This monstrous piscine humanoid has a scaly hide of dark grayish-blue. Its muscular arms end in webbed claws.

ARGOS	CR 3

XP 800
NE Medium monstrous humanoid (aquatic, extraplanar)
Init +1; **Senses** blindsense 60 ft., darkvision 60 ft.; **Perception** +8

AC 17, touch 11, flat-footed 16 (+1 Dex, +6 natural)
hp 30 (4d10+8)
Fort +5; **Ref** +5; **Will** +5
Immune poison; effects of the River Styx; **Resist** electricity 10
Weakness light sensitivity

Speed 30 ft., swim 60 ft.
Melee spear +7 (1d8+4), bite +2 (1d4+3) or 2 claws +7 (1d4+3), bite +7 (1d4+3)

Str 16, **Dex** 13, **Con** 15, **Int** 14, **Wis** 13, **Cha** 12
Base Atk +4; **CMB** +7; **CMD** 18
Feats Great Fortitude, Power Attack
Skills Diplomacy +3, Intimidate +8, Knowledge (planes) +4, Perception +8, Stealth +8, Survival +8, Swim +18
Languages Aquan, Argos, Common
SQ amphibious

Environment any (River Styx)
Organization Solitary, pair, team (5–8), patrol (11–20 plus 1 lieutenant of 5th level), band (20–80 plus 100% noncombatants, 1 lieutenant of 5th level and 1 chieftain of 6th level per 20 adults), or tribe (70–160 plus 100% noncombatants, 1 lieutenant of 5th level per 20 adults, 1 chieftain of 6th level per 40 adults, 9 guards of 6th level, 1–4 water priestesses of 4th–7th level, 1 priestess of 8th level, 1 priest-king of 7th–9th level)
Treasure standard (spear, other treasure)

Believed by some to be far-distant relatives of the sahuagin, the argos are an aggressive race of aquatic creature that dwell in the depths of the River Styx living in great underwater castles and cities. Argosian cities and strongholds are constructed of stone and coral. The argos are a highly superstitious race, not really trusting arcane magic, but reveling in the miracles of divine magic and what it can do. Most argosian towns, cities, and strongholds have a temple at the center. Some have several temples; one larger one dedicated to the Drowning Lord and several smaller temples dedicated to the lesser aquatic deities. Rulers in argosian society are known as priest-kings, and all are mid- to high-level clerics. These individuals are revered by all argos and many consider them to be the living embodiment of their deity. To kill an argosian priest or priestess is punishable by death. In some argosian societies, even merely offending a priest or priestess brings swift and harsh punishment.

The typical argos stand 6 feet tall and weigh just over 200 pounds. Its hide is scaly grayish-blue shading to light colors on its chest. A long dark gray fin runs from the crown of its head to its lower back. Its clawed hands and feet are both webbed, and its eyes are the color of soot. Females stand just less than 6 feet tall and are usually lighter in color. Argos mate once every few years generally, and gestation lasts about 6 months. Young are born live and are light gray in color, reaching maturity within 15 months. An argos typically lives to about 40 years of age. The typical argos diet consists of shark, small fish, seaweed and undersea plants and humanoid flesh.

Argos are particularly fond of humans, elves, aquatic elves, and merfolk; the latter being considered a delicacy. Squid is never eaten by an argos; the animal being considered sacred and the favored animal of the Drowning Lord.

In combat, an argos prefers to fight with a spear and its vicious bite. If disarmed or simply by choice, an argos can fight with its webbed claws to rend and slash its foes. When battling, an argos prefers to fight in the water where it has the advantage. Favored tactics include swooping down on prey from above or swimming up beneath prey and attacking from surprise. When attacking seaside towns civilizations, argos raiding bands attack at night and can number up to 80 individuals. They prefer to swarm their opponents and attack using their great numbers to overwhelm their opponents. They use the same general tactics when attacking seagoing vessels as well, swarming their targets and crushing them under the onslaught. Prisoners are rarely taken in such raids as most land-based life cannot breathe underwater or survive the memory-draining power of the River Styx. Some argosian cities do use magic however to sustain air breathing slaves and prisoners. These are rare, as most prisoners are slain and devoured within a few hours.

Astral Spider

This giant silvery spider has ten legs, and a glossy silver abdomen with tiny black streaks that seem to move and sway on their own.

ASTRAL SPIDER	CR 8

XP 4,800
N Large outsider
Init +7; **Senses** darkvision 60 ft., tremorsense 60 ft.; **Perception** +25

AC 22, touch 12, flat-footed 19 (+3 Dex, +10 natural, −1 size)
hp 104 (11d10+44)
Fort +11; **Ref** +12; **Will** +6

Speed 40 ft., climb 40 ft.
Melee 4 legs +15 (1d6+5), bite +15 (1d8+5 plus poison)
Space 10 ft.; **Reach** 5 ft.
Special Attacks web (+13 ranged, DC 23, 16 hp)

Str 20, **Dex** 17, **Con** 18, **Int** 2, **Wis** 13, **Cha** 11
Base Atk +11; **CMB** +17; **CMD** 30 (42 vs. trip)
Feats Improved Initiative, Iron Will, Lightning Reflexes, Lunge, Power Attack, Skill Focus (Perception)
Skills Climb +25, Perception +25, Stealth +17 (+21 in webs); **Racial Modifiers** +12 Climb, +4 Perception, +4 Stealth (+8 in webs)
SQ strong webs

Environment any (Astral Plane)
Organization solitary or band (2–5)
Treasure incidental

Poison (Ex) Bite—injury; *save* DC 21 Fort; *frequency* 1/round for 8 rounds; *effect* 1d4 Con; *cure* 2 consecutive saves. The save DC is Constitution-based and gains a +2 racial bonus.
Strong Webs (Ex) An astral spider's webs gain a +4 bonus to the DC to break or escape, and have +50% hit points.

Astral spiders are ambush hunters that dwell on the Astral Plane, using their silvery webs to capture and entangle prey. They make their lairs wherever they can on their endless plane; using dead planar travelers (that aren't devoured), bits of planar refuse, bits of solid matter, and anything else they can cobble together. An astral spider's lair can stretch over several hundred feet.

A typical lair contains a single female astral spider who several times a year lays up to 30 eggs at a time. These eggs are wrapped tightly in the spider's webs and attached to some part of the lair. Within 6–8 weeks, the eggs hatch, the newborn astral spiders using their sharpened mandibles to tear through the eggs and webbing. Most hatchlings don't survive, being eaten by other astral spiders, astral sharks, or some other denizen of the plane. Those that do reach adulthood, journey off into the Astral Plane a few months after hatching.

Astral spiders sustain themselves on a diet of other creatures, particularly astral sharks and planar travelers. When food is scarce, an astral spider can enter a state of semi-hibernation, remaining motionless in its web without food for months at a time.

An astral spider is about 8 feet long with a glossy silver body covered in tiny, dancing black streaks. Its ten legs are glossy silver and its eyes appear as small dots of black ink. The creature's mandibles are slightly oversized and dull silver in color. Its underside is dull silver, fading to a dull grayish-silver near the spider's rear legs. Older astral spiders have completely gray undersides.

An astral spider rarely initiates combat and simply lies in wait, motionless, in its webs. When it detects movement, it scuttles out and attacks. In combat, an astral spider rears on its back six legs and slashes its foes with its front four legs, following quickly with its deadly bite. Particularly bothersome opponents are webbed and immobilized with the spider moving into bite its trapped foe quickly. Slain prey and webbed prey are carried back to its lair and fed to the young. Portions of the prey not devoured are webbed and worked into solid makeup of the lair.

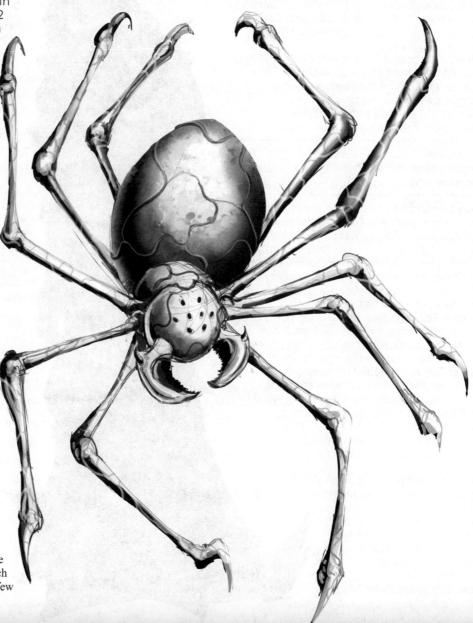

Aswang

This hideous creature wears rags and has long unkempt black hair, filthy claws, bloodshot eyes, and a long black snake-like tongue.

ASWANG	CR 6

XP 2,400
CE Medium undead
Init +8; **Senses** corpse scent 100 ft., darkvision 60 ft.; **Perception** +14

AC 21, touch 14, flat-footed 17 (+4 Dex, +7 natural)
hp 60 (8d8+16 plus 8)
Fort +4; **Ref** +6; **Will** +7
Defensive Abilities channel resistance +4; **DR** 10/cold iron;
Immune undead traits; **Resist** cold 10
Weaknesses vulnerability to garlic

Speed 40 ft.
Melee 2 claws +8 (1d4+2 plus grab), bite +8 (1d6+2/18–20)
Special Attacks blood drain, deceiving sound, devour heart

Str 15, **Dex** 18, **Con** —, **Int** 13, **Wis** 13, **Cha** 15
Base Atk +6; **CMB** +8 (+12 grapple); **CMD** 22
Feats Alertness, Improved Initiative, Power Attack, Toughness
Skills Acrobatics +8, Climb +9, Craft +8, Disguise +13, Knowledge (any) +5, Perception +14, Stealth +19; **Racial Modifiers** +4 Stealth
Languages Common, plus any one
SQ change shape (human, *alter self*, or black dog, *beast shape I*)

Environment any
Organization solitary
Treasure none

Blood Drain (Su) An aswang can suck blood from a grappled opponent; if the aswang establishes or maintains a pin, it drains blood, dealing 1d4 points of Constitution damage. The aswang heals 5 hit points or gains 5 temporary hit points for 1 hour (up to a maximum number of temporary hit points equal to its full normal hit points) each round it drains blood.
Corpse Scent (Ex) An aswang can detect corporeal undead within 100 feet. It can detect fresh corpses (creatures killed within the last two hours) to a range of one mile.
Deceiving Sound (Su) An aswang can produce a 'tik-tik' sound from its throat that seemingly originates from up to 100 feet away from the aswang's actual location. Creatures hearing this sound can attempt a DC 16 Perception check to pinpoint the aswang's true location.
Devour Heart (Ex) An aswang's bite attack threatens a critical hit on an 18–20. If an aswang kills a foe with a critical hit, it can tear out the victim's heart as a free action. An aswang that devours a victim's heart gains a +4 bonus to Strength for 1 hour.

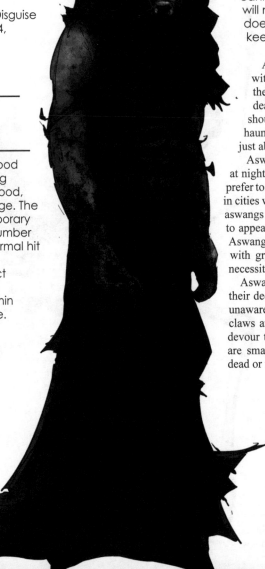

Detecting an Aswang

One method of detecting a nearby aswang is through the use of exotic oils made from mammal fat mixed with rare herbs. The mixture is then *blessed* by a cleric of 6th level or higher. Whenever an aswang (even one currently using its change shape ability) approaches within 50 feet of the blessed mixture, the concoction boils and bubbles, and quickly fades to a dark brown color. This mixture is good for a single use and lasts three weeks if sealed in an air-tight container and unused.

Devouring multiple hearts does not increase this bonus. Such a victim cannot be restored to life by a *raise dead* spell (though *resurrection* and *true resurrection* can still revive the victim). Any creature that witnesses this event must succeed on a DC 16 Will save or be shaken 1d4 rounds. The save DC is Charisma-based.
Vulnerability to Garlic (Ex) Aswangs cannot tolerate the odor of garlic, and will not enter an area laced with it. It doesn't harm an aswang—it merely keeps it at bay.

Aswangs are extremely malevolent undead with a taste for blood. These creatures drink the blood of both the living and the recently dead; including devouring the victim's heart should it still be intact. Aswangs generally haunt graveyards and ruins, but can be found just about anywhere.

Aswangs sleep during the day and venture out at night. Sunlight doesn't harm aswangs; they just prefer to hunt at night. Many aswangs prefer to dwell in cities where they have their pick of victims. These aswangs make use of their shapechanging ability to appear human and blend in with the population. Aswangs sleep on grave dirt or in coffins filled with grave dirt. Sages debate whether this is by necessity or simply a ritual performed by aswangs.

Aswangs disorient potential victims by using their deceiving sound ability hoping to catch them unaware. In combat, aswangs attack with their claws and nasty bite. Aswangs that kill their foes devour the heart, though not during combat. They are smart enough to wait until all opponents are dead or fleeing.

Aurochs, Northlands

This massive ox is as tall as a man at the shoulders. Its coat is black with a pale stripe down its spine. Great lyre-shaped horns sweep forward from its bony brow.

NORTHLANDS AUROCHS (DIRE KINE)　　CR 7

XP 3,200
N Huge animal
Init +0; **Senses** low-light vision, scent; **Perception** +20

AC 20, touch 8, flat-footed 20 (+12 natural, −2 size)
hp 105 (10d8+50 plus 10)
Fort +14; **Ref** +7; **Will** +4

Speed 40 ft.
Melee gore +16 (2d8+15)
Space 15 ft.; **Reach** 10 ft.
Special Attacks powerful charge (gore +18, 4d8+15), stampede, trample (2d8+15, DC 25)

Str 30, **Dex** 10, **Con** 21, **Int** 2, **Wis** 13, **Cha** 7
Base Atk +7; **CMB** +19; **CMD** 29 (33 vs. trip)
Feats Endurance, Great Fortitude, Toughness, Skill Focus (Perception), Weapon Focus (gore)
Skills Perception +20

Environment Northlands forests and plains
Organization solitary, pair, or herd (3–12)
Treasure none

Stampede (Ex) A frightened herd of aurochs (3 or more) flees as a group in a random direction (but always away from the perceived source of danger). They literally run over (as an overrun that does not provoke attacks of opportunity) anything of size Gargantuan or smaller that is in their path, but no CMB check is necessary, and the target cannot choose to let them pass without taking any damage. The stampede deals 5d6 points of damage for every two aurochs in the herd (rounded up). Any victims of the stampede can make a DC 25 Reflex save for half damage. The save DC is Strength-based.

These massive aurochs (singular and plural) are prehistoric cattle that once roamed the plains and forests of the world in vast herds but are now on the verge of extinction, being found only in the primeval forests and remote places of the Northlands where their horns are prized trophies of the hunt—though many a hunter has fallen beneath their spearlike horns and crushing hooves in the attempt. Massive beasts, these prehistoric aurochs have been used as symbols of fertility and strength for many cults down through the ages appearing in decoration from the crudest cave paintings to ornate temples. When captured they command a high price for use in the arenas of cosmopolitan regions, though they often take a heavy toll among the matadors who face them.

Northlands aurochs stand 6 feet or more high at the withers with their heads rising 2 feet above that. Their characteristic lyre-shaped horns extend upward another 2 feet. They grow up to 18 feet long and can weigh as much as 8,000 pounds. Males have a black coat with a pale stripe down the spine, and females and calves have a reddish coat. A light load for a Northlands aurochs is up to 3,200 pounds; a medium load 3,201–6,400 pounds; and a heavy load 6,401–9,600 pounds. An aurochs can drag 48,000 pounds.

Credit
Original author Greg A. Vaughan/Kenneth Spencer
Originally appearing in *Northlands Saga 3: The Death Curse of Sven Oakenfist* (© Frog God Games/Kenneth Spencer, 2011)

Baba Yaga

This hideous crone has brownish-green flesh, a large nose and razor-sharp teeth.

BABA YAGA	CR 10

XP 9,600
NE Medium monstrous humanoid
Init +8; **Senses** darkvision 60 ft.; **Perception** +27
Aura fear (30 ft., DC 20)

AC 22, touch 14, flat-footed 18 (+4 Dex, +8 natural)
hp 114 (12d10+48)
Fort +8; **Ref** +12; **Will** +14
DR 10/cold iron and magic; **Immune** charm, fear, sleep;
Resist cold 10, fire 10; **SR** 22

Speed 30 ft.
Melee 2 claws +17 (1d6+5 plus grab), bite +17 (1d8+5)
Special Attacks decaying hex (DC 22), evil eye (DC 22), rend (2d6+7)
Spells Prepared (CL 12th; melee touch +17, ranged touch +16):
6th—*greater dispel magic, flesh to stone* (DC 22), *mass suggestion* (DC 22)
5th—*dominate person* (DC 21), *feeblemind* (DC 21), *hold monster* (DC 21), *summon monster V*
4th—*enervation, ice storm, poison* (DC 20), *scrying* (DC 20)
3rd—*bestow curse* (DC 19), *dispel magic, fly* (DC 19), *screech* (DC 19), *spit venom* (DC 19)
2nd—*alter self, death knell* (DC 18), *enthrall* (DC 18), *hold person* (DC 18), *touch of idiocy, web* (DC 18)
1st—*cause fear* (DC 17), *charm person* (DC 17), *dancing lantern, mage armor* (DC 17), *obscuring mist, sleep* (DC 17)
0 (at will)—*bleed* (DC 16), *dancing lights, putrefy food and drink* (DC 16), *touch of fatigue* (DC 16)

Str 20, **Dex** 19, **Con** 19, **Int** 23, **Wis** 18, **Cha** 19
Base Atk +12; **CMB** +17 (+21 grapple); **CMD** 31
Feats Alertness, Combat Casting, Empower Spell, Improved Initiative, Iron Will, Quicken Spell
Skills Bluff +16, Intimidate +19, Knowledge (arcana) +18, Knowledge (nature) +22, Knowledge (planes) +18, Perception +27, Sense Motive +20, Spellcraft +18, Stealth +19 (+27 in swamps), Use Magical Device +16; **Racial Modifiers** +4 Knowledge (nature), +4 Perception, +8 Stealth in swamps
Languages Abyssal, Common, Draconic, Giant, Infernal, Sylvan
SQ swamp stride

Environment temperate swamps
Organization solitary or coven (3)
Treasure standard

Aura of Fear (Su) This aura functions as a *fear* spell (CL 12th). A creature that successfully saves against the baba yaga's aura is unaffected by the same baba yaga's aura for one day. This is a mind-affecting effect. The save DC is Charisma-based. A baba yaga can suppress or restart this aura as a free action.
Evil Eye (Su) As a standard action, a baba yaga can crush the will of a foe within 30 feet that she can see. The target must succeed on a DC 22 Will save or take a –4 penalty on attack rolls, saving throws, and skill checks until the evil eye is removed. This is a curse effect. The save DC is Intelligence-based. A creature currently affected by a baba yaga's evil eye cannot be affected again (by the same or a different

baba yaga).
Decaying Hex (Su) As a standard action, a baba yaga can place a hex on any living creature within 60 feet. If the creature fails a DC 22 Fortitude save it takes 3d6 points of damage plus 2d6 bleed damage. A creature that fails its save by 5 or more also takes 1d2 points of Constitution damage. The bleeding can be stopped with a DC 15 Heal check or through the application of any magical healing. The save DC is Intelligence-based.
Spells A baba yaga casts spells as a 12th-level witch (*Pathfinder Roleplaying Game Advanced Player's Guide*). They do not gain access to any other witch abilities.
Swamp Stride (Ex) A baba yaga can move through bogs and quicksand without penalty at its normal speed.

Long thought to be a solitary or unique being (similar to the medusa), sages and scholars have come to believe the baba yaga are in fact a race of evil crones related to the hag race. Perhaps this theory is accurate, or perhaps it is what the true Baba Yaga wants the world to believe; no one is quite sure what is true and what isn't when it comes to the baba yaga.

A baba yaga makes its home deep in the darkest and most remote swamps and fens. There in the center of the swamp is her home: a large wooden hut perched atop two tall and muscular chicken legs. The hut is believed to be highly magical, ten times larger on the inside than it appears outside, and possibly contain portals to other planes. It is also believed by some to be some sort of construct or golem, though no proof of such claims exists. Surrounding the hut is a small dark picket fence which holds the skulls of the baba yaga's victims. The hut can lower itself to the ground so the baba yaga can enter, but it only functions if she chants, and it only functions for the baba yaga that dwells there. No other creature has figured out how to control the baba yaga's hut.

Adventurers who have seen a baba yaga on the move say she moves through her swampy lair at in a giant mortar, steering it with a large pestle in one hand, and using a magic broom to sweep all traces of her passing with the other. This mortar, rumors say, can only be driven by a baba yaga or high level spellcaster, but again, no one is certain what the truth is.

A baba yaga appears as a slightly hunched, old, and hideously ugly crone, with a large nose, long sharp teeth, and hands that end in wicked claws. She dresses in loose fitting ugly brown cloaks. When moving about in civilized areas, a baba yaga often pulls the hood of her cloak over her head, walks slowly, and carries a crooked and rotting walking stick.

Baboonwere

This lithe creature has the head of a baboon, a fur-covered body, and sharpened fangs that glisten with fresh blood.

BABOONWERE	CR 2

XP 600
CE Medium magical beast (shapechanger)
Init +3; **Senses** darkvision 60 ft., low-light vision, scent; **Perception** +5

AC 16, touch 13, flat-footed 13 (+2 armor, +3 Dex, +1 natural)
hp 15 (2d10+4)
Fort +5; **Ref** +6; **Will** +1
DR 5/cold iron

Speed 30 ft.
Melee longsword +5 (1d8+1), bite +0 (1d6 plus disease) or bite +5 (1d6+1 plus disease)
Special Attacks weapon intuition

Str 13, **Dex** 17, **Con** 14, **Int** 11, **Wis** 12, **Cha** 12
Base Atk +2; **CMB** +3; **CMD** 16
Feats Weapon Finesse
Skills Acrobatics +5, Bluff +4, Climb +3, Perception +5, Stealth +7, Survival +4; **Racial Modifiers** +2 Acrobatics, +2 Bluff, +2 Climb, +2 Survival
Languages Common
SQ baboon empathy, change shape

Environment warm forests and plains
Organization solitary, pair, gang (1–2 plus 6–10 baboons), or troop (3–6 plus 10–20 baboons)
Treasure standard (leather armor, longsword, other treasure)

Baboon Empathy (Ex) A baboonwere can communicate and empathize with baboons, and can use Bluff as if it were Diplomacy to change a baboon's attitude, receiving a +4 racial bonus to do so.
Change Shape (Su) A baboonwere has three forms. Its natural form is that of a baboon, but it can also take the form of a human or human-baboon hybrid. A baboonwere's human form is fixed—it cannot assume different human forms. A baboonwere can only use its diseased bite in hybrid or baboon form. In baboon form, it functions as a baboon. In its hybrid form, a baboonwere can make a bite attack as a secondary attack, while in human form it lacks its bite entirely. A baboonwere can shift into any of its three alternate forms as a move action. Equipment does not meld with the new form between human and hybrid forms but does between those forms and its baboon form.
Disease (Ex) *Filth Fever:* Bite—injury; *save* DC 13 Fort; *onset* 1d3 days; *frequency* 1/day; *effect* 1d3 Dex damage and 1d3 Con damage; *cure* 2 consecutive saves. The save DC is Constitution-based.
Weapon Intuition (Ex) A baboonwere is proficient with simple and martial melee weapons.

Baboonweres are evil baboons born with the ability to assume human or hybrid human form. Baboonweres are most often found among normal baboons, though some prefer to maintain their human form and live amongst ordinary people in small towns and villages. Usually when the livestock and cattle begin turning up missing or slain is when the baboonwere moves on, before the finger of suspicion is pointed its way.

In its hybrid form, a baboonwere stands just over 5 feet tall and weighs roughly 130 pounds. Its hair tends to be either light brown or dark brown. Eyes are always brown.

Baboonweres fight with weapons, usually longswords, short swords, and spears or crossbows and a diseased bite. Slain foes are dragged back to their lairs and eaten at the baboonwere's leisure.

Baboonweres are frequently found among normal baboons and are indistinguishable from them when in animal form. The statistics for a standard baboon may be found in the *Pathfinder Roleplaying Game Bestiary 2*.

Banshee, Lesser

*A beautiful , ghostlike elven woman beckons you closer, ever closer.
The air seems to chill as she opens her mouth...*

BANSHEE, LESSER	CR 13

XP 25,600
NE Medium undead (incorporeal)
Init +11; **Senses** darkvision 60 ft., lifesense; **Perception** +24

AC 23, touch 23, flat-footed 15 (+7 deflection, +5 Dex +1
dodge)
hp 142 (15d8+75)
Fort +10; **Ref** +12; **Will** +13
Defensive Abilities incorporeal traits; **Immune** undead traits
Weaknesses sunlight powerlessness

Speed fly 60 ft. (perfect)
Melee incorporeal touch +18 (1d6 plus energy drain)
Special Attacks create spawn, energy drain (1 level, DC 22),
wail (DC 24)

Str —, **Dex** 24, **Con** —, **Int** 16, **Wis** 18, **Cha** 20
Base Atk +10; **CMB** +18; **CMD** 41(cannot be grappled
or tripped)
Feats Ability Focus (wail), Combat Reflexes, Dodge,
Flyby Attack, Improved Initiative, Mobility, Spring Attack,
Weapon Finesse
Skills Diplomacy +20, Fly +33, Intimidate +23, Knowledge
(arcane) +21, Perception +24, Sense Motive +22, Stealth
+25; **Racial Modifiers** +2 Perception
Languages Common, Elven

Environment any (usually tombs)
Organization solitary or rarely pair
Treasure none

Create Spawn (Su) The spirit of any female humanoid
that is slain by a lesser t's death wail or energy drain rises
to become a banshee in 1d4 rounds. Similarly, any male
humanoid slain by a banshee's death wail or energy drain
rises to become a dread wraith in 1d4 rounds.
Lifesense (Ex) Lesser banshee's can detect living creatures
within 60 feet, as if they possessed the blindsight ability. In
addition, the lesser banshee senses the strength and life-
force of the creature, as the spell deathwatch.
Sunlight Powerlessness (Ex) A banshee is powerless in natural
sunlight (not merely a daylight spell) and flees from it,
typically by hiding within a solid object. A banshee caught
in sunlight cannot attack or use its wail and can take only a
single standard or move action in a round.
Unnatural Aura (Su) Animals can sense the aura of a lesser
banshee at a distance of 30 feet. The animal will not willingly
near a lesser banshee, and panics if forced to do so.
Wail (Su) A lesser banshee may let loose a wail so horrible
that those within 30 feet must make a DC 24 Fortitude save
or die. The lesser banshee may only use her death wail at
night, and no more than twice per day. After using this
ability a lesser banshee must wait for 1d6 rounds before
using it again. The save is Charisma-based, and includes the
bonus from the Ability Focus feat.

Lesser banshees are the spirits of departed women (especially of
elven heritage) that were cruel and evil in life. Lesser banshees appear
as ghostly, translucent figures, and bear the same beauty they possessed
in life. Lesser banshees attack with their incorporeal touch, and drain
the energy of their foes. They are most widely known for their horrible

keening (death wail), and fondness for attacking from solid objects.

Lesser banshees cling to areas they were familiar with in life; many
lesser banshees may be found in dark forests or rolling moors; rarely, their
incorporeal nature allows them to travel to new places, and such creatures
become interred in dungeons or mausoleums, completely unaware of
where they are or why they are there. This infuriates the banshees even
more, and makes them far deadlier opponents.

Credit
Original author William Loran
Christensen
Originally appearing in *Fane of the
Fallen* (© Frog God Games/ William
Loran Christensen, 2010)

Battlehulk

A massive block of stone rolls ponderously forward on great stone rollers. Iron plates armor this stone monstrosity, the front of which is studded with spikes of iron, adamantine and stone. Great stone clubs capped in iron sprout from loopholes in the sides like the arms of a giant. The top of this huge structure is a platform surrounded by stone merlons to provide cover for any defenders riding upon it. At the back edge of this platform extend two chains that end in great stone spheres that spin on a pivoted base and lay waste to anyone behind the mobile fortress.

BATTLEHULK	CR 13

XP 25,600
N Huge construct (good)
Init −4; **Senses** darkvision 60 ft., low-light vision; **Perception** +0

AC 27, touch 4, flat-footed 27 (+2 armor, −4 Dex, +21 natural, −2 size)
hp 177 (25d10+40)
Fort +8; **Ref** +4; **Will** +8
DR 15/adamantine; **Immune** acid, cold, electricity, fire, construct traits (+40 hp); **SR** 20

Speed 10 ft.; charge
Melee ram +38 (4d8+22) and 4 slams +38 (2d10+15)
Space 15 ft.; **Reach** 5 ft. (10 ft. with slams)
Special Attacks bull rush, charge, ram, sweep, trample (8d8+44, DC 37)

Str 40, **Dex** 3, **Con** —, **Int** —, **Wis** 11, **Cha** 1
Base Atk +25; **CMB** +42 (+46 bull rush); **CMD** 48 (52 vs. bull rush, can't be tripped)
Feats Greater Bull Rush[B], Improved Bull Rush[B]

Environment any relatively flat and dry terrain

Organization solitary
Treasure none

Bull Rush (Ex) If the battlehulk is charging it can opt to make a bull rush attack without provoking an attack of opportunity. If the bull rush is successful, the defender is automatically pushed back the distance that the battlehulk moves forward past his position. The battlehulk does not require a check result of 5 or more higher than the defender's check result to determine how far back the defender can be pushed. The battlehulk can bull rush as many opponents as occupy the squares in its path of travel with the usual −4 penalty to additional combat maneuver checks.

Charge (Ex) Each round a battlehulk double moves in a straight line, it adds an additional 10 ft. to its speed as its weight and inertia propel it forward. It can reach a maximum speed of 80 feet in this way. A battlehulk can stop after charging only by striking an unyielding obstacle (like a mountain) or by gradually slowing. It can reduce its speed by 10 feet per round as it slows its momentum. A battlehulk can only turn when going at a speed of 30 feet or less. If traveling downhill on a steep slope, the battlehulk accelerates twice as fast (i.e. it goes from 10 feet, to 30 feet, to 50 feet, etc.) and decelerate twice as slow (i.e. it takes 2 rounds to decelerate from 80 feet to 70 feet and so on). Likewise if traveling up hill on a steep slope it decelerates twice as fast and accelerates twice as slow.

Immunities (Ex) A battlehulk is immune to acid, cold, electricity, and fire and confers this immunity to anyone sealed within its inner compartment.

Ram (Ex) The ram attack of the battlehulk is with the ironplated and spike-studded front face. The damage this

attack deals is considered both piercing and bludgeoning. Because of the different metal compositions used in the spikes and enchantments placed on this front facing, this attack is both cold iron and adamantine and is considered magic and good-aligned for the purpose of overcoming damage reduction. This attack is particularly useful against evil outsiders.

Sweep (Ex) As a full round action a battlehulk can make a bull rush attack with each of its slamming arms on targets within range without provoking attacks of opportunity. Each stone arm is considered a Large creature for this purpose and has a combat maneuver bonus of +45. The flail on the back is also capable of making this bull rush attack on any targets atop the platform (roll separately for each target). Anyone moved off the platform results in a 15-foot fall to the ground below for 1d6 points of damage.

Battlehulks are constructs crafted for war. They were created by the Army of Light to roll over enemy lines, smash enemy fortifications and, if necessary, fight toe-to-toe with even the mightiest balor demon.

It resembles a squat stone building surmounting massive stone rollers that provide it mobility. From embrasures in the sides (one on each side and one in back) project long stone arms capped in iron that the construct uses for slam attacks. In addition at the upper edge of the back is a massive swivel-mounted double flail that also provides a slam attack.

The front is studded with many spikes for ramming opponents. Defenders can ride atop the platform and obtain cover from its merlons while firing down on enemy troops. Normally they would lower a rope or ladder to allow other riders on — otherwise it requires a DC 25 Climb check (DC 35 if the battlehulk is moving). The battlehulk is able to reach those atop it with its flail slam if enemies reach that position, though not with its club slams.

In the center of the platform is a secret door (DC 25 Perception check to locate) leading to an interior chamber large enough to hold two Medium creatures. This compartment is sealed against water and air and holds enough air to supply two Medium creatures for 10 minutes before the door must be opened again or suffocation begins. Ordinarily the controller would ride here. Anyone opening this door other than the controller must make a DC 40 Strength check or deal 60 points of damage against a Hardness 8. These hit points are not deducted from the battlehulk's total. Slaying the controller does not stop the battlehulk, which continues to carry out the controller's last command.

A battlehulk is a 15-foot cube atop three 5-foot diameter stone rollers. It weighs about 50,000 pounds.

A battlehulk is nonintelligent and has no forms of communication, taking direction telepathically from its controller. It rolls with a grinding rumble, crushing anything in its path. Despite its bulk it is able to maneuver well since its rollers are able to swivel individually to some extent.

A battlehulk is a terror to behold in combat, and very few will willingly stand against one. Entire enemy formations are often routed by the mere presence of a battlehulk on the field. Against obstacles and large masses of troops, the battlehulk usually attempts its bull rush, ram, and trample attacks, flailing with its slamming arms at any who linger near. Against smaller groups it divides its slam attacks against those within range and focuses its ram and trample attacks at those who appear to be inflicting the most damage.

Construction

A battlehulk is constructed from a single block of granite and exotic metals and processes that cost 10,000 gp. When created it is attuned to an amulet or ring that is worn by a controller who can command the battlehulk telepathically within a quarter mile.

BATTLEHULK
CL 18th; **Price** 250,000 gp

CONSTRUCTION
Requirements Craft Construct, *bull's strength, geas/quest, limited wish, polymorph any object, align weapon,* creator must be caster level 18th; **Skill** Craft (sculptures) or (stonemasonry) DC 18; **Cost** 70,000 gp.

Credit
Original author Greg A. Vaughan
Originally appearing in *Slumbering Tsar* (© Frog God Games/ Greg A. Vaughan, 2012)

Bear, Shadow Dire

A looming shadow like that of a massive bear with claws like sickles rises before you.

SHADOW DIRE BEAR	CR 10

XP 9,600
CE Large undead (incorporeal)
Init +5; **Senses** darkvision 60 ft.; **Perception** +11

AC (incorporeal) 13, touch 13, flat-footed 11 (+2 deflection, +1 Dex, +1 dodge, –1 size) or
AC (partially corporeal) 18, touch 11, flat-footed 16 (+1 Dex, +1 dodge, +7 natural, –1 size)
hp 90 (12d8+24 plus 12)
Fort +6; **Ref** +5; **Will** +9
Defensive Abilities channel resistance +2, incorporeal; **Immune** undead traits

Speed fly 40 ft. (good)
Melee 3 incorporeal touches +10 (1d6 Strength damage) or claw +19 (1d6+10 plus grab) and bite +18 (1d8+10)
Space 10 ft.; **Reach** 5 ft.
Special Attacks create spawn

Str 31, **Dex** 13, **Con** —, **Int** 2, **Wis** 12, **Cha** 14
Base Atk +9; **CMB** +11 (incorporeal) or +20 (partially corporeal); **CMD** 24 (incorporeal) or 32 (partially corporeal)
Feats Dodge, Improved Initiative, Skill Focus (Perception), Toughness, Weapon Focus (claw), Weapon Focus (incorporeal touch)
Skills Fly +10, Perception +11, Stealth +4 (+8 dim light); **Racial Modifiers** +4 Stealth in dim light (–4 in bright light)
SQ partially corporeal

Environment any
Organization solitary
Treasure none

Create Spawn (Su) Any animal reduced to Strength 0 by a shadow dire bear becomes a shadow animal within 1d4 rounds. It is not under the control of its killer but attacks all living targets immediately.
Grab (Ex) While partially corporeal, a shadow dire bear that hits with a claw attack can then attempt to start a grapple as a free action without provoking an attack of opportunity. The grapple is lost if the shadow dire bear becomes incorporeal again. If the shadow sire bear gains a hold, it automatically deals bite damage each round that the hold is maintained.
Partially Corporeal (Su) As a move action a shadow dire bear can become partially corporeal without provoking attacks of opportunity. It can likewise resume its incorporeal state as a move action without provoking attacks of opportunity. While in its partially corporeal state the shadow dire bear benefits from its natural armor and its Strength bonus for attacks and damage. In this state its attacks have a 20% chance to ignore natural armor, armor, and shields. Likewise, though attacks against it with magic weapons can hit normally, it can ignore damage from attacks with normal weapons from a corporeal source 50% of the time. It does not retain any of the other incorporeal traits while in this state.
Strength Damage (Su) The touch of a shadow dire bear while incorporeal deals 1d6 points of Strength damage to a living creature. This is a negative energy effect. A creature dies if this Strength damage equals or exceeds its actual Strength score.

A strange incarnation of sentient darkness and feral rage, this is an incorporeal form of a dire bear that resembles its earthly form in all other respects. Its origin lies in the strange result of a shadow's create spawn ability affecting an animal. How such an outcome occurred is anyone's guess, but sages in the lore of undeath have been unable to recreate it since. It is difficult to see in dark or gloomy places but is clearly visible in bright illumination.

Like a dire bear the shadow dire bear is over 12 feet long, but it is weightless except when partially corporeal when it weighs about 1,000 lb. A shadow dire bear attacks aggressively like its living counterparts with its incorporeal claws and bite alternating this with its grab and tearing claws as it becomes partially corporeal.

Credit
Original author Greg A. Vaughan
Originally appearing in *Slumbering Tsar* (© Frog God Games/ Greg A. Vaughan, 2012)

Beetle, Ravager

This creature is covered in a jet black carapace with whitish markings crisscrossing its back and gold-tinted wing covers.

RAVAGER BEETLE	CR 2

XP 600
N Medium vermin
Init +0; **Senses** darkvision 60 ft., tremorsense 60 ft.; **Perception** +0

AC 19, touch 10, flat-footed 19 (+9 natural)
hp 26 (4d8+8)
Fort +6; **Ref** +1; **Will** +1
Immune mind-affecting effects

Speed 30 ft., fly 20 ft. (poor)
Melee bite +6 (1d8+4 plus poison and grab)

Str 16, **Dex** 10, **Con** 14, **Int** —, **Wis** 10, **Cha** 6
Base Atk +3; **CMB** +6; **CMD** 16 (24 vs. trip)
Skills Fly −4

Environment temperate forests
Organization solitary, pair, cluster (3–8) or nest (9–20)
Treasure none

Gnaw (Ex) A ravager beetle that is grappling a foe and chooses to damage the foe with an additional grapple check deals twice its normal bite damage (2d8+8 points of damage for most ravager beetles), in addition to injecting an additional dose of poison with each successful check.
Poison (Ex) Bite—injury; *save* DC 14 Fort; *frequency* 1/round for 6 rounds; *effect* 1d2 Constitution damage and excruciating pain (−2 penalty on attack rolls, checks, and saves); *cure* 1 save. Multiple bites do not result in cumulative penalties to attack rolls, checks, and saves. Apply the penalties only once for the duration of the poison. The save DC is Constitution-based.

Ravager beetles are omnivorous beetles found in temperate or warm forests, hills, and swamps. While generally sustaining themselves on a diet of foliage and grasses, they sometimes scavenge the remains of creatures killed by other predators.

Like most beetles, a ravager has a thick plated carapace and two large mandibles it uses to crush and chew its food. Its carapace is black in color with several white streaks crisscrossing it. Its mandibles are dark bluish-black. Its wing covers are black with hints of gold. A typical ravager beetle is about 4 feet long.

Ravagers have a single life cycle that spans an entire year. Females generally lay 4–8 eggs in soft earth or soil and within two weeks the larva emerges. Young are almost always born in the warmer spring and early summer months. Young are noncombatants and rely solely on their mother for protection and food, feeding generally for 10 days before entering the pupa stage. After about 20 days, the pupae become adults.

Ravager beetles are generally scavengers by nature, and rarely attack, except in times when food is scarce. Even then, they usually limit their attacks to weakened, sleeping, wounded, or otherwise incapacitated prey. When attacking, ravager beetles lock onto an opponent with their mandibles and continue biting and crushing the target until it is dead.

Beetle, Stench

This beetle is about the size of a small dog and has a mottled green carapace with darker legs fading to black near the ends. Its mandibles are dull brown.

STENCH BEETLE	CR 1/2

XP 200
N Small vermin
Init +0; **Senses** darkvision 60 ft.; **Perception** +0
Aura stench (DC 11, 10 rounds)

AC 14, touch 11, flat-footed 14 (+3 natural, +1 size)
hp 9 (2d8)
Fort +3; **Ref** +0; **Will** +0
Immune mind-affecting effects

Speed 30 ft., fly 30 ft. (poor)
Melee bite +2 (1d4)
Special Attacks death throes

Str 10, **Dex** 11, **Con** 11, **Int** —, **Wis** 10, **Cha** 6
Base Atk +1; **CMB** +0; **CMD** 10 (18 vs. trip)
Skills Fly -2

Environment temperate forests or plains
Organization cluster (3–6) or colony (7–16)
Treasure none

Death Throes (Ex) When a stench beetle dies violently, its body splits open and releases a deluge of nauseating fluids and gasses. Creatures within 10 feet must make DC 13 Fortitude save or be nauseated for 1d4 rounds and sickened for 1d6+2 minutes thereafter. The save DC is Constitution-based and includes a +2 racial bonus.

Stench beetles are small, nocturnal hunters that sustain themselves on a diet of grains, fruits, vegetables, and leaves. In civilized lands they are considered a nuisance for the damage they cause, especially in larger groups, to crops and farmlands. If faced with extreme hunger, stench beetles eat cattle, small game animals, and the occasional child that wanders too far into the forests.

Stench beetles make their lairs in large hollow logs and fallen trees. A typical lair can contain almost twenty of these creatures with half that number in noncombatant young. Females lay up to a dozen eggs at a given time, usually once per year. Eggs are laid on leaves, and the female chews the ends of the leaves so it curls and folds around the eggs, concealing them from predators and protecting the eggs from the elements. Young go from larvae to adulthood in the span of a year. When they reach adulthood most stench beetles leave the lair.

Stench beetles attack with their bite, seeking retreat if combat goes against them.

Blaze Boa

This enormous, muscular snake has crimson scales and emerald eyes. Its charcoal tongue flicks rapidly as it slithers forward.

BLAZE BOA	CR 6

XP 2,400
N Large magical beast
Init +3; **Senses** darkvision 60 ft., low-light vision, scent; **Perception** +14

AC 21, touch 13, flat-footed 17 (+3 Dex, +1 dodge, +8 natural, −1 size)
hp 85 (9d10+27 plus 9)
Fort +9; **Ref** +9; **Will** +4
DR 5/magic; **Resist** fire 30

Speed 30 ft., climb 20 ft., swim 20 ft.
Melee bite +16 (2d6+10/19–20 plus grab)
Space 10 ft.; **Reach** 5 ft.
Special Attacks constrict (2d6+10 plus conflagration)

Str 25, **Dex** 17, **Con** 16, **Int** 2, **Wis** 12, **Cha** 6
Base Atk +9; **CMB** +17 (+21 grapple); **CMD** 31 (can't be tripped)
Feats Dodge, Improved Critical (bite), Skill Focus (Perception), Toughness, Weapon Focus (bite)
Skills Acrobatics +17, Climb +15, Perception +14, Stealth +9, Swim +15;
Racial Modifiers +8 Acrobatics, +4 Perception, +4 Stealth

Environment warm forests and marshes
Organization solitary or pair
Treasure incidental

Conflagration (Su) A blaze boa that has an opponent wrapped in its coils can ignite its body as a free action. This deals 2d6 points of fire damage (in addition to constriction damage) to the grappled target each round the grapple persists. Once the grapple ends, the blaze boa's fire burns out. A blaze boa can stop and restart this ability as a free action (once per turn), but can only use it if it is grappling a foe.

Blaze boas are dangerous constrictor snakes found in jungles, warm forests, and swamplands. From the treetops they survey the area, ever watching for potential prey. These creatures sustain themselves on insects, wild animals, and small humanoids (particularly halflings and goblins). Cannibalism is not unknown among blaze boas.

Blaze boas reproduce on average, once per year, with the female giving birth to live young after a gestation period of roughly 8–9 months. The female can birth up to twenty newborns at one time. Blaze boas are dark red in color when newborn. Young reach maturity within two years.

Blaze boas can reach lengths of 40 feet or more, though the average blaze boa is 10–15 feet long and weighs 150 pounds. Its body is a crimson colored background overlaid with dark red blotches. Its eyes are emerald and set high on its head. Its tongue is the color of charcoal. Faint wisps of smoke seem to rise from the body of a blaze boa.

Blaze boas lurk in treetops or just beneath the surface of the water, waiting for prey to come close. When prey is detected, a blaze boa strikes from its hiding place, wrapping the creature in its deadly coils. Prey that proves resistant to its constriction attack is subjected to the blaze boa's conflagration ability. Slain prey is either devoured immediately or carried back to the creature's lair to feed the young.

Blood Orchid

This beast has three downward curving "petals" of flesh with a dark, pebbly outer hide and a pallid whitish underside. The petals end with split tip, and converge at the blood orchid's center. On its underside at the center dangle a swarm of writhing pallid tentacles: 16 manipulator arms and eight thinner tendrils with red eyes at the ends. At the center of these tentacles is a sphincter-shaped mouth at the end of a flexible trunk one foot long and six inches in diameter. At the apex of the creature there is another cluster of eye tendrils.

BLOOD ORCHID — CR 5

XP 1,600
LE Large aberration
Init +5; **Senses** all-around vision, darkvision 60 ft.; **Perception** +15
AC 18, touch 10, flat-footed 17 (+1 Dex, +8 natural, −1 size)

hp 52 (7d8+21)
Fort +5; **Ref** +5; **Will** +8
Immune sonic; **Resist** acid 10, cold 10, electricity 10, fire 10

Speed 5 ft., fly 30 ft. (good)
Melee 6 tentacles +7 (1d3+2 plus grab plus poison)
Space 10 ft.; **Reach** 5 ft.
Special Attacks blood drain

Str 15, **Dex** 12, **Con** 16, **Int** 11, **Wis** 12, **Cha** 13
Base Atk +5; **CMB** +8 (+12 grapple); **CMD** 19
Feats Improved Initiative, Iron Will, Lightning Reflexes, Weapon Focus (tentacle)
Skills Fly +7, Intimidate +10, Knowledge (dungeoneering) +10, Perception +15, Stealth +7; **Racial Modifiers** +4 Perception
SQ telepathic link

Environment underground
Organization solitary, brood (3–8), or colony (9–20)
Treasure standard

All-Around Vision (Ex) A blood orchid sees in all directions at once. It cannot be flanked.
Blood Drain (Ex) On a successful grapple check with two or more tentacles against a single foe a blood orchid can pull the grappled creature to the mouth on its underside as a free action that does not provoke an attack of opportunity. The mouth latches on and drains blood from the victim. Each round it maintains its grapple, the blood orchid automatically deals 1d4 points of bite damage and 1 point of Constitution damage as it drains its victim's blood.

Poison (Ex) Tentacle—injury; save DC 16 Fort; frequency 1/round for 4 rounds; effect unconsciousness; cure 1 save.
Telepathic Bond (Ex) Blood orchids communicate through a non-magical telepathic bond. They can sense emotions in other blood orchids at a distance of 100 ft. or less, and emotions in other creatures at a range of five feet. They can communicate mentally with each other through full telepathy at a distance of 20 ft. or less, and can share knowledge very rapidly when touching each other.

BLOOD ORCHID SAVANT — CR 6

XP 2,400
Blood orchid sorcerer 4
LE Large aberration
Init +6; **Senses** all-around vision, darkvision 60 ft.; **Perception** +21

AC 19, touch 11, flat-footed 17 (+2 Dex, +8 natural, −1 size)
hp 71 (7d8+14 plus 4d6+8 plus 4)
Fort +5; **Ref** +7; **Will** +14
Immune sonic; **Resist** acid 10, cold 10, electricity 10, fire 10

Speed 5 ft., fly 30 ft. (good)
Melee 6 tentacles +9 (1d3+2 plus grab plus poison)
Space 10 ft.; **Reach** 5 ft.
Special Attacks blood drain
Bloodline Spell-Like Abilities (CL 4th; ranged touch +9): 7/day—acidic ray (1d6+1)
Spells Known (CL 4th; melee touch +9, ranged touch +9):
2nd (4/day)—touch of idiocy
1st (7/day)—burning hands, cure light wounds, magic missile, shield
0 (at will)—daze, detect magic, flare, light, mage hand, resistance
Bloodline Aberrant

Str 15, **Dex** 14, **Con** 14, **Int** 13, **Wis** 16, **Cha** 18
Base Atk +7; **CMB** +10 (+14 grapple); **CMD** 22
Feats Combat Casting, Eschew Materials[B], Extend Spell, Improved Initiative, Iron Will, Lightning Reflexes, Weapon Focus (tentacle)
Skills Fly +9, Intimidate +13, Knowledge (arcana) +12, Knowledge (dungeoneering) +11, Perception +21, Spellcraft +10, Stealth +9; **Racial Modifiers** +4 Perception
SQ telepathic link

All-Around Vision (Ex) A blood orchid sees in all directions at once. It cannot be flanked.
Blood Drain (Ex) On a successful grapple check with two or more tentacles against a single foe a blood orchid can pull the grappled creature to the mouth on its underside as a

free action that does not provoke an attack of opportunity. The mouth latches on and drains blood from the victim. Each round it maintains its grapple, the blood orchid automatically deals 1d4 points of bite damage and 1 point of Constitution damage as it drains its victim's blood.

Poison (Ex) Tentacle—injury; *save* DC 17 Fort; *frequency* 1/round for 4 rounds; *effect* unconsciousness; *cure* 1 save.

Spells: The blood orchid savant replaces its bloodline bonus spells with the following: *cure light wounds* (3rd), *cure moderate wounds* (5th), *cure serious wounds* (7th). Also, blood orchid savants do not cast spells in the same way most creatures do. Their spells require no verbal or material components to be cast, though somatic components (tentacle writhing) is still required.

Telepathic Bond (Ex) Blood orchids communicate through a non-magical telepathic bond. They can sense emotions in other blood orchids at a distance of 100 ft. or less, and emotions in other creatures at a range of five feet. They can communicate mentally with each other through full telepathy at a distance of 20 ft. or less, and can share knowledge very rapidly when touching each other.

BLOOD ORCHID GRAND SAVANT — CR 9

XP 6,400
Blood orchid sorcerer 7
LE Huge aberration
Init +5; **Senses** all-around vision, darkvision 60 ft.; **Perception** +20

AC 22, touch 12, flat-footed 20 (+2 deflection, +1 Dex, +1 dodge, +10 natural, –2 size)
hp 119 (7d8+28 plus 7d6+28 plus 7)
Fort +8; **Ref** +7; **Will** +15
Immune sonic; **Resist** acid 10, cold 10, electricity 10, fire 10

Speed 5 ft., fly 30 ft. (good)
Melee 6 tentacles +14 (1d3+6 plus grab plus poison)
Space 10 ft.; **Reach** 5 ft.
Special Attacks blood drain
Bloodline Spell-Like Abilities (CL 7th; ranged touch +8):
8/day—*acidic ray* (1d6+1)
Spells Known (CL 7th; melee touch +13, ranged touch +8):
3rd (5/day)—*lightning bolt* (DC 18), *vampiric touch*
2nd (7/day)—*cure moderate wounds*, *false life*, *scorching ray*, *touch of idiocy*
1st (8/day)—*burning hands*, *color spray* (DC 16), *cure light wounds*, *mage armor*, *magic missile*, *shield*
0 (at will)—*daze*, *dancing lights*, *detect magic*, *flare*, *light*, *mage hand*, *resistance*
Bloodline Aberrant

Str 23, **Dex** 13, **Con** 18, **Int** 13, **Wis** 16, **Cha** 20
Base Atk +8; **CMB** +15 (+19 grapple); **CMD** 26
Feats Arcane Strike, Combat Casting[B], Dodge, Eschew Materials[B], Extend Spell, Improved Initiative, Iron Will, Lightning Reflexes, Weapon Focus (tentacle)
Skills Fly +7, Intimidate +14, Knowledge (arcana) +14, Knowledge (dungeoneering) +11, Perception +20, Spellcraft +12, Stealth +8; **Racial Modifiers** +4 Perception
SQ telepathic link
Gear *ring of protection +2*

All-Around Vision (Ex) A blood orchid sees in all directions at once. It cannot be flanked.

Blood Drain (Ex) On a successful grapple check with two or more tentacles against a single foe a blood orchid can pull the grappled creature to the mouth on its underside as a free action that does not provoke an attack of opportunity. The mouth latches on and drains blood from the victim. Each round it maintains its grapple, the blood orchid automatically deals 1d4 points of bite damage and 1 point of Constitution damage as it drains its victim's blood.

Poison (Ex) Tentacle—injury; *save* DC 21 Fort; *frequency* 1/round for 4 rounds; *effect* unconsciousness; *cure* 1 save.

Spells: The blood orchid savant replaces its bloodline bonus spells with the following: *cure light wounds* (3rd), *cure moderate wounds* (5th), *cure serious wounds* (7th). Also, blood orchid savants do not cast spells in the same way most creatures do. Their spells require no verbal or material components to be cast, though somatic components (tentacle writhing) is still required.

Telepathic Bond (Ex) Blood orchids communicate through a non-magical telepathic bond. They can sense emotions in other blood orchids at a distance of 100 ft. or less, and emotions in other creatures at a range of five feet. They can communicate mentally with each other through full telepathy at a distance of 20 ft. or less, and can share knowledge very rapidly when touching each other.

Blood orchids are territorial, xenophobic, and possessive. They rarely form alliances with other creatures, as their alien mindset keeps them from forming any common ground. They regard other races as aberrant and not to be trusted, even other lawful creatures.

Communication for blood orchids is through a means of empathy/telepathy. They have no sense of hearing, which helps render them immune to sonic effects. The blood orchid can close its outer petals downward and rest on the ground, where it resembles a rocky nodule or fungus of some kind.

Blood orchids occasionally develop sorcerous talents, and transform into savants. When their abilities have reached a certain level, they can evolve into a grand savant. Normally each colony of blood orchids is led by a single grand savant, and another cannot evolve while one is present. Typically, a blood orchid savant ready to become a grand savant leaves the colony with a few followers, and set out to establish a new brood elsewhere.

Credit
Originally appearing in Rappan Athuk Reloaded
(© Necromancer Games, 2006)

Bloodsoaker Vine

The vines dangling from the treetops are about as thick as a halfling's leg. They sway gently and almost innocently in the breeze, but the wicked barbs along their lengths glisten unwholesomely with a reddish liquid. The smell of decaying flesh is unmistakable.

BLOODSOAKER VINE   CR 9

XP 6,400
N Large plant (extraplanar)
Init +0; **Senses** blindsight 60 ft., tremorsense 60 ft.; **Perception** +9

AC 19, touch 9, flat-footed 19 (+10 natural, −1 size)
hp 115 (11d8+55 plus 11)
Fort +14; **Ref** +3; **Will** +6
DR 10/slashing; **Immune** plant traits

Speed 10 ft., climb 10 ft.
Melee 6 tendrils +14 (1d8+6 plus bleed)
Space 10 ft.; **Reach** 10 ft.
Special Attacks bleed (1d6), rend (2 tendrils, 1d8+9)

Str 22, **Dex** 10, **Con** 21, **Int** 2, **Wis** 12, **Cha** 6
Base Atk +8; **CMB** +15; **CMD** 25 (can't be tripped)
Feats Great Fortitude, Iron Will, Power Attack, Toughness, Vital Strike, Weapon Focus (tendril)
Skills Climb +14, Perception +9, Stealth +5

Environment temperate forests or marshes
Organization solitary or colony (2–5)
Treasure incidental

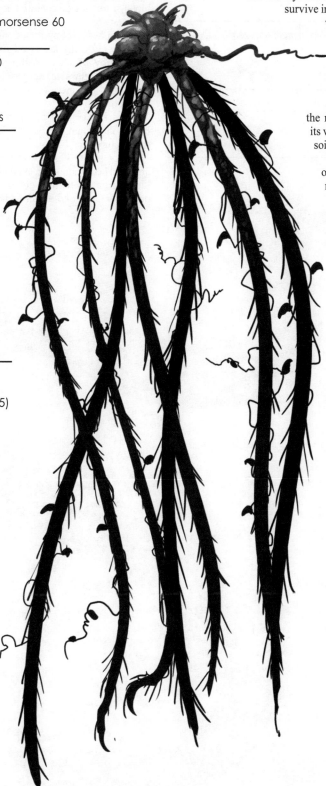

The bloodsoaker vine is a horrid plant that is believed to have its origins in the blood-stained fields of the Plane of Agony. Some unknown botanist–perhaps one of the N'gathau themselves–supposedly spliced an unknown root from that dismal place with the assassin vine to create this monstrosity. Several other theories as to this plant's origin abound, but this one is the most widely accepted.

The root system of the bloodsoaker vine needs blood to survive in the same manner as other plants need water. The vine provides nourishment for itself and the host tree from which it dangles by shredding unfortunate forest travelers into easily degraded bits. The trees benefit from the meaty compost while the bloodsoaker vine–true to the name–hungrily feeds on the blood of its victim and any that saturates the nearby soil.

A typical bloodsoaker vine is a mass of roots, vines, and tendrils. Coloration ranges from deep greens to various browns, and all colors in between. The bloodsoaker vine eventually changes colors to better match its surroundings the longer it remains in one location.

Ironically, the bloodsoaker vine produces an orchid-like flower thought by many to be among the most beautiful in creation. Far above the carnage below, where its tendrils break the forest canopy, delicate pink blossoms spread their petals and nourish birds and insects with sweet-smelling nectar.

Bloodworm

This creature appears to be a large semi-translucent worm about 15 feet long. Pale red stripes line its segmented body.

BLOODWORM	CR 4

XP 1,200
N Large vermin
Init +0; **Senses** bloodsense 120 ft., darkvision 60 ft., tremorsense 60 ft.; **Perception** +0

AC 15, touch 9, flat-footed 15 (+6 natural, −1 size)
hp 45 (6d8+18)
Fort +8; **Ref** +2; **Will** +2
Immune mind-affecting effects

Speed 20 ft., burrow 10 ft., swim 20 ft.
Melee bite +8 (2d6+7 plus bleed)
Space 10 ft.; **Reach** 5 ft.
Special Attacks bleed (1d6)

Str 21, **Dex** 10, **Con** 17, **Int** —, **Wis** 10, **Cha** 2
Base Atk +4;
CMB +10; **CMD** 20 (can't be tripped)
Skills Swim +13

Environment temperate and warm coastlines and underground
Organization solitary or gang (2–5)
Treasure incidental

Bloodsense (Ex) When a bloodworm bites an opponent, it secretes a pheromone that mixes with the blood and that can be detected by other bloodworms to a range of 120 ft. This functions on both land and in water.

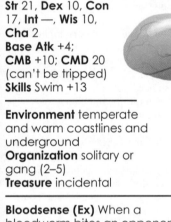

Bloodworms are carnivorous hunters with voracious appetites, and though not aquatic by nature, prefer a diet of fish, especially smaller sharks and dolphins, shellfish, and the occasional swimmer. Hunting occurs whenever the bloodworm is hungry–day or night.

A bloodworm's lair is beneath the ground, usually in soft earth near the shoreline of lakes and streams. A typical lair is at least as deep as the bloodworm is long and terminates in a large round chamber. Here the bloodworm dine on captured prey and spawn during mating season.

Bloodworms mate during the late summer months. Young are born alive and kept wet by secretions from the larger bloodworms as well as water from nearby lakes and rivers. The young do not hunt yet and are cared for by the adults. Within a few months the young are strong enough to fend for themselves and do so, going out on their own.

Bloodworms are pale and slightly pink in color. They can grow to a length of 40 feet or more, though most average about 12–15 feet long. The red stripes seen along its body are actually a combination of its bodily fluids and the fluids of recently devoured prey flowing through the creature.

A bloodworm lies in wait for its prey, most often just beneath the silt and sand near shorelines. When it detects a potential meal, the bloodworm lunges from its hiding spot, striking with its extended proboscis. Slain prey is dragged into its lair and devoured.

Boarfolk

A group of large, wild-pig-faced humanoids snort derisively and head towards you. They do not appear to be friendly at all.

BOARFOLK	CR 10

XP 9,600
N Large magical beast
Init +3; **Senses** darkvision 60 ft., low-light vision, scent; **Perception** +17

AC 18, touch 12, flat-footed 15 (+3 Dex, +6 natural, −1 size)
hp 126 (13d10+42 plus 13)
Fort +12; **Ref** +11; **Will** +5
Defensive Abilities ferocity

Speed 40 ft.
Melee greatclub +20/+15 (1d10+10), gore +20 (2d6+10)
Space 10 ft.; **Reach** 10 ft.
Special Attacks trample (1d6+10, DC 23)

Str 24, **Dex** 16, **Con** 18, **Int** 6, **Wis** 8, **Cha** 8
Base Atk +13; **CMB** +21 (+23 sunder); **CMD** 34 (36 vs. sunder)
Feats Cleave, Great Cleave, Improved Sunder, Iron Will, Martial Weapon Proficiency (greatclub), Power Attack, Toughness
Skills Perception +6, Stealth +6, Swim +15
Languages boarfolk
SQ rage (32 rounds/day)
Gear Greatclubs

Environment temperate forest
Organization solitary, pair, or club (4–9)
Treasure no coins; 50% goods

Boarfolk are giant humanoids standing some 9 to 10 feet tall, weighing nearly 700 pounds. They possess boar-like features, including large tusks that protrude from their mouths.

Boarfolk are created by the sorceress, Circe, on the Isle of the Phoenix, in the Land of the Dead. There she uses her powers to transmute travelers that are unfortunate enough to cross her path. Once transmuted the boarfolk grow enthralled by her beauty and charisma, and serve her without question.

Boarfolk speak an offshoot of Common, but so thickly accented as to make it a separate language.

The boarfolk live in nomadic, tribal fashion. Should the influence of Circe ever depart, the boarfolk would turn to infighting and barbaric tribal law; the strongest would rule, and the rest of the boarfollk would split into warring tribes.

Credit
Original author William Loran Christensen
Originally appearing in *Fane of the Fallen* (© Frog God Games/ William Loran Christensen, 2010)

Bone Crawler

Unarmored, the bone crawler is a fleshy disc-shaped lump approximately six ft. in diameter, with a slightly concave top. The bottom curves downward, and ends with a circular mouth at its nadir. From the central mass sprout several dozen tentacles, each specialized to perform different functions: stubby muscular ones provide movement, thin graceful tendrils are tipped with sensory organs, and the long, limber whipfronds are used as a means of attack and manipulation. The flesh of a bone crawler ranges from olive green to slate grey to jet black. When it is encased in bone armor, the bone crawler appears much different. When still, it resembles a 15 ft. diameter mound of bones, piled haphazardly together. A canny observer may note fleshy tendrils or roots webbed through the mass. Once it begins to move, the armored crawler is a whirling nightmare of interlocked bones forming a 15 ft. diameter central mass, with bony tentacles extending out from it in all directions.

BONE CRAWLER	CR 12

XP 19,200
N Huge aberration
Init +3; **Senses** blindsight 60 ft.; **Perception** +15

AC 11, touch 11, flat-footed 8 (+3 Dex, –2 size) or
AC 18, touch 8, flat-footed 18 (+10 natural armor, –2 size) in bone armor
hp 114 (12d8+60)
Fort +9; **Ref** +9; **Will** +10
Defensive Abilities bone armor, cannot be flanked; **SR** 23

Speed 20 ft. in bone armor (30 ft. base), climb 10 ft.
Melee up to 12 bone blades +16 (1d8+8/19–20) and/or up to 12 whipfronds +15 (1d4+8)
Space 15 ft.; **Reach** 10 ft.
Special Attacks bone blades, whipfronds, whirling frenzy

Str 26, **Dex** 16, **Con** 21, **Int** 9, **Wis** 15, **Cha** 9
Base Atk +9; **CMB** +19; **CMD** 32
Feats Cleave, Improved Critical (bone blade), Lightning Reflexes, Lunge, Power Attack, Weapon Focus (bone blade)
Skills Acrobatics +11, Climb +25 (+15 in bone armor), Disguise +5 (+15 disguised as mound of bones), Perception +15, Stealth +8; **Racial Modifiers** when in bone armor, a bone crawler gains a +10 on disguise checks to resemble a mound of bones, and takes a –10 armor check penalty on Climb checks
Languages Aklo

Environment underground
Organization solitary
Treasure standard

Bone Armor (Ex) The bone crawler is normally encountered encased in a shell of iron-hard bones. This shell has a hardness of 10, takes half damage from energy attacks (except sonic attacks) and has hit points equal to 10 x (HD + 1). Bone armor weighs 1 pound per hit point. It can take damage like any object, though it receives the bone crawler's saving throws and spell resistance. Unlike carried objects, area of effect attacks require the bone crawler to roll a separate saving throw for its bone armor, even if it makes the saving throw itself. Spell resistance is checked just once for the overall creature and its armor, however. While it bears bone armor, the bone crawler

receives no bonus to AC for its Dexterity. After the first 10 hit points of damage, every 10 hit points worth of bone armor provides the bone crawler with one bone blade that it can use in melee as described below. As its armor receives damage, it likewise loses these bone blades. The last 10 hit points of bone armor represent those protecting the main body itself; until the armor is destroyed, the central body is considered to have total cover. A bone crawler can repair its armor by absorbing new bones into its mass. This requires a 24-hour period while enzymes secreted by specialized tendrils harden the bone. The number of hit points gained depends on the size of the skeleton or bone collection absorbed: a Tiny skeleton repairs 1 hit point, a Small skeleton 1d4 hit points, a Medium skeleton 2d4 hit points, and Large and larger skeletons 4d4 hit points. Note that skeletons of Huge size and larger contain many bones that are too large for the bone crawler to absorb effectively into its mass, which is why the hit points gained do not increase after Large size.

Bone Blade (Ex) The bone crawler has a number of bony limbs that it can manipulate with its whipfronds. When attacking with these, it gains its full attack bonus as a primary weapon attack. It can only attack a creature or creatures in a single 5 ft. square with a maximum of 4 bone blades at once. Sunder attacks directed at bone blades do damage to the creature's bone armor (see above).

Whipfrond (Ex) The bone crawler's primary attacking tentacles are called whipfronds. It has one whipfrond per hit die. A whipfrond can be severed with a successful Sunder attack with a slashing weapon that inflicts, in a single blow, a number of points of damage equal to or greater than the bone crawler's hit dice. Whipfronds cannot be sundered while encased in bone armor; the armor must be destroyed first. As with the bone blades, the bone crawler can only attack a single 5 ft. square area with up to 4 whipfronds at a time, no more.

Whirling Frenzy (Ex) As a full round action the bone crawler may whirl its bone blades around it in a swirling storm of sharpened edges. This attack inflicts 1d8+4 points of damage per three bone blades used (round down) on anyone within the bone crawler's reach. A DC 19 Reflex save is allowed to take only half damage from this attack; alternately, a targeted creature may opt instead to make an attack of opportunity against the bone crawler instead. The save DC is Dexterity-based.

The bone crawler is an unusual aberration that girds itself with hardened bones, fused together and manipulated by lenticular limbs called whipfronds, to serve as both a weapon and a defense.

Bone crawlers exist by attacking and killing just about anything they can come to grips with. They feast upon the flesh of their enemies, and then integrate the bones of their prey into their armor, repairing any damage it has sustained. Some bone crawlers have been known to seek out crypts and graveyards, exhuming bodies for their bones.

Bone crawlers understand and may speak Aklo, but rarely converse with their victims.

Credit

Originally appearing in *Rappan Athuk Reloaded* (© Necromancer Games, 2006)

Bone Delver

This rotting humanoid wears tattered rags that hang loosely about its twisted and hunched form. Its face is twisted into a visage of pain and rage, and its clawed hands clutch the tools of its trade—a shovel and a lantern that glows with an eerie red hue.

BONE DELVER	CR 2

XP 600
CE Medium undead
Init +3; **Senses** darkvision 60 ft.; **Perception** +6
Aura grave light (10 ft.)

AC 16, touch 13, flat-footed 13 (+3 Dex, +3 natural)
hp 13 (2d8+4); fast healing 2
Fort +2; **Ref** +3; **Will** +4
Immune undead traits

Speed 30 ft.
Melee shovel +4 (1d6+1 plus disease) or 2 claws +4 (1d4+1 plus disease)
Special Attacks grave light, scream of agony

Str 13, **Dex** 16, **Con** —, **Int** 10, **Wis** 13, **Cha** 14
Base Atk +1; **CMB** +2; **CMD** 15
Feats Weapon Finesse
Skills Disable Device +9, Knowledge (local) +2, Perception +6, Stealth +10; **Racial Modifiers** +4 Disable Device, +2 Stealth
Languages Common
SQ shovel

Environment any land
Organization solitary or crew (2–5)
Treasure standard (shovel, *bone delver's lantern*, thieves' tools, other treasure)

Disease (Ex) *Filth Fever:* claws or shovel—injury; *save* DC 13 Fort; *onset* 1d3 days; *frequency* 1/day; *effect* 1d3 Dex damage and 1d3 Con damage; *cure* 2 consecutive saves. The save DC is Charisma-based.
Grave Light (Su) A bone delver's lantern sheds light in a 10-foot radius. Living creatures within the area take 1 point of damage each round. Additionally, a bone delver's fast healing only works when it is within 10 feet of its lantern. The lantern can be extinguished with a *bless* spell (it relights after 1 hour) or attacked and destroyed (hardness 5, hp 10). This lantern functions only for the bone delver to which it belongs. In the hands of living creatures it functions differently (see below).
Scream of Agony (Su) A bone delver can unleash a bone-chilling shriek that affects all who hear it within 30 feet. An affected creature must make a DC 13 Will save or be shaken for 1d4+2 rounds. Creatures with more than 4 HD are unaffected by this attack. Creatures that successfully save are immune to the scream of agony of that bone delver for one day. The save DC is Charisma-based.

Bone Delver Lantern

Aura moderate divination; **CL** 6th
Slot hand; **Price** 4,000 gp; **Weight** 2 lbs.

The lanterns bone delvers perpetually carry are formerly mundane hooded lanterns that were infused with negative energy in the same way as their unliving bearers. In between the hours of dusk and dawn, a *bone delver lantern* glows with a red glowing light and continually emanates an effect that functions as *detect undead* (CL 6th). In addition, it increases the effectiveness of negative energy channeling by +2. This +2 bonus adds to damage done (or healed) by a negative energy burst, and increases the Will save for the Command Undead feat by +2.

The *bone delver lantern* is completely powerless during daylight hours, and does not show an aura if *detect magic* is cast on it during that time. A *bone delver lantern* is an innately evil creation, and generates one negative level in any good creature that carries it. This negative level cannot be removed until the good-aligned creature gets rid of the *lantern*. The *lantern* must be taken from a bone delver before the creature is destroyed in order for the item to retain any power.

Requirements special; a *bone delver lantern* cannot be crafted as they are spontaneously created when a slain grave robber rises as a bone delver.

Shovel A bone delver suffers no penalties on attack rolls when wielding a shovel as a weapon.

Cemeteries and graveyards are well known for their concentration of negative energy and it is this, rather than the mere presence of the buried dead, that can cause all manner of creatures to rise from their graves to haunt the living. A few braves souls make their gruesome livelyhood by preying on graves, digging up the treasures and riches sometimes laid to rest with their owners. Thes graverobbers are detested by most civilized societies for their callous nature, and all too often would be graverobbers fall foul to the unliving denizens of the graveyard.

Bone delvers were in life graverobbers that died whilst performing their nefarious tasks. Some may have inadvertently awoken undead creatures in their graves, others were outwitted by cunning traps placed in well protected mausoleums. Bone delvers usually appear as hunched, shambling humanoids with faces twisted into a visage of pain and rage. They visibly carry the wounds that caused their demise. Bone delvers forever carry the tools of their trade—a lantern and a shovel, though lockpicks are also commonly found on their walking corpses. The lantern still burns, though with an unnatural and eerie red glowing light.

A bone delver initiatite its attack by uttering a chilling scream of terribly agony, rage, and frustration that transcensds death itself. Those not affected by the scream are made targets of melee attacks with the creature's shovel or filthy claws.

Boobrie

This creature stands taller than a normal human and resembles a crane with rich, black feathers that fade to dull gray on its undercarriage. Its bill is long, slightly curved, and serrated. Its feet are sharp and sport wicked talons that resemble twisted, almost humanoid clawed hands.

BOOBRIE	CR 5

XP 1,600
N Large magical beast (aquatic)
Init +2; **Senses** darkvision 60 ft., low-light vision; **Perception** +8

AC 17, touch 11, flat-footed 15 (+2 Dex, +6 natural, −1 size)
hp 67 (9d10+18)
Fort +8; **Ref** +8; **Will** +5
Immune poison
Weakness marsh bound

Speed 30 ft., swim 30 ft.
Melee 2 claws +11 (1d8+3/19–20), bite +11 (2d6+3)
Space 10 ft.; **Reach** 10 ft.
Special Attacks wail

Str 17, **Dex** 15, **Con** 15, **Int** 3, **Wis** 14, **Cha** 12
Base Atk +9; **CMB** +13; **CMD** 25
Feats Ability Focus (wail), Alertness, Improved Critical (claw), Power Attack, Swim-By Attack
Skills Perception +8, Stealth +7, Swim +16
Languages Common
SQ amphibious, change shape

Environment temperate marshes
Organization solitary or flock (3–6 plus 100% noncombatants)
Treasure none

Change Shape (Su) A boobrie can assume the form of a Large heavy warhorse as a standard action. In this form, it can run on top of water (including deep water such as rivers and lakes) and marshy ground as if it were solid, flat terrain. The boobrie is still marsh bound in this form and suffers the normal penalties if it moves too far from its environment.
Marsh Bound (Ex) A boobrie can survive away from its marshy home for 1 hour per 2 points of Constitution. After that, refer to the drowning rules.
Wail (Su) Once every 2d4 rounds as a standard action, a boobrie can emit an eerie wail that deals 4d6 points of sonic damage to all creatures within 40 feet that hear it. A DC 18 Fortitude save reduces the damage by half. Further, a creature failing its save is paralyzed for 2d4 rounds. This is a sonic mind-affecting attack. A creature that

successfully saves is immune to the wail of that boobrie for one day. The save DC is Constitution-based and includes a +2 bonus from the boobrie's Ability Focus feat.

The boobrie, or marsh terror, is a quick-moving, malign, flightless bird found haunting desolate and overgrown swamps, wetlands, and marshes. It is carnivorous by nature and feasts on a diet of crocodile meat, fish, and humans (the last of which is one of its favorite meals). When food is scarce, boobrie flocks often war with each other, eating the fallen and the slain.

A boobrie flock dwells in thick, overgrown (and usually well-hidden) marsh groves. A typical flock consists of more males than females and a number of young equal to the combined total of adult boobries. A single dominate male acts as the leader of the flock and commands the others of the flock in carrying out particular tasks. Boobrie flocks sometimes settle near (but not too near) human settlements and conduct raids into the settlements, stealing livestock, children, and even lone adults.

Boobries speak broken Common and their own language of hoots, croaks, and clicks.

Boobries are vicious creatures with voracious appetites. They are almost always hungry and usually attack prey on sight. A boobrie attacks with two sharpened talons and a nasty bite from its serrated bill. Slain prey is dragged to the lair and given to the young who promptly tear it to shreds, devouring as much of the kill as they can. Leftovers are simply discarded and left to rot or discarded for other scavengers to claim.

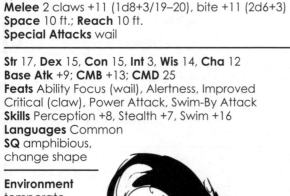
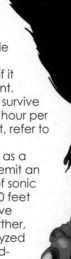

Borsin

A borsin is a creature with the head, arms, and upper body of an ape joined to the body and legs of a quadruped. The lower half may be that of a boar, equine, or hound; these may be a race of battle-beasts magically crossbred in antiquity.

BORSIN	CR 3

XP 800
N Medium monstrous humanoid
Init +6; **Senses** darkvision 60 ft.; **Perception** +7

AC 13, touch 12, flat-footed 11 (+2 Dex, +1 natural)
hp 30 (4d10+8)
Fort +3; **Ref** +6; **Will** +6

Speed 45 ft.
Melee 2 claws +8 (1d6+4) and bite +3 (1d4+4)
Special Attacks rend (2 claws, 1d6+6)

Str 18, **Dex** 14, **Con** 15, **Int** 7, **Wis** 14, **Cha** 12
Base Atk +4; **CMB** +8; **CMD** 20 (24 against trip)
Feats Fleet, Improved Initiative, Run[B]
Skills Intimidate +6, Perception +7, Survival +9
Languages Aklo

Environment temperate forest or plains
Organization solitary, pair or tribe (3–12 plus 1 8HD leader)
Treasure none

A borsin is a savage, cunning beast capable of problem-solving and setting crude traps. They do not use weapons or tools, or carry treasure, although pack leaders will drape themselves in the skins and furs of creatures they have killed – including humans and adventurers.

Borsin form packs led by the strongest member. They attack with two claws and a bite, and use pack tactics to drive opponents and prey into traps, kill zones, or natural hazards such as cliffs and ravines. Borsin packs stake out their territory by making small cairns topped with the skulls of their kills, and patrol their borders regularly. Borsin are omnivorous and hardy, capable of surviving on plant matter, yet enjoying a fresh kill.

Borsin speak Aklo, but rarely speak with those outside of their own tribe.

Credit
Original author Scott Wylie Roberts, "Myrystyr";
Pathfinder conversion by Skeeter Green
Originally appearing in *Jungle Ruins of Madaro-Shanti* (© Frog God Games, 2010)

Bronze Minotaur

This massive bronze figure is shaped as a common minotaur, although its sheer bulk and slow movements bely it is an automaton of some kind.

BRONZE MINOTAUR	CR 11

XP 12,800
N Large construct
Init −1; **Senses** darkvision 60 ft., low-light vision; **Perception** +0

AC 26, touch 8, flat-footed 26 (−1 Dex, +18 natural, −1 size)
hp 107 (14d10+30)
Fort +4; **Ref** +3; **Will** +4
DR 5/adamantine; **Immune** construct traits (+30 hp), magic

Speed 20 ft.
Melee large greataxe +23/+18/+13 (3d6+13/×3)
Space 10 ft.; **Reach** 10 ft.
Special Attacks breathe fire (4d6, DC 17)

Str 28, **Dex** 9, **Con** —, **Int** —, **Wis** 11, **Cha** 1
Base Atk +14; **CMB** +24; **CMD** 33

Environment any
Organization solitary
Treasure none

Immunity to Magic (Ex) A bronze minotaur is immune to any spell or spell-like ability that allows spell resistance. In addition, certain spells and effects function differently against the creature, as noted: A magical attack that deals electricity damage slows a bronze minotaur (as the *slow* spell) for three rounds with no saving throw. A magical attack that deals fire damage breaks any *slow* effect on the bronze minotaur and heals one point of damage for every three points of damage the attack would otherwise deal. If the amount of healing would cause the bronze minotaur to exceed its full normal hit points, it gains any excess as temporary hit points. A bronze minotaur gets no saving throw against fire attacks.
Breath Fire (Su) A bronze minotaur can breathe fire as a free action on the first round of combat and every other round thereafter. A bronze minotaur's fiery breath shoots from its mouth in a 30 foot cone inflicting 4d6 damage. A DC 17 Reflex save can reduce the damage by half. The save DC is Constitution based.

Tall, dark and powerfully built, the bronze minotaur is an intimidating sight. Standing over 8 feet tall, and weighing nearly 4,000 pounds, it is a massive and impressive guardian.

Bronze minotaurs can understand simple commands from their creators. They follow these orders unswervingly.

Construction

A bronze minotaur is constructed from 5,000 pounds of bronze, forged with rare minerals and oils casting at least 10,000 gp.

BRONZE MINOTAUR
CL 16th; **Price** 120,000 gp

CONSTRUCTION
Requirements Craft Construct, *burning hands, geas/quest, limited wish, polymorph any object,* creator

must be caster level 16th; **Skill** Craft (blacksmithing) DC 18; **Cost** 60,000 gp.

Credit

Original author Mark R. Shipley
Originally appearing in *The Black Monastery* (© Frog God Games/ Mark R. Shipley, 2011)

Bucentaur

This hulking brute has the lower torso of a powerful black bull and the upper torso of a powerfully built man with the head of a bull.

BUCENTAUR	CR 6

XP 2,400
CE Large monstrous humanoid
Init +1; **Senses** darkvision 60 ft.; **Perception** +14

AC 16, touch 10, flat-footed 15 (+1 Dex, +6 natural, −1 size)
hp 68 (8d10+24)
Fort +7; **Ref** +7; **Will** +7
Defensive Abilities natural cunning

Speed 40 ft.
Melee greataxe +12/+7 (3d6+7), 2 hooves +7 (1d6+5), gore +7 (1d6+5)
Space 10 ft.; **Reach** 5 ft.
Special Attacks powerful charge (gore +12, 2d6+7)

Str 21, **Dex** 12, **Con** 16, **Int** 8, **Wis** 12, **Cha** 10
Base Atk +8; **CMB** +14; **CMD** 25 (29 vs. trip)
Feats Great Fortitude, Improved Bull Rush, Power Attack, Run
Skills Intimidate +9, Perception +14, Stealth +6, Survival +14; **Racial Modifiers** +4 Perception, +4 Survival
Languages Giant

Environment temperate forests and plains or underground
Organization solitary, pair, band (3–6), or herd (7–16 plus leader of 10th–12th level)
Treasure standard (greataxe, other treasure)

Natural Cunning (Ex) Although bucentaurs are not especially intelligent, they possess innate cunning and logical ability. This gives them immunity to *maze* spells and prevents them from ever becoming lost. Further, they are never caught flat-footed.

These beings, also known as mantaurs or bulltaurs are the progeny of a minotaur and a heifer, though rarely (1% chance) one is born to normal minotaurs. Bucentaurs are considered to be a blessing by many minotaur clans, and are often raised by minotaur priests to be kings and rulers of a minotaur tribe. Their battle prowess is legendary, the skulls of many heroes adorning the walls of their pen.

Bucentaurs make their home in desolate forests and ruins, generally away from civilized races. They are fiercely territorial, attacking any who trespass their realm, including other bucentaur clans on occasion. Hunts are a standard occasion and can see up to six or eight of these creatures strike out to capture and kill large game.

Bucentaurs stand almost 8 feet tall and weigh over 2,200

pounds. Skin colors vary widely, but most tend to be darker colors such as blacks or blackish-blue. Eyes are almost always dark. Bucentaurs typically live to 50 years of age.

Bucentaurs are straightforward combatants, bull rushing and goring foes before cutting them down with their greataxes. They are savage creatures, and rarely flee from a fight, preferring to inflict as much damage as possible on their foes before the need to escape.

Burning Ghat

A humanoid figure stands swathed in smoke, its distinct features obliterated by the charred and blackened flesh. Ash perpetually trails from the creature as it moves and small patches of burnt skin flake from its body. Its eyes are small dots of brilliant crimson fire.

BURNING GHAT	CR 3

XP 800
CE medium undead (fire)
Init +2; **Senses** darkvision 60 ft.; **Perception** +9

AC 16, touch 12, flat-footed 14 (+2 Dex, +4 natural)
hp 26 (4d8+8)
Fort +3; **Ref** +3; **Will** +6
DR 5/magic; **Immune** fire, undead traits
Weaknesses vulnerability to cold

Speed 30 ft.
Melee 2 claws +5 (1d4+1 plus burn)
Special Attacks burn (2d6, DC 14), burning blood, fire burst

Str 13, **Dex** 15, **Con** —, **Int** 13, **Wis** 14, **Cha** 14
Base Atk +3; **CMB** +4; **CMD** 16
Feats Blind-Fight, Weapon Finesse
Skills Climb +8, Escape Artist +6, Intimidate +9, Perception +9, Stealth +9
Languages Common
SQ odor

Environment any
Organization solitary or gang (2–4)
Treasure standard

Burning Blood (Su) When a burning ghat takes damage from a slashing or piercing weapon, its flesh bursts open and sprays the attacker with a mixture of burning fluids. The attacker must succeed on a DC 14 Reflex save or take 1d6 points of fire damage. The save DC is Charisma-based.
Fire Burst (Ex) Once per day, a burning ghat can unleash a burst of flames in a 20-foot radius centered on itself. Creatures caught in the burst take 4d6 points of fire damage. A successful DC 14 Reflex save reduces the damage by half. The burning ghat is slowed (as the *slow* spell) for 1d4 rounds after using this ability. The save DC is Charisma-based.
Odor (Ex) A burning ghat reeks of charred flesh, which can be detected at a range of 30 feet with a DC 10 Perception check. Creatures with the scent ability automatically detect its presence as soon as they come within 60 feet of a burning ghat.

The burning ghat is a rare form of undead created in areas of unusually high negative energy when a living creature is put to death by fire for a crime it did not commit. Utterly twisted and maddened by its fate, a burning ghat is a fearsome creature, consumed with a hatred for the living and seeking to end life wherever it finds it. The distinct and pungent stench of burnt flesh is often the harbinger of a burning ghat's arrival and is easily noticeable within 30 feet of the creature. They can often still be found wearing the clothes they wore as they burned to death, if the garments survived the flames, though a burning ghat of any great age will usually have none.

Burning ghats inhabit remote areas near places where they were put to death. They are not bound to this area as some undead seem to be, but they seldom wander more than a mile or so away from their death site. Most encounters are with a lone burning ghat, but occassionally when more than one innocent has been put to the flames, a pack of these creatures can be found. Burning ghats are nocturnal pack hunters, feasting on the charred flesh of those they encounter and kill. They are seldom found with other undead, preferring to keep company with their own kind or operating alone.

A typical burning ghat is 6 feet tall and weighs 150 pounds. A burning ghat can communicate in the Common tongue and any other language it knew in life. Its voice crackles and hisses like a freshly-stoked fire.

A burning ghat attacks with its claws, seeking to slay any living creature it encounters. A burning ghat's claws heats the blood of living creatures upon contact, causing great pain as it sizzles and boils away into the air. It favors burning its victims to death but is content to rend them apart if they should prove immune to fire.

Carrion Claw

This insect-like horror has six large, spear-like legs and a poison bite. It crawls about on hundreds of legs, using its six spears to impale victims which it then bites. It resembles a centipede. Its body is covered with tiny hair-like barbs that allow this creature to grapple a man sized or smaller opponent.

CARRION CLAW	CR 6

XP 2,400
NE Large magical beast
Init +6; **Senses** darkvision 60 ft., low-light vision; **Perception** +6
AC 14, touch 11, flat-footed 12 (+2 Dex, +3 natural, –1 size)

hp 51 (6d10+12 plus 6)
Fort +7; **Ref** +7; **Will** +3
Weaknesses light sensitivity, vulnerable to magical light

Speed 40 ft., climb 40 ft.
Melee 6 claws +10 (1d6+4 plus grab), bite +9 (1d3+4 plus paralysis)
Space 10 ft.; **Reach** 5 ft.
Special Attacks hatred of elves (+1 to hit and damage), paralysis (1d4 hours, DC 15)

Str 18, **Dex** 14, **Con** 14, **Int** 4, **Wis** 12, **Cha** 11
Base Atk +6; **CMB** +11 (+15 grapple); **CMD** 23 (can't be tripped)
Feats Improved Initiative, Toughness, Weapon Focus (claw)
Skills Climb +17, Perception +6, Stealth +11; **Racial Modifiers** +8 Stealth
SQ superior climbing

Environment underground or temperate forest
Organization solitary, gang (2–5) or fist (5–30)
Treasure incidental

Superior Climbing (Ex) A carrion claw need not make Climb checks to traverse a vertical or horizontal surface (even upside down). It retains its Dexterity bonus to Armor Class while climbing, and opponents get no special bonus to their attacks against it. It cannot, however, use the run action while climbing.

Vulnerable to Magical Light (Ex) A carrion claw that is the target of a spell with the light descriptor must succeed on a Will save or be dazed for 1 round. The Will save DC is equal to 10 + the spell level + the caster's key ability.

Carrion claws have a preferential taste for elf flesh, and seek to attack and eat elves before other opponents. It does not like halfling flesh, and kills but does not devour halflings.

The creature can climb any surface, even hanging upside down from the ceiling if desired. The carrion claw is terrified of and hates magical light.

Carrion claws hunt in packs, with one claw feigning injury on a floor, while the rest of its pack circle prey along the walls and ceiling to drop and attack with surprise.

Carrion claws are used by drow to hunt down elves frequenting their underground lairs. Forward posts of the dark elves usually have up to a dozen carrion claws used for shock troops against elven incursions.

Credit

Original author John Bentley Webb
Originally appearing in *Rappan Athuk* (© Frog God Games/John Bentley Webb, 2012)

Cavern Crawler

This creature appears to be a wild mix of giant centipede and slate gray reptile.

CAVERN CRAWLER	CR 4

XP 1,200
N Medium magical beast
Init +2; **Senses** darkvision 60 ft., low-light vision;
Perception +10

AC 20, touch 12, flat-footed 18 (+2 Dex, +8 natural)
hp 51 (6d10+18)
Fort +8; **Ref** +7; **Will** +3

Speed 30 ft., climb 30 ft.
Melee bite +11 (1d8+6 plus disease)

Str 19, **Dex** 15, **Con** 17, **Int** 2, **Wis** 12, **Cha** 6
Base Atk +6; **CMB** +10; **CMD** 22 (34 vs. trip)
Feats Power Attack, Skill Focus (Perception),
Weapon Focus (bite)
Skills Climb +22, Perception +10; **Racial
Modifiers** +4 Climb

Environment any underground
Organization solitary, gang (2–5), or
swarm (6–12)
Treasure none

Disease (Ex) *Cavern Sickness*:
Bite—injury; *save DC 16 Fort;
onset* 1 minute; *frequency* 1
day; *effect* 1d2 Str damage
and –2 penalty on all attack
rolls, checks, and saves
while underground; *cure* 2
consecutive saves. *Note:*
Failing two consecutive saves
results in the victim being
affected as if by a *confusion*
spell for the duration of
the disease. The save DC is
Constitution-based.

Cavern crawlers are subterranean creatures that make their lairs in narrow pits and shafts, feeding on cave rats, monstrous centipedes and spiders, and other such underground denizens. They are feared by subterranean dwellers for their toxic bite which causes its victims to become delusional or lost in deep dark cavern recesses.

Cavern crawlers lair in areas where food is plentiful; when their source of food runs out, they move the entire lair to a new area, digging new tunnels and chambers as needed by the nest. A cavern crawler can go roughly a week without food before it begins to exhibit signs of starvation. Many resort to cannibalism before that happens however. A cavern crawler nest consists of a single female and several male workers and soldiers. The workers hunt for and supply needed food for the nest while the soldiers guard the female and young. The female lays 10–20 eggs at one time which are buried beneath the ground in a special chamber dug off the main chamber of the lair. Eggs hatch 60–90 days after incubation and young reach maturity in about 12 months.

A cavern crawler has a reptilian head similar to that of an iguana and eighteen short clawed legs on each side of its body which allows it to climb on any rocky surface with ease. Its body is slate gray and lighter on the underside. Its legs are covered in short bristles of dark gray or black. A typical cavern crawler can reach lengths of 6 feet or more. Some species up to 12 feet long are rumored to have been encountered by unsuspecting adventurers, but these reports have yet to be confirmed.

A cavern crawler attacks from ambush, clinging to stalactites or overhangs and dropping on its unsuspecting prey. The target is subjected to repeated bites and dragged to a safe place before being devoured by the cavern crawler.

Char Shambler

The humanoid creature looks like a mass of charred skin, burned black and hard with cracks showing raw, red flesh beneath. Visible waves of heat rise from this creature and a miasma of foul smoke seems to follow its every shuffling step, and the stench of scorched flesh and acrid smoke clings to its flesh.

CHAR SHAMBLER — CR 11

XP 12,800
CE Medium magical beast (fire)
Init +4; **Senses** darkvision 60 ft., low-light vision; **Perception** +7
Aura desecrating aura (20 ft.), smoke cloud (10 ft., DC 24), stench (10 ft., DC 22, 1d8 rounds)
AC 25, touch 10, flat-footed 25 (+15 natural)

hp 147 (14d10+70)
Fort +14; **Ref** +9; **Will** +6
Immune fire
Weaknesses vulnerability to cold

Speed 20 ft.
Melee bite +19 (1d6+4 plus 1d6 fire), 2 claws +18 (1d4+4 plus 1d6 fire plus grab)
Special Attacks burning touch

Str 18, **Dex** 10, **Con** 20, **Int** 7, **Wis** 10, **Cha** 12
Base Atk +14; **CMB** +18 (+22 grapple); **CMD** 28
Feats Ability Focus (smoke cloud), Cleave, Improved Initiative, Iron Will, Power Attack, Skill Focus (Stealth), Weapon Focus (bite)
Skills Intimidate +6, Perception +7, Stealth +11
Languages Undercommon (cannot speak)

Environment any land or underground near cities
Organization solitary or pair
Treasure none

Burning Touch (Su) A char shambler that wins a grapple check establishes a hold, latching onto the opponent's body and automatically doing bite damage each round that the hold is maintained. In addition the fire damage from the bite attack increases from 1d6 on the first round to 3d6 points of damage on the third round. As the char shambler makes this attack it slowly begins charring its opponent. If it kills an opponent in this manner, the victim's flesh and tissues are completely charred away while the char shambler inhales the resulting smoke for its sustenance. It then devours the scorched and crumbling bones in 1d4 rounds.
Desecrating Aura (Su) Through the sheer foulness of its presence, a char shambler emits an aura within a 20-foot radius similar in effect to the secondary function of a *desecrate* spell (i.e. cutting off an area's connection to a non-associated deity and countering *consecrate*). This effect does not offer any bonuses to undead within the radius. Furthermore, it counters and dispels spells with the good descriptor within its area as if it was casting *dispel magic* as a 5th-level wizard.
Smoke Cloud (Ex) In addition to its stench, a char shambler continually gives off a cloud of acrid smoke from its scorched flesh. This cloud likewise affects all within 10 feet of the char shambler. The smoke provides concealment (20% miss chance) to those within the cloud and they must make a Fortitude save each round (DC 24, +1 per previous check) or spend that round coughing and choking. This is saving throw in addition to the sickening effects of the char shambler's stench. A character who chokes for 2 consecutive rounds takes 1d6 points of nonlethal damage. The save DC is Constitution-based and includes a +2 bonus from its Ability Focus feat. A char shambler is immune to the effects of smoke (its own or otherwise) and ignores the concealment it provides as well.

A char shambler is the result of a failed experiment to create a creature known as a charfiend (see *Creature Collection* by **Sword and Sorcery Studios**) from some base stock. The only documented examples come from the work of the lich Saca-Baroo and his experiments with the silid race (see *The Tome of Horrors Complete* by **Frog God Games**), but other examples may exist.

As described, a char shambler's skin is charred and broken, and the creature lives in constant searing pain from the failed process that created it. It typically stands 6 to 7 feet tall and weighs 300 pounds. Its face is a mask of charred flesh hiding the appearance of the original creature. This tough, charred shell provides it with good natural armor.

Whether a char shambler can speak or not is unknown, as none have ever been known to. They do respond to commands in Common when under magical compulsion or a similar condition.

A char shambler's existence is typically occupied by its never-ending desire to feed, and its actions tend to follow this course. When prey is spotted, it tries to disperse its enemies with its stench and smoke cloud so that it can focus on capturing and feeding on one individual without distractions.

Credit
Original author Greg A. Vaughan
Originally appearing in *Slumbering Tsar* (© Frog God Games/ Greg A. Vaughan, 2012)

Chike (Croc Folk)

This green-scaled reptilian humanoid is powerfully built and has the head of a crocodile.

CHIKE	CR 2

XP 600
NE Large humanoid (reptilian)
Init +0; **Senses** low-light vision; **Perception** +8

AC 11, touch 9, flat-footed 11 (+2 natural, −1 size)
hp 30 (4d8+12)
Fort +7; **Ref** +1; **Will** +1

Speed 30 ft., swim 30 ft.
Melee battleaxe +6 (2d6+4), bite +1 (1d8+2) or 2 claws +6 (1d6+4), bite +6 (1d8+4)
Space 10 ft.; **Reach** 10 ft.

Str 18, **Dex** 11, **Con** 16, **Int** 7, **Wis** 10, **Cha** 11
Base Atk +3; **CMB** +8; **CMD** 18
Feats Power Attack, Skill Focus (Perception)
Skills Perception +8, Stealth −2 (+6 in water), Swim +13;
Racial Modifiers +4 Perception, +8 Stealth in water
Languages Chike
SQ crocodile empathy, hold breath

Environment temperate and warm marshes and rivers
Organization solitary, pair, raiding party (3–6 plus 2–3 crocodiles), band (7–12), or tribe (20–40 plus 4–6 crocodiles plus 1–2 dire crocodiles)
Treasure standard (battleaxe, other treasure)

Crocodile Empathy (Ex) A chike can communicate and empathize with crocodiles and dire crocodiles. They can use Diplomacy to alter such an animal's attitude, and when doing so gain a +4 racial bonus on the check.
Hold Breath (Ex) A chike can hold its breath for a number of rounds equal to 4 times its Constitution score before it risks drowning.

Chike are savage crocodilian humanoids (called Crocfolk by other races) that make their homes deep within swamps and marshlands. They are believed to be descended from or related to actual crocodiles, though scholars cannot find a link between the two somewhat related creatures. Chike usually live in small tribal villages of up to 40 individuals led by a tribal leader (usually the strongest of the group). Buildings are constructed of whatever natural resources and materials the chike can find. Larger tribes also have one or two shamans in their midst. Chike are extremely territorial, generally sharing their domain only with actual crocodiles. Some tribes however do associate with marsh-dwelling races such as lizardfolk engaging in trade and allying against common enemies.

Chike are diurnal hunters, preferring the heat of the day vs. the cold and darkness of night. Favored meals include birds, fish, humans, goblins, and reptiles (including other chike if food truly becomes scarce). Being cold-blooded, a chike's metabolism allows it to survive up to 3 months without eating.

Chike males stand over 8 feet tall while females stand just about 8 feet tall on average. Greenish-brown scales cover the chike's back while their sides and underbellies are generally smooth and lighter in color. Chike reproduce on average once per year with the female laying up to six eggs at a time. Eggs are buried deep within their muddy lair in a special incubation hut. The female spends most of her time with the eggs until they hatch. Both the eggs and young are protected by all adults in the tribe. Females fight to the death to protect their eggs and young.

Chike are feared by many other races for their brutality and savagery in battle. These creatures prefer to use weapons and a fearsome bite, but particularly savage chike forego weapons and simply rend their opponents to pieces using their powerful claws. When hunting, chike submerge in water, leaving only their eyes and snout exposed. When their quarry moves within range, chike spring to attack. Though chike possess tails, they do not normally use them in combat.

Chuul-Ttaen

A thick armored shell protects this Abyssal-dwelling lobster-like creature. Tiny glowing-red eyes gleam above a mouth full of writhing tentacles.

CHUUL-TTAEN	CR 9

XP 6,400
CE Large aberration (aquatic)
Init +7; **Senses** blindsight 60 ft.; darkvision 60 ft.;
Perception +19
AC 22, touch 12, flat-footed 19 (+3 Dex, +10 natural, –1 size)

hp 138 (14d8+56)
Fort +8; **Ref** +7; **Will** +11
Defensive Abilities darkvision camouflage; **Immune** poison
Weakness light blindness

Speed 30 ft., swim 20 ft.
Melee 2 claws +17 (2d6+7 plus grab)
Space 10 ft.; **Reach** 5 ft.
Special Attacks constrict (3d6+7), larvae spray, paralytic tentacles

Str 25, **Dex** 16, **Con** 18, **Int** 10, **Wis** 14, **Cha** 5
Base Atk +10; **CMB** +18 (+22 grapple); **CMD** 31 (35 vs. trip)
Feats Ability Focus (paralysis), Alertness, Blind-Fight, Combat Reflexes, Improved Initiative, Improved Natural Attack (claw), Weapon Focus (claw)
Skills Knowledge (nature) +10, Perception +23, Sense Motive +11, Stealth +13, Swim +32
Languages Common, Undercommon
SQ amphibious

Environment warm subterranean lakes and rivers
Organization solitary, pair, or pack (3–6)
Treasure standard

Darkvision Camouflage (Ex) A chuul-ttaen is virtually impossible to detect solely using darkvision. A chuul-ttaen is considered invisible (+40 Stealth or +20 Stealth when moving) when encountered in the dark by a creature using darkvision. In lit areas, a chuul-ttaen appears as a ghostly white surface-dwelling chuul.
Larvae Spray (Ex) Once per week as a free action, a female chuul-ttaen can release a spray (15-foot cone) of minute barbed larvae. The initial blast deals 1d8 points of damage and injects larvae into the opponent's body. The affected creature must succeed on a DC 23 Fortitude save to avoid implantation. The save DC is Constitution based. If a chuul-ttaen implants larvae into a paralyzed or otherwise helpless creature, it gets no saving throw. The larvae pupate over the course of 10 days. The host becomes increasing ill suffering a –1 to Strength, Constitution and Dexterity each day of the pupation (–10 maximum) as the pupae absorb nutrients. At the end of the 10 day gestation, 2d4 Diminutive chuul-ttaen burst from the host, killing it in the process. A *remove disease* or *heal* spell rids a victim of the larvae/pupae as does a DC 25 Heal check. If the check fails, the healer can try again, but each attempt (successful or not) deals 1d4 points of damage to the patient. The ability score damage heals normally after the larvae/pupae have been removed.

Paralytic Tentacles (Ex) A chuul-ttaen can transfer a grappled victim from a claw to its tentacles as a move action. The tentacles grapple with the same strength as the claw but deal no damage, instead exuding a paralytic secretion. Anyone held in the tentacles must succeed on a DC 23 Fortitude save each round on the chuul-ttaen's turn or be paralyzed for 6 rounds. The save DC is Constitution-based. While held in the tentacles, paralyzed or not, a victim automatically takes 1d8+7 points of damage each round from the creature's mandibles.

Chuul-ttaens are similar to their normal chuul cousins, possessing many of the same skills, attacks and defenses.

The ttaen versions are said to swim in the cold depths of the world and only find their way to the surface when summoned by particularly vile wizards. Others claim they are simply underground albino versions of a normal chuul – albeit a more intelligent and deadly monstrosity. The heavily armored chuul-ttaens are excellent swimmers, and often rise up from the depths to grab land-bound creatures in their claws and tentacles.

Some scholars say the ttaen addition to their names is a designation of royalty or a higher ranking in chuul society, although this has not been confirmed.

The ttaens are able to communicate more easily with other races via a raspy Common speech. Chuul-ttaens have little interest in conversation, however, and are much more likely to attack before asking questions. Only extremely powerful foes give them pause and might warrant words before weapons.

Underground races fear the chuul-ttaens, claiming the hideous creatures were bred to wipe out all life in the tunnels under the land. They are perfect assassins and even the deadly drow fear these versions that can hide from darkvision.

Credit

Original author Gary Schotter & Jeff Harkness
Originally appearing in *Splinters of Faith Adventure 8: Pains of Scalded Glass* (© Frog God Games/ Gary Schotter & Jeff Harkness, 2011)

Cimota

A figure materializes out of the surrounding shadows. It has the black cloak and cowl of a monk, floating in the air with no visible body. Menacing green eyes glare from inside the dark hood.

CIMOTA	CR 4

XP 1,200
LE Medium undead
Init +7; **Senses** darkvision 60 ft., lifesense; **Perception** +10
Aura unnatural aura (30 ft.)

AC 18, touch 13, flat-footed 15 (+5 natural, +3 Dex)
hp 47 (5d8+25)
Fort +6; **Ref** +4; **Will** +6
Defensive Abilities channel resistance +2, displacement, unholy existence; **Immune** cold, electricity, undead traits; **SR** 12

Speed fly 60 ft. (good)
Melee 2 claws +6 (1d6+3/19–20)
Special Attack manifestation

Str 16, **Dex** 16, **Con** —, **Int** 14, **Wis** 14, **Cha** 21
Base Atk +3; **CMB** +6; **CMD** 19
Feats Combat Reflexes, Improved Initiative, Weapon Finesse
Skills Diplomacy +10, Fly +7, Intimidate +13, Knowledge (planes) +7, Perception +10, Sense Motive +10, Stealth +11
Languages Common, Infernal

Environment any
Organization solitary, pair, or haunt (3–6)
Treasure standard

Displacement (Su) Cimota manifest on the Prime Material Plane as a shifting cloud of shadows that coalesce into their cloaked and hooded forms. On any round that a cimota first manifests (see below), its shifting forms affect it as a displacement spell. Attacks on a cimota at this time have a 50% miss chance as if the cimota had total concealment. Unlike actual total concealment, this displacement does not prevent enemies from targeting a cimota normally. This effect is canceled one round after a cimota manifests, or if a cimota takes any action in its new locale.
Lifesense (Su) A cimota notices and locates living creatures within 60 ft., just as if it possessed the blindsight ability.
Manifestation (Su) As a standard action, a cimota can transport itself via planar travel from any point on the Prime Material Plane to another point within its defined area, or within 300 ft. of the artifact to which it is bound. A cimota may also lurk on the Negative Material Plane, prepared to manifest on the Prime Material if certain conditions are met, such as trespassers entering the area they are doomed to guard. A cimota cannot attack or move in the same round in which it manifests, although it may manifest as partial surprise action before initiative. A cimota benefits from displacement (see above) on the round in which it first manifests.
Unholy Existence (Su) Although it is possible to temporarily destroy a cimota's physical form, it will return in 1d6 days, manifesting again to continue its unholy existence. The only way to permanently destroy a cimota is to disrupt its existence by consecrating the ground to which it is tied or the destruction of the artifact to which it is bound. Sometimes, significant alteration of an unholy place, such as demolition of an evil temple or burning a haunted forest, could cause cimota to fade away permanently.

Although their physical forms may be damaged by normal attacks, their unholy existence grants them SR 17. Because cimota exist partially on the Negative Material Plane they are subject to banishment or other spells that affect outsiders.
Unnatural Aura (Su) Animals do not willingly approach within 30 ft. of a cimota unless a master makes a DC 25 Handle Animal, Ride, or wild empathy check. This aura takes effect when a cimota manifests on the Prime Material Plane. Animals that come within 30 ft. of a place where cimota are lurking on the Negative Material Plane, or an artifact to which a cimota is bound; Will be uneasy and show signs of disquiet.

GUARDIAN CIMOTA	CR 6

XP 2,400
LE Medium undead
Init +8; **Senses** darkvision 60 ft., lifesense; **Perception** +13
Aura unnatural aura (30 ft.)

AC 20, touch 14, flat-footed 16 (+6 natural, +4 Dex)
hp 85 (8d8+48)
Fort +8; **Ref** +7; **Will** +8
Defensive Abilities channel resistance +4, displacement, unholy existence; **Immune** cold, electricity, undead traits; **SR** 15

Speed fly 60 ft. (good)
Melee 2 scimitars +11 (1d6+4 plus 1d6 negative energy/18–20, evil-aligned)
Special Attack manifestation, superior two-weapon fighting

Str 18, **Dex** 16, **Con** —, **Int** 14, **Wis** 14, **Cha** 22
Base Atk +6; **CMB** +10; **CMD** 20
Feats Combat Reflexes, Improved Initiative, Lightning Reflexes, Weapon Focus (scimitar)
Skills Diplomacy +13 Fly +12, Intimidate +17, Knowledge (planes) +10, Perception +13, Sense Motive +13, Stealth +13
Languages Common, Infernal

Environment any
Organization solitary or pair
Treasure standard

Displacement (Su) Cimota manifest on the Prime Material Plane as a shifting cloud of shadows that coalesce into their cloaked and hooded forms. On any round that a cimota first manifests (see below), its shifting forms affect it as a displacement spell. Attacks on a cimota at this time have a 50% miss chance as if the cimota had total concealment. Unlike actual total concealment, this displacement does not prevent enemies from targeting a cimota normally. This effect is canceled one round after a cimota manifests, or if a cimota takes any action in its new locale.
Lifesense (Su) A cimota notices and locates living creatures within 60 feet, just as if it possessed the blindsight ability.
Manifestation (Su) As a standard action, a cimota can transport itself via planar travel from any point on the Prime Material Plane to another point within its defined area, or within 300 feet of the artifact to which it is bound. A cimota may also lurk on the Negative Material Plane, prepared to manifest on the Prime Material if certain conditions are met, such as trespassers entering the area they are doomed to guard. A cimota cannot attack or move in the same round in which it manifests, although it may manifest as partial

surprise action before initiative. A cimota benefits from displacement (see above) on the round in which it first manifests.

Superior Two-Weapon Fighting (Ex) A black skeleton usually fights with a short sword in each hand. Because of its magical nature, its Two-Weapon Fighting feat allows it to attack with both weapons at no penalty.

Unholy Existence (Su) Although it is possible to temporarily destroy a cimota's physical form, it will return in 1d6 days, manifesting again to continue its unholy existence. The only way to permanently destroy a cimota is to disrupt its existence by consecrating the ground to which it is tied or the destruction of the artifact to which it is bound. Sometimes, significant alteration of an unholy place, such as demolition of an evil temple or burning a haunted forest, could cause cimota to fade away permanently. Although their physical forms may be damaged by normal attacks, their unholy existence grants them spell resistance 17. Because cimota exist partially on the Negative Material Plane they are subject to banishment or other spells that affect outsiders.

Unnatural Aura (Su) Animals do not willingly approach within 30 feet of a cimota unless a master makes a DC 25 Handle Animal, Ride, or wild empathy check. This aura takes effect when a cimota manifests on the Prime Material Plane. Animals that come within 30 feet of a place where cimota are lurking on the Negative Material Plane, or an artifact to which a cimota is bound; Will be uneasy and show signs of disquiet.

HIGH CIMOTA — CR 9

XP 6,400
LE Medium undead
Init +8; **Senses** darkvision 60 ft., lifesense; **Perception** +20
Aura unnatural aura (30 ft.)

AC 21, touch 14, flat-footed 17 (+7 natural, +4 Dex)
hp 141 (14d8+84)
Fort +10; **Ref** +10; **Will** +12
Defensive Abilities channel resistance +4, displacement, undead traits, unholy existence; **Immune** cold, electricity; **SR** 17

Speed fly 60 ft. (good)
Melee 2 scimitars +15 (1d6+4 plus 1d6 electrical/15–20, evil-aligned)
Special Attack dark fury, manifestation, superior two-weapon fighting

Str 18, **Dex** 18, **Con** —, **Int** 14, **Wis** 16, **Cha** 22
Base Atk +10; **CMB** +14; **CMD** 28
Feats Combat Reflexes, Improved Critical (scimitar), Improved Initiative, Lightning Reflexes, Improved Lightning Reflexes, Two-Weapon Fighting, Weapon Focus (scimitar)
Skills Diplomacy +20, Fly +13, Intimidate +23, Knowledge (planes) +16, Perception +20 Sense Motive +20, Stealth +19

Languages Common, Infernal

Environment any
Organization solitary
Treasure standard

Dark Fury (Su) As a free action a high cimota may generate a field of negative energy in the form of black lightning. A high cimota may use this power at the start of combat and every 1d3 rounds thereafter. This field of energy may take the form of black lightning either in a 20 ft. radius ball around the high cimota or as a 100 foot line extending from the high cimota's invisible fingertips. Dark fury inflicts 6d6 negative energy damage on any living creature in its area of effect unless it succeeds on a DC 19 Reflex save. This save is charisma based. Undead, constructs and other non-living objects are not affected by dark fury.

Displacement (Su) Cimota manifest on the Prime Material Plane as a shifting cloud of shadows that coalesce into their cloaked and hooded forms. On any round that a cimota first manifests (see below), its shifting forms affect it as a displacement spell. Attacks on a cimota at this time have a 50% miss chance as if the cimota had total concealment. Unlike actual total concealment, this displacement does not prevent enemies from targeting a cimota normally. This effect is canceled one round after a cimota manifests, or if a cimota takes any action in its new locale.

Manifestation (Su) As a standard action, a cimota can transport itself via planar travel from any point on the Prime Material Plane to another point within its defined area, or within 300 feet of the artifact to which it is bound. A cimota may also lurk on the Negative Material Plane, prepared to manifest on the Prime Material if certain conditions are met, such as trespassers entering the area they are doomed to guard. A cimota cannot attack or move in the same round in which it manifests, although it may manifest as partial surprise action before initiative. A cimota benefits from displacement (see above) on the round in which it first manifests.

Lifesense (Su) A cimota notices and locates living creatures

41

within 60 feet, just as if it possessed the blindsight ability.

Superior Two-Weapon Fighting (Ex) A black skeleton usually fights with a short sword in each hand. Because of its magical nature, its Two-Weapon Fighting feat allows it to attack with both weapons at no penalty.

Unholy Existence (Su) Although it is possible to temporarily destroy a cimota's physical form, it will return in 1d6 days, manifesting again to continue its unholy existence. The only way to permanently destroy a cimota is to disrupt its existence by consecrating the ground to which it is tied or the destruction of the artifact to which it is bound. Sometimes, significant alteration of an unholy place, such as demolition of an evil temple or burning a haunted forest, could cause cimota to fade away permanently. Although their physical forms may be damaged by normal attacks, their unholy existence grants them spell resistance 17. Because cimota exist partially on the Negative Material Plane they are subject to banishment or other spells that affect outsiders.

Unnatural Aura (Su) Animals do not willingly approach within 30 feet of a cimota unless a master makes a DC 25 Handle Animal, Ride, or wild empathy check. This aura takes effect when a cimota manifests on the Prime Material Plane. Animals that come within 30 feet of a place where cimota are lurking on the Negative Material Plane, or an artifact to which a cimota is bound; Will be uneasy and show signs of disquiet.

Cimota are the physical manifestations of evil thoughts and actions. They exist on the Negative Material Plane, manifesting in the Prime Material as cloaked figures. Their existence is always tied to a specific area or artifact that is imbued with ancient and highly malevolent evil. A cimota is able to manifest itself anywhere within an accursed locale that has given it life, or within 300 feet of an evil artifact to which it is attached.

The physical form of a cimota is a floating figure in a monk's cassock. Green eyes glow deep within their raised cowls, but their bodies are entirely invisible. See *invisibility*, *true sight*, or some similar ability to see invisible objects will reveal a ghostly, black human figure within the cimota's cloak. Cimota are manifestations of evil that may be touched like any other creature. They take damage from normal weapons. Their unnatural existence allows them to fly on the Prime Material Plane just like an incorporeal creature, except that they cannot pass through solid objects. When a cimota is destroyed in combat only a few shreds of tattered black cloth remain to show that they ever existed.

Cimota are bound to repeat the evil thoughts and actions that created them. When they manifest they will endlessly repeat the deeds that spawned them. So, for instance, a group of cimota may haunt a ruined temple, re-enacting evil rituals. Cimota may guard an unholy site such as a city, forest or building. They will fight to the death to defend these places. Cimota who are bound to an artifact may act out the intentions of that artifact. A cimota might follow the owner of an artifact, for instance, slaying the owner's friends and associates while keeping its existence a secret. Within the parameters of their creation, cimota are capable of strategy, deception and intelligent tactics.

Cimota are created by evil energy. Their supernatural nature gives them the ability to fight with two fists or two weapons without penalty, each attack landing with the force and accuracy of a single weapon attack. Cimota attacks are either a rake of invisible claws or a blow from a fist. They are capable of delivering slashing or bludgeoning blows as needed.

Cimota are capable of speaking Common and Infernal. Their voices are either hollow, ringing and unnatural, or malevolent whispers. Most often cimota use their voices to chant or to shout out dire condemnations at intruders. They do not parley and they never negotiate unless it is to deceive mortals to their deaths.

Credit
Original author Mark R. Shipley
Originally appearing in *The Black Monastery* (© Frog God Games/ Mark R. Shipley, 2011)

Cinder Knight

This intimidating figure stands unmoving, an immense sword clutched in its hands. Wisps of smoke rise from its blackened armor.

CINDER KNIGHT	CR 11

XP 12,800
N Medium outsider (elemental, extraplanar, fire)
Init +3; **Senses** darkvision 60 ft.; **Perception** +19
Aura heat (10 ft., 1d6 fire)

AC 26, touch 11, flat-footed 25 (+9 armor, +1 Dex, +6 natural)
hp 142 (15d10+60)
Fort +15; **Ref** +8; **Will** +12
Immune elemental traits, fire; **SR** 21
Weaknesses vulnerability to cold

Speed 30 ft. (40 ft. unarmored)
Melee mwk greatsword +24/+19/+14 (2d6+10 plus 1d6 fire) or 2 slams +22 (1d4+7 plus 1d6 fire)

Str 24, **Dex** 16, **Con** 18, **Int** 11, **Wis** 12, **Cha** 11
Base Atk +15; **CMB** +22; **CMD** 35
Feats Cleave, Critical Focus, Great Cleave, Great Fortitude, Iron Will, Power Attack, Vital Strike, Weapon Focus (greatsword)
Skills Diplomacy +18, Intimidate +18, Knowledge (planes) +18, Perception +19, Sense Motive +19, Survival +19
Languages Common, Ignan

Environment any (Plane of Fire)
Organization solitary
Treasure standard (full plate armor, masterwork greatsword, other treasure)

Cinder knights are elemental creatures composed completely of fire and encased in suits of irremovable armor. Over time, the armor adheres to the cinder knight's form, and the armor chars and blackens as the flames of the cinder knight's body scorch and burns it. Cinder knights dwell on the Plane of Fire among other fire elementals and creatures. The creature's true origins are unknown, but some believe the cinder knight to be an advanced form of fire elemental or perhaps a fire elemental punished for some transgression.

A cinder knight stands over 6 feet tall and weighs 200 pounds (without its armor, its true form weighs less). The creature's true form is never seen, for when a cinder knight dies, its fires extinguish, and it vanishes in wisps of smoke, leaving only its armor behind. The armor is extremely hot to the touch and deals 1d6 points of fire damage to any creature touching it. One hour after a cinder knight dies, the armor, while still warm, can be handled without taking damage.

A cinder knight rarely attacks using natural attacks, preferring the use of weapons in combat. Greatswords are the most common weapon, followed by mauls, longswords, and flails. Regardless of the weapon used, a cinder knight deals fire damage with its fire attack (a product of the creature itself and not the weapon).

Cobalt Viper

This creature appears to be a metallic blue-scaled snake with crystal eyes. Its forked red tongue flicks from its fanged mouth.

COBALT VIPER — CR 4

XP 1,200
N Medium magical beast (extraplanar)
Init +7; **Senses** darkvision 60 ft., low-light vision, scent;
Perception +11
Aura poison (10 ft., DC 17)

AC 18, touch 13, flat-footed 15 (+3 Dex, +5 natural)
hp 42 (5d10+15)
Fort +7; **Ref** +7; **Will** +3

Speed 30 ft., climb 20 ft., swim 20 ft.
Melee bite +9 (1d8+1 plus poison)

Str 12, **Dex** 17, **Con** 16, **Int** 2, **Wis** 14, **Cha** 10
Base Atk +5; **CMB** +6; **CMD** 19 (can't be tripped)
Feats Improved Initiative, Weapon Finesse, Weapon Focus (bite)
Skills Acrobatics +15, Climb +15, Perception +11, Stealth +11, Swim +11; **Racial Modifiers** +8 Acrobatics, +4 Perception, +4 Stealth; Dexterity modifies Climb and Swim

Environment any (Plane of Molten Skies)
Organization solitary, pair, or nest (3–6)
Treasure incidental

Poison (Ex) Bite—injury; *save* DC 17 Fort; *frequency* 1/round for 6 rounds; *effect* 1d3 Con damage; *cure* 2 consecutive saves. The save DC is Constitution-based and includes a +2 racial bonus.
Poison Aura (Ex) A cobalt viper's poison is so potent, that it exudes it in an aura around its body. A creature that starts its turn within the area is subjected to the cobalt viper's poison. The poison from this aura is weaker than its bite however, and deals only 1 point of Con damage (instead of 1d3 Con damage).

GIANT COBALT VIPER — CR 7

XP 3,200
N Large magical beast (extraplanar)
Init +7; **Senses** darkvision 60 ft., low-light vision, scent;
Perception +14
Aura poison (20 ft., DC 17)

AC 22, touch 12, flat-footed 19 (+3 Dex, +10 natural, −1 size)
hp 104 (11d10+44)
Fort +11; **Ref** +10; **Will** +6

Speed 30 ft., climb 20 ft., swim 20 ft.
Melee bite +17 (2d6+9 plus poison)
Space 10 ft.; **Reach** 5 ft.

Str 22, **Dex** 17, **Con** 18, **Int** 2, **Wis** 17, **Cha** 12
Base Atk +11; **CMB** +18; **CMD** 31 (can't be tripped)
Feats Improved Initiative, Power Attack, Skill Focus (Stealth), Vital Strike, Weapon Finesse, Weapon Focus (bite)
Skills Acrobatics +16, Climb +19, Perception +14, Stealth +12, Swim +14; **Racial Modifiers** +8 Acrobatics, +4 Perception, +4 Stealth

Environment any (Plane of Molten Skies)
Organization solitary, pair, or nest (3–6)
Treasure incidental

Poison (Ex) Bite—injury; *save* DC 21 Fort; *frequency* 1/round for 6 rounds; *effect* 1d6 Con damage; *cure* 2 consecutive saves. The save DC is Constitution-based and includes a +2 racial bonus.
Poison Aura (Ex) A cobalt viper's poison is so potent, that it exudes it in an aura around its body. A creature that starts its turn within the area is subjected to the cobalt viper's poison. The poison from this aura is weaker than its bite however, and deals only 1d2 points of Con damage (instead of 1d6 Con damage).

Cobalt vipers are poisonous snakes found on the Plane of Molten Skies. Whatever magic transported the Steel Garden to that realm is thought to have brought the vipers here as well. They are indigenous to the Garden and are virtually unknown outside of it.

A cobalt viper appears to be constructed of metal; in fact its scales are actually a composite of the steel found within the Steel Garden and normal snake scales. How exactly these creatures came to exist is unknown. A typical cobalt viper is about 5 feet long though species up to 12 feet long or more have been sighted. Cobalt vipers are sometimes hunted by intelligent races for their scales. The scales are taken and fashioned into various pieces of jewelry or used to adorn armor and weapons.

Cobalt vipers are highly aggressive predators that prefer to attack from ambush. Normally, a cobalt viper trails its prey allowing its poison aura to sap the target's strength. After its prey is sufficiently weakened, the cobalt viper lunges from its hiding place and strikes.

Conshee

This creature appears to be a tiny, hairless, gray-skinned humanoid with leathery wings, small horns, and bulbous crimson eyes.

CONSHEE	CR 1/3

XP 135
CN Tiny fey
Init +2; **Senses** *detect evil, detect good*, low-light vision; **Perception** +7

AC 16 touch 14, flat-footed 14 (+2 Dex, +2 natural, +2 size)
hp 3 (1d6)
Fort +0; **Ref** +4; **Will** +3
DR 4/cold iron

Speed 30 ft., fly 50 ft. (perfect)
Melee dagger +0 (1d2–2)
Ranged short bow +4 (1d3–2)
Space 2–1/2 ft.; **Reach** 0 ft.

Spell-Like Abilities (CL 5th):
Constant—*detect evil, detect good*
3/day—*faerie fire, light, silent image* (DC 12)
2/day—*blink, entangle* (DC 12), *invisibility* (DC 13), *levitate*
1/day—*fear* (DC 15), *silence* (DC 13), *warp wood* (DC 13)

Str 6, **Dex** 15, **Con** 11, **Int** 12, **Wis** 13, **Cha** 13
Base Atk +0; **CMB** +0; **CMD** 12
Feats Alertness
Skills Bluff +5, Diplomacy +5, Escape Artist +6, Fly +18, Perception +7, Sleight of Hand +6, Stealth +14
Languages Common, Sylvan

Environment any underground
Organization troop (3–6), band (7–12), or swarm (13–22)
Treasure standard (dagger, shortbow with 20 arrows, other treasure)

Conshee make their homes in large, open subterranean caverns far from the surface world. They spend most of their days mining, collecting minerals, or simply enjoying the natural beauty of their surroundings. Conshee don't take intrusions lightly and are moved to anger quickly when their homes are threatened. The conshee have an intense dislike for mites (see the *Tome of Horrors Complete*) and generally attack them on sight. Captured mites are killed almost immediately; very rarely are they ever taken prisoner. Mites seem to dislike the conshee equally as much, though captured conshee are often kept as slaves or sold back to their conshee clan or family.

Conshee prefer ambush tactics to straight-forward combat, attacking at range with their short bows and spell-like abilities. Some conshee also use daggers, saps, and other such weapons, allowing them to attack quickly and often times unnoticed. Conshee also employ a wide array of traps, snares, and pitfalls to injure, confuse, or capture would-be opponents. The corridors and passages leading to a conshee lair are often rife with all manner of such traps and pitfalls. Conshee often employ natural poisons as well, taken from the various plants, leaves, and underground flowers near their lairs.

An adult conshee stands about 2 feet tall. It is a small lithe creature with grayish skin, a hairless body, and two leathery bat-like wings growing from its back. Its hands end in claws, though they are not strong enough to use in combat.

Seemingly made of red vapor, the crimson mist is an outstanding stealth hunter. The crimson death is vaguely humanoid in appearance, with arms, torso and a head being discernible. The creature has no distinct facial features, other than 2 glowing points where eyes should be.

CRIMSON DEATH — CR 10

XP 9,600
NE Medium aberration
Init +8; **Senses** darkvision 60 ft.; **Perception** +29

AC 24, touch 14, flat-footed 20 (+4 Dex, +10 natural)
hp 127 (17d8+51)
Fort +10; **Ref** +11; **Will** +15
DR 5/magic and silver; **SR** 21

Speed 60 ft. (30 ft. after feeding)
Melee 2 tentacles +17 (1d6 plus engulf)
Special Attacks engulf (DC 18, 1d6 plus 1d6 Con)

Str 11, **Dex** 18, **Con** 16, **Int** 17, **Wis** 16, **Cha** 16
Base Atk +12; **CMB** +16; **CMD** 26
Feats Agile Maneuvers, Great Fortitude, Improved Initiative, Iron Will, Lightning Reflexes, Skill Focus (Perception), Skill Focus (Stealth), Weapon Finesse, Weapon Focus (tentacles)
Skills Climb +20, Escape Artist +24, Knowledge (dungeoneering) +23, Perception +29, Stealth +30 (+42 in mist or fog), Survival +23, Swim +20; **Racial Modifiers** +12 Stealth in mist or fog
Languages Aklo (can't speak)
SQ susceptibility

Environment swamp or underground

Organization solitary
Treasure incidental

Engulf (Ex) When a crimson death strikes a target with one of its tentacles, it can immediately make an engulf attack, including moving into the opponent's square. Targeted creatures can make attacks of opportunity against the crimson death, but if they do so, they are not entitled to a saving throw against the engulf attack. Those who do not attempt attacks of opportunity can attempt a Reflex (DC 18) save to avoid being engulfed—on a success, they are pushed back or aside (target's choice) as the crimson death moves forward. Engulfed opponents gain the pinned condition, are in danger of suffocating, are trapped within the crimson death's body until they are no longer pinned, and suffer 1d6 points of damage and 1d6 points of Constitution damage every round. A victim reduced to 0 Constitution dies. The save DC is Strength-based.

Susceptibility (Ex) After draining its victim's Constitution, the crimson death, sated from its feeding, moves at half its normal speed, loses its racial bonus to Stealth checks (because it flushes crimson, hence the name), and suffers a −4 circumstance penalty to AC. These effects last for 1 hour.

A crimson death attacks from ambush, usually hiding in naturally occurring fog and waiting for potential prey to wander close. Often times, a crimson death uses sound (imitating cries for help, for example) in an attempt to lure a victim into its grasp.

A crimson death can understand Aklo, although it does not speak.

Credit
Originally appearing in *Rappan Athuk Reloaded* (© Necromancer Games, 2006)

46

Crysolax

This creature looks like a horrible amalgam of a centipede and a praying mantis made out of translucent white crystal with brilliant multifaceted blue eyes.

CRYSOLAX   CR 15

XP 51,200
LE Huge outsider (earth, elemental, extraplanar)
Init +7; **Senses** darkvision 60 ft.; **Perception** +24
Aura scintillating aura (20 ft.; DC 20 Will)

AC 27, touch 11, flat-footed 24 (+3 Dex, +16 natural, –2 size)
hp 172 (15d10+90)
Fort +17; **Ref** +12; **Will** +7
DR 10/magic and bludgeoning; **Immune** blindness, light-based effects; **Resist** cold 10, electricity 10, fire 10; **SR** 26
Weakness vulnerable to sonic

Speed 50 ft.
Melee 2 claws +22 (1d8+8/19–20 plus grab), bite +21 (2d6+8 plus 1d6 Dex damage)
Space 15 ft.; **Reach** 10 ft.
Special Attacks petrifying bite, scintillating aura

Str 27, **Dex** 16, **Con** 22, **Int** 12, **Wis** 14, **Cha** 16
Base Atk +15; **CMB** +25 (+29 grapple); **CMD** 38 (50 vs. trip)
Feats Ability Focus (petrifying bite), Alertness, Improved Critical (claw), Improved Initiative, Power Attack, Weapon Focus (claw), Great Fortitude, Vital Strike
Skills Acrobatics +21, Climb +26, Escape Artist +21, Knowledge (planes) +19, Perception +24, Sense Motive +4, Stealth +13, Survival +20
Languages Common, Terran

Environment any (Plane of Earth)
Organization solitary or carat (2–4)
Treasure incidental coins and items; twice standard gemstones

Petrifying Bite (Ex) The bite of a crysolax deals 1d6 points of Dexterity damage. A creature reduced to Dex 0 is turned to crystal (as the *stone to flesh* spell) permanently if it fails a DC 25 Fortitude save. The save DC is Constitution-based and includes a +2 bonus from the crysolax's Ability Focus feat.
Scintillating Aura (Ex) As long as there is a light source present within 30 feet of it, the crysolax constantly radiates an aura that duplicates the effects of a *rainbow pattern* spell (CL 15th). The save is Charisma-based.

A terrifying predator native to the Plane of Earth (and also a pocket dimension known as the Demiplane of Crystal), the crysolax is a hunter, active most often during the daylight hours. During the day, natural sunlight refracts from the crysolax causing it to appear to be a multitude of different colors. It uses this natural sunlight to activate its aura when hunting or in combat.

A crysolax spends its days hunting creatures native to the Plane of Earth, while at night, the creature is usually found in its lair, a large and complex maze of twisting corridors, caverns, and spiraling tunnels located deep within the rocky earth of its native plane. A crysolax lair usually consists of 2–4 adults and twice that number in smaller noncombatant crysolax. The female lays 4–8 large crystal eggs usually once per year. These eggs usually hatch within 60 days and a crysolax reaches maturity within two years. Its lair is also scattered with any treasure it may have gathered. Though not a creature known for collecting treasure, a crysolax is quite fond of gemstones, and as such a large amount of said treasure usually can be found in its lair. While a crysolax has no need to eat, some do enjoy ingesting certain gemstone (the exact type seems to vary between each crysolax).

A crysolax attacks with its bite, attempting to petrify the strongest opponents first. It also rakes and slashes with its razor-sharp claws or grabs a foe and repeatedly subjects it to its bite attack, knowing that eventually the victim will succumb to its petrifying nature.

Daochyn

This creature resembles a manta-ray in general outline. It is a bat-like, with a long, powerful tail and membranous "wings" with which it effortlessly darts through the water. The mouth of a creature is wide, like a shark's, and contains multiple rows of razor-sharp serrated teeth. The tip of each wing ends in cruel-looking claws.

DAOCHYN	CR 5

XP 1,600
N Medium outsider (extraplanar, water)
Init +3; **Senses** darkvision 60 ft.; **Perception** +12

AC 20, touch 14, flat-footed 16 (+3 Dex, +1 dodge, +6 natural)
hp 76 (8d10+32)
Fort +10; **Ref** +9; **Will** +3
DR 5/magic; **Immune** cold

Speed swim 50 ft.
Melee bite +11 (1d6+3), 2 claws +11 (1d4+3), tail slap +6 (1d6+1) or tongue +11 (desalination and grab)
Special Attacks desalination

Str 17, **Dex** 16, **Con** 18, **Int** 7, **Wis** 12, **Cha** 12
Base Atk +8; **CMB** +11 (+15 grapple); **CMD** 25 (can't be tripped)
Feats Dodge, Lunge, Mobility, Power Attack
Skills Knowledge (planes) +9, Perception +12, Stealth +14 (+22 in water), Swim +22; **Racial Modifiers** +8 Stealth in water

Environment any (Plane of Water)
Organization solitary, pair, or pod (4–12)
Treasure none

Desalination (Ex) The touch of a daochyn's tongue wicks away salt and other vital minerals from a living opponent, dealing 1d2 points of Constitution damage. A daochyn that is grappling with its tongue automatically deals this damage each round to the grappled opponent for as long as it maintains the grapple. A daochyn that is grappling an opponent with its tongue cannot use its bite attack.

The daochyns (or sea phantoms), are creatures from the Plane of Water. It is uncertain how the daochyns manage to cross from their home plane to the Material Plane. Sailors' legends say that in the middle of the deepest ocean there is a massive waterspout that is the nexus of a permanent gate between this world and the Plane of Water. This waterspout has never been documented or proven to exist, however, so that tale remains in doubt. The most powerful daochyns are sometimes worshipped as gods by seafaring creatures such as sahuagin and some clans of merfolk.

Daochyns are in a constant state of motion and never stop swimming. Generally an encounter is with a solitary creature, though some do travel in pods or family units of up to twelve creatures. Sages are not sure how daochyns procreate but encounters with young have been reported (though these encounters could in fact be with smaller adult daochyns

rather than young).

On the Plane of Water daochyns sustain themselves on a diet of small elemental fish and other creatures. On the Material Plane, daochyns eat a variety of foods ranging from aquatic plants to fish to those swimmers unlucky enough to run across a hungry sea phantom.

A typical daochyn is 5 feet long and weighs 150 pounds.

In combat, a daochyn lashes out with its tongue, attempting to weaken stronger opponents with its desalination attack, while attacking other opponents with its tail and raking claws. An opponent that gets too close is subjected to a bite from its massive jaws. A daochyn has the ability to alter its coloration to appear almost transparent while in water and does so if attacking from ambush or attempting to flee.

Dark Custodian

A dark robed and hooded figure moves across the floor effortlessly, almost as if floating. Its hands are tucked away in the sleeves of its cassock, and where its face should be is only the blackness of the pit.

DARK CUSTODIAN	CR 9

XP 6,400
NE Medium undead (incorporeal)
Init +7; **Senses** darkvision 60 ft., lifesense 60 ft.; **Perception** +25
Aura unnatural aura (30 ft.)

AC 16, touch 16, flat-footed 12 (+2 deflection, +3 Dex, +1 dodge)
hp 91 (14d8+28)
Fort +6; **Ref** +7; **Will** +11
Defensive Abilities channel resistance +4, incorporeal;
Immune undead traits
Weaknesses sunlight powerlessness

Speed fly 80 ft. (perfect)
Melee incorporeal touch +13 (1d8 plus energy drain and incorporeal grab)
Special Attacks devour, energy drain (1 level, DC 19), silence of the grave

Str 20, **Dex** 16, **Con** —, **Int** 14, **Wis** 14, **Cha** 15
Base Atk +10; **CMB** +15 (+19 grapple); **CMD** 31
Feats Blind-Fight, Dodge, Improved Initiative, Mobility, Skill Focus (Perception), Spring Attack, Weapon Finesse
Skills Fly +28, Intimidate +19, Knowledge (religion) +19, Perception +25, Spellcraft +19, Stealth +20
Languages Abyssal, Common, Infernal

Environment any
Organization solitary, gang (2–4), or swarm (6–11)
Treasure none

Devour (Su) Any living creature that is pinned by a dark custodian's grapple gains two negative levels per round that the hold is maintained rather than the standard one negative level of its energy drain. Any creature slain by the dark custodian's energy drain is left a steaming, bloody skeleton, all of its soft tissues having been consumed by the undead.
Incorporeal Grab (Su) If a dark custodian hits with an incorporeal touch, it can then attempt to start a grapple as a free action without provoking an attack of opportunity. During the course of this grapple, the dark custodian becomes partially corporeal and its opponent becomes partially incorporeal. This has no game effect other than allowing the dark custodian to use its Strength bonus in its CMB. If it wins the grapple, it establishes a hold at which point its opponent becomes completely incorporeal, as well, along with the dark custodian. The dark custodian automatically begins to devour the held opponent each round he is held. The opponent remains incorporeal until he manages to break the grapple at which time he becomes immediately corporeal. If this occurs within a solid object, the opponent

is forcefully ejected from the object's nearest surface, and the opponent takes 1d6 points of damage in the process. The dark custodian must then try to hit with its incorporeal touch attack again to try to reestablish the grapple. Once the dark custodian has an opponent pinned, it attempts to drag him away to devour him in peace. **Lifesense (Su)** A dark custodian notices and locates living creatures within 60 feet, just as if it possessed the blindsight ability. It also senses the strength of their life force automatically, as if it had cast *deathwatch*. Walls less than 5 feet thick are no impediment to this ability.
Silence of the Grave (Su) As a standard action a dark custodian can use its silence of the grave ability. This creates a *silence* effect as the spell in a 20-foot radius for 7 rounds. This silent zone acts as a *desecrate* spell giving the dark custodian a +1 profane bonus on attack rolls, damage rolls and saving throws, as well as, imposing a –3 profane penalty on turn checks. Any living creature within the area of affect must succeed on a DC 19 Will save or become dazed for 1 round. A new save is allowed each round. This is a sonic mind-affecting compulsion effect. Because it takes place in an area of *silence*, it cannot be counteracted by bardic music. A creature that successfully saves cannot be affected by the *daze* effect of the same dark custodian's silence of the grave for 24 hours. The save DC is Charisma-based.
Sunlight Powerlessness (Ex) Dark custodians are powerless in natural sunlight (not merely a *daylight* spell) and flee from it. A dark custodian caught in sunlight cannot attack and can take only a single move action or attack action in a round.
Unnatural Aura (Su) Animals, whether wild or domesticated, can sense the unnatural presence of a dark custodian at a distance of 30 feet. They do not willingly approach nearer than that and panic if forced to do so; they remain panicked as long as they are within that range.

Dark custodians are the undead remains of evil clerics tasked to remain behind after death and guard the sacred places of their vile worship. They hate all living things and seek to devour any who come within their guarded precincts. They do not require these feedings for sustenance but rather merely take pleasure in the carnage and brutality.

A dark custodian's true form is hidden beneath its ghostly burnoose with a lightless black void where its face should be. Only in combat are its hands seen, appearing pale with thickened, clawlike nails. They understand the languages they knew in life, but cannot speak.

A dark custodian prefers to attack from ambush, leaping through a solid wall to make an incorporeal grab before dragging its prey back through with it. When attacking in groups they usually surround their prey and use their silence of the grave abilities before trying to grab and drag individual opponents in different directions to be consumed.

Credit
Original author Greg A. Vaughan
Originally appearing in *Slumbering Tsar* (© Frog God Games/ Greg A. Vaughan, 2012)

Deathstroke Serpent

This gigantic serpent has dark green and black mottled scales. There appears to be a hint of intelligence behind its pale gray eyes.

DEATHSTROKE SERPENT	CR 12

XP 19,200
CE Huge magical beast
Init +5; **Senses** darkvision 60 ft., low-light vision, scent, *see invisibility*; **Perception** +19

AC 25, touch 10, flat-footed 23 (+1 Dex, +1 dodge, +15 natural, −2 size)
hp 161 (14d10+70 plus 14)
Fort +14; **Ref** +10; **Will** +6
DR 10/cold iron; **Resist** cold 10, electricity 10, fire 10; **SR** 23

Speed 20 ft., climb 20 ft., swim 20 ft.
Melee bite +24 (3d6+16/19–20 plus grab)
Space 15 ft.; **Reach** 10 ft.
Special Attacks constrict (3d6+16)
Spell-Like Abilities (CL 14th; melee touch +23, ranged touch +13):
Constant—*see invisibility*
At will—*detect good, detect magic*
3/day—*lightning bolt* (DC 15), *magic circle against good, unholy aura* (DC 20), *unholy blight* (DC 16), *wall of fire*
1/day—*blasphemy* (DC 19), *desecrate, greater teleport* (self plus 50 lbs. of objects only)

Str 33, **Dex** 13, **Con** 20, **Int** 12, **Wis** 14, **Cha** 14
Base Atk +14; **CMB** +27 (+31 grapple); **CMD** 39 (can't be tripped)
Feats Dodge, Improved Critical (bite), Improved Initiative, Power Attack, Skill Focus (Perception), Toughness, Weapon Focus (bite)
Skills Acrobatics +19, Climb +25, Knowledge (any) +8, Knowledge (arcana) +3, Knowledge (planes) +8, Knowledge (religion) +3, Perception +19, Stealth +7, Swim +19; **Racial Modifiers** +8 Acrobatics, +4 Perception, +4 Stealth
Languages Common, Undercommon

Environment temperate and warm lands and underground
Organization solitary
Treasure standard

Deathstroke serpents are greatly feared predators found dwelling in forests, jungles, marshes, and bogs. These creatures generally sustain themselves on a diet of large game and other animals, but eat anything readily available, including humanoids if the opportunity presents itself. These creatures are generally solitary, so mating and reproduction information is unknown, though scholars assume these rituals mimic other serpentine creatures.

Deathstrokes, because of their intelligence and cunning are often worshipped by scaly humanoids as gods or quasi-deities. The deathstroke does nothing to dismiss these beliefs as the worshippers keep it supplied with a steady supply of animal and humanoid sacrifices.

Deathstroke serpents can reach lengths of 50 feet. Colorations may also vary depending on climate and habit, but most deathstrokes are dark green with mottled scales. Deathstroke serpents spend large parts of their days sleeping, being mostly active at night. Prey is often ambushed and killed, and then returned to the deathstroke's lair to be devoured. After feeding, deathstrokes can sleep for up to one week.

A deathstroke serpent attacks by biting and grabbing its opponent. A grappled foe is quickly wrapped in its coils and constricted, while remaining foes are assaulted by the deathstroke's lightning bolts and blasphemy spell-like abilities.

Defender Globe

This small glowing orb radiates light similar to that of a lantern. Small filaments of electrical energy dance across its illuminated surface.

DEFENDER GLOBE	CR 3

XP 800
N Small outsider (elemental, native)
Init +3; **Senses** darkvision 60 ft.; **Perception** +8

AC 17, touch 17, flat-footed 13 (+2 deflection, +3 Dex, +1 dodge, +1 size)
hp 26 (4d10+4)
Fort +2; **Ref** +7; **Will** +5
Defensive Abilities awareness, defensive aura; **Immune** electricity; **Resist** cold 10, fire 10

Speed 5 ft., 40 ft. fly (perfect)
Ranged electrical bolt +8 (2d6 electricity)
Spell-Like Abilities (CL 4th):
Continuous—*light*

Str 4, **Dex** 16, **Con** 12, **Int** 4, **Wis** 12, **Cha** 14
Base Atk +4; **CMB** +0; **CMD** 16 (can't be tripped)
Feats Dodge, Mobility
Skills Fly +20, Knowledge (planes) +4, Perception +8

Environment any
Organization solitary
Treasure incidental

Awareness (Ex) A defender globe cannot be surprised or flanked.
Defensive Aura (Ex) A defender globe adds its Charisma bonus to its AC and CMD as a deflection bonus.
Flight (Su) A defender globe can cease or resume flight as a free action. The ability is supernatural, so it becomes ineffective in an *antimagic field*, and the defender globe loses its ability to fly for as long as the antimagic effect persists.

This small outsider is bound by spellcasters using the *summon monster III* or *lesser planar binding* spells, serving for up to 1 day per caster level. Using more powerful incantations can bind the globes for longer periods (GM's discretion).

They can understand, but not speak, any language spoken by their summoner. The summoned globes can understand simple orders, and carries out their last order until destroyed or dismissed.

Credit
Originally appearing in *Rappan Athuk* (© Frog God Games, 2012)

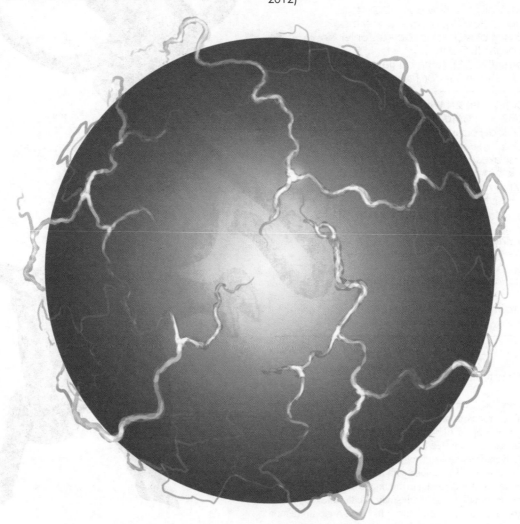

Demon, Ciratto

This powerful entity has the lower torso of a black horse and the upper torso of a charcoal-colored humanoid. Its eyes blaze the color of fire and two downward curving horns protrude from its head. Four long, sinewy snakes seem to grow from the humanoid back of this creature.

CIRATTO	CR 16

XP 76,800
CE Large outsider (chaotic, demon, evil, extraplanar)
Init +5; **Senses** darkvision 60 ft., *see invisibility*; **Perception** +24
Aura *unholy aura* (DC 24)

AC 29, touch 14, flat-footed 24 (+5 Dex, +15 natural, −1 size)
hp 187 (15d10+105)
Fort +12; **Ref** +14; **Will** +17
DR 10/good; **Immune** electricity, poison; **Resist** acid 10, cold 10, fire 10; **SR** 27

Speed 60 ft.
Melee mwk heavy mace +23/+18/+13 (2d6+8/19–20), 4 snakes +18 (1d6 plus poison), 2 hooves +17 (1d6+8)
Ranged composite longbow +19/+14/+9 (2d6+8)
Space 10 ft.; **Reach** 5 ft.
Spell-Like Abilities (CL 15th; melee touch +22, ranged touch +19):
Constant—*see invisibility*, *unholy aura* (DC 24)
At will—*call lightning* (DC 19), *greater dispel magic*, *greater teleport* (self plus 50 lbs. of objects only), *slow* (DC 19), *unholy blight* (DC 20)
1/day—*blasphemy* (DC 23), summon (level 5, 1 ciratto 20%, 1 nalfeshnee 35%, or 1d6 glabrezus 60%)

Str 27, **Dex** 21, **Con** 25, **Int** 21, **Wis** 22, **Cha** 22
Base Atk +15; **CMB** +24; **CMD** 39 (43 vs. trip)
Feats Cleave, Critical Focus, Great Cleave, Improved Critical (heavy mace), Iron Will, Power Attack, Vital Strike, Weapon Focus (snakes)
Skills Bluff +24, Diplomacy +24, Escape Artist +20, Intimidate +24, Knowledge (arcana) +20, Knowledge (planes) +23, Perception +24, Sense Motive +24, Stealth +23, Survival +24, Use Magical Device +24
Languages Abyssal, Celestial, Common, Draconic, telepathy 100 ft.

Environment any (Abyss)
Organization solitary or troop (1 ciratto and 1–4 glabrezu)
Treasure standard (masterwork heavy mace, composite longbow, other treasure)

Poison (Ex) Bite—injury; *save* DC 24 Fort; *frequency* 1/round for 6 rounds; *effect* 1d2 Constitution damage; *cure* 2 saves. The save DC is Constitution-based.

Ciratto demons are bred for combat, and as such are often found leading other demonic troops in battle. Cirattos can be found on any of the Abyssal layers in the employ of numerous lords and nobles. When not carrying out the orders of their master, they often spend their time hunting lesser demons and adventurers foolish enough to wander into the Abyss.

Ciratto demons are centaur-like demons with the lower torso of a black horse and the upper torso of a dark-skinned demon. Its head sports two large gray horns and its mouth is lined with small needle-like teeth. Four large poisonous dark mottled vipers grow from its back. A ciratto demon stands over 8 feet tall and weighs around 2,500 pounds.

Ciratto demons enjoy wading into battle. They attack with an array

of weapons including maces, morningstars, and spiked clubs. In combat, they quickly close ranks with their opponents after unleashing a barrage of spell-like abilities so they can use their hooves and poisonous snakes. Slain foes are usually devoured immediately. Those not eaten, or parts of creatures not eaten, are left for scavengers. Ciratto, while they enjoy hunting devils, never eat their flesh, finding it disgusting to both smell and taste.

Demon, Kytha

This powerful creature has bluish-black scaly skin, a triangular head, large ruby-colored eyes, and two downward-curving horns. Its mouth is filled with needle-sharp fangs, and a small ridge of spines runs from the crown of its head to the small of its back.

DEMON, KYTHA	CR 9

XP 6,400
CE Medium outsider (chaotic, demon, evil, extraplanar)
Init +7; **Senses** darkvision 60 ft.; **Perception** +22

AC 23, touch 13, flat-footed 20 (+3 Dex, +10 natural)
hp 112 (9d10+54 plus 9)
Fort +12; **Ref** +6; **Will** +8
DR 10/cold iron or good; **Immune** electricity, poison; **Resist** acid 10, cold 10, fire 10; **SR** 20

Speed 40 ft.
Melee 2 claws +16 (1d6+7), bite +16 (1d8+10/19–20), tongue +16 (1d6+7 plus poison)
Spell-Like Abilities (CL 9th; melee touch +16, ranged touch +12):
At will—*deeper darkness, greater teleport* (self plus 50 lbs. of objects only)
3/day—*enervation, silence* (DC 15)
1/day—*mass hold person* (DC 20), summon (level 4, 1 kytha 40% or 1d2 babaus 30%)

Str 24, **Dex** 16, **Con** 22, **Int** 12, **Wis** 14, **Cha** 16
Base Atk +9; **CMB** +16; **CMD** 29
Feats Blind-Fight, Cleave, Improved Initiative, Power Attack, Toughness[B], Vital Strike
Skills Bluff +15, Diplomacy +15, Intimidate +19, Knowledge (planes) +13, Perception +22, Sense Motive +14, Stealth +15;
Racial Modifiers +4 Intimidate, +8 Perception
Languages Abyssal, Abyssal, Celestial, Celestial, Draconic, Draconic, telepathy 100 ft.

Environment any (Abyss)
Organization solitary or gang (2–4)
Treasure standard

Poison (Ex) tongue—injury; *save* DC 18 Fort; *frequency* 1 round for 8 rounds; *effect* 1d6 Strength damage, creatures reduced to Str 0 suffocate; *cure* 2 saves. The save DC is Constitution-based.
Serrated Bite (Ex) A kytha's bite always deals 1–1/2 its Strength modifier on damage rolls and threatens a critical hit on a roll of 19–20.

Kytha are lesser demons found throughout the various layers of the Abyss. Though native to just about all of the Abyssal planes, they generally avoid those steeped in cold and ice (they have no particular vulnerability to cold; they just don't like it).

Kytha are often employed by the Abyssal dukes and nobles as ground troops and soldiers in their battles against one another and against interlopers from other planes. The kytha's love of blood and battle greatly enhances their usefulness in the eyes of many of the Abyssal nobility.

When not serving in the rank-and-file of some Abyssal noble's army, these monsters are found roaming the various Abyssal planes hunting and tracking down food, which to a kytha is just about anything it can catch and kill. It has a great fondness for the flesh of minor demons (dretch for example) and humans. Captured prey is usually devoured on the spot; rarely does a kytha kill something and save it for later.

A kytha stands about 7 feet tall and weighs around 300 pounds. Its skin is usually blue-black or solid black, and its eyes red. The fin-like spines running down its back are coal black.

Upon entering combat, a kytha often frightens its opponents as it seemingly changes into a mindless killing machine; roaring and growling, drooling and hissing, as it circles its prey. A kytha attacks with its wickedly-sharp claws and with its envenomed tongue. Kytha enjoy combat, especially against creatures weaker than themselves, and so they never flee unless facing overwhelming odds. Many kytha however, equate fleeing with cowardice and choose to fight to the death, no matter the odds.

Demon, Tatarux

This massive creature stands well over 10 feet tall. Its lower torso is covered in black fur and its powerful legs end in cloven hooves. The monster's eyes are black with white pupils and its mouth is filled with serrated teeth.

TATARUX	CR 13

XP 25,600
CE Large outsider (chaotic, demon, evil, extraplanar)
Init +8; **Senses** darkvision 60 ft.; **Perception** +19
Aura *unholy aura* (DC 22)

AC 28, touch 13, flat-footed 24 (+4 Dex, +15 natural, –1 size)
hp 188 (13d10+117)
Fort +19; **Ref** +8; **Will** +13
DR 10/good; **Immune** electricity, poison; **Resist** acid 10, cold 10, fire 10; **SR** 24

Speed 40 ft.
Melee 2 claws +22 (2d6+10 plus bleed), bite +22 (2d8+10/19–20)
Space 10 ft.; **Reach** 10 ft.
Special Attacks bleed (2d6), rend (2 claws, 2d6+15)
Spell-Like Abilities (CL 13th; melee touch +22, ranged touch +16):
Constant—*unholy aura* (DC 22)
At will—*detect good, greater dispel magic, greater teleport* (self plus 50 lbs. of objects only)
3/day—*blasphemy* (DC 21), *bull's strength*
1/day—*fire storm* (DC 22), *haste,* summon (level 5, tatarux, 25%, 1d4 vrocks 40%, or 1d4 gulazu 40%)

Str 30, **Dex** 18, **Con** 28, **Int** 16, **Wis** 16, **Cha** 18
Base Atk +13; **CMB** +24; **CMD** 38
Feats Awesome Blow, Great Fortitude, Improved Bull Rush, Improved Critical (bite), Improved Initiative, Iron Will, Power Attack
Skills Bluff +20, Diplomacy +20, Escape Artist +20, Intimidate +20, Knowledge (planes) +19, Perception +19, Sense Motive +19, Stealth +20, Survival +19
Languages Abyssal, Celestial, Draconic, telepathy 100 ft.

Environment any (Abyss)
Organization solitary or band (1–2 plus 2–5 vrocks)
Treasure standard

The bestial tatarux spends its days roaming the Abyss, always on the hunt. This ferocious creature relishes the blood of battle and the cries of its enemies as they fall to this monstrous creature. Though they can be found on any Abyssal plane, they prefer layers with mires and swamps or overgrown jungles. These layers offer more places for their enemies to hide, and more excitement when the

tatarux hunts them down and finally slays them.

Though quite intelligent, the tatarux prefers to embrace its animalistic side and is rarely found leading other demons. Most of their time is spent hunting, feeding, or resting. They do have an affinity for vrocks and both races can often be found hunting together.

A tatarux stands 12 feet tall and weighs just over 4,000 pounds. Its body is dark, usually black, and its fur is always black and often caked with the dried blood of those it has slain. These demons are manifested from the souls of murders and cold-blooded killers who died without remorse.

Tatarux demons charge into combat first by unleashing a *fire storm* on their foes, followed quickly by *blasphemy*. Creatures left standing are put to the tatarux's claws and ripped to pieces. Against powerful opponents, they use *bull's strength* and *haste* to deal maximum damage.

Demonic Mist

This cloud of sickly green mist seems to move as if it were alive.

DEMONIC MIST	CR 5

XP 1,600
CE Medium outsider (chaotic, evil, extraplanar)
Init +9; **Senses** darkvision 60 ft.; Perception +9

AC 16, touch 16, flat-footed 10 (+5 Dex, +1 dodge)
hp 47 (5d10+20)
Fort +8; **Ref** +9; **Will** +2
Defensive Abilities amorphous; **DR** 5/magic; **Immune** acid, cold; **Resist** fire 10; **SR** 16
Weaknesses vulnerability to wind

Speed fly 50 ft. (perfect)
Melee touch +10 (5d6)
Special Attacks psychic crush
Spell-Like Abilities (CL 5th; melee touch +10):
At will—*detect magic*
2/day—*enervation, vampiric touch*
1/day—*cause fear* (DC 14), *confusion* (DC 17)

Str —, **Dex** 21, **Con** 18, **Int** 11, **Wis** 13, **Cha** 16
Base Atk +5; **CMB** +5; **CMD** 21 (can't be tripped)
Feats Dodge, Improved Initiative, Weapon Finesse
Skills Acrobatics +13, Escape Artist +13, Fly +21, Knowledge (planes) +8, Perception +9, Stealth +13 (+21 in fog or mist); **Racial Modifiers** +8 Stealth in fog or mist
Languages Abyssal, Common; telepathy 100 ft.
SQ gaseous

Environment any (Abyss)
Organization solitary, pair, or gang (3–6)
Treasure standard

Gaseous (Ex) A demonic mist can pass through small holes, even cracks, without reducing its speed. It cannot enter water or other liquid. It has no Strength score, and cannot manipulate objects.
Psychic Crush (Su) Three times per day, as a standard action, a demonic mist can attempt to crush the mind of a single creature within 40 feet. The target must make a DC 15 Will save or take 3d6 points of damage and become sickened for 1d4+1 rounds. This is a mind-affecting effect. The save DC is Charisma-based.
Vulnerability to Wind (Ex) A demonic mist is treated as a Tiny creature for the purposes of determining the effects high wind has upon it.

Some scholars and sages believe a demonic mist is the incomplete manifestation of a demon on the Material Plane. Others conjecture it is a representation of chaos unleashed by the denizens of the Abyss. Whatever the true nature of its origin, a demonic mist is a creature wholly chaotic and evil. When encountered on the Material Plane it is most often in areas of consecrated ground such as graveyards, temples, and holy sites. In their native environment, demonic mists are found haunting the most putrid and disgusting of the Abyssal planes. Those planes covered with oozes, mires, fens, and swamps are favored by these creatures. Demonic mists have voracious appetites and always seem to be on the hunt. They are carnivorous creatures devouring just about anything they came across. Once a demonic mist slays its prey, it moves over the body and rapidly digests it, draining blood and body fluids, and leaving nothing more than a dried husk.

A demonic mist's semi-solid body is composed of a strange, sickly green and ever-shifting mist. It can change its color to a semi-translucent whitish smoke, thereby blending in and hiding in areas of normal fog and mist. When hiding in this way, a demonic mist seeks to quickly close ground with its target and attack from ambush, unleashing its psychic crush and enervating attacks at the closest and strongest opponents.

Demonic mists are often found in the employ of clerics dedicated to the demonic lords (particularly Tsathogga and Jubilex), serving as temple guards or assassins.

Devil, Dantalion (Duke of Hell)

This creature appears to be a handsome human with deep reddish-brown skin, dark hair, and fiery yellow eyes. It stands about 9 feet tall and wears robes of gold and black. Its small black horns and snake-like barbed tail betray its true origins.

DANTALION (DUKE OF HELL) — CR 24

XP 1,230,000
LE Large outsider (devil, evil, extraplanar, lawful)
Init +12; **Senses** darkvision 60 ft., *detect magic, detect thoughts,* see in darkness, *see invisibility*; **Perception** +34

AC 40, touch 25, flat-footed 32 (+8 Dex, +15 natural, –1 size, +8 profane)
hp 356 (23d10+230); regeneration 10 (good weapons, good spells)
Fort +19; **Ref** +17; **Will** +19
DR 15/good and silver; **Immune** fire, poison; **Resist** acid 10, cold 10; **SR** 35

Speed 40 ft.
Melee +4 *unholy heavy mace* +37/+32/+27/+22 (2d6+14) and tail sting +32 (1d6+10 plus poison)
Space 10 ft.; **Reach** 10 ft.
Spell-Like Abilities (CL 23rd; melee touch +32, ranged touch +35):
Constant—*detect magic, see invisibility*
At will—*blasphemy* (DC 25), *detect thoughts* (DC 20), *fireball* (DC 21), *greater dispel magic, greater scrying* (DC 25), *greater teleport* (self plus 50 lbs. of objects only), *hold person* (DC 21), *lightning bolt* (DC 21), *magic circle against good, mass charm monster* (DC 26), *power word blind, suggestion* (DC 21), *touch of idiocy, trap the soul* (DC 26), *unholy aura* (DC 26), *wall of fire, web* (DC 20)
3/day—*baleful polymorph* (DC 23), *energy drain* (DC 27), *flame strike* (DC 23), *heat metal* (DC 20), *meteor swarm* (DC 27), *persistent image* (DC 23), *phantasmal killer* (DC 22)
1/day—*harm* (DC 24), *power word kill, summon* (level 9, 1d8+3 barbed devils, 100%; 1d4 pit fiends, 90%)

Str 31, **Dex** 26, **Con** 31, **Int** 27, **Wis** 27, **Cha** 26
Base Atk +23; **CMB** +34; **CMD** 52
Feats Blind-Fight, Cleave, Combat Casting, Deceitful, Empower Spell, Great Fortitude, Improved Initiative, Iron Will, Power Attack, Quicken Spell-Like Ability (*fireball*), Vital Strike, Weapon Focus (mace)
Skills Bluff +36, Climb +36, Diplomacy +34, Disguise +33, Intimidate +34, Knowledge (arcana) +31, Knowledge (planes) +34, Knowledge (religion) +34, Perception +34, Sense Motive +34, Spellcraft +31, Stealth +34, Survival +34, Use Magical Device +31
Languages Abyssal, Celestial, Common, Draconic, Giant, Infernal, telepathy 100 ft.

Environment any (Nine Hells)
Organization solitary or troupe (Dantalion plus 4–12 barbed devils)
Treasure triple standard (+4 *unholy heavy mace*, other treasure)

Poison (Ex) Tail sting—injury; *save* DC 31 Fort; *frequency* 1/round for 10 rounds; *effect* 1d8 Constitution damage; *cure* 3 consecutive saves. The save DC is Constitution-based.

Dantalion is a Duke of Hell and commands 30 legions of barbed devils in service to Baalzebul, Lord of the Seventh Hell. He is a highly charismatic creature and rules by wits and wile more than by might and power. Those who know him however, know he is capable of much more than he appears, and none, especially those serving him, dare cross him.

Dantalion once served as viceroy to Lucifer, millennia ago when Lucifer ruled the Nine Hells. When the battle for rulership came, Dantalion first showed loyalty to his master and fought against the armies of Asmodeus and Mephistopheles. Feeling the tide turning, Dantalion betrayed Lucifer at crucial moment in the war and switched allegiances, forever pledging fealty to Asmodeus. When the war ended, Asmodeus rewarded him by appointing him Duke under Baalzebul. Lucifer, now an outcast, would like nothing more than to see Dantalion's devilish smile wiped from his face and his head at the end of Alastor's greataxe.

Dantalion's fortified black stone keep rests atop a craggy mountain within the seventh Hell. Many barbed devils guard the only passage leading to his castle, killing any who do not have Dantalion's permission to traverse the road. A large company of barbed devils, rumored to be several hundred in number, make their home beneath the keep. There they stand guard, awaiting Dantalion's orders should the castle walls ever be sieged.

Devouring Mist

This drifting nightmare resembles a cloud of dark red vapor about 10 ft. in diameter.

DEVOURING MIST	CR 10

XP 9,600
NE Large undead (swarm)
Init +4; **Senses** darkvision 60 ft.; **Perception** +26

AC 14, touch 14, flat-footed 9 (+4 Dex, +1 dodge, –1 size)
hp 133 (14d12+42)
Fort +9; **Ref** +10; **Will** +12
Defensive Abilities channel resistance +4, swarm traits;
Immune undead traits, weapon damage; **SR** 24
Weaknesses swarm traits

Speed fly 40 ft. (perfect)
Melee swarm (blood drain)
Space 10 ft.; **Reach** 0 ft.
Special Attacks create spawn, distraction (DC 20)

Str 1, **Dex** 19, **Con** —, **Int** 8, **Wis** 16, **Cha** 16
Base Atk +10; **CMB** —; **CMD** —
Feats Dodge, Great Fortitude, Improved Channel Resistance, Lightning Reflexes, Mobility, Skill Focus (Perception), Skill Focus (Stealth)
Skills Fly +27, Perception +26, Stealth +23 (+33 in the Bloodways); **Racial Modifiers** +10 circumstance bonus on Stealth checks while in the red mists of the Bloodways

Environment underground (the Bloodways)
Organization solitary
Treasure none

Blood Drain (Ex) Creatures in the devouring mist's space at the end of its movement each round take 1d4 points of Constitution damage as it siphons blood out of the victim's body. For every point so drained, the devouring mist heals 5 hit points of damage. Creatures without blood take no damage from the devouring mist.
Create Spawn (Su) Any creature slain by a devouring mist rises as a vampire spawn in 1d4 days, unless the remains are *blessed*. If the victim had more than 5 hit dice, there is a 1% chance per hit die that it arises as a full-fledged vampire instead, or a 5% chance per hit die if the victim was of the humanoid type.

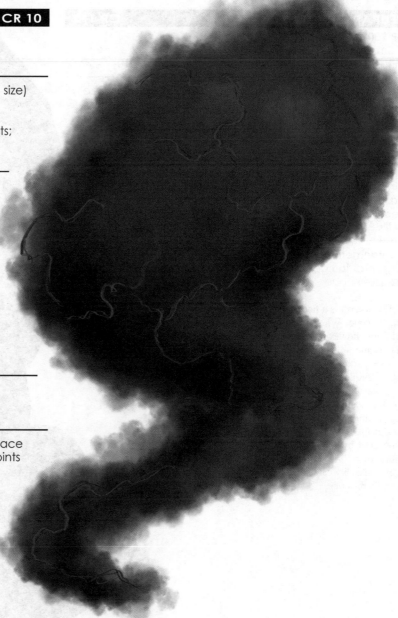

Spawned of the dreams of the Bloodwraith, devouring mists are undead composed of equal parts blood and malice, wedded together by negative energy. They drift the halls of the Bloodways, looking for living prey to feed on and torment. When they strike, they surround their enemies and draw their blood from their bodies.

Devouring mists are possessed of a malicious cunning. They are quite capable of blending into the mists of the Bloodways so as to take their prey unaware. They may also follow creatures for a time and attack when they are distracted or preoccupied. A devouring mist may even stalk its prey over hours or even days, striking again and again, in effect milking them of blood.

Devouring mists do not speak, nor can they be communicated with.

Credit
Originally appearing in *Rappan Athuk Reloaded* (© Necromancer Games, 2006)

Dinosaur, Euparkeria

This grayish-green reptile is about the size of a small dog. Its snout is long and its mouth is filled with needle-like teeth.

EUPARKERIA   CR 1/2

XP 200
N Small animal
Init +2; **Senses** low-light vision, scent; **Perception** +10

AC 14, touch 13, flat-footed 12 (+2 Dex, +1 natural, +1 size)
hp 13 (2d8+4)
Fort +7; **Ref** +5; **Will** +1

Speed 40 ft.
Melee bite +3 (1d4+1), 2 claws (1d3+1)

Str 12, **Dex** 15, **Con** 14, **Int** 2, **Wis** 12, **Cha** 8
Base Atk +1; **CMB** +1; **CMD** 13
Feats Great Fortitude
Skills Perception +10; **Racial Modifiers** +4 Perception

Environment any land
Organization gang (2–4) or pack (5–12)
Treasure none

Euparkeria is a nocturnal carnivore, feeding on insects and small game. When moving, it usually moves on all fours; however, when running or in combat, it stands and fights on its back legs.

A euparkeria can reach lengths of 3 feet or more. Skin coloration is gray or grayish-green.

When attacking prey, the euparkeria stands on its hind legs and attacks with a vicious bite. Its front legs feature a small thumb-like claw that it uses to slash its opponents. Much like other small dinosaurs, by itself the euparkeria doesn't pose much of a threat. In large numbers however, they can easily catch and kill prey much larger than themselves.

Dinosaur, Gorgosaurus

This huge reptile has small two-fingered forelimbs, strong powerful legs, and an enormous mouth filled with rows of sharp teeth.

GROGOSAURUS	CR 7

XP 3,200
N Huge animal
Init +5; **Senses** low-light vision, scent; **Perception** +30

AC 19, touch 9, flat-footed 18 (+1 Dex, +10 natural, −2 size)
hp 105 (14d8+42)
Fort +12; **Ref** +10; **Will** +7

Speed 40 ft.
Melee bite +15 (3d6+14/19–20 plus grab)
Space 15 ft.; **Reach** 15 ft.
Special Attacks swallow whole (2d6+7, AC 15, 10 hp)

Str 25, **Dex** 13, **Con** 16, **Int** 2, **Wis** 12, **Cha** 10
Base Atk +10; **CMB** +19 (+23 grapple); **CMD** 30
Feats Critical Focus, Diehard, Endurance, Improved Critical (bite), Improved Initiative, Iron Will, Skill Focus (Perception)
Skills Perception +30; **Racial Modifiers** +6 Perception
SQ powerful bite

Environment warm plains and shorelines
Organization solitary or pack (2–4)
Treasure none

Powerful Bite (Ex) A gorgosaurus applies twice its Strength modifier to bite damage.

A gorgosaurus is about 28 feet long from snout to tail and weighs almost 6,000 pounds. Its coloration can vary from dark shades of green to various shades of gray. Its diet consists of anything it can catch and kill, including large animals such as mastodons and mammoths, brontosauruses, and other such creatures.

A gorgosaurus's tactics are simple: charge, bite, swallow.

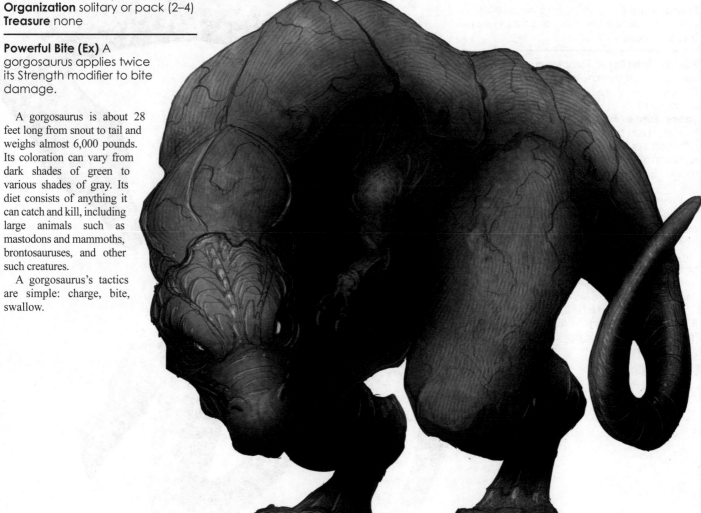

Dinosaur, Nothosaurus

This grayish-blue reptile has a long sleek body, webbed feet, and long jaws that open to reveal needle-like teeth.

NOTHOSAURUS	CR 6

XP 2,400
N Large animal
Init +6; **Senses** low-light vision, scent; **Perception** +13

AC 17, touch 11, flat-footed 15 (+2 Dex, +6 natural, −1 size)
hp 76 (9d8+36)
Fort +12; **Ref** +8; **Will** +4

Speed 10 ft., swim 40 ft.
Melee bite +12 (2d6+9 plus grab)
Space 10 ft.; **Reach** 5 ft.

Str 22, **Dex** 15, **Con** 18, **Int** 2, **Wis** 12, **Cha** 6
Base Atk +6; **CMB** +13 (+17 grapple); **CMD** 25 (can't be tripped)
Feats Great Fortitude, Improved Initiative, Skill Focus (Perception), Swim-By Attack, Weapon Focus (bite)
Skills Perception +13, Stealth +3 (+11 in water), Swim +18;
Racial Modifiers +8 Stealth in water
SQ hold breath, speed surge

Environment temperate and warm aquatic
Organization solitary, pair, or school (3–6)
Treasure none

Hold Breath (Ex) A nothosaurus can hold its breath for a number of minutes equal to 6 times its Constitution score before it risks drowning.
Speed Surge (Ex) Three times per day as a swift action, a nothosaurus may take an additional move action in that round.

A nothosaurus is about 13 feet long and grayish-blue in color. When swimming, its uses its webbed feet, fin-like tail, and powerful legs to propel it through the water. It sustains itself on a diet of fish, seals, walruses, and other marine animals. The nothosaurus breathes air and moves slowly on land, rarely venturing far away from the shoreline. When not hunting, a nothosaurus often suns itself on large rocks.

Nothosaurus is an ambush hunter, moving quietly through the water as it sneaks up on its prey. As the nothosaurus draws closer, it uses its speed surge to close rapidly and grab the prey with its powerful jaws.

Dinosaur, Podokesaurus

This small bipedal reptile has a long, narrow head and sharp, curved teeth.

PODOKESAURUS	CR 1/3

XP 135
N Tiny animal
Init +8; **Senses** low-light vision, scent; **Perception** +4

AC 17, touch 16, flat-footed 13 (+4 Dex, +1 natural, +2 size)
hp 6 (1d8+2)
Fort +4; **Ref** +6; **Will** +0

Speed 60 ft.
Melee bite +1 (1d3–1), 2 claws +1 (1d2–1)
Space 1/2 ft.; **Reach** 0 ft.
Special Attacks pounce

Str 8, **Dex** 19, **Con** 14, **Int** 2, **Wis** 11, **Cha** 5
Base Atk +0; **CMB** +2; **CMD** 11
Feats Improved Initiative, Run[B]
Skills Perception +4

Environment warm forests
Organization gang (5–12) or pack (13–24)
Treasure none

Podokesaurus are small, swift-footed pack hunters that feast on a diet of meat, often attacking prey much larger than themselves. In such instances, they use their overwhelming numbers to bring their quarry down.

An adult podokesaurus stands about 1 foot tall and is around 3 feet long. Its long tail acts as a counterweight to keep it upright when it is running at a high rate of speed. Skin color varies slightly, but is usually varying shades of browns and grays. Its teeth are curved and serrated to aid in tearing meat for consumption.

A lone podokesaurus isn't much of a threat, especially to larger opponents. In large numbers however, these creatures become extremely dangerous, using pack and swarming tactics to attack. Prey that attempts to escape is easily run down by the swarming podokesaurus.

Dire Animals

Dire animals are large, feral looking animals. They are not just bigger versions of normal animals, however. On the whole, dire animals are bigger, stronger, faster, and much more aggressive than their normal counterparts.

Scholars are uncertain as to the origins of dire animals. Some maintain nature caused animals to adapt to the ever-changing world around them, while others insist dire animals are a regression to a more savage time.

Dire Fox

This giant fox has dark red fur and a mouthful of white glistening fangs.

DIRE FOX	CR 2

XP 600
N Medium animal
Init +4; **Senses** low-light vision, scent; **Perception** +11

AC 20, touch 14, flat-footed 16 (+4 Dex, +6 natural)
hp 34 (4d8+16)
Fort +10; **Ref** +8; **Will** +4

Speed 50 ft.
Melee bite +7 (1d6+4)

Str 16, **Dex** 19, **Con** 18, **Int** 2, **Wis** 16, **Cha** 10
Base Atk +3; **CMB** +6; **CMD** 20 (24 vs. trip)
Feats Great Fortitude, Weapon Finesse
Skills Acrobatics +6, Perception +11, Stealth +13, Survival +8;
Racial Modifiers +2 Acrobatics, +4 Perception, +4 Stealth, +4 Survival

Environment cold and temperate forests and plains
Organization solitary
Treasure none

Dire foxes are larger and fiercer versions of the normal fox. They are solitary creatures whose hunting grounds can cover up to 10 square miles.

Dire foxes spend about one-third of their day hunting for food. They are excellent hunters and have no problem attacking and bringing down large prey. They are omnivorous and feast on a diet of rodents, dire rodents (such as dire rats), insects and giant insects, and various plants and herbs. If food is scarce, dire foxes live off of carrion until their food supply increases. Mating season varies depending on climate. Dire foxes found in colder climates mate during the late winter and early spring months. Those found in warmer climates mate during the winter. This is the only time more than one dire fox will be encountered and such encounters consist of one male and at least one female (two females sometimes). If pups are present, there will be 2d6 of them. Young dire foxes reach maturity at about 10 months of age and leave the den to claim their own hunting territory which can be up to 250 miles away from their birthplace.

Dire foxes are about 5 feet long and have yellowish-red or reddish-brown fur. A strip of black fur runs across their shoulders and down the center of their backs. The dire fox's underbelly is white more often than not, but a gray underbelly is not uncommon. Dire foxes have thick, bushy tails with the same color fur as their body. The tail ends in a black or white bushy tip. The lower legs of a dire fox are either black or white and their eyes are yellow. A rare breed of dire fox has silver or silver-black fur.

A dire fox prefers to sneak up on its prey and catch it unaware. When it spots a potential meal, the dire fox stands motionless, waiting for its target to move closer. When its prey is within range, it leaps out and attacks. If cornered, dire foxes fight to the death.

Dire Mastiff

This large black hound is about the size of a small horse.

DIRE MASTIFF	CR 3

XP 800
N Large animal
Init +2; **Senses** low-light vision, scent; **Perception** +9

AC 15, touch 11, flat-footed 13 (+2 Dex, +4 natural, −1 size)
hp 42 (5d8+20)
Fort +8; **Ref** +6; **Will** +2

Speed 50 ft.
Melee bite +7 (1d8+6 plus trip)
Space 10 ft.; **Reach** 5 ft.

Str 19, **Dex** 15, **Con** 18, **Int** 2, **Wis** 12, **Cha** 10
Base Atk +3; **CMB** +8; **CMD** 20 (24 vs. trip)
Feats Power Attack, Skill Focus (Perception), Weapon Focus (bite)
Skills Acrobatics +7 (+11 jumping), Perception +9, Survival +2 (+6 scent tracking); **Racial Modifiers** +4 Acrobatics when jumping, +4 Survival when tracking by scent

Environment any
Organization solitary, pair, or pack (3–12)
Treasure none

Dire mastiffs are the domestic equivalent of dire wolves. They are large, vicious canines highly prized for their ability to track and kill opponents much larger than themselves. Domesticated dire mastiffs are often trained and outfitted for war in spiked, studded leather armor. Orcs often use trained dire mastiffs in warfare.

Dire mastiffs are much like wolves, and in the wild, they commingle in packs of up to twelve. The dominant male is always the leader, though other males frequently challenge for the position. Such exchanges, while violent, rarely result in death. The loser of the contest simply submits to the victor and acknowledges it as the new pack leader.

Dire mastiffs are carnivores and their diet consists of just about any animal or creature they can catch and kill. Favorite meals include leopards, skunks, horses, and rodents. They rarely devour humanoid flesh, but will do so if food is scarce. Kills are often carried back to the lair and distributed among the pups and females.

Dire mastiffs breed twice a year, usually every 6 months. The

Perception, +4 Stealth

Environment cold or temperate forests and plains
Organization solitary, pair, or herd (10–50 deer plus 1 dire stag per 10 deer)
Treasure none

Dire stags are impressive creatures found in all but the warmest regions. Most inhabit forests and plains, though some often roam more rugged territory. Dire stags are aggressive giant versions of male deer.

Dire stag are nocturnal creatures and exist on a diet of leaves, vines, ivy, and meat, the latter consisting of rodents and small animals (rabbits, moles, pigs, and wolves). A typical male's territory covers a range of 5 square miles. Dire stags mark territorial boundaries by digging holes with their antlers. Such holes can measure up to 6 feet wide and 3 feet deep. They often thrash the ground throughout their territory, stirring up the leaves and underbrush, to further define their territory.

Dire stags are solitary creatures, but sometimes band together, usually during mating or rutting season. During rutting season, a dire stag gathers up to 12 female deer in its territory. Mating season is usually late fall and gestation typically lasts 8 months. Newborn are nursed by the females and are dependent on their mother for the first few months of their lives. Young are slowly weaned over a period of 6 months and reach maturity by 18 months.

A dire stag stands 6 feet at the shoulder and about 12 feet long with its weight exceeding 1,000 pounds. Its antlers average up to 8 feet wide, though some of the largest dire stag have antlers reaching up to 12 feet wide. Its coat varies in color from brown to brownish-white to black, with its underbelly being lighter, and usually white. Its antlers are brown or black. Dire stags are hunted for their meat as well as their tough hides. A reasonably intact dire stag hide is worth 500 gp or more.

Dire stags are aggressive animals and rarely back down from a challenge. They unleash a guttural, blood-curdling bleat before attacking. This serves to warn the females and young as well as potential aggressors. Dire stags almost never retreat, preferring to fight to the death against a foe.

A dire stag attacks with its antlers, goring its opponent, or it rears onto its hind legs and slashes with its hooves. Most dire stags fight to the death to protect their young.

actual month or time varies depending on climate, terrain, and other environmental factors. Gestation lasts about 4 months after which time the female gives birth to 1d3+3 pups. Pups depend on their mother or the hunters of a pack to feed them and rarely journey out on their own until they reach 4 months of age. Dire mastiffs reach maturity around 8 months after birth.

Before attacking, the hair on the neck of a dire mastiff rises, its ears fold back, its tail stiffens, and it bears its sharpened teeth, through which a low growl is often heard. A dire mastiff rushes its opponent and bites ferociously with its powerful jaws.

Dire Stag

This gigantic stag stands as tall as a human at the shoulders and has antlers that are almost twice that long.

DIRE STAG	CR 3

XP 800
N Large animal
Init +3; **Senses** low-light vision, scent; **Perception** +12

AC 17, touch 13, flat-footed 13 (+3 Dex, +1 dodge, +4 natural, –1 size)
hp 42 (5d8+20)
Fort +8; **Ref** +9; **Will** +3

Speed 40 ft.
Melee gore +7 (1d8+5), 2 hooves +5 (1d6+2)
Space 10 ft.; **Reach** 5 ft.

Str 21, **Dex** 17, **Con** 18, **Int** 2, **Wis** 15, **Cha** 10
Base Atk +3; **CMB** +9; **CMD** 23 (27 vs. trip)
Feats Dodge, Lightning Reflexes, Multiattack[B], Run
Skills Perception +12, Stealth +8; **Racial Modifiers** +4

Dobie

This sylvan creature resembles a 5-foot tall elf with brownish-tan skin, large pointed ears, and brown eyes.

DOBIE	CR 4

XP 1,200
CN Medium fey
Init +7; Senses low-light vision; Perception +11

AC 17, touch 14, flat-footed 13 (+3 Dex, +1 dodge, +3 natural)
hp 33 (6d6+12)
Fort +4; Ref +8; Will +9
DR 5/cold iron
Weaknesses vulnerability to fire

Speed 30 ft.
Melee longsword +4 (1d8+1/19–20)

Str 12, Dex 16, Con 14, Int 12, Wis 15, Cha 15
Base Atk +3; CMB +4; CMD 18
Feats Dodge, Improved Initiative, Iron Will
Skills Bluff +11, Craft (any one) +7, Diplomacy +8, Escape Artist +12, Handle Animal +5, Knowledge (nature) +10, Perception +11, Perform (dancing) +8, Stealth +12
Languages Common, Sylvan
SQ size alteration

Environment temperate forests
Organization solitary or pair
Treasure standard (longsword, other treasure)

Size Alteration (Su) At will as a standard action, a dobie can change its size between Medium and Large. Weapons, armor, and other objects on the dobie's person grow proportionally when it changes sizes (objects revert to normal size one round after a dobie releases them). When a dobie becomes Large, its speed increases to 40 feet, it gains +6 Strength, –2 Dexterity, and +4 Constitution, and takes a –1 size penalty to AC.

A dobie can use this ability only in its natural environment. If a dobie leaves its natural environment while enlarged, it immediately reverts to its normal size. Additionally, an enlarged dobie that takes 10 points of fire damage or more from a single fire effect immediately reverts to its normal size. It cannot enlarge itself again for 3 rounds after being hit by a fire effect.

Dobies are forest creatures believed by some to be the offspring of a spriggan and a dryad, though most learned sages brush this off as simple folklore. They are generally good-natured creatures and aid good-aligned or neutral creatures in need. Creatures they encounter destroying their forests or slaughtering its denizens are attacked almost immediately without question.

Dobies build their homes deep within the forests they protect. Though their homes are generally secluded so prying eyes

don't disturb them, they always fashion them in such a way that allows the dobie to keep a watchful eye on its domain at all times. Dobies are solitary creatures; if more than one is encountered they are likely a mated pair. Dobies mate for life.

Dobies stand about 5 feet tall but can alter their size to attain heights of 10 feet. They dress in brightly colored clothes and overcoats of green, brown, red, and tan. Dobies can live to be 600 years old, generally reaching maturity around age 100.

Dobies enlarge themselves at the start of combat, seeking to gain any advantage they can over their enemies, attacking with both weapons and spell-like abilities. If the battle is going against a dobie, it uses its summon ability to bring forest creatures to its aid and to cover its escape.

DOBIE (ENLARGED)	CR 4

XP 1,200
CN Large fey
Init +6; Senses low-light vision; Perception +11

AC 15, touch 12, flat-footed 12 (+2 Dex, +1 dodge, +3 natural, –1 size)
hp 45 (6d6+24)
Fort +6; Ref +7; Will +9
DR 5/cold iron
Weaknesses vulnerability to fire

Speed 40 ft.
Melee longsword +6 (2d6+4/19–20)
Space 10 ft.; Reach 10 ft.

Str 18, Dex 14, Con 18, Int 12, Wis 15, Cha 15
Base Atk +3; CMB +8; CMD 21
Feats Dodge, Improved Initiative, Iron Will
Skills Bluff +11, Craft (any one) +7, Diplomacy +8, Escape Artist +11, Handle Animal +5, Knowledge (nature) +10, Perception +11, Perform +8, Stealth +7
Languages Common, Sylvan
SQ size alteration

Environment temperate forests
Organization solitary or pair
Treasure standard (longsword, other treasure)

Domovoi

This small hairy humanoid has pointed ears, a long dirty beard, and wields a short sword in its wicked clawed hands.

DOMOVOI	CR 4

XP 1,200
CE Small fey
Init +4; **Senses** darkvision 60 ft., low-light vision; **Perception** +8

AC 18, touch 15, flat-footed 14 (+4 Dex, +3 natural, +1 size)
hp 26 (4d6+8 plus 4)
Fort +3; **Ref** +8; **Will** +5
DR 5/cold iron; **SR** 15

Speed 30 ft., climb 20 ft.
Melee short sword +7 (1d4+1), bite +2 (1d4) or 2 claws +7 (1d3+1 plus grab), bite +7 (1d4)
Special Attacks sneak attack (2d6), telekinesis
Spell-Like Abilities (CL 4th; melee touch +4, ranged touch +7):
At will—*dancing lights, prestidigitation* (DC 11)
3/day—*heat metal* (DC 13), *sleep* (DC 12), *snare*

Str 13, **Dex** 18, **Con** 15, **Int** 11, **Wis** 12, **Cha** 13
Base Atk +2; **CMB** +2 (+6 grapple); **CMD** 16
Feats Toughness, Weapon Finesse
Skills Acrobatics +11, Climb +14, Craft (any one) +7, Escape Artist +9, Intimidate +5, Perception +8, Stealth +15
Languages Sylvan, Undercommon
SQ knocker spirit

Environment any urban or underground
Organization solitary or gang (2–5)
Treasure standard (short sword, other treasure)

Knocker Spirit (Su) A domovoi killed by violence rises in 1 hour as a poltergeist.
Telekinesis (Su) As a standard action once per turn, a domovoi can use telekinesis. This ability functions as the *telekinesis* spell with a CL equal to the domovoi's Hit Dice (CL 4th for most domovoi). A typical domovoi has a ranged attack roll of +5 when using telekinesis to hurl objects or creatures, and can use this ability on objects or creatures of up to 75 pounds. If a domovoi attempts to hurl a creature with this ability, that creature can resist the effect with a successful DC 13 Will save. The save DC is Strength-based.

Domovoi are wicked fey found at the forests' edge, in underground caves, and in small cities and towns, usually dwelling in ruined buildings or in attics and crawlspaces of occupied residences. They are capricious and violent creatures and take great delight in inflicting harm on those that cross them—and sometimes on those that don't.

Domovoi stand just over 2 feet tall and weigh around 60 pounds. Their clothes are usually dirty and smelly, but other than that seem to be well kept (no holes, no tears, for example). The creature's hair is dark and wildly unkempt. Males have long dirty beards the same color as their hair. No females or young domovoi have been encountered.

Domovoi prefer to attack from ambush, startling their opponents with sudden attacks and catching them unaware. A favored tactic is to stay hidden and assault a target with random objects through the use of the domovoi's telekinesis.

Dracohydra

Five dragon-like heads of varying colors rise from the sleek, serpentine body of this hideous monster.

DRACOHYDRA	CR 10

XP 9,600
N Huge magical beast
Init +1; **Senses** darkvision 60 ft., low-light vision, scent; **Perception** +12

AC 20, touch 9, flat-footed 19 (+1 Dex, +11 natural, –2 size)
hp 105 (10d10+50); fast healing 10
Fort +11; **Ref** +10; **Will** +5
Defensive Abilities all-around vision; **Resist** acid 10, cold 10, electricity 10, fire 10

Speed 30 ft., swim 20 ft.
Melee 5 bites +14 (2d6+5/19–20)
Space 15 ft.; **Reach** 10 ft.
Special Attacks 5 breath weapons (30-ft. cone, DC 19, 4d6 damage; see text), savage bite

Str 21, **Dex** 12, **Con** 19, **Int** 6, **Wis** 11, **Cha** 12
Base Atk +10; **CMB** +17; **CMD** 28 (can't be tripped)
Feats Combat Reflexes, Iron Will, Lightning Reflexes, Lunge, Toughness, Weapon Focus (bite)[B]
Skills Intimidate +6, Perception +12, Swim +13; **Racial Modifiers** +4 Perception
Languages Common, Draconic
SQ hydra traits, regenerate head

Environment any
Organization solitary
Treasure double standard

Breath Weapon (Su) Each of a dracohydra's heads has a single breath weapon. To determine each head's color and the associated breath weapon, choose from or roll on the table below.

1d10	Head Color	Breath Weapon
1–2	Black	Acid
3–4	Blue	Electricity
5–6	Green	Acid
7–8	Red	Fire
9–10	White	Cold

Fast Healing (Ex) A dracohydra's fast healing applies only to damage inflicted on the dracohydra's body.
Hydra Traits (Ex) A dracohydra can be killed by severing its heads or slaying its body. Any attack that is not an attempt to sever a head affects the body, including area attacks or attacks that cause piercing or bludgeoning damage. To sever a head, an opponent must make a sunder attempt with a slashing weapon targeting a head. A head is considered a separate weapon with hardness 0 and 10 hit points. To sever a head, an opponent must inflict enough damage to reduce the head's hit points to 0 or less. Severing a head deals 10 points of damage to the dracohydra's body. A dracohydra can't attack with a severed head, but takes no other penalties.
Regenerate Head (Ex) When a dracohydra's head is destroyed, two heads regrow in 1d4 rounds. The heads are of the same color as the one that was severed. A dracohydra cannot have more than 10 heads at any one time. To prevent new heads from growing, at least 5 points of

acid or fire damage (after overcoming the dracohydra's resistances) must be dealt to the stump (a touch attack to hit) before they appear. Acid or fire damage from area attacks can affect stumps and the body simultaneously. A dracohydra doesn't die from losing its heads until all are cut off and the stumps seared by acid or fire.

Savage Bite (Ex) A dracohydra applies 1–1/2 times its Strength bonus to damage dealt with its bite attack, and it threatens a critical hit on a 19–20.

Believed to be either the mating of a hydra and a dragon or the offspring of a draconic deity, the dracohydra is truly a fearsome monster. Most intelligent creatures do their best to avoid trespassing on a dracohydra's domain for these creatures are extremely territorial, even more so than some dragons. Dracohydras prefer lairing in remote locations such as mountaintops and ruins, far away from civilization and far away from adventurous treasure seekers.

Dracohydras, while solitary, often make pacts with local humanoids; most often orcs, gnolls, and hobgoblins. Generally these pacts are lopsided deals that favor the dracohydra: give it food and it won't eat your village. Such food usually consists of herd animals or cattle, and sometimes humanoids if necessary to sate the dracohydra's voracious appetite. Humanoid sacrifices usually take the form of slaves or prisoners, but if either of those is in low numbers, tribes have been known to sacrifice their own to appease a dracohydra.

Betraying their draconic origin, dracohydras amass treasure in great quantities. Most treasures are left strewn about the lair, but some, such as rare gemstones and small trinkets are devoured by dracohydras.

Dracohydras do not associate with other dracohydras, hydras, or dragons. Hydras are particularly reviled for unknown reasons, and are attacked on sight and slaughtered, their bodies being almost completely devoured by a dracohydra.

A dracohydra's body is usually dark gray or dark grayish-blue. Its dragon-like heads are scaled and vary in color blending into the body at the neckline. A dracohydra's eyes are always sapphire blue, regardless of the color of the dragon's head.

Dragon, Gray

Steam emanates from the nostrils and mouth of this slate gray dragon.

GRAY DRAGON

NE dragon (water)

CR 2; **Size** Tiny; **Hit Dice** 3d12
Speed 60 ft., swim 40 ft.
Natural Armor +4; **Breath Weapon** line, 2d6 fire
Str 11, **Dex** 16, **Con** 13, **Int** 9, **Wis** 11, **Cha** 9

Environment warm coastlines
Organization solitary
Treasure triple standard

Breath Weapon (Su) A gray dragon's breath weapon is a superheated line of steam.

Gray dragons are evil dragons that inhabit mountains and hills near coastlines. They have little regard for other races and often enslave others to do their bidding. Adult and older gray dragons are rarely found without a retinue of humanoid slaves. Gray dragons mate for life and a single mated pair often terrorizes nearby villages, laying waste to those that oppose the dragon's will.

AGE CATEGORY	SPECIAL ABILITIES	CASTER LEVEL
Wyrmling	immunity to poison	—
Very Young	water breathing	—
Young	change shape, fog cloud	—
Juvenile	create water	1st
Young Adult	DR 5/magic, spell resistance	3rd
Adult	corrupt water, frightful presence	5th
Mature Adult	DR 10/magic	7th
Old	control winds	9th
Very Old	DR 15/magic	11th
Ancient	control water	13th
Wyrm	DR 20/magic	15th
Great Wyrm	—	17th

Change Shape (Su) A young or older gray dragon can take any animal or humanoid form 3/day as if using *polymorph*.
Corrupt Water (Sp) Once per day an adult or older gray dragon can stagnate 10 cubic feet of still water, making it foul and unable to support water-breathing life. The ability spoils liquids containing water. Liquid-based magic items (such as potions) and items in a creature's possession must succeed on a Will save (DC 19) or become ruined. This ability is the equivalent of a 1st-level spell. Its range is 180 ft.
Spell-Like Abilities (Sp)
A gray dragon gains the following spell-like abilities, usable at will upon reaching the listed age category.
• Young—*fog cloud*;
• Juvenile—*create water*;
• Old—*control winds*;
• Ancient—*control water*;
Water Breathing (Ex) A gray dragon breathes water and can use its breath weapon, spells, and abilities underwater.

WYRMLING GRAY DRAGON   CR 2

XP 600
NE Tiny dragon (water)
Init +7; **Senses** dragon senses; **Perception** +6

AC 19, touch 15, flat-footed 16 (+3 Dex, +4 natural, +2 size)
hp 22 (3d12+3)
Fort +4; **Ref** +8; **Will** +3
Immune paralysis, sleep

Speed 60 ft., fly 100 ft. (average), swim 40 ft.
Melee 2 claws +5 (1d3), bite +5 (1d4)
Space 1/2 ft.; **Reach** 0 ft. (5 ft. with bite)
Special Attacks breath weapon (30-ft. line, 2d6 fire; DC 12 Ref half)

Str 11, **Dex** 16, **Con** 13, **Int** 9, **Wis** 11, **Cha** 9
Base Atk +3; **CMB** +4; **CMD** 14 (18 vs. trip)
Feats Improved Initiative, Lightning Reflexes
Skills Bluff +5, Fly +13, Intimidate +5, Perception +6, Stealth +17, Swim +8
Languages Draconic

VERY YOUNG GRAY DRAGON   CR 4

XP 1,200
NE Small dragon (water)
Init +6; **Senses** dragon senses; **Perception** +11

AC 20, touch 13, flat-footed 18 (+2 Dex, +7 natural, +1 size)
hp 42 (5d12+10)
Fort +6; **Ref** +8; **Will** +5
Immune paralysis, sleep

Speed 60 ft., fly 150 ft. (average), swim 40 ft.
Melee 2 claws +8 (1d4+2), bite +8 (1d6+3)
Space 5 ft.; **Reach** 5 ft. (10 ft. with bite)
Special Attacks breath weapon (40-ft. line, 4d6 fire; DC 14 Ref half)

Str 15, **Dex** 14, **Con** 15, **Int** 11, **Wis** 13, **Cha** 11
Base Atk +5; **CMB** +6; **CMD** 18 (22 vs. trip)
Feats Alertness, Improved Initiative, Lightning Reflexes
Skills Bluff +8, Fly +12, Intimidate +8, Knowledge (local) +7, Perception +11, Sense Motive +3, Stealth +14, Swim +14
Languages Draconic

YOUNG GRAY DRAGON   CR 6

XP 2,400
NE Medium dragon (water)
Init +6; **Senses** dragon senses; **Perception** +13

AC 22, touch 12, flat-footed 20 (+2 Dex, +10 natural)
hp 66 (7d12+21)
Fort +8; **Ref** +9; **Will** +6
Immune paralysis, sleep

Speed 60 ft., fly 150 ft. (average), swim 40 ft.
Melee 2 claws +11 (1d6+4), bite +11 (1d8+6), 2 wings +11 (1d4+2)
Space 5 ft.; **Reach** 5 ft. (10 ft. with bite)
Special Attacks breath weapon (60-ft. line, 6d6 fire; DC 16 Ref half)

Str 19, **Dex** 14, **Con** 17, **Int** 11, **Wis** 13, **Cha** 11
Base Atk +7; **CMB** +11; **CMD** 23 (27 vs. trip)
Feats Alertness, Improved Initiative, Lightning Reflexes, Multiattack
Skills Bluff +10, Fly +12, Intimidate +10, Knowledge (local) +8, Perception +13, Sense Motive +3, Stealth +12, Swim +17
Languages Draconic

JUVENILE GRAY DRAGON — CR 7

XP 3,200
NE Medium dragon (water)
Init +6; **Senses** dragon senses; **Perception** +16

AC 25, touch 12, flat-footed 23 (+2 Dex, +13 natural)
hp 94 (9d12+36)
Fort +10; **Ref** +10; **Will** +8
Immune paralysis, sleep

Speed 60 ft., fly 150 ft. (average), swim 40 ft.
Melee 2 claws +14 (1d6+5), bite +15 (1d8+7), 2 wings +14 (1d4+5)
Space 5 ft.; **Reach** 5 ft. (10 ft. with bite)
Special Attacks breath weapon (60-ft. line, 8d6 fire; DC 18 Ref half)
Spells Known (CL 1st; melee touch +13, ranged touch +11):
1st (4/day)—*protection from good, obscuring mist*
0 (at will)—*dancing lights, detect magic, ray of frost, resistance*

Str 21, **Dex** 14, **Con** 19, **Int** 13, **Wis** 15, **Cha** 13
Base Atk +9; **CMB** +14; **CMD** 26 (30 vs. trip)
Feats Alertness, Improved Initiative, Lightning Reflexes, Multiattack, Weapon Focus (bite)
Skills Bluff +13, Fly +14, Intimidate +13, Knowledge (local) +13, Perception +16, Sense Motive +4, Stealth +14, Swim +25
Languages Common, Draconic

YOUNG ADULT GRAY DRAGON — CR 9

XP 6,400
NE Large dragon (water)
Init +5; **Senses** dragon senses; **Perception** +18

AC 26, touch 10, flat-footed 25 (+1 Dex, +16 natural, −1 size)
hp 115 (11d12+44)
Fort +11; **Ref** +10; **Will** +9
Immune paralysis, sleep; **SR** 20

Speed 60 ft., fly 200 ft. (average), swim 40 ft.
Melee 2 claws +16 (1d8+6), bite +17 (2d6+9), 2 wings +14 (1d6+3), tail slap +14 (1d8+9)
Space 10 ft.; **Reach** 5 ft. (10 ft. with bite)
Special Attacks breath weapon (80-ft. line, 10d6 fire; DC 19 Ref half)
Spells Known (CL 3rd; melee touch +16, ranged touch +11):
1st (6/day)—*burning hands* (DC 12), *protection from good, obscuring mist*
0 (at will)—*acid splash, dancing lights, detect magic, ray of frost, resistance*

Str 23, **Dex** 12, **Con** 19, **Int** 13, **Wis** 15, **Cha** 13
Base Atk +11; **CMB** +18; **CMD** 29 (33 vs. trip)
Feats Alertness, Improved Initiative, Lightning Reflexes, Multiattack, Power Attack, Weapon Focus (bite)
Skills Bluff +15, Fly +13, Intimidate +15, Knowledge (local) +15, Perception +20, Sense Motive +4,

Stealth +11, Swim +28
Languages Common, Draconic

ADULT GRAY DRAGON   CR 10

XP 9,600
NE Large dragon (water)
Init +5; **Senses** dragon senses; **Perception** +21
Aura frightful presence (180 ft., DC 18)

AC 29, touch 10, flat-footed 28 (+1 Dex, +19 natural, –1 size)
hp 149 (13d12+65)
Fort +13; **Ref** +11; **Will** +11
Immune paralysis, sleep; **SR** 21

Speed 60 ft., fly 200 ft. (average), swim 40 ft.
Melee 2 claws +19 (1d8+7), bite +20 (2d6+10/19–20), 2 wings +17 (1d6+3), tail slap +17 (1d8+10)
Space 10 ft.; **Reach** 5 ft. (10 ft. with bite)
Special Attacks breath weapon (80-ft. line, 12d6 fire; DC 21 Ref half)
Spells Known (CL 5th; melee touch +19, ranged touch +13):
2nd (5/day)—*blur, eagle's splendor*
1st (7/day)—*burning hands* (DC 13), *magic missile, obscuring mist, protection from good*
0 (at will)—*acid splash, dancing lights, detect magic, light, ray of frost, resistance*

Str 25, **Dex** 12, **Con** 21, **Int** 15, **Wis** 17, **Cha** 15
Base Atk +13; **CMB** +21; **CMD** 32 (36 vs. trip)
Feats Alertness, Improved Critical (bite), Improved Initiative, Lightning Reflexes, Multiattack, Power Attack, Weapon Focus (bite)
Skills Bluff +18, Fly +15, Intimidate +18, Knowledge (local) +18, Perception +23, Sense Motive +23, Stealth +13, Swim +31
Languages Aquan, Common, Draconic

MATURE GRAY DRAGON   CR 11

XP 12,800
NE Large dragon (water)
Init +5; **Senses** dragon senses; **Perception** +23
Aura frightful presence (210 ft., DC 19)

AC 32, touch 10, flat-footed 31 (+1 Dex, +22 natural, –1 size)
hp 172 (15d12+75)
Fort +14; **Ref** +12; **Will** +12
Immune paralysis, sleep; **SR** 22

Speed 60 ft., fly 200 ft. (average), swim 40 ft.
Melee 2 claws +22 (1d8+8), bite +23 (2d6+12/19–20), 2 wings +20 (1d6+4), tail slap +20 (1d8+8)
Space 10 ft.; **Reach** 5 ft. (10 ft. with bite)
Special Attacks breath weapon (80-ft. line, 14d6 fire; DC 22 Ref half)
Spells Known (CL 7th; melee touch +22, ranged touch +15):
3rd (4/day)—*dispel magic, gaseous form*
2nd (7/day)—*blur, eagle's splendor, locate object*
1st (7/day)—*burning hands* (DC 13), *magic missile, obscuring mist, protection from good, shield*
0 (at will)—*acid splash, dancing lights, detect magic, light, ray of frost, read magic, resistance*

Str 27, **Dex** 12, **Con** 21, **Int** 15, **Wis** 17, **Cha** 15
Base Atk +15; **CMB** +24; **CMD** 35 (39 vs. trip)
Feats Alertness, Flyby Attack, Improved Critical (bite), Improved Initiative, Lightning Reflexes, Multiattack, Power Attack, Weapon Focus (bite)
Skills Bluff +20, Fly +17, Intimidate +20, Knowledge (local) +20, Perception +25, Sense Motive +25, Stealth +15, Swim +34
Languages Aquan, Common, Draconic

OLD GRAY DRAGON   CR 13

XP 25,600
NE Huge dragon (water)
Init +4; **Senses** dragon senses; **Perception** +26
Aura frightful presence (240 ft., DC 21)

AC 33, touch 8, flat-footed 33 (+25 natural, –2 size)
hp 212 (17d12+102)
Fort +16; **Ref** +12; **Will** +14
Immune paralysis, sleep; **SR** 24

Speed 60 ft., fly 200 ft. (average), swim 40 ft.
Melee 2 claws +24 (2d6+9), bite +25 (2d8+13/19–20), 2 wings +22 (1d8+4), tail slap +22 (2d6+13)
Space 15 ft.; **Reach** 10 ft. (15 ft. with bite)
Special Attacks breath weapon (100-ft. line, 16d6 fire; DC 24 Ref half)
Spells Known (CL 9th; melee touch +24, ranged touch +15):
4th (4/day)—*dimension door, greater invisibility*
3rd (7/day)—*dispel magic, gaseous form, protection from energy*
2nd (7/day)—*blur, eagle's splendor, locate object, mirror image*
1st (7/day)—*burning hands* (DC 14), *magic missile, protection from good, obscuring mist, shield*
0 (at will)—*acid splash, dancing lights, detect magic, light, mage hand, ray of frost, read magic, resistance*

Str 29, **Dex** 10, **Con** 23, **Int** 17, **Wis** 19, **Cha** 17
Base Atk +17; **CMB** +28; **CMD** 38 (42 vs. trip)
Feats Alertness, Cleave, Flyby Attack, Improved Critical (bite), Improved Initiative, Lightning Reflexes, Multiattack, Power Attack, Weapon Focus (bite)
Skills Bluff +23, Fly +16, Intimidate +23, Knowledge (local) +23, Perception +28, Sense Motive +28, Spellcraft +23, Stealth +12, Swim +37
Languages Aquan, Common, Draconic, Giant

VERY OLD GRAY DRAGON   CR 14

XP 36,400
NE Huge dragon (water)
Init +4; **Senses** dragon senses; **Perception** +28
Aura frightful presence (270 ft., DC 22)

AC 36, touch 8, flat-footed 36 (+28 natural, –2 size)
hp 237 (19d12+114)
Fort +17; **Ref** +13; **Will** +17
Immune paralysis, sleep; **SR** 25

Speed 60 ft., fly 200 ft. (average), swim 40 ft.
Melee 2 claws +27 (2d6+10), bite +28 (2d8+15/19–20), 2 wings +25 (1d8+5), tail slap +25 (2d6+15)
Space 15 ft.; **Reach** 10 ft. (15 ft. with bite)
Special Attacks breath weapon (100-ft. line, 18d6 fire; DC 25 Ref half)
Spells Known (CL 11th; melee touch +27, ranged touch +17):
5th (4/day)—*cloudkill* (DC 18), *telekinesis*
4th (6/day)—*dimension door, greater invisibility, scrying* (DC 17)
3rd (7/day)—*dispel magic, gaseous form, protection from energy, ray of exhaustion* (DC 16)
2nd (7/day)—*blur, eagle's splendor, gust of wind* (DC 15), *locate object, mirror image*
1st (7/day)—*burning hands* (DC 14), *magic missile, protection from good, obscuring mist, shield*
0 (at will)—*acid splash, dancing lights, detect magic, light, mage hand, ray of frost, read magic, resistance, touch of fatigue* (DC 14)

Str 31, **Dex** 10, **Con** 23, **Int** 17, **Wis** 19, **Cha** 17

Base Atk +19; **CMB** +31; **CMD** 41 (45 vs. trip)
Feats Alertness, Cleave, Flyby Attack, Improved Critical (bite), Improved Initiative, Iron Will, Lightning Reflexes, Multiattack, Power Attack, Weapon Focus (bite)
Skills Bluff +25, Fly +18, Intimidate +25, Knowledge (local) +25, Perception +30, Sense Motive +30, Spellcraft +25, Stealth +14, Swim +40
Languages Aquan, Common, Draconic, Giant

ANCIENT GRAY DRAGON   CR 15

XP 51,200
NE Huge dragon (water)
Init +4; **Senses** dragon senses; **Perception** +31
Aura frightful presence (300 ft., DC 24)

AC 39, touch 8, flat-footed 39 (+31 natural, –2 size)
hp 283 (21d12+147)
Fort +19; **Ref** +14; **Will** +19
Immune paralysis, sleep; **SR** 26

Speed 60 ft., fly 200 ft. (average), swim 40 ft.
Melee 2 claws +30 (2d6+11), bite +31 (2d8+16/19–20), 2 wings +28 (1d8+5), tail slap +28 (2d6+11)
Space 15 ft.; **Reach** 10 ft. (15 ft. with bite)
Special Attacks breath weapon (100-ft. line, 20d6 fire; DC 27 Ref half)
Spells Known (CL 13th; melee touch +30, ranged touch +19):
6th (4/day)—flesh to stone (DC 20), move earth
5th (6/day)—cloudkill (DC 19), telekinesis, transmute rock to mud
4th (7/day)—dimension door, greater invisibility, scrying (DC 18), stoneskin
3rd (7/day)—dispel magic, gaseous form, protection from energy, ray of exhaustion (DC 17)
2nd (7/day)— blur, eagle's splendor, gust of wind (DC 16), locate object, mirror image
1st (7/day)—burning hands (DC 15), magic missile, protection from good, obscuring mist, shield
0 (at will)—acid splash, dancing lights, detect magic, light, ray of frost, read magic, resistance, touch of fatigue (DC 14)

Str 33, **Dex** 10, **Con** 25, **Int** 19, **Wis** 21, **Cha** 19
Base Atk +21; **CMB** +34; **CMD** 44 (48 vs. trip)
Feats Alertness, Cleave, Flyby Attack, Great Cleave, Improved Critical (bite), Improved Initiative, Iron Will, Lightning Reflexes, Multiattack, Power Attack, Weapon Focus (bite)
Skills Bluff +28, Fly +20, Intimidate +28, Knowledge (arcana) +28, Knowledge (local) +28, Perception +33, Sense Motive +33, Spellcraft +28, Stealth +16, Swim +43
Languages Abyssal, Aquan, Common, Draconic, Giant

WYRM GRAY DRAGON   CR 16

XP 76,800
NE Huge dragon (water)
Init +3; **Senses** dragon senses; **Perception** +33
Aura frightful presence (330 ft., DC 25)

AC 41, touch 7, flat-footed 41 (–1 Dex, +34 natural, –2 size)
hp 310 (23d12+161)
Fort +20; **Ref** +14; **Will** +20
Immune paralysis, sleep; **SR** 27

Speed 60 ft., fly 200 ft. (average), swim 40 ft.
Melee 2 claws +33 (2d6+12), bite +34 (2d8+18/19–20), 2 wings +31 (1d8+6), tail slap +31 (2d6+18)
Space 15 ft.; **Reach** 10 ft. (15 ft. with bite)
Special Attacks breath weapon (100-ft. line, 22d6 fire; DC 28 Ref half)
Spells Known (CL 15th; melee touch +33, ranged touch +20):
7th (4/day)—power word blind, waves of exhaustion
6th (6/day)—flesh to stone (DC 20), greater heroism, move earth

5th (6/day)—cloudkill (DC 18), telekinesis, transmute rock to mud, wall of stone
4th (7/day)—dimension door, greater invisibility, scrying (DC 18), stoneskin
3rd (7/day)—dispel magic, gaseous form, protection from energy, ray of exhaustion (DC 17)
2nd (7/day)— blur, eagle's splendor, gust of wind (DC 16), locate object, mirror image
1st (7/day)—burning hands (DC 15), magic missile, protection from good, obscuring mist, shield
0 (at will)—acid splash, dancing lights, detect magic, light, ray of frost, read magic, resistance, touch of fatigue (DC 14)

Str 35, **Dex** 8, **Con** 25, **Int** 19, **Wis** 21, **Cha** 19
Base Atk +23; **CMB** +37; **CMD** 46 (50 vs. trip)
Feats Alertness, Cleave, Flyby Attack, Great Cleave, Improved Critical (bite), Improved Initiative, Iron Will, Lightning Reflexes, Multiattack, Power Attack, Vital Strike, Weapon Focus (bite)
Skills Bluff +30, Fly +21, Intimidate +30, Knowledge (arcana) +30, Knowledge (local) +30, Perception +35, Sense Motive +35, Spellcraft +30, Stealth +17, Swim +46
Languages Abyssal, Aquan, Common, Draconic, Giant

GREAT WYRM GRAY DRAGON   CR 18

XP 153,600
NE Gargantuan dragon (water)
Init +3; **Senses** dragon senses; **Perception** +36
Aura frightful presence (360 ft., DC 27)

AC 42, touch 5, flat-footed 42 (–1 Dex, +37 natural, –4 size)
hp 362 (25d12+200)
Fort +22; **Ref** +15; **Will** +22
Immune paralysis, sleep; **SR** 29

Speed 60 ft., fly 250 ft. (average), swim 40 ft.
Melee 2 claws +34 (2d6+13), bite +35 (2d8+19/19–20), 2 wings +32 (2d6+6), tail slap +32 (2d8+19)
Space 20 ft.; **Reach** 15 ft. (20 ft. with bite)
Special Attacks breath weapon (120-ft. line, 24d6 fire; DC 30 Ref half)
Spells Known (CL 17th; melee touch +34, ranged touch +20):
8th (4/day)—horrid wilting (DC 23), moment of prescience
7th (6/day)—limited wish, power word blind, waves of exhaustion
6th (6/day)—flesh to stone (DC 21), greater heroism, move earth
5th (7/day)—cloudkill (DC 20), telekinesis, transmute rock to mud, wall of stone
4th (7/day)—dimension door, greater invisibility, scrying (DC 19), stoneskin
3rd (7/day)—dispel magic, gaseous form, protection from energy, ray of exhaustion (DC 18)
2nd (7/day)—blur, eagle's splendor, gust of wind (DC 17), locate object, mirror image
1st (8/day)—burning hands (DC 16), magic missile, protection from good, obscuring mist, shield
0 (at will)—acid splash, dancing lights, detect magic, light, mage hand, ray of frost, read magic, resistance, touch of fatigue (DC 15)

Str 37, **Dex** 8, **Con** 27, **Int** 21, **Wis** 23, **Cha** 21
Base Atk +25; **CMB** +42; **CMD** 51 (55 vs. trip)
Feats Alertness, Cleave, Flyby Attack, Great Cleave, Improved Critical (bite), Improved Initiative, Improved Vital Strike, Iron Will, Lightning Reflexes, Multiattack, Power Attack, Vital Strike, Weapon Focus (bite)
Skills Bluff +33, Fly +21, Intimidate +33, Knowledge (arcana) +33, Knowledge (local) +33, Knowledge (nature) +33, Perception +38, Sense Motive +38, Spellcraft +33, Stealth +15, Swim +49, Use Magical Device +33
Languages Abyssal, Aquan, Common, Draconic, Giant, Infernal

Drake, Brine

This creature resembles a giant eel with a draconic head and a mouth full of razor-sharp teeth. The creature's head has small pectoral and caudal fins. A sail-like dorsal fin runs from the base of its skull to the tip of its tail.

BRINE DRAKE	CR 9

XP 6,400
NE Large dragon (aquatic)
Init +6; **Senses** darkvision 60 ft., low-light vision, scent;
Perception +14

AC 23, touch 11, flat-footed 21 (+2 Dex, +12 natural, –1 size)
hp 105 (10d12+40)
Fort +11; **Ref** +11; **Will** +8
Immune paralysis, sleep

Speed 20 ft., swim 60 ft.
Melee bite +14 (2d6+5/19–20 plus grab), tail slap +9 (1d8+2)
Space 10 ft.; **Reach** 10 ft.
Special Attacks constrict (2d6+7), maelstrom, watery breath

Str 21, **Dex** 15, **Con** 18, **Int** 8, **Wis** 12, **Cha** 12
Base Atk +10; **CMB** +16; **CMD** 28 (can't be tripped)
Feats Improved Initiative, Lightning Reflexes, Power Attack, Skill Focus (Stealth), Swim-By Attack
Skills Intimidate +14, Perception +14, Stealth +17, Survival +14, Swim +26
Languages Draconic
SQ amphibious, speed surge

Environment any oceans
Organization solitary, pair, or wing (3–8)
Treasure standard

Maelstrom (Ex) Once per day, as a standard action, a brine drake can create a whirlpool within 100 feet. The whirlpool is 50 feet deep and covers a 30-foot radius at its top. Ships and creatures of the brine drake's size or smaller that come into contact with the whirlpool must succeed on a DC 19 check (Swim check for creatures, Profession [sailor] check for ships) or be pulled into the swirling waters and trapped, spinning around the whirlpool and taking 6d6 points of bludgeoning damage initially and 3d6 points of bludgeoning damage for another 1d6 rounds at which point the whirlpool dissipates. A brine dragon is immune to the effects of its own maelstrom. The check DC is Constitution-based.
Savage Bite (Ex) A brine drake applies 1-1/2 times its Strength bonus to damage dealt with its bite attack, and it threatens a critical hit on a 19-20.
Speed Surge (Ex) Three times per day as a swift action, a brine drake may draw on its draconic heritage for a boost of strength and speed to take an additional move action in that round.
Watery Breath (Su) Once per round, as a standard action, a brine drake can unleash a blast of salt water in a 60-foot cone. Creatures caught in the area take 7d6 points of bludgeoning damage (DC 19 Reflex half). Once a brine drake has used its watery breath, it cannot use it again for 1d6 rounds. The save DC is Constitution-based.

Brine drakes are often confused with sea dragons and have a similar appearance to their much larger, and deadlier cousins. Like true sea dragons, brine drakes are the bane of major shipping lanes, lying in shallow water near the surface and attacking small lightly armed vessels and hunting lesser creatures.

Brine drakes make their homes in underwater caverns and the hulls of sunken vessels large enough to handle their huge size. What treasures they scour from the depths of the sea are piled within their caverns.

Brine drakes thankfully mate only once every few years, with a female producing a clutch of two to six eggs. Eggs hatch within 8 months and young reach maturity in roughly 5 years. Brine drakes are over 12 feet long and weigh around 1,600 pounds. They live up to 300 years.

Brine drakes attack from beneath whenever possible, rising from the waters at great speed, latching their jaws around their target and coiling themselves around other prey or crushing the hulls of vessels under 30 feet in length. Brine drakes drive other creatures away with slaps of its deadly tail.

Drake, Storm

This powerful dragon is dull gray in color and sports massive wings. Its mouth is lined with razor-sharp fangs the length of daggers.

A storm drake is merciless in combat, biting and slashing its foes with its dagger-like teeth and claws. An ambush hunter by nature, a storm drake's approach is usually foreshadowed by a sudden shift in the weather from clear or slightly overcast skies to dark skies and storms.

STORM DRAKE	CR 7

XP 3,200
LE Large dragon (air)
Init +5; **Senses** darkvision 60 ft., low-light vision, scent, storm vision; **Perception** +12

AC 20, touch 10, flat-footed 19 (+1 Dex, +10 natural, −1 size)
hp 84 (8d12+32)
Fort +10; **Ref** +7; **Will** +9
Immune paralysis, sleep; **Resist** electricity 20

Speed 30 ft., fly 60 ft. (average)
Melee bite +13 (2d6+6/19–20), 2 claws +13 (1d6+6)
Space 10 ft.; **Reach** 10 ft.
Special Attacks lightning breath, savage bite
Spell-Like Abilities (CL 8th):
3/day—*call lightning* (DC 14), *fog cloud*, *obscuring mist*, *sleet storm*
1/day—*control weather*, *control winds* (DC 16)

Str 22, **Dex** 13, **Con** 18, **Int** 8, **Wis** 12, **Cha** 13
Base Atk +8; **CMB** +15; **CMD** 26
Feats Flyby Attack, Improved Initiative, Iron Will, Power Attack
Skills Fly +10, Intimidate +12, Knowledge (nature) +6, Perception +12, Stealth +8, Survival +8
Languages Draconic
SQ speed surge

Environment temperate mountains
Organization solitary, pair, or wing (3–8)
Treasure standard

Lightning Breath (Su) A storm drake can, as a standard action, breathe a ball of electricity that explodes upon contact with a solid surface or target. This attack has a range of 100 feet and deals 7d6 points of electricity damage (DC 18 Reflex half) to all creatures within a 20-foot radius spread. Once a storm drake has used its lightning breath, it cannot do so again for 1d6 rounds. The save DC is Constitution-based.
Savage Bite (Ex) A storm drake applies 1-1/2 times its Strength bonus to damage dealt with its bite attack, and it threatens a critical hit on a 19-20.
Speed Surge (Ex) Three times per day as a swift action, a storm drake may draw on its draconic heritage for a boost of strength and speed to take an additional move action in that round.
Storm Vision (Ex) A storm drake can see through fog, clouds, and similar obscuring effects with perfect clarity, including areas affected by spells such as *obscuring mist* and *fog cloud*.

Storm drakes are fierce creatures that make their lairs high atop storm-ravaged mountains. From here, they can survey their territory, and dive to the attack when a potential meal is spotted. Favored meals include humanoids of all kinds, and large game such as deer, elk, and moose.

Storm drakes are generally 20 feet long from nose to tail and weigh over 3,000 pounds. Colors range from dark, dull gray to slate gray mottled with lighter grays. Claws and talons are black and its eyes are the color of dark storm clouds. Storm drakes typically live 300 years.

Drake, Vile

This sleek dragon is black in color with graceful wings and a horned head. Sizzling acid drips from its toothy maw.

VILE DRAKE	CR 8

XP 4,800
CE Large dragon (water)
Init +6; **Senses** darkvision 60 ft., low-light vision, scent;
Perception +15

AC 20, touch 11, flat-footed 18 (+2 Dex, +9 natural, −1 size)
hp 94 (9d12+36)
Fort +10; **Ref** +10; **Will** +6
Immune paralysis, sleep; **Resist** acid 20

Speed 30 ft., fly 50 ft. (average), swim 20 ft.
Melee bite +13 (2d6+5/19–20 plus disease), 2 claws +13 (1d6+5)
Space 10 ft.; **Reach** 10 ft.
Special Attacks acid breath, disease, savage bite

Str 21, **Dex** 14, **Con** 18, **Int** 8, **Wis** 10, **Cha** 12
Base Atk +9; **CMB** +15; **CMD** 27
Feats Flyby Attack, Improved Initiative, Lightning Reflexes, Power Attack, Skill Focus (Perception)
Skills Fly +12, Intimidate +13, Perception +15, Stealth +10, Survival +7, Swim +21
Languages Draconic
SQ speed surge, swamp stride, water breathing

Environment temperate and warm marshes
Organization solitary, pair, or wing (3–8)
Treasure standard

Acid Breath (Su) A vile drake can, as a standard action, spit a ball of liquid that explodes into a cloud of acid. This attack has a range of 60 feet and deals 6d6 points of acid damage (DC 17 Reflex half) to all creatures in a 20-foot radius spread. Additionally, a creature that fails its save takes 3d6 points of acid damage one round after failing its save. Once a vile drake has used its acid breath, it cannot do so again for 1d6 rounds. The save DC is Constitution-based.

Disease (Su) *Marsh Sickness*: Bite—injury; *save* DC 17 Fort; *onset* 1 day; *frequency* 1/day; *effect* 1d3 Con and 1d3 Int damage. A creature whose Int score drops below 12 as a result of marsh sickness acts as if affected by a *confusion* spell (CL 9th) until the disease is cured; *cure* 2 saves. The save DC is Constitution-based.

Savage Bite (Ex) A vile drake applies 1-1/2 times its Strength bonus to damage dealt with its bite attack, and it threatens a critical hit at a 19-20.

Speed Surge (Ex) Three times per day as a swift action, a vile drake may draw on its draconic heritage for a boost of strength and speed to take an additional move action in that round.

Swamp Stride (Ex) A vile drake can move through bogs and quicksand without penalty at its normal speed.

Water Breathing (Ex) A vile drake can breathe underwater indefinitely and can freely use its acid breath and other abilities while submerged.

Vile drakes prey upon those creatures unlucky enough to find themselves caught in the drake's territory. Travelers, fishermen, crocodiles, lizardfolk, and chikes (see their entry in this book) are the usual victims and subsequent meals of vile drakes. Prey that is not devoured immediately is carried back to their swampy lairs and stored under the muck and mud for later consumption.

Vile drakes are about 9 feet long and weigh close to 800 pounds. Their scales are usually black or dark gray, with lighter colors present on their undersides. Eyes are always dark in color. Vile drakes mate for life with the female laying a clutch of up to five eggs once per year. Eggs are laid in the mud and buried to hide them from predators and poachers. Eggs hatch within 9 months. Young reach maturity rapidly, usually within 3 years. Vile drakes, on average, live up to 200 years.

Vile drakes often stalk their prey for miles before attacking. They are generally pack hunters and so encounters with a solitary vile drake are rare. When they spring to attack, vile drakes open with their breath weapon, and then rush in to bite with their nasty fangs.

Drakeling, Flame

This tiny creature looks like a miniature red dragon.

FLAME DRAKELING	CR 2

XP 600
N Tiny dragon (fire)
Init +3; **Senses** darkvision 60 ft., low-light vision, scent;
Perception +7

AC 18, touch 15, flat-footed 15 (+3 Dex, +3 natural, +2 size)
hp 22 (3d12+3)
Fort +4; **Ref** +6; **Will** +4
Immune fire, paralysis, sleep
Weaknesses vulnerability to cold

Speed 20 ft., fly 40 ft. (poor)
Melee bite +8 (1d6–2 plus 1d4 fire)
Space 1/2 ft.; **Reach** 0 ft.
Special Attacks fire breath, heat generation

Str 6, **Dex** 17, **Con** 12, **Int** 6, **Wis** 13, **Cha** 8
Base Atk +3; **CMB** +4; **CMD** 12
Feats Flyby Attack, Weapon Finesse
Skills Fly +9, Intimidate +5, Perception +7, Stealth +17
Languages Draconic

Environment warm hills and mountains
Organization solitary, pair, or band (3–6)
Treasure standard

Fire Breath (Su) A flame drakeling can, as a standard action, spit a line of liquid fire to a range of 20 feet. A creature struck takes 2d6 points of fire damage (DC 12 Reflex half). Further, a creature that fails its save catches on fire and takes 1d6 points of fire damage each round until the flames are extinguished. Once a flame drakeling uses its fire breath, it cannot do so again for 1d4 rounds. The save DC is Constitution-based.

Heat Generation (Su) As a free action, a flame drakeling can increase its body temperature to extreme levels. Creatures attacking the flame drakeling with natural weapons or touching the flame drakeling take 1d4 points of fire damage each round of contact.

Fire drakelings are believed to somehow be related to red dragons or flame drakes, but scholars have yet to find any connection linking the races together. Fire drakelings are generally docile creatures and make their lairs near active volcanoes. They are active during the day most of the time, feeding on insects and small game.

Flame drakelings are about 12 inches long and weigh close to 70 pounds. Scales are varying hues of red, with darker scales running the length of the drakelings back and wings. Females and males are indistinguishable from one another. Flame drakelings mate twice per year with the female laying a small clutch of 4–6 eggs in the lair. eggs incubate for up to 8 months before hatching, and hatchlings reach maturity within 2 years. Flame drakelings live up to 150 years on average.

Flame drakelings generally shun combat with larger foes, seeking refuge among the hills and mountains where their opponents can't reach them. If cornered or defending their young, flame drakelings attack with a vicious bite and surprisingly potent breath weapon.

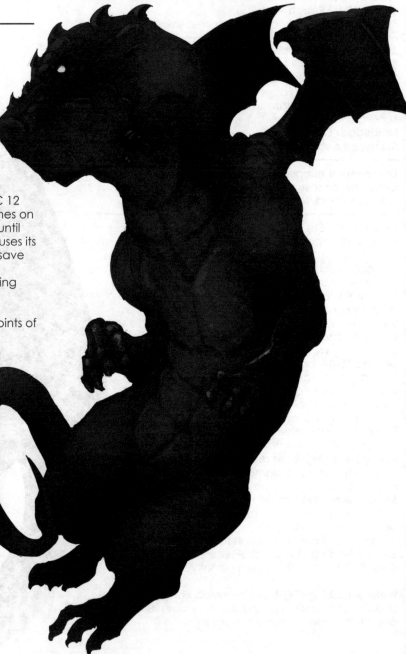

Drakeling, Frost

This miniature dragon has dull blue scales and long wings with ice blue tipped claws.

FROST DRAKELING	CR 3

XP 800
N Tiny dragon (cold)
Init +3; **Senses** darkvision 60 ft., low-light vision, scent; **Perception** +7

AC 17, touch 15, flat-footed 14 (+3 Dex, +2 natural, +2 size)
hp 25 (3d12+6)
Fort +5; **Ref** +6; **Will** +4
Immune cold, paralysis, sleep
Weaknesses vulnerability to fire

Speed 20 ft., burrow 20 ft., fly 40 ft. (poor)
Melee bite +8 (1d6–1 plus 1d4 cold)
Space 1/2 ft.; **Reach** 0 ft.
Special Attacks icy breath, cold generation

Str 8, **Dex** 17, **Con** 14, **Int** 6, **Wis** 13, **Cha** 8
Base Atk +3; **CMB** +4; **CMD** 13
Feats Flyby Attack, Weapon Finesse
Skills Climb +4, Fly +8, Intimidate +4, Perception +7, Stealth +17
Languages Draconic
SQ icewalking

Environment cold hills and mountains
Organization solitary or band (2–4)
Treasure standard

Cold Generation (Su) As a free action, a frost drakeling can decrease its body temperature to extreme levels. Creatures attacking the frost drakeling with natural weapons or touching the frost drakeling take 1d4 points of cold damage each round of contact.

Icewalking (Ex) This ability works like *spider climb*, but the surfaces the frost drakeling climbs must be icy. It can move across icy surfaces without penalty and does not need to make Acrobatics checks to run or charge on ice.

Icy Breath (Su) A frost drakeling can, as a standard action, spit a line of freezing ice to a range of 20 feet. A creature struck takes 3d6 points of cold damage (DC 13 Reflex half). Further, a creature that fails its save is slowed (as the *slow* spell) for 1d4 rounds. Once a frost drakeling uses its icy breath, it cannot use it again for 1d4 rounds. The save DC is Constitution-based.

Frost drakelings are, like their counterparts the flame drakelings, believed to be related to or an offshoot of dragons or drakes (in this case white dragons or frost drakes). As with the flame drakelings however, scholars find nothing linking the races together.

Frost drakelings are diurnal hunters and feed upon small game found in their artic territories. Frost drakelings hunts are known to span several miles from their lair, especially if tracking game. Prey is killed and dragged back to their lair (usually a frigid cave complex set into the side of a mountain out of reach of other predators).

Frost drakelings are about 18 inches long and weigh 50 pounds. Their scales are dull blue with some frost drakelings having white blotches on their bodies. Wings are long and thin and usually icy blue in color. Eyes are deep, rich blue in color. Frost drakelings mate for life and when reproducing, the female lays a small clutch of one to three eggs. Eggs are small, frail, and sapphire blue in color, resembling large gemstones. The eggs hatch within 6 months, and young reach maturity within 2 years. Frost drakelings live up to 120 years on average.

Frost drakelings, unlike other drakelings, do not shy away from combat. When confronted, the creature unleashes its frigid breath weapon and swoops in to attack with its bite.

Dreadweed

This humanoid figure appears to be comprised of a tangle of roots and vines.

DREADWEED	CR 8

XP 4,800
CE Medium plant
Init +7; **Senses** low-light vision, tremorsense 60 ft.; **Perception** +9
Aura enervating aura (10 ft., DC 19)

AC 22, touch 14, flat-footed 18 (+3 Dex, +1 dodge, +8 natural)
hp 76 (8d8+40)
Fort +11; **Ref** +5; **Will** +4
Defensive Abilities negative energy affinity; **DR** 10/magic or good; **Immune** plant traits

---

Speed 30 ft.
Melee bite +10 (1d8+4 plus poison)
Ranged 4 vines +10 (1d6+4 plus 1d4 negative energy plus pull)
Space 5 ft.; **Reach** 5 ft. (20 ft. with vine)
Special Attacks enervating ray, pull (vine, 5 ft.)

Str 18, **Dex** 17, **Con** 21, **Int** 4, **Wis** 14, **Cha** 15
Base Atk +6; **CMB** +10 (+14 with pull); **CMD** 24
Feats Combat Reflexes, Dodge, Improved Initiative, Weapon Focus (vine)
Skills Perception +9, Stealth +10

Environment any temperate or warm land
Organization solitary or cluster (2–8)
Treasure incidental

Enervating Aura (Su) Negative energy weeps from a dreadweed's form. Living creatures in the area take 2d6 points of negative energy damage each round. A successful DC 19 Fortitude save negates the damage that round. A new save must be made each round. The save DC is Constitution-based.

Enervating Ray (Su) Once per round and no more than three times per day, as a standard action, a dreadweed can fire a ray of negative energy at a single target to a range of 30 feet. This ray functions as an *enervation* spell (CL 8th). Each time a dreadweed uses this ray, it suppresses its enervating aura for 1d4 rounds.

Poison (Ex) Bite—injury; *save* DC 19 Fort; *frequency* 1/round for 6 rounds; *effect* 1d4 Con damage; *cure* 1 save. The save DC is Constitution-based.

Vines (Ex) A dreadweed can extend up to four vines from its body at a time, launching them to a maximum range of 20 feet. A dreadweed's attacks with its vines resolve as ranged touch attacks. These vines are quite strong, but can be severed by any amount of slashing damage (a vine is AC 20).If a dreadweed uses its pull ability to pull a target within reach of its bite attack, it can immediately make a free bite attack with a +4 bonus on its attack roll against that target.

A dreadweed is a strange plant creature that grows on unholy ground. Infused with negative energy, it feeds on any living creature it encounters. A dreadweed never stops growing as long as it is able to find food, so in the right cursed soil these plants can grow to truly monstrous proportions. At rest, a dreadweed resembles a matted, chaotic tangle of vines and undergrowth, filled with old sticks, briars, thistles, and nettles. Once roused, however, the dreadweed pulls together into a vaguely humanoid shape and emits a chilling aura that saps the life from living creatures.

A dreadweed is about 6 feet tall but only weighs 75 pounds.

A dreadweed attacks with its vine-like tentacles, tearing at its prey and injecting a powerful poisonous sap with its bite attack. It often attacks in ambush, leaping towards its victim in a swirl of lashes. During battle, a dreadweed can focus its negative energy aura into a powerful ray that further damages its foes.

Dune Horror

This gigantic sand-colored scorpion-like creature has two large claws, a long tail ending in a massive stinger, and a long thick neck that ends in a large snake-like head.

DUNE HORROR	CR 13

XP 25,600
N Huge magical beast
Init +4; **Senses** darkvision 60 ft., low-light vision, tremorsense 60 ft.; **Perception** +21

AC 24, touch 8, flat-footed 24 (+16 natural, –2 size)
hp 168 (16d10+80)
Fort +17; **Ref** +10; **Will** +7
DR 10/magic; **Immune** mind-affecting effects; **Resist** fire 20; **SR** 24

Speed 40 ft., burrow 30 ft.
Melee 2 claws +25 (1d8+10 plus grab), bite +25 (2d6+10/19–20 plus poison), sting +25 (1d8+10 plus poison)
Space 15 ft.; **Reach** 15 ft.
Special Attacks constrict (1d8+10), rapid sting

Str 31, **Dex** 10, **Con** 21, **Int** 2, **Wis** 14, **Cha** 10
Base Atk +16; **CMB** +28 (+32 grapple); **CMD** 38 (50 vs. trip)
Feats Awesome Blow, Great Fortitude, Improved Bull Rush, Improved Critical (bite), Improved Initiative, Power Attack, Weapon Focus (bite, sting), Weapon Focus (claw)[B]
Skills Climb +14, Perception +21, Stealth +11; **Racial Modifiers** +4 Climb, +8 Perception, +8 Stealth

---

Environment warm deserts
Organization solitary
Treasure incidental

Poison (Ex) Bite or Sting—injury; *save* DC 23 Fort; *frequency* 1/round for 6 rounds; *effect* 1d4 Strength damage and 1d4 Constitution damage; *cure* 3 consecutive saves. The save DC is Constitution-based.
Rapid Sting (Ex) A dune horror can make one additional attack in a round with its sting as a swift action.

The dune horror is a massive and vicious creature that makes its lair in the warmer regions of the world, usually deserts, but occasionally underground. A typical underground lair is a large rocky cave while those living aboveground dwell beneath the sand and earth. Dune horrors sustain themselves on a diet of plants such as mosses or cacti and meat, such as preferring larger animals and humanoids, including giants to other sources of meat.

A typical dune horror is 20 feet long with a light brown carapace. Its legs and claws are dark brown, growing darker near the ends. Its tail is dark brown as well, and the stinger black. The dune horror's serpentine neck is covered in light brown scales and its eyes are ruby-colored. Males and females are indistinguishable from one another, save the females are sometimes smaller. A typical female dune horror lays 2–16 eggs once every few years, with the eggs usually hatching 90–100 days later. Juvenile dune horrors are dark brown in color and are blind for the first month of their life. They mature rapidly, reaching adulthood within 6 months. Dune horrors generally live for 20 years.

Dune horrors prefer to attack from ambush, often hiding just beneath the surface waiting for prey to come close. When prey is detected, the dune horror springs to the attack, rending its prey with its claws, stinging it with its deadly stinger, and biting it with its serpentine fanged maw. Grabbed prey is stung to death and devoured. Dune horrors do not collect treasure; any treasure found within its lair is the remnants of a previous meal.

Dwarf, Frost

This stocky humanoid is about 4 feet tall with bright blue eyes and long bluish-white hair.

FROST DWARF	CR 1

XP 400
CN (evil tendencies) Medium humanoid (cold, dwarf)
Init +0; **Senses** darkvision 60 ft.; **Perception** +1

AC 13, touch 10, flat-footed 13 (+2 armor, +1 natural)
hp 13 (2d8+4)
Fort +5; **Ref** +0; **Will** +1
Immune cold
Weaknesses vulnerability to fire

Speed 20 ft.
Melee battleaxe +3 (1d8+1 plus 1d4 cold)
Special Attacks breath weapon (20-ft. line, 2d6 cold damage; DC 13 Ref half, 3/day)

Str 13, **Dex** 10, **Con** 14, **Int** 11, **Wis** 13, **Cha** 6
Base Atk +1; **CMB** +2; **CMD** 12
Feats Weapon Focus (battleaxe)
Skills Craft (any) +5, Perception +1, Stealth +0 (+4 in snow), Survival +6; **Racial Modifiers** +4 Stealth in snow
Languages Common, Dwarf, Giant
SQ dwarf traits

Environment cold mountains
Organization Team (2–4), squad (9–16 plus 3 3rd-level sergeants and 1 leader of 3rd-8th level), or clan (30–100 plus 30% non-combatants plus 1 3rd level sergeant per 10 adults, 5 5th-level lieutenants, and 3 7th level captains), or jarldom (2–6 clans plus one jarl or king of level 10+)
Treasure standard (leather, battleaxe, other treasure)

Cold (Su) When a frost dwarf is in a cold climate, it deals an extra 1d4 points of cold damage with both weapons and natural attacks. This does not function if the frost dwarf is in temperate or warmer climates.

Frost dwarves are chaotic and untamed as the glacial expanses which they inhabit. Often they have lairs hidden deep beneath snow and ice packs burrowed deep into the living stone where they plunder for gemstones and metals as any other dwarf. Skilled crafters, frost dwarves trade freely with frost giants, constructing many of their massive weapons and armor in exchange for loot and protection. They are typically disliked and dismissed by their "true" dwarven kin who consider them to be abominations or worse.

Frost dwarves are known for their rudeness and coarse sense of humor. They are however famed for their skill at craftsmanship and the enchantment of strange and unusual magical items. Most typically frost dwarves are worshippers of Thrym and enjoy his taste in puzzles and conundrums. Frost dwarf traps are legendary amongst the frozen wastes of the world.

Frost dwarves are proficient combatants and make use of their natural surroundings to their advantage. They assault enemies with crossbows from distance and use their battleaxe to crush charges. They enjoy surprise and prefer to attack using dirty tricks such as unleashing avalanches upon unsuspecting travelers, then pick through their frozen carcasses for loot. Higher level frost dwarves often ride winter wolves as mounts. It is not uncommon for 1–2 of the beasts to be in the company of a frost dwarf squad.

Frost Dwarf Society

Frost dwarves are commonly found serving frost giant masters. In their own nations they elect a king from the ruling clans. This jarl rules for life though does not necessarily establish any form of dynasty. Frost dwarf clans organize themselves loosely after the fashion of their mountain and hill dwarf cousins, but are more tribal in nature. Frost dwarves keep a semblance of military titles amongst the various clans. Frost dwarves are attuned to the use of magic and many of their leaders are powerful wizards or clerics. They are equally likely to be barbarians.

There are no frost dwarf females. Frost dwarves are born to the union of a frost dwarf and dwarf (any), human, gnome, or frost or hill giant. Any child conceived from such a union is always born a frost dwarf male and reaches full size within a matter of weeks. Frost dwarf children are often abandoned near known frost dwarf communities where it is expected they will be found and cared for or claimed by their father's clan. Frost dwarves are often shunned by their maternal parent as an abomination, especially among hill and mountain dwarves who likely banish the mother from their halls if she survives the child's birth. The exception to this rule is that of frost dwarves born to frost giant and jotun mothers. In frost giant culture, frost dwarves are considered a sign of good luck. They are however still sent to live amongst others of their kind until they reach the age of maturity, which is about 50 years old, when they are welcomed back amongst the frost giants who sired them.

Ebony Horse

This large horse has black skin, a black mane, and inky-black hooves.

EBONY HORSE	CR 6

XP 2,400
N Large outsider (extraplanar, native)
Init +4; **Senses** darkvision 60 ft., low-light vision; **Perception** +16

AC 19, touch 13, flat-footed 15 (+4 Dex, +6 natural, –1 size)
hp 84 (8d10+40)
Fort +7; **Ref** +10; **Will** +9

Speed 50 ft., fly 90 ft. (good)
Melee 2 hooves +7 (1d6+2), bite +12 (1d8+5)
Space 10 ft.; **Reach** 5 ft.
Spell-Like Abilities (CL 8th):
1/day— *plane shift* (self plus five others to elemental planes, Astral Plane, or Material Plane only)

Str 20, **Dex** 18, **Con** 21, **Int** 13, **Wis** 17, **Cha** 11
Base Atk +8; **CMB** +14; **CMD** 28 (32 vs. trip)
Feats Alertness, Endurance, Flyby Attack, Run
Skills Fly +17, Intimidate +11, Knowledge (planes) +12, Perception +16, Sense Motive +16, Stealth +11, Survival +14
Languages Common, any two elemental languages (Aquan, Auran, Ignan, Terran), any one planar language (Abyssal, Celestial, Infernal)
SQ elemental endurance

Environment warm and temperate plains
Organization solitary or herd (2–4)
Treasure none

Elemental Endurance (Ex) An ebony horse can remain on the Planes of Air, Earth, Fire, or Water for up to 24 hours at a time. An ebony horse can extend this protection to its rider and up to four of the rider's allies in a 30 foot radius around itself. If the ebony and horse and any protected allies move more than 30 feet apart, the protection ends for that individual and cannot be regained for 24 hours. If the ebony horse is killed, this protection ends immediately. Failure to return to the Material Plane before that time expires causes an ebony horse to take 1 point of damage per additional hour spent on the elemental plane, until it dies or returns to the Material Plane. Other creatures protected by elemental endurance suffer damage normally from the elemental plane when that time expires.

Ebony horses are massive stallions prized for their loyalty, running speed, their ability to fly, and their ability to enter the various elemental planes unharmed. These creatures are often used by genies, demons, devils, and others due to their innate ability to withstand the various planar atmospheres and survive unharmed while simultaneously extending this protection to others.

Ebony horses are generally solitary creatures but on very rare occasions a small herd of these creatures may be encountered. When not traveling the many planes of existence, ebony horses spend their time roaming vast grasslands on the Material Plane. They do not associate with normal horses or other steeds, preferring to keep company with their own.

Ebony horses kick with their front hooves and lash out with a nasty bite when forced into combat. They are strong-willed and brave creatures, rarely backing down when confronted. They are, however, smart enough to know when the battle is lost and take to the air in such times. An ebony horse is fiercely loyal creature to its rider and, if on a hostile plane and protecting a rider with its elemental endurance ability, it will not flee and end this protection, even fighting to its death if necessary. Ebony horses have no known enemies, but tend to show aggression around nightmares. While no known enmity exists between the two, combat is as likely to occur as is no confrontation at all.

Larger ebony horses (10 HD, Huge size) are known to exist and are used extensively by the seraphs (see the *Genie, Seraph* entry in this book) in their ongoing wars with the efreet.

Edon

This creature resembles a small hairy ape-like humanoid with long muscular arms that end in slightly oversized clawed hands.

EDON	CR 1

XP 400
N Small magical beast
Init +2; **Senses** darkvision 60 ft., low-light vision; **Perception** +5
Aura stench (DC 13, 1d4 rounds)

AC 14, touch 13, flat-footed 12 (+2 Dex, +1 natural, +1 size)
hp 15 (2d10+4)
Fort +5; **Ref** +5; **Will** +1
Immune sonic

Speed 30 ft., climb 20 ft.; brachiate
Melee 2 claws +5 (1d3+1), bite +5 (1d4+1)

Str 12, **Dex** 15, **Con** 14, **Int** 4, **Wis** 12, **Cha** 8
Base Atk +2; **CMB** +2; **CMD** 14
Feats Weapon Finesse
Skills Acrobatics +10, Climb +13, Perception +5;
Racial Modifiers +4 Acrobatics, +4 Climb
Languages Sylvan (can't speak)
SQ deaf

Environment warm or temperate forests
Organization gang (2–5) or pack (6–11)
Treasure standard

Brachiate (Ex) An edon can move its climb speed through treetops by leaping from tree to tree so long as the trees are no more than 10 feet apart and the creature's hands are empty.
Deaf (Ex) An edon is deaf and automatically fails any Perception check based on sound. It is immune to any effect that requires the target be able to hear.
Stench Aura (Ex) An edon's stench aura affects only humans and halflings, and creatures with the scent special ability. All other creatures are immune to its effects. An edon can suppress its stench for 1d2 hours by rubbing juniper berries on its body. Doing so negates the aura for the duration.

Edons are forest-dwelling creatures with a great fondness for human and halfling flesh. At first glance they appear to be monkeys or small apes with powerful arms and sharp claws. They are territorial creatures that dine on mosses, leaves, small forest animals, and of course their favorite meal: humans and halflings. Edons are active during the day and rest in their treetop lairs at night.

An edon stands about 3 feet tall and weighs around 60 pounds. Its fur is brown or brownish-gray and its eyes are gray. An edon has a lifespan of roughly 50 years.

Edons are completely deaf and do not speak, though they do seem to understand the Sylvan tongue. They communicate with others of their kind through body motion and sign language.

Edons attack by hiding among the treetops and dropping on unsuspecting prey. They are relentless in their attacks, slashing and biting their foe until it is dead. Edons realize they are not the strongest or largest creatures, so they rely on their sheer numbers to gang up on their foes. Recent encounters with packs of edons have led to stories of pack leaders who appear to be smarter than the average edon and who employ traps such as tripwires and deadfalls to catch or disable their prey.

Eel, Fire

This eel is about 10 feet long and roughly one foot thick. It has a broad, triangular head and dark gray scales.

FIRE EEL	CR 5

XP 1,600
N Large magical beast (aquatic)
Init +6; **Senses** darkvision 60 ft., low-light vision; **Perception** +7

AC 19, touch 11, flat-footed 17 (+2 Dex, +8 natural, −1 size)
hp 51 (6d10+18)
Fort +8; **Ref** +9; **Will** +4
Resist fire 20

Speed swim 40 ft.
Melee bite +12 (2d6+9 plus grab)
Space 10 ft.; **Reach** 5 ft.
Special Attacks fire shroud

Str 22, **Dex** 14, **Con** 16, **Int** 2, **Wis** 14, **Cha** 11
Base Atk +6; **CMB** +13 (+16 grapple); **CMD** 25 (can't be tripped)
Feats Improved Initiative, Lightning Reflexes, Weapon Focus (bite)
Skills Escape Artist +10, Perception +7, Stealth +3, Swim +19; **Racial Modifiers** +8 Escape Artist

Environment temperate and warm oceans
Organization solitary, pair, or nest (3–10)
Treasure incidental

Fire Shroud (Ex) A fire eel constantly secretes highly flammable oil from its body. Upon contact with the air, the oil bursts into flames. The oil normally burns for 1 minute before extinguishing itself. Anyone contacting the burning oil takes 3d6 points of fire damage. Underwater, a fire eel can release this oil quickly (as a swift action) in a 10-foot radius around its body. The oil automatically ignites at the start of the fire eel's next turn. It deals the same fire damage as above, but only burns for 5 rounds underwater. A fire eel can ignite its oil once per minute in this way.

Fire eels are a beautiful but dangerous species of aquatic beast that secrete and can ignite an oily residue on their skin to drive away predators and attract a mate. The flames emitted by a fire eel can be green, blue, red, or violet, or even a pattern of these colors, depending on the individual eel. Fire eels can be particularly dangerous to seagoing vessels during their mating season, when they come to the surface en masse to perform fiery courtship rituals, and are more aggressive than usual.

Fire eels are at home in both saltwater and freshwater, and live in groups of up to 10 eels. A fire eel lair consists of a number of long and winding tunnels burrowed into sand, rocks, or mud in shallow water. These tunnels eventually empty into a large central chamber. Fire eels, normally non-aggressive, become highly aggressive if their lair is threatened.

Fire eels are normally inoffensive, and avoid combat if possible. However, if they are attacked, grabbed, or if it is their mating season, they become more aggressive, and use their fire shroud to ward off attacks while they bite relentlessly until their opponents are driven away.

Ekimmu

This spectral figure moves forward, its face bent and twisted in anguish.

EKIMMU	CR 7

XP 3,200
CE Medium undead (incorporeal)
Init +7; **Senses** darkvision 60 ft., lifesense 60 ft.; **Perception** +13
Aura unnatural aura (30 ft.)

AC 19, touch 19, flat-footed 15 (+5 deflection, +1 dodge, +3 Dex)
hp 84 (8d8+40 plus 8)
Fort +7; **Ref** +5; **Will** +10
Defensive Abilities channel resistance +4, incorporeal, rejuvenation; **Immune** undead traits

Speed fly 30 ft. (perfect)
Melee incorporeal touch +9 (7d6, DC 19 Fort half)
Special Attacks malevolence, paralyzing howl

Str —, **Dex** 16, **Con** —, **Int** 14, **Wis** 14, **Cha** 21
Base Atk +6; **CMB** +9; **CMD** 28
Feats Ability Focus (malevolence)[B], Dodge, Improved Initiative, Iron Will, Toughness
Skills Fly +22, Intimidate +16, Knowledge (local) +10, Perception +13, Sense Motive +13, Stealth +14
Languages Common

Environment any
Organization solitary
Treasure none

Incorporeal Touch (Su) By passing part of its incorporeal body through a foe's body as a standard action, the ekimmu inflicts 7d6 damage. This damage is not negative energy—it manifests in the form of physical wounds and aches from supernatural aging. Creatures immune to magical aging are immune to this damage, but otherwise the damage bypasses all forms of damage reduction. A Fortitude save halves the damage inflicted.
Lifesense (Su) An ekimmu notices and locates living creatures within 60 feet, just as if it possessed the blindsight ability.
Malevolence (Su) The ekimmu's jealousy of the living is particularly potent. Once per round, the ekimmu can merge its body with a creature on the Material Plane. This ability is similar to a *magic jar* spell (CL 8th), except that it does not require a receptacle. To use this ability, the ekimmu must be adjacent to the target. The target can resist the attack with a successful DC 21 Will save. A creature that successfully saves is immune to that same ekimmu's malevolence for one day. The save DC is Charisma-based and includes a +2 bonus from the ekimmu's Ability Focus feat.
Paralyzing Howl (Su) At will, an ekimmu can let out a fearsome howl that paralyzes all within a 30 feet radius for 1d4+1 rounds unless they succeed on a DC 19 Will save. A creature that successfully saves is immune to that ekimmu's howl for one day. The save DC is Charisma-based.
Rejuvenation (Su) In most cases, it's difficult to destroy an ekimmu through simple combat: the "destroyed" spirit restores itself in 2d6 days. Even the most powerful spells are usually only temporary solutions. The only way to permanently destroy an ekimmu is to determine the reason for its existence and set right whatever prevents it from entering the underworld.
Unnatural Aura (Su) Animals do not willingly approach within 30 feet of an ekimmu, unless a master makes a DC 25 Handle Animal, Ride, or wild empathy check.

An ekimmu is the evil ghost of one who has been denied entrance to the underworld and is doomed to wander the earth. It is greatly feared, for it attaches itself quite easily to virtually any living person regardless of whether that person has been acquainted with the dead one. Once it has possessed a living host, it is very difficult to exorcise.

An ekimmu roams the lands near where it was killed. Though it is not bound to the area, it feels a sense of connection to it and rarely wanders more than a few miles from it. An ekimmu has no permanent lair and wanders its realm perpetually, always on the move.

An ekimmu roams the earth, seeking victims to possess and using its hosts to bring misfortune and death to the living. Its howling in the night is often the only warning of its approach. In battle, it uses its array of abilities to defeat and destroy its opponents, opening combat with its paralyzing howl and then using its malevolence to attack a target it deems weak-willed and open for possession.

Elemental Lords

For every type of elemental, there is a ruler, a huge elemental of massive size and strength that holds dominion over its own kind. These rulers are often worshipped by elementals and some are even worshipped by cults on the Material Plane. At the GM's discretion, clerics who worship an elemental ruler gains access to one elemental domain related to the elemental lord, plus another domain. Suggested domains are below.

Command Elementals (Su) As a standard action, an elemental lord can attempt to gain control of any elemental creature of the same element within 100 feet. Elementals receive a Will save to negate the effect. The DC for this Will save is equal to 10 + 1/2 the elemental lord's + its Charisma modifier. Elementals that make their save are immune to the command of that elemental lord for one day. Elementals that fail their saves fall under the elemental lord's control, obeying its commands to the best of their ability. An elemental lord does not need to concentrate to maintain control over commanded elementals.

Once commanded, an elemental serves until either it dies, the elemental lord dies, the elemental lord dismisses it, or the summoning magic ends (if the elemental was summoned). An elemental lord can command any number of elementals, so long as their total Hit Dice do not exceed twice the elemental lord's Hit Dice. If an elemental creature is under the control of another creature, the elemental lord can attempt an opposed Charisma check to gain control of the elemental.

Elemental Lord	Element	Domains
Inder	Fire	Fire, Healing
Lypso	Water	Water, Travel
Onyst	Earth	Earth, Strength
Susir	Air	Air, Weather

Inder (Lord of Fire Elementals)

This creature appears to be a 20-foot tall column of fire, vaguely humanoid in shape.

INDER	CR 23

XP 820,000
N Huge outsider (elemental, extraplanar, fire)
Init +17; **Senses** darkvision 60 ft.; **Perception** +50
Aura searing heat (30 ft., DC 37)

AC 34, touch 22, flat-footed 20 (+13 Dex, +1 dodge, +12 natural, −2 size)
hp 500 (40d10+280)
Fort +31; **Ref** +35; **Will** +22
DR 15/—; **Immune** elemental traits, fire; **SR** 34
Weaknesses vulnerability to cold

Speed 60 ft.
Melee 2 slams +51 (4d6+12 plus burn)
Space 15 ft.; **Reach** 15 ft.
Special Attacks burn (4d6, DC 37), command fire elementals (DC 37)
Spell-Like Abilities (CL 20th; melee touch +50, ranged touch +51):
At will—*detect magic, dispel magic, greater teleport* (self plus 50 lbs. of objects only), *heat metal* (DC 19), *scorching ray*
3/day—*fire storm* (DC 25), *fireball* (DC 20), *flame strike* (DC 22), *wall of fire*
1/day—*incendiary cloud* (DC 25), summon (level 9, 1d2 elder fire elementals, 1d4 greater fire elementals, 1d4 efreet, or 4–8 salamanders 100%)

Str 35, **Dex** 37, **Con** 24, **Int** 22, **Wis** 24, **Cha** 24
Base Atk +40; **CMB** +54; **CMD** 78
Feats Blind-Fight, Cleave, Combat Expertise, Combat Reflexes, Critical Focus, Dodge, Great Cleave, Great Fortitude, Improved Initiative, Improved Vital Strike, Iron Will, Lightning Stance, Lunge, Mobility, Power Attack, Spring Attack, Vital Strike, Weapon Finesse, Whirlwind Attack, Wind Stance
Skills Acrobatics +56, Climb +52, Diplomacy +47, Escape Artist +53, Intimidate +50, Knowledge (arcana) +49, Knowledge (planes) +49, Knowledge (religion) +49, Perception +50, Sense Motive +50, Stealth +48, Survival +47
Languages Aquan, Auran, Common, Ignan, Terran; telepathy 100 ft.

Environment any (Plane of Fire)
Organization solitary or band (Inder plus 2–4 greater fire elementals)
Treasure triple standard

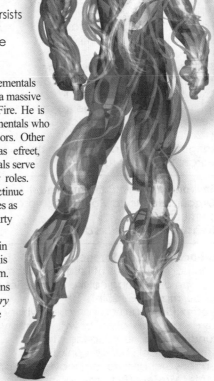

Searing Heat (Ex) Any creature that starts its turn within 30 feet of Inder must succeed on a DC 37 Fortitude save or take 2d8 points of fire damage. Anyone striking Inder with a natural weapon or unarmed strike takes 4d6 points of fire damage (DC 37 Reflex save for half). A creature that grapples Inder or is grappled by Inder takes 4d6 points of fire damage each round the grapple persists (DC 37 Reflex save for half). The save DCs are Constitution-based.

Inder rules over fire elementals and makes his home within a massive fiery lake on the Plane of Fire. He is attended by 4 elder fire elementals who serve in his court as advisors. Other fire-based creatures such as efreet, azer, and lesser fire elementals serve him in the court in minor roles. Inder also keeps a large retinue of female fire-based creatures as his harem, having over thirty wives at last count.

Inder rarely engages in battle, preferring to let his fire elementals fight for him. If forced however, he opens with a *fireball, incendiary cloud,* and *fire storm,* before summoning creatures to his aid. When facing a large number of opponents, he often rides a red dragon of largest size into battle.

Lypso (Lord of Water Elementals)

This massive creature appears to be a gigantic crashing wave. No other features are discernible on its form.

LYPSO	CR 23

XP 820,000
N Huge outsider (elemental, extraplanar, water)
Init +11; **Senses** darkvision 60 ft.; **Perception** +50

AC 32, touch 16, flat-footed 24 (+7 Dex, +1 dodge, +16 natural, –2 size)
hp 540 (40d10+320)
Fort +32; **Ref** +31; **Will** +22
DR 15/—; **Immune** elemental traits; **SR** 34

Speed 30 ft., swim 100 ft.
Melee 2 slams +55 (4d6+16/19–20)
Space 15 ft.; **Reach** 15 ft.
Special Attacks command water elementals (DC 37), drench, vortex (DC 46), water mastery
Spell-Like Abilities (CL 20th; melee touch +54, ranged touch +45):
At will—*control water* (DC 23), *create water, detect magic, dispel magic, fog cloud, greater teleport* (self plus 50 lbs. of objects only)
3/day—*cone of cold* (DC 22), *horrid wilting* (DC 25), *ice storm*
1/day— summon (level 9, 1d2 elder water elementals, 1d4 greater water elementals, 1d4 marid, or 20–40 sahuagin 100%)

Str 43, **Dex** 25, **Con** 27, **Int** 22, **Wis** 24, **Cha** 24
Base Atk +40; **CMB** +58; **CMD** 76
Feats Blind-Fight, Cleave, Combat Expertise, Critical Focus, Dodge, Great Cleave, Great Fortitude, Improved Bull Rush, Improved Critical (slam), Improved Initiative, Improved Sunder, Improved Vital Strike, Iron Will, Lightning Reflexes, Mobility, Power Attack, Spring Attack, SwimBy Attack, Vital Strike, Weapon Focus (slam)
Skills Acrobatics +50, Diplomacy +47, Escape Artist +47, Intimidate +50, Knowledge (arcana) +49, Knowledge (planes) +49, Knowledge (religion) +49, Perception +50, Sense Motive +50, Stealth +42, Survival +47, Swim +67
Languages Aquan, Auran, Common, Ignan, Terran; telepathy 100 ft.

Environment any (Plane of Water)
Organization solitary or band (Lypso plus 2–4 greater water elementals)
Treasure triple standard

Drench (Ex) Lypso's touch puts out nonmagical flames of Large size or smaller. He can dispel magical fire he touches as *dispel magic* (CL 20th).
Vortex (Su) Lypso can create a whirlpool as a standard action, at will. This ability functions identically to the whirlwind special attack, but can only form underwater and cannot leave the water.
Water Mastery (Ex) Lypso gains a +1 bonus

on attack and damage rolls if both he and his opponent are touching water. If the opponent or Lypso is touching the ground, Lypso takes a –4 penalty on attack and damage rolls. These modifiers apply to bull rush and overrun maneuvers, whether Lypso is initiating or resisting these kinds of attacks.

Lypso rules over water elementals and those who call the Plane of Water home. His lair is a massive cavern deep within the Plane of Water. His court consists of water elementals, water weirds, and marid. His most trusted advisor is a marid of ancient age and power. Lypso keeps an "aviary" of water mephitis for his amusement as well. Legends tell of a great enmity between Lypso and Inder, the Lord of Fire Elementals, and that a great elemental war is brewing between the two. This same legend reveals that Lypso and Inder are brothers. Whether this is truth or not is currently unknown.

In combat, Lypso uses his vortex attack and horrid wilting attack to begin battle. Creatures that survive are subjected to his ice storm ability as well as a pummeling by his powerful slam attacks. If outclassed, Lypso summons water creatures, or a small army of sahuagin to his aid.

Onyst (Lord of Earth Elementals)

This 15-foot tall hulking humanoid appears to have been chiseled from stone. Its face is mostly featureless though dark recesses seem to function as eyes.

ONYST	CR 24

XP 1,230,000
N Huge outsider (earth, elemental, extraplanar)
Init +2; **Senses** darkvision 60 ft., tremorsense 60 ft.; **Perception** +49

AC 37, touch 11, flat-footed 34 (+2 Dex, +1 dodge, +26 natural, –2 size)
hp 660 (40d10+440)
Fort +35; **Ref** +24; **Will** +21
DR 15/—; **Immune** elemental traits; **SR** 35

Speed 30 ft., burrow 30 ft.; earth glide
Melee 2 slams +58 (4d8+19/19–20)
Space 15 ft.; **Reach** 15 ft.
Special Attacks command earth elementals (DC 36), earth mastery
Spell-Like Abilities (CL 20th; melee touch +57, ranged touch +40):
At will—*detect magic, dispel magic, greater teleport* (self plus 50 lbs. of objects only), *soften earth and stone, stone shape*
3/day—*flesh to stone* (DC 22), *move earth, wall of stone* (DC 21)
1/day—*earthquake* (DC 24), *summon* (level 9, 1d2 elder earth elementals, 1d4 greater earth elementals, 1d4 shaitan, or 4–8 xorn 100%)

Str 49, **Dex** 14, **Con** 32, **Int** 20, **Wis** 22, **Cha** 22
Base Atk +40; **CMB** +61; **CMD** 74
Feats Awesome Blow, Blind-Fight, Cleave, Critical Focus, Dodge, Great Cleave, Great Fortitude, Greater Bull Rush, Greater Overrun, Greater Sunder, Improved Bull Rush, Improved Critical (slam), Improved Overrun, Improved Sunder, Improved Vital Strike, Iron Will, Lunge, Power Attack, Vital Strike, Weapon Focus (slam)
Skills Climb +62, Diplomacy +46, Intimidate +46, Knowledge (arcana) +48, Knowledge (dungeoneering) +48, Knowledge (planes) +48, Knowledge (religion) +45, Perception +49, Sense Motive +49, Stealth +37, Survival +49
Languages Aquan, Auran, Common, Ignan, Terran; telepathy 100 ft.

Environment any (Plane of Earth)
Organization solitary or band (Onyst plus 2–4 greater earth elementals)
Treasure triple standard

Earth Glide (Ex) Onyst can pass through stone, dirt, or almost any other sort of earth except metal as easily as a fish swims through water. If protected against fire damage, he can even glide through lava. His burrowing leaves behind no tunnel or hole, nor does it create any ripple or other sign of his presence. A *move earth* spell cast on an area containing him flings him back 30 feet, stunning him for 1 round unless he succeeds on a DC 15 Fortitude save.

Earth Mastery (Ex) Onyst gains a +1 bonus on attack and damage rolls if both he and his foe are touching the ground. If an opponent is airborne or waterborne, Onyst takes a –4 penalty on attack and damage rolls. These modifiers apply to bull rush and overrun maneuvers, whether Onyst is initiating or resisting these kinds of attacks. (These modifiers are not included in the statistics block.)

Onyst makes his home in a gigantic complex of caverns hollowed into the side of an enormous mountain of stone on the Plane of Earth. He is constantly attended by various earth elementals, stone giants, and xorn. He has a blue dragon of advanced age; some say the dragon serves as advisor and counsel, others say it is nothing more than a pet.

In battle, Onyst likes to pound his foes with his enormous fists. Creatures that prove meddlesome are turned to stone and then pulverized, their remains scattered to the winds.

Susir (Lord of Air Elementals)

This enormous cloud-like creature has no discernible features as it spins into cyclone form.

SUSIR	CR 23

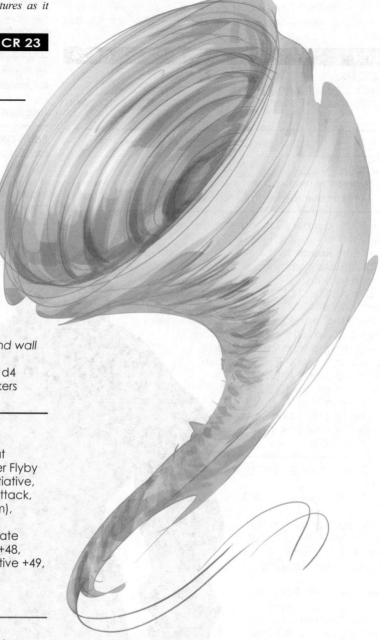

XP 820,000
N Huge outsider (air, elemental, extraplanar)
Init +18; **Senses** darkvision 60 ft.; **Perception** +49

AC 35, touch 23, flat-footed 20 (+14 Dex, +1 dodge, +12 natural, –2 size)
hp 500 (40d10+280)
Fort +31; **Ref** +38; **Will** +21
Defensive Abilities air mastery; **DR** 15/—; **Immune** elemental traits; **SR** 34

Speed fly 120 ft. (perfect)
Melee 2 slams +53 (4d6+14)
Space 15 ft.; **Reach** 15 ft.
Special Attacks command air elementals (DC 36), whirlwind (DC 44)
Spell-Like Abilities (CL 20th; melee touch +52, ranged touch +52):
At will—*control winds* (DC 21), *detect magic*, *dispel magic*, *greater teleport* (self plus 50 lbs. of objects only), *gust of wind* (DC 18), *obscuring mist*
3/day—*chain lightning* (DC 22), *control weather*, *wind wall* (DC 19)
1/day— summon (level 9, 1d2 elder air elementals, 1d4 greater air elementals, 1d4 djinn, or 4–8 invisible stalkers 100%)

Str 39, **Dex** 38, **Con** 24, **Int** 20, **Wis** 22, **Cha** 22
Base Atk +40; **CMB** +56; **CMD** 81
Feats Blind-Fight, Cleave, Combat Expertise, Combat Reflexes, Critical Focus, Dodge, Flyby Attack, Greater Flyby Attack, Great Cleave, Great Fortitude, Improved Initiative, Iron Will, Lightning Reflexes, Lunge, Mobility, Power Attack, Spring Attack, Weapon Finesse, Weapon Focus (slam), Whirlwind Attack
Skills Acrobatics +57, Diplomacy +46, Fly +61, Intimidate +46, Knowledge (arcana) +48, Knowledge (planes) +48, Knowledge (religion) +48, Perception +49, Sense Motive +49, Stealth +49, Survival +49
Languages Aquan, Auran, Common, Ignan, Terran; telepathy 100 ft.

Environment any (Plane of Air)
Organization solitary or band (Susir plus 2–4 greater air elementals)
Treasure triple standard

Air Mastery (Ex) Airborne creatures take a –1 penalty on attack and damage rolls against Susir.

Susir makes his home hidden among the fog and clouds of the Plane of Air. His great airy palace is formed of the same material as the Plane itself and swirls and shifts across the great expanse of the Plane of Air. Within his palace dwell air elementals of all sizes and ages, invisible stalkers, will-o-wisps, and an array of other air-based creatures.

Susir dislikes combat, believing it a boring and mundane activity. If forced into battle however, he attacks first using his chain lighting attacks, followed by his whirlwind.

Elemental, Salt

This crystalline humanoid is slightly translucent and light gray in color. Its head has no discernible features and its power arms end in massive fists.

SALT ELEMENTAL

Languages Terran

Environment any (Plane of Earth)
Organization solitary, pair, or gang (3–8)
Treasure none

Dehydration Aura (Su) A salt elemental's aura draws moisture from an area centered on itself. Living creatures within range take damage (damage is detailed with each elemental) each round they remain in the area. A successful Fortitude save reduces the damage by half. This effect is especially devastating to plants, animals, and aquatic creatures, which take a –4 penalty on their saving throws. The save DC is Constitution-based.

Earth Mastery (Ex) A salt elemental gains a +1 bonus on attack and damage rolls if both it and its foe are touching the ground. If an opponent is airborne or waterborne, the elemental takes a –4 penalty on attack and damage rolls. These modifiers apply to bull rush and overrun maneuvers, whether the elemental is initiating or resisting these kinds of attacks. (These modifiers are not included in the statistics block.)

Salt Poisoning (Ex) Anyone hit by a salt elemental's claw attack is sickened for 3 rounds + 1 round per Hit Dice of the salt elemental. A successful Fortitude save negates this effect. The save DC is Constitution-based.

Vulnerability to Water (Ex) A salt elemental submerged in water that covers at least half its body takes 1d6 points of damage each round until it escapes. Damage from water-based attacks (such as the slam attack of a water elemental) deal +50% damage to a salt elemental.

Size	Height	Weight
Small	4 ft.	60 lbs.
Medium	8 ft.	560 lbs.
Large	16 ft.	4,500 lbs.
Huge	20 ft.	25,000 lbs.
Greater	26 ft.	30,000 lbs.
Elder	32 ft.	36,000 lbs.

SMALL SALT ELEMENTAL   CR 1/2

XP 200
N Small outsider (earth, elemental, extraplanar)
Init +4; **Senses** darkvision 60 ft.; **Perception** +4
Aura dehydration (10 ft., DC 10, 1d4)

AC 16, touch 11, flat-footed 16 (+5 natural, +1 size)
hp 5 (1d10)
Fort +2; **Ref** +0; **Will** +2
Immune elemental traits
Weaknesses vulnerability to water

Speed 20 ft.
Melee claw +3 (1d4+1 plus salt poisoning)
Special Attacks salt poisoning (4 rounds, DC 10)

Str 13, **Dex** 10, **Con** 11, **Int** 4, **Wis** 11, **Cha** 11
Base Atk +1; **CMB** +1; **CMD** 11

Feats Power Attack
Skills Climb +5, Perception +4, Stealth +8

MEDIUM SALT ELEMENTAL   CR 2

XP 600
N Medium outsider (earth, elemental, extraplanar)
Init +0; **Senses** darkvision 60 ft.; **Perception** +6
Aura dehydration (10 ft., DC 12, 1d6)

AC 17, touch 10, flat-footed 17 (+7 natural)
hp 19 (3d10+3)
Fort +4; **Ref** +1; **Will** +3
Immune elemental traits
Weaknesses vulnerability to water

Speed 20 ft.
Melee claw +5 (1d6+3 slashing plus salt poisoning)
Special Attacks salt poisoning (6 rounds, DC 12)

Str 15, **Dex** 10, **Con** 13, **Int** 4, **Wis** 11, **Cha** 11
Base Atk +3; **CMB** +5; **CMD** 15
Feats Cleave, Power Attack
Skills Climb +8, Perception +6, Stealth +6

LARGE SALT ELEMENTAL — CR 4

XP 1,200
N Large outsider (earth, elemental, extraplanar)
Init +0; **Senses** darkvision 60 ft.; **Perception** +9
Aura dehydration (10 ft., DC 15, 1d8)

AC 17, touch 9, flat-footed 17 (+8 natural, –1 size)
hp 45 (6d10+12)
Fort +7; **Ref** +2; **Will** +5
DR 5/—; **Immune** elemental traits
Weaknesses vulnerability to water

Speed 20 ft.
Melee 2 claws +9 (1d8+4 slashing plus salt poisoning)
Space 10 ft.; **Reach** 10 ft.
Special Attacks salt poisoning (9 rounds, DC 15)

Str 18, **Dex** 10, **Con** 15, **Int** 6, **Wis** 11, **Cha** 11
Base Atk +6; **CMB** +11; **CMD** 21
Feats Cleave, Great Cleave, Power Attack
Skills Climb +13, Knowledge (dungeoneering) +4, Knowledge (planes) +4, Perception +9, Stealth +5

HUGE SALT ELEMENTAL — CR 6

XP 2,400
N Huge outsider (earth, elemental, extraplanar)
Init +0; **Senses** darkvision 60 ft.; **Perception** +11
Aura dehydration (20 ft., DC 17, 2d6)

AC 18, touch 9, flat-footed 17 (+1 dodge, +9 natural, –2 size)
hp 68 (8d10+24)
Fort +9; **Ref** +2; **Will** +6
DR 5/—; **Immune** elemental traits
Weaknesses vulnerability to water

Speed 20 ft.
Melee 2 claws +11 (2d6+5 plus salt poisoning)
Space 15 ft.; **Reach** 15 ft.
Special Attacks salt poisoning (11 rounds, DC 17)

Str 21, **Dex** 10, **Con** 17, **Int** 6, **Wis** 11, **Cha** 11
Base Atk +8; **CMB** +15; **CMD** 26
Feats Cleave, Dodge^B, Endurance, Great Cleave, Mobility, Power Attack
Skills Climb +16, Knowledge (dungeoneering) +5, Knowledge (planes) +5, Perception +11, Stealth +3

GREATER SALT ELEMENTAL — CR 8

XP 4,800
N Huge outsider (earth, elemental, extraplanar)
Init +0; **Senses** darkvision 60 ft.; **Perception** +13
Aura dehydration (20 ft., DC 19, 2d8)

AC 20, touch 10, flat-footed 18 (+1 Dex, +1 dodge, +10 natural, –2 size)
hp 95 (10d10+40)
Fort +11; **Ref** +4; **Will** +7
DR 10/—; **Immune** elemental traits
Weaknesses vulnerability to water

Speed 20 ft.
Melee 2 claws +14 (2d8+6 plus salt poisoning)
Space 15 ft.; **Reach** 15 ft.
Special Attacks salt poisoning (13 rounds, DC 19)

Str 23, **Dex** 13, **Con** 19, **Int** 6, **Wis** 11, **Cha** 11
Base Atk +10; **CMB** +18; **CMD** 29
Feats Cleave, Dodge, Great Cleave, Mobility, Power Attack
Skills Climb +17, Knowledge (dungeoneering) +8, Knowledge (planes) +7, Perception +13, Stealth +5

ELDER SALT ELEMENTAL — CR 10

XP 9,600
N Huge outsider (earth, elemental, extraplanar)
Init +0; **Senses** darkvision 60 ft.; **Perception** +15
Aura dehydration (20 ft., DC 20, 2d10)

AC 22, touch 10, flat-footed 20 (+1 Dex, +12 natural, –2 size)
hp 114 (12d10+48)
Fort +12; **Ref** +5; **Will** +8
DR 10/—; **Immune** elemental traits
Weaknesses vulnerability to water

Speed 20 ft.
Melee 2 claws +18 (2d8+7 plus salt poisoning)
Space 15 ft.; **Reach** 15 ft.
Special Attacks salt poisoning (15 rounds, DC 20)

Str 25, **Dex** 13, **Con** 19, **Int** 10, **Wis** 11, **Cha** 11
Base Atk +12; **CMB** +21; **CMD** 33
Feats Cleave, Great Cleave, Improved Bull Rush, Power Attack, Step Up, Weapon Focus (claws)
Skills Climb +22, Intimidate +12, Knowledge (dungeoneering) +15, Knowledge (planes) +15, Perception +15, Stealth +8

Salt elementals inhabit regions rich in salt upon the Plane of Earth. Some believe they originated on a pocket plane somewhere near the energy planes and Plane of Water; perhaps an Elemental Plane of Salt. Salt elementals, avoid large expanses of water at all costs, knowing exposure to such a large quantity spells disaster.

Salt elementals spend most of their time wandering their realm and often make forays into other planes (except the Plane of Water), seeking creatures on which to feed. They are particularly fond of plants, which are extremely vulnerable to their dehydrating ability.

A salt elemental generally appears as a humanoid with no discernible features, though they can take other forms, and some do, preferring to appear in the shape of large animals or giant vermin (usually beetles).

Elemental, Smoke

A black cloud of acrid smoke drifts ahead.

SMOKE ELEMENTAL

Languages Auran

Environment any (Plane of Air, Plane of Fire, or Plane of Smoke)
Organization solitary, pair, or gang (3–8)
Treasure none

Air Mastery (Ex) Airborne creatures take a −1 penalty on attack and damage rolls against a smoke elemental.
Burn (Ex) A smoke elemental's burn DC includes a −2 racial penalty, as their fires don't burn as hot as a true fire elemental's flames.
Engulf (Ex) A smoke elemental can engulf creatures of its size or smaller into its smoky form as part of a standard action. It cannot make any other attack in which it engulfs. The smoke elemental merely has to move over its opponents, affecting as many as it can cover. Targeted creatures can make attacks of opportunity against the creature, but if they do so, they are not entitled to a saving throw against the engulf attack. Those who do not attempt attacks of opportunity can attempt a Reflex save to avoid being engulfed—on a success, they move back or aside (target's choice). The smoke obscures all sight, including darkvision, beyond 5 feet and grants concealment to creatures inside the cloud from attacks by opponents that are not adjacent to them.

Engulfed opponents do not gain the pinned condition and may move normally. Each round a creature begins its turn engulfed, it suffers from burning eyes (−2 on attack rolls and Perception checks) and takes 3d6 points of fire damage from smoke inhalation. The penalties and damage continue for a number of rounds equal to the smoke elemental's Hit Dice even after escaping the engulf. A creature can make a Fortitude save (DC is listed with each elemental) to end the penalties and damage. The save DCs are Constitution-based.
Gaseous (Ex) A smoke elemental can pass through small holes or narrow openings without reducing its speed.
Vulnerability to Wind (Ex) A smoke elemental is treated as two sizes smaller for purposes of determining the effects high wind has upon it.

Size	Height	Weight
Small	4 ft.	1 lbs.
Medium	8 ft.	2 lbs.
Large	16 ft.	4 lbs.
Huge	20 ft.	6 lbs.
Greater	26 ft.	7 lbs.
Elder	32 ft	8 lbs.

SMALL SMOKE ELEMENTAL · CR 1
XP 400
N Small outsider (air, elemental, extraplanar, fire)
Init +2; **Senses** darkvision 60 ft.; **Perception** +5

AC 16, touch 13, flat-footed 14 (+2 Dex, +3 natural, +1 size)
hp 11 (2d10)
Fort +3; **Ref** +5; **Will** +0
Defensive Abilities air mastery, amorphous; **Immune** elemental traits, fire
Weaknesses vulnerability to cold, vulnerability to wind

Speed fly 80 ft. (perfect)

Melee slam +3 (1d4 plus burn)
Special Attacks burn (1d3, DC 9), engulf (DC 11)

Str 11, **Dex** 15, **Con** 11, **Int** 4, **Wis** 11, **Cha** 11
Base Atk +2; **CMB** +1; **CMD** 13 (can't be tripped)
Feats Flyby Attack
Skills Fly +17, Perception +5, Stealth +11 (+19 in smoke or fog); **Racial Modifiers** +8 Stealth in smoke or fog
SQ gaseous

MEDIUM SMOKE ELEMENTAL · CR 3
XP 800
N Medium outsider (air, elemental, extraplanar, fire)
Init +8; **Senses** darkvision 60 ft.; **Perception** +7

AC 17, touch 14, flat-footed 13 (+4 Dex, +3 natural)
hp 30 (4d10+8)
Fort +6; **Ref** +8; **Will** +1
Defensive Abilities air mastery, amorphous; **Immune** elemental traits, fire
Weaknesses vulnerability to cold, vulnerability to wind

Speed fly 80 ft. (perfect)
Melee slam +5 (1d6+1 plus burn)
Special Attacks burn (1d4, DC 11), engulf (DC 13)

Str 13, **Dex** 19, **Con** 14, **Int** 4, **Wis** 11, **Cha** 11
Base Atk +4; **CMB** +5; **CMD** 19 (can't be tripped)
Feats Flyby Attack, Improved Initiative
Skills Fly +19, Perception +7, Stealth +11 (+19 in smoke or fog); **Racial Modifiers** +8 Stealth in smoke or fog
SQ gaseous

LARGE SMOKE ELEMENTAL · CR 5
XP 1,600
N Large outsider (air, elemental, extraplanar, fire)
Init +10; **Senses** darkvision 60 ft.; **Perception** +11

AC 19, touch 15, flat-footed 13 (+6 Dex, +4 natural, -1 size)
hp 60 (8d10+16)
Fort +8; **Ref** +12; **Will** +2
Defensive Abilities air mastery, amorphous; **DR** 5/—; **Immune** elemental traits, fire
Weaknesses vulnerability to cold, vulnerability to wind

Speed fly 80 ft. (perfect)
Melee 2 slams +13 (1d8+3 plus burn)
Space 10 ft.; **Reach** 10 ft.
Special Attacks burn (1d6, DC 15), engulf (DC 17)

Str 16, **Dex** 23, **Con** 15, **Int** 6, **Wis** 11, **Cha** 11
Base Atk +8; **CMB** +12; **CMD** 28 (can't be tripped)
Feats Combat Reflexes, Flyby Attack, Improved Initiative, Weapon Finesse
Skills Escape Artist +17, Fly +23, Perception +11, Stealth +13 (+21 in smoke or fog); **Racial Modifiers** +8 Stealth in smoke or fog
SQ gaseous

HUGE SMOKE ELEMENTAL · CR 7
XP 3,200
N Huge outsider (air, elemental, extraplanar, fire)
Init +12; **Senses** darkvision 60 ft.; **Perception** +13

AC 22, touch 17, flat-footed 13 (+1 dodge, +8 Dex, +5 natural, −2 size)

hp 85 (10d10+30)
Fort +10; **Ref** +15; **Will** +3
Defensive Abilities air mastery, amorphous;
DR 5/—; **Immune** elemental traits, fire
Weaknesses vulnerability to cold,
vulnerability to wind

Speed fly 80 ft. (perfect)
Melee 2 slams +16 (2d6+5 plus burn)
Space 15 ft.; **Reach** 15 ft.
Special Attacks burn (1d8, DC 18), engulf (DC 20)

Str 20, **Dex** 27, **Con** 17, **Int** 6, **Wis** 11, **Cha** 11
Base Atk +10; **CMB** +17; **CMD** 36 (can't be
tripped)
Feats Combat Reflexes, Dodge, Flyby Attack,
Improved Initiative, Weapon Finesse
Skills Escape Artist +21, Fly +25, Perception
+13, Stealth +13 (+21 in smoke or fog); **Racial
Modifiers** +8 Stealth in smoke or fog
SQ gaseous

GREATER SMOKE ELEMENTAL CR 9
XP 6,400
N Huge outsider (air, elemental,
extraplanar, fire)
Init +13; **Senses** darkvision 60 ft.;
Perception +16

AC 24, touch 18, flat-footed 14 (+1
dodge, +9 Dex, +6 natural, –2 size)
hp 123 (13d10+52)
Fort +12; **Ref** +17; **Will** +4
Defensive Abilities air mastery,
amorphous; **DR** 10/—; **Immune** elemental
traits, fire
Weaknesses vulnerability to cold,
vulnerability to wind

Speed fly 80 ft. (perfect)
Melee 2 slams +20 (2d8+7 plus burn)
Space 15 ft.; **Reach** 15 ft.
Special Attacks burn (2d6, DC 18), engulf (DC 23)

Str 24, **Dex** 29, **Con** 18, **Int** 8, **Wis** 11, **Cha** 11
Base Atk +13; **CMB** +22; **CMD** 42 (can't be tripped)
Feats Blind-Fight, Combat Reflexes, Dodge, Flyby Attack,
Improved Initiative, Mobility, Weapon Finesse
Skills Escape Artist +25, Fly +29, Intimidate +16, Perception
+16, Stealth +17 (+25 in smoke or fog); **Racial Modifiers** +8
Stealth in smoke or fog
SQ gaseous

ELDER SMOKE ELEMENTAL CR 11
XP 12,800
N Huge outsider (air, elemental, extraplanar, fire)
Init +14; **Senses** darkvision 60 ft.; **Perception** +19

AC 27, touch 19, flat-footed 16 (+1 dodge, +10 Dex, +8
natural, –2 size)
hp 152 (16d10+64)
Fort +14; **Ref** +20; **Will** +5
Defensive Abilities air mastery, amorphous; **DR** 10/—;
Immune elemental traits, fire
Weaknesses vulnerability to cold, vulnerability to wind

Speed fly 80 ft. (perfect)
Melee 2 slams +24 (2d8+8 plus burn)
Space 15 ft.; **Reach** 15 ft.

Special Attacks burn (2d8, DC 24), engulf (DC 26)

Str 27, **Dex** 31, **Con** 18, **Int** 10, **Wis** 11, **Cha** 11
Base Atk +16; **CMB** +26; **CMD** 47 (can't be tripped)
Feats Blind-Fight, Combat Reflexes, Dodge, Flyby Attack,
Improved Initiative, Mobility, Spring Attack, Weapon Finesse
Skills Escape Artist +29, Fly +33, Intimidate +19, Knowledge
(planes) +19, Perception +19, Stealth +21 (+29 in smoke or
fog); **Racial Modifiers** +8 Stealth in smoke or fog
SQ gaseous

Smoke elementals are creatures of elemental smoke: part fire, part air. Where the Elemental Plane of Air meets the Elemental Plane of Fire lies a para-elemental plane, that of Elemental Smoke. It is from that black clouded region that these creatures hail.

Smoke elementals spend most of their time on their home plane, only occasionally venturing into the Elemental Planes of Air or Fire. Rarely do they ever enter the Material Plane unless called by a spellcaster.

A smoke elemental appears as a cloud of black smoke or thick fog. No discernible features can be seen in its form, though it can reshape itself at will to form two large eyes and a mouth of empty darkness (which serve no purpose other than to perhaps startle onlookers).

Elemental, Wood

Wood elementals appear as twiggy, wooden beings, with long, elf-like ears and curious features. They are quite strong, although slow moving and deliberate. Wood elementals encountered are always huge beings, and it is not known if smaller versions exist.

WOOD ELEMENTAL	CR 16

XP 76,800
N Huge outsider (elemental, native)
Init +3; **Senses** darkvision 60 ft.; **Perception** +24 (+28 in forests)

AC 26, touch 7, flat-footed 26 (–1 Dex, +19 natural, –2 size)
hp 252 (21d10+105)
Fort +17; **Ref** +6; **Will** +15
DR 15/slashing; **Immune** elemental traits
Weakness vulnerability to fire

Speed 30 ft.
Melee 2 slams +33 (3d6+13/19–20)
Space 15 ft.; **Reach** 15 ft.
Special Attacks *flesh to wood* (touch +32, DC 21), forest mastery

Str 37, **Dex** 8, **Con** 21, **Int** 14, **Wis** 12, **Cha** 12
Base Atk +21; **CMB** +36 (+38 sunder); **CMD** 45 (47 vs. sunder)
Feats Awesome Blow, Bleeding Critical, Cleave, Critical Focus, Improved Bull Rush[B], Improved Critical (slam), Improved Initiative, Improved Natural Attack (slam), Improved Sunder, Iron Will, Power Attack, Weapon Focus (slam)
Skills Intimidate +21, Knowledge (history) +12, Knowledge (local) +25, Knowledge (nature) +25, Knowledge (the planes) +25, Perception +24 (+28 in forests), Sense Motive +24 , Stealth +12 (+28 in forests), Survival +24;
Racial Modifiers +4 Perception and +16 Stealth in forests
Languages Sylvan

Environment any forest or jungle (Prime Material Plane)
Organization solitary, pair or stand (3–6)
Treasure none

Flesh to Wood (Su) Once every 1d4 rounds a wood elemental may attempt to turn flesh to wood with a successful touch attack. A DC 21 Fortitude save negates. The save is Constitution-based. This malady cannot be remedied short of a *wish, miracle,* or Dobrynya the druid's intervention.
Forest Mastery (Ex) A wood elemental gains a +1 bonus to both attack and damage rolls if she and her opponent are both in a forested area. This ability has been added in to the above stat block.

Wood elementals serve as protectors of the forest, and each forest usually has one, while great primeval forests may boast several. Wood elementals spend most of their time in a euphoric slumber, waking only when their forest is in danger. At these times the wood elemental moves forth to seek and destroy that which threatens the forest. At times they are known to ally with factions that work to protect and save the forest, especially elves. Wood elementals attack with a slam attack, as their limbs are strong and powerful, much like those of a treants.

Huge wood elementals stand 16 to 24 feet tall, with a 3 foot to 7 foot trunk, weighing 1,500 to 4,000 pounds. Wood elementals typically replicate the look of the native trees of their forest; some wood elementals appear as mighty oaks, some as maples, birch, pine or majestic cedar trees. More exotic species are certainly possible (tiger wood, ipe, etc.).

Credit

Original author William Loran Christensen
Originally appearing in *Fane of the Fallen* (© Frog God Games/ William Loran Christensen, 2010)

Emberleaf

This small flowering plant has dark green leaves shot through with crimson. Several small bright yellow flowers are sprinkled around its form.

EMBERLEAF	CR 4

XP 1,200
N Small plant
Init +6; **Senses** blindsight 60 ft., scent; **Perception** +4
Aura heat (10 ft., 1d6 fire)

AC 16, touch 13, flat-footed 14 (+2 Dex, +3 natural, +1 size)
hp 51 (6d8+24)
Fort +9; **Ref** +4; **Will** +3
Defensive Abilities fire healing; **Immune** fire, plant traits
Weaknesses vulnerability to cold

Speed 20 ft., climb 20 ft.
Melee 2 tendrils +7 (1d6+2 plus 1d6 fire)
Special Attacks ring of fire

Str 14, **Dex** 15, **Con** 19, **Int** 6, **Wis** 12, **Cha** 7
Base Atk +4; **CMB** +5; **CMD** 17 (21 vs. trip)
Feats Combat Reflexes, Improved Initiative, Skill Focus (Perception)
Skills Climb +10, Perception +4, Stealth +15
Languages Sylvan (can't speak)

Environment temperate forests
Organization solitary or patch (2–4)
Treasure incidental

Fire Healing (Ex) An emberleaf subjected to fire damage regains 1 hit point for every 3 points of damage the attack would have otherwise dealt.
Heat Aura (Ex) An emberleaf can suppress or restart its heat aura as a free action. If it uses its ring of fire ability, its heat aura automatically dissipates and it cannot restart it again for 1 hour.
Ring of Fire (Su) Once per day as a standard action, an emberleaf can create an immobile, blazing ring of fire in a 30-foot radius around its form. This fire is similar to a *wall of fire* spell. The ring of fire is 20 feet tall, and deals 2d6 points of fire damage to creatures within 10 feet of it. Those beyond 10 feet but within 20 feet take 1d6 points of fire damage. Creatures passing through the ring take 3d6 points of fire damage. The ring deals this damage when it appears, and to all creatures in the area on the emberleaf's turn each round. The ring of fire lasts a number of rounds equal to the emberleaf's Hit Dice (6 rounds for a standard emberleaf). The emberleaf cannot use this ability to invoke its fire healing.

The emberleaf is a sentient plant found deep within darkened and desolate forests where it preys on insects and other small game animals. Often times, an emberleaf makes its lair near trails or roads that wend their way through the forests in hopes of catching a larger meal passing through.

An emberleaf appears as a small flowering plant with various yellow, sweet smelling flowers. It typical grows no taller than two or three feet and when at rest resembles an ordinary plant. The creature is active during the day and rests during the nighttime hours. During warmer months, the creature is more active, while during cooler months and winter, the creature is dormant most of the time. An emberleaf can go up to one month without eating.

Emberleafs do not actively hunt prey. Rather, they wait for their prey to come to them. The sweet smelling flowers and aroma given off by the flowers usually attracts insects and small game who unknowingly wander into range of the emberleaf's tendrils. Particularly tough opponents are subjected to its heat aura. If extremely hungry, an emberleaf uses its ring of fire attack to prevent its prey from escaping.

Fachan

This hideous creature is a bizarre giant that has a single leg, one arm that sprouts from the middle of its chest, and one eye in the middle of its forehead.

FACHAN	CR 6

XP 2,400
NE Large humanoid (giant)
Init −1; **Senses** darkvision 60 ft., low-light vision; **Perception** +0

AC 18, touch 8, flat-footed 18 (−1 Dex, +10 natural, −1 size)
hp 73 (7d8+35 plus 7)
Fort +10; **Ref** +1; **Will** +4; +4 vs. fear effects
DR 5/—

Speed 30 ft.
Melee greatclub +12 (2d8+10) or slam +11 (2d6+10)
Space 10 ft.; **Reach** 10 ft.
Special Attacks horrific visage, powerful grip

Str 25, **Dex** 9, **Con** 20, **Int** 6, **Wis** 10, **Cha** 12
Base Atk +5; **CMB** +13; **CMD** 22 (can't be tripped)
Feats Cleave, Great Cleave, Improved Bull Rush[B], Iron Will, Power Attack, Toughness[B], Weapon Focus (greatclub)[B]
Skills Intimidate +11
Languages Giant
SQ one-legged stance

Environment any land
Organization solitary, gang (2–5), or tribe (10–30)
Treasure standard (greatclub, other treasure)

Horrific Visage (Ex) Any creature within 30 feet viewing a fachan must succeed on a DC 16 Will save or be shaken for 1d4+2 rounds. A creature that makes its save is immune to the horrific visage of that fachan for one day. The save DC is Charisma-based and includes a +2 racial bonus.
One-Legged Stance (Ex) Fachans are surprisingly nimble while hopping on their single leg. This unusual mode of movement allows the fachans to ignore the effects of difficult terrain on movement and makes it impossible to trip.
Powerful Grip (Ex) A fachan can wield a two-handed weapon in its single hand, gaining all the usual benefits for wielding a two-handed weapon.

Fachans are foul-tempered and foul-smelling beasts with a taste for human flesh. Despite having only one leg and arm, they are extremely agile. Having only one eye does not hamper their vision any more than one leg hampers their mobility. Some sages believe fachans are an offshoot of one of the giant races while others believe fachans are the deformed offspring of a failed hill giant and ogre or cyclops mating. These creatures are shunned by other giant races, except hill giants with whom they have a distant but tolerable relationship. They rarely associate with other races for any reason.

Fachans take up residence wherever they can find a warm, dry spot. They are not against building huts and hovels when they must, but they prefer the convenience of driving out the residents of an existing structure and claiming it as their own. They are most often encountered in wastelands and swamps. Fachan villages can consist of up to 30 individuals plus 30% noncombatant young. Fachan leaders are always fighters or barbarians.

Fachans stand 12 feet tall and weigh 1,000 pounds. Their hair is unkempt and matted. Skin tone is usually bronze or brown, and their hair is dark.

A fachan makes for an odd opponent at best. It most often attempts a bull rush against its largest foe in the first round of combat, and tries to avoid spellcasters. After this, it moves in with its melee attacks.

Firebird

A majestic bird about 8 feet long swoops overhead. Its feathers shine like silver and gold and its eyes are the color of crystals.

FIREBIRD	CR 8

XP 4,800
NG Large magical beast
Init +6; **Senses** darkvision 60 ft., low-light vision; **Perception** +15

AC 20, touch 11, flat-footed 18 (+2 Dex, +9 natural, −1 size)
hp 85 (9d10+36)
Fort +10; **Ref** +8; **Will** +7
Defensive Abilities *magic circle against evil*; **DR** 10/evil;
Resist cold 10, fire 10; **SR** 19

Speed 30 ft., fly 70 ft. (good)
Melee 2 claws +13 (1d8+5), bite +13 (2d6+5), 2 wings +11 (1d6+2)
Space 10 ft.; **Reach** 5 ft.
Special Attacks blinding brilliance, breath weapon (60-ft. cone, 5d6 fire damage; DC 18 Ref half, every 1d4 rounds)
Spell-Like Abilities (CL 9th):
Constant—*magic circle against evil*
At will—*detect evil*, *flare* (DC 12)
3/day—*cure moderate wounds* (DC 14), *hold person* (DC 15; evil creatures only)
1/day—*fire shield*, *sunburst* (DC 20)

Str 21, **Dex** 15, **Con** 19, **Int** 15, **Wis** 14, **Cha** 15
Base Atk +9; **CMB** +15; **CMD** 27
Feats Alertness, Flyby Attack, Improved Initiative, Iron Will, Multiattack
Skills Diplomacy +11, Fly +8, Heal +11, Knowledge (any one) +11, Perception +15, Sense Motive +8; **Racial Modifiers** +4 Perception
Languages Auran, Celestial, Common, Sylvan
SQ chant

Environment temperate forests
Organization solitary or pair
Treasure standard

Blinding Brilliance (Su) At will as a swift action, a firebird can increase the light output of its tail feathers so they radiate brilliant yellow light in a 100-toot radius. Creatures in the affected area must succeed on a DC 18 Fortitude save or be blinded for 2d4 rounds. The save DC is Constitution-based.
Chant (Su) By chanting for one full round, a firebird can create any one of the following effects: *cure serious wounds, remove blindness/deafness, remove disease, remove fear,* or *slow poison.* Each is usable once per round at will, but a single creature can only gain the benefit of each one once per day. Each functions as the spell of the same name with a caster level equal to the firebird's Hit Dice.

Firebirds are considered by many to be good luck. Sighting one on a journey is considered to be a boon (unless of course you are evil, in which case it is deemed bad luck to see a firebird). Firebirds are thought of as protectors and guardians of the forest and often befriend elves,

dryads, and druids and can sometimes be found in the company of such creatures. They dislike orcs, goblins, and any who would despoil and destroy the forests.

These creatures roost in great caves far away from civilized lands and are usually only seen in the early morning or evening hours. Once a month firebirds take to the night sky at the stroke of midnight. To the casual observer a firebird in the night sky appears to be a shooting star or comet flying across the sky.

Firebirds claim vast amounts of territory as their own, protecting this domain from evil, and also using it as their own personal hunting ground. Such domains often overlap with other firebirds (which suits each just fine as they share the duties of guardianship over the overlapping territory). Firebirds live on a diet of game animals, fruits, nuts, and berries.

A firebird appears as a large bird about 8 feet long with golden and silver feathers. A majestic crest of gold runs from its head, along its back, and disappears into its tail feathers. Its beak and claws are the color of pearls and its eyes shine like crystal.

Firebirds almost always attack evil-aligned creatures and those that would despoil their forests. They prefer to fight from the air and always enter battle with their *magic circle against evil* in effect. A firebird usually begins combat using its blinding brilliance, followed quickly by its breath weapon. Foes that continue to press the fight are *held* (if evil) or subjected to a *sunburst*.

Fisherman

This large humanoid stands over 10 feet tall, and is clad in the garb of a mundane fisherman. Its eyes glow with an eerie blue light and its grizzled face is trimmed with a gnarled beard from which scuttle small crabs, fish, and shrimp.

FISHERMAN	CR 15

XP 51,200
LE Large outsider (aquatic, evil, lawful, native)
Init +2; **Senses** darkvision 60 ft., *deathwatch* 15 miles, weather sense 30 miles; **Perception** +23

AC 21, touch 11, flat-footed 19 (+2 Dex, +10 natural, –1 size)
hp 202 (15d10+120)
Fort +13; **Ref** +11; **Will** +16
DR 15/magic; **Immune** cold; **Resist** electricity 10, fire 10; **SR** 26

Speed 40 ft., swim 30 ft.
Melee *+3 boat hook* +26/+21/+16 (1d8+13) or *+3 boat hook* +22/+17/+12 (1d8+9), *+3 boat hook* +22 (1d6+9) or *+3 boat hook* +22/+17/+12 (1d8+9), *+3 gaff hook* +22 (1d8+9)
Ranged net +16 (entangle)
Space 10 ft.; **Reach** 10 ft.
Spell-Like Abilities (CL 15th):
Constant — *deathwatch* (15 mile radius), *freedom of movement* (underwater)
1/day—*summon nature's ally V*
Spells Prepared (CL 9th; melee touch +23, ranged touch +16):
5th—*slay living* (DC 20, x2)
4th—*control water, spell immunity, unholy blight* (DC 19)
3rd—*bestow curse* (DC 18), *deeper darkness, magic circle against good, water walk*
2nd—*align weapon, darkness, death knell* (DC 17), *enthrall* (DC 17), *silence* (DC 17)
1st—*bane* (DC 16), *command* (DC 16), *curse water* x2, *obscuring mist, sanctuary* (DC 16)
0—*bleed* (DC 15), *create water, detect magic, mending*

Str 28, **Dex** 15, **Con** 26, **Int** 15, **Wis** 21, **Cha** 20
Base Atk +15; **CMB** +25; **CMD** 37
Feats Cleave, Diehard, Endurance, Great Cleave, Iron Will, Power Attack, Two-Weapon Fighting, Vital Strike
Skills Bluff +23, Craft (any) +20, Diplomacy +23, Intimidate +23, Knowledge (local) +20, Perception +23, Sense Motive +23, Swim +35
Languages Aquan, Sylvan
SQ amphibious, create soul cage, exotic weapons, gambling

Environment any aquatic
Organization solitary
Treasure standard (*+3 boat hook, +3 gaff hook*, net, other treasure)

Create *Soul Cage* (Su) Using debris that floats to the bottom of the ocean, a fisherman can construct a *soul cage*. The soul cage is a magical construction that, through its crafting, has been endowed with a *trap the* *soul* spell. The spell requires no material components other than the debris from which it is created. The magic of the *soul cage* only functions for fishermen and the souls remain trapped for as long as the fisherman wishes and remains on the Material Plane. Usually, only upon the death of the fisherman may the trapped souls be released. A *soul cage* can hold up to six souls at any given time.

Deathwatch (Sp) A fisherman makes constant use of the spell *deathwatch*, as cast by a 15th level cleric. The range of a fisherman's *deathwatch* is 1 mile per hit die, allowing it to sense the life state of any creature within its territory. This ability can be negated, but the fisherman can reactivate it the next round as a free action.

Exotic Weapons (Ex) A fisherman is proficient in the use of the boat hook and gaff hook.

Gambling (Ex) Fishermen are fond of games and gambling and should one be offered a fair chance of odds, he may find a wager impossible to resist. In this way, it may be possible to bargain for the release of the soul of a companion or loved one. Although evil, fishermen are bound by a personal code and honor the terms of a wager if they lose.

Spells Fishermen cast divine spells as 9th-level clerics. They do not gain access to domains or other cleric abilities.

Weather Sense (Su) A fisherman always knows the condition of the weather within a 30 mile radius, even if he is currently underwater.

The fisherman is a rare creature not often encountered by the mortals of the material world. Sages and scholars often postulate these aquatic spirits may hail from some other plane of existence, whilst others assume the fisherman is some strange form of undead, the powerful soul of a legendary seaman fated to lurk in the depths of the ocean. Sailors know only that they are to be feared. Although they do not often engage in melee combat, many have found to their own detriment that fishermen are quite skilled. Fighting with a variety of maritime tools and weapons, fishermen favor boathooks, gaff hooks, and nets to ensnare and slay those who intrude upon their habitat. All fishermen seem to be male — no female of the species has ever been witnessed by any sailor. They are powerful creatures who enjoy tormenting seafarers and work hard to collect the souls of those who die at the hands of the sea. At the bottom of the ocean they may be found tending to devices called soul cages that resemble ordinary lobster traps, though they are used to imprison the spirits of the drowned. The territory of a fisherman can extend over a dozen miles from its lair.

Fishermen stand between 11 and 12 feet tall and weigh 1,600 pounds.

When a fisherman detects a great storm at sea, or is otherwise aware that sailors are meeting watery deaths, it rises to the surface in order to start collecting as many of the souls as it can. An individual fisherman may tend to as many as 3d6 *soul cages*, each containing the incarcerated spirits of 1d6 unfortunate sailors, all of which have met their deaths through storm, shipwreck, or some other maritime disaster. Those slain by intentional violence are left to wander the depths by the fisherman. They are very competitive with others of their kind but occasionally they swap souls to enhance their own collections.

Special Weapons

Boat Hook: A boat hook resembles a quarterstaff with a barbed hook at one end. Sailors use boat hooks to snag mooring lines and pull in small boats. Because a boat hook is not intended to be used as a weapon, it requires the Exotic Weapon Proficiency to be used in that capacity. A boat hook is a double weapon. The damage is given as hook/staff.

Cost 6 gp; *Small* 1d4/1d3, *Medium* 1d6/1d4, *Large* 1d8/1d6; *Critical* x2; *Weight* 5 lb.; *Type* Bludgeoning/Piercing.

Gaff Hook: A gaff hook is a curved metallic hook with a cross bar. Gaff hooks are used by fishermen to lift heavy catches into their boats. Because a gaff hook is not intended to be used as a weapon, it requires the Exotic Weapon Proficiency to be used in that capacity.

Cost 4 gp; *Small* 1d4, *Medium* 1d6, *Large* 1d8; *Critical* x2; *Weight* 3 lb.; *Type* Piercing.

Flayed Angel

This once angelic being has been reduced to a twisted mass of oozing, raw flesh and muscle tissue, every bit of the skin having been stripped away from the body. The neck ends at a jagged stump, and the tattered, shredded remains of once-beautiful wings extend behind it.

FLAYED ANGEL	CR 16

XP 76,800
NE Large undead (extraplanar)
Init +8; **Senses** blindsight 120 ft.; **Perception** +18

AC 32, touch 24, flat-footed 27 (+4 Dex, +1 dodge, +8 natural, +10 profane, −1 size)
hp 252 (24d8+120 plus 24)
Fort +17; **Ref** +14; **Will** +19
Defensive Abilities channel resistance +6, profane presence; **DR** 10/evil; **Immune** acid, undead traits; **SR** 27

Speed 40 ft.
Melee 2 slams +25 (2d6+7/19–20 plus 2d6 acid)
Space 10 ft.; **Reach** 10 ft.
Special Attacks gout of blood, rend (2 slams, 3d6+10 plus 2d6 acid)

Str 25, **Dex** 18, **Con** —, **Int** 6, **Wis** 16, **Cha** 21
Base Atk +18; **CMB** +26; **CMD** 51
Feats Cleave, Dodge, Great Fortitude, Improved Critical (slam), Improved Initiative, Improved Natural Attack (slam), Mobility, Power Attack, Skill Focus (Acrobatics), Spring Attack, Toughness, Weapon Focus (slam)
Skills Acrobatics +34 (+46 jump), Climb +22, Perception +18; **Racial Modifiers** +8 Acrobatics to jump

Environment any
Organization solitary
Treasure none

Gout of Blood (Ex) Whenever a flayed angel is physically struck in battle, the impact causes a spray of acidic blood to fly off the creature at anyone within 5 feet. Anyone in the area of affect must make a DC 24 Reflex save or take 1d6 points of acid damage from this splatter. The save DC is Dexterity-based.
Profane Presence (Su) The existence of a flayed angel is such an anathema to the order of the multiverse that its very presence is a profanity of nature. This presence provides it with a +10 profane bonus to Armor Class and a +2 profane bonus to its saves.

On some rare occasions when an extremely powerful angel is captured, tortured to death and subjected to particularly vile rituals, dark gods of evil will intervene and prevent that being's essence from returning to its celestial home, instead trapping it within the mutilated corpse as a horrifyingly profane undead abomination. Such creations are anathema to the heavenly hosts and are actively hunted down by angles and archons whenever their existence is discovered. They seek to erase the stain upon the forces of good by the perversion of such a champion and to release its essence back to its rightful plane.

A flayed angel is horribly mutilated, its skin flayed away, its wings crippled, and its head removed. The preparation ritual also involves the introduction of an acidic embalming fluid that mingles with the blood left in its body as a continually-leaking, caustic brew.

A flayed angel stands around 8 feet tall due to the removal of its head and weighs about 450 pounds.

Flayed angels have lost most of their original battle prowess becoming little more than lumbering death dealers. However, they are still quite agile and, as former flyers of great renown, are still expert jumpers. They often climb to a higher position in order to leap down on their foes and attack in a sad caricature of their former ability to swoop down upon enemies from above. Regardless, their attacks soon devolve into brutish attempts to rend their foes into unrecognizable hunks of meat.

They strangely retain their inherent damage reduction that can only be overcome by evil-aligned weapons, often making them difficult and confusing foes. Their natural attacks are no longer considered good-aligned for the purpose of overcoming damage reduction.

The acidic blood mixture that continually oozes through their bodies splatters upon a foe on a successful melee hit and deals acid damage as well.

Credit

Original author Greg A. Vaughan
Originally appearing in *Slumbering Tsar* (© Frog God Games/ Greg A. Vaughan, 2012)

Fountain Fungus

This appears to be a large fountain covered in vines and mold.

FOUNTAIN FUNGUS	CR 8

XP 4,800
N Large plant
Init +5; **Senses** blindsight 60 ft., low-light vision; **Perception** +9

AC 20, touch 10, flat-footed 19 (+1 Dex, +10 natural, –1 size)
hp 114 (12d8+60)
Fort +15; **Ref** +5; **Will** +5
Immune plant traits; **Resist** acid 20

Speed 10 ft.
Melee 2 tendrils +16 (1d6+7 plus grab), bite +15 (2d6+10)
Space 10 ft.; **Reach** 10 ft. (20 ft. with tendril)
Special Attacks acid fountain, swallow whole (4d6 acid damage, AC 15, 11 hp)

Str 25, **Dex** 13, **Con** 20, **Int** 1, **Wis** 12, **Cha** 6
Base Atk +9; **CMB** +17 (+21 grapple); **CMD** 28 (can't be tripped)
Feats Cleave, Great Fortitude, Improved Initiative, Power Attack, Skill Focus (Stealth), Weapon Focus (tendril)
Skills Perception +9, Stealth +10 (+18 in undergrowth); **Racial Modifiers** +8 Stealth in undergrowth
SQ camouflage

Environment any non-cold
Organization solitary
Treasure incidental

Acid Fountain (Ex) As a standard action every 1d4 rounds, a fountain fungus can spray acid into the air. This acid quickly falls and covers a 10-foot-radius burst around the fountain fungus. Creatures in the area take 7d6 points of acid damage. A DC 21 Reflex save reduces the damage by half. The save is Constitution-based.
Camouflage (Ex) Since a fountain fungus looks like a normal moss-covered fountain when at rest, a DC 20 Perception check is required to notice it before it attacks for the first time. Anyone with ranks in Survival or Knowledge (nature) can use either of those skills instead of Perception to notice the plant.

A fountain fungus is a semi-intelligent plant creature that enjoys luring other creatures to their doom and then devouring them. While it appears to be an ordinary fountain carved of stone and covered with mold and vegetation, the fountain fungus is 100% vegetable matter through and through. The gray coloration of its central body lends to its deception.

Fountain funguses can be found just about anywhere save the coldest of climates. Many are encountered underground as these creatures seem to have a particular like for the dampness and darkness that dungeons and caverns provide. Fountain funguses subsist on a diet of blood, so regardless of where they lair, they always make sure a supply of fresh food is readily available (e.g., a popular dungeon perhaps where adventurers like to explore). When a fountain fungus's food supply dwindles it simply rolls itself into a ball and moves to another location.

A fountain fungus is about 10 feet in diameter. Its central body is stone gray with many vines, leaves, and mushroom-like growths of varying greens covering it. Somewhere in this tangled mass are four tentacles that look like thick rugged vines.

A fountain fungus's tactics are simple: spray acid on foes, slap and whip foes with its tendrils, and finally grab an opponent and attempt to swallow it. Creatures killed by a fountain fungus are wrapped in its vines and pulled into its body. The fountain fungus spends the next few days absorbing all fluids and nutrients from its prey before ejecting a dried out husk of its victim onto the ground.

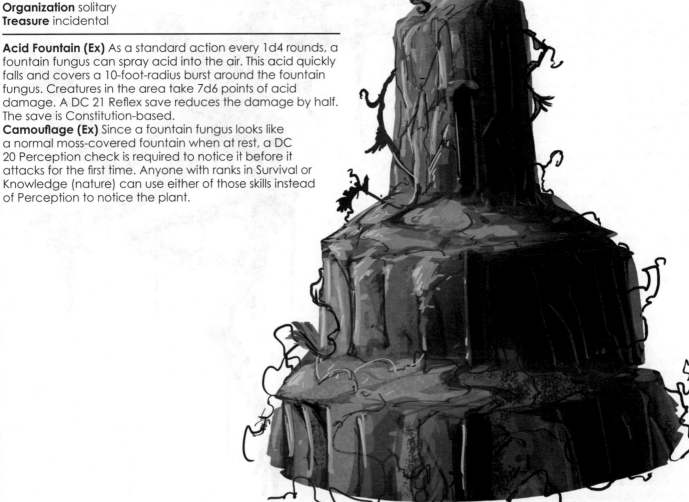

Fungus Man

These small, non-aggressive plant-men appear to be mobile toadstools, with brightly colored caps, stubby arms and thick, trunk-like legs. They do not speak, but they hold up their hands in a sign of peace or supplication.

FUNGUS MAN	CR 2

XP 600
N Small plant
Init +2; **Senses** low-light vision; **Perception** +9

AC 15, touch 13, flat-footed 13 (+2 Dex, +2 natural, +1 size)
hp 16 (3d8+3)
Fort +4; **Ref** +3; **Will** +2
DR 5/slashing or piercing; **Immune** poison, plant traits,
Resist cold 5
Weaknesses vulnerable to fire

Speed 20 ft.
Melee slam +5 (1d3–2)
Special Attacks spore cloud

Str 6, **Dex** 15, **Con** 13, **Int** 9, **Wis** 12, **Cha** 10
Base Atk +2; **CMB** +3; **CMD** 11
Feats Agile Maneuvers, Skill Focus (Perception), Weapon Finesse[B]
Skills Perception +9, Stealth +10

Environment underground
Organization pod (4–16), branch (17–30), colony (30+, plus a fungus man king)
Treasure incidental

Spore Cloud (Ex) Once per round as a standard action, a fungus man can release a cloud of noxious spores. All living creatures within 5 ft. must make a DC 12 Fortitude save or become nauseated for 1d4+1 rounds. The save DC is Constitution-based. This is a poison effect, and once a creature successfully saves it is immune to the spore cloud of that particular fungus man for 24 hours.

FUNGUS MAN KING	CR 4

XP 1,200
Male giant fungus man
N Medium plant
Init +1; **Senses** low-light vision; **Perception** +12

AC 16, touch 11, flat-footed 15 (+1 Dex, +5 natural)
hp 45 (6d8+18)
Fort +8; **Ref** +3; **Will** +5
DR 5/slashing or piercing; **Immune** poison, plant traits,
Resist cold 5
Weaknesses vulnerable to fire

Speed 20 ft.
Melee slam +5 (1d4)
Special Attacks spore cloud

Str 10, **Dex** 13, **Con** 17, **Int** 9, **Wis** 12, **Cha** 10
Base Atk +4; **CMB** +5; **CMD** 15
Feats Agile Maneuvers, Iron Will, Skill Focus (Perception), Weapon Finesse[B]
Skills Perception +12, Stealth +5

Environment underground
Organization solitary or colony (with 30+ fungus men)
Treasure incidental

Spore Cloud (Ex) Once per round as a standard action,

a fungus man can release a cloud of noxious spores. All living creatures within 5 ft. must make a DC 16 Fortitude save or become nauseated for 1d4+1 rounds. The save DC is Constitution-based. This is a poison effect, and once a creature successfully saves it is immune to the spore cloud of that particular fungus man for 24 hours.

Fungus men are an extremely peaceful and easy-going race of intelligent plants. They are bipedal, in a squat, humanoid fashion. The fungus men are sexless, and reproduce by means of spore clouds. They lack the appendages for fine manipulation of objects, but are quite dexterous in their own way. The fungus men are fiercely loyal to their fungus man king, and attack immediately if it is threatened.

Fungus men do not communicate by verbal means; they have learned to deal with outsiders by using hand gestures and supplicating movements. They communicate with each other by pheromones and spores release.

Fungus men cohabitate in enclaves throughout the underdark, farming lichen and mosses to trade with other races for soil and excrement (their sources of food). Some fungus man colonies keep "domesticated" giant lizards available to replenish their dung fields and for pack animal uses. Fungus man colonies are not hostile towards each other; neither do they work together in any societal fashion.

Credit

Originally appearing in *Rappan Athuk Reloaded* (© Necromancer Games, 2006)

Galley Beggar

This creature looks like a translucent, headless, skeletal humanoid wrapped in a tattered black shroud. Tucked under its arm is its rotting and seemingly lifeless head. The creature floats a few feet above the ground.

GALLEY BEGGAR	CR 8

XP 4,800
CE Medium undead (incorporeal)
Init +6; **Senses** darkvision 60 ft.; **Perception** +19
Aura frightful presence (40 ft., DC 18)

AC 16, touch 16, flat-footed 13 (+3 deflection, +1 dodge, +2 Dex)
hp 85 (10d8+30 plus 10)
Fort +6; **Ref** +7; **Will** +8
Defensive Abilities channel resistance +4, incorporeal;
Immune undead traits

Speed fly 50 ft. (perfect)
Melee incorporeal touch +9 (5d6+3, DC 18 Fort half) or incorporeal drain +9 (1d4 Cha drain)
Special Attacks annihilating wail, draining touch, unholy touch

Str —, **Dex** 15, **Con** —, **Int** 13, **Wis** 13, **Cha** 16
Base Atk +7; **CMB** +9; **CMD** 25
Feats Alertness, Dodge, Improved Initiative, Lightning Reflexes, Toughness
Skills Bluff +8, Diplomacy +8, Fly +23, Intimidate +16, Knowledge (any) +6, Perception +19, Sense Motive +11, Stealth +18; **Racial Modifiers** +8 Perception, +8 Stealth
Languages Common

Environment any
Organization solitary
Treasure none

Annihilating Wail (Su) Once per minute, a galley beggar can emit a piercing and heart-stopping scream that affects all creatures within 60 feet that hear it. Affected creatures must make a DC 18 Fortitude save. Those making their save are blinded for 1d4+4 rounds. Those failing their save take 10d6 points of damage. A creature that makes its save is immune to the annihilating wail of that galley beggar for one day. The save DC is Charisma-based.
Draining Touch (Su) The incorporeal touch of a galley beggar drains 1d4 points of Charisma. On a successful attack, the galley beggar also heals 5 points of damage to itself.
Incorporeal Touch (Su) By passing part of its incorporeal body through a foe's body as a standard action, the galley begger inflicts 5d6+3 damage. This damage is not negative energy—it manifests in the form of physical wounds and aches from supernatural aging. Creatures immune to magical aging are immune to this damage, but otherwise the damage bypasses all forms of damage reduction. A Fortitude save halves the damage inflicted.
Unholy Touch (Su) A galley beggar adds its Charisma modifier to damage for its incorporeal touch attack.

Galley beggars are the ghostly remains of travelers who met their demise before their journey was complete. Therefore most encounters with galley beggars occur on roads and paths between cities and towns. A galley beggar generally haunts a single area of no more than 1 square mile, and though it is not tied to the area, it rarely ever ventures far from the place where it died.

A galley beggar is a hateful creature, unhappy and resentful of its current state of unlife. It seeks nothing more than to kill any living creature it encounters.

Galley beggars are believed to speak Common and at least one other language, though sages are unsure of this as no galley beggar has ever conversed with a living creature (or at least conversed with any living creature that lived to tell about it).

A galley beggar begins combat the instant it encounters a living creature. It opens a battle using its annihilating wail if any opponent is within range by extending a skeletal arm and showing its severed head to its foes. If no opponent is within range the galley beggar moves in and uses its annihilating wail as soon as possible. It follows this with its incorporeal or draining touch.

Gargoyle, Spitting

A grotesque winged humanoid, it has a stony hide and wickedly-pointed horns. Its mouth is a gaping "O" like a water spout, and its chin is stained with a green patina of corrosion.

SPITTING GARGOYLE	CR 5

XP 1,600
CE Medium monstrous humanoid (earth)
Init +2; **Senses** darkvision 60 ft.; **Perception** +10

AC 16, touch 12, flat-footed 14 (+2 Dex, +4 natural)
hp 52 (5d10+20 plus 5)
Fort +5; **Ref** +6; **Will** +4
DR 10/magic

Speed 40 ft., fly 60 ft. (average)
Melee 2 claws +7 (1d6+2), bite +7 (1d4+2), gore +7 (1d4+2)
Special Attacks acid spit

Str 15, **Dex** 14, **Con** 18, **Int** 10, **Wis** 11, **Cha** 7
Base Atk +5; **CMB** +7; **CMD** 19
Feats Hover, Skill Focus (Fly), Toughness
Skills Fly +13, Perception +10, Stealth +12 (+16 stony environs), Survival +8; **Racial Modifiers** +2 Perception, +2 Stealth (+6 in stony environs)
Languages Common, Terran

SQ freeze

Environment any
Organization solitary, pair, or nasty (5–16)
Treasure standard

Acid Spit (Ex) 30-foot line, once every 4 rounds, damage 3d6 acid, Reflex DC 16 half. The save DC is Constitution based.
Freeze (Ex) A spitting gargoyle can hold itself so still it appears to be a statue. A spitting gargoyle that uses freeze can take 20 on its Stealth check to hide in plain sight as a stone statue.

Like its cousin the common gargoyle, spitting gargoyles are cruel creatures taking great delight in torturing others just to watch their suffering. Before closing to attack with their melee attacks, spitting gargoyles often dive to use their acid spit attacks initially to soften up their targets. Other than the variations mentioned here, they in all other ways conform to the standard gargoyle as detailed in the *Pathfinder Roleplaying Game Bestiary*.

Credit

Original author Greg A. Vaughan
Originally appearing in *Slumbering Tsar* (© Frog God Games/ Greg A. Vaughan, 2012)

Gelatinous Emperor

This large, reddish-brown amorphous blob moves slowly forward.

GELATINOUS EMPEROR	CR 17

XP 102,400
CE Huge ooze (chaotic, evil, extraplanar)
Init +4; **Senses** blindsight 60 ft.; **Perception** +23

AC 29, touch 8, flat-footed 29 (+21 natural, –2 size)
hp 256 (19d8+171)
Fort +17; **Ref** +8; **Will** +10
DR 10/magic and good; **Immune** acid, electricity, ooze traits; **Resist** cold 10, fire 10; **SR** 28

Speed 20 ft., climb 20 ft.
Melee 2 tentacles +23 (2d8+10 plus 2d8 acid)
Space 15 ft.; **Reach** 15 ft.
Special Attacks spew acid, trample (2d8+15 plus 2d8 acid, DC 29)
Spell-Like Abilities (CL 15th):
1/day—*summon* (level 7, 1d4 black puddings 100%, 1d4 gelatinous cubes 100%, or 1d2 15 HD black puddings 50%)

Str 31, **Dex** 10, **Con** 28, **Int** 10, **Wis** 15, **Cha** 13
Base Atk +14; **CMB** +26; **CMD** 36 (can't be tripped)
Feats Alertness, Critical Focus, Great Fortitude, Improved Initiative, Iron Will, Lightning Reflexes, Power Attack, Skill Focus (Perception), Staggering Critical, Weapon Focus (tentacle)
Skills Climb +27, Perception +23, Sense Motive +4, Stealth +1, Swim +19
Languages Abyssal (cannot speak)

Environment any (Abyss)
Organization solitary or gang (1 emperor plus 2–5 advanced black puddings)
Treasure none

Acid (Ex) A gelatinous emperor's acid does not harm metal or stone.
Spew Acid (Ex) A gelatinous emperor can, as a standard action, spew forth acid in a 30-foot line at a single target. A creature struck takes 12d6 points of acid damage. A DC 28 Reflex save reduces the damage by half. Once a gelatinous emperor has spewed acid, it cannot do so again for 1d4 rounds. The save DC is Constitution-based.

Gelatinous emperors are intelligent, foul oozes found in the court of Jubilex. What purpose and in what capacity they serve the Faceless Lord is anyone's guess. From his Abyssal plane they strike out, devouring anything and everything they run across. They are eternal hunters, always moving and always hungry. When a gelatinous emperor slips into the Material Plane it quickly ravages the area leaving it devoid of all life. Thankfully these creatures are not often found on the Material Plane.

A gelatinous emperor is believed to be a foul mix of gelatinous cube, gray ooze, black pudding, and all other manner of puddings and oozes meshed together by Jubilex, either for some nefarious purpose or for nothing more than his sheer amusement. Sages believe the latter to be the truer of the two theories.

A gelatinous emperor attacks by forming multiple pseudopods from its amorphous body and lashing out at its opponents. If the emperor can maneuver its opponents into a tight group it employs its trample attack, crushing as many of its foes in one move as possible.

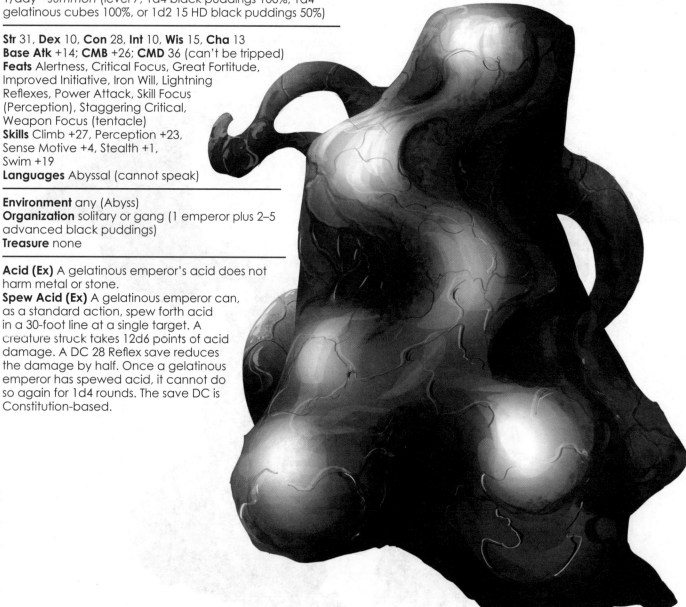

Genie, Seraph

This creature resembles a ten foot tall human with brick-red skin and coal-black hair, long and braided.

GENIE, SERAPH	CR 8

XP 4,800
NG Large outsider (extraplanar, fire)
Init +8; **Senses** darkvision 60 ft.; **Perception** +15

AC 20, touch 14, flat-footed 15 (+4 Dex, +1 dodge, +6 natural, −1 size)
hp 95 (10d10+40)
Fort +7; **Ref** +11; **Will** +9
Immune fire
Weaknesses vulnerability to cold

Speed 40 ft., fly 30 ft. (perfect)
Melee mwk scimitar +14/+9 (1d8+4 plus 1d6 fire) or 2 slams +13 (1d8+4 plus 1d6 fire)
Space 10 ft.; **Reach** 10 ft.
Special Attacks fire burst, heat
Spell-Like Abilities (CL 12th; melee touch +13, ranged touch +13):
Constant—*detect evil, detect magic*
At will—*flame blade, plane shift* (willing targets to elemental planes, Astral Plane, or Material Plane only), *produce flame, pyrotechnics* (DC 15)
3/day—*fireball* (DC 16), *flame strike* (DC 18), *invisibility* (self only), *see invisibility, wall of fire*
1/day—*fire storm* (DC 21), *wish* (to non-genies only)

Str 19, **Dex** 18, **Con** 18, **Int** 14, **Wis** 15, **Cha** 17
Base Atk +10; **CMB** +15; **CMD** 30
Feats Combat Casting, Combat Reflexes, Dodge, Improved Initiative[B], Mobility, Power Attack
Skills Craft (any one) +15, Diplomacy +16, Fly +23, Knowledge (planes) +15, Perception +15, Sense Motive +15, Spellcraft +15, Stealth +13
Languages Celestial, Common, Ignan, telepathy 100 ft.

Environment any (Plane of Fire)
Organization solitary, pair, company (3–6), or band (7–12)
Treasure standard (masterwork scimitar, other treasure)

Fire Burst (Su) Once every 1d4 rounds as a standard action, a seraph can emit a blast of elemental fire in a 30-foot-radius burst. Creatures in the area take 8d6 points of fire damage. A successful DC 19 Reflex save reduces the damage by half. The save DC is Constitution-based.
Heat (Ex) A seraph generates so much heat that its mere touch deals an additional 1d6 points of fire damage. A seraph's metallic weapons also conduct this heat. A seraph can start or stop this ability as a free action once per round on its turn.

The seraphs are genies from the Plane of Fire, and the sworn enemies of the efreet. A violent war between the two genie races has spanned centuries and spilled into an uncountable number of planes. Any encounter between a seraph and an efreeti sparks a battle that only ends when one or the other is killed. Those that aid the efreeti are treated by seraphs as if they were efreeti themselves; no mercy is shown in battle to an ally of the hated fire genies. The seraphs often align themselves with djinn as they both share the efreeti as a common enemy.

A seraph prefers to use its spell-like abilities over melee weapons in combat, often allowing its opponents to move in close so the seraph can unleash its fire burst. A seraph facing overwhelming odds in battle attempts to flee; covering its escape by turning invisible or erecting a *wall of fire* between itself and its enemies. When battling efreet, a seraph often employs cold-based magic weapons such as *frost scimitars* and *icy burst spears*.

A typical seraph stands 10 feet tall and weighs about 1,500 pounds.

Some seraphs are noble, known as beys or caliphs. A noble seraph has 14 Hit Dice and gains the following spell-like abilities: 3/day—*fire seeds, heat metal*; 1/day—*elemental swarm* (fire elementals only), *greater invisibility*. A noble seraph's caster level for its spell-like abilities is 16th. Noble seraphs are CR 10.

Ghaggurath

This massive creature appears to be a pile of brownish-gray flesh covered in large eyes. Eight long tentacles sprout from its body, each ending in a mouth lined with sharpened fangs. Its large central mass is amoeba-like and oozes a foul-smelling liquid.

GHAGGURATH	CR 18

XP 153,600
N Huge aberration
Init +5; **Senses** all-around vision, darkvision 60 ft., tremorsense 60 ft.; **Perception** +36

AC 31, touch 13, flat-footed 26 (+5 Dex, +18 natural, –2 size)
hp 304 (21d8+210)
Fort +19; **Ref** +12; **Will** +20
Defensive Abilities resistant to poison; **DR** 15/—; **Immune** charm, fear, paralysis, sleep; **Resist** acid 20, cold 20, fire 20, sonic 20; **SR** 29

Speed 20 ft., climb 20 ft.
Melee 8 bites +27 (2d6+13/19–20 plus grab)
Ranged 4 thrall worms +18 (1d8 plus poison)
Space 15 ft.; **Reach** 15 ft. (30 ft. with tentacle)
Special Attacks thrall

Str 37, **Dex** 21, **Con** 30, **Int** 24, **Wis** 22, **Cha** 21
Base Atk +15; **CMB** +30 (+34 grapple); **CMD** 45 (can't be tripped)
Feats Bleeding Critical, Cleave, Combat Reflexes, Critical Focus, Endurance, Great Fortitude, Improved Critical (bite), Iron Will, Power Attack, Skill Focus (Perception), Weapon Focus (bite)
Skills Bluff +26, Climb +45, Escape Artist +29, Intimidate +29, Knowledge (any) +31, Knowledge (history) +28, Knowledge (planes) +28, Perception +36, Sense Motive +27, Stealth +21, Survival +30, Swim +22
Languages Abyssal, Common, Giant, Goblin, Infernal, Terran, Undercommon; telepathy 100 ft.

Environment any underground
Organization solitary
Treasure double standard

Poison (Ex) Thrall worm—injury; *save* DC 30 Fort; *frequency* 1/round for 6 rounds; *effect* 1d6 Wisdom damage; *cure* 2 consecutive saves. The save DC is Constitution-based.
Resistance to Poison (Ex) A ghaggurath is highly resistant to poison. Whenever it makes a saving throw against poison, it can roll its save twice, keeping the better result.
Spittle (Ex) In lieu of biting, a tentacle mouth can eject a fleshy worm, called a thrall worm, at a single target to a range of 50 feet. A target that is hit is automatically bitten by the worm and subjected to the ghaggurath's poison. Regardless of which head fires the worm, a ghaggurath can launch only 24 such worms in any 24-hour period.

When a thrall worm strikes its target, it quickly burrows into the target's body. This worm can be safely removed with a successful DC 30 Heal check or by the application of a *cure* spell; otherwise removing the worm deals an extra 1d6 points of damage to the target. After 1d4 rounds, the worm works its way so deep into the target's body that it can only be removed by cutting open the area (dealing 1d8 points of damage to the victim) before attempting a Heal check or casting a *cure* spell. A *remove disease* spell destroys the worm if the caster succeeds on a caster level check against DC 30. As long as a thrall worm remains inside a target, the target cannot heal the Wisdom damage dealt by the ghaggurath's poison. A creature can only ever have one thrall worm inside

it at one time; it can however be attacked by and bitten by multiple thrall worms. The check DCs are Constitution-based.
Thrall (Su) A victim whose Wisdom score drops to 0 from the ghaggurath's poison is automatically dominated (as by a *dominate monster* spell, CL 20th). This effect lasts until the thrall worm is removed and at least 1 point of Wisdom is restored. The ghaggurath does not have to concentrate each day to maintain this effect, and a dominated creature does not receive a save to break the effects. If the ghaggurath is slain, any thrall under its command fall unconscious and remain so until the thrall worm is removed and at least 1 point of Wisdom is restored.

The ghaggurath is a massive subterranean creature feared for its ability to enslave others to its will, and feared for its ability to devour just about anything it desires. Though the ghaggurath has a seemingly endless hunger, it can in fact go up to 6 months without a meal; its body enters a sort of hibernation to sustain the creature. During this time, many creatures assume the ghaggurath is vulnerable; it isn't. Though the creature appears to be hibernating, it is completely aware of its surroundings. Many would-be predators and foolish adventurers have stumbled upon a hibernating ghaggurath assuming it unaware, only to become the creature's next meal.

Resourceful adventurers who have braved the subterranean worlds tell of huge cities governed by ghagguraths and whose entire populations are enslaved and under command of these creatures. Other tales speak of an underground race of humans that worship the ghaggurath as deities. Most subterranean races fear these creatures and avoid them at all costs.

In combat, a ghaggurath lashes out with its tentacles, the mouths biting and gnashing its opponents. A grabbed foe is held and subjected to multiple bites. Stronger opponents, particularly spellcasters, are of great interest to a ghaggurath, and it usually subjects such opponents to its thrall worms, attempting to bring them under its control. Controlled spellcasters are forced to do the ghaggurath's bidding or carried back to their great underground cities, enslaved, and experimented upon. Eventually, when a ghaggurath grows weary of the creature, it devours it.

Ghirru

This undead creature's flesh is burned and charred and hangs loosely about its form. The stench of burnt flesh permeates the air as it draws closer.

A ghirru attacks with its claws and bite, attempting to grab its prey and set it on fire. A grappled creature is held and incinerated, then promptly devoured by the ghirru.

GHIRRU	CR 9

XP 6,400
LE Large undead (extraplanar, fire)
Init +3; **Senses** darkvision 60 ft.; **Perception** +19

AC 23, touch 13, flat-footed 19 (+3 Dex, +1 dodge, +10 natural, −1 size)
hp 95 (10d8+50)
Fort +10; **Ref** +6; **Will** +9
DR 5/good; **Immune** fire, undead traits
Weaknesses vulnerability to cold

Speed 30 ft.
Melee 2 claws +15 (1d8+8 plus burn and grab), bite +14 (2d6+8 plus burn)
Space 10 ft.; **Reach** 10 ft.
Special Attacks burn (1d8, DC 20)

Str 27, **Dex** 17, **Con** —, **Int** 12, **Wis** 14, **Cha** 20
Base Atk +7; **CMB** +16 (+20 grapple); **CMD** 30
Feats Cleave, Dodge, Great Fortitude, Power Attack, Weapon Focus (claws)
Skills Bluff +15, Intimidate +18, Perception +19, Sense Motive +15, Stealth +12; **Racial Modifiers** +4 Perception
Languages Aquan, Auran, Common, Ignan, Terran
SQ change shape (flame-spawned dire wolf; does not detect as undead in this form; *beast shape II*), genie-kin

---

Environment any (Plane of Fire)
Organization solitary or pack (2–6)
Treasure standard

Burn (Ex) A ghirru deals burn damage each round it grapples. A creature that catches on fire cannot extinguish the flames until it first escapes the grapple.
Change Shape (Su) A ghirru can assume the shape of a Large flame-spawned dire wolf. A flame-spawned dire wolf is an 8 HD dire wolf with the following abilities: immunity to fire, vulnerability to cold, deals 1d6 points of fire damage with its bite attack.
Genie-kin (Ex) For all race-related effects (such as a ranger's favored enemy), a ghirru is considered a genie even though its type is undead.

Ghirru are undead efreet, returned to the land of the living by efreeti necromancers through foul and dark magic. A ghirru closely resembles its original efreeti form, save its flesh is charred and hangs loosely about it, sometimes falling off in pieces as the creature moves.

Ghirru haunt cemeteries, ruins, ancient temples to the efreet gods, and other such places. Legend speaks of a large lair of these creatures led by a sorcerer of vast power hidden somewhere beneath the fabled City of Brass. None have found this secret lair thus far. And few go looking for it.

Ghirru have a taste for genie flesh, particularly djinn and marid, though the latter is often hard to come by on the Plane of Fire. When hunting on the Material Plane, ghirru are found in warmer lands, often near extinct volcanoes and other such warm places.

A ghirru stands 12 feet tall and weighs around 1,500 pounds. Its skin is charred and burned, though in a few places the original crimson color shines through. Its body constantly emanates small wisps of smoke, and the smell of burnt flesh lingers in the air around the creature.

Giant, Coral

This towering humanoid has reddish skin and long, dark hair. It is clad in loose-fitting clothes and carries a massive trident.

CORAL GIANT   CR 9

XP 6,400
CN Large humanoid (giant)
Init +2; **Senses** darkvision 60 ft., low-light vision; **Perception** +13

AC 23, touch 12, flat-footed 20 (+2 Dex, +1 dodge, +11 natural, −1 size)
hp 123 (13d8+65)
Fort +13; **Ref** +6, **Will** +5
Defensive Abilities rock catching; **Resist** cold 20

Speed 40 ft., swim 40 ft.
Melee mwk trident +17/+12 (2d6+10) or 2 slams +15 (1d8+7)
Ranged rock +11 (1d8+10)
Space 10 ft.; **Reach** 10 ft.
Special Attacks rock throwing (150 ft.), water mastery

Str 25, **Dex** 14, **Con** 21, **Int** 11, **Wis** 12, **Cha** 10
Base Atk +9; **CMB** +17; **CMD** 30
Feats Alertness, Cleave, Dodge, Intimidating Prowess, Power Attack, Skill Focus (Perception), Weapon Focus (trident)
Skills Craft (jewelry) +9, Intimidate +14, Perception +13, Sense Motive +3, Survival +10, Swim +21
Languages Giant
SQ amphibious, water stride

Environment temperate and warm aquatic
Organization solitary, gang (2–5), hunting party (6–9), or clan (10–20 plus 1 fighter chief of 5th level, and 11–20 sharks)
Treasure standard (masterwork trident, other treasure)

Water Mastery (Ex) A coral giant gains a +1 bonus on attack and damage rolls if both it and its opponent are touching water. If the opponent or the coral giant is touching the ground, the coral giant takes a −4 penalty on attack and damage rolls. These modifiers apply to bull rush and overrun maneuvers, whether the coral giant is initiating or resisting these kinds of attacks.

Water Stride (Ex) A coral giant suffers no penalties for fighting in or under water (as if affected by a *freedom of movement* spell).

Coral giants are 12-foot tall humanoids that dwell beneath the waves. They make their homes in great undersea castles constructed of stone. They are generally peaceful creatures and spend their days fishing and tending to their coral farms. Their diet typically consists of undersea plants, fish, and the like, with occasional forays onto land to hunt large game. Trade with other intelligent races is common, with coral giant jewelry being prized by many races. These creatures are on generally good terms with merfolk, tritons, storm giants, and humans. Wars are waged against the sahuagin, krakens, and aboleths, the latter being a particularly hated foe.

Coral giant homes are most always constructed of smooth stone and contain large, open expanses and rooms. Their homes usually contain a few rooms constructed for air-breathers so land-based visitors can move about somewhat freely. Homes are deep under the waters, but no so deep as to be inaccessible to other races looking to trade and bargain. Though coral giants can survive in any waters, they prefer temperate or warm environments to cold temperatures. They can also freely breathe air, but prefer life underwater to land.

Coral giants are, on average, 12 feet tall and weigh 1,500 pounds. Females tend to be slightly smaller and lighter than males. Skin tones vary in color but are always some shade of coral. Hair color varies from deep blacks to light reds. On very rare occasions, a coral giant is encountered that has white hair. Coral giant's eyes are usually dark blue or green. They can live to be 400 years old. Coral giant leaders are typically fighters or barbarians, though a few are rangers. Druids and clerics are common among coral giants; other spellcasting classes are not.

Coral giants fight with massive tridents in combat, fiercely protecting their territory and young. Creatures not driven off are slaughtered and left for scavenging fish to feed upon.

Giant, Crag

This muscular giant has dark brown skin and wild, long, black hair. It wields a huge club in its massive hands.

CRAG GIANT	CR 11

XP 12,800
CE Large humanoid (giant)
Init +0; **Senses** darkvision 60 ft., low-light vision; **Perception** +14

AC 25, touch 9, flat-footed 25 (+16 natural, –1 size)
hp 133 (14d8+70)
Fort +14; **Ref** +4; **Will** +7
Defensive Abilities rock catching

Speed 40 ft., climb 30 ft.
Melee greatclub +18/+13 (2d8+13) or 2 slams +18 (1d8+9)
Ranged rock +10 (2d8+13)
Space 10 ft.; **Reach** 10 ft.
Special Attacks earth mastery, rock throwing (180 ft.)
Spell-Like Abilities (CL 14th):
1/day—*earthquake* (DC 19), *summon monster VII* (earth elementals only)

Str 29, **Dex** 10, **Con** 21, **Int** 10, **Wis** 12, **Cha** 12
Base Atk +10; **CMB** +20; **CMD** 30
Feats Awesome Blow, Cleave, Improved Bull Rush, Improved Sunder, Intimidating Prowess, Iron Will, Marital Weapon Proficiency (greatclub)ᴮ, Power Attack
Skills Climb +24, Intimidate +20, Perception +14, Stealth +2, Survival +5
Languages Giant
SQ stonecunning

Environment any mountains
Organization solitary, gang (2–5), band (4–8), or tribe (10–20 plus 40% noncombatants, 1–2 elders, and 4–8 gargoyles)
Treasure standard (greatclub, other treasure)

Earth Mastery (Ex) A crag giant gains a +1 bonus on attack and damage rolls if both it and its foe are touching the ground. If an opponent is airborne or waterborne, the crag giant takes a –4 penalty on attack and damage rolls. These modifiers apply to bull rush and overrun maneuvers, whether the crag giant is initiating or resisting these kinds of attacks. (These modifiers are not included in the statistics block.)
Stonecunning (Ex) This ability functions as the dwarf's stonecunning ability.

Crag giants are malicious and capricious giants found inhabiting mountains and hills. They are highly territorial and attack most any creatures that wander into their lands. Bestial creatures are slaughtered and served as food while humanoids, especially dwarves, orcs, and humans are enslaved and forced into manual labor serving the crag giants and their ilk. When labor is in short supply and high demand, crag giant hunting parties venture forth, raiding nearby civilized lands and capturing whatever humanoids they can. Slave trade is common between crag giants, other giant races, and drow.

Crag giants stand 11 feet in height, and typical weigh around 1,100 pounds.

Skin color is almost always dark brown, but some slate gray crag giants have been encountered. Hair on both males and females tends to be long and worn in ponytails. Hair color ranges from black to brown to red. Eyes are usually brown or green. Crag giants generally live to be 250 years old.

Crag giants are violent creatures and wade headlong into combat, swinging their massive clubs or smashing their foes with their great fists. If interlopers are detected early and crag giants have the high ground, they bombard their foes with rocks, moving in to mop up any survivors.

Giant, Jotun

This large muscular humanoid has frost-white skin, bright blue eyes, and bluish-white hair.

JOTUN	CR 11

XP 12,800
CE Large humanoid (cold, giant)
Init +0; **Senses** low-light vision; **Perception** +15

AC 23, touch 9, flat-footed 23 (+4 armor, +10 natural, –1 size)
hp 152 (16d8+80)
Fort +15; **Ref** +5; **Will** +7
Defensive Abilities rock catching; **Immune** cold
Weaknesses vulnerability to fire

Speed 40 ft.
Melee mwk greataxe +22/+17/+12 (3d6+15) or 2 slams +21 (1d6+10)
Ranged rock +11 (1d8+15)
Space 10 ft.; **Reach** 10 ft.
Special Attacks rock throwing (120 ft.)
Spell-Like Abilities (CL 16th):
3/day—*alter self*
1/day—*enlarge person* (self only), *major image* (DC 14), *reduce person* (self only)

Str 31, **Dex** 10, **Con** 21, **Int** 14, **Wis** 14, **Cha** 12
Base Atk +12; **CMB** +23; **CMD** 33
Feats Cleave, Critical Focus, Great Cleave, Improved Overrun, Improved Sunder, Martial Weapon Proficiency (greataxe), Power Attack, Skill Focus (Stealth)
Skills Climb +22, Craft (any) +11, Diplomacy +9, Intimidate +14, Knowledge (any) +10, Knowledge (local) +8, Perception +15, Stealth +6 (+12 in snow); **Racial Modifiers** +6 Stealth in snow
Languages Common, Giant

Environment cold mountains
Organization Solitary, gang (2–4), band (2–4 plus 2–8 frost giants plus 1 wizard or cleric of 3rd–5th level), hunting/raiding party (3–6 plus 3–9 frost giants plus 1 cleric or wizard of 4th–8th level plus 2–4 winter wolves and 2–3 ogres), or tribe (10–20 plus 15–30 frost giants plus 35% noncombatants plus 1 wizard, cleric, or sorcerer of 6th or 10th level plus 12–30 winter wolves, 12–22 ogres, and 1–2 young white dragons)
Treasure standard (masterwork chain shirt, masterwork greataxe, other treasure)

Jotuns are the purest blooded of the frost giant race, from which all other frost giants sprang. As brutal as their lesser cousins, they are also highly intelligent, possessing the knowledge of ancient runes with which they may tap into great magical powers. The jotun lineage is said to go back to that of the elder gods, with some jotun females having been the mothers of demigods still worshipped by various races to this day. Jotuns are held as nobility amongst normal frost giant tribes, who obey them as the true children of the frost giant god.

Jotuns love games of chance, puzzles and conundrums. The sometimes offer prisoners such a game to win their freedom; of course, the jotun frequently cheat at these games, taking perverse pleasure in doing so.

Unlike normal frost giants, Jotuns have a taste for finery, not usually found amongst their lesser cousins. They prefer masterwork and magical gear as well as finely tailored furs to the sloppy filth of normal frost giants. Truly ancient jotuns rival titans in size and the power of their illusions.

A jotun's skin is white as snow and their eyes glitter like blue diamonds. Their hair color ranges from red, yellow, blue-grey and even white. Females of the species are quite beautiful and have been known to seduce human men to their death with their feminine wiles. Jotun females are frequently sorcerers.

Adult males stand 15–17 feet tall and weigh between 2,800 and 3,200 lbs. Females are only slightly smaller averaging 14–16 feet in height. Jotuns' have a potential lifespan of over 1,000 years and continue to grow in size and magical prowess throughout the span of their lives.

It is not uncommon for a jotun to have a few levels of sorcerer, wizard (Illusionist) or cleric as well as their natural powers and abilities.

A jotun prefers to conceal itself with powerful illusions and take its enemies by surprise, attacking one opponent at a time until all are subdued or slain. When ganged up on by greater numbers of smaller foes it overruns them, stomping its opponents into the snow, slaughtering them before they have a chance to rise. When threatened with death, a jotun may attempt to flee or barter for its life.

Gibbering Abomination

This massive fleshy conglomeration is covered with madly staring eyes, gaping mouths in screaming faces, and pulsing orifices exuding foul-smelling substances.

GIBBERING ABOMINATION	CR 13

XP 25,600
CE Large aberration
Init +7; **Senses** all-around vision, darkvision 60 ft., tremorsense 60 ft.; **Perception** +18

AC 22, touch 12, flat-footed 19 (+3 Dex, +10 natural, −1 size)
hp 162 (13d8+91 plus 13); fast healing 3
Fort +13; **Ref** +9; **Will** +8
Defensive Abilities amorphous; **DR** 10/bludgeoning; **Immune** critical hits, nausea, pain, precision damage, sickening; **Resist** electricity 10, sonic 10

Speed 10 ft., climb 10 ft.
Melee 6 bites +12 (1d8+4 plus grab /19–20)
Space 10 ft.; **Reach** 5 ft.
Special Attacks arcane frenzy, blood drain, disruptive cacophony
Spell-like Abilities (CL 13th; ranged touch +12):
At will—*blur, confusion* (single target only, DC 18), *daze monster* (no HD limit, DC 16), *dispel magic, enfeeblement* (as ray but no ranged attack required, DC 15), *fear* (single target only DC 18), *freedom of movement, freezing ray* (as *scorching ray* but cold damage) *overland flight, telekinesis* (325 pounds max, DC 19)

Str 18, **Dex** 16, **Con** 25, **Int** 10, **Wis** 6, **Cha** 19
Base Atk +9; **CMB** +14 (+18

grapple); **CMD** 27 (can't be tripped)
Feats Combat Reflexes, Endurance[B], Great Fortitude[B], Improved Critical (bite), Improved Initiative, Iron Will, Lightning Reflexes, Toughness, Weapon Focus (bite)
Skills Climb +11, Fly +8, Knowledge (dungeoneering) +8, Perception +18, Spellcraft +12, Stealth +14, Survival +9; **Racial Modifiers** +4 Perception
Languages Aklo
SQ deathless

Environment forest or underground
Organization solitary
Treasure standard

All-around Vision (Ex) A gibbering abomination sees in all directions at once. It cannot be flanked List special ability info here.
Amorphous (Ex) A gibbering abomination's body is malleable and shapeless. It is immune to precision damage (like sneak attacks) and critical hits, and can move through an area as small as one-quarter its space without squeezing or one-eighth its space when squeezing.
Arcane Frenzy (Ex) A gibbering abomination is capable of using its spell-like abilities more frequently than other creatures. It may use a single spell-like ability each round as a swift action, two spell-like abilities as a standard action, or four spell-like abilities as a full-round action; it may not choose to do more than one of these in the same round, and cannot use this ability in the same round it uses Disruptive Cacophony. When engaging in an arcane frenzy, the gibbering abomination may use the same spell-like ability multiple times, but may not use the same spell-like ability against the same target twice in one round. If more than one spell-like ability is used, the specific spell-like

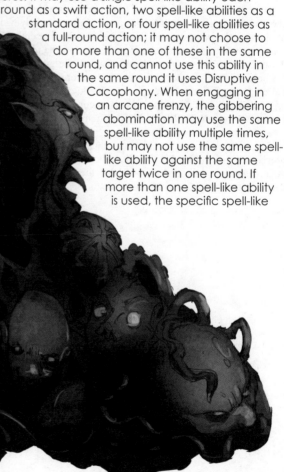

abilities and their targets must be determined before any effects are determined, including saves and attack rolls.

Blood Drain (Ex) On a successful grapple check after grabbing, several of the creature's mouths attach to its target. Each round it maintains its grapple, the gibbering abomination automatically deals 3d6+12 points of bite damage and 1 point of Constitution damage as it drains its victim's blood.

Deathless (Su) When a gibbering abomination is slain, it is not truly dead, and 1 hour later it returns to life at 0 hit points, allowing fast healing thereafter to resume healing it. A gibbering abomination can be permanently destroyed only with death magic or complete incineration of its remains (such as dumping it into a pool of magma).

Disruptive Cacophony (Su) As a free action the gibbering abomination may produce a horrible quasi-arcane chanting that is highly disruptive to nearby magic effects. Any creature that can clearly hear this chanting (maximum range 100 ft.) must make a concentration check (DC 20 plus level of spell) to successfully cast a spell or use a spell-like ability. The check DC is Charisma-based. A gibbering abomination that uses this ability may not use any of its spell-like abilities on its current turn, or until the start of its next turn.

Pain Immunity (Ex) Because the gibbering abomination is already in incredible pain, it is immune to any effect or condition caused as a result of extreme pain or agony. This ability does not protect it against any physical damage it might suffer as well, however.

A horrifying expanse of fused faces and parts of faces, the gibbering abomination is the result of foul arcane experiments studying the creation of chimerical creatures. It bears a close superficial resemblance to a gibbering mouther or lesser gibbering orb, and may be mistaken for one of those, but they are no true relation. Instead, the gibbering abomination has been cobbled together from the faces and organs of dozens of humanoid creatures; its innards are a bizarre tangle of brains, hearts, and other organs. The gibbering abomination is in constant pain as a result of the process that created it, haunted by half-remembered memories from the creatures it was composed from.

Gibbering abominations have clear memories of the experiments and procedures they suffered in their formation, and value nothing more than their own personal freedom. Beyond that, their constant anguish has given them a hateful attitude toward other creatures.

Gibbering Abomination Variants

As the result of the twisted experiments that created them, no two gibbering abominations have the same selection of spell-like abilities. The abilities listed in the stat block above are merely an example of a typical specimen—if such a term could be applied to a creature as bizarre as this.

When creating new gibbering abominations, use the following guidelines to assist in assigning spell-like abilities to the creature:

1. The abomination should have between 8 and 12 spell-like abilities, with a combined total spell level of 38–45.
2. Roughly half the spell-like abilities should be derived from 1st to 3rd–level spells, and the other half 4th to 6th–level spells. Just one should be of 7th to 9th level; the higher level that spell is, the more it should be a non-primary combat spell effect.
3. Any spell with an area effect should be changed to affect a single target only with a range of Close. Similarly, any spell that would normally generate a ray effect no longer needs a ranged touch attack to hit, but if the spell would normally generate multiple rays, any additional rays are lost.
4. Any caps for maximum hit dice of creatures affected should be removed, but other level-dependent caps, such as maximum number of dice of damage, should remain.
5. Do not use spell-like abilities with casting times greater than one standard action, such as most summoning spells.
6. In general, it is best to pick spell-like abilities with a balance of offensive, defensive, tactical, and utilitarian spell effects. However, creating a gibbering abomination focused for a particular task is certainly possible, as the mad beings who created it may have designed it with just such a purpose in mind.

Credit
Originally appearing in *Rappan Athuk* (© Frog God Games, 2012)

Gibbering Orb

These great masses of floating amorphous flesh appear to be covered in bloodshot, weeping eyes and disgustingly vile mouths. The gibbering orb is a pulsing mass of sickly greyish-green flesh, roughly 20 ft. in diameter. The orb distends and undulates as it flies, seeming to spasm through the air rather than fly. The creature does not seem to have a top or bottom, nor does it have any form of appendages for handling objects.

GIBBERING ORB	CR 27

XP 3,276,800
CE Huge aberration
Init +16; **Senses** darkvision 60 ft.; **Perception** +37

AC 48, touch 32, flat-footed 36 (+12 Dex, +12 insight, +16 natural, –2 size)
hp 337 (27d8+216)
Fort +17; **Ref** +21; **Will** +24
Defensive Abilities all-around vision; **DR** 10/epic; **Immune** critical hits, flanking; **SR** 37

Speed 5 ft., fly 20 ft. (good)
Melee 12 bites +30 (2d8+11/19–20 plus grab)
Ranged 24 eye rays +31 touch
Space 15 ft.; **Reach** 10 ft.
Special Attacks eye rays, gibbering (60 ft.; DC 29 Will), steal spell, steal spell-like ability, swallow whole (4d8 constriction damage plus 3d10 acid damage, AC 18, hp 33)
Spell-like Abilities (CL 27th; save DC 16 + spell level):
At will—two stolen spells or spell-like abilities per round

Str 32, **Dex** 35, **Con** 27, **Int** 40, **Wis** 24, **Cha** 22
Base Atk +20; **CMB** +33 (+37 to grapple); **CMD** 55 (can't be tripped)
Feats Bleeding Critical, Critical Focus, Die Hard, Endurance, Flyby Attack, Greater Vital Strike, Improved Critical, Improved Critical (bite), Improved Initiative, Improved Vital Strike, Iron Will, Vital Strike, Weapon Focus (eye ray), Weapon Focus (bite)
Skills Acrobatics +42, Bluff +33, Diplomacy +33, Escape Artist +42, Fly +42, Heal +34, Intimidate +36, Knowledge (arcana) +45, Knowledge (dungeoneering) +42, Knowledge (history) +42, Knowledge (local) +42, Knowledge (planes) +45, Knowledge (religion) +27, Linguistics +42, Perception +41, Sense Motive +34, Spellcraft +45, Stealth +34, Survival +37, Use Magic Device +33; **Racial Modifiers** +4 Perception
Languages all
SQ flight

Environment any

Organization solitary
Treasure standard

Eye Rays (Su) Two dozen of the eyes can each produce a magical ray each round, with each eye emulating a spell from among the list of spells below (CL 27th). The save DCs, where applicable, are 16 + spell level. A gibbering orb has no directional limitations on where it can point its eye rays, because the eyes orbiting around its body drift and float wherever needed. However, a gibbering orb can never aim more than five rays at any single target, due to limitations of aiming. All rays have a range of 150 ft. Each of these effects functions as a ray, regardless of the normal parameters of the spell it resembles. That is, each is usable against a single target and requires a ranged touch attack. The eye rays are: *cone of cold, disintegrate, dominate monster, energy drain, feeblemind, finger of death, flesh to stone, greater dispel magic, harm, hold monster, horrid wilting, implosion, inflict critical wounds, lightning bolt, magic missile, mage's disjunction, irresistible dance, baleful polymorph, power word blind, power word kill, power word stun, prismatic spray, slay living,* and *temporal stasis.*

Flight (Ex) The gibbering orb's body is naturally buoyant. This buoyancy allows it to fly as the spell, as a free action, at a speed of 20 ft. This buoyancy also grants it a permanent *feather fall* effect with personal range.

Gibbering (Su) The cacophony of speech emanating from the scores of mouths that make up the orb forces all within 60 ft. of the creature to succeed at a DC 29 Will save each round or suffer the effects of an *insanity* spell.

Steal Spell/Steal Spell-Like Ability (Su) When a creature dies by being swallowed whole (or when a creature killed by the gibbering orb in some other fashion is eaten by it), the gibbering orb absorbs the creature's known spells, prepared spells, and spell-like abilities. The orb can use any two of those abilities per round as a free action. Each originates from an eye that is not producing an eye ray (see above) that round. Stolen spells and spell-like abilities are lost after 24 hours.

These great harbingers of insanity and chaos are fortunately very rare indeed. Locked away by whatever powers preserve order and sanity, the gibbering orbs occasionally make their way to the civilized world to satiate its ravenous hunger for sentient beings. While the gibbering orb looks like a mass of chaotic, insanely impossible flesh, it is a clever and very intelligent adversary. If any being is so foolish as to attack a gibbering orb, it hurls itself at its foes with complete abandon, somehow making tactical decisions despite its completely random approach to destruction.

Gibbering orbs speak all languages, and frequently speak in several tongues at once to disorient their opponents. Gibbering orbs are incapable of speaking in a non-dominant role, their egos are too vast.

Gibbering orbs are 20 feet or more in diameter, weighing at least 8,000 pounds. Their coloration varies from a sickly, mottled gray to luminescent green or deep magenta at random intervals. The orbs flesh spasms and twitches constantly, and the entire surface is covered in eyes, mouths and other incomprehensible appendages. The orb has no obvious top or bottom; as it hovers, the entire mass continuously rotates so no one side is ever in direct contact with opponents for longer than a few seconds.

Gibbering orbs are planar travelers; fortunately, they grow bored of one place quickly. The only time gibbering orbs maintain a residence for long in any one place is if they are guarding some location for their own amusement, or if they are stranded or bound to a location. Woe to those who stumble upon an orb that cannot leave of its own free will!

Gibbering orbs in combat are forces of nature. They attack with seeming abandon, although they are incredibly intelligent, their ego does not allow them to comprehend the concept other being are as powerful as they are. Gibbering orbs consume there foes fully, drawing them into their various mouths; thus, any treasure found with a gibbering orb is one the inside of the creature.

Gibbering orbs are never found together. It is unknown how they reproduce, and such an event would most likely take place in a very secluded lair.

Credit
Originally appearing in *Rappan Athuk* (© Frog God Games, 2012)

Gibbering Orb, Lesser

These hideous masses of floating flesh appear to be covered with staring eyes and hungry mouths. The lesser gibbering orb is a pulsing mass of sickly greyish-green flesh, roughly 8 ft. in diameter. The orb seems to fly in starts and fits, but this is a ruse, for the creature is nimble for its bulk. It may be a distant cousin to the eye of the deep or similarly-orbed entities.

LESSER GIBBERING ORB	CR 11

XP 12,800
CE Large aberration
Init +7; **Senses** darkvision 60 ft.; **Perception** +23

AC 20, touch 12, flat-footed 17 (+3 Dex, +8 natural, −1 size)
hp 91 (14d8+42)
Fort +7; **Ref** +7; **Will** +13
Defensive Abilities all-around vision; **Immune** critical hits, flanking; **SR** 21

Speed 5 ft., fly 30 ft. (good)

Melee 6 bites +12 (1d8+3 plus grab)
Ranged 6 eye rays +13 touch
Space 10 ft.; **Reach** 5 ft.
Special Attacks eye rays, gibbering (60 ft.; DC 23 Will), steal spell, steal spell-like ability, swallow whole (1d8 acid damage, AC 14, hp 9)
Spell-like Abilities (CL 14th; save DC 16 + spell level)
Constant—*fly*
At will—one stolen spell or spell-like ability per round

Str 16, **Dex** 17, **Con** 17, **Int** 20, **Wis** 14, **Cha** 22
Base Atk +10; **CMB** +14 (+18 grapple); **CMD** 27 (can't be tripped)
Feats Diehard, Endurance, Flyby Attack, Improved Initiative, Iron Will, Vital Strike, Weapon Focus (eye ray)
Skills Acrobatics +20, Fly +22, Intimidate +23, Knowledge (arcana) +22, Knowledge (dungeoneering) +19, Linguistics +19, Perception +23, Sense Motive +16, Stealth +19; **Racial**

Lesser Gibbering Orb Eye Rays

Lesser gibbering orbs are an immature or offshoot form of the great and terrible aberrations that are known to inhabit the dark recesses of the world. Created in some manner of magical nightmare, the orbs are as different as their underground realms. If the GM so desires, these additional eye powers are presented as possible replacements.

Eye Rays (Su) Six of the eyes can each produce a magical ray each round, with each eye emulating a spell from among the list of spells below as if cast by a 14th-level caster. The save DCs, where applicable, are 16 + spell level. A gibbering orb has no directional limitations on where it can point its eye rays, because the eyes orbiting around its body drift and float wherever needed. However, a gibbering orb can never aim more than three rays at any single target, due to limitations of aiming. All rays have a range of 80 feet. Each of these effects functions as a ray, regardless of the normal parameters of the spell it resembles. That is, each is usable against a single target and requires a ranged touch attack.

A lesser gibbering orb can have up to 6 eye rays, each based on a 0–3rd level cleric or sorcerer spell. The rays can be determined by the GM or rolled randomly on the table below.

ROLL	EYE RAY
1	acid arrow
2	blindness/deafness
3	chill touch
4	color spray
5	daze monster
6	dispel magic
7	flaming sphere
8	glitterdust
9	grease
10	hypnotism
11	hypnotic pattern
12	inflict light wounds
13	inflict moderate wounds
14	magic missile
15	ray of enfeeblement
16	ray of frost
17	shatter
18	sleep
19	slow
20	touch of fatigue

Modifiers +4 Perception
Languages all
SQ flight

Environment any
Organization solitary or occulum (2–3)
Treasure standard

Eye Rays (Su) Six of the eyes can produce a magical ray per round, with each eye emulating a spell from among the list of spells below as if cast by a 14th-level caster. The save DCs, where applicable, are 16 + spell level. A gibbering orb has no directional limitations on where it can point its eye rays, because the eyes orbiting around its body drift and float wherever needed. However, a gibbering orb can never aim more than three rays at any single target, due to limitations of aiming. All rays have a range of 80 feet. Each of these effects functions as a ray, regardless of the normal parameters of the spell it resembles. That is, each is usable against a single target and requires a ranged touch attack. The eye rays are: *daze monster, dispel magic, flaming sphere, inflict moderate wounds, magic missile,* and *ray of enfeeblement*. The save DC is Charisma-based.
Flight (Sp) The gibbering orb's body is naturally buoyant. This buoyancy allows it to cast *fly*, as the spell, as a free action, at a speed of 30 ft. This buoyancy also grants it a permanent *feather fall* effect with personal range.
Gibbering (Su) As a free action, no more than once per 1d4 rounds, a gibbering orb can emit a cacophony of maddening sound. All creatures other than gibbering mouthers and gibbering orbs within 60 feet must succeed on a DC 23 Will save or be confused for 1d4 rounds. This is a mind-affecting compulsion insanity effect. A creature that saves cannot be affected by the same orb's gibbering for 24 hours. The save DC is Charisma-based.
Steal Spell/Steal Spell-Like Ability (Su) When a creature dies by being swallowed whole (or when a creature killed by the gibbering orb in some other fashion is eaten by it), the gibbering orb absorbs the creature's known spells, prepared spells, and spell-like abilities. The orb can use any one of those abilities per round as a free action. Each originates from an eye that is not producing an eye ray (see above) that round. Stolen spells and spell-like abilities are lost after 24 hours.

The lesser gibbering orb is either a smaller or younger version of the gibbering orb, or so similar it makes no difference for naming purposes. These odd beasts are not quite the force of nature their larger brethren are, but they are every bit as chaotic and hungry as the larger version. These creatures are very distinct, and no two lesser gibbering orbs encountered are the same, if the encounter is survived at all!

The gibbering orb has the ability to bite its foes by extending a pseudopod with one of its mouths protruding from the end. The orb can extend two of these at any one foe, or a total of six in any given round. At the same time, the legions of eyes have the ability to cast a host of spells at a rapid rate.

Like their larger kin, lesser gibbering orbs speak any language, and constantly babble and gurgle unintelligible gibberish to confuse and disorient their foes.

Credit
Originally appearing in *Rappan Athuk* (© Frog God Games, 2012)

Glacial Haunt

This humanoid has pale white skin and is partially covered in ice and snow. Its hair appears stiff and frozen, glittering with small particles of ice. Its eyes are deep blue and show no signs of life.

GLACIAL HAUNT	CR 2

XP 600
CE Medium undead (cold)
Init +2; **Senses** darkvision 60 ft., lifesense 100 ft.; **Perception** +8
Aura bitter cold (10 ft.)

AC 17, touch 13, flat-footed 14 (+1 dodge, +2 Dex, +4 natural)
hp 22 (4d8+4)
Fort +2; **Ref** +3; **Will** +5
Defensive Abilities channel resistance +2; **Immune** cold, undead traits
Weaknesses vulnerability to fire

Speed 30 ft., burrow 20 ft. (ice and snow only); snow glide
Melee slam +6 (1d4+3 plus heat drain)

Str 14, **Dex** 15, **Con** —, **Int** 8, **Wis** 12, **Cha** 13
Base Atk +3; **CMB** +5; **CMD** 18
Feats Dodge, Weapon Focus (slam)
Skills Climb +9, Perception +8, Stealth +9
Languages Common

Environment cold lands
Organization solitary or gang (2–5)
Treasure none

Bitter Cold (Ex) A glacial haunt radiates intense cold in a 10-foot radius. Creatures in or entering the area take 1d2 points of cold damage each round.
Heat Drain (Su) A glacial haunt's slam attack drains away body heat from living creatures. This attack deals 1d4 points of Strength damage to a living creature. This is a negative energy effect. A creature freezes to death if this Strength damage equals or exceeds its actual Strength score.
Lifesense (Ex) A glacial haunt can detect living creatures within 100 feet by the heat their bodies radiate. This includes invisible creatures.
Snow Glide (Ex) A burrowing glacial haunt can pass through ice and snow as easily as a fish swims through water. Its burrowing leaves behind no tunnel or hole, nor does it create any ripple or other sign of its presence.

The icy wastes sometimes grant unlife to those who freeze to death at her unforgiving hands. The result is a glacial haunt, the utter bane of the unwary traveler, for the glacial haunt is drawn to the heat of all sources, be it from magic, fires, or the warmth given off by living creatures. Glacial haunts spend most of their time wandering their frigid domains seeking to kill and devour anything they encounter. When winter spreads her icy embrace to other lands, the glacial haunt's hunting grounds increase.

A glacial haunt is 6 feet tall and weighs about 165 pounds. It is usually dressed in the attire it wore at the time of its death, though much of it has rotted or fallen away. Glacial haunts seem to understand, and possibly be able to speak, the Common tongue, but no encounters with these creatures has born any hard evidence of this. Multiple glacial haunts in a single encounter is rare and believed to come about when a group of adventurers succumb to the cold and perish together. Others have speculated that glacial haunts actually reproduce by melting and then splitting into two identical creatures.

Glacial haunts detest living creatures and attack them on sight. A favored tactic of glacial haunts is to burrow into the snow when it detects living creatures in its domain, and then spring from ambush to assault them when they move near. Glacial haunts batter their foes with their fists, seeking to destroy them by literally smashing the life from them.

Gloom Haunt

A vaguely humanoid shape composed of darkness rises from the shadows.

GLOOM HAUNT	CR 5

XP 1,600
CE Medium undead (incorporeal)
Init +7; **Senses** darkvision 60 ft., see in darkness; **Perception** +13

AC 18, touch 18, flat-footed 15 (+5 deflection, +3 Dex)
hp 57 (6d8+30)
Fort +7; **Ref** +5; **Will** +7
Defensive Abilities incorporeal, channel resistance +2, shadowy resolve; **Immune** undead traits

Speed fly 50 ft. (good)
Melee incorporeal touch +7 (3d6+5 plus pain touch)
Special Attacks shadow mastery

Str —, **Dex** 17, **Con** —, **Int** 14, **Wis** 14, **Cha** 20
Base Atk +4; **CMB** +7; **CMD** 25
Feats Alertness, Flyby Attack, Improved Initiative
Skills Fly +16, Intimidate +14, Knowledge (any one) +8, Perception +13, Sense Motive +13, Stealth +12 (+16 in dim light, +8 in bright light); **Racial Modifiers** +4 Stealth in dim light (–4 in bright light)
SQ creeping shadows

Environment any
Organization solitary or gang (gloom haunt plus 2–4 shadows)
Treasure standard

Creeping Shadows (Su) Once per day, a gloom haunt can emanate an inky darkness in a 30-foot-radius burst as a standard action. This functions as a *deeper darkness* spell (CL 6th).
Incorporeal Touch (Su) By passing part of its incorporeal body through a foe's body as a standard action, the gloom haunt inflicts 7d6 damage. This damage is not negative energy—it manifests in the form of physical wounds and aches from supernatural aging. Creatures immune to magical aging are immune to this damage, but otherwise the damage bypasses all forms of damage reduction. A Fortitude save halves the damage inflicted.
Pain Touch (Su) A gloom haunt adds its Charisma modifier on damage rolls with its incorporeal touch. Additionally, the touch of a gloom haunt sends a wave of intense pain through the opponent's body. A creature touched must succeed on a DC 18 Fortitude save or be stunned for 1 round and shaken for 1d4+2 rounds thereafter. The save DC is Charisma-based.
Shadow Mastery (Su) A gloom haunt is a creature of darkness. In areas of total darkness (including that created by its creeping shadows ability), a gloom haunt gains a +2 racial bonus on attack rolls, saves, and checks. These bonuses are not included in the statistics block.
Shadowy Resolve (Su) In areas of shadowy illumination or total darkness, a gloom haunts channel resistance increases to +4.

Gloom haunts are believed to somehow be related to shadows though most learned scholars agree that people simply relate them to shadows because of their resemblance to said creatures. In actuality, gloom haunts are different creatures, unrelated to the aforementioned undead at all. While both prefer areas of gloom and darkness, and both seem to be formed of shadowstuff, that's where the similarities end.

Gloom haunts are vile evil creatures, who seem to have no ties to the living (i.e., scholars cannot find any reasonable explanation as to why they exist), though a few learned sages believe gloom haunts to be the spiritual remains of paladins who were sacrificed by evil clerics to their vile and dark gods. Gloom haunts are found haunting graves, dungeons, and catacombs. These creatures detest light (though they are not harmed by it) and move about at night when their natural coloration and abilities help them the most.

A gloom haunt appears as a humanoid-shaped somewhat translucent creature formed of darkness. Two small pinpoints of red light function as eyes. A gloom haunt does not speak or utter any sounds.

Gloom haunts use their ability to hide in shadows to wait for living creatures to come close. When such a creature does, glooms haunt leap to the attack.

Golem, Crystalline

A man-size biped made entirely of what looks like glass or crystal moves forward, the light reflecting off is faceted form in a dizzying array.

CRYSTALLINE GOLEM	CR 5

XP 1,600
N Medium construct
Init −1; **Senses** darkvision 60 ft., low-light vision;
Perception +0

AC 17, touch 9, flat-footed 17 (−1 Dex, +8 natural)
hp 44 (8d10+20)
Fort +2; **Ref** +1; **Will** +2
DR 5/adamantine; **Immune** construct traits (+20 hp),
electricity, fire, magic
Weakness vulnerability to sonic

Speed 30 ft.
Melee 2 slams +11 (1d6+3)
Special Attacks crystalline destruction

Str 16, **Dex** 9, **Con** —, **Int** —, **Wis** 11, **Cha** 1
Base Atk +8; **CMB** +11; **CMD** 20

Environment any
Organization solitary
Treasure none

Crystalline Destruction (Ex) When reduced to 0 hit points, a crystal golem shatters in an explosion of jagged shards of rock. All creatures within a 10-foot burst take 3d6 points of slashing damage and 2d6 points of bludgeoning damage; a DC 13 Reflex save halves the damage. The save DC is Constitution-based.

Immunity to Magic (Ex) A crystal golem is immune to any spell or spell-like ability that allows spell resistance, with the exception of spells and spell-like abilities that have the sonic descriptor. In addition, certain spells and effects function differently against the creature, as noted: A *transmute rock to mud* spell slows a crystalline golem (as the *slow* spell) for 2d6 rounds, with no saving throw, while *transmute mud to rock* heals all of its lost hit points. A *stone to flesh* spell does not actually change the golem's structure but negates its damage reduction and immunity to magic for 1 full round.

Crystalline golems are man-shaped growths of crystal, animated by a powerful wizard and possessed of rudimentary intelligence. They attack by clubbing with their rock-like fists. These are comparably quite a weak form of golem, but the process of creating them is not as arduous as for the other sorts.

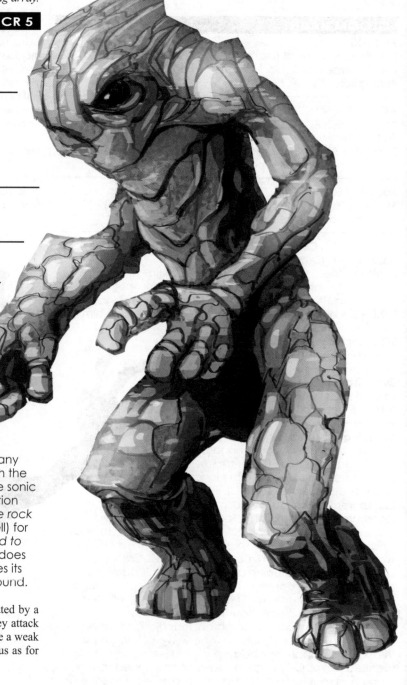

Construction

Crystalline golems are created out of fine quartz or other crystal weighing 1,200 pounds, and worth 3,000 gp. The crystal is shaped into a man-size form, and infused with electricity to spark its animation.

CRYSTALLINE GOLEM
CL 8th; **Price** 6,000 gp

CONSTRUCTION
Requirements Craft Construct, *geas/quest*, *limited wish*, *shocking grasp*, creator must be caster level 8th; **Skill**; **Cost** 3,000 gp

Credit
Original author Matthew J. Finch
Originally appearing in *The Spire of Iron and Crystal* (© Frog God Games/Matthew J. Finch, 2011)

Golem, Necromantic

This creature looks like a large, rotting humanoid whose body has been stitched together with cord, wires, and string.

NECROMANTIC GOLEM	CR 8

XP 4,800
N Large construct
Init +0; **Senses** darkvision 60 ft., low-light vision; **Perception** +1

AC 21, touch 9, flat-footed 21 (+12 natural, –1 size)
hp 90 (11d10+30)
Fort +3; **Ref** +3; **Will** +4
DR 5/adamantine; **Immune** construct traits (+30 hp), magic

Speed 30 ft.
Melee 2 slams +14 (2d6+4 plus 1d6 negative energy)
Space 10 ft.; **Reach** 10 ft.
Special Attacks enervating ray, unholy blast

Str 18, **Dex** 10, **Con** —, **Int** —, **Wis** 12, **Cha** 1
Base Atk +11; **CMB** +16; **CMD** 26
SQ rejuvenation

Environment any
Organization solitary
Treasure none

Enervating Ray (Su) Once per day, a necromantic golem can unleash a ray of negative energy in a 30-foot line. A creature struck must make a DC 17 Fortitude save or gain 2d4 negative levels. Even on a successful save, the victim gains 1d4 negative levels. Assuming the target survives, it regains lost levels after 11 hours have passed. Negative levels from a necromantic golem do not have a chance of becoming permanent. The save DC is Constitution-based and includes a +2 racial bonus.

Immunity to Magic (Ex) A necromantic golem is immune to any spell or spell-like ability that allows spell resistance. In addition, certain spells and effects function differently against the creature, as noted: A magical attack that heals living creatures slows a necromantic golem (as the *slow* spell) for 2d6 rounds (no save). A magical attack that deals negative energy damage breaks any *slow* effect on the golem and heals 1 point of damage for every 3 points of damage the attack would otherwise deal. If the amount of healing would cause the golem to exceed its full normal hit points, it gains any excess as temporary hit points. A necromantic golem gets no saving throw against attacks that deal negative energy damage. A *raise dead* spell deals 6d6 points of damage to a necromantic golem. A necromantic golem gets no saving throw against this effect. A *resurrection* or *true resurrection* spell negates its DR and immunity to magic for 1 minute. In an area affected by a *hallow* spell, a necromantic golem takes a –2 penalty on attack rolls, damage rolls, checks, and saves, and a –2 penalty to AC. In areas affected by an *unhallow* spell, a necromantic golem gains a +2 bonus on attack rolls, damage rolls, checks, and saves, and a +2 bonus to AC.

Rejuvenation (Su) A necromantic golem heals 1 hit point every hour up to its maximum hit points. If reduced to 0 hit points or less, the golem continues to heal. A necromantic golem can be permanently destroyed by reducing it to 0 hit points or less, casting a *hallow* spell on the corpse, and dousing the golem with holy water.

Unholy Blast (Su) As a free action once every 1d4+1 rounds, a necromantic golem can unleash a blast of negative energy in a 20-foot cone. Creatures caught in the area take 6d6 points of negative energy damage (good-aligned outsiders caught in the area take 6d8 points of negative energy damage). A DC 15 Reflex save reduces the damage by half. The save DC is Constitution-based.

A necromantic golem resembles a flesh golem, and is often times mistaken for said creature. It is assembled in much the same way as a flesh golem is (humanoid body parts stitched together into a single form), and infused with negative energy during the construction process.

A necromantic golem stands 8 feet tall and weighs around 500 pounds. Its sickly greenish flesh is drawn tight around its frame in areas and rotted completely away in others. Its form weeps fluids from various sores and injuries. A necromantic golem wields no weapons and wears whatever its creator gives it, usually ragged clothing and nothing more.

A necromantic golem cannot speak, though it does seem to understand basic commands spoken in the Common tongue.

In combat, a necromantic golem attacks with its unholy blast and powerful slam attacks, usually opening battle with its enervating ray. It is relentless and fights to the death unless otherwise instructed by its creator. A necromantic golem moves and walks with a stiff gait.

Construction

The pieces of a necromantic golem must come from normal humanoid corpses that have not decayed significantly. Assembly requires a minimum of six different bodies—one for each limb, the torso (including head), and the brain. In some cases, more bodies may be necessary. Special unguents and bindings worth 500 gp are also required. Note that creating a necromantic golem requires casting a spell with the evil descriptor.

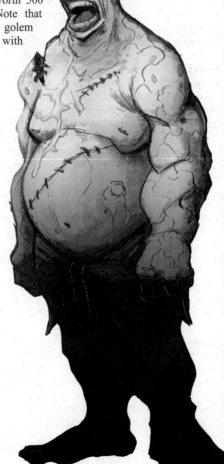

NECROMANTIC GOLEM
CL 10th;
Price 24,500 gp

CONSTRUCTION
Requirements Craft Construct, *animate dead, bull's strength, enervation, geas/quest, limited wish,* creator must be caster level 10th;
Skill Craft (leather) or Heal DC 15;
Cost 12,000 gp

Golem, Philosopher

This creature appears as a nine-foot tall humanoid crafted from lapis lazuli. It has a regal bearing and wields a rod of platinum in its hand.

PHILOSOPHER GOLEM	CR 9

XP 6,400
N (usually; but any) Large construct
Init +0; **Senses** darkvision 60 ft., low-light vision; **Perception** +14

AC 20, touch 9, flat-footed 20 (+11 natural, −1 size)
hp 112 (15d10+30)
Fort +5; **Ref** +5; **Will** +9
DR 10/adamantine; **Immune** construct traits (+30 hp), magic

Speed 30 ft.
Melee platinum rod +19/+14 (1d8+5) or 2 slams +19 (2d6+5)
Space 10 ft.; **Reach** 10 ft.
Special Attacks spells
Spells Known (CL 7th; melee touch +19, ranged touch +14):
3rd (4/day)—*lightning bolt* (DC 15), *sleet storm*
2nd (7/day)—*flaming sphere* (DC 14), *invisibility*, *web* (DC 14)
1st (7/day)—*burning hands* (DC 13), *charm person* (DC 13), *detect secret doors*, *ray of enfeeblement* (DC 13), *true strike*
0 (at will)—*bleed* (DC 12), *dancing lights*, *detect magic*, *flare* (DC 12), *mage hand*, *read magic*, *touch of fatigue* (DC 12)

Str 20, **Dex** 11, **Con** —, **Int** 15, **Wis** 15, **Cha** 15
Base Atk +15; **CMB** +21; **CMD** 31
Feats Alertness, Combat Casting, Craft Construct[B], Craft Wondrous Item, Extend Spell, Iron Will, Maximize Spell, Power Attack, Quicken Spell
Skills Craft (any one) +12, Knowledge (any one) +12, Knowledge (arcana) +12, Perception +14, Sense Motive +4, Spellcraft +12, Use Magical Device +12
Languages Common, plus two others

Environment any
Organization solitary
Treasure platinum rod (1,500 gp)

Immunity to Magic (Ex) A philosopher golem is immune to any spell or spell-like ability that allows spell resistance. In addition, certain spells and effects function differently against the creature as noted: A *shatter* spell deals damage to a philosopher golem as if it were a crystalline creature. A *keen edge* spell affects a philosopher golem's slam attacks as if they were slashing weapons. A magical attack that deals cold damage slows a philosopher golem (as the *slow* spell) for 3 rounds (no saving throw). A magical attack that deals fire damage ends any *slow* effect on the golem and heals 1 point of damage for each 3 points of damage the attack would otherwise deal. If the amount of healing would cause the golem to exceed its full normal hit points, it gains any excess as temporary hit points. A philosopher golem gets no saving throw against fire effects.
Spells When a philosopher golem is created, it is programmed with spells. The creator can add as many or as few spells as desired up to the limit of the golem's caster level. A philosopher golem has a caster level equal to one-half its Hit Dice. A philosopher golem does not require any spell components or focuses to cast its spells, and once a spell is cast, it is expended until the golem recharges it. To recharge its expended spells, a philosopher golem must remain idle (resting, more or less) for 8 hours.

The philosopher golem is a completely self-aware construct, designed as an aid to powerful spellcasters. The philosopher golem is subservient to its master but acts more as a companion and confidant, having its own mind as to choices of right and wrong or good and evil. Philosopher golems are often used as proxies in the crafting of dangerous magical items by their creators who use the philosopher golem in the handling of volatile spell

components or in the acquisition of reagents from hostile environments. Philosopher golems can, or so it is rumored, teach other spellcasters the spells they have programmed if the spellcaster is of sufficient level to cast the spell. A philosopher golem cannot change its programmed spells, but its creator or another spellcaster can. Spells can be added, removed, or changed by the creator or another spellcaster.

Philosopher golems are most often found in the employ of wizards, sorcerers, and clerics. In combat, philosopher golem uses its programmed spells and powerful slam attacks to dispatch its foes. It can also attack with its platinum rod (treat as a club).

Reprogramming a Philosopher Golem

A spellcaster can add, remove, or change the philosopher golem's programmed spells.

Adding a New Programmed Spell

The following rules apply when adding a new spell to an existing philosopher golem.

The philosopher golem must have available spell slots. A golem has as many spell slots as would a spellcaster equal to its caster level.

A new spell can only be added in a spell slot of the spell's level or higher.

The spellcaster must be able to cast the spell to be added and must have access to it (that is, it must appear on his spell list and he must have access to it via spellbook, prepared spell or known spell, scroll, etc.)

Adding a new spell takes 1 hour per spell level and the spellcaster must expend a number of gold pieces equal to the spell's level x the philosopher golem's caster level x 500 gp. 0th level spells cost one-half this price. The spellcaster makes a Spellcraft check (DC 20 if the spellcaster is the golem's creator; DC 25 if not + the spell's level). If successful, the new spell is added to the golem. If the check fails, both time and cost are wasted.

Removing a Programmed Spell

Removing a programmed spell from a philosopher golem takes 1 hour per spell level and requires a DC 20 Spellcraft check. Modify the DC as follows (add all that apply).

Circumstance	DC
Spellcaster is not the golem's creator	+5
Spell doesn't appear on spellcaster's list (or doesn't know the spell)	+5
Spell is of a higher level than spellcaster can cast	+5 per level over

If the Spellcraft check succeeds, the spell is removed. If the check fails, the spell is not removed. The spellcaster can try again, but the DC to remove that spell increases by +5 each time he fails this check.

Changing a Programmed Spell

Changing a spell requires the spellcaster to first remove the spell (using the rules above), and then add the spell to the golem (using the rules above).

Construction

A philosopher golem's body is chiseled from a single block of lapis lazuli, weighing at least 2,000 pounds. The lapis lazuli must be of exceptional quality, and costs 10,000 gp.

PHILOSOPHER GOLEM
CL 14th; **Price** 64,000 gp

CONSTRUCTION
Requirements Craft Construct, *antimagic field, geas/quest, limited wish,* all of the spells the creator wants to program into the philosopher golem, creator must be caster level 14th; **Skill** Craft (sculpting) or Craft (jewelrymaking) DC 17; **Cost** 37,000 gp

Golem, Skiff

This unusual river skiff is constructed of finely-crafted wood. On the bow of the ship stands a statue of a skeletal figure dressed in a hooded black robe. Its hand clutches a long staff.

SKIFF GOLEM	**CR 11**

XP 12,800
N Huge construct (extraplanar)
Init −2; **Senses** darkvision 60 ft., low-light vision; **Perception** +0

AC 21, touch 6, flat-footed 21 (−2 Dex, +15 natural, −2 size)
hp 122 (15d10+40)
Fort +5; **Ref** +3; **Will** +5
DR 10/adamantine; **Immune** construct traits (+40 hp), magic; **Resist** fire 20

Speed 40 ft., swim 50 ft.
Melee quarterstaff +23/+18/+13 (2d6+15 plus paralysis)
Space 15 ft.; **Reach** 10 ft.
Special Attacks breath weapon (30-ft. cone, 7d6 electricity damage; DC 17 Ref half, usable five times/day), man overboard, paralysis (2d4 rounds, DC 17)
Spell-Like Abilities (CL 15th):
1/day—*passwall*, summon (level 8, 1d4 charonadaemons 35%)

Str 31, **Dex** 6, **Con** —, **Int** —, **Wis** 11, **Cha** 11
Base Atk +15; **CMB** +27; **CMD** 35 (can't be tripped)
Skills Swim +18
Languages Abyssal, Common, Infernal (cannot speak any)

Environment any (lower planes)
Organization solitary
Treasure none

Immunity to Magic (Ex) A skill golem is immune to any spell or spell-like ability that allows spell resistance. In addition, certain spells and effects function differently against the creature, as noted: *Warp wood* or *wood shape* slows a skiff golem (as the slow spell) for 2d6 rounds (no save). A magical attack that deals cold damage breaks any slow effect on the skiff golem and heals 1 point of damage for every 3 points of damage the attack would otherwise deal. If the amount of healing would cause the golem to exceed its full normal hit points, it gains any excess as temporary hit points. A skiff golem gets no saving throw against attacks that deal cold damage. *Repel wood* drives the skiff golem back 30 feet and deals 2d12 points of damage to it (no save). *Ironwood* heals a skiff golem of all its lost hit points.
Man Overboard (Ex) A skiff golem can rock itself violently back and forth as a move action, causing all those onboard to fall into the water (which if on the River Styx could be a very bad thing indeed). A creature can attempt to maintain its footing and grab onto the skiff golem by succeeding on a DC 27 Acrobatics check. The check DC is Strength-based.

Crafted by Charon, the Boatman of the Lower Planes and his servants, these creatures serve as an automated means of transportation across the Styx. A rider's destination need merely be whispered in the golem's ear and payment dropped into a nearby container on the skiff. When these conditions are met, the skiff sets out immediately at full speed, polling across water and land alike with otherworldly determination.

If attacked, or if travelers attempt to board the skiff without first paying, a skiff golem attacks with its ebon staff and breath weapon (the skeletal figure pivots to face its opponents). If it manages to paralyze an opponent with its staff, it attempts to knock that foe from its skiff into the waiting waters. If threatened with destruction, the skiff golem summons several charonadaemons to its aid or makes haste to retreat, poling thru rock, stone, magical obstructions, water and fire if necessary.

Construction

The construction of a skiff golem is a closely guarded secret, known only to Charon and some of his most loyal servants.

Golem, Spontaneous — Ossuary Golem

A massive amalgamation of jagged bones bears a multitude of wickedly clawed arms and a head formed of numerous skulls held in place together. It moves quickly on its many limbs before rising to its full height of 12 feet and bringing its four skeletal arms to bear.

OSSUARY GOLEM	CR 11

XP 12,800
N Large construct
Init +4; **Senses** darkvision 60 ft., low-light vision;
Perception +20
AC 23, touch 9, flat-footed 23 (+14 natural, −1 size)

hp 96 (12d10+30)
Fort +4; **Ref** +6; **Will** +6
Defensive Abilities disassemble;
DR 10/adamantine and bludgeoning; **Immune** construct traits (+30 hp), magic

Speed 40 ft.
Melee 4 slams +18 (2d10+6 plus wounding)
Space 10 ft.; **Reach** 10 ft.
Special Attacks wounding

Str 22, **Dex** 10, **Con** —, **Int** 2, **Wis** 14, **Cha** 10
Base Atk +12; **CMB** +19; **CMD** 29 (37 vs. trip)
Feats Cleave, Improved Initiative, Lightning Reflexes, Power Attack, Skill Focus (Perception), Weapon Focus (slam)
Skills Disguise +0 (+20 as pile of bones), Perception +20, Stealth −4 (+26 among other bones); **Racial Modifiers** +20 Disguise as pile of bones, +30 Stealth when among other bones such as battlefields, catacombs, etc.

Environment any
Organization solitary
Treasure none

Disassemble (Ex) When at rest with no living prey nearby, an ossuary golem as a free action separates into its component skeletons that lie inert in true death. In this form it is immune to all damage short of disintegration. As a free action, an ossuary golem can reassemble into its conglomerate form to attack. While living prey is nearby, an ossuary golem will not use its disassemble ability. Use of this ability does not provoke attacks of opportunity.
Immunity to Magic (Ex) An ossuary golem is immune to any spell or spell-like ability that allows spell resistance. In addition, certain spells and effects function differently against the creature as noted: An *animate dead* spell causes several of the golem's bones to temporarily fall away from its body which slows (as the *slow* spell) the golem for 1d4 rounds. A *raise dead* spell with a successful touch attack deals 5d6 points of damage. A *resurrection* spell with a successful touch attack deals 1d6 points of damage per caster level (15d6 maximum). A *speak with dead* spell stuns the golem for 1 round as the spirits of the many deceased temporarily confuse it while vying for control of their individual bodies. A *true resurrection* spell with a successful touch attack deals 10 points of damage per caster level to a maximum of 150 points at 15th level (as the *harm* spell).
Wounding (Ex) The jagged, bony claws of an ossuary golem function as *wounding* weapons, dealing 1 point of bleed damage per hit. Bleeding creatures take the bleed damage at the start of their turns. Bleeding can be stopped by a DC 15 Heal check or through the application of any spell that cures hit point damage. A critical hit does not multiply the bleed damage. Creatures immune to critical hits are immune to this bleed damage.

Spontaneous golems are constructs, much like the more common golem varieties, but they have no creator and are completely independent. A place of great pain, great fear, or great sorrow may, if conditions are just right, become the birthplace of one of these hideous, soulless things. These rare and possibly unique creatures possess a degree of cunning spurring them on in whatever violent impulse takes them.

Ossuary golems form only after many souls were slain in some catastrophic calamity and large quantities of intact bone lie exposed for long periods of time.

An ossuary golem cannot speak. It walks with a spindly though agile gait. Composed entirely of dry bones calcified into hardened rods, it weighs only 200 pounds.

An ossuary golem is vicious in combat raking with its many claws leaving horrid wounds in their wake. Typically it focuses its multitude of attacks on a single opponent until the target is reduced to bloody ribbons before moving on to another. Based on the Spontaneous Golem type from *Creature Collection III: Savage Bestiary* by **Sword & Sorcery Studio**.

Credit
Original author Greg A. Vaughan
Originally appearing in *Slumbering Tsar*
(© Frog God Games/ Greg A. Vaughan, 2012)

Grave Mount

This eerie black warhorse is rotting and decaying; its skeleton exposed in many places across its body. Its eyes burn red and its jet black mane is falling out in clumps.

GRAVE MONUT	CR 4

XP 1,200
LE Large undead
Init +6; **Senses** darkvision 60 ft., scent; **Perception** +10
Aura frightful presence (30 ft., DC 14)

AC 20, touch 11, flat-footed 18 (+2 Dex, +9 natural, −1 size)
hp 33 (6d8+6)
Fort +3; **Ref** +4; **Will** +6
DR 10/magic; **Immune** undead traits

Speed 30 ft.
Melee bite +7 (1d8+4 plus bleed), 2 hooves +5 (1d8+2)
Space 10 ft.; **Reach** 5 ft.
Special Attacks bleed (1d4), breath weapon (30-ft. cone, DC 14 Fort, *tomb fever*, usable 3/day)

Str 18, **Dex** 15, **Con** —, **Int** 12, **Wis** 12, **Cha** 13
Base Atk +4; **CMB** +9; **CMD** 21 (25 vs. trip)
Feats Improved Initiative, Multiattack, Run
Skills Bluff +7, Intimidate +10, Perception +10, Sense Motive +10, Stealth +7
Languages Common (can't speak)

Environment any land
Organization solitary
Treasure none

Disease (Su) *Tomb Fever*—inhaled; *save* DC 14 Fort, *onset* 1d6 days, *frequency* 1/day, *effect* 1d4 Dex damage and 1d4 Con damage, *cure* 2 consecutive saves. The DC is Charisma-based.

The grave mount is the insult to all that is good and holy when a paladin's steed is returned from the dead to wreak havoc upon the world. These undead creatures are rare and usually created when a death knight rises from the grave to ride the steed he owned in his former life, though a few necromancers are also able to raise a grave mount given time and study.

Grave mounts stand 5 to 6 feet tall at the shoulder and weigh between 800 and 1,000 pounds.

A grave mount begins melee with its breath weapon. Once engaged, it uses its hooves and bite attack to battle its opponents.

Grey Spirit

The lone female figure is clad in long, flowing grey robes and scarves which whip around her wildly even in the absence of a strong wind. Her head is covered by a wrapped veil, shielding her face from those who would see it.

GREY SPIRIT	CR 5

XP 1,600
NE Medium undead (incorporeal)
Init +3; **Senses** darkvision 60 ft.; **Perception** +12
Aura frightful presence (30 ft., DC 17)

AC 17, touch 17, flat-footed 14 (+4 deflection, +3 Dex)
hp 51 (6d8+24)
Fort +6; **Ref** +5; **Will** +5
Defensive Abilities channel resistance +4, incorporeal, rejuvenation; **Immune** undead traits

Speed fly 30 ft. (perfect)
Melee incorporeal touch +8 (2d6 cold plus energy drain)
Special Attacks energy drain (1 level, DC 17), ravages of death gaze

Str —, **Dex** 16, **Con** —, **Int** 11, **Wis** 11, **Cha** 18
Base Atk +4; **CMB** +7; **CMD** 24
Feats Ability Focus (gaze), Skill Focus (Perception), Weapon Focus (incorporeal touch)
Skills Fly +11, Intimidate +13, Perception +12, Sense Motive +9, Stealth +12
Languages Common
SQ harbinger

Environment any land
Organization solitary
Treasure none

Harbinger (Su) The appearance of a grey spirit is usually a harbinger of some future catastrophe, such as a great storm or a shipwreck. Such events occur within 1d6 days of the sighting of a grey spirit. Note that the grey spirit does not cause this catastrophe, rather she predicts it.

Ravages of Death Gaze (Su) Any living creature that sees the face of a grey spirit suddenly knows her pain, frustration, and rage, and has glimpse of the anguish of what it is like to die broken hearted. Any opponent experiencing this tragic emotion must succeed on a DC 19 Will save or be stunned for 2d6 rounds. A creature stunned by a grey spirit is wrought with despair, weeping and wailing uncontrollably. A *calm emotions* spell ends this effect. This is a mind-affecting effect. A creature who succeeds on the save cannot be affected by the same grey spirit's gaze for one day. The save DC is Charisma-based and includes a +2 bonus from the grey spirit's Ability Focus feat.

Rejuvenation (Su) In most cases, it's difficult to destroy a grey spirit through simple combat: the "destroyed" spirit restores itself in 2d4 days. Even the most powerful spells are usually only temporary solutions. The only way to permanently destroy a grey spirit is to confront her with irrefutable evidence of her loved one's death. The exact means varies with each spirit and may require a good deal of research, and should be created specifically for each different grey spirit by the GM.

Many a sailor who ventures out into the trackless sea is destined never to look again on the loved ones he left behind. Either death or the lure of foreign lands keeps them from returning to those who wait patiently for them. A grey spirit, usually female, is the shade of someone who died heartbroken and alone, pining away on shore and ultimately dying of a broken heart while waiting for the return of a loved one from across the sea.

A grey spirit attacks any creature that approaches her, her rage and frustration at having lost her loved one knowing no bounds. In melee, a grey spirit fails wildly with her ghostly arms and hands, screaming and cursing all the while. If an opponent proves to be particularly strong, a grey spirit pulls aside the cowl that covers her face.

Gribbon

This wicked little creature looks like an oversized monkey with leathery bat wings. It clutches a needle-like dagger in its claws.

GRIBBON	CR 1/2

XP 200
NE Small monstrous humanoid
Init +3; **Senses** darkvision 60 ft.; **Perception** +4

AC 15, touch 14, flat-footed 12 (+3 Dex, +1 natural, +1 size)
hp 6 (1d10+1)
Fort +1; **Ref** +5; **Will** +2

Speed 30 ft., fly 30 ft. (poor)
Melee dagger +3 (1d3+1/19–20) or 2 claws +3 (1d3+1 plus grab)
Ranged dart +5 (1d3+1)
Special Attacks coordinated attack, grab (Medium)

Str 12, **Dex** 16, **Con** 13, **Int** 10, **Wis** 10, **Cha** 11
Base Atk +1; **CMB** +1 (+5 grapple); **CMD** 14
Feats Flyby Attack
Skills Climb +5, Fly +5, Perception +4, Stealth +11 (+15 in forests); **Racial Modifiers** +4 Stealth in forests

Environment temperate forests
Organization gang (2–5), band (6–11), or tribe (10–100 plus champion of 3rd level per 20 adults, 1 priestess of 3rd–5th level, 1 sorceress leader of 5th–8th level, and 2–8 wolves)
Treasure standard (dagger, dart, other treasure)

Coordinated Attack (Ex) When making a combat maneuver check, a gribbon gains a +2 bonus on its CMB check for the first gribbon adjacent to it, and an additional +1 bonus on CMB checks for each additional adjacent gribbon.

Gribbons, at first glance, resemble large monkeys with bat wings. Closer examination, however, reveals facial features of a more human than simian nature. Their bodies are covered in a coarse, brown fur, and their hands end in powerful and sharp claws. These creatures are fiercely territorial and prefer to swoop down from the treetops and assault trespassers without warning. Though they greatly prefer forests, gribbons have been known to reside in caves and caverns, especially those higher up with outcroppings where they can perch and survey their territory.

Gribbons are equally as likely to attack their opponents with weapons (preferring daggers and darts, though sometimes employing short swords) as they are with their claws. Their favorite tactic is to grab an opponent, fly above the ground and drop it.

Grimlock

This hulking stone gray humanoid is dressed in rags and torn clothes, and grips a sharpened axe in its hands. Its hair is filthy and dark, and its eyes are clouded milky white.

GRIMLOCK	CR 1

XP 400
NE Medium monstrous humanoid
Init +1; **Senses** blindsight 40 ft., scent; **Perception** +9

AC 15, touch 11, flat-footed 14 (+1 Dex, +4 natural)
hp 15 (2d10+4)
Fort +2; **Ref** +4; **Will** +2
Immune gaze attacks, illusions, visual effects
Weaknesses blindness

Speed 30 ft.
Melee battleaxe +4 (1d8+2) or 2 slams +4 (1d4+2)

Str 15, **Dex** 13, **Con** 14, **Int** 10, **Wis** 8, **Cha** 6
Base Atk +2; **CMB** +4; **CMD** 15
Feats Alertness[B], Skill Focus (Perception)
Skills Climb +7, Perception +9, Sense Motive +1, Stealth +6 (+14 in stony environs), Survival +4; **Racial Modifiers** +8 Stealth in stony environs
Languages Grimlock, Undercommon

Environment any underground
Organization Gang (2–4), hunting party (5–8), pack (10–20), or tribe (10–60 plus 1 leader of 3rd–5th level per 10 adults)
Treasure standard (battleaxe, other treasure)

Grimlocks are evil and foul subterranean dwellers believed to be descendants of an ancient human race. Legends speak of long ago wars between various races that drove humans underground. For a while, they survived on what food they could forage, but eventually turned to cannibalism; beginning with small underground animals such as rats and other rodents, and eventually turning to aboveground raids on other races. Grimlocks dine on humanoid flesh and blood (with humans and dwarves being their favorite meals). They are primitive creatures, living in tribal communities of up to 60 or more individuals in underground caves and tunnels. Raiding and hunting bands often venture to the surface world to attack nearby settlements, capturing or killing those they encounter and returning to their lair to feast upon their spoils. Raids such as these are always conducted at night under the cover of darkness when grimlocks have the advantage. Grimlocks detest sunlight but are not harmed by it.

When not raiding the surface world, grimlocks often battle with other subterranean races including drow, dwarves, duergar, and even other grimlock tribes. Such battles can consist of outright warfare, but most of the time the battles are simple raids into other underground lairs to procure food (usually human or dwarven slaves kept by the other underground races). When engaged in wars with other races, grimlock leaders often ride basilisks into battle. Some larger grimlock lairs often have at least one medusa in midst as well.

A grimlock stands 5 to 6 feet tall and weighs 150 to 200 pounds. Its skin is slate gray and its hair is oily and matted. The creature emanates a stench that most others find nauseating, yet to a grimlock, it's a means of identification, for each scent is unique to a grimlock. Such fine distinctions are noticeable to other grimlocks, and possibly other creatures with a strong olfactory sense.

Due to their lack of sight, grimlocks prefer melee to ranged combat and close on enemies quickly when engaged. They attack with their menacing axes or powerful slams, slashing or pummeling their foes until their opponents are dead. Opponents that attempt to flee are run down and killed. Grimlocks that fall in combat are "honored" by being carried off the field of battle and devoured by their own.

Recent forays into underground caverns and caves by an intrepid band of adventurers speak of another race of grimlocks, civilized, and non-cannibalistic. These same adventurers speak of a large underground city full of these creatures. Whether these are truly advanced grimlocks or another race entirely is yet to be confirmed.

Grimshrike

A gaunt, gargoyle-like figure passes silently overhead. It has bat-like wings, long, cruel talons, and its eyes seem to burn with a cold white fire. Two serpentine tails, ten feet long, trail behind the creature as it wheels around and dives to attack.

GRIMSHRIKE	CR 4

XP 1,200
NE Medium undead (extraplanar)
Init +1; **Senses** darkvision 60 ft.; **Perception** +8

AC 16, touch 11, flat-footed 15 (+1 Dex, +5 natural)
hp 37 (5d8+15)
Fort +4; **Ref** +2; **Will** +6
DR 5/darkwood; **Immune** undead traits

Speed 30 ft., fly 40 ft. (good)
Melee 2 claws +6 (1d6+3), bite +6 (1d8+3), 2 tail slaps +4 (1d6+1)
Special Attacks negative energy breath, gaze of lost souls

Str 17, **Dex** 12, **Con** —, **Int** 8, **Wis** 14, **Cha** 16
Base Atk +3; **CMB** +6; **CMD** 17
Feats Command Undead, Flyby Attack, Multiattack
Skills Fly +11, Intimidate +9, Knowledge (arcana) +5, Perception +8, Stealth +7
Languages Abyssal, Common, Infernal, Grimshrike

Environment any
Organization solitary, pair, or flight (3–12)
Treasure standard

Negative Energy Breath (Su) Once per round and no more than 6 times per day, as a standard action, a grimshrike can exhale a 30-foot cone of negative energy that functions as the channel negative energy ability of an evil cleric whose level equals the grimshrike's Hit Dice. This cone deals 3d6 points of damage to living creatures (DC 15 Will save for half) or heals 3d6 points of damage on undead creatures in the area (no save). If a grimshrike takes levels in a class that provides the channel energy ability, its racial Hit Dice stack with the levels of that class for the purposes of determining the damage dealt or healed and the save DC. This ability counts as the channel energy class ability for any feat that requires it. The save DC is Charisma-based.
Gaze of Lost Souls (Su) Creatures meeting a grimshrike's gaze must succeed on a DC 15 Will save or take 1d4 points of Wisdom damage and be paralyzed 1d4 rounds. The save DC is Charisma-based. This is a gaze effect.

Grimshrikes are native to a dark demiplane about which little is known other than its terrible history. The place was once vibrant and full of life every bit as diverse and beautiful as the Material Plane. Centuries ago, however, all that changed. Something rent the boundaries between that placid demiplane and the Negative Energy Plane. Dark energies spilled forth unchecked,

fouling the very essence of which the demiplane was created. In a matter of hours, all life in that plane ceased to exist. The primary inhabitants of the demiplane, a race of twin-tailed gargoyles, were reanimated as the tortured servants of the nightshades. Grimshrikes are often given as rewards to powerful necromancers who have performed some service of the nightshades. An army of zombies or skeletons is made all the more frightening by presence of grimshrikes urging them on and bolstering their strength.

A grimshrike is about 7 feet tall and weighs 350 pounds.

To look into the eyes of a grimshrike is to invite madness. A grimshrike is forever tortured by the horrible vision of death and agony that befell its home plane. It can temporarily relieve itself of the vision by mentally transferring the vision into the mind of a living victim with but a gaze. A grimshrike attacks first with its gaze, attempting to bring down the most powerful opponents as quickly as possible. In combat, it concentrates its attacks on clerics and paladins first, before moving to fighters and arcane spellcasters. In melee, a grimshrike tries to remain out of reach of its opponent, lashing with its tails or further weakening its opponent with its foul breath weapon.

Hag Nymph

This hideous, bent crone has sickly green skin, thin dark green hair and hands that end in wicked claws with filthy nails.

HAG NYMPH	CR 10

XP 9,600
CE Medium fey
Init +5; **Senses** darkvision 60 ft., low-light vision; **Perception** +16

AC 25, touch 21, flat-footed 19 (+1 dodge, +5 Dex, +4 natural, +5 profane)
hp 75 (10d6+40)
Fort +12; **Ref** +17; **Will** +15
DR 10/cold iron; **Resist** cold 10, fire 10; **SR** 21

Speed 30 ft.
Melee 2 claws +11 (1d6+2)
Special Attacks profane beauty, spells
Spell-Like Abilities (CL 10th; melee touch +10, ranged touch +10):
Constant—*detect good, detect magic*
At will—*alter self, inflict light wounds* (DC 16)
3/day—*inflict serious wounds* (DC 18)
1/day—*baleful polymorph* (DC 20), *summon* (level 7, 1d3 shadow demons 50%)
Spells Known (CL 10th; melee touch +10, ranged touch +10):
5th (4/day)—*beast shape III*
4th (6/day)—*bestow curse* (DC 19), *greater invisibility*
3rd (7/day)—*fly, haste* (DC 18), *lightning bolt* (DC 18)
2nd (7/day)—*blindness/deafness* (DC 17), *fog cloud, ghoul touch* (DC 17), *spider climb* (DC 17)
1st (8/day)—*cause fear* (DC 16), *charm person* (DC 16), *chill touch* (DC 16), *disguise self, ray of enfeeblement* (DC 16)
0 (at will)—*acid splash, bleed* (DC 15), *daze* (DC 15), *flare* (DC 15), *ghost sound* (DC 15), *open/close, prestidigitation* (DC 15), *read magic, touch of fatigue* (DC 15)

Str 15, **Dex** 21, **Con** 18, **Int** 16, **Wis** 17, **Cha** 21
Base Atk +5; **CMB** +10; **CMD** 28
Feats Agile Maneuvers, Combat Casting, Dodge, Weapon Finesse, Weapon Focus (claw)
Skills Bluff +18, Diplomacy +16, Escape Artist +18, Handle Animal +11, Intimidate +15, Knowledge (nature) +12, Knowledge (planes) +13, Perception +16, Sense Motive +16, Stealth +18
Languages Common, Draconic, Giant, Sylvan
SQ profane grace

Environment temperate and cold forests
Organization solitary or coven (3 hag nymphs)
Treasure standard

Profane Beauty (Su) This ability affects all humanoids within 30 feet of a hag nymph. Those who look directly at a hag nymph must succeed on a DC 20 Fortitude save or take 2d4 points of Strength damage. A hag nymph can suppress or resume this ability as a free action. A creature that saves or fails its save cannot be affected by the same hag nymph's profane beauty for one day. The save DC is Charisma-based.
Profane Grace (Su) A hag nymph adds her Charisma modifier as a racial bonus on all her saving throws, and as a profane bonus to her Armor Class.
Spells A hag nymph casts spells as a 10th-level sorcerer, and does not need any material components.

The true origins of the hag nymph are cloaked in secrecy. Tales speak of a band of nymphs that blasphemed their goddess and were punished for dare offending her. Other legends say the hag nymph is the resulting offspring of a demon and nymph. Regardless, these creatures are vile and evil and take great pleasure in tormenting others.

Hag nymphs live deep within dark forests in huts composed of mud and timber. These huts are well constructed and littered with the rotting remains of creatures they devour. Hag nymphs relish the taste of humanoid flesh, but sustain themselves on a diet of forest animals when humanoids are scarce. Forays under the cover of darkness into towns on the edge of the forest are not unheard of. In such raids, children are the most likely victims as they are easier to carry away.

Hag nymphs stand 6 feet tall and weigh 150 pounds. Their frames are somewhat emaciated, almost corpse-like in appearance. Their clothes usually carry the bloodstains of previous victims. Hag nymphs live for 150 years.

Hag nymphs attack from range bombarding their foes with an array of spells. Slain opponents are dragged to the hag nymph's lair and devoured at her leisure. Occasionally hag nymphs seek to capture rather than kill their opponents. Such opponents are taken prisoner and used as slaves by the hag nymphs, performing manual labor for them or being used as blood sacrifices in dark rituals.

Hedon

This creature resembles an ugly elf with the lower torso of a giant bird. Its legs are the clawed talons of a falcon, covered in sickly greenish-brown feathers. Its hands end in wicked claws with dirty brown nails. A forked black tongue dances across the creature's lips, revealing a mouth of sharpened fangs.

HEDON	CR 3

XP 800
CE Medium fey
Init +6; **Senses** low-light vision; **Perception** +8

AC 14, touch 12, flat-footed 12 (+2 Dex, +2 natural)
hp 16 (3d6+6)
Fort +5; **Ref** +5; **Will** +5
DR 5/cold iron

Speed 30 ft.
Melee 2 claws +2 (1d4+1 plus grab)
Special Attacks rake (2 claws, 1d6+1)
Spell-Like Abilities (CL 3rd; melee touch +2, ranged touch +3):
Constant—*detect good, speak with animals*
3/day—*entangle* (DC 13), *heat metal* (DC 14), *scare* (DC 14), *shatter* (DC 14), *shocking grasp*
1/day—*snare*

Str 12, **Dex** 15, **Con** 14, **Int** 10, **Wis** 14, **Cha** 15
Base Atk +1; **CMB** +2 (+6 grapple); **CMD** 14
Feats Great Fortitude, Improved Initiative
Skills Bluff +8, Escape Artist +8, Knowledge (nature) +6, Perception +8, Perform (dancing) +8, Stealth +8
Languages Common, Sylvan, *speak with animals*

Environment temperate forests
Organization solitary or gang (2–5)
Treasure standard

The origins of the hedon are shrouded in mystery but many sages and scholars believe the creatures to be the union of a harpy and an elf or a harpy and some fey creature. Other sages dispute these claims and believe the hedon are the result of a curse laid on an entire community of fey creatures by a vengeful annis or hag.

Hedons are malevolent and violent fey creatures that dwell in darkened forests found on the fringes of civilization. They take great delight in tormenting travelers and townsfolk and always lair near heavily traveled roads or paths and communities. Many hedons sneak into nearby towns under the cover of darkness and slaughter livestock or kidnap children (because they are easier to carry and control than adults).

Hedons lair in caverns, caves, or nests built from branches, straw, twigs, and so on. Lairs are always kept well hidden away from prying eyes and are difficult to locate by all but the best of scouts and trackers. A typical hedon lair contains 2–4 adults and an equal number of noncombatant young. Mating season for hedons is year round and the female lays a clutch of 1d4 eggs. The eggs hatch after about 3 months and young reach maturity within 2 or 3 years.

A hedon appears as a tan-skinned elf with the lower torso of a hawk or falcon. It rarely wears clothes, but should it choose to do so (and some do, especially to hide their appearance when they attempt to move through a populated area without drawing undue attention to themselves), it usually dons a long hooded cloak or robe of green, gray, or brown. Hedons rarely carry weapons, preferring to fight with their claws.

A hedon attacks with its spell-like abilities, targeting the strongest perceived foes first. It quickly follows this barrage with melee by grabbing its foe and raking with its clawed feet.

Hellwidow

This massive long-legged giant spider is crimson in color with dull red, barely visible, hourglass-shaped markings on its underside.

HELLWIDOW	CR 8

XP 4,800
LE Large magical beast (extraplanar)
Init +7; **Senses** darkvision 60 ft., low-light vision, tremorsense 60 ft.; **Perception** +8

AC 22, touch 12, flat-footed 19 (+3 Dex, +10 natural, –1 size)
hp 95 (10d10+40)
Fort +13; **Ref** +12; **Will** +5
Defensive Abilities venom resistance; **DR** 10/silver; **Immune** fire; **Resist** acid 10, cold 10

Speed 40 ft., climb 30 ft.
Melee bite +17 (2d8+10 plus 1d6 fire and poison)
Space 10 ft.; **Reach** 5 ft.
Special Attacks fiery webs, web (+12 ranged, DC 19, 10 hp)

Str 24, **Dex** 17, **Con** 18, **Int** 7, **Wis** 15, **Cha** 12
Base Atk +10; **CMB** +18; **CMD** 31 (39 vs. trip)
Feats Great Fortitude, Improved Initiative, Lightning Reflexes, Skill Focus (Stealth), Weapon Focus (bite)
Skills Climb +22, Perception +8, Stealth +8
Languages Infernal (can't speak)

Environment any (Nine Hells)
Organization solitary, pair, or gang (3–6)
Treasure incidental

Fiery Webs (Ex) The hellwidow can set any of its webs on fire as a free action at the start of its turn merely by touching the webbing. Creatures caught in the webs when they catch fire take 2d6 points of fire damage each round until they escape. After escaping, creatures continue taking this damage each round unless they succeed on a DC 15 Reflex save. A new save can be made each round to extinguish the fire.
Poison (Ex) Bite—injury; *save* DC 23 Fort; *frequency* 1/ round for 6 rounds; *effect* 1d4 Constitution damage plus 1d6 fire damage and staggered; *cure* 2 saves. The save DC is Constitution-based and includes a +4 racial bonus.
Venom Resistance (Ex) Hellwidows gain a +4 racial bonus on saving throws against spider venom.

Hellwidows are giant spiders that make their home within the Nine Hells. They are believed to be the result of diabolical experiments that crossed giant black widows with devils. These creatures, while possibly related to black widows, are much more cunning and intelligent. Hellwidows dwell on the warmer planes of Hell's layers, generally avoiding the colder lower planes. Giant web-filled caverns serve as their lairs. When encountered on the Material Plane, it is most often in thick forests or caverns in warmer climates. Evil spellcasters occasionally summon a hellwidow to the Material Plane and strike a bargain with the creature offering food, treasure, or the like in return for some service (usually guarding a location or killing a particular enemy).

Hellwidows are roughly 9 feet long and weighs nearly 1,000 pounds, with males being slightly smaller than females. Hellwidows mate several times per year with the female laying up to 100 eggs in a single dull gray egg sac. The eggs hatch within 30 days, with only about 25% of the young surviving. Young are blood red in color with dull yellow stripes on their abdomens. Young mature rapidly, reaching adulthood within six months.

Hellwidows are carnivores and prey on various types of other creatures, including lesser devils, fiendish insects, and even other hellwidows. Prey is quickly cocooned in the hellwidow's webbing, set on fire, and then bitten repeatedly until it succumbs to the widow's poison. Once the prey is dead, the hellwidow carries it back to its lair to be devoured. Hellwidows prefer to hunt by ambush; usually hiding in dark corners within their webs. When they detect movement, such as a creature becoming entangled in their webs, they quickly move to strike.

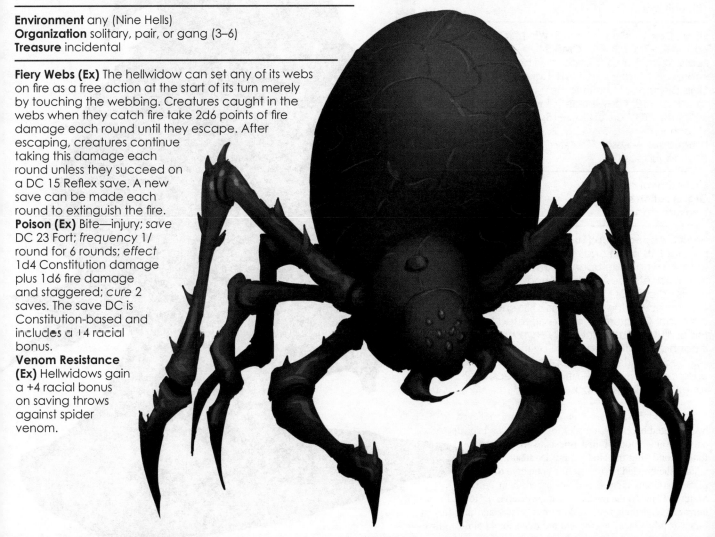

Hooded Horror

This creature looks like a humanoid dressed in a tattered and rotting brownish-black hooded robe. Its head and face are obscured by the hood, though its eyes seem to flash the color of blood.

HOODED HORROR	CR 8

XP 4,800
CE Medium undead
Init +7; **Senses** darkvision 60 ft., *detect thoughts, true seeing*;
Perception +15
Aura horrific appearance (30 ft.)

AC 24, touch 14, flat-footed 20 (+3 Dex, +1 dodge, +10 natural)
hp 75 (10d8+30)
Fort +6; **Ref** +8; **Will** +11
Defensive Abilities channel resistance +4; **DR** 10/magic;
Immune undead traits

Speed 30 ft.
Melee 2 claws +10 (1d8+3)
Special Attacks desiccating breath (40-ft. cone, 8d6 negative energy damage; DC 20 Will half, usable every 1d4 rounds), horrific appearance
Spell-Like Abilities (CL 10th):
Constant—*detect thoughts* (DC 15), *true seeing*
1/day—*blasphemy* (DC 20), *charm monster* (DC 18), *unholy blight* (DC 17)

Str 16, **Dex** 16, **Con** —, **Int** 15, **Wis** 15, **Cha** 16
Base Atk +7; **CMB** +10; **CMD** 24
Feats Ability Focus (desiccating breath), Dodge, Improved Initiative, Iron Will, Lightning Reflexes
Skills Disguise +11, Intimidate +16, Knowledge (arcana) +10, Knowledge (planes) +7, Knowledge (religion) +10, Perception +15, Sense Motive +15, Stealth +16
Languages Abyssal, Celestial, Common (can't speak any languages)

Environment any
Organization solitary
Treasure standard

Horrific Appearance (Su) A hooded horror can pull back its hood and reveal its skeletal visage to those who gaze upon it. Anyone within 30 feet who sets eyes upon the hooded horror must succeed on a DC 18 Will save or be instantly weakened, taking 1d6 points of Strength damage. Creatures that are affected by this ability or that successfully save against it cannot be affected again by the same hooded horror's horrific appearance for one day. This is a mind-affecting effect. The save DC is Charisma-based.

A hooded horror is an undead creature believed to have been created by Orcus in order to subjugate and corrupt paladins and good-aligned priests. Though often found wandering the Undead Lord's great abyssal palace, the hooded horror itself is not native to that plane, as Orcus created and unleashed them on the Material Plane (if the legends are to be believed). Hooded horrors spend their time seeking out priests and paladins in order to fulfill their desires and are often found amidst graveyards, ruined temples to good-aligned deities, and other such places where its chosen targets might be encountered.

A hooded horror appears as a rotting and skeletal humanoid cloaked in a brownish-black hooded robe. Its eyes are deep sockets, pitch black with a small pinpoint of red light. Its hands end in razor-sharp talons.

Hooded horrors understand Abyssal, Celestial, and Common, but do not appear to speak any of these languages. Methods of communication with (and between) these creatures is unknown.

A hooded horror begins an encounter by revealing its desiccated countenance to its foes thereby invoking fear in those that see it. Creatures that succeed on their save are then assaulted by the creature's breath weapon and filthy claws. If it can, the hooded horror attempts to charm and bring under its control any paladins and good-aligned priests it encounters. Other good-aligned creatures that oppose the hooded horror are simply destroyed.

Horde, Zombie

A stumbling crush of moaning, reaching bodies comes towards you. Empty eyes seek you out, each staggering footstep bringing the deathless mass closer. Straining to grasp you, this group of zombies are so tightly packed together it seems to be a single mass of undead, flailing limbs.

ZOMBIE HORDE	CR 14

XP 38,400
NE Colossal undead (horde)
Init +0; **Senses** darkvision 60 ft.; **Perception** +0

AC 13, touch 2, flat-footed 13 (+11 natural, –8 size)
hp 110 (20d8 plus 20)
Fort +6; **Ref** +6; **Will** +12
Defensive Abilities half damage from piercing weapons; **DR** 10/slashing; **Immune** undead traits

Speed 30 ft.
Melee horde attack (6d6)
Space 30 ft.; **Reach** 5 ft.
Special Attacks feral rage, rend (+3d6)

Str 22, **Dex** 10, **Con** —, **Int** —, **Wis** 10, **Cha** 10
Base Atk +15; **CMB** +29; **CMD** 39 (can't be tripped)
Feats Improved Overrun[B], Toughness[B]
Skills Stealth –16

Environment any
Organization solitary, mass (2–4 hordes), or apocalypse (5+ hordes)
Treasure none

Feral Rage (Ex) The horde attacks as a ruthless mob, intent only on tearing apart those that fall into their clutches. This frenzy prevents them from using any sort of tactics, and frees them from any form of control by other beings. However, the sheer force of the wave attack allows them to deal 6d6 points of damage to any creature whose space they occupy at the end of their move. This ability is lost if the horde is broken up.

Horde Traits (Ex) Hordes are not so called because of the size of the group but rather the size of the creatures that compose the horde. Unlike normal swarms, hordes are composed of Medium creatures which are usually a normal version of a creature but otherwise behave in a swarmlike manner. There are usually around 50 creatures in a horde. The net effect is that they take only half damage from piercing weapons but take normal damage from other weapons. In addition when the swarm is reduced to 0 hit points or lower and breaks up, unless the damage was dealt by area-affecting attacks, then 2d6 surviving members of the horde continue their attack, though now only as individual creatures. Otherwise, a horde conforms to all of the other swarm traits as described in the *Pathfinder Roleplaying Game Bestiary*.

Rend (EX) Due to the grasping and clawing nature of the zombie horde attack, any time the horde does more than 20 points of damage, add 3d6 slashing damage from the additional pulling and tearing. This ability is lost if the swarm is broken up.

Zombies are one of the most used and abused of the mindless undead. Singly, a zombie may be dealt with by experienced adventurers. When gathered together in a horde, these mindless creatures are a terror to behold. Packed together as tightly as they are, they appear as one solid mass of decaying flesh and sinuous limbs.

The flailing nature of the zombie horde's limbs allow the throng to grasp and tear at opponents, dealing rend damage in addition to their base attack. Any time the horde is in an opponent's square, the target risks being completely overrun by the horde

If the horde takes enough individual damage to break it up, up to a dozen of the creatures continue on their rampage of destruction, until finally they too must be slain.

Credit
Originally appearing in *Rappan Athuk* (© Frog God Games, 2012)

Horse, Rhianna

This horse is shorter and less elegantly muscled than most other riding breeds. It has a shaggy brown coat and a long, thick mane.

HORSE, RHIANNA	CR 1

XP 400
N Large animal
Init +1; **Senses** low-light vision, scent; **Perception** +6

AC 14, touch 10, flat-footed 13 (+1 Dex, +4 natural, –1 size)
hp 16 (3d8+3)
Fort +6; **Ref** +4; **Will** +2
Weakness encumbrance penalty

Speed 60 ft.
Melee 2 hooves –1 (1d4+1)
Space 10 ft.; **Reach** 5 ft.

Str 16, **Dex** 13, **Con** 17, **Int** 2, **Wis** 13, **Cha** 6
Base Atk +2; **CMB** +6; **CMD** 17 (21 vs. trip)
Feats Endurance, Nimble Moves, Run[B]
Skills Acrobatics +5 (+9 to balance), Perception +6; **Racial Modifiers** +4 Acrobatics to balance
SQ dexterous, docile, hardy

Environment temperate plains
Organization solitary, pair, or herd (3–30)
Treasure none

Dexterous (Ex) Rhiannas convey a +2 bonus to their riders' Ride checks to avoid obstacles.
Docile (Ex) Unless specifically trained for combat (see the Handle Animal skill), a Rhianna's hooves are treated as secondary attacks.
Encumbrance Penalty (Ex) Rhiannas lose the benefits of the Run feat whenever they are encumbered. They may still run at 4 times their speed with light encumbrance (up to 228 lbs.), and 3 times their speed with medium (459 lbs.) or heavy (690 lbs.) encumbrance.
Hardy (Ex) Rhiannas are extremely durable creatures. Unlike with other mounts, anytime a hustle, forced march or spurred movement would do damage to these horses, they are allowed a Constitution save to negate the damage.

Domesticated Rhiannas retain the notable traits of their wild ancestors: small size, endurance and sure-footedness. They are especially popular with woodsmen — those who opt for mounted travels — due to their hardiness, dexterity and companionship. Most homesteaders choose the Rhianna breed as well, as they are equally suited to long-distance rides over varied terrain and drawing a market cart over rutted roads. Only the heaviest farm labors, such as breaking sod, spring plowing and pulling stumps, are reserved for larger draft horses, and many of the farmers of the valley make do with Rhiannas alone.

Rhianna horses differ from other light warhorses in several ways. Although they are similar in build to warhorses, they cannot fight with a rider. While their speed is the same, they do not perform as well when heavily loaded. Due to their evolution in a valley littered with obstacles such as trees, streams, boulders and scrub growth, they are extremely agile and adept at negotiating obstacles. They are resistant to damage incurred by fatigue, and may be pushed harder and for longer periods of time without the risk of injury. Because of their intolerance for encumbrance, Rhiannas make ideal mounts for lightly armed and armored heroes. Even encumbered, their ability to increase their speed for short distances gives them an advantage over common riding horses. This is especially useful when difficult terrain disallows running and charging.

Credit
Original author Nathan Douglas Paul
Originally appearing in *The Eamonvale Incursion*
(© Necromancer Games, 2008)

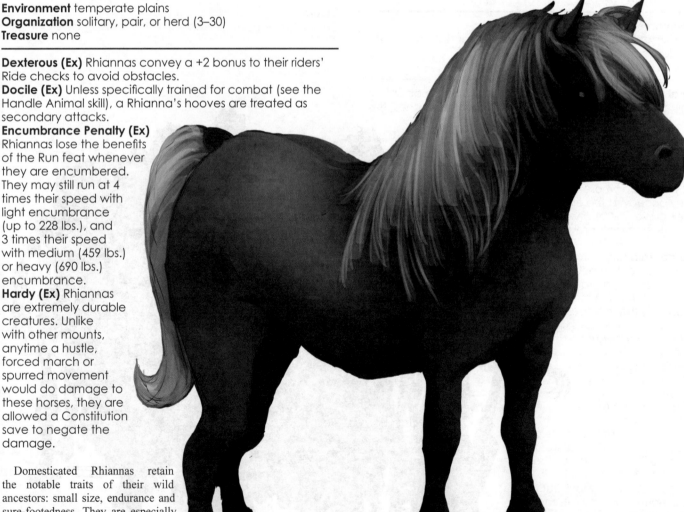

Inphidians

Somewhere in humanities lost eons a race of malformed serpentine humanoids rose, now known as inphidians. While the truth of their origins has been long forgotten, most sages subscribe to one of two theories. The first states the creatures are the failed results of horrific experiments performed by the dark and nameless sorcerers of an ancient snake cult in their attempts to ensorcel their followers. The second theory contends the inphidians were once a cult of snake worshippers cursed by an ancient snake-god for some transgression against the ethos. Whatever the truth, it appears as of late that the inphidians have evolved into true race, beyond the machinations of arcane experiments or curses. While several known species exist, recent reports describe encounters with yet unidentified inphidians, and others are sure to surface as encounters with the race grow more frequent.

All inphidians, regardless of the subspecies, have viper heads in place of their hands. The creatures use these in combat to deliver a powerful bite that injects the victim with poison. Inphidians, particularly the craftsmen, wear special gloves called inphidian gauntlets that let them use their hands like any other humanoid with five digits (including an opposing thumb) uses its hands.

Inphidians trade with other races, particularly evil underground races such as derro, driders, and drow. Trade usually takes the form of crafted goods, food, or slaves. Inphidian craftsmen are some of the finest known distillers of poisons, venoms, and antitoxins. Their products are highly sought after by all manner of poison-using races.

An important aspect of any inphidian community is religion. The inphidian race as a whole worships the Great Serpent (Hassith-Kaa). Little is known of this religion or the priests of the Great Serpent. Inphidian clerics can choose from any of the two following domains: Evil, Serpent, Strength, and Trickery.

Inphidian, Death's Head

This tall slender humanoid is dressed in dark-colored robes. Its body is covered in dull blue-green scales with whorls of reddish-brown. Its head is viper-like and its arms end in snake-like hands. It clutches a long wooden staff tipped with a ruby-encrusted snake's skull.

DEATH'S HEAD INPHIDIAN	CR 5

XP 1,600
NE Medium monstrous humanoid (reptilian)
Init +7; **Senses** darkvision 60 ft., scent; **Perception** +16

AC 21, touch 13, flat-footed 18 (+3 Dex, +8 natural)
hp 68 (8d10+24)
Fort +7; **Ref** +9; **Will** +11

Speed 40 ft.
Melee quarterstaff +12/+7 (1d6+4 plus poison or grab) or 2 snake-hands +13 (1d8+4 plus bleed and poison)
Special Attacks bleed (1d4), death's head staff
Spell-Like Abilities (CL 8th):
Constant--*speak with snakes* (as *speak with animals*, but snakes only)
3/day—*cause fear* (DC 15), *suggestion* (DC 17)
1/day—*accelerate poison* (DC 16; see sidebar), *snake staff* (see sidebar)

Str 18, **Dex** 17, **Con** 17, **Int** 19, **Wis** 20, **Cha** 18
Base Atk +8; **CMB** +12 (+16 grapple with staff); **CMD** 25
Feats Blind-Fight, Great Fortitude, Improved Initiative, Weapon Focus (snake-hands)
Skills Acrobatics +7, Bluff +8, Climb +11, Diplomacy +12, Intimidate +15, Knowledge (history) +8, Knowledge (religion) +11, Perception +16, Sense Motive +9, Stealth +14, Survival +16

Serpent Domain

Granted Powers Over time, your devotion bestows you with serpentine traits. As the great serpent, you can hypnotize prey with your gaze. You also slowly develop an immunity to poison.

Serpent's Gaze (Su) As a full-round action, you can attempt a gaze attack to hypnotize a single opponent with 30 feet (as per a *hypnotism* spell). You can use this ability a number of times per day equal to 3 + your Wisdom modifier.

Poison Resistance (Ex) At 8th level, whenever you make a saving throw against poison, you can roll twice, taking the better result. At 12th level, you gain immunity to poison.

Domain Spells 1st—*magic fang*; 2nd—*summon swarm* (snakes only); 3rd—*greater magic fang*; 4th—*charm monster*; 5th—*animal growth*; 6th—*irresistible dance*; 7th—*creeping doom* (Tiny snakes); 8th—*animal shapes* (snake forms only); 9th—*summon nature's ally IX* (snakes only)

Languages Common, Inphidian, Sylvan, Undercommon, *speak with snakes*
SQ snake empathy

Environment warm forests and plains or underground
Organization band (1 death's head inphidian plus 1–2 rattler inphidians) or troupe (1 death's head inphidian plus 1 night adder inphidian, 1–2 rattler inphidians, and 3–4 giant vipers)
Treasure standard

Poison (Ex) Bite—injury; *save* DC 21 Fort; *frequency* 1/round for 6 rounds; *effect* 1d4 Con damage; *cure* 2 consecutive saves. The save DC is Constitution-based and includes a +4 racial bonus.
Snake Empathy (Ex) Snakes, including giant snakes, do not

Accelerate poison

School transmutation; **Level** druid 2, ranger 2, sorcerer/wizard 2
Casting Time 1 standard action
Components V, S, M (a thorn)
Range touch
Target creature touched
Duration instantaneous
Saving Throw Fortitude negates; **Spell Resistance** yes

You hasten the onset of poison in the target. If the poison normally has an onset time, its effects begin immediately. If the poison has no onset time, its frequency is doubled, requiring two saving throws and inflicting damage twice per round or minute, though its duration is halved. *Accelerate poison* does not change the cure condition for the poison. If the target is affected by more than one poison, you may choose which is affected if you administered the poison; otherwise, randomly determine which poison is affected.

Snake Staff

School transmutation; **Level** cleric 5, druid 5
Casting Time 1 standard action
Components V, S, M (a knife suitable for whittling)
Range medium (100 ft. + 10 ft./level)
Target 1 or more pieces of wood, no two of which can be more than 30 ft. apart
Duration 1 round/level
Saving Throw Will negates (object); **Spell Resistance** yes (object)

With a long hissing whisper, you transform ordinary pieces of wood into various sorts of snakes that immediately attack your foes. As long as the snakes remain within sight, you can direct their actions telepathically as a free action. You can only apply this spell to wooden objects not in a creature's possession or not part of a larger structure or plant. Each time you cast this spell you can create a number of snakes equal to your caster level. More powerful snakes take up more than one of your available total, as noted below. See snake statistics and advanced and giant simple templates.

Venomous Snake: A stick or piece of firewood (counts as 1 snake).

Constrictor Snake: A staff or tree branch (counts as 2 snakes).

Advanced Venomous Snake: A stick or piece of firewood (counts as 2 snakes).

Advanced Constrictor Snake: A staff or tree branch (counts as 3 snakes).

Advanced Giant Venomous Snake: A log or pile of debris (counts as 4 snakes).

Advanced Giant Constrictor Snake: A fallen tree or a large pile of debris (counts as 5 snakes).

willingly attack a death's head inphidian, though they can be forced to do so by magic. If the death's head inphidian attacks a snake, its protection against that creature ends.
Death's Head Staff (Ex) The staff of a death's head inphidian can hold poisons in a specially crafted chamber inside the jewel encrusted snake skull. The chamber holds enough poison to deliver three doses. Most death's head inphidians fill the chamber with their own poison (use the stats above).

In lieu of poisoning an opponent struck by the staff, a death's head can command its staff to grapple and constrict its target. When a foe is successfully hit by the staff, the death's head inphidian can make an immediate grapple check as a free action. If successful, the opponent is pinned and takes 1d6+6 points of bludgeoning damage each round until it escapes. (Use the death's head inphidian's statistics above to resolve the grapple and escape.) This staff functions only in the hands of a death's head inphidian. In the hands of any other creature, it acts as a normal quarterstaff. The gem-encrusted snake skull is worth a total of 1,000–3,000 gp.

Death's head inphidians may not be the strongest or largest of the inphidian races, but they certainly are the most feared and respected; hence the reason the death's head is the leader of an inphidian nest. These creatures rule by fear and maintain tight control over their nest. Rules, commands, judgments, and punishments are all meted out by a death's head and all come quickly. As a death's head ages and draws near the end of its life, its position is often challenged by other death's heads, all vying for control of the inphidian nest. Such challenges generally end in the death of all but one death's head inphidian, who becomes the new leader of the nest, after the current leader dies (which is often times aided by the death's head in waiting). For this reason, as a death's head ages, it is rarely ever encountered alone, always having a retinue of other inphidians or giant snakes around it at all times.

A typical death's head inphidian stands 6 feet tall and weighs 180 pounds. Its dull blue-green scales darken and fade as it ages. A death's head has an average lifespan of 50 years.

A death's head in combat is a fearsome creature, having many tools at its disposal—and it uses all of them to the best of its ability. It usually opens combat with its spell-like abilities (*suggestion* or *cause fear*) and then launches into melee with its snake hands and staff. A poisoned foe is subjected to its accelerated poison spell-like ability. If overwhelmed, a death's head uses its *snake staff* ability to occupy its opponents while it makes its escape.

Inphidian, Gray-Scale

This hulking brute is covered in slate gray scales. It has the head of a giant venomous snake, and its long, muscular arms end in large snake heads where its hands should be.

GRAY-SCALE INPHIDIAN	CR 6

XP 2,400
NE Large monstrous humanoid (reptilian)
Init −1; **Senses** darkvision 60 ft.; **Perception** +12

AC 17, touch 8, flat-footed 17 (−1 Dex, +9 natural, −1 size)
hp 76 (8d10+32)
Fort +6; **Ref** +5; **Will** +7

Speed 30 ft., climb 30 ft., swim 20 ft.
Melee 2 snake-hands +13 (1d8+6 plus poison and grab), bite +13 (2d6+6/19–20 plus poison)
Space 10 ft.; **Reach** 10 ft.

Str 22, **Dex** 8, **Con** 18, **Int** 6, **Wis** 12, **Cha** 12
Base Atk +8; **CMB** +15 (+19 grapple); **CMD** 24
Feats Cleave, Improved Critical (bite), Power Attack,

Uncontrolled Rage
Skills Climb +14, Intimidate +8, Perception +12, Stealth +2, Swim +14
Languages Inphidian
SQ magic bane (see text)

Environment warm forests and plains or underground
Organization solitary or gang (1 gray-scale inphidian plus 2–3 cobra-back inphidians)
Treasure incidental

Magic Bane (Ex) There is a 50% chance that any gray-scale encountered has this ability. It grants the gray-scale a +2 bonus on attack and damage rolls against spellcasters. A gray-scale with this special ability also takes a –2 penalty on all saves against spells and spell-like abilities.
Poison (Ex) Bite—injury; *save* DC 20 Fort; *frequency* 1/round for 6 rounds; *effect* 1d4 Str and 1d4 Con; *cure* 2 consecutive saves. The save DC is Constitution-based and includes a +2 racial bonus.
Uncontrolled Rage Uncontrolled Rage is a new feat detailed in the appendix.

The gray-scale inphidian (also called the abomination inphidian) is the result of a magical experiment gone awry. Foul, dark magic brought down by inphidian sorcerers on others of their race resulted in this creature; the strongest of the inphidian race perhaps, but also the most weak-minded and slowest. Most gray-scales seemingly have no memories of their past life or the tortures inflicted on them; those that do however, have both a hatred and fear for magic and those that wield it.

Gray-scales are considered by many inphidian nests to be dangerous, unstable, and an abomination against the race, particularly the gray-scales with the magic bane quality. These feelings, often times come from inphidian night adders (some of whom likely assisted in helping the gray-scale into its current state). Most often, gray-scales are shunned by their inphidian nest and cast out, left to wander the world and survive on their own, by whatever means they can. In some instances, a gray-scale stays with its nest, never fully accepted by many of the other inphidians, but tolerated, feared and respected for their battle skills. In these cases, one or more gray-scales serve as guards for the nest, or the muscle for an inphidian raiding party.

A gray-scale inphidian appears as an 8-foot tall hulking and slightly hunched humanoid with slate gray scales, the head of a giant viper with elongated fangs and red eyes, and the distinguishing inphidian characteristic: the heads of vipers in place of its hands. They shun wearing both armor and clothing. Gray-scales understand the Inphidian language, but seemingly have trouble speaking it; communicating in a slow and broken tone.

Perhaps a side-effect

of the experiments conducted on them, or perhaps by design, but no sightings of female gray-scales have ever been reported. Likewise, gray-scales appear to be sterile, unable to reproduce with others of the inphidian race.

In battle, a gray-scale inphidian prefers to overwhelm its opponents with its pure strength instead of attacking from ambush. It lashes out with both snake hands followed closely with a vicious bite from its viper head. A grabbed opponent is repeatedly bitten by the gray-scale until either it is dead or wounded enough to be out of the fight. The gray-scale then turns its attention to another opponent. If faced with a spellcasting opponent, it usually focuses all attention in the spellcaster's direction, even pushing through other opponents to get to the spellcaster.

Jolly Jelly

This creature appears to be a bright pink ooze speckled with spots of green, yellow, and blue. Scattered across the body of the ooze are small spiracles through which it apparently breathes.

JOLLY JELLY	CR 5

XP 1,600
N Medium ooze
Init –5; **Senses** blindsight 60 ft.; **Perception** –5
Aura gloom (30 ft., DC 14)

AC 10, touch 5, flat-footed 10 (–5 Dex, +5 natural)
hp 63 (6d8+36)
Fort +8; **Ref** –3; **Will** –3
Immune fire, ooze traits

Speed 30 ft.
Melee 3 slams +6 (1d6+2)
Special Attacks pheromones

Str 14, **Dex** 1, **Con** 22, **Int** —, **Wis** 1, **Cha** 12
Base Atk +4; **CMB** +6; **CMD** 11 (can't be tripped)

Environment temperate land
Organization solitary
Treasure none

Aura of Gloom (Su) Any living creature that comes within 30 feet of a jolly jelly must succeed on a DC 14 Will save or take 1d2 points of Charisma damage. A new save must be made each round the creature remains in the area. A creature that takes 6 or more points of Charisma damage from this attack is automatically affected as if by a *rage* spell (CL 6th) with the exception that it cannot tell friend from foe. The affected creature remains enraged until it moves more than 30 feet away from the jolly jelly. There is no save against the *rage* effect. This is a mind-affecting effect. The save DC is Charisma-based.

Pheromones (Ex) Once per day, as a swift action, a jolly jelly can emit a cloud of pheromones containing the distilled essence of the positive emotions the jelly has consumed. This cloud covers a 20-foot-radius burst around the jelly. Living creatures in the cloud must succeed on a DC 19 Fortitude save or be affected as by a *hideous laughter* spell (CL 6th) for 2d4 rounds. The save DC is Constitution-based.

Jolly jellies are psychic vampires which feed on positive emotion. The mere presence of a jolly jelly causes living creatures in its vicinity to become dour and petulant. Often the victims of a jolly jelly descend into violence against one another as all traces of happiness and mirth are drained away by the creature. A jolly jelly needs no nourishment other than the emotions it drains from its victims. A jolly jelly can go several months between meals before the effects of starvation are noticed.

Jolly jellies are mostly active during sunrise and sunset, even underground. During daylight hours they are sedentary in their lair which if aboveground is usually under fallen trees or hollowed logs. Underground, jolly jellies dwell in damp caves and caverns.

Jolly jellies vary in size, but a typical specimen is 5 feet across and weighs 100 pounds. A jolly jelly that has recently eaten (usually within the last 4 hours) is flushed with a deeper pink hue than one that hasn't.

Unlike most oozes, a jolly jelly has no acid with which it can attack. Its only means of physical defense are slams from its multi-colored pseudopods. As a last-ditch defense, a jolly jelly can emit a cloud of pheromones containing the mirth it has absorbed from its victims. It is this laughter-inducing cloud that gave the jolly jelly its name.

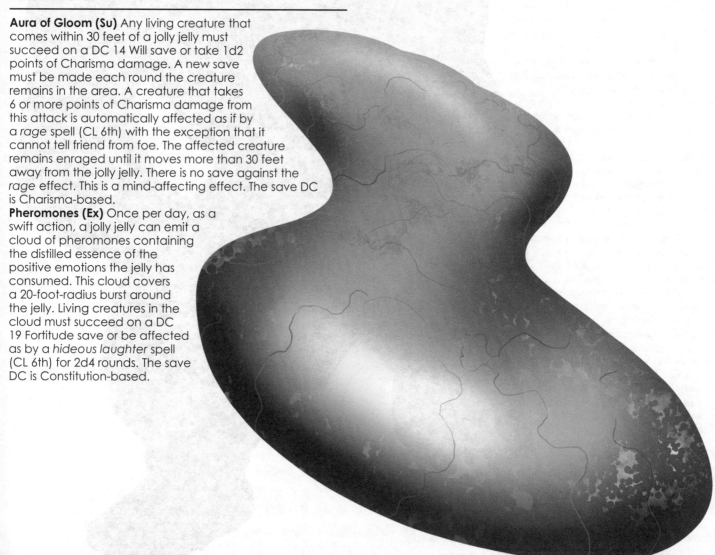

Jynx

This creature resembles a 3-foot tall elf with slightly longer ears and a pair of glittering insect-like wings. Its clothes are varying shades of green, and the creature carries a small short sword.

JYNX	CR 2

XP 600
CN Small fey
Init +4; **Senses** low-light vision; **Perception** +7

AC 17, touch 16, flat-footed 12 (+4 Dex, +1 dodge, +1 natural, +1 size)
hp 9 (2d6+2)
Fort +1; **Ref** +7; **Will** +5
DR 5/cold iron; **Immune** electricity; **SR** 13

Speed 30 ft., fly 80 ft. (perfect)
Melee short sword +6 (1d4–2)
Ranged shortbow +6 (1d4–2)
Special Attacks jinxed
Spell-Like Abilities (CL 6th; melee touch +0, ranged touch +5):
Constant—*detect evil, detect good, detect magic*
At will—*dancing lights, daze* (DC 13)
1/day—*color spray* (DC 14), *detect thoughts* (DC 15), *dispel magic, entangle* (DC 14), *misdirection* (DC 15), *ventriloquism* (DC 14)

Str 7, **Dex** 18, **Con** 12, **Int** 15, **Wis** 14, **Cha** 16
Base Atk +1; **CMB** –2; **CMD** 13
Feats Dodge, Weapon Finesse[B]
Skills Acrobatics +9, Bluff +8, Escape Artist +9, Fly +19, Knowledge (nature) +7, Perception +7, Sense Motive +7, Stealth +13
Languages Common, Sylvan

Environment temperate forests
Organization solitary, gang (2–4), or band (6–11)
Treasure standard (short sword, short bow, other treasure)

Jinxed (Su) As a standard action, a jynx can place a curse on a single creature within 30 feet. A DC 14 Will save negates the effect. On a failed save, the target is permanently cursed. The victim of the curse takes a –2 penalty on all attack rolls, saving throws, and checks until the curse is removed. A creature can only be affected by a single jynx at one time. This is a curse effect. The save DC is Charisma-based.

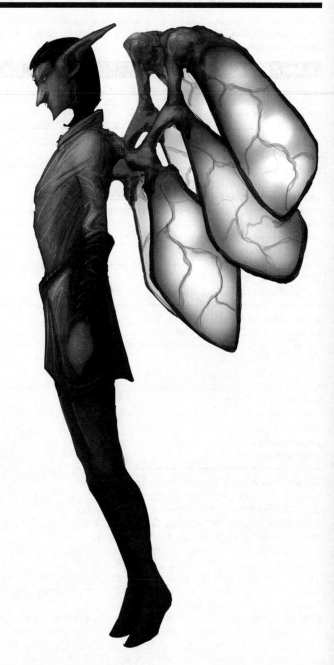

Jynx are small whimsical, fun-loving forest fey thought to be an offshoot of the elven race. They live in small moss-covered caves within their forests, with such caves often being located near well-travelled roads and paths, but still well hidden from prying eyes. This location makes it much easier for the jynx to partake in one of their favorite pastimes—leading travelers astray. Jynx rarely try to harm the target of their pranks; they simply delight in sewing confusion and watching the target's reactions to such events. Those that despoil the forests on the other hand, are led astray and often led into jynx-placed traps that seek to maim or even kill such creatures.

Jynx have good relations with other forest-dwelling humanoids and creatures (elves, sprites, pixies, etc.) and can often be found in their midst. They are on good terms with neutral and good-aligned druids and rangers as well.

A typical jynx stands around 3 feet tall and weighs about 40 pounds. Skin color is usually tan and hair color varies wildly from the deepest blacks to the brightest blondes. Eyes are most often deep blue or dark green. A jynx's lifespan is about 300 years.

Jynx tend to avoid melee combat, preferring to assault their enemies with their spell-like abilities and shortbows.

Kamarupa

This floating nightmare has twisted facial features that are filled with hatred for the living. Their voices sound like the screaming wind, and their forms are insubstantial.

KAMARUPA	CR 7

CE Medium undead (incorporeal)
Init +7; **Senses** darkvision 60 ft., low-light vision;
Perception +16

AC 16, touch 16, flat-footed 12 (+2 deflection, +3 Dex, +1 dodge)
hp 65 (10d8)
Fort +5; **Ref** +8; **Will** +12
Defensive abilities +4 channel resistance, incorporeal, unnatural aura; **Immune** undead traits
Weakness Powerless in sunlight

Speed 40 ft., fly 80 ft. (perfect)
Melee incorporeal touch +10 (2d6 plus death touch)
Space 5 ft.; **Reach** 5 ft.
Special Attacks death touch, gaze attack, *nightmare*

Str —, **Dex** 16, **Con** —, **Int** 14, **Wis** 16, **Cha** 15
Base Atk +7; **CMB** +10; **CMD** 26
Feats Dodge, Improved Initiative, Iron Will, Lightning Reflexes, Toughness
Skills Fly +24, Intimidate +16, Knowledge (history) +12, Knowledge (religion) +10, Perception +16, Sense Motive +11, Stealth +16

Environment any
Organization solitary
Treasure none

Death Touch (Su): Creatures hit by a kamarupa's incorporeal touch must make a DC 17 Fort save or die as the touch stops the heart. Even if the save is successful, the creature suffers 2d6 points of damage as the kamarupa clutches its heart. Often, a creature surviving a touch attack acquires a harmless trait or characteristic for 2d4 months. Traits can be a white streak of hair, a nervous twitch, pale complexion or dilated eyes. The save DC is Charisma-based.
Frightful Gaze (Su): A kamarupa's glance creates dread in living beings, at a range of up to 30 feet. Creatures meeting the gaze must make a DC 17 Fortitude save or become panicked for 3d4 rounds. Even if successful, the subject becomes shaken for 1d4 rounds. The save DC is Charisma-based.
Nightmare (Su): Once per night, a kamarupa places a *nightmare* on one creature it has encountered. They prefer to send the *nightmare* to particularly powerful opponents or priests night after night until the opponent dies. The target can resist the attack with a DC 17 Will save. A creature that drops any possession (while panicked) near the kamarupa suffers a –4 penalty to the save until the item is recovered. A creature that successfully saves is immune to the *nightmare* for 24 hours. The save DC is Charisma-based.
Powerless in Sunlight (Ex): Kamarupas are powerless in natural sunlight (not merely a *daylight* spell) and flee before it. A kamarupa caught in sunlight cannot attack and can take only a single move action each round. Kamarupas lose one-third of their hit points each round spent in direct sunlight.

Unnatural Aura (Su): Animals sense the kamarupa's unnatural presence at 30 feet. They panic if forced to get closer and remain panicked while within range.

A kamarupa appears as a mockery of its former fleshbound life. Its hollow eyes and mouth are black voids, and its facial features twist and stretch into a nightmarish appearance. Kamarupa are the distorted souls of evil priests betrayed and sacrificed to their deity.

Kamarupas are highly intelligent and communicate in voices similar to the screaming wind. They hate life and light. A kamarupa is roughly human-sized and weightless. A kamarupa attacks with its heart-stopping touch. It uses its incorporeal nature to move through walls, ceilings and floors to attack.

Credit

Original author Gary Schotter & Jeff Harkness
Originally appearing in *Splinters of Faith Adventure 5: Eclipse of the Hearth* (© Frog God Games/ Gary Schotter & Jeff Harkness, 2010)

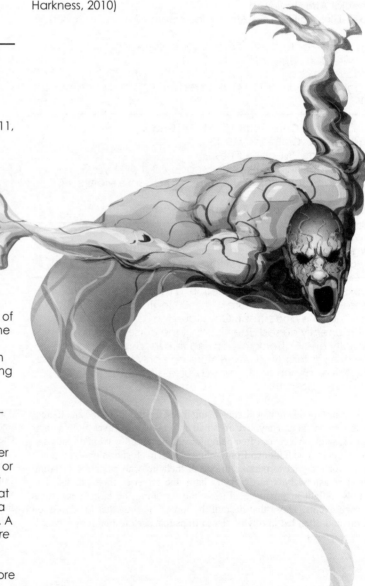

Kapre

This humanoid creature has dark brown skin, the color of tree bark and long black hair.

KAPRE	CR 2

XP 600
N Medium fey
Init +1; **Senses** low-light vision; **Perception** +10

AC 15, touch 11, flat-footed 14 (+1 Dex, +4 natural)
hp 18 (4d6+4)
Fort +2; **Ref** +7; **Will** +5
DR 5/cold iron; **SR** 13

Speed 30 ft., climb 20 ft.
Melee club +4 (1d6+2) or 2 claws +4 (1d4+2)
Spell-Like Abilities (CL 4th):
At will—*dancing lights, ventriloquism* (DC 13)
3/day—*confusion* (DC 16)
1/day—*dispel magic, entangle* (DC 13)

Str 15, **Dex** 13, **Con** 13, **Int** 10, **Wis** 12, **Cha** 14
Base Atk +2; **CMB** +4; **CMD** 15
Feats Alertness, Lightning Reflexes
Skills Bluff +7, Climb +15, Escape Artist +6, Knowledge (nature) +5, Perception +10, Perform (singing) +9, Sense Motive +3, Stealth +8, Survival +5
Languages Common, Sylvan
SQ woodland stride

Environment temperate and warm forests
Organization solitary or gang (2–5)
Treasure standard (club, other treasure)

Woodland Stride (Ex) A kapre can move through any sort of undergrowth (such as natural thorns, briars, overgrown areas, and similar terrain) at its normal speed and without taking damage or suffering any other impairment. However, thorns, briars, and overgrown areas that have been magically manipulated to impede motion still affect it.

Kapres are peaceful forest- and mountain-dwelling creatures that make their homes in the dense, thick treetops of large trees. If threatened or provoked, however, kapres do not hesitate to fight (especially if their lair or young are threatened). They exist on a diet of plants, small forest game, and nuts and berries. They are adept hunters and fishermen and prefer rabbit, deer, and boar above all other meats. Though they appear to some to be primitive savages, kapres do not eat humanoids and have no love for human flesh. (Rumors speak of a degenerative race of kapres who do in fact enjoy the taste of flesh; these rumors are believed to be stories told by other humanoid races to their children in order to keep them from wandering into the forests alone.)

Kapres stand about 7 feet tall with dark hair and dark skin. Clothes are usually well maintained and match the color of their surroundings. Kapres live for up to 250 years.

In battle, a kapre uses its confusion and then attacks with a large wooden club, or if unarmed, slashes with its claws. It seeks to drive off its foes rather than kill them if possible. If a battle goes against a kapre, it attempts to take to the trees and flee. If its homeland, mate, or young are threatened however, it fights to the death. Some kapre also wear magical belts that grant them the ability of invisibility.

Kapre Belt

This is a thick leather belt, well-made and tailored. By activating the power of the belt, the wearer gains the benefits of *invisibility* for up to 5 minutes per day. The usage need not be consecutive.

Faint illusion; **CL** 5th; Craft Wondrous Item, *invisibility*; **Price** 12,500 gp; **Weight** 1 lb.

Knight Gaunt

This desiccated creature resembles a once proud knight fallen from grace. Its armor reveals its former station. The creature's eyes burn red and its hands end in wicked claws.

KNIGHT GAUNT	CR 3

XP 800
CE Medium undead
Init +1; **Senses** darkvision 60 ft.; **Perception** +8

AC 21, touch 11, flat-footed 20 (+6 armor, +1 Dex, +4 natural)
hp 26 (4d8+8)
Fort +3; **Ref** +2; **Will** +5
Immune undead traits; **Resist** cold 10; **SR** 14

Speed 20 ft. (base 30 ft.)
Melee longsword +6 (1d8+3 plus bleed) or 2 claws +5 (1d4+2 plus bleed)
Special Attacks bleed (1d4), smite good, weapon attunement

Str 15, **Dex** 12, **Con** —, **Int** 11, **Wis** 13, **Cha** 15
Base Atk +3; **CMB** +5; **CMD** 16
Feats Cleave, Power Attack
Skills Intimidate +9, Perception +8, Ride +0, Stealth +3
Languages Common

Environment any
Organization solitary or troop (2–8)
Treasure standard (chainmail armor, longsword, other treasure)

Smite Good (Su) Once per day, a knight gaunt can smite good. As a swift action, the knight gaunt chooses one target within sight. If this target is good, the knight gaunt adds its Charisma bonus on its attack rolls and adds its Hit Dice on all damage rolls made against that target. If the target is an outsider with the good subtype or a good-aligned creature with levels of cleric of paladin, the bonus to damage on the first successful attack is doubled. Regardless of the target, smite good attacks automatically bypass any DR the creature might possess. Additionally, the knight gaunt gains a deflection bonus equal to its Charisma bonus to AC against attacks made by the target of the smite. The smite good remains in effect until the target of the smite is dead or until 24 hours have passed.
Weapon Attunement (Su) A knight gaunt gains a +1 bonus on attack rolls and damage rolls with any melee weapon it wields. Additionally, it gains the bleed special attack with any melee weapon it wields.

A knight gaunt is an undead creature created when a paladin falls in battle. Other than a few fleeting thoughts perhaps of the martial training they received in life, these creatures have no memories of their former lives. A knight gaunt often wears the armor it wore in life and wields the weapons it carried into its last battle before rising as undead.

Knight gaunts are most often found in the employ of death knights serving as companions or knights-in-training. Others wander the world seeking out goodness wherever they find it, squashing it beneath their steel-booted heel and putting the righteous to their blades. Paladins and clerics of good alignment are hated by many knight gaunts for they represent everything the knight gaunt isn't, and perhaps once was or once strived to be.

A typical knight gaunt stands 6 feet tall and weighs 180 pounds. It wears the armor it wore when alive and still carries the weapons it wielded in life. Its skin is ash gray in color and its eyes are milky white with fiery red pupils.

A knight gaunt fights with bladed weapons in battle, preferring longswords, greatswords, and axes to all others. Only when disarmed does it resort to using its claws. A knight gaunt that retains its mount (that is undead now as well) or procures some undead steed to carry it into battle wields a lance in addition to its other weapons. In battle, a knight gaunt is relentless, attacking with its blades until all of its foes are vanquished.

Korog

The Korog resemble tall men, but with a head somewhat like that of a hairless horse with long teeth, and smoldering, malevolent eyes.

KOROG	CR 4

XP 1,200
LE Medium humanoid (korog)
Init +2; **Senses** darkvision 90 ft.; **Perception** +4

AC 16, touch 12, flat-footed 14 (+1 armor, +2 Dex, +3 natural)
hp 28 (4d8+4)
Fort +2; **Ref** +3; **Will** +6

Speed 30 ft.
Melee unarmed strike +5 (1d3+2)

Str 15, **Dex** 15, **Con** 13, **Int** 18, **Wis** 11, **Cha** 8
Base Atk +3; **CMB** +5; **CMD** 17
Feats Improved Iron Will, Iron Will
Skills Craft (any) +13, Disable Device +8, Knowledge (dungeoneering) +8, Knowledge (engineering) +8, Perception +4, Profession (scientist) +7
Languages Terran, Undercommon
Combat Gear *wand of hold person* (CL7th; 5 charges; DC 15); **Other Gear** masterwork tools, leather work apron, 1d6 gp.

Environment any (underground)
Organization solitary or consortium (2–8)
Treasure standard (*wand of hold person*, other treasure)

The Korog resemble tall men, but with a head somewhat like that of a hairless horse with long teeth, and smoldering, malevolent eyes. Standing between 6 and 7 feet tall, The korog are typically quite thin, weighing around 150 to 180 pounds. They possess horse-hooves, and natural coloration is dull grays and light browns.

Various Korog "castes" exist, with differing abilities, but adventurers most frequently encounter the technician and warrior castes.

All Korog technicians carry a silver wand with them at all times for self-defense. These wands can be used by non-Korogs, but they carry only five charges and can only be recharged in the Korog laboratories beneath the earth. Korog warriors may use any weapon or armor, butprefer exotic weapons and light armor.

The Korog are the ancient race of beings from which the wizard Iomnogoron evolved (see *The Spire of Iron and Crystal* from **Frog God Games** for more information). Few yet live, but some of these still continue very limited operations in the deep, dark places beneath the earth, collecting surface essences for their machinations in deep underground strongholds.

IOMNOGORON, KOROG SCIENTIST	CR 12

XP 19,200
Male korog scientist sorcerer 10
LE Large humanoid (korog)
Init +0; **Senses** darkvision 120 ft.; **Perception** +13

AC 16, touch 10, flat-footed 16 (+6 natural)
hp 80 (4d8+4 plus 12d6+16)
Fort +8; **Ref** +5; **Will** +14

Defensive Abilities protean resistance (+4), reality wrinkle (12 rounds); **Resist** acid 10

Speed 10 ft.
Melee 2 tentacles +14/+9 (1d6+4 plus grab)
Special Attacks protoplasm (7/day)
Spells Known (CL 12th; melee touch +13, ranged touch +9):
6th (3/day)—*flesh to stone* (DC 22)
5th (5/day)—*baleful polymorph* (DC 21), *major creation*ᴮ, *suffocation* (DC 19)*
4th (7/day)—*confusion* (DC 18)ᴮ, *detonate* (DC 18)*, *greater invisibility*, *stone shape*
3rd (7/day)—*deep slumber* (DC 17), *dispel magic*, *gaseous form*ᴮ, *haste*, *seek thoughts* (DC 17)*
2nd (7/day)—*blindness/deafness* (DC 16), *blur*ᴮ, *hideous laughter* (DC 16), *levitate* (DC 18), *resist energy*, *share language**
1st (7/day)—*break* (DC 15)*, *charm person* (DC 15), *entropic shield*ᴮ, *ray of enfeeblement* (DC 15), *reduce person* (DC 17), *vanish**
0 (at will)—*acid splash* (DC 15), *arcane mark*, *bleed* (DC 15), *detect magic*, *detect poison*, *mage hand*, *message*, *open/close*, *touch of fatigue* (DC 15)
Bloodline Protean*

Str 18, **Dex** 10, **Con** 13, **Int** 3, **Wis** 11, **Cha** 18
Base Atk +9; **CMB** +14 (+18 grapple); **CMD** 24 (cannot be tripped)
Feats Deepsight*, Extend Spell, Great Fortitude, Improved Great Fortitude, Improved Iron Will, Greater Spell Focus (transmutation), Iron Will, Spell Focus (transmutation), Spell Penetration
Skills Perception +16
Languages Terran, Undercommon (does not speak)
SQ bloodline arcana

Environment any (underground)
Organization solitary
Treasure standard
Pathfinder Roleplaying Game Advanced Player's Guide

Iomnogoron is a desiccated, almost skeletal creature encased in a huge pillar-like glob of transparent ooze, combining korog technology with his massive sorcerous abilities. He is dependent on this ooze-prison for his almost immortal lifespan.

The creature is no longer sane, but is cunning and still evidences a dangerous intelligence. Iomnogoron can cast spells at the same time his outer ooze attacks with its two tentacles.

SPECIAL: Due to Iomnogoron's insanity, his concentration score is reduced by half. While he may use his tentacles and spells in the same round, he has only a 50% chance of doing so, due to his lack of coherent thought.

Credit
Original author Matthew J. Finch
Originally appearing in *The Spire of Iron and Crystal* (© Frog God Games/Matthew J. Finch, 2011)

Kulgreer

This is a macabre creature, possessing no evident features common to other living creatures such as a cranium, appendages, or eyes. It has a long, conical body and a horrific gaping maw.

KULGREER	CR 16

XP 76,800
N Gargantuan aberration (aquatic)
Init +4; **Senses** blindsight 120 ft., darkvision 60 ft.; **Perception** +27

AC 22, touch 6, flat-footed 22 (+16 natural, −4 size)
hp 252 (24d8+144)
Fort +16; **Ref** +10; **Will** +16
DR 20/magic; **SR** 27

Speed swim 50 ft.
Melee slam +27 (4d6+18/19–20)
Space 20 ft.; **Reach** 15 ft.
Special Attacks vortex

Str 34, **Dex** 10, **Con** 22, **Int** 10, **Wis** 11, **Cha** 14
Base Atk +18; **CMB** +34; **CMD** 44 (can't be tripped)
Feats Awesome Blow, Cleave, Great Cleave, Great Fortitude, Improved Bull Rush, Improved Critical (slam), Improved Initiative, Iron Will, Lightning Reflexes, Power Attack, Skill Focus (Swim), Weapon Focus (slam)
Skills Escape Artist +15, Intimidate +29, Knowledge (arcana) +12, Perception +27, Swim +53
Languages Common (can't speak)

Environment any oceans
Organization solitary
Treasure none

Vortex (Su) Three times per day, a kulgreer can create a powerful, self-contained whirlpool within its conical frame. This lasts for 1d6+6 rounds. Huge and smaller creatures within 20 feet of the kulgreer must succeed on a DC 34 Swim check or be yanked into the 30-foot diameter mouth of the whirlpool. As the whirlpool spirals through the kulgreer's frame, creatures inside are thrashed violently about taking 2d6+18 points of damage each round. A successful DC 34 Reflex save or DC 34 Swim check negates the damage for that round and allows the trapped creature to escape. The save DCs are Strength-based.
During the final round of the vortex's duration, any creatures still trapped are pulled through the sphere of dim, white light in the kulgreer's tapered outlet. Such creatures must succeed on a DC 28 Fortitude save or take 12d6 points of damage. Those succeeding on their save take only half damage and are forcibly ejected from the kulgreer and flung 40 feet away. There is a 5% chance that any ejected creature is instead sent to a random plane of existence (GM's choice as to which one). The save DC is Constitution-based.

The kulgreer is a massive, abominable being of the deep sea that creates powerful whirlpools inside its funnel-like body. It has a 30 foot long, conical body resembling a funnel, beginning in a wide mouth 30 feet in diameter, and tapering into a 5 foot diameter outlet of dim, white light.

The kulgreer navigates the depths in a non-cognizant state, pointed-end first; its conical body gradually rotates and propels itself forward subconsciously, amassing various creatures into its frame as it passes through. If awakened from this state, the kulgreer is generally violent. It is popular belief that creatures sucked into the kulgreer's funnel-like body are teleported to another plane of existence.

Though not consciously aggressive, the circumstances presented through a kulgreer's presence inevitably lead to conflict. If provoked, the kulgreer typically tramples its opponent in a fit of sudden sentience and conclude in the use of its supernatural ability.

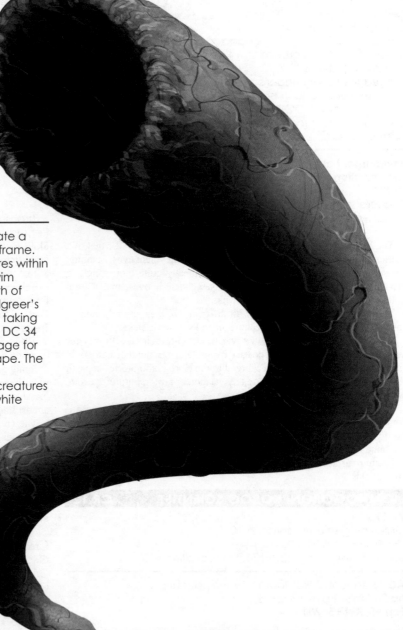

Lamprey, Burrowing

This eel-like creature has leathery-looking skin almost black in color. No discernible features are present on its form.

BURROWING LAMPREY	CR 2

XP 600
N Small magical beast (aquatic)
Init +6; **Senses** darkvision 60 ft., low-light vision; **Perception** +5

AC 15, touch 13, flat-footed 13 (+2 Dex, +2 natural, +1 size)
hp 8 (1d10+3)
Fort +5; **Ref** +4; **Will** +1

Speed 5 ft., swim 30 ft.
Melee bite +4 (1d4 plus attach plus poison)
Special Attacks attach, flesh burrow, poison

Str 10, **Dex** 15, **Con** 16, **Int** 1, **Wis** 12, **Cha** 2
Base Atk +1; **CMB** +0 (+8 grapple when attached); **CMD** 12 (can't be tripped)
Feats Improved Initiative, Weapon Finesse[B]
Skills Escape Artist +10, Perception +5, Swim +8; **Racial Modifiers** +8 Escape Artist
SQ amphibious

Environment temperate and warm aquatic
Organization cluster (2–5) or swarm (6–20)
Treasure none

Attach (Ex) When a burrowing lamprey hits with a bite attack, its suckered mouth latches onto the target, anchoring it in place. An attached burrowing lamprey is effectively grappling its prey. The burrowing lamprey loses its Dexterity bonus to AC and has an AC of 13, but holds on with great tenacity. A burrowing lamprey has a +8 racial bonus to maintain its grapple on a foe once it is attached. An attached burrowing lamprey can be struck with a weapon or grappled itself—if its prey manages to win a grapple check or Escape Artist check against it, the burrowing lamprey is removed.

Flesh Burrow (Ex) At the start of its next turn, the round after it attaches to its prey, a burrowing lamprey burrows into the target's flesh and subjects it to its poison. Applying flame to the point of entry deals 1d6 points of fire damage to both the host and the burrowing lamprey. Cutting the lamprey out works, but the longer the lamprey remains in the host, the more damage this method does. Cutting a lamprey out requires a slashing weapon and a DC 20 Heal check, and deals 1d6 points of damage to the host per round the lamprey has been inside it. If the Heal check succeeds, one lamprey is removed. *Remove disease* instantly kills any burrowing lampreys inside a host.

Poison (Ex) Flesh burrow—injury; *save* DC 14 Fort; *effect* 1d2 Constitution damage; *cure* —. The save DC is Constitution-based. The lamprey's poison liquefies the host's organs. A successful saving throw can prevent Con damage for that round, but the only cure is to remove the burrowing lamprey from the host.

The burrowing lamprey is an eel-like fish that attaches to its prey, and then burrows into its body, feasting on blood and the rich vital organs. They are a danger to fish and aquatic mammals, and can be as deadly as a school of piranha when encountered in large numbers. Burrowing lampreys resemble eels three to four feet long, with sphincter-like mouths positioned within hardened cartilaginous beaks.

Although they are usually marine creatures, burrowing lampreys breed in coastal freshwater swamps and rivers, and thus can be found in both fresh and saltwater environments.

They prefer to either ambush prey by hiding along the ocean floor or in rocky crevices, or swarm around a target if traveling in numbers. However, it is possible that they can be encountered inside a dead creature's remains, feeding on its vital organs.

Medium- and large-sized burrowing lampreys are less common, but sometimes found in the deeper sea, where they may attack large sharks or even small whales.

Burrowing lampreys seek out targets at least equal to their size category, and up to three sizes larger, if they can, though a starving lamprey attacks just about anything. They attack with their bite, then immediately attempt to burrow into their victim.

Leonine

This muscular creature has the upper torso of a golden-skinned human with long flowing braided hair and the lower torso of a powerful lion. Its massive fists clutch tightly around a wicked-looking spear.

LEONINE	CR 4

XP 1,200
NE (sometimes LE) Large monstrous humanoid
Init +6; **Senses** darkvision 60 ft., scent; **Perception** +14

AC 16, touch 11, flat-footed 14 (+2 Dex, +5 natural, –1 size)
hp 51 (6d10+18)
Fort +7; **Ref** +7; **Will** +7

Speed 40 ft.
Melee spear +9/+4 (2d6+6), 2 fore-claws +9 (1d4+4) or 2 claws +9 (1d4+4), 2 fore-claws +9 (1d4+4)
Space 10 ft.; **Reach** 5 ft.
Special Attacks pounce
Spell-Like Abilities (CL 6th):
Constant—*speak with animals* (lions and dire lions only)

Str 19, **Dex** 15, **Con** 16, **Int** 10, **Wis** 14, **Cha** 10
Base Atk +6; **CMB** +11; **CMD** 23 (27 vs. trip)
Feats Great Fortitude, Improved Initiative, Skill Focus (Perception)
Skills Acrobatics +12, Diplomacy +2, Intimidate +7, Perception +14, Stealth +11; **Racial Modifiers** +4 Acrobatics, +4 Stealth
Languages Leonine
SQ feline passivism

Environment warm plains and forests
Organization solitary, pair, hunting party (3–8 plus 1–4 lions), or pride (10–20 plus 4–6 lions)
Treasure standard (spear, other treasure)

Feline Passivism (Ex) Lions (including dire lions) do not willingly attack a leonine, though they can be forced to do so through magic. If a leonine attacks a lion or dire lion, its protection against that creature ends.

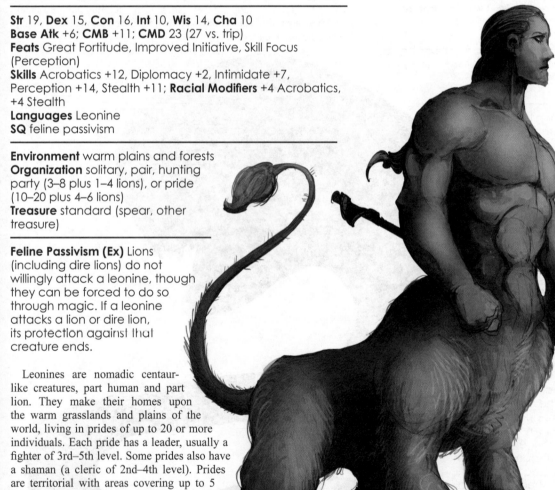

Leonines are nomadic centaur-like creatures, part human and part lion. They make their homes upon the warm grasslands and plains of the world, living in prides of up to 20 or more individuals. Each pride has a leader, usually a fighter of 3rd–5th level. Some prides also have a shaman (a cleric of 2nd–4th level). Prides are territorial with areas covering up to 5 square miles. Prides generally do not encroach on another's territory. In cases where territories overlap, bloody battles are fought between the prides with the victors claiming rights to the area.

Some particularly evil leonine prides worship Gorson, the Blood Duke (see *The Tome of Horrors Complete* by **Frog God Games** for details), and sacrifice captured humanoids to him. These prides feel a connection to Gorson and some believe he is the progenitor of the first leonines.

A leonine stands 7 feet tall and can reach lengths of up to 10 feet long. Average weigh is around 700 pounds. Males sport long, flowing hair of black or brown and usually wear it braided. A strip of hair runs from the base of its neck, down its back, and blends into its lion-like body. Females are slightly smaller than males, wear their hair shorter, and do not have the strip of hair running down their back. While females generally take care of the young, they are just as fierce and effective in combat as males. Young leonines are born live and reach maturity within three years. If the young are threatened, the entire pride fights to protect them.

Leonines fight with wicked, slightly curved spears and their forepaws. If disarmed, they can slash with their clawed hands. They attack from ambush when hunting, often tracking their quarry for several miles before springing to the attack. Leonines have a longstanding hatred for the tabaxi race and kill them on sight.

Leviathan

This is a tremendous sea creature, resembling a whale of gigantic proportions. Its humped back stands like a mountain, and its massive eye is nearly as large as a sailing ship. Its cavernous blowhole spews forth a jet of water like a cyclone.

LEVIATHAN	CR 19

XP 204,800
N Colossal magical beast
Init –2; **Senses** darkvision 60 ft., low-light vision; **Perception** +27

AC 30, touch 0, flat-footed 30 (–2 Dex, +30 natural, –8 size)
hp 310 (20d10+200)
Fort +24; **Ref** +10; **Will** +12
DR 20/magic; **Immune** cold, electricity; **Resist** fire 20, sonic 20; **SR** 30

Speed swim 60 ft.
Melee bite +34 (6d6+22/19–20), tail slap +29 (4d6+11)
Space 30 ft.; **Reach** 20 ft.
Special Attacks capsize, smashing breach, swallow whole (6d8+22 acid damage, AC 25, 31 hp), tail storm, whale song
Spell-Like Abilities (CL 20th):
3/day—*control weather, summon nature's ally IX* (aquatic animals only)

Str 54, **Dex** 6, **Con** 30, **Int** 18, **Wis** 18, **Cha** 21
Base Atk +20; **CMB** +50; **CMD** 58 (can't be tripped)
Feats Augment Summoning[B], Critical Focus, Diehard, Endurance, Great Fortitude, Improved Bull Rush, Improved Critical (bite), Iron Will, Power Attack, Skill Focus (Swim), Staggering Critical
Skills Knowledge (any one) +24, Knowledge (local) +24, Knowledge (nature) +24, Perception +27, Stealth +5, Swim +59
Languages Aquan
SQ hold breath

Environment any oceans
Organization solitary
Treasure standard

Smashing Breach (Ex) As a full-round action, a leviathan can make a special charge attack against creatures on the surface of the water. At the end of its charge, the leviathan breaches, then slams down onto the target with incredible force. Any Huge or smaller creatures in the leviathan's space must make a DC 30 Reflex save or take 4d8+33 points of bludgeoning damage and be forced into the nearest square that is adjacent to the whale. This breach automatically attempts to capsize any boats caught wholly or partially in this area. The save DC is Constitution-based.
Tail Storm (Ex) As a full-round action, a leviathan can raise its massive tail and bring it crashing down into the water, causing a massive wave that sinks ships in the area. The resulting wave fans out from the leviathan's tail in a 100-foot cone. Huge or smaller ships caught in the area and within 10 feet of the leviathan's tail automatically sink. Creatures in the water and within 10 feet of the leviathan's tail take 4d6+22 points bludgeoning damage. A successful DC 42 Reflex save reduces the damage by half. Additionally, a creature that fails its save is pushed 6d6 x 10 feet away. Huge or smaller ships more than 10 feet away within the area must succeed on a Profession (sailor) check or capsize. The DC of this check is 42, decreasing by 5 for every 10 feet from the leviathan a ship is. The DC increases by a cumulative +5 for each size smaller than Huge a ship is. The save and base check DC is Strength-based.

Whale Song (Su) As a swift action, a leviathan can unleash a song that is so deep and of such low frequency that the vibrations alone have adverse effects on living creatures. Any living creature within 100 feet of a singing leviathan must succeed on a DC 30 Fortitude save or be stunned for 1d6 rounds. A creature that succeeds on its save is unaffected by that leviathan's whale song for one day. This song is more felt than heard, and can be detected by creatures up to 10 miles away. Creatures capable of detecting extremely low-frequency sounds (e.g. dolphins, whales, other leviathans) can detect this song up to 100 miles away. The save DC is Constitution-based.

Legend holds that there is but one leviathan in every ocean in the world, each creature being the undisputed sovereign of its domain. Smaller leviathans control the seas, whilst the tiniest—still massive by any measure—lurk in a few secluded bays within the lonelier parts of the world. Completely unopposed by any other creature, they dominate their realms. When a leviathan grows to such size that it can no longer be supported by its territory, it challenges another larger in size, seeking to gain mastery of its sea or ocean. Failure in this challenge results in death but if it overcomes its rival, the leviathan assumes sovereignty of the domain. Battles between these titanic creatures are an awesome sight to behold, for tidal waves and hurricanes erupt, devastating nearby coastal settlements.

Leviathans are over 500 feet long and weigh many hundreds of tons.

Leviathans are seldom stirred to anger and only attack to defend themselves from opponents who can truly harm them—a rare occurrence indeed. They strike with their massive tail or by biting. A leviathan is so immense that it cannot bite any creature smaller than Huge; such small prey is simply swallowed whole. Any enemy flanking a leviathan from behind is attacked with a devastating tail slap or subjected to the leviathan's tail storm attack.

Lightning Bladder

A roiling, bubble-like creature slowly oozes its way towards you, tiny surges of electricity arc through its semi-transparent form, and an acrid stench surrounds the creature like a cloud.

LIGHTNING BLADDER	CR 4

XP 1,200
N Medium ooze
Init –5; **Senses** blindsight 60 ft.; **Perception** –5

AC 5, touch 5, flat-footed 5 (–5 Dex)
hp 50 (4d8+32)
Fort +9; **Ref** –4; **Will** –4
Defensive Abilities ooze traits; **Immune** cold, electricity, fire

Speed 10 ft., swim 30 ft.
Melee slam +6 (1d6+4 plus 1d6 acid)
Special Attacks acid, electrical discharge

Str 16, **Dex** 1, **Con** 26, **Int** —, **Wis** 1, **Cha** 1
Base Atk +3; **CMB** +6; **CMD** 11 (can't be tripped)

Environment any (underground)
Organization solitary
Treasure none

Acid (Ex) The corrosive acid that covers a lightning bladder dissolves metals and organic material, but not stone. Each slam attack deals 1d6 additional acid damage. Armor or clothing worn by a creature touched by a lightning bladder takes the same amount of acid damage unless the wearer succeeds on a DC 20 Reflex saving throw. A wooden or metal weapon that strikes the creature takes 1d6 acid damage unless the weapon's wielder succeeds on a DC 20 Reflex save. The bladder's touch deals 12 points of acid damage per round to wooden or metal objects, but the bladder must remain in contact with the material for 1 full round in order to deal this damage. The save DCs are Constitution-based.

Electrical Discharge (Ex) Any hit scored against a lightning bladder with a piercing or slashing weapon opens a hole in the creature's acidic membrane, through which lightning-like charges of electricity will blast out each subsequent combat round. These bolts of lightning inflict 2d6 points of damage against a randomly determined opponent (DC 15 Reflex save for half damage). The bladder can have any number of such openings before it is eventually killed from the damage.

Lightning bladders are a form of ooze, contained within a thin, membranous skin; they resemble massive, half-filled blue water balloons some 5–6 feet in diameter.

The inside of the creature is charged with immense electrical potential, clearly visible as lightning-like flashes and forks within the bluish-hued interior of the shapeless mass. The exterior membrane is highly acidic, and the creature will attack by slumping up against its opponents to slam them. The more dangerous aspect of a lightning bladder, however, is what happens when a pointed or cutting weapon pierces its outer membrane, releasing the inner electrical charge.

Credit
Original author Matthew J. Finch
Originally appearing in *The Spire of Iron and Crystal* (© Frog God Games/Matthew J. Finch, 2011)

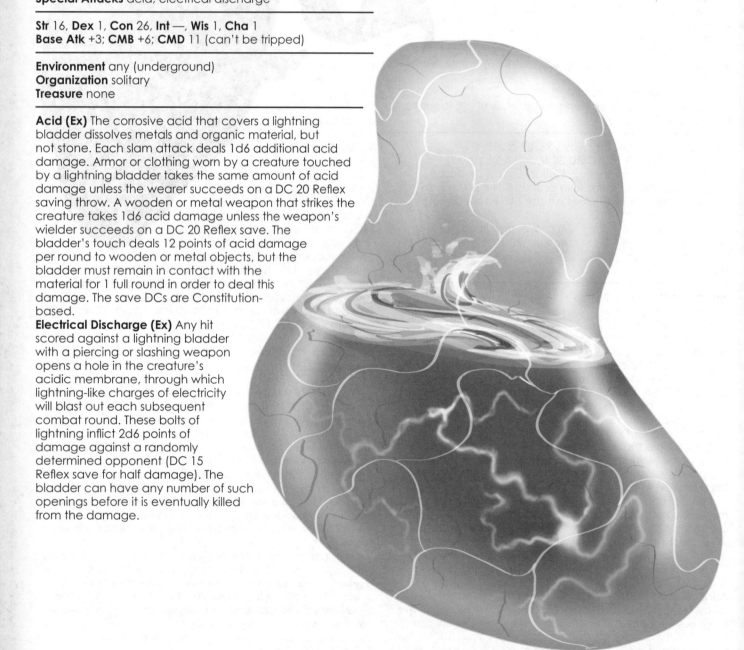

Lightning Lamprey

Lightning lampreys are floating, eel-like creatures about 3 ft. long that are covered in static electricity, with arcs and bolts of tiny lightning flying off in all directions.

LIGHTNING LAMPREY	CR 2

XP 600
N Small magical beast
Init +1; **Senses** blindsight 30 ft.; **Perception** +0

AC 12, touch 12, flat-footed 11 (+1 Dex, +1 size)
hp 25 (3d10+6)
Fort +5; **Ref** +4; **Will** +1
Immune mind-affecting effects

Speed 5 ft., fly 30 ft. (good)
Melee bite +4 (1d2 plus 1d6 electrical)

Str 11, **Dex** 12, **Con** 14, **Int** –, **Wis** 10, **Cha** 1
Base Atk +3; **CMB** +2; **CMD** 13 (can't be tripped)
Skills Fly +7, Stealth +5 (+13 in clouds);
Racial Modifiers +8 Stealth in clouds

Environment any
Organization solitary or schools (2–20)
Treasure none

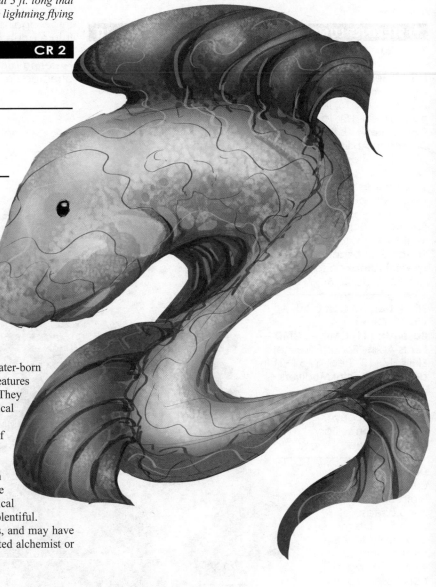

These strange, flying leeches are very similar to their water-born kin; they are roughly 3 feet long, thin grayish-blue creatures with tiny arcs of electricity playing over their bodies. They constantly twitch and writhe, as if receiving electrical stimulation throughout their bodies.

Schools of lightning lampreys drift along in the wake of storm clouds, feeding upon powerful electrical currents and lightning. They are not normally encountered away from electrical storms (some may sniff their way down from higher altitudes if lightning is actually striking the ground). However, they might be found in unusual magical environments where electrical discharges or lightning is plentiful.

Their bodies are extremely good electrical conductors, and may have uses in magical experiments (value 200 gp to an interested alchemist or wizard).

Credit
Original author Matthew J. Finch
Originally appearing in *The Spire of Iron and Crystal* (© Frog God Games/Matthew J. Finch, 2011)

Living Disease

A cloud rises before you like a dark smear in the air, the smell of death in its wake.

FESTERING LUNG — CR 10

XP 9,600
N Medium vermin (swarm)
Init +5; **Senses** lifesense 60 ft.; **Perception** +0

AC 15, touch 15, flat-footed 10 (+5 Dex)
hp 52 (15d8–15); fast healing 10
Fort +8; **Ref** +10; **Will** +5
Defensive Abilities evasion; **Immune** mind-affecting effects, weapon damage, swarm traits, vermin traits
Weaknesses swarm traits, vulnerability to *remove disease*

Speed fly 10 ft. (perfect)
Melee swarm (disease)
Space 5 ft.; **Reach** 0 ft.
Special Attacks disease, distraction (DC 16)

Str —, **Dex** 20, **Con** 8, **Int** —, **Wis** 10, **Cha** 1
Base Atk +11; **CMB** —; **CMD** —
Feats Ability Focus (disease)[B]
Skills Fly +13, Stealth +5 (+21 in darkness); **Racial Modifiers** +16 Stealth in darkness

Environment any
Organization solitary
Treasure none

Disease (Ex) Any creature whose space is occupied by the living disease at the end of its move is exposed to the form of disease of which the swarm is composed. Such a creature must succeed at a Fortitude save each round that it is in the swarm or take ability damage for that round as indicated under the disease type. There is no incubation period for this type of exposure and its method of delivery is irrelevant due to the sheer concentration of disease organisms present. Even after a creature leaves the area of a swarm, it must make the appropriate Fortitude save or continue to take ability damage each day as indicated by the disease. At this point two successful saving throws in a row indicate that the creature has fought off the disease and recovers, taking no more damage. However, the disease can be contracted again through regular exposure or another encounter with a living disease. Once a creature has made a successful saving throw against the disease of a living disease, it is immune to future bouts of disease of that particular living disease for 1 year.

Festering Lung: This infection gets into the lungs of the affected creature and begins to break down the respiratory system, producing choking and copious amounts of bloody phlegm. It saps the strength from the victim due to poor oxygenation and renders him unable to speak or make any vocal noises two days after contraction. Creatures that do not breathe are immune to festering lung.

Festering Lung: Swarm—inhaled; *save* DC 24 Fort; *onset* immediate; *frequency* 1/day; *effect* 1d4 Str damage and 1d4 Con damage; *cure* 2 consecutive saves. The save DC is Dexterity-based.

Evasion (Ex) Due to its composition of billions of highly resilient microscopic organisms, if it makes a Reflex saving throw against an attack that normally deals half damage on a successful save, a living disease instead takes no damage. It is identical to the rogue ability of the same name.

Lifesense (Ex) The overpowering drive to propagate itself gives a living disease the ability to notice and locate living creatures within 60 feet, just as if it possessed the blindsight ability.

Vulnerability to *Remove Disease* (Ex) If a *remove disease* is cast on a living disease or a victim currently in a space occupied by a living disease and the living disease fails a Fortitude save against the spell, it deals 5d10 points of damage to the living disease. A creature that has *remove disease* cast on it is not cured unless outside of the swarm's area when the spell is cast or unless the living disease was destroyed by the casting of the spell. Otherwise, an infected creature will require an additional *remove disease* upon leaving the living disease's space if it contracted the disease while within.

BLACK ROT — CR 16

XP 76,800
N Medium vermin (swarm)
Init +5; **Senses** lifesense 60 ft.; **Perception** +0

AC 15, touch 15, flat-footed 10 (+5 Dex)
hp 108 (24d8); fast healing 10
Fort +14; **Ref** +13; **Will** +8
Defensive Abilities evasion; **Immune** mind-affecting effects, weapon damage, swarm traits, vermin traits

Weaknesses swarm traits, vulnerability to *remove disease*

Speed fly 10 ft. (perfect)
Melee swarm (disease)
Space 5 ft.; **Reach** 0 ft.
Special Attacks disease, distraction (DC 22)

Str —, **Dex** 21, **Con** 10, **Int** —, **Wis** 10, **Cha** 1
Base Atk +18; **CMB** —; **CMD** —
Feats Ability Focus (disease)[B]
Skills Fly +13, Stealth +5 (+21 in darkness); **Racial Modifiers** +16 Stealth in darkness

Environment any
Organization solitary
Treasure none

Disease (Ex) *Black Rot:* This highly infectious disease affects the skin and muscles of the victim, creating an accelerated gangrenous process that turns the affected tissue black and eats it away. For every 4 points of Con damage sustained by the victim, a random limb is lost and can only be recovered by *regeneration* or similar magic. *Black Rot:* Swarm—contact; *save* DC 29 Fort; *onset* immediate; *frequency* 1/day; *effect* 1d6 Con damage, 1d6 Dex damage, and 1d3 Cha damage; *cure* 2 consecutive saves. The save DC is Dexterity-based.

Living diseases are swarms of microscopic organisms, harmful bacteria or viruses that have supernaturally gained limited sentience as a cohesive swarm under certain exceedingly foul or magical conditions. They seek out hosts through which to propagate their contagion. Though they are considered swarms, their individual components are so small as to be invisible to unaided sight, exponentially smaller than even Fine creatures, and they are thus considered one Medium creature. They are only visible at all due to the sheer number of individual organisms that comprise the swarm; literally billions of them make up a single living disease.

Living diseases offer no resistance to items or creatures entering their midst and cannot be physically felt. They make no sound whatsoever. A living disease in the dark is terrible indeed, as there is no indication it is present until its effects are first felt.

Living diseases neither see nor sleep. Their movements are by pure instinct, and they locate potential hosts with their lifesense. Because of their resilience and extremely high reproductive rate, the microorganisms of a living disease give it fast healing 10.

Though extremely rare, there are many different kinds of living diseases — potentially as many kinds as there are diseases. Two in particular are described here: festering lung and black rot.

A living disease seeks to surround any potential host it senses. It instinctively avoids undead, oozes, plants and constructs, which do not make suitable hosts for the spreading of disease. Unlike normal swarms, a living disease does not deal physical damage. Instead it exposes any creature whose space it occupies at the end of its move to its form of disease.

Credit

Original author Greg A. Vaughan
Originally appearing in *Slumbering Tsar* (© Frog God Games/ Greg A. Vaughan, 2012)

Living Monolith

This massive creature appears to be an amorphous column of flesh coated in a thick, bubbling slime. Several large maws litter its form, each filled with sharpened teeth. Many long tentacles whip and flail about its body.

LIVING MONOLITH	CR 13

XP 25,600
N Gargantuan ooze
Init –2; **Senses** blindsight 120 ft., tremorsense 120 ft.; **Perception** –5

AC 24, touch 4, flat-footed 24 (-2 Dex, +20 natural, –4 size)
hp 225 (18d8+144); regeneration 10 (fire)
Fort +14; **Ref** +4; **Will** +1
DR 10/—; **Immune** acid, electricity, ooze traits; **Resist** cold 20; **SR** 24

Speed 5 ft.
Melee 4 tentacles +20 (2d6+11 plus 2d6 acid and grab) or bite +20 (4d8+24 plus 2d6 acid; only against grabbed foe)
Space 20 ft.; **Reach** 20 ft.
Special Attacks spawn offspring, swallow whole (6d8 acid damage, AC 20, 20 hp)

Str 32, **Dex** 6, **Con** 26, **Int** —, **Wis** 1, **Cha** 1
Base Atk +13; **CMB** +28 (+32 grapple); **CMD** 36 (can't be tripped)

Environment underground
Organization solitary
Treasure standard

Acid (Ex) A living monolith secrets a digestive acid that dissolves organic material and metal quickly, but does not affect stone. Each time a creature suffers damage from a living monolith's acid, its clothing and armor take the same amount of damage from the acid. A DC 27 Reflex save prevents damage to clothing and armor. A metal or wooden weapon that strikes a living monolith takes 2d6 points of acid damage unless the weapon's wielder succeeds on a DC 27 Reflex save. If a living monolith remains in contact with a wooden or metal object for 1 full round, it inflicts 27 points of acid damage (no save) to the object. The save DCs are Constitution-based.

Spawn Offspring (Ex) Every 1d4 rounds, a living monolith spawns 1d6 crawling offspring from its form, but 1d6 of these are instantly destroyed or reabsorbed by the living monolith. (See the Crawling Offspring entry below.)

Tentacles (Ex) A living monolith can transfer a grabbed opponent from a tentacle to one of its mouths as a move action.

The living monolith, sometimes called a monolith of fecundity, is a slow-moving pillar of amorphous flesh dripping with slime. Along its gigantic bulk are several gaping mouths and writhing pseudopods. This loathsome being is usually brought forth by the summoning spells of clerics who worship perverse fertility deities.

At irregular intervals its flesh breaks open and instantly regenerates as the living monolith spawns twisted offspring that crawl and slither away from its progenitor. Some of these spawn are instantly disintegrated by the acidic slime dripping from the monolith or torn to pieces by pseudopods and ravenous mouths, but a few scuttle away and survive (see the crawling offspring entry).

A living monolith thrashes mindlessly at opponents with its tentacles. When disturbed, it constantly seeps its acidic slime which is as likely to destroy its crawling offspring as inflicting damage on opponents. An opponent unlucky enough to be grabbed by a flailing tentacle is shoved into one of the living monolith's maws and swallowed whole, subjected to the monster's deadly digestive acids.

Living Monolith (Crawling Offspring)

Crawling Offspring

This slime-covered humanoid lurches forward, its frame twisted, eyes bulging.

CRAWLING OFFSPRING	CR 5

XP 1,600
N Small aberration
Init +0; **Senses** blindsight 60 ft., darkvision 60 ft.; **Perception** +9

AC 16, touch 11, flat-footed 16 (+5 natural, +1 size)
hp 60 (8d8+16 plus 8); fast healing 2
Fort +6; **Ref** +2; **Will** +8

Speed 30 ft.
Melee slam +10 (1d3+4)
Special Attacks varies (see below)

Str 16, **Dex** 11, **Con** 14, **Int** 3, **Wis** 10, **Cha** 11
Base Atk +6; **CMB** +8; **CMD** 18
Feats Alertness, Great Fortitude, Iron Will, Toughness
Skills Climb +10, Perception +9

Environment any
Organization pack (4–6) or swarm (7–12)
Treasure none

Crawling offspring are mindless creatures spawned from a living monolith. There is great variety in the form and appearance of the crawling offspring; such as bulging eyes, flapping wings, writhing tentacles, slime-covered pseudopods, and so on.

Most crawling offspring are destroyed and re-absorbed by the living monolith they were spawned from, but those few that escape wander or crawl about seeking prey. A crawling offspring attempts to devour the nearest living creature it detects.

Each crawling offspring is unique; roll on the Crawling Offspring Features table to determine the special attack of each.

Crawling Offspring Features

Roll 1d6 to determine the crawling offspring's special ability.

1	Spit Acid (20-ft. line, 2d6 acid damage, Reflex DC 16 half)
2	Rotting Touch (1d3 Con damage)
3	Tentacle Attack (10-ft reach, 1d3+3 damage, in addition to slam attack)
4	Regeneration (5 [fire]; replaces fast healing)
5	Flight (fly 30 ft., average maneuverability)
6	No special feature

Lizard, Giant Forest

This giant lizard has brown and green markings on its body, a long, thick tail, and a blunt snout that opens to reveal a mouth full of strong, thick teeth.

GIANT FOREST LIZARD	CR 5

XP 1,600
N Large animal
Init +6; **Senses** low-light vision, scent; **Perception** +11

AC 19, touch 11, flat-footed 17 (+2 Dex, +8 natural, –1 size)
hp 68 (8d8+32)
Fort +12; **Ref** +8; **Will** +3

Speed 30 ft., climb 20 ft.
Melee bite +12 (2d6+9 plus poison)
Space 10 ft.; **Reach** 5 ft.

Str 23, **Dex** 15, **Con** 19, **Int** 2, **Wis** 12, **Cha** 10
Base Atk +6; **CMB** +13; **CMD** 25 (29 vs. trip)
Feats Great Fortitude, Improved Initiative, Skill Focus (Perception), Weapon Focus (bite)
Skills Acrobatics +6 (+14 jumping), Climb +18, Perception +11, Stealth +3 (+7 in undergrowth); **Racial Modifiers** +8 Acrobatics when jumping, +4 Stealth in undergrowth
SQ powerful leaper

Environment temperate forests
Organization solitary or pack (2–5)
Treasure none

Poison (Ex) Bite—injury; *save* DC 18 Fort; *frequency* 1/round for 6 rounds; *effect* 1d4 Dexterity damage; *cure* 2 saves. The save DC is Constitution-based.
Powerful Leaper (Ex) A giant forest lizard uses its Strength to modify Acrobatics checks made to jump, and it has a +8 racial bonus on Acrobatics checks made to jump.

Giant forest lizards are carnivorous animals that dwell in overgrown forests, making their lairs in hidden caves and passages. These creatures are highly territorial, nocturnal and spend most of the day sleeping in their lair or sunning themselves on large tree limbs where the sun breaks through the treetops. Giant forest lizards dine on other forest animals, consuming almost anything they find. When food is scarce, they scavenge as well. A typical giant forest lizard's territory covers several square miles.

A giant forest lizard is 9 feet long and weighs nearly 2,000 pounds. Its coloration and markings are browns and greens, allowing it to adapt and hide in the forests. These creatures mate but once a year with the female depositing up to four eggs in the lair. Eggs hatch within 3 months and young reach maturity within 10 months. Forest lizards can live to be 20 years old.

When hunting, a giant forest lizard perches within the trees on strong, overhanging limbs. When potential prey passes beneath it, it drops to the ground and attacks. Prey that is killed is carried back to its lair and eaten or saved for later consumption. In combat, or when warning other creatures that have entered its territory, the giant forest lizard vocalizes, emitting a deep, rolling hissing sound.

Lizard, Lava

This massive lizard is dark cherry red with a pale yellow underbelly.

LAVA LIZARD	CR 8

XP 4,800
N Large magical beast
Init +5; **Senses** darkvision 60 ft., low-light vision, scent;
Perception +11
Aura heat (10 ft., DC 18)

AC 20, touch 10, flat-footed 19 (+1 Dex, +10
natural, −1 size)
hp 94 (9d10+36 plus 9)
Fort +12; **Ref** +9; **Will** +5
Immune fire; **Resist** cold 20

Speed 30 ft., climb 20 ft., swim 20 ft.
Melee bite +14 (3d8+7 plus burn)
Space 10 ft.; **Reach** 5 ft.
Special Attacks burn (2d6, DC 18), heated flesh

Str 21, **Dex** 13, **Con** 19, **Int** 2, **Wis** 14, **Cha** 10
Base Atk +9; **CMB** +15; **CMD** 26 (30 vs. trip)
Feats Great Fortitude, Improved Initiative, Lightning Reflexes,
Skill Focus (Perception), Toughness[B], Weapon Focus (bite)
Skills Climb +18, Perception +11, Stealth +2, Swim +18
SQ lava affinity

Environment warm mountains
Organization solitary, pair, or band (3–8)
Treasure none

Heat Aura (Ex) A lava lizard radiates heat, and
any creature that starts its turn within 10 feet of
a lava lizard must succeed on a DC 18 Fortitude
save or take 1d6 points of fire damage. The save
DC is Constitution-based.
Heated Flesh (Ex) Any metal weapon
striking a lava lizard must succeed at
a DC 18 Fortitude save or take 3d6
points of fire damage. Wooden
weapons take double damage.
Damage caused to weapons in this
manner is not halved, but hardness
does help prevent some of the damage
dealt. Unarmed and natural attacks made
against the lava lizard deal 2d6 points of fire damage to the
attacker. The save DC is Constitution-based.
Lava Affinity (Ex) A lava lizard can breathe and swim while
submerged in lava and magma.

Lava lizards make their lairs in or near active volcanoes, spending
their days swimming in the boiling magma. These creatures have few
predators, save for some red dragons and fire giants. Lava lizards prefer
to hunt during the day and sustain themselves on a diet of large game
animals or whatever happens to wander close to their lair. Most prey is
killed and carried back to the lair to be devoured later. Lava lizards often
store their prey in magma pools as they prefer high temperature food.

Lava lizards are about 10 feet long and weigh around 600 pounds. Their
skin is always a shade of cherry red and their eyes are pale yellow. These
creatures reproduce once per year on average with the female laying 4
to 6 large reddish eggs. These eggs are usually tucked away beneath a
lava pool to not only incubate them, but also deter predators. Eggs hatch
within 60 days and young reach maturity with 3 years. Lava lizards live
about 100 years.

Lava lizards generally avoid combat unless provoked, threatened, or
hunting. In combat they assault their prey with their bite attempting to
incinerate it as quickly as possible. Lava lizards that are outmatched flee if
possible, seeking refuge in nearby magma pools or lava tubes where most
attackers dare not venture.

Lupin

This dog-headed humanoid has dirty, matted dark fur and appears slightly taller than the average human.

LUPIN	CR 2

XP 600
LE Medium humanoid (lupin)
Init +1; **Senses** darkvision 60 ft., scent; **Perception** +6

AC 16, touch 11, flat-footed 15 (+2 armor, +1 Dex, +2 natural, +1 shield)
hp 22 (4d8+4)
Fort +5; **Ref** +2; **Will** +1

Speed 30 ft.
Melee longsword +5 (1d8+2) and bite +5 (1d6+2)
Ranged longbow +4 (1d8/x3)

Str 15, **Dex** 12, **Con** 13, **Int** 10, **Wis** 11, **Cha** 12
Base Atk +3; **CMB** +5; **CMD** 16
Feats Alertness, Power Attack
Skills Perception +6, Sense Motive +2, Stealth +3, Survival +5 (+9 scent tracking); **Racial Modifiers** +4 Survival when tracking by scent
Languages Gnoll, Lupin

Environment temperate and warm plains or desert
Organization solitary, pair, hunting party (2–5 lupins and 1–2 dogs), band (10–100 adults plus 50% noncombatant children, 1 sergeant of 5th level per 20 adults, 1 leader of 6th–8th level, and 5–8 dogs or wolves), or tribe (20–200 plus 1 sergeant of 5th level per 20 adults, 1 or 2 lieutenants of 6th or 7th level, 1 leader of 8th–10th level, 7–12 dogs, and 4–7 wolves)
Treasure standard (leather armor, light wooden shield, longsword, longbow, 20 arrows, other treasure)

Lupins are dog-headed humanoids standing over 6 feet tall with grayish skin and dark, usually filthy and matted fur. These creatures have an excellent sense of smell, and their tracking ability is often times unmatched. Lupins are colorblind and see only in shades of gray.

These creatures are believed to be related to both gnolls and flinds though sages have never found a true link tying the races together. These canine humanoids are carnivorous nocturnal pack hunters and relish in the hunt, often toying with their prey before taking it down. Though savage by some standards, lupins are still considered to be more organized and civilized than their cousins the gnolls.

Lupin tribes form loose alliances with nearby tribes and settlements, sometimes offering protection to weaker tribes (such as those composed of goblins or kobolds) in exchange for gold, food, and anything else the tribe feels it needs. Lupins are generally on good terms with all the goblinoid races as well as minotaurs, orcs, and the occasional ogre or hill giant tribe. Human settlements sometimes form an alliance with a nearby lupin tribe as well; out of mutual need, or out of fear. The other humanoid races, dwarves, elves, gnomes, are generally treated with tolerance, but few alliances between lupins and these races are known to exist. Elves are often viewed as a weak race and, any such alliance between a lupin tribe and elven settlement is extremely shaky at best. Halflings are the single race the lupins detest (Sages are uncertain as to the exact reasons for this hatred). Halflings are killed on sight, carried back to the lupins' lair, and fed to the lupin pups. Other times, halflings are captured and hunted for sport by the lupins, and then fed to

the pups afterward. Halfling settlements when found are ravaged and burned to the ground. Halfling temples and holy grounds are desecrated and defaced, the priests of these places torn to shreds, their bodies littered about the ruined temples and grounds.

Lupins are savage and ferocious in battle, attacking with longswords and a vicious bite. Their battle tactics are well-organized and focused, usually concentrating on the single strongest opponent, and only moving to the next target, when that opponent falls. When overwhelmed and outnumbered, lupins resort to ambush and hit-and-run tactics. In large scale battles, lupins often employ gnolls and flinds (and occasionally, but rarely, goblins and kobolds) as shock troops.

Lupin leaders are generally rangers or fighters. Lupin females generally take the role of caregiver in a lupin tribe, staying out of battles and tending to the pups. Some however, seem more skilled in the magical arts than their male counterparts, and sometimes take up the path of the sorcerer. Clerics are highly regarded among lupin tribes and often serve as counselors to the tribal leaders. Religion among lupin tribes is scattered and generally varies from tribe to tribe. Lupins do not seem to have just one god they call their own. Each tribe pays homage to its own god, usually one of the arch-devils.

Lucifer, Belial, Geryon, Moloch, and Asmodeus seem to be the most prevalent.

Lurker Wraith

A diaphanous, almost translucent curtain blows on a nonexistent breeze towards you. It spreads its folds wide as it approaches as if to envelop you.

LURKER WRAITH	CR 10

XP 9,600
NE Large undead
Init +5; **Senses** darkvision 60 ft.; **Perception** +11

AC 18, touch 10, flat-footed 17 (+1 Dex, +8 natural, −1 size)
hp 112 (15d8+30 plus 15)
Fort +7; **Ref** +8; **Will** +9
Defensive Abilities amorphous, channel resistance +4; **DR** 10/silver and piercing or slashing; **Immune** undead traits
Weaknesses sunlight powerlessness, vulnerability to fire

Speed fly 40 ft. (average)
Melee buffet +20 (2d4+15 plus 1d6 Con drain and grab)
Space 10 ft.; **Reach** 5 ft.
Special Attacks create spawn, smother

Str 30, **Dex** 12, **Con** —, **Int** 6, **Wis** 11, **Cha** 14
Base Atk +11; **CMB** +22 (+26 grapple); **CMD** 33 (can't be tripped)
Feats Blind-Fight, Deceitful, Hover, Improved Initiative, Lightning Reflexes, Skill Focus (Perception), Skill Focus (Stealth), Toughness
Skills Bluff +8, Disguise +12 (+20 as curtain, wall hanging or textile), Fly +3, Perception +11, Stealth +25; **Racial Modifiers** +4 Stealth, +8 Disguise as curtain, wall hanging or textile

Environment any
Organization solitary or pair
Treasure none

Amorphous (Ex) Lurking wraiths are immune to precision damage (like sneak attacks) and critical hits, and can move through an area as small as one-quarter their space without squeezing or one-eighth their space when squeezing.
Constitution Drain (Su) Creatures hit by a lurker wraith's buffet attack must succeed on a DC 19 Fortitude save or take 1d6 points of Constitution drain. On each such successful attack, the lurker wraith gains 5 temporary hit points. The save DC is Charisma-based.
Create Spawn (Su) A humanoid slain by either a lurker wraith's Constitution drain or smother attack becomes a ghoul in 1d4 rounds. Spawn are not under the command of the lurker wraith (which typically ignores them), but they do instinctively protect their creator. They do not possess any of the abilities they had in life. A humanoid of 4 Hit Dice or more rises as a ghast, not a ghoul.
Smother (Ex) When a lurker wraith grapples a target, it continues its Constitution drain each round (though the victim is still allowed a save each round). In addition it forms an airtight seal around its prey. A grappled target cannot speak or cast spells with verbal components and must hold its breath (see "Suffocation" in Chapter 13 of the Pathfinder Roleplaying Game).
Sunlight Powerlessness (Ex) A lurker wraith caught in sunlight cannot attack and is staggered.

If there is an undead form of the aberrations known as lurkers, this is surely it. They have a gauzy appearance and resemble some thin cloth, though close inspection reveals they are quite durable and thick with a certain translucence. They often disguise themselves as tapestries or curtains in order to lure the unwary into their smothering embrace. Sometimes they roll themselves up to appear as innocuous bolts of cloth before unfurling and revealing the true horror. They tend to lurk in subterranean areas or within ruins where they avoid rays of direct sunlight.

A lurker wraith is about 10 feet long by 10 feet wide and approximately 1/4 inch thick. They weigh less than 50 pounds. Lurker wraiths typically disguise themselves as ordinary textiles and then try to attack prey with surprise by buffeting them and attempting to smother.

There are often a few stray ghouls lairing near where lurker wraiths dwell — past victims that will come to defend their creator.

Credit
Original author Greg A. Vaughan
Originally appearing in *Slumbering Tsar* (© Frog God Games/Greg A. Vaughan, 2012)

Lycanthrope, Werewolverine

Howling out of the taiga comes a ferocious humanoid creature covered in thick grey fur. Its hands are tipped in long claws.

WEREWOLVERINE (HUMAN FORM)   CR 3

XP 800
Human natural werewolverine barbarian 3 (*Pathfinder Roleplaying Game Core Rulebook*)
CN Medium humanoid (human, shapechanger)
Init +1; **Senses** low-light vision, scent; **Perception** +7

AC 13, touch 9, flat-footed 11 (+3 armor, +1 Dex, –2 rage, +1 shield)
hp 43 (3d12+12 plus 6)
Fort +7; **Ref** +2; **Will** +4
Defensive Abilities uncanny dodge

Speed 40 ft.
Melee battleaxe +8 (1d8+5/x3)
Ranged throwing axe +4 (1d6+5)
Special Attacks rage (10 rounds), rage power (intimidating glare)

Str 21, **Dex** 13, **Con** 18, **Int** 8, **Wis** 12, **Cha** 10
Base Atk +3; **CMB** +8; **CMD** 19
Feats Power Attack, Skill Focus (Intimidate), Toughness
Skills Climb +9, Intimidate +9, Perception +7, Survival +7
Languages Common
SQ change shape (human, hybrid, and wolverine; *polymorph*), fast movement, trap sense +1, lycanthropic empathy (badgers and wolverines)

Environment cold forests
Organization solitary, pair, family (3–6), pack (6–10), or troupe (11–20)
Treasure NPC gear (battleaxe, 2 daggers, 2 throwing axes, studded leather armor, small wooden shield, other gear)

WEREWOLVERINE (HYBRID FORM)   CR 3

XP 800
Human natural werewolverine barbarian 3 (*Pathfinder Roleplaying Game Core Rulebook*)
CN Medium humanoid (human, shapechanger)
Init +1; **Senses** low-light vision, scent; **Perception** +7

AC 17, touch 9, flat-footed 15 (+3 armor, +1 Dex, +4 natural, –2 rage, +1 shield)
hp 46 (3d12+15 plus 6)
Fort +8; **Ref** +2; **Will** +4
Defensive Abilities uncanny dodge; **DR** 10/silver

Speed 40 ft.
Melee battleaxe +9 (1d8+6/x3), or 2 claws +9 (1d6+6), bite +9 (1d4+6 plus curse of lycanthropy; DC 15)
Ranged throwing axe +4 (1d6+6)
Special Attacks rage (10 rounds), rage power (intimidating glare)

Str 23, **Dex** 13, **Con** 20, **Int** 8, **Wis** 12, **Cha** 10
Base Atk +3; **CMB** +8; **CMD** 19

Feats Power Attack, Skill Focus (Intimidate), Toughness
Skills Climb +12, Intimidate +9, Perception +7, Survival +7
Languages Common
SQ change shape (human, hybrid, and wolverine; *polymorph*), fast movement, trap sense +1, lycanthropic empathy (badgers and wolverines)

Rage (Ex) A werewolverine in hybrid or animal form that takes damage in combat flies into a rage on its next turn, clawing and biting madly until either it or its opponent is dead. The creature cannot end its rage voluntarily.

In their humanoid forms, werewolverines are wiry, muscular folk with broad shoulders and powerful hands. Their faces are almost always contorted into a twitchy sneer. Quick to anger and slow to calm, werewolverines are seemingly always on the brink of a powerful emotional outburst. When angered, a werewolverine screams and howls in a raspy voice that speaks of violent, primal rage.

Instinctively brutal, werewolverines make the ideal strong-arms for bandit gangs.

Note that the statistics presented here for werewolverines assume that the creatures are in their barbarian rage — if the creatures are encountered at another time, simply adjust their statistics accordingly.

Credit

Original author Nathan Douglas Paul
Originally appearing in *The Eamonvale Incursion* (© Necromancer Games, 2008)

Malkeen

This large cat resembles a brown-furred leopard.

MALKEEN	CR 6

XP 2,400
N Large magical beast
Init +6; **Senses** darkvision 60 ft., low-light
vision; **Perception** +10

AC 16, touch 12, flat-footed 13 (+2 Dex,
+1 dodge, +4 natural, −1 size)
hp 76 (8d10+32)
Fort +10; **Ref** +8; **Will** +4
Immune mind-affecting effects

Speed 40 ft.
Melee 2 claws +13 (1d6+5), bite +12 (1d8+5)
Space 10 ft.; **Reach** 5 ft.
Special Attacks mind blast, pounce, rake (2 claws +13,
1d6+5)

Str 21, **Dex** 15, **Con** 18, **Int** 6, **Wis** 14, **Cha** 12
Base Atk +8; **CMB** +14; **CMD** 27 (31 vs. trip)
Feats Dodge, Improved Initiative, Skill Focus (Perception),
Weapon Focus (claw)
Skills Acrobatics +11, Perception +10, Stealth +7 (+11 in
marshes), Swim +10; **Racial Modifiers** +4 Acrobatics, +4
Stealth (+8 in marshes)
Languages Common; telepathy 100 ft.

Environment temperate and warm marshes
Organization solitary or pair
Treasure standard

Mind Blast (Su) As a standard action, a malkeen can
deliver a massive blast of mental energy at a single
target within 50 feet. The target must succeed on
a DC 15 Will save or take 6d6 points of damage.
A malkeen can use this ability once every 1d6
rounds. The save DC is Charisma-based.

   Malkeens are intelligent, ferocious swamp cats that closely
resemble dark furred leopards. These creatures are extremely
territorial with the average malkeen's territory covering 10 square
miles or more. Creatures entering its territory are stalked and watched
from afar before the malkeen moves in to attack. Malkeens are generally
passive creatures and only attack if threatened or hungry. They are
carnivores and dine on creatures such as alligators, marsh reptiles, marsh
birds, and wild game.

   Malkeens reach lengths of 12 feet or more and weigh up to 5,500
pounds. Malkeens can live for up to 50 years.

   Malkeens are ambush hunters and sneak up on their prey before
lunging to attack. These creatures almost always open combat with their
mind blast attack, attempting to kill or disable their opponent as quickly
as possible. After that, opponents left standing are assaulted by claws and
bites.

Mandrake, Deadly

This creature appears as a tiny humanoid, brownish-green in color with a large flowering plant growing from its head.

DEADLY MANDRAKE	CR 2

XP 600
N Tiny plant
Init +4; **Senses** low-light vision, tremorsense 60 ft.; **Perception** +7

AC 17, touch 16, flat-footed 13 (+4 Dex, +1 natural, +2 size)
hp 16 (3d8+3)
Fort +4; **Ref** +5; **Will** +2
DR 5/cold iron; **Immune** plant traits; **SR** 13

Speed 30 ft., burrow 10 ft.
Melee 2 claws +8 (1d2–2)
Space 1/2 ft.; **Reach** 0 ft.
Special Attacks death scream
Spell-Like Abilities (CL 6th):
At will—*dancing lights, ghost sound* (DC 13), *prestidigitation* (DC 13)
3/day—*lesser confusion* (DC 14), *hypnotism* (DC 14)
1/day—*hallucinatory terrain* (DC 17), *sleep* (DC 14)

Str 6, **Dex** 18, **Con** 13, **Int** 10, **Wis** 13, **Cha** 16
Base Atk +2; **CMB** +4; **CMD** 12
Feats Alertness, Weapon Finesse
Skills Acrobatics +5, Escape Artist +5, Knowledge (nature) +1, Perception +7, Perform (sing) +4, Sense Motive +3, Stealth +16 (+24 in vegetation); **Racial Modifiers** +8 in vegetation
Languages Common, Sylvan

Environment temperate forests
Organization solitary or grove (2–6)
Treasure standard

Death Scream (Su) Once per minute, a deadly mandrake may scream as a full-round action. The scream lasts until the beginning of its next turn. All creatures within 40 feet of the deadly mandrake when it begins its scream, as well as those that end their turn within the area, must succeed on a DC 14 Fortitude save. (This save is only required once per scream.) Creatures under the effects of a fear effect take a –2 penalty on this save. Creatures that make their save are sickened for 1d2 rounds. Those that fail their save take 20 points of damage. If a screaming mandrake is damaged during a scream, it must make a Will save (DC 15 + damage taken) to maintain the scream; otherwise it ends. This is a sonic death effect. The save DC is Charisma-based.

Deadly mandrakes are mischievous plant creatures believed to be part plant and part fey. They relish in playing tricks on those passing through their domain. These tricks are always more playful than harmful, at least to the deadly mandrake. Most such tricks take the form of lights or weird sounds meant to distract and confuse travelers.

Deadly mandrakes sustain themselves on a diet of tree bark, leaves, and berries, and are most active during the day. At night they burrow into the ground to rest. Often times, a deadly mandrake burrows just far enough into the ground to cover its body, leaving the flower on top of its head exposed. Little else is known of these creatures thus far.

Deadly mandrakes, despite their name, are generally inoffensive unless disturbed. If disturbed or forced into battle, deadly mandrakes use their death scream immediately in an attempt to end the confrontation as quickly as possible. Creatures that resist are subjected to *sleep, lesser confusion*, or *hypnotism*. They can attack with their claws if needed, but rarely do so.

Any deadly mandrake killed has a 1% chance of returning in 1d4 days as a mandragora. If the deadly mandrake's body is doused with demon ichor (from a demon CR 6 or above), or a deadly mandrake is killed by a demon CR 6 or above, the chance rises to 10%. Using a deadly mandrake in the alchemical creation of a mandragora lowers the Craft (alchemy) DC from 25 to 20. (See the *Pathfinder Roleplaying Game Bestiary 2* "Mandragora", for details on the mandragora and the creation of a mandragora.)

Megaswarm, Dire Rat

A squirming horde of vicious rats the size of small dogs streams forward. They have coarse, spiky fur, feral eyes, and jagged, yellowed teeth. They surge ahead in a roiling mass of filth and stench.

DIRE RAT MEGASWARM   CR 5

XP 1,600
N Small animal (megaswarm)
Init +7; **Senses** low-light vision, scent; **Perception** +11

AC 14, touch 14, flat-footed 11 (+3 Dex, +1 size)
hp 52 (8d8+8 plus 8)
Fort +9; **Ref** +9; **Will** +3
Defensive Abilities half damage from piercing weapons

Speed 40 ft., climb 20 ft., swim 20 ft.
Melee swarm (2d6 plus disease)
Space 10 ft.; **Reach** 0 ft.
Special Attacks disease, distraction (DC 15)

Str 10, **Dex** 17, **Con** 13, **Int** 2, **Wis** 13, **Cha** 4
Base Atk +6; **CMB** —; **CMD** —
Feats Great Fortitude, Improved Initiative, Skill Focus (Perception), Toughness
Skills Climb +11, Perception +11, Stealth +14, Swim +11; **Racial Modifiers** uses Dex to modify Climb and Swim

Environment any urban
Organization solitary, pack (2–4 megaswarms), infestation (7–12 megaswarms)
Treasure none

Disease (Ex) *Filth fever*: Swarm—injury; *save* DC 15 Fort; *onset* 1d3 days; *frequency* 1/day; *effect* 1d3 Dex damage and 1d3 Con damage; *cure* 2 consecutive saves. The save DC is Constitution-based.

Megaswarm Traits (Ex) Megaswarms are not so called because of the size of the swarm but rather the size of the creatures that compose the swarm. Unlike normal swarms, megaswarms are composed of Small creatures which are usually a megafauna version of a normal swarm and otherwise behave in a swarmlike manner. There are usually around 100 creatures in a megaswarm. The net effect is that they take only half damage from piercing weapons but take normal damage from other weapons. In addition when the swarm is reduced to 0 hit points or lower and breaks up, unless the damage was dealt by area-affecting attacks, then 2d6 surviving members of the megaswarm continue their attack, though now only as individual creatures. Otherwise, a megaswarm conforms to all of the other swarm traits as described in the *Pathfinder Roleplaying Game Bestiary*.

Much like a swarm of ordinary rats, a dire rat swarm is composed of a teeming mass of disease-ridden dire rats intent on feeding on whatever

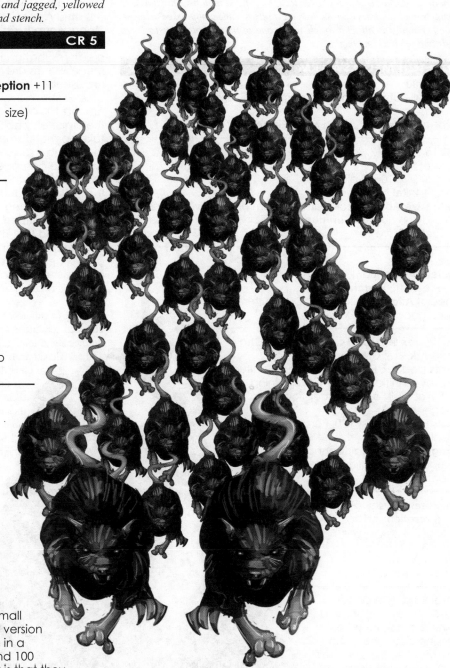

they can catch. A dire rat swarm usually exists in abandoned ruins or city dumps where there is a plentiful food supply and a lack of significant predators.

A dire rat swarm seeks to overrun and attack any warm-blooded prey it encounters. It typically ignores undead and other creatures that are not warm-blooded.

Credit
Original author Greg A. Vaughan
Originally appearing in *Slumbering Tsar* (© Frog God Games/ Greg A. Vaughan, 2012)

Megaswarm, Dretch

A roiling mass of rubbery skin and flailing limbs surges towards you. Demonic eyes stare at you above slack, fang-filled mouths. This horde is comprised of small creatures with pale, hairless hide compressed so close together that it is difficult to tell where one of these rabid monstrosities ends and the next one begins.

DRETCH MEGASWARM	CR 12

XP 19,200
CE Small outsider (chaotic, demon, evil, extraplanar, megaswarm)
Init +4; **Senses** darkvision 60 ft.; **Perception** +25

AC 15, touch 12, flat-footed 13 (+1 dodge, +3 natural, +1 size)
hp 136 (16d10+32 plus 16)
Fort +14; **Ref** +7; **Will** +12
Defensive Abilities half damage from piercing weapons; **DR** 5/cold iron or good; **Immune** electricity, poison; **Resist** acid 10, cold 10, fire 10

Speed 20 ft.
Melee swarm (6d6)
Space 10 ft.; **Reach** 0 ft.
Special Attacks distraction (DC 20), feral rage, smite good

Str 12, **Dex** 10, **Con** 14, **Int** 5, **Wis** 11, **Cha** 11
Base Atk +16; **CMB** —; **CMD** —
Feats Dodge[B], Endurance, Great Fortitude, Improved Initiative, Iron Will, Lightning Reflexes, Skill Focus (Perception), Stealthy, Toughness
Skills Escape Artist +20, Perception +25, Stealth +23
Languages Abyssal (cannot speak); telepathy 100 ft. (limited to Abyssal-speaking targets)

Environment any (Abyss)
Organization solitary, pack (2–4 megaswarms), infestation (7–12 megaswarms)
Treasure none

Feral Rage (Ex) Dretch megaswarms attack in a mindless mob intent only tearing apart those that fall into their clutches. This frenzy prevents them from using any of their regularly-available spell-like or summoning abilities. However, the wild abandon of their attack allows them to deal 6d6 points of damage to any creature whose space they occupy at the end of their move rather than the 4d6 typical for a swarm of their HD. This ability is lost if the swarm is broken up.

Megaswarm Traits (Ex) Megaswarms are not so called because of the size of the swarm but rather the size of the creatures that compose the swarm. Unlike normal swarms, megaswarms are composed of Small creatures which are usually a megafauna version of a normal swarm and otherwise behave in a swarmlike manner. There are usually around 100 creatures in a megaswarm. The net effect is that they take only half damage from piercing weapons but take normal damage from other weapons. In addition when the swarm is reduced to 0 hit points or lower and breaks up, unless the damage was dealt by area-affecting attacks, then 2d6 surviving members of the megaswarm continue their attack, though now only as individual creatures. Otherwise, a megaswarm conforms to all of the other swarm traits as described in the *Pathfinder RPG Bestiary*.

Smite Good (Su) The collective chaos and evil concentrated in the existence of a dretch megaswarm allows the swarm deal extra damage equal to its HD (+16) once per day against a good foe. This ability is lost if the swarm is broken up.

The lowly dretch are the most moblike of the demons and in certain crowded conditions actually develop a pack mentality and form a swarm. In their rabid mob, dretch swarms lose their ability to communicate with others telepathically, though they can still receive the telepathic commands of other demons to guide them in their attacks.

If the swarm breaks up, then surviving dretches continue their attacks, though now as individual creatures regaining their normal abilities and tactics (see *Pathfinder Roleplaying Game Bestiary*) and losing their feral rage.

Like individual dretches, dretch megaswarms rely on their sheer numbers when attacking. Unlike individuals, though, megaswarms are not cowardly and attack in a maddened frenzy regardless of the damage they are taking or the stoutness of the adversity. Their own mob mentality prods them on so that the commanding presence of a more powerful demon is not required to motivate them.

A dretch megaswarm's natural attacks are treated as chaotic-aligned and evil-aligned for the purpose of overcoming damage reduction.

Credit
Original author Greg A. Vaughan Originally appearing in *Slumbering Tsar* (© Frog God Games/ Greg A. Vaughan, 2012)

Mimic, Undead

Two sinewy tentacles sprout from what appears to be an ancient and slime-covered chest.

UNDEAD MIMIC	CR 6

XP 2,400
NE Medium undead (shapechanger)
Init +5; **Senses** darkvision 60 ft.; **Perception** +15

AC 17, touch 11, flat-footed 16 (+1 Dex, +6 natural)
hp 59 (7d8+21 plus 7)
Fort +5; **Ref** +5; **Will** +7
Immune acid, undead traits

Speed 10 ft.
Melee slam +11 (1d8+7 plus adhesive)
Special Attacks constrict (1d8+7), soul drain, weeping discharge

Str 21, **Dex** 12, **Con** —, **Int** 12, **Wis** 14, **Cha** 16
Base Atk +5; **CMB** +10; **CMD** 21 (can't be tripped)
Feats Improved Initiative, Lightning Reflexes, Skill Focus (Perception), Toughness[B], Weapon Focus (slam)
Skills Climb +15, Disguise +13 (+33 when mimicking objects), Knowledge (dungeoneering) +8, Perception +15, Stealth +11; **Racial Modifiers** +20 Disguise when mimicking objects
Languages Common
SQ mimic object

Environment any
Organization solitary
Treasure incidental

Adhesive (Ex) An undead mimic exudes a thick slime that acts as a powerful adhesive, holding fast any creatures or items that touch it. An adhesive-covered undead mimic automatically grapples any creature it hits with its slam attack. Opponents so grappled cannot get free while the undead mimic is alive without removing the adhesive first. A weapon that strikes an adhesive-coated undead mimic is stuck fast unless the wielder succeeds on a DC 18 Reflex save. A successful DC 18 Strength check is needed to pry off a stuck weapon. Strong alcohol or *universal solvent* dissolves the adhesive, but the undead mimic can still grapple normally. An undead mimic can dissolve its adhesive at will, and the substance breaks down 5 rounds after the creature is destroyed. The save DC is Strength-based.
Mimic Object (Ex) An undead mimic can assume the general shape of any Medium object, such as a massive chest, a stout bed, or a door. The creature cannot substantially alter its size, though. An undead mimic's body is hard and has a rough texture, no matter what appearance it might present. An undead mimic gains a +20 racial bonus on Disguise checks when imitating an object in this manner. Disguise is always a class skill for an undead mimic.
Soul Drain (Su) An undead mimic can take a move action to devour the soul of an adjacent creature it has recently (within the last hour) killed. A creature whose soul is drained cannot be restored to life until the undead mimic containing its soul is destroyed. Each time an undead mimic drains a soul it gains 1d8 temporary hit points and gains a +2 bonus to Strength for 1 hour. These bonuses stack with themselves. After 24 hours, the soul is completely devoured, and the deceased creature cannot be brought back to life

via *raise dead* (*resurrection* and more powerful effects work normally though the undead mimic must still be destroyed before this magic works).
Weeping Discharge (Ex) An undead mimic constantly leaks and oozes its foul adhesive in a 20-foot-radius area around its body. The area quickly becomes coated in the fluids and is considered difficult terrain. Undead mimics are not hampered by this secretion (their own or that of another undead mimic). The slimy coating lasts for 1 hour before becoming inert.

Undead mimics are believed to be the result of experimentation on mimics by insane necromancers. What possessed them to create an undead version of a truly horrid creature is beyond most scholars' comprehension.

Undead mimics, unlike standard mimics, are evil, poisoned by the necromantic magic that created them. They desire flesh and blood and dine on the souls of those they slay.

Undead mimics do not associate with standard mimics (or most other creatures for that matter). Often times, an undead mimic is found in the employ of an evil necromancer, possibly the one that created it.

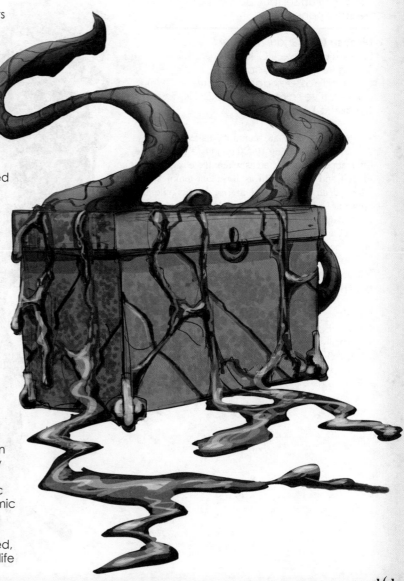

Monkey, Ghoul

Filthy, emaciated beasts, ghoul monkeys are depraved examples of harmless animals saturated in evil.

GHOUL MONKEY	CR 1

XP 400
CE small undead
Init +2; **Senses** darkvision 60 ft.; Perception +7

AC 15, touch 13, flat-footed 13 (+2 Dex, +2 natural, +1 size)
hp 13 (2d8+4)
Fort +2; **Ref** +2; **Will** +5
Immune undead traits

Speed 30 ft., climb 30 ft.
Melee bite +4 (1d2+1 plus disease) and 2 claws +4 (1d2+1 plus disease)

Str 12, **Dex** 15, **Con** —, **Int** 10, **Wis** 14, **Cha** 14
Base Atk +1; **CMB** +1; **CMD** 13
Feats Weapon Finesse
Skills Acrobatics +4, Climb +14, Perception +7, Stealth +11

Environment warm jungles
Organization solitary, pair, or pack (4–12)
Treasure none

Disease (Su) *Ghoul Monkey Fever*: Bite—injury; *save* DC 13 Fort; *onset* 1 day; *frequency* 1/day; *effect* 1d2 Con and 1d2 Dex damage; *cure* 2 consecutive saves. The save DC is Charisma-based.

Ghoul monkeys are cunning, undead monkeys 2–3 feet tall, weighing 10–20 pounds. These monkeys often appear in jungle areas where there is great residue of evil and chaos, such as forgotten temples or altars where dead monkeys might rise in this vile form of undeath. Unlike "human-type" ghouls, their bite does not cause paralysis.

They extremely vulnerable to holy water (2d6 damage) and to being turned (no channel resistance).

Ghoul monkeys lose the social drive of normal monkeys, but occasionally group together when the draw of evil is powerful enough.

Credit
Original author Scott Casper
Originally appearing in *Jungle Ruins of Madaro-Shanti* (© Frog God Games, 2010)

Monkey, Spire

The Spire Monkey is a two-headed, six-armed monkey that lives on roofs (spires and minarets are preferred) and high in the treetops. In some tropical countries they are tolerated in cities as messengers of the gods, and roam temples with impunity.

SPIRE MONKEY	CR 1/4

XP 100
N Tiny animal
Init +2; **Senses** low-light vision; **Perception** +5

AC 14, touch 14, flat-footed 12 (+2 Dex, +2 size)
hp 4 (1d8)
Fort +2; **Ref** +4; **Will** +1

Speed 30 ft., climb 30 ft.
Melee 2 claws +4 melee (1d3–1) and bite –1 (1d3–1)
Space 2–1/2 ft.; **Reach** 0 ft.

Str 8, **Dex** 15, **Con** 10, **Int** 2, **Wis** 12, **Cha** 5
Base Atk +0; **CMB** –3; **CMD** 9
Feats Weapon Finesse
Skills Acrobatics +10, Climb +10, Perception +5;
Racial Modifiers +8 Acrobatics, uses Dex for Climb checks

Environment warm jungles
Organization solitary, pair, or clan (3–14)
Treasure none

Omnivorous and foul-tempered, spire monkeys race from rooftop to rooftop and steal food (and occasionally loose coins or trinkets) from the streets below. Spire monkeys attack by clawing, as well as by throwing rocks or other small objects (such as roof tiles), and can divide their attacks between two opponents. They can climb as fast as they can run, and leap from tree to tree or building to building.

Credit

Original author Scott Wylie Roberts, "Myrystyr"; Pathfinder conversion by Skeeter Green
Originally appearing in *Jungle Ruins of Madaro-Shanti*
(© Frog God Games, 2010)

Mordnaissant

Floating before you is a horrid, shriveled human fetus nested within a translucent sphere of dark energy. Its jet-black eyes glitter with intensity as it twitches and spasms slightly, as if in great pain.

MORDNAISSANT	CR 7

XP 3,200
NE Tiny undead
Init +6; **Senses** darkvision 60 ft., lifesense; **Perception** +18

AC 20, touch 20, flat-footed 18 (+6 deflection, +2 Dex, +2 size,)
hp 94 (9d8+54)
Fort +9; **Ref** +5; **Will** +10
Defensive Abilities channel resistance +2, shield of agony; **Immune** undead traits

Speed 5 ft. (cannot run), fly 50 ft. (perfect)
Melee 2 claws +10 (1d2–4)
Ranged *lash of fury* +11/+6
Space 2–1/2 ft.; **Reach** 0 ft. (30 ft. with *lash*)
Special Attacks death curse, lash of fury, pain wail

Str 3, **Dex** 14, **Con** —, **Int** 7, **Wis** 18, **Cha** 23
Base Atk +6; **CMB** +6; **CMD** 18
Feats Ability Focus (lash of fury), Improved Initiative, Skill Focus (Perception), Weapon Finesse, Weapon Focus (ray)
Skills Fly +19, Perception +18, Stealth +21

Environment any
Organization solitary, twins, or litter (3–8)
Treasure none

Death Curse (Su) As a final cruel jest to the individual that puts a mordnaissant out of its misery, the slayer must make a DC 20 Will save or suffer from a terrible curse that reduces all subsequent experience points awarded by 50%. The save DC is Charisma-based.
Lash of Fury (Su) The mordnaissant can lash out with its negative energy powers and directly attack the vitality of living creatures, in the form of a twisting stream of black energy. The mordnaissant must make a ranged touch attack against its target as an attack action. If the ray hits, the victim must make a DC 22 Fortitude save for half damage or duration, depending on the specific effect chosen by the mordnaissant. The save DC is Charisma-based. The *lash of fury* has a range of 30 ft. with no range increment. The mordnaissant can pick from three possible lashes; it must make its choice prior to rolling the attack. The three options are: *whip the flesh* (as *inflict moderate wounds*, 2d8+9 damage), *whip the mind* (1d4 points of Intelligence damage), or *whip the soul* (stun 1d4+1 rounds). A critical hit doubles the damage rolled or the duration, in the case of *whip the soul*.
Lifesense (Su) A mordnaissant notices and locates living creatures within 60 ft., just as if it possessed the blindsight ability.
Pain Wail (Su) As a swift action, the mordnaissant can produce a terrible wailing sound that reflects the pain it experiences every moment of its existence. All living creatures within 20 ft. must make a DC 20 Will save or be dazed for one round. For every 20 points of damage the mordnaissant takes, the save DC increases by +1.
Shield of Agony (Su) A mordnaissant harnesses the pain of its existence to shield it. It adds its Charisma modifier as a deflection bonus to its AC and CMD.

Occasionally when a gravid woman dies violently in a place infused with unholy or negative energies, the unborn child within her does not perish, but instead continues to grow, vitalized by dark power, until it is capable of clawing its way free from its dead mother. This horrible creature, known as a mordnaissant, lives an existence of eternal pain, loneliness and suffering, relived only by its ability to inflict harm on those around it. Mordnaissants avoid bright light if they can, though they suffer no ill effects from it.

Credit
Originally appearing in *Rappan Athuk Reloaded* (© Necromancer Games, 2006)

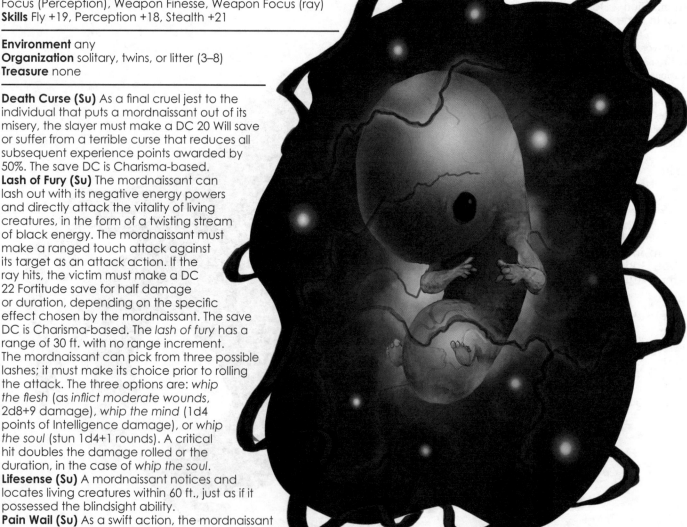

Mummy, Asp

This humanoid is wrapped in loose-fitting and dirty bandages. Clutched in each powerful fist and wrapped around the creature's arms is a long black snake. Several more snakes slither in and out of its bandages and across the creature's body.

ASP MUMMY	CR 8

XP 4,800
LE Medium undead
Init +0; **Senses** darkvision 60 ft.; **Perception** +21
Aura despair (30 ft., paralyzed for 1d4 rounds; DC 18 Will negates)

AC 22, touch 10, flat-footed 22 (+12 natural)
hp 85 (10d8+40)
Fort +6; **Ref** +3; **Will** +11
DR 5/—; **Immune** undead traits
Weaknesses vulnerability to fire

Speed 30 ft.
Melee slam +16 (2d6+8 plus mummy rot), snakes +10 (1d6+8 plus poison)
Special Attacks asp storm, writhing snakes

Str 26, **Dex** 10, **Con** —, **Int** 8, **Wis** 15, **Cha** 17
Base Atk +7; **CMB** +15; **CMD** 25
Feats Iron Will, Power Attack, Skill Focus (Perception), Toughness, Weapon Focus (slam)
Skills Intimidate +16, Perception +21, Stealth +17; **Racial Modifiers** +4 Stealth
Languages Common

Environment any
Organization solitary, pair, or court (3–6)
Treasure standard

Asp Storm (Su) Once per day, as a standard action, an asp mummy can call down a deluge of poisonous asps. The rain of asps functions as a venomous snake swarm (see below).
Despair (Su) All creatures within a 30-foot radius that see an asp mummy must make a DC 18 Will save or be paralyzed by fear for 1d4 rounds. Whether or not the save is successful, that creature cannot be affected again by the same asp mummy's despair ability for one day. This is a paralysis and a mind-affecting fear affect. The save DC is Charisma-based.
Mummy Rot (Su) Curse and disease—slam; *save* DC 18 Fort; *onset* 1 minute; *frequency* 1/day; *effect* 1d6 Con and 1d6 Cha; *cure* —. Mummy rot is both a curse and disease and can only be cured if the curse is first removed, at which point the disease can be magically removed. Even after the curse element of mummy rot is lifted, a creature suffering from it cannot recover naturally over time. Anyone casting a conjuration (healing) spell on the afflicted creature must succeed on a DC 20 caster level check, or the spell is wasted and the healing has no effect. Anyone who dies from mummy rot turns to dust and cannot be raised without a *resurrection* or greater magic. The save DC is Charisma-based.
Poison (Ex) Snake Bite—injury; *save* DC 20 Fort; *frequency* 1/round for 6 rounds; *effect* 1d3

Con damage; *cure* 2 consecutive saves. The save DC is Charisma-based and includes a +2 racial bonus.
Writhing Snakes (Ex) When a creature adjacent to an asp mummy makes a melee attack against it, that creature must succeed on a DC 18 Reflex save or be subjected to the asp mummy's poison as the many snakes slithering in and out of the its bandages spring and bite. The save DC is Charisma-based.

Similar in many respects to standard mummies, asp mummies are created to guard tombs of regal kings and nobles. Some believe these creatures even have a spark of the divine mixed in with their creation and are appointed by the gods themselves to watch over their favored followers. Asp mummies are known to be favored as guardians among the followers of Set.

The creation of an asp mummy follows the same procedure as a standard mummy, save that many small asps are placed into the hollowed corpse along with the herbs and flowers.

Asp Swarm

The statistics for the asp swarm are taken from the *Pathfinder Roleplaying Game Bestiary 3* (Venomous Snake Swarm entry). See that book for more information.

ASP SWARM	CR 4

XP 1,200
N Tiny animal (swarm)
Init +7; **Senses** low-light vision, scent; **Perception** +13

AC 17, touch 15, flat-footed 14 (+3 Dex, +2 natural, +2 size)
hp 37 (5d8+15)
Fort +7; **Ref** +9; **Will** +2
Defensive Abilities swarm traits

Speed 20 ft., climb 20 ft., swim 10 ft.
Melee swarm (1d6 plus distraction and poison)
Space 10 ft.; **Reach** 0 ft.
Special Attacks distraction (DC 15)

Str 9, **Dex** 16, **Con** 17, **Int** 1, **Wis** 12, **Cha** 2
Base Atk +3; **CMB** +4; **CMD** 13 (can't be tripped)
Feats Improved Initiative, Lightning Reflexes, Skill Focus (Perception)
Skills Acrobatics +7 (+3 when jumping), Climb +15, Perception +13, Stealth +19, Swim +11; **Racial Modifiers** +4 Perception, +4 Stealth; uses Dex to modify Climb and Swim

Environment any
Organization solitary, nest (2-4 swarms), or knot (5-7 swarms)
Treasure none

Poison (Ex) Swarm—injury; *save* DC 17 Fort; *frequency* 1/round for 6 rounds; *effect* 1d3 Con damage; *cure* 2 consecutive saves. The save DC is Constitution-based and includes a +2 racial bonus.

Naga, Death

A death naga is an undead snake covered in rotting or tattered scales flowing down its sinuous body from its humanoid head. A horrible stench emanates from the naga's snake body as its tattered skin is a husk containing rotted organs and entrails. Their eyes are missing, hollow voids in their female faces. A few lack flesh completely and appear as skeletal snakes with leering skull heads. Many have loose vertebrae jutting from the tips of their tails to create bone rattles.

DEATH NAGA	CR 12

XP 19,200
LE Large undead
Init +3; **Senses** darkvision 60 ft.; **Perception** +17

AC 24, touch 18, flat-footed 16 (+4 deflection, +3 Dex, +1 dodge, +7 natural, −1 size)
hp 85 (12d8+48)
Fort +8; **Ref** +9; **Will** +11
Defensive Abilities infernal blessing; **Immune** undead immunities

Speed 40 ft.
Melee bite +15 (1d8+4), sting +12 (2d4+4 plus poison)
Space 10 ft.; **Reach** 5 ft. (10 ft. with sting)
Special Attacks atrophic breath (DC 22)
Spells Known (CL 9th; melee touch +12, ranged touch +11):
4th (5/day)—*greater invisibility, stoneskin*
3rd (7/day)—*displacement, haste, lightning bolt* (DC 17)
2nd (7/day)—*cat's grace, command undead, scorching ray, web*
1st (7/day)—*mage armor, magic missile, ray of enfeeblement* (DC 15), *shield, silent image*
0 (At will)—*daze* (DC 15), *detect magic, ghost sound, light, mage hand, open/close, ray of frost, read magic*

Str 19, **Dex** 17, **Con** —, **Int** 16, **Wis** 17, **Cha** 19
Base Atk +9; **CMB** +14; **CMD** 32 (can't be tripped)
Feats Ability Focus (atrophic breath), Alertness, Combat Casting, Dodge, Eschew Materials[B], Lightning Reflexes, Stealthy
Skills Bluff +13, Diplomacy +13, Escape Artist +17, Intimidate +13, Knowledge (arcana) +15, Perception +17, Sense Motive +17, Spellcraft +15, Stealth +17
Languages Common, Infernal

Environment any underground
Organization solitary or nest (2–4)
Treasure standard

Atrophic Breath (Su) Once every 1d4 rounds, death nagas can blast opponents with a 60-ft. cone of deteriorating negative energy. The blast deals 12d6 points of unholy and negative energy damage (half of each). In addition, those within the cone gain one negative level. A Reflex DC 22 save halves the damage and prevents the negative level. Undead remain unharmed within the cone but gain 2d4x5 temporary hit points for 1 hour. The save DC is Charisma-based.

Infernal Blessing (Su) A death naga adds her Charisma modifier as a deflection bonus to her armor class.

Naga Venin Poison (Ex) Sting—injury; *save* DC 20 Fort; *frequency* 1 round (2d4 rounds); *effect* 1d2 Constitution damage; *cure* 2 consecutive saves.

Spells Death nagas cast spells as 9th-level sorcerers with access to the divine domains of Death and Destruction as sorcerer spells.

Death nagas are what remains of dark or spirit nagas slain by powerful negative energy. It is unknown why or how these nagas return as undead versions of their former selves. They often dominate ruins and remote regions using zombies and skeleton minions. Death nagas often ally themselves with powerful undead. Death nagas speak Common and any languages known in life.

Credit

Original author Gary Schotter & Jeff Harkness
Originally appearing in *Splinters of Faith Adventure 10: Remorse of Life* (© Frog God Games/ Gary Schotter & Jeff Harkness, 2011)

Naga, Ha-Naga

This enormous snake-like creature has the head of a gigantic humanoid.

HA-NAGA	CR 16

XP 76,800
CE Huge aberration
Init +10; **Senses** darkvision 60 ft., *see invisibility*; **Perception** +35

AC 31, touch 15, flat-footed 24 (+6 Dex, +1 dodge, +16 natural, −2 size)
hp 250 (20d8+160)
Fort +14; **Ref** +14; **Will** +20
DR 10/magic; **Immune** charm, sleep; **Resist** cold 20, fire 20; **SR** 27

Speed 50 ft., fly 80 ft. (good)
Melee bite +21 (2d8+8), sting +21 (1d8+8 plus poison), tail slap +19 (2d6+4 plus grab)
Space 15 ft.; **Reach** 10 ft.
Special Attacks charming gaze, constrict (2d6+8), poison
Spell-Like Abilities (CL 15th):
Constant—*see invisibility*
3/day—*plane shift* (self plus willing targets only)
Spells Known (CL 15th; melee touch +21, ranged touch +19):
7th (5/day)—*finger of death* (DC 24), *prismatic spray* (DC 24)
6th (7/day)—*chain lightning* (DC 23), *summon monster VI*, *true seeing*
5th (7/day)—*baleful polymorph* (DC 22), *feeblemind* (DC 22), *symbol of sleep* (DC 22), *teleport* (DC 22)
4th (7/day)—*bestow curse* (DC 21), *fear* (DC 21), *greater invisibility*, *wall of fire*
3rd (8/day)—*dispel magic*, *hold person* (DC 20), *magic circle against good*, *sleet storm*
2nd (8/day)—*blindness-deafness* (DC 19), *blur*, *gust of wind* (DC 19), *invisibility*, *shatter* (DC 19)
1st (8/day)—*chill touch* (DC 18), *mage armor*, *magic missile*, *protection from good* (DC 18), *true strike*
0 (at will)—*acid splash*, *bleed* (DC 17), *daze* (DC 17), *detect magic*, *flare* (DC 17), *message*, *open/close*, *read magic*, *touch of fatigue* (DC 17)

Str 27, **Dex** 23, **Con** 26, **Int** 24, **Wis** 26, **Cha** 24
Base Atk +15; **CMB** +25 (+29 grapple); **CMD** 42 (can't be tripped)
Feats Alertness, Combat Casting, Combat Reflexes, Dodge, Eschew Materials, Flyby Attack, Improved Initiative, Lightning Reflexes, Mobility, Multiattack
Skills Acrobatics +25, Bluff +27, Diplomacy +27, Fly +24, Intimidate +25, Knowledge (arcana) +30, Knowledge (nobility) +27, Knowledge (planes) +27, Perception +35, Sense Motive +32, Spellcraft +30, Stealth +21 (+29 blending);
Racial Modifiers +8 Stealth blend with surroundings
Languages Abyssal, Celestial, Common, Draconic, Giant, Infernal, any one elemental language (Aquan, Auran, Ignan, Terran)

Environment temperate and warm lands and underground
Organization solitary
Treasure double standard

Charming Gaze (Su) This ability functions as a *charm monster* spell (CL 20th); 90 feet; DC 27 Will negates. The save DC is Charisma-based.
Poison (Ex) Sting—injury; *save* DC 28 Fort; *frequency* 1/round for 6 rounds; *effect* 1d6 Con damage; *cure* 2 consecutive saves. The save DC is Constitution-based.

The ha-naga is a stronger, fiercer version of the more common naga that spends its time moving from plane to plane, engaging in diplomacy, courtly intrigues and plotting, and even hunting (both for sport and for food). These creatures are known for their voracious appetites, eating anything, both alive or dead, except for others of their own kind (even in times of starvation).

Ha-nagas lair in deep, dark caves or ruins, far away from most civilized lands. A typical ha-naga lair is a twisted maze of tunnels and chambers with multiple entry and exit points, all camouflaged and trapped with both mundane and magical traps.

Ha-nagas are generally solitary creatures but can occasionally be encountered with other nagas of evil disposition. These creatures sometimes make truces with local evil humanoids (gnolls, inphidians especially, or hobgoblins) allowing the humanoids to serve them or in some cases even worship them as gods, and exchanging gifts and treasure for knowledge, food, and other goods.

A typical ha-naga stretches over 20 feet and weighs over 600 pounds. Larger versions are known to exist. They are stronger and smarter than the ha-naga presented here. One unique ha-naga of Colossal size, Sss'ashisth, dwells in the fabled City of Brass, spending his days in the court of the Sultan. (See the *City of Brass* boxed set from **Necromancer Games** for details.)

Naga, Hanu-Naga

Hanu-nagas are a predominantly tropical and subtropical form of naga; rather than a human-headed giant snake, hanu-nagas have a feral monkey head upon a great serpentine body.

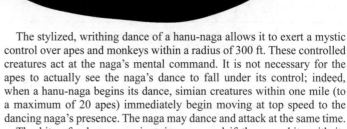

HANU-NAGA	CR 4

XP 1,200
CE Large aberration
Init +4; **Senses** darkvision 60 ft.; **Perception** +7

AC 17, touch 13, flat-footed 13 (+4 Dex, +4 natural, −1 size)
hp 47 (5d8+25)
Fort +6; **Ref** +5; **Will** +5

Speed 30 ft., climb 20 ft.
Melee bite +8 (1d6+5 plus poison and constrict)
Ranged spit +6 touch (poison)
Space 10 ft.; **Reach** 5 ft.
Special Attacks *call monkey dance*, constrict (1d6+7), control simians

Str 21, **Dex** 18, **Con** 20, **Int** 10, **Wis** 12, **Cha** 18
Base Atk +3; **CMB** +9; **CMD** 23 (can't be tripped)
Feats Acrobatic, Diehard, Endurance
Skills Acrobatics +15, Climb +17, Escape Artist +10, Intimidate +11, Perception +7, Stealth +8, Survival +7; **Racial Modifiers** +4 Acrobatics, +4 Climb
Languages Aklo, common, speak with simians

Call Monkey Dance (Su)
A hanu-naga *calls* 1d6 ghoul monkeys every 1d4 rounds as a 9th-level sorcerer. The *call* lasts as long as the hanu-naga performs its swaying dance. The naga may use the *dance* 3/day.
Control Simians (Su) The hanu-naga may *command* any simian within 60 ft. (no save).
Poison (Ex) Bite—injury or spit—contact; *save* DC 17 Fort; *frequency* 1/round for 6 rounds; *effect* 1d2 Con damage; *cure* 2 consecutive saves. The save DC is Constitution-based.
Spit (Ex) A hanu-naga can spit its venom up to 30 feet as a standard action. This is a ranged touch attack with no range increment. Opponents hit by this attack must make successful saves (see above) to avoid the effect.

The Hanu-nagas lair in jungles and rainforests, haunting forgotten temples and ancient ruins, where many are worshipped by tribes of wild monkeys and/or apes. The most intelligent of hanu-nagas may have followings of tribesmen or cavemen.

The stylized, writhing dance of a hanu-naga allows it to exert a mystic control over apes and monkeys within a radius of 300 ft. These controlled creatures act at the naga's mental command. It is not necessary for the apes to actually see the naga's dance to fall under its control; indeed, when a hanu-naga begins its dance, simian creatures within one mile (to a maximum of 20 apes) immediately begin moving at top speed to the dancing naga's presence. The naga may dance and attack at the same time.

The bite of a hanu-naga is poisonous, and if the naga hits with its constricting attack it inflicts automatic damage of 1d6 per round until killed.

Credit
Original author Scott Casper
Originally appearing in *Jungle Ruins of Madaro-Shanti* (© Frog God Games, 2010)

Narwhal

This creature appears as a large bluish-white whale with white blotches on its skin. A horn, as long as a man grows from its head.

NARWHAL	CR 4

XP 1,200
NG Large magical beast
Init +2; **Senses** darkvision 60 ft., low-light vision, tremorsense 60 ft.; **Perception** +12

AC 15, touch 11, flat-footed 13 (+2 Dex, +4 natural, –1 size)
hp 42 (5d10+15)
Fort +7; **Ref** +6; **Will** +3
DR 10/evil; **SR** 15 (against spells cast by evil-aligned creatures only)

Speed swim 50 ft.
Melee gore +10 (2d6+5) or slam +9 (1d8+5)
Space 10 ft.; **Reach** 5 ft.
Spell-Like Abilities (CL 5th):
At will—*aid, detect evil, magic circle against evil*
3/day—*bless weapon, bless, prayer*

Str 21, **Dex** 15, **Con** 17, **Int** 6, **Wis** 14, **Cha** 12
Base Atk +5; **CMB** +11; **CMD** 23 (can't be tripped)
Feats Alertness, Swim-By Attack, Weapon Focus (gore)
Skills Perception +12, Swim +13
Languages Celestial, Common (can't speak any)
SQ ghost form, hold breath

Environment cold and temperate oceans
Organization solitary, pair, or pod (3–6 plus 6–12 noncombatant young)
Treasure none

Ghost Form (Su) Once per day, a narwhal can assume an ethereal form. This functions as the *etherealness* spell (CL 10th).

A narwhal (sometimes called a ghost whale or sea unicorn) is a good-aligned creature found swimming throughout the world's oceans. Most narwhals prefer colder waters and as such will be more commonly encountered in arctic environments. These creatures do not like warm waters and are never encountered in such places.

Mistakenly, many who encounter a narwhal believe it to have a horn growing from its head. Closer inspection reveals this to be false however. The horn is actually a single tooth that grows straight from the creature's mouth and can reach lengths of 10 feet or more. Narwhals use this horn to defend themselves and their young.

Narwhals spend the majority of their time swimming through the oceans feasting upon smaller sea life and plants (including coral, one of their favorite meals). A typical narwhal school consists of 2–6 adults and twice as many (noncombatant) young. Young narwhals lack the horn that adults have (though by age 2 it has grown in).

Narwhals typically average 10 to 12 feet in length, though they can grow to a length of 15 feet. A typical narwhal weighs up to 1-1/2 tons. Narwhals understand Celestial and Common but cannot speak.

Narwhals are generally non-aggressive creatures only entering battle when threatened, when their pod is threatened, or when it sees a good-aligned creature in trouble. Upon entering battle, a narwhal uses its horn to spear and impale its enemies. When aiding good-aligned creatures (or facing evil-aligned creatures on its own), a narwhal uses its *bless* and *magic circle* spell-like abilities to aid itself and its allies.

Necro-Phantom

This creature appears to be a rotting corpse dressed in dirty and torn clothing. Its hair is unkempt, its nails long and filthy. Its eyes show no semblance of life but glow with an eerie pale green light.

NECRO-PHANTOM	CR 3

XP 800
CE Medium undead
Init +1; **Senses** darkvision 60 ft., sense necromancy 60 ft.; **Perception** +11

AC 15, touch 11, flat-footed 14 (+1 Dex, +4 natural)
hp 26 (4d8+8)
Fort +3; **Ref** +2; **Will** +5
Defensive Abilities channel resistance +2, resist the grave; **DR** 5/magic; **Immune** undead traits

Speed 30 ft.
Melee 2 claws +7 (1d6+3 plus 1d4 Con damage), bite +6 (1d6+3)
Special Attacks grave touch

Str 16, **Dex** 13, **Con** —, **Int** 10, **Wis** 12, **Cha** 14
Base Atk +3; **CMB** +6; **CMD** 17
Feats Skill Focus (Perception), Weapon Focus (claw)
Skills Climb +8, Intimidate +9, Perception +11, Spellcraft +5, Stealth +8
Languages Common

Environment any
Organization solitary or gang (2–5)
Treasure none

Grave Touch (Su) The claws of a necro-phantom deal 1d4 points of Constitution damage (DC 14 Will save negates). A successful critical hit causes 1d4 points of Constitution damage and 1 point of Constitution drain (instead of double Constitution damage). With each successful attack, a necro-phantom gains 5 temporary hit points. The save DC is Charisma-based.
Resist the Grave (Ex) A necro-phantom gains a +4 racial bonus on saving throws against spells and spell-like abilities from the school of Necromancy.
Sense Necromancy (Su) A necro-phantom can attempt a Spellcraft check to identify a spell being cast within a 60-foot radius (DC 15 + spell level). The necro-phantom gains a +4 racial bonus on its check if the spell is from the school of Necromancy.

A creature that dies (either of its own accord or one that is killed) in an area poisoned by necromantic magic sometimes returns to the land of the living as a necro-phantom, an evil undead creature with a hatred for all things living, especially those who dabble in necromancy. Necro-phantoms are found haunting cemeteries, temples, mausoleums, and any other place necromantic magic is or was once prevalent. Often more than one necro-phantom is encountered; some strange effect of the magic that created them seems to draw these creatures to one another.

A necro-phantom appears as a rotting desiccated corpse still dressed in the clothing it wore in life (though it is now tattered and worn). Its nails are filthy and long and its teeth are broken. Each necro-phantom varies in height from 5 feet to almost 7 feet tall and weighs anywhere from 100 pounds to over 200 pounds. Necro-phantoms can speak Common, but seldom bother unless they are cursing a necromancy-wielding opponent.

Necro-phantoms attack their opponents by raking and slashing with their claws. A necro-phantom engaged in battle with a spellcaster uses its sense magic ability to attempt to identify any spell being cast. If it detects a necromancy spell, it focuses its attention on that spellcaster, ignoring all other opponents until the necromancy-wielding caster flees or is dead. If one necro-phantom out of a group successfully identifies a necromancy spell, it signals to the others of its kind and all move to attack the spellcaster.

Neomimic

This creature is grey-green blob of what appears to be human flesh. It shudders, and then begins growing arms and legs as it assumes a humanoid shape.

NEOMIMIC	CR 5

XP 1,600
NE Medium aberration
Init +6; **Senses** darkvision 60 ft.; **Perception** +12

AC 18, touch 12, flat-footed 16 (+2 Dex, +6 natural)
hp 52 (7d8+21)
Fort +5; **Ref** +6; **Will** +7
Defensive Abilities amorphous; **Immune** acid

Speed 30 ft.
Melee slam +10 (1d8+6 plus adhesive) or 2 slams (1d8+6 plus adhesive)

Str 19, **Dex** 14, **Con** 17, **Int** 13, **Wis** 15, **Cha** 13
Base Atk +5; **CMB** +9; **CMD** 21
Feats Armor Proficiency (Light, Medium)[B], Improved Initiative, Lightning Reflexes, Martial Weapon Proficiency[B], Skill Focus (Stealth), Weapon Focus (slam)
Skills Climb +14, Disguise +8, Intimidate +9, Knowledge (dungeoneering) +8, Perception +12, Stealth +13
Languages Common
SQ change shape (small, medium, or large creature; *alter self*, *beast shape III*, and *plant shape I*)

Environment any land and underground
Organization solitary
Treasure none

Adhesive (Ex) A neomimic exudes a thick slime that acts as a powerful adhesive, holding fast any creatures or items that touch it. An adhesive-covered neomimic automatically grapples any creature it hits with its slam attack. Opponents so grappled cannot get free while the neomimic is alive without removing the adhesive first. A weapon that strikes an adhesive-coated neomimic is stuck fast unless the wielder succeeds on a DC 17 Reflex save. A successful DC 17 Strength check is needed to pry off a stuck weapon. Strong alcohol or universal solvent dissolves the adhesive, but the neomimic can still grapple normally. A neomimic can dissolve its adhesive at will, and the substance breaks down 5 rounds after the creature dies. The save DC is Strength-based.

Alter Physique (Ex) At will as a standard action, a neomimic can alter its physical structure to affect its physique. A neomimic can shift points between its Strength, Dexterity, or Constitution by reducing one or more of the scores while raising one or more by the same amount. The neomimic can shift no more than 12 points at one time and no score can be raised or lowered by more than 10 points. For example, a neomimic can reduce its Strength from 19 to 10 while increasing its Dexterity from 14 to 18. It could not, however, decrease its Strength to less than 9, or increase its Dexterity to greater than 24. These changes remain in effect until the neomimic uses this ability again.

Unlike its lesser kin, the skin of a neomimic is soft and fleshy, and it cannot substantially alter its texture to appear as wood or stone. When taking the form of a creature of any kind, a neomimic cannot assume the form of a specific individual. Anyone who examines the neomimic can detect the ruse with a successful Perception check opposed by the neomimic's Disguise check.

The neomimic is thought by sages to be an advanced species of mimic perhaps from some distant future or unknown plane. Neomimics may also be somehow related to doppelgangers, but any such relationship has not been proven.

In its natural state, a neomimic is an amorphous blob of fleshy substance approximately 5 feet across. Its skin is the color of dead tissue, a sickening grey-green hue tinged here and there with what appears to be healthy human skin. Like normal mimics, a neomimic can assume nearly any shape it can conceive. A neomimic often takes humanoid form, however, and rarely resorts to taking the shape of inanimate objects.

A neomimic in its natural form is 6 feet tall and weighs 200 pounds.

In its natural form or the form of an inanimate object, a neomimic pounds its opponent with powerful fist-shaped pseudopods in much the same way as a normal mimic. While in the form of a creature, however, a neomimic strives to fight as much as possible like the creature it is emulating.

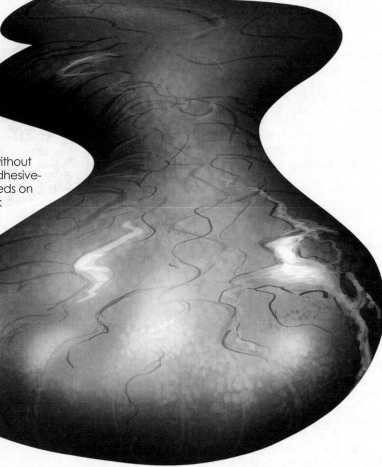

Niserie

Reclining on a rock in the surf is a gorgeous and voluptuous female humanoid with long golden hair, pearly white skin, and blue eyes. She is clad in soft, silk-like cloth of white and gold.

NISERIE	CR 7

XP 3,200
CN Medium fey (water)
Init +6; **Senses** low-light vision; **Perception** +9

AC 13, touch 13, flat-footed 10 (+2 Dex, +1 dodge)
hp 22 (4d6+8)
Fort +5; **Ref** +6; **Will** +6
Defensive Abilities water form; **SR** 18

Speed 30 ft., swim 40 ft.
Melee dagger +2 (1d4)
Spell-Like Abilities (CL 7th):
At will—*control water* (DC 20), *fog cloud*, *water breathing* (on another)
Spells Prepared (CL 7th; melee touch +2, ranged touch +4):
4th—*unholy blight* (DC 16)
3rd—*bestow curse* (DC 15), *remove curse*
2nd—*bear's endurance* (DC 14), *cure moderate wounds*, *silence* (DC 14), *sound burst* (DC 14)
1st—*bane* (DC 13), *comprehend languages*, *cure light wounds*, *doom* (DC 13), *obscuring mist*
0—*bleed* (DC 12), *create water*, *purify food and drink* (DC 12), *resistance* (DC 12)

Str 10, **Dex** 14, **Con** 14, **Int** 12, **Wis** 15, **Cha** 18
Base Atk +2; **CMB** +2; **CMD** 15
Feats Dodge[B], Great Fortitude, Improved Initiative
Skills Bluff +11, Diplomacy +11, Knowledge (local) +8, Knowledge (nature) +8, Perception +9, Sense Motive +9, Sleight of Hand +7, Stealth +7 (+15 in water), Swim +8; **Racial Modifiers** +8 Stealth in water
Languages Aquan, Sylvan
SQ amphibious

Environment any aquatic
Organization solitary, pair, or gang (3–6)
Treasure standard (dagger, other treasure)

Spells Niserie can cast divine spells as 7th-level clerics. They do not gain access to domains or other cleric abilities.
Water Form (Ex) As a standard action, a niserie can turn into a mobile pool of water. This functions like *gaseous form*, except that the niserie cannot fly in this form. It retains its own base speed, and its swim speed doubles to 80 feet. The niserie can remain in her water form for a number of minutes equal to twice her Constitution bonus and can end this ability as a standard action.

A spell with the cold descriptor inflicts no damage on a niserie in its water form, but instead automatically *slows* the creature as per the spell for 1d6 rounds or until she leaves her water form.

A spell with the electricity, fire, or sonic descriptor inflicts normal damage on a niserie in its water form.

Niserie (also called undine or true undine) are playful and mischievous fey. On occasion they are malicious, taking great pleasure in luring sailors to their watery graves. Also known as sea nymphs, niserie prefer trickery to combat and flee if presented with overwhelming odds.

Niserie stand from 5 to 6 feet tall and weigh around 130 pounds. They are always female; there are no male niserie (that scholars are aware of). While most niserie have golden hair, the rare niserie has seaweed green hair with moss green eyes.

If forced into combat, a niserie defends herself with her spell-like abilities and dagger, seeking escape at the earliest convenience by changing into water and flowing away.

Nithu

This creature appears to be a semi-translucent and ever-shifting mass of protoplasm floating a few feet above the ground. Four long and sinewy tentacles writhe and sway from its form. It has no other discernible features.

NITHU	CR 6

XP 2,400
NE Large aberration
Init +5; **Senses** darkvision 60 ft.; **Perception** +18
Aura stench (DC 17, 1d6 rounds)

AC 21, touch 14, flat-footed 16 (+5 Dex, +7 natural, −1 size)
hp 60 (8d8+24)
Fort +5; **Ref** +7; **Will** +8
DR 10/magic; **Resist** cold 10, fire 10

Speed fly 40 ft. (good)
Melee 4 tentacles +10 (1d8+3 plus grab)
Space 10 ft.; **Reach** 10 ft.
Special Attacks constrict (1d6+3), disease

Str 16, **Dex** 21, **Con** 16, **Int** 11, **Wis** 14, **Cha** 12
Base Atk +6; **CMB** +10 (+14 grapple); **CMD** 25 (can't be tripped)
Feats Alertness, Combat Reflexes, Skill Focus (Perception), Weapon Finesse
Skills Fly +16, Intimidate +10, Perception +18, Stealth +10, Survival +11
Languages Common (cannot speak)

Environment temperate forests or marshes
Organization solitary
Treasure incidental

Disease (Ex) A creature hit by two or more tentacles in the same round is subjected to *mire blindness.*
Mire Blindness tentacle—injury; *save* DC 17 Fort; *onset* 1 day; *frequency* 1/day; *effect* blindness and 1d3 Constitution damage; *cure* 2 consecutive saves. A creature that fails two saving throws is rendered permanently blinded. The save DC is Constitution-based.

Nithus are evil monsters that dwell deep within darkened swamps, bogs, mires, and marshes. These creatures sustain themselves on a diet of swamp creatures: alligators, fish, and adventurers and just about anything else that enters their domain. Slain prey is either devoured immediately or dragged back to the nithu's lair where it is slowly devoured over the course of a few days. A nithu's lair is a well-hidden and dark cave, cavern, or other such place. Nithus occasionally make truces with nearby humanoids (particularly orcs, gnolls, and goblins) in exchange for a steady supply of food (victims).

Nithus are solitary creatures and extremely territorial, even fighting their own kind for control of an area. No encounters of multiple nithus have been recorded. Sages are unsure how (and if) nithu reproduce. They appear to be sexless creatures and no young have ever been encountered. A typical nithu has a lifespan of 20 years. As a nithu ages, its color shifts from translucent light gray to a darker, but still semi-translucent gray. Its tentacles, usually the same color as the body change colors as well.

A nithu cares little to nothing for treasure; thus, any treasure found in or around its lair is typically all that remains of those who have fallen prey to the creature's insatiable hunger.

The nithu is an ambush hunter, preferring to lay in wait for potential prey to pass near. A nithu picks and chooses its targets carefully. The creature's average intelligence is enough to let it to know when it is outmanned and outclassed; thus it prefers to attack the lone straggler or a party member who may have become lost in the monster's swampy lair. Unless extremely hungry, an nithu doesn't attack a large group of creatures unless it itself is threatened and attacked first or unless it is assured of victory.

Noble Steed

The horse has a sturdy body and long, powerful legs. It has an extremely long tail, nearly reaching the ground. Its mane is also unusually long and flows back from its head and neck in long, graceful locks. The huge hooves of the animal let loose a small shower of sparks as it runs.

NOBLE STEED	**CR 4**

XP 1,200
N Large magical beast
Init +4; **Senses** darkvision 60 ft., low-light vision; **Perception** +10

AC 19, touch 13, flat-footed 15 (+4 Dex, +6 natural, −1 size)
hp 52 (5d10+25)
Fort +9; **Ref** +8; **Will** +4

Speed 70 ft., fly 70 ft. (perfect)
Melee 2 hooves +10 (1d6+5), bite +9 (1d4+5)
Space 10 ft.; **Reach** 5 ft.

Str 20, **Dex** 18, **Con** 21, **Int** 4, **Wis** 17, **Cha** 11
Base Atk +5; **CMB** +11; **CMD** 25 (29 vs. trip)
Feats Endurance, Run[B], Skill Focus (Fly), Weapon Focus (hoof)
Skills Fly +17, Perception +10
Languages Auran (can't speak)

Environment any land
Organization solitary, mated pair, family (solitary mare plus 1–3 foals), or herd (5–20)
Treasure none

Flight (Su) A noble steed's ability to fly is magical in nature, and becomes ineffective in an *antimagic field*. The noble steed loses the ability to fly for as long as the antimagic effect persists or for as long as it remains in the area.

Noble steeds are highly prized as mounts. They are about the same size as warhorses, but have leaner musculature and long, flowing manes and tails. Noble steeds are incredibly fast, and can even run on air. In the wild, noble steeds can often be found associating with normal horses and pegasuses.

Adult wild noble steeds are incapable of being tamed; these animals must be raised as foals in captivity if they are to be tamed. Domesticated adult noble steeds can cost as much as 800 gp when they can be found. Noble steed foals cost around 400 gp.

Noble steeds can vary in color just as standard horses do. Most tend toward lighter shades however, with slightly darker manes and tails. Noble steeds can breed with normal horses. The offspring however is always a normal horse. Only the mating of two noble steeds produces another noble steed. Noble steeds can live up to 50–60 years.

Noble steeds are generally docile and avoid combat if possible. If the family or herd is threatened however, the males move to attack while females move to protect the young. Much like their mundane counterparts, noble steeds attack with a combination of hooves and biting. If combat goes against them, noble steeds can usually outrun their foes or can take to the air and flee.

Ommoth

This twelve-foot long creature resembles a giant scorpion with four menacing pincers and dual stingers.

OMMOTH	CR 5

XP 1,600
N Large magical beast
Init +4; **Senses** darkvision 60 ft., low-light vision, tremorsense 120 ft.; **Perception** +14

AC 18, touch 9, flat-footed 18 (+9 natural, −1 size)
hp 59 (7d10+21)
Fort +10; **Ref** +5; **Will** +2

Speed 40 ft.
Melee 4 claws +13 (1d6+6 plus grab), 2 stings +13 (1d6+6 plus poison)
Space 10 ft.; **Reach** 10 ft.
Special Attacks constrict (1d6+6)

Str 23, **Dex** 10, **Con** 16, **Int** 2, **Wis** 10, **Cha** 2
Base Atk +7; **CMB** +14 (+18 grapple); **CMD** 24 (36 vs. trip)
Feats Great Fortitude, Improved Initiative, Power Attack, Weapon Focus (claw)
Skills Climb +11, Perception +14, Stealth +5; **Racial Modifiers** +8 Perception, +4 Stealth

Environment warm or temperate deserts, forests, plains, or underground
Organization solitary, pair, hunting band (3–6)
Treasure incidental

Poison (Ex) Sting—injury; *save* DC 18 Fort; *frequency* 1/round for 6 rounds; *effect* 1d4 Strength damage; *cure* 1 save. The save DC is Constitution-based and includes a +2 racial bonus.

Ommoth are diurnal hunters that dine on giant insects and rodents; and the occasional adventurer that wanders too close to their nest. Hunting bands consist of both male and female ommoth with the strongest male being the leader of the pack. Favored prey of an ommoth includes large game, humanoids, and the occasional giant scorpion. Prey is always killed and carried back to the lair to be devoured or fed to the young. Young ommoth remain in the lair for three to six months generally, before dispersing into the world. A typical ommoth can live up to 30 years.

An ommoth lair is an underground burrow, either of their devising or an existing and abandoned burrow created by some other burrowing creatures. An existing burrow is often reconfigured to consist of a single long passageway that empties into a large main chamber. Here in the main chamber is the ommoth's nest. Any other passageways and chambers are sealed off by the ommoth with dirt, rocks, debris, and anything else it can find.

An ommoth is highly aggressive and attacks any creature that wanders into its territory. If cornered or threatened, it responds by rearing its claws and poising its tail overhead. Creatures that continue to harass the ommoth are met

with a series of tail stings and claw attacks. An ommoth flees if confronted by a superior opponent, but if the nest is threatened, it fights to the death.

An ommoth appears as a twelve foot long giant scorpion with four large claws, two long tails that each end in a wicked stinger, and a carapace of reddish-brown or black. It has one set of eyes on the front of its head and two other pairs just behind those on the sides of its head. The creature has two sets of serrated mandibles that help in rending its food. Its forelegs are slightly longer and thinner than its others legs and it uses these to detect prey and explore its surroundings. Some species have white or tan markings on their undersides or white bands on their forelegs.

Ooze, Ebon

This is a jet-black, loathsome mass in a roughly spherical shape that slithers forward with a wet slurping sound.

EBON OOZE	CR 6

XP 2,400
NE Huge ooze
Init +2; **Senses** blindsight 60 ft.; **Perception** +2

AC 6, touch 6, flat-footed 6 (–2 Dex, –2 size)
hp 100 (8d8+56 plus 8)
Fort +9; **Ref** +2; **Will** +4
Defensive Abilities negative energy affinity; **Immune** acid, disease, ooze traits, sonic

Speed 20 ft., swim 20 ft.
Melee slam +12 (3d6+10 plus 2d6 acid plus grab)
Space 15 ft.; **Reach** 10 ft.
Special Attacks disease (slimy doom, DC 21)

Str 24, **Dex** 7, **Con** 24, **Int** 8, **Wis** 14, **Cha** 3
Base Atk +6; **CMB** +15 (+19 to grapple); **CMD** 23 (can't be tripped)
Feats Improved Initiative, Lightning Reflexes, Skill Focus (Stealth), Toughness[B], Weapon Focus (slam)
Skills Stealth +1

Environment underground
Organization solitary

Treasure standard

Negative Energy Affinity (Ex) An ebon ooze is healed by negative energy attacks, and harmed by positive energy, as if it were undead.
Slimy Doom (Ex) Slam—injury; *save* DC 21 Fort; *onset* 1 day; *frequency* 1 day; *effect* 1d4 Con damage; *cure* 2 consecutive saves.

The ebon ooze is a cousin of the black pudding. It has an affinity for negative energy, and tends to dwell in locations near undead and evil priests. Unlike most oozes, an ebon ooze is intelligent, and takes great pleasure in stalking and devouring living creatures. Although it is not harmed by sunlight, the ebon ooze finds it painful, and usually takes shelter in a dark, shady location if outdoors during the day.

Ebon oozes are ambush predators, using terrain to their advantage to conceal itself until prey draws near. If it feels it clearly outmatches its prey, an ebon ooze may choose to forego grabbing and killing it outright, instead stalking and toying with it. However, when facing a clearly superior opponent, the ebon ooze is not afraid to retreat, and generally tries to have some means of escape should a fight go against it, such as a deep, narrow crevice or the bottom of a deep pool.

Credit
Originally appearing in *Rappan Athuk Reloaded* (© Necromancer Games, 2006)

Ooze, Spawn of Jubilex

This humanoid creature wears chain armor and wields a gleaming battleaxe. Its entire form drips with viscous black slime.

SPAWN OF JUIBLEX	CR 6

XP 2,400
CE Medium ooze (extraplanar)
Init +3; **Senses** darkvision 60 ft.; **Perception** +9

AC 18, touch 9, flat-footed 18 (+6 armor, −1 Dex, +3 natural)
hp 80 (7d8+49); fast healing 5
Fort +9; **Ref** +1; **Will** +4
Defensive Abilities amorphous; **DR** 5/magic; **Immune** acid, ooze traits; **Resist** fire 10

Speed 20 ft. (30 ft. unarmored)
Melee mwk greataxe +10 (1d12+6 plus 1d6 acid) or 2 slams +9 (1d6+4 plus 1d6 acid)
Special Attacks death throes

Str 18, **Dex** 8, **Con** 24, **Int** 10, **Wis** 10, **Cha** 6
Base Atk +5; **CMB** +9; **CMD** 18
Feats Alertness, Blind-Fight, Improved Initiative, Iron Will
Skills Perception +9, Sense Motive +2, Stealth +6

Environment any (Abyss)
Organization solitary or warband (2–7)
Treasure standard (chainmail armor, masterwork greataxe, other treasure)

Acid (Ex) A spawn of Jubilex's acid does not harm metal or stone.
Death Throes (Ex) When a spawn of Jubilex is slain, it melts into a pool of caustic acid that quickly covers a 10-foot by 10-foot square area. Creatures within or entering the area must succeed on a DC 20 Fortitude save or take 2d6 points of acid damage each round they remain in the area. The save DC is Constitution-based.

Spawn of Jubilex were once human creatures corrupted by foul and dark rituals at the hands of Jubilex the Faceless Lord. The first known sighting of these creatures was in the Citadel (see *G5 Chaos Rising*, by **Necromancer Games**) when Jubilex used his power to corrupt a group of dwarves (known now as The Corrupted). Using his dark magic, Jubilex slayed the dwarves, liquefied their remains, and reanimated them as his spawn.

Spawn are not mindless, but do not retain much of their former lives. Fleeting memories perhaps, but nothing else seems to remain. These creatures are hateful and attack anything they encounter.

Spawn look as they did in their former lives, save they are covered in a thick, black slime that constantly weeps from their bodies.

Spawn attack with weapons, favoring weapons they used in their former life. These creatures rarely retreat from battle, their ever-consuming hatred driving them to their own destruction.

Oozeanderthal

Oozeanderthals are humanoid host beings that have been magically altered in a terrifying fashion. These host creatures are coated in a slimy substance about an inch thick, a product of ancient and forgotten magic. The bones of their forearms have been magically grown outward from the skin, and drastically elongated, with the fingers extending out into foot-long, semi-crystallized claws.

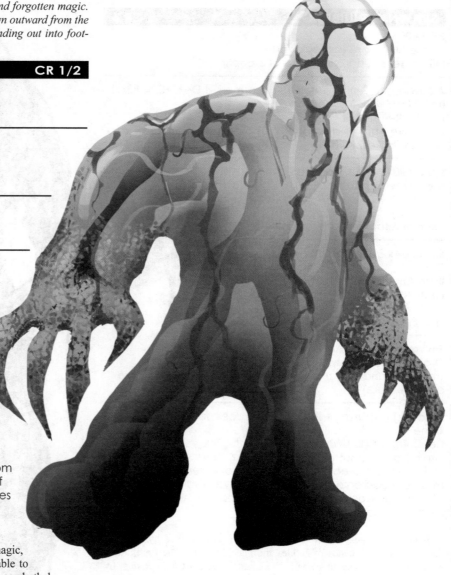

OOZEANDERTHAL   CR 1/2

XP 200
NE Medium undead
Init +0; **Senses** darkvision 60 ft.; **Perception** +0

AC 12, touch 10, flat-footed 12 (+2 natural)
hp 22 (3d8+3)
Fort +1; **Ref** +1; **Will** +3
Immune electricity, turning

Speed 30 ft.
Melee 2 claws +5 (1d6+4 plus toxic ooze)
Special Attacks toxic ooze (DC 15)

Str 17, **Dex** 10, **Con** —, **Int** —, **Wis** 10, **Cha** 10
Base Atk +2; **CMB** +5; **CMD** 15
Feats Toughness[B]
SQ ooze coating

Environment any
Organization solitary or clan (2–7)
Treasure standard

Ooze Coating (Su) Oozeanderthals are entirely covered in slime approximately 1 in. thick. This slime is highly toxic to others and if an oozeanderthal rakes an opponent with its slime-covered claws the victim must make a DC 15 Fortitude save or fall twitching to the ground for 1d6 rounds from muscle spasms. The nonconductive nature of the ooze surrounding an oozeanderthal makes it immune to electrical damage. The save is Strength-based

Undead creatures created from a lost form of magic, the oozeanderthals are truly horrible wretches. Not able to leave the mortal realm, the host body inside an oozeanderthal dies slowly to feed the enveloping slime. The power of the sustaining slime is enough to retain the oozeanderthal in a zombie-like existence for many years, although it weakens and deteriorates over the centuries. Oozeanderthals are completely non-intelligent and use straightforward tactics.

Credit
Original author Matthew J. Finch
Originally appearing in *The Spire of Iron and Crystal* (© Frog God Games/Matthew J. Finch, 2011)

Peg Powler

This creature appears to be a bent, ugly crone with sickly green skin and sharp teeth.

PEG POWLER	CR 3

XP 800
CE Medium monstrous humanoid (aquatic)
Init +3; **Senses** darkvision 60 ft.; **Perception** +9

AC 17, touch 13, flat-footed 14 (+3 Dex, +4 natural)
hp 38 (4d10+16)
Fort +5; **Ref** +7; **Will** +6
DR 5/cold iron; **Immune** charm, sleep

Speed 30 ft., swim 40 ft.
Melee 2 claws +8 (1d6+4 plus grab)
Special Attacks rend (2d6+6)

Str 18, **Dex** 16, **Con** 18, **Int** 13, **Wis** 14, **Cha** 15
Base Atk +4; **CMB** +8 (+12 grapple); **CMD** 21
Feats Power Attack, Skill Focus (Stealth)
Skills Bluff +10, Intimidate +9, Perception +9, Stealth +13, Swim +19; **Racial Modifiers** +4 Bluff
Languages Common, Giant
SQ amphibious, sound mimicry (voices)

Environment any aquatic
Organization solitary or gang (2–5)
Treasure standard

A peg powler appears as an old crone, believed to be distantly related to the various hags (particularly sea hags). The creature makes its home on the bottom of rivers and lakes, but spends most of its time near the shore where it attempts to lure fishermen, children, and sometimes even animals to their watery graves. Though it can sustain itself on a diet of seaweed, kelp, and various underwater plants, the peg powler prefers the taste of flesh and blood. Stories told, perhaps only to scare children, speak of swarms of peg powlers journeying far inland when their shoreline food supplies run scarce. These stories tell of entire villages being destroyed and every single inhabitant devoured by the ravenous peg powler swarm.

Peg powlers tolerate the presence of sea hags, but there is no love lost between the two races. Stories speak of some peg powlers enjoying the taste of a sea hag's flesh over that of any other creature. This doesn't sit well with sea hags who have heard this tale.

A peg powler appears as an emaciated woman with sickly green skin wearing tattered rags. Her hair, wild and unkempt, is usually brown or black. Her eyes are gray and appear almost pupiless. A typical peg powler stands roughly 6 feet tall and weighs 140 pounds.

A peg powler attacks with its claws, attempting to grab its foe, and drag it into its watery lair. A favored tactic of the peg powler is to hide near the riverbanks, grab an unsuspecting foe as it passes by, and then drag it into the water where it is drowned.

Pestilential Cadaver

This creature appears to be an animated corpse composed of mismatched body parts, crudely stitched together. Maggots and worms writhe from its rotting form.

PESTILENTIAL CADAVER	CR 7

XP 3,200
N Medium construct
Init +1; **Senses** darkvision 60 ft., low-light vision; **Perception** +6
Aura disease (30 ft., DC 15)

AC 19, touch 11, flat-footed 18 (+1 Dex, +8 natural)
hp 64 (8d10+20); fast healing 5
Fort +2; **Ref** +3; **Will** +2
DR 5/magic; **Immune** construct traits (+20 hp), magic

Speed 30 ft.
Melee 2 slams +12 (1d8+3 plus sickness)
Special Attacks disease aura, sickness

Str 16, **Dex** 12, **Con** —, **Int** 10, **Wis** 10, **Cha** 12
Base Atk +8; **CMB** +11; **CMD** 22
Feats Ability Focus (disease), Alertness, Stealthy, Weapon Focus (slam)
Skills Disguise +7, Escape Artist +3, Perception +6, Stealth +13; **Racial Modifiers** +4 Stealth
Languages Abyssal, Common, Infernal (cannot speak any languages)

Environment any
Organization solitary
Treasure none

Disease Aura (Ex) A pestilential cadaver exudes a putrid aura in a 30-foot radius around itself. Creatures entering or caught in the area must succeed on a DC 15 Fortitude save or contract one of the diseases listed on the table below. A creature that saves is immune to the disease aura of that pestilential cadaver for one day. The save DC is Charisma-based.

1D8	DISEASE
1	Blinding sickness
2	Cackle fever
3	Filth fever
4	Mindfire
5	Red ache
6	Shakes
7	Slimy doom
8	Roll twice, ignoring any results of 8

Fast Healing (Ex) A pestilential cadaver's fast healing only works if it is within 30 feet of a fresh corpse. A fresh corpse is defined as any living creature killed within the last 24 hours.
Immunity to Magic (Ex) A pestilential cadaver is immune to any spell or spell-like ability that allows spell resistance. In addition, certain spells and effects function differently against the creature, as noted: A magical attack that deals fire damage dazes a pestilential

cadaver (as the *daze* spell) for 3 rounds (no save). A magical attack that inflicts disease heals the cadaver of 1d6 hit points per level of the spellcaster. A *remove disease* spell deals 1d6 points of damage per caster level (maximum 10d6) to a pestilential cadaver. The creature can attempt a Fortitude save to reduce the damage by half. A *heal* spell functions as a *harm* spell against a pestilential cadaver.
Sickness (Ex) A living creature hit by a pestilential cadaver's slam attack must succeed on a DC 15 Fortitude save or become sickened for 2d6 rounds. A creature that fails its save by 5 or more is must immediately attempt another DC 15 Fortitude save or be subjected to one of the diseases above just as if it had been affected by the cadaver's aura. A creature that succeeds on the second Fortitude save is not subject to the disease effects of this ability for one day, even if it fails any subsequent Fortitude saves by 5 or more. The save DC is Charisma-based.

The pestilential cadaver is literally a walking disease, a construct formed from the bodies of those who died of plague and fever. It is ever active, seeking to spread its contagion to all who live. It rots constantly, losing flesh to decomposition, but gaining material from those it slays.

Although it moves awkwardly, in fits and jerks, the pestilential cadaver is as swift and dexterous as a healthy man, even capable of running (though it rarely does so). It stands about 6 feet in height, and weighs roughly 150 pounds.

The pestilential cadaver engages in combat primarily as a means of infecting new victims and absorbing their diseased remains once it slays them. It is a straightforward combatant, deadly even to those it does not touch.

Petrified Horror

A revolting stack of carnage stands before you. Its delicate silhouette belies the true horror that it is. It is as if someone carved a human-sized sculpture from the still-living flesh, bone and muscle of a much-larger creature, and then somehow gave that figure life.

PETRIFIED HORROR	CR 15

XP 51,200
N Medium construct
Init +8; **Senses** blindsight 60 ft.; **Perception** +0
Aura frightful presence (60 ft., DC 20)

AC 24, touch 14, flat-footed 20 (+4 Dex, +10 natural)
hp 140 (20d10+30)
Fort +6; **Ref** +10; **Will** +6
DR 5/adamantine; **Immune** construct traits (+30 hp), magic

Speed 30 ft.
Melee 2 slams +25 (2d6+5)
Special Attacks bloodstorm

Str 21, **Dex** 19, **Con** —, **Int** —, **Wis** 11, **Cha** 10
Base Atk +20; **CMB** +25; **CMD** 39
Feats Improved Initiative[B]

Environment any
Organization solitary
Treasure none

Bloodstorm (Su) A petrified horror can create a bloodstorm effect (as the spell) centered upon itself as a free action once every 2 minutes. The bloodstorm forms a whirlwind of blood in a column 25 feet in diameter and 40 feet high. The effect has a duration of 12 rounds, requiring those within to make a DC 20 Reflex save to avoid being blinded while they remain within the whirlwind and for 2d6 rounds after leaving it and a DC 20 Will save to avoid becoming panicked if less than 8 HD or frightened if 8 HD or above for the duration of the effect. Furthermore, creatures fighting within the bloodstorm or ranged attacks passing through it take –4 penalty on attack rolls Finally, the blood is slightly acidic and deals 1d4 points of acid damage per round. The petrified horror is immune to the effects of the bloodstorm, including the attack penalties, and the whirlwind remains centered on the petrified horror even if it moves. The save DCs are Constitution-based.

Full details of the *bloodstorm* spell can be found in *Relics & Rituals* by **Sword & Sorcery Studios**.

The name of the petrified horror belies the true nature of this hideous construct. For while it is true that the construct is crafted from the petrified remains of a Large creature, it is not until the new Medium statue is returned to flesh from its prison of stone that the horror is unleashed. Until then it just resembles an ordinary statue in whatever shape it was sculpted to be and is incapable of action.

This can be quite disconcerting when a delicate ballerina statue suddenly becomes a lumbering pile of bleeding meat and bone. Creators of these creatures often use them like time bombs, inert until freed by the spells of an inquisitive intruder or as part of a trap activated by the intruders. They instinctively recognize and avoid harming their creator but have no compunctions about destroying anything and anyone else they see.

In statue form, a typical specimen stands 5 to 8 feet tall and, being composed of solid stone, weighs anywhere from 1,000 to 1,800 pounds. Despite being a typical statue, it does give off a moderate aura of transmutation. When the creator or someone else casts *stone to flesh* or *break enchantment* the construct transforms to flesh and weighs 300 to 500 pounds depending on its height. As a construct it is does not require a Fortitude save to survive the transformation. Because the petrified horror is constructed from a larger creature, it gains the bonus hit points of a size Large construct rather than a Medium. Because it has no actual eyes, it sees through blindsight rather than with the traditional darkvision and low-light vision of a construct.

Despite its lumbering appearance, a petrified horror's newly crafted form is quite quick and agile. It moves with a discernable squishing noise and leaves a trail of blood and ichor wherever it goes.

Petrified horrors are incapable of speech and do not understand or heed commands.

Petrified horrors are typically left in out-of-the-way places by their creators, so when activated the damages they cause can be minimized. Once released from its stony imprisonment petrified horrors immediately go into a rampage destroying all they see, preferring living creatures over inanimate objects but content to demolish even inanimate objects if that is all there is. As part of their programming, they rush directly into the center of whatever group is nearest to them (bull rushing if necessary) while flailing with their fists. Once they are in amongst their foes, they use their bloodstorm ability as they continue to fight.

Construction

A petrified horror is carved from the petrified form of a Large creature which usually costs 10,000 gp to procure. Special masterwork tools for this process worth 500 gp are also required and are ruined in the creation process. Sculpting the body from the base material requires a DC 25 Craft (sculptures) check. Failure means that the petrified creature's form has been cracked and ruined and a new Large petrified creature must be procured.

PETRIFIED HORROR
CL 14th; **Price** 110,000 gp

CONSTRUCTION
Requirements Craft Construct, *animate dead, bloodstorm, flesh to stone, geas/quest, limited wish,* caster must be at least 14th level; **Skill** Craft (sculptures) DC 25; **Cost** 65,500 gp.

Credit
Original author Greg A. Vaughan
Originally appearing in *Slumbering Tsar* (© Frog God Games/ Greg A. Vaughan, 2012)

Piranha

Perhaps no creature of the water is feared more than the piranha. Lightning speed, coupled with vicious teeth and a pack-slaughter mentality place this predator firmly at the top of the food chain. Whether swarming together to take down larger prey, or developing wings to attack land creatures, the ravenous piranha cannot be stopped.

GIANT FLYING PIRANHA   CR 2

XP 600
N Small animal (aquatic)
Init +2; **Senses** low-light vision, scent; **Perception** +3

AC 13, touch 13, flat-footed 11 (+2 Dex, +1 size)
hp 18 (3d8)
Fort +3; **Ref** +5; **Will** +2

Speed swim 50 ft., fly 20 ft. (poor)
Melee bite +6 (1d4–2 plus 2 bleed)
Special Attacks bleed (2)

Str 7, **Dex** 15, **Con** 11, **Int** 1, **Wis** 12, **Cha** 2
Base Atk +3; **CMB** –1; **CMD** 12 (cannot be tripped)
Feats Alertness, Weapon Finesse[B]
Skills Fly +6, Perception +3, Swim +10; **Racial Modifiers** +8 to Swim, uses Dex for Swim

Environment any warm saltwater
Organization solitary or cloud (2–20)
Treasure none

Larger cousins to the standard piranha, the giant flying piranha is vicious fish between 2–3 feet in length, with a silver-gray coloration along the dorsal spine; brighter colors in red, orange, and yellow decorate the underbelly. Rows of tightly packed teeth give the piranha is distinctive underbite, with the individual teeth being 1 inch in length, and broadly arrowhead-shaped. Some humanoid tribes prize the giant teeth for use in weapons and tools.

Giant piranha usually attack intruders while in the water, but may attempt to strike an unwary victim walking near the water's edge. The giant piranha's goal is to get prey in or very near water. While they can fly for short periods, the giant piranha do cannot leave the water for long before they being to suffocate (see suffocation rules in the *Pathfinder Roleplaying Games Core Rulebook*).

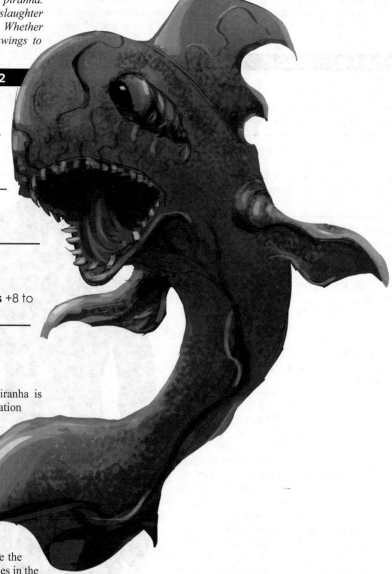

PIRANHA SWARM   CR 4

XP 1,200
N Tiny animal (aquatic, swarm)
Init +3; **Senses** low-light vision, scent; **Perception** +6

AC 15, touch 15, flat-footed 12 (+3 Dex, +2 size)
hp 28 (5d8)
Fort +4; **Ref** +7; **Will** +2

Speed swim 70 ft.
Melee swarm (1d6 plus bleed)
Special Attacks bleed (2 points), distraction (DC 12)

Str 3, **Dex** 16, **Con** 11, **Int** 1, **Wis** 12, **Cha** 2
Base Atk +3; **CMB** -3; **CMD** 10 (cannot be tripped)
Feats Alertness, Skill Focus (perception), Skill Focus (swim),
Weapon Finesse[B]
Skills Perception +6, Swim +22; **Racial Modifiers** +8 to Swim, use Dex for Swim

Environment any warm saltwater
Organization solitary or mass (2–4 swarms)
Treasure none

This large grouping of piranha is a fearsome sight. While individual piranha are frightening enough, the piranha swarm attacks as a single-minded mass of predatory fish. With lining speed, a piranha swarm can strip the flesh of a Large creature in seconds.

Credit

Original author Scott Casper
Originally appearing in *Jungle Ruins of Madaro-Shanti* (© Frog God Games, 2010)

Plant Guardian

The plant guardians are, as their name suggests, the self-proclaimed protectors and wardens of regions of unspoiled wilderness. There are several species of plant guardians, the most well-known of which is the treant. There is at least one type of plant guardian for every imaginable environment.

Plant guardians prefer to watch potential foes carefully before attacking. They often charge suddenly from cover to trample the despoilers of their environment. If sorely pressed, they animate plants as reinforcements.

Plant Guardian

Animate Plants (Sp) A plant guardian can animate any plants of the same type within 180 feet at will, controlling up to two such plants at a time. It takes 1 full round for the plant to uproot itself, after which it moves at a speed of 10 feet and fights as a plant of the same type as the one animating it (exceptions are noted in each entry below), gaining the plant guardian's vulnerability to fire. If the plant guardian that animated it terminates the animation, moves out of range, or is incapacitated, the plant immediately takes root wherever it is and returns to its normal state.

Double Damage against Objects (Ex) A plant guardian or animated tree that makes a full attack against an object or structure deals double damage.

Plantspeech (Ex) A plant guardian has the ability to converse with plants as if subject to a continual *speak with plants* spell, and most plants greet them with an attitude of friendly or helpful.

Algant

A large tentacle rises from this gigantic mass of seaweed.

ALGANT	CR 7

XP 3,200
NG Huge plant (aquatic)
Init +2; **Senses** blindsense 60 ft., tremorsense 120 ft.; **Perception** +11

AC 20, touch 10, flat-footed 18 (+2 Dex, +10 natural, -2 size)
hp 95 (10d8+50)
Fort +12; **Ref** +5; **Will** +7
DR 10/slashing; **Immune** plant traits
Weaknesses vulnerability to fire

Speed 10 ft., swim 30 ft.
Melee slam +12 (2d6+10/19–20 plus grab)
Space 15 ft., **Reach** 10 ft.

Str 25, **Dex** 14, **Con** 21, **Int** 12, **Wis** 15, **Cha** 12
Base Atk +7; **CMB** +16 (+20 grapple); **CMD** 28
Feats Alertness, Endurance, Improved Critical (slam)B, Iron Will, Power Attack, Swim-By Attack
Skills Diplomacy +7, Intimidate +7, Knowledge (nature) +7, Perception +11, Sense Motive +8, Stealth +1 (+17 in native environs), Swim +15; **Racial Modifiers** +16 Stealth in native environment
Languages Algant, Aquan, Common
SQ amphibious, animate plants, double damage against objects, plantspeech

Environment any freshwater
Organization solitary or patch (2–7)
Treasure standard

Engulf (Ex) An algant can simply engulf Huge or smaller creatures in its path as a standard action. It cannot make a slam attack during the round in which it engulfs. The algant merely has to move over the opponents, affecting as many as it can cover. Opponents can make attacks of opportunity against the creature, but if they do so they are not entitled to a saving throw. Those who do not attempt attacks of opportunity can attempt a DC 22 Reflex save to avoid being engulfed—in a success, they are pushed back or aside (opponent's choice) as the creature moves forward. Engulfed creatures are subject to an automatic slam attack each round, gain the pinned condition, are in danger of drowning, and are trapped within the algant's body until they are no longer pinned. The save DC is Strength-based.

The algants are the plant guardians of the water. An algant resembles a large mass of algae and dwells in freshwater.

Cactant

This creature appears to be a gigantic animated cactus covered in many sharp needles.

CACTANT	CR 6

XP 2,400
CG Huge plant
Init +2; **Senses** low-light vision; **Perception** +14

AC 19, touch 10, flat-footed 17 (+2 Dex, +9 natural, –2 size)
hp 76 (9d8+36)
Fort +10; **Ref** +5; **Will** +7
DR 10/slashing; **Immune** plant traits
Weaknesses vulnerability to fire

Speed 30 ft.
Melee 2 slams +11 (1d8+7 plus bleed)
Ranged rock +7 (2d6+10)
Space 15 ft.; **Reach** 15 ft.
Special Attacks bleed (1d4), needles, needle storm, rock throwing (150 ft.)

Str 25, **Dex** 14, **Con** 19, **Int** 12, **Wis** 15, **Cha** 12
Base Atk +6; **CMB** +15; **CMD** 27
Feats Alertness, Cleave, Iron Will, Power Attack, Skill Focus (Perception)
Skills Diplomacy +5, Intimidate +5, Knowledge (nature) +5, Perception +14, Sense Motive +7, Stealth +1, Survival +6
Languages Cactant, Common, Sylvan
SQ animate plants, double damage against objects, plantspeech

Environment warm deserts
Organization solitary or grove (2–7)
Treasure standard

Needles (Ex) The body and limbs of a cactant are covered in the characteristic needles of a cactus, and deal 1d4 bleed damage with a slam attack. Any creature grappling a cactant or attacking it with a natural weapon automatically takes bleed damage.

Needle Storm (Ex) Once per round as a standard action, a cactant can release a hail of needles in a 30-foot-radius burst. Creatures caught in the area take 7d6 points of piercing damage and 2d4 bleed damage. A successful DC 18 Reflex save reduces the damage by half and negates the bleed damage. A cactant can use this ability once every 1d4 rounds, and no more than five times per day. The save DC is Constitution-based.

The cactants are the plant guardians of hot, dry deserts. A cactant resembles a large saguaro cactus with thick arms.

Sargassant

A variant of the algant is the sargassant. It resembles a large floating mass of sargassum weed and dwells in saltwater environments.

Banyant

This animated tree has many large branches that writhe and thrash about it.

BANYANT	CR 9

XP 6,400
CG Huge plant
Init –1; **Senses** low-light vision; **Perception** +13

AC 19, touch 7, flat-footed 19 (–1 Dex, +12 natural, –2 size)
hp 114 (12d8+60)
Fort +15; **Ref** +3; **Will** +8
DR 10/slashing; **Immune** plant traits
Weaknesses vulnerability to fire

Speed 20 ft.
Melee 4 slams +14 (1d8+7/19–20)
Ranged rock +7 (2d6+10)
Space 15 ft.; **Reach** 15 ft.
Special Attacks rock throwing (150 ft.)

Str 25, **Dex** 8, **Con** 21, **Int** 12, **Wis** 14, **Cha** 12
Base Atk +9; **CMB** +18; **CMD** 27
Feats Alertness, Cleave, Great Fortitude, Improved Critical (slam), Iron Will, Power Attack
Skills Diplomacy +7, Intimidate +7, Knowledge (nature) +7, Perception +13, Sense Motive +8, Stealth –2 (+14 in native environs), Survival +6; **Racial Modifiers** +16 Stealth in native environment
Languages Banyant, Common, Sylvan
SQ animate plants, double damage against objects, plantspeech

Environment warm plains
Organization solitary or grove (2–7)
Treasure standard

The banyants are the plant guardians of warm plains such as savannas and equatorial grasslands. A banyant resembles a banyan tree.

Plantoid

This creature is a floating sphere of moss with several red eyes that are randomly spaced over the surface of the sphere, looking out through eyelid-like gaps.

PLANTOID	CR 4

XP 1,200
N Medium plant (extraplanar)
Init +1; **Senses** low-light vision; **Perception** +11

AC 14, touch 12, flat-footed 12 (+1 Dex, +1 dodge, +2 natural)
hp 42 (5d8+10)
Fort +6; **Ref** +2; **Will** +4
Immune bludgeoning damage, plant traits

Speed fly 40 ft. (perfect)
Melee 4 tendrils +3 (1d4–1 plus grab)
Space 5 ft.; **Reach** 5 ft. (10 ft. with tendrils)
Special Attacks control, create servitor, moss tendrils (+1 to grapple per tendril)

Str 8, **Dex** 13, **Con** 14, **Int** 12, **Wis** 16, **Cha** 16
Base Atk +3; **CMB** +2 (+6 grapple); **CMD** 14 (can't be tripped)
Feats Dodge, Mobility, Weapon Focus (tendrils)
Skills Fly +14, Knowledge (planes) +6, Perception +11, Stealth +7
Languages Plantoid
SQ alien plant

Environment any
Organization group (1–8 plus one servitor per plantoid)
Treasure none

Alien Plant (Ex): Plantoids are extradimensional fungi, and have the same class skills as aberrations.

Moss Tendrils (Ex) A plantoid lashes out with several mossy tendrils when it attacks, gaining a +1 bonus on its grapple check for each tendril that hit its opponent.

Control (Ex) The tendrils of a plantoid inject a mind-controlling substance, which it injects as a free action as part of its grapple check. Anyone touched by the mossy tendrils must succeed on a DC 15 Will save or fall under control of the plantoid. This otherwise acts like the *dominate person* spell except that the plantoid must touch the target and it functions on any Medium humanoid or monstrous humanoid. Control lasts for as long as the plantoid maintains contact. The victim also gets another saving throw to resist as described under the *dominate person* spell, and once every 4 hours after control is initiated. The save DC is Charisma-based.

Create Servitor (Ex) Anyone who remains controlled by a plantoid for more than 24 hours becomes a plantoid servitor, all human reason irrevocably lost. A plantoid can only control and transform a single creature or servitor at a time.

Plantoids are creatures from another dimension or plane of existence, occasionally summoned forth into the Material Plane. The eyes are not magical, but the long strands of moss trailing after the plantoid have a very dangerous ability to enslave anyone caught within them. The soft, mossy consistency of plantoids makes these creatures immune to blunt weapons. The plantoids can snap their mossy beards out like whips, attempting to touch a potential victim.

Plantoid King

It is rumored that plantoid "Kings" exist, with 10 HD and a limited immunity to both spells (SR 11+ CR) and non-magic weapons (DR 5/magic).

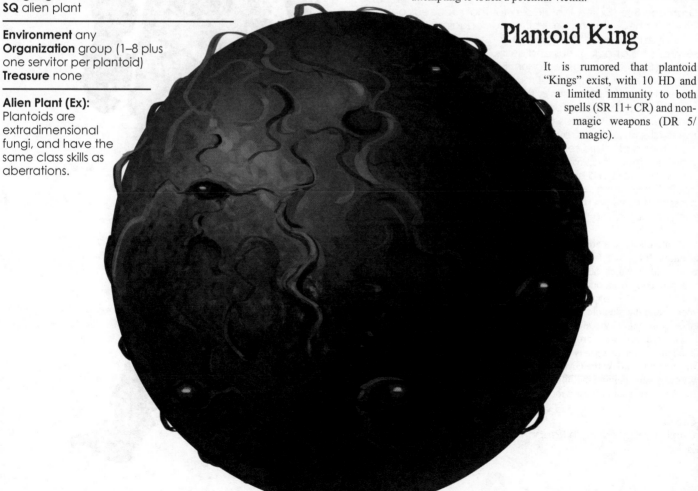

Plantoid Servitor

These shambling humanoids resemble green-skinned zombies with glowing red eyes, their heads draped with moss.

PLANTOID	CR 2

XP 600
N Medium plant
Init +0; **Senses** low-light vision; **Perception** +4

AC 14, touch 10, flat-footed 14 (+4 natural)
hp 22 (3d8+6 plus 3)
Fort +5; **Ref** +1; **Will** +1
Immune plant traits

Speed 40 ft.
Melee 2 slams +4 (1d4+2 plus grab)
Special Attacks grab and bite (melee +4, 1d3+2 plus poison), poison

Str 14, **Dex** 11, **Con** 14, **Int** 2, **Wis** 11, **Cha** 1
Base Atk +2; **CMB** +4 (+8 grapple); **CMD** 14
Feats Endurance, Die Hard[B], Toughness
Skills Perception +4, Stealth +5
Combat Gear special (see description)

Environment any
Organization solitary, gang (2–5)
Treasure special (see description)

Grab and Bite (Ex) A plantoid servitor that succeeds on a grapple check can make a bite attack against its opponent as an immediate action. This attack uses the plantoid servitor's full attack bonus and deals 1d3+2 damage.
Poison (Ex) *Transformative Poison:* Bite—injury; *save* DC 13 Fort; *frequency* 1/round for 4 rounds; *effect* special; *cure* 1 save. On the first failed save, the victim is paralyzed for 1d6 rounds. On the second failed saving throw, moss rapidly grows on all skin surfaces. The victim gets a +2 bonus on the third saving throw, but if the third save fails the victim becomes a plantoid servitor under the control of the nearest plantoid. There is a 25% chance that the victim becomes a new plantoid in a hideous transformation that takes 24 hours. If the victim succeeds on his third saving throw, the moss that grew on him withers and dies and falls away within a few minutes. The save DC is Constiution-based.

Plantoid servitors are humans (and their ilk) who have fallen prey to a plantoid. It is possible for a plantoid servitor to operate independently of a plantoid, in which case the eyes will not glow. Plantoid servitors acting independently from one of the plantoid masters are capable of following only the simplest of instructions, such as "attack anyone entering this room," and the plantoid is not able to give further instructions until it can once again gain physical contact with the plantoid servitor.

Plantoid servitors drop any held equipment when they are first dominated, but retain any worn gear such as armor, backpacks, capes, rings, and so on. At the GM's discretion, a plantoid servitor may still be wearing—and gaining the full benefit of—any special worn gear or magic items it possessed in its previous life.

Credit
Originally appearing in *Rappan Athuk* (© Frog God Games, 2012)

Proto-Creature

You can tell that this creature was once something else, but it has somehow been horribly misshapen. It still retains a vaguely humanoid form, but it now consists of a terrible conglomeration of exposed organs and bone, gnarled limbs, corded muscles with patches of strange, pebbly flesh and eyes and mouths in unnatural locations.

PROTO-CREATURE   CR 8

XP 4,800
NE Medium monstrous humanoid
Init −1; **Senses** darkvision 60 ft.; **Perception** +13

AC 21, touch 9, flat-footed 21 (−1 Dex, +12 natural)
hp 125 (10d10+60 plus 10); fast healing 10
Fort +11; **Ref** +6; **Will** +7
Defensive Abilities ferocity; **Immune** acid, electricity, critical hits, nonlethal damage, sneak attacks

Speed 30 ft.
Melee 2 slams +16 (1d6+5 plus grab)
Special Attacks acidic sweat (1d6 acid)

Str 20, **Dex** 9, **Con** 22, **Int** 6, **Wis** 10, **Cha** 5
Base Atk +10; **CMB** +15 (+19 grapple); **CMD** 24
Feats Cleave, Great Fortitude, Power Attack, Toughness, Weapon Focus (slam)
Skills Perception +13, Survival +13
Languages Common (cannot speak)

Acidic Sweat (Ex) The metabolism and biology of a protocreature has been so corrupted, that unidentifiable caustic fluids now course through its body instead of the traditional humors. In the third round of combat or heavy exertion, a proto-creature begins to secrete this fluid through the pores of its skin as sweat. Anyone physically touching a protocreature (not including with a weapon or other object) or who is hit by a slam attack after this sweating begins takes 1d6 acid damage. An opponent that is grappled by a proto-creature takes double this damage each round that the grapple is maintained. A living proto-creature continues to sweat this substance for 10 minutes following the completion of the battle or other activity that initiated it.

GIANT PROTO-CREATURE   CR 12

XP 19,200
NE Large monstrous humanoid
Init −1; **Senses** darkvision 60 ft.; **Perception** +17

AC 26, touch 8, flat-footed 26 (−1 Dex, +18 natural, −1 size)
hp 203 (14d10+112 plus 14); fast healing 10
Fort +14; **Ref** +8; **Will** +9
Defensive Abilities ferocity; **Immune** acid, electricity, critical hits, nonlethal damage, sneak attacks

Speed 30 ft.
Melee 2 slams +21 (2d6+7 plus grab)

Space 10 ft.; **Reach** 10 ft.
Special Attacks acidic sweat (2d6 acid)

Str 24, **Dex** 8, **Con** 26, **Int** 6, **Wis** 10, **Cha** 5
Base Atk +14; **CMB** +22 (+26 grapple); **CMD** 31
Feats Cleave, Great Cleave, Great Fortitude, Improved Natural Attack (slam), Power Attack, Toughness, Weapon Focus (slam)
Skills Perception +17, Survival +17
Languages Common (cannot speak)

Acidic Sweat (Ex) The acid damage from a giant proto-creature is 2d6 points of damage.

Proto-creatures are the results of the failed early experiments with *protomatter* by the Disciples of Orcus in their attempts to create ever better and more powerful servants and warriors. The proto-creatures proved to be too dumb and too difficult to control. Rather than destroy the beasts, they were instead placed in suspended animation and secreted away at various locations in case a use should ever be found with them.

All proto-creatures encountered to date have come from either humanoid or giant stock. Proto-creatures stand about 7 feet tall and weigh as much as 350 pounds. Giant proto-creatures are up to 12 feet tall and 1,500 pounds.

The secret of their accidental creation has been lost, and proto-creatures cannot propagate their own species, so their dwindling numbers are limited to those that were first created by the Disciples of Orcus.

Proto-creatures exist in constant pain. The only thing that distracts them from this pain is the release of combat. Therefore, they always seek to engage other creatures in combat upon first sighting them. The fact that these opponents also serve as their source of food is a merely a convenient byproduct. A proto-creature's body has been so warped and twisted by the experiments that created it, that it no longer has a recognizable physiology. This combined with its extreme resilience makes it immune to acid and electricity as well as sneak attacks, critical hits, and nonlethal damage.

In combat, a proto-creatures prefers to focus its attacks on a single opponent, grappling and subjecting the victim to its acidic sweat as soon as it begins to flow. They have been known to be fooled into dropping a victim who goes limp and plays dead in order to move onto other opponents. Such a subterfuge requires a Bluff check opposed to the proto-creature's Sense Motive.

Credit

Original author Greg A. Vaughan
Originally appearing in *Slumbering Tsar* (© Frog God Games/ Greg A. Vaughan, 2012)

Rakewood

Poking up through the leaf litter is a rounded hump of green, woody fungus. Waving in the air are three dull brown tendrils oozing a foul-smelling sap.

RAKEWOOD	CR 9

XP 6,400
N Large plant
Init +0; **Senses** blindsight 60 ft., tremorsense 60 ft.; **Perception** +9

AC 24, touch 9, flat-footed 24 (+15 natural, –1 size)
hp 115 (11d8+66)
Fort +13; **Ref** +3; **t** +4
DR 10/slashing or piercing; **Immune** plant traits

Speed 20 ft.
Melee 3 slams +16 (1d8+8 plus grab), bite +16 (2d6+8/19–20)
Space 10 ft.; **Reach** 10 ft.
Special Attacks spores, swallow whole (3d6 acid damage, AC 17, 11 hp)

Str 26, **Dex** 10, **Con** 23, **Int** 1, **Wis** 12, **Cha** 11
Base Atk +8; **CMB** +17 (+21 grapple); **CMD** 27 (can't be tripped)
Feats Cleave, Improved Critical (bite), Power Attack, Step Up, Weapon Focus (bite, slam)
Skills Perception +9, Stealth +5 (+13 in undergrowth); **Racial Modifiers** +8 Stealth in undergrowth

Environment temperate forests
Organization solitary or grove (2–5)
Treasure incidental

Spores (Ex) As a standard action once every 1d6 rounds, a rakewood can release a cloud of deadly spores in a 20-foot-radius burst. Creatures caught in the cloud must succeed on a DC 21 Fortitude save or be paralyzed for 2d4 rounds. Creatures succeeding their save are sickened for 1d4 rounds instead. The cloud lasts for 1 round before dispersing. The save DC is Constitution-based.

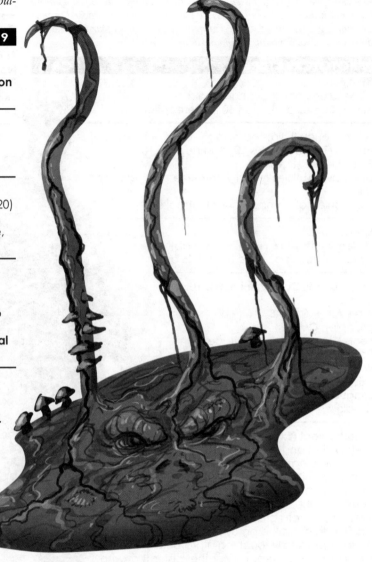

A rakewood is a barely sentient plant creature that lives deep within old-growth forests. It consists of a filthy, spheroid fungal mass with a ring of three brown tendrils at the top. The tendrils surround a sphincter-like mouth lined with razor-sharp spiny teeth. Although it can move of its own accord through the use of finger-like cilia at its base, a rakewood rarely moves once it has settled itself. Rakewoods live on decaying plant matter, and generally they are content to let the world go by as the soak up nutrients from the leaf litter. In less productive seasons such as winter, rakewoods supplement their diet with animal flesh.

Rakewoods are about 10 feet long and weigh 1,000 pounds. Coloration can vary from rakewood to rakewood, but most are dark green in color and covered in various fungi and molds. When at rest, a rakewood's tendrils appear to be tree roots or large, thick vines.

A rakewood enters combat by releasing its cloud of paralytic spores. Any opponents left standing are then pummeled with its slam attacks. A grappled or paralyzed opponent is pulled into its maw to be swallowed.

Rat-Ghouls

The foulest form of common vermin, rat-ghouls are abnormally large rats that have been infused with necrotic energy, either from proximity to a source of foulness, or feasting upon necrotic flesh.

RAT-GHOULS	CR 1

XP 135
N Small undead
Init +3; **Senses** low-light vision, scent; **Perception** +4

AC 14, touch 14, flat-footed 11 (+3 Dex, +1 size)
hp 4 (1d8)
Fort +2; **Ref** +3; **Will** +3
Immune undead traits

Speed 40 ft., climb 20 ft., swim 20 ft.
Melee bite +1 (1d4 plus disease)
Special Attacks disease, paralysis (1d4 rounds, DC 10, elves are immune to this effect)

Str 10, **Dex** 17, **Con** —, **Int** 2, **Wis** 13, **Cha** 10
Base Atk +0; **CMB** −1; **CMD** 12 (16 vs. trip)
Feats Skill Focus (Perception)
Skills Climb +11, Perception +4, Stealth +11, Swim +11; **Racial Modifiers** uses Dex to modify Climb and Swim

Environment any
Organization solitary or flood (2–40)
Treasure none

Disease (Ex) *Filth fever*: Bite—injury; *save* DC 10 Fort; *onset* 1d3 days; *frequency* 1/day; *effect* 1d3 Dex damage and 1d3 Con damage; *cure* 2 consecutive saves. The save DC is Charisma-based.

Resembling giant rats with desiccated, leathery skin, and patches of missing fur and flesh, the rat-ghoul is created when normal or dire rats feast on undead flesh, or being inundated with black magic or necrotic forces. Rat-ghouls may be found in any evil area, and they act much as normal rats in their typical environments.

Rat-ghouls retain a spark of their former rat intelligence. They tend to stay in packs, looking to feast on flesh and detritus. If no "normal" food is available, the rat-ghouls begin feasting on each other, and then possibly even themselves, so strong is their hunger.

Rat-ghouls attack en masse, and attempt to overrun their opponents. Rat-ghouls that successfully take an opponent to the ground swarm and eat the creature as soon as possible. Rat-ghouls retain the ability to paralyze foes as normal ghouls.

Credit

Original author James C. Boney
Originally appearing in *Dread Saecaroth*
(© Frog God Games, 2011)

Ravager

The Ravager has three possible forms, and corresponding descriptions:

The Crawler: This enormous creature stands 18 ft. high at the shoulders and has a body 30 ft. long. Its body is long and narrow, with eight stubby legs ending in ebon claws the size of large falchions. Its mouth is filled with sharp black teeth, and its eyes are jet-black orbs the size of dinner platters, set above a delicate muzzle like that of a bulldog. The body is hairless, covered with a thick, leathery crimson hide.

The Brawler: Towering 35 ft. high is a massive, apelike creature, resting on two sets of powerfully muscled legs. A third set of arms, thick and corded with muscle, bulges out from its massive shoulders, ending with massive black claws. The mouth is filled with jagged black teeth, and glistening black eyes are set over a wide muzzle. Its skin is deep red, somewhat lighter on the underbelly.

The Flier: With a crack and boom, this creature spreads a pair of great leathery wings over 50 ft. in span. Its body is lean and covered with rippling muscle beneath a thick, leathery crimson hide. Its claws and teeth are black, as are its eyes.

THE RAVAGER (CRAWLER FORM) — CR 30

XP 9,830,400
N Gargantuan magical beast
Init +7; **Senses** darkvision 120 ft., low-light vision, scent, tremorsense 60 ft.; **Perception** +45

AC 45, touch 13, flat-footed 38 (+7 Dex, +32 natural, −4 size)
hp 857 (35d10+630 plus 35); regeneration 20 (epic-level weapons and artifacts), vampiric healing
Fort +39; **Ref** +26; **Will** +20
Defensive Abilities magic disruption (1–4 on d20); **DR** 30/epic; **Immune** energy drain; **Resist** death, energy 20

Speed 50 ft., burrow 20 ft.
Melee bite +46 (6d6+15/19–20/x3), 4 claws +46 (4d6+15/15–20)
Space 20 ft.; **Reach** 15 ft.
Special Attacks trample (4d6+22, DC 42)

Str 40, **Dex** 24, **Con** 46, **Int** 6, **Wis** 25, **Cha** 24
Base Atk +35; **CMB** +54; **CMD** 71 (75 vs. trip)
Feats Cleave, Combat Reflexes, Critical Focus, Great Cleave, Great Fortitude, Improved Critical (bite), Improved Critical (claw), Improved Natural Armor (x4), Improved Natural Attack (bite), Improved Natural Attack (claw), Improved Vital Strike, Iron Will, Power Attack, Toughness, Vital Strike
Skills Perception +45
SQ form-shifting

Environment any
Organization solitary
Treasure none

THE RAVAGER (BRAWLER FORM) — CR 30

XP 9,830,400
N Gargantuan magical beast
Init +7; **Senses** darkvision 120 ft., low-light vision, scent, tremorsense 60 ft.; **Perception** +45

AC 45, touch 13, flat-footed 38 (+7 Dex, +32 natural, −4 size)
hp 612 (35d10+385 plus 35); regeneration 20 (epic-level weapons and artifacts), vampiric healing
Fort +32; **Ref** +26; **Will** +20
Defensive Abilities magic disruption (1–4 on d20); **DR** 30/epic; **Immune** energy drain; **Resist** death, energy 20

Speed 70 ft.
Melee bite +51 (3d8+20/x3), 2 claws +51 (3d8+20/15–20)
Space 20 ft.; **Reach** 20 ft.
Special Attacks trample (3d8+30, DC 45)

Str 50, **Dex** 24, **Con** 32, **Int** 6, **Wis** 25, **Cha** 24
Base Atk +35; **CMB** +59; **CMD** 76
Feats Awesome Blow, Cleave, Combat Reflexes, Critical Focus, Great Cleave, Great Fortitude, Improved Critical (claw), Improved Natural Armor (x4), Improved Natural Attack (claw) (x2), Improved Sunder, Iron Will, Power Attack, Toughness, Vital Strike
Skills Perception +45
SQ form-shifting

Environment any
Organization solitary

Treasure none

THE RAVAGER (FLIER FORM)   CR 30

XP 9,830,400
N Gargantuan magical beast
Init +14; **Senses** darkvision 120 ft., low-light vision, scent, tremorsense 60 ft.; **Perception** +45

AC 52, touch 20, flat-footed 38 (+14 Dex, +32 natural, −4 size)
hp 612 (35d10+385 plus 35); regeneration 20 (epic-level weapons and artifacts), vampiric healing
Fort +34; **Ref** +33; **Will** +20
Defensive Abilities magic disruption (1–4 on d20); **DR** 30/epic; **Immune** energy drain; **Resist** death, energy 20

Speed 20 ft., fly 140 ft. (good)
Melee bite +46 (6d8+15/x3), 2 claws +46 (2d8+15/18–20)
Space 20 ft.; **Reach** 15 ft.

Str 40, **Dex** 38, **Con** 32, **Int** 6, **Wis** 25, **Cha** 24
Base Atk +35; **CMB** +54; **CMD** 78
Feats Cleave, Combat Reflexes, Critical Focus, Flyby Attack, Great Cleave, Great Fortitude, Hover, Improved Natural Attack (bite) (x2), Improved Natural Armor (x4), Improved Vital Strike, Iron Will, Power Attack, Snatch[B], Toughness, Vital Strike
Skills Perception +45
SQ form-shifting

Environment any
Organization solitary
Treasure none

Death Resistance (Ex) The Ravager possesses an innate resistance to effects that would kill or permanently incapacitate it, including petrification and imprisonment. Against such effects it is considered to automatically make any required saving throws.
Energy Resistance (Ex) The Ravager possesses energy resistance against *all* forms of energy attack (fire, cold, electricity, acid, and sonic).
Form-Shifting (Ex) The Ravager can physically alter its physiology to take on one of the three listed forms: the crawler, the brawler, or the flier. Doing so takes one minute, and during this period it cannot take any other actions, though it is not considered helpless.
Magic Disruption (Su) Every time the Ravager comes into contact with a spell or spell-like or supernatural effect, there is a chance as indicated above that the magic does not affect it. In the case of ongoing effects, a new check is made each round.
Regeneration (Ex) The Ravager and its brood treat all damage as subdual, except damage from epic-level weapons and artifacts.
Trample (Ex) The Ravager gains its vampiric healing ability on this damage where appropriate. The Ravager does not have this ability in its flier form. Instead, it gains Snatch as a bonus feat.
Vampiric Healing (Su) Whenever the Ravager hits with a melee attack, it is healed hit points equal to half the damage it inflicts on its opponent. This ability cannot heal it above its natural maximum hit points. This ability extends to its trample special attack, where applicable.

The Ravager was created eons ago by a primeval race of beings who believed in the unity of three forces: body, mind, and spirit. In their ongoing war with another race of savages, they created several weapons of terrible power. The greatest of these is the living beast known only as the Ravager.

This beast was given incredible vitality, and the power to manipulate its

own body to assume a form most advantageous to it: a crawling weasel-like form that can burrow, a hulking apelike humanoid form with greater reach and strength, and a winged form to allow it greater mobility and agility.

After being used once or twice on the battlefield, those who created it realized its awesome danger and contained it in the strongest prison they could devise, suspended in time until it would once again be needed.

However, due to the subsequent influence of Orcus near the vault where the Ravager was contained, the wards were damaged, and a taint of evil infected its quarantine. This has resulted in it reproducing asexually, and has granted the ravager an astonishing capacity for growth. For every week that it lives, it permanently gains 1 hit die. There is no known limit to how far this advancement can go before it either devastates the planet it lives on or collapses under its own weight.

RAVAGER SPAWN (CRAWLER FORM) — CR 20

XP 307,200
N Huge magical beast
Init +5; **Senses** darkvision 120 ft., low-light vision, scent, tremorsense 60 ft.; **Perception** +40

AC 40, touch 13, flat-footed 35 (+5 Dex, +27 natural, –2 size)
hp 495 (30d10+300 plus 30); regeneration 5 (epic-level weapons and artifacts), vampiric healing
Fort +29; **Ref** +22; **Will** +19
Defensive Abilities magic disruption (1 on d20); **DR** 15/epic; **Immune** energy drain; **Resist** death, energy 5

Speed 40 ft., burrow 10 ft.
Melee bite +37 (3d8+9/19–20/x3), 4 claws +37 (2d8+9/18–20)
Space 15 ft.; **Reach** 10 ft.

Str 28, **Dex** 20, **Con** 30, **Int** 5, **Wis** 25, **Cha** 18
Base Atk +30; **CMB** +41 (+43 to bull rush); **CMD** 56 (58 vs. bull rush, 60 vs. trip)
Feats Cleave, Combat Reflexes, Critical Focus, Great Cleave, Great Fortitude, Improved Bull Rush, Improved Critical (bite), Improved Natural Armor (x3), Improved Natural Attack (bite), Improved Natural Attack (claw), Iron Will, Power Attack, Toughness
Skills Perception +40
SQ form-shifting

Environment any
Organization solitary or brood (2–8)
Treasure none

RAVAGER SPAWN (BRAWLER FORM) — CR 20

XP 307,200
N Huge magical beast
Init +5; **Senses** darkvision 120 ft., low-light vision, scent, tremorsense 60 ft.; **Perception** +26

AC 37, touch 13, flat-footed 32 (+5 Dex, +24 natural, –2 size)
hp 405 (30d10+210 plus 30); regeneration 5 (epic-level weapons and artifacts), vampiric healing
Fort +26; **Ref** +22; **Will** +19
Defensive Abilities magic disruption (1 on d20); **DR** 15/epic; **Immune** energy drain; **Resist** death, energy 5

Speed 50 ft.
Melee bite +40 (3d6+12/x3), 2 claws +40 (1d12+12/15–20)
Space 15 ft.; **Reach** 15 ft.

Str 34, **Dex** 20, **Con** 24, **Int** 5, **Wis** 25, **Cha** 18
Base Atk +30; **CMB** +43 (+45 to bull rush); **CMD** 58 (60 vs. bull rush)
Feats Awesome Blow, Cleave, Combat Reflexes, Critical Focus, Great Fortitude, Greater Vital Strike, Improved Bull Rush, Improved Critical (claw), Improved Vital Strike, Iron Will, Power Attack, Staggering Critical, Stunning Critical, Toughness, Vital Strike
Skills Perception +40
SQ form-shifting

Environment any
Organization solitary or brood (2–8)
Treasure none

RAVAGER SPAWN (FLIER FORM) — CR 20

XP 307,200
N Huge magical beast
Init +8; **Senses** darkvision 120 ft., low-light vision, scent, tremorsense 60 ft.; **Perception** +18

AC 40, touch 16, flat-footed 32 (+8 Dex, +24 natural, –2 size)
hp 405 (30d10+210 plus 30); regeneration 5 (epic-level weapons and artifacts), vampiric healing
Fort +25; **Ref** +27; **Will** +19
Defensive Abilities magic disruption (1 on d20); **DR** 15/epic; **Immune** energy drain; **Resist** death, energy 5

Speed 20 ft., fly 100 ft. (good)
Melee bite +37 (3d6+9/x3), 2 claws +37 (1d12+9/18–20)
Space 15 ft.; **Reach** 10 ft.

Str 28, **Dex** 26, **Con** 24, **Int** 5, **Wis** 25, **Cha** 18
Base Atk +30; **CMB** +41; **CMD** 59
Feats Cleave, Combat Reflexes, Critical Focus, Endurance, Flyby Attack, Great Fortitude, Hover, Iron Will, Lightning Reflexes, Lunge, Power Attack, Skill Focus (Fly), Snatch, Toughness, Wingover
Skills Fly +22, Perception +18
SQ form-shifting

Environment any
Organization solitary or brood (2–8)
Treasure none

Death Resistance (Ex) A Ravager spawn possesses an innate resistance to effects that would kill or permanently incapacitate it, including petrification and imprisonment. Against such effects it is considered to automatically make any required saving throws.
Energy Resistance (Ex) A Ravager spawn possesses energy resistance against all forms of energy attack (fire, cold, electricity, acid, and sonic).
Form-Shifting (Ex) A Ravager spawn can physically alter its physiology to take on one of the three listed forms: the crawler, the brawler, or the flier. Doing so takes one minute, and during this period it cannot take any other actions, though it is not considered helpless.
Magic Disruption (Su) Every time a Ravager spawn comes into contact with a spell or spell-like or supernatural effect, there is a chance as indicated above that the magic does not affect it. In the case of ongoing effects, a new check is made each round.
Regeneration (Ex) A Ravager spawn treats all damage as subdual, except damage from epic-level weapons and artifacts.
Vampiric Healing (Su) Whenever a Ravager spawn hits with a melee attack, it is healed hit points equal to half the damage it inflicts on its opponent. This ability cannot heal it above its natural maximum hit points. This ability extends to its trample special attack, where applicable.

Credit
Originally appearing in Rappan Athuk Reloaded (© Necromancer Games, 2006)

Salamander, Ice

This creature has the scaled upper torso of a humanoid, a snake-like head, and the lower body of a four-legged lizard with thick powerful legs. Its scales are icy blue and the creature's underbelly is white.

ICE SALAMANDER	CR 5

XP 1,600
CE Medium outsider (air, cold, extraplanar, water)
Init +5; **Senses** darkvision 60 ft.; **Perception** +12
Aura bitter cold (10 ft.)

AC 18, touch 11, flat-footed 17 (+1 Dex, +7 natural)
hp 59 (7d10+21)
Fort +8; **Ref** +6; **Will** +4
DR 10/magic; **Immune** cold
Weaknesses vulnerability to fire

Speed 30 ft., burrow 20 ft. (ice and snow only)
Melee spear +11/+6 (1d8+4/x3 plus 1d6 cold) or 2 claws +10 (1d6+3 plus 1d6 cold)

Str 16, **Dex** 12, **Con** 16, **Int** 12, **Wis** 15, **Cha** 12
Base Atk +7; **CMB** +10; **CMD** 21 (25 vs. trip)
Feats Cleave, Improved Initiative, Power Attack, Weapon Focus (spear)
Skills Bluff +11, Intimidate +11, Knowledge (planes) +11, Perception +12, Sense Motive +12, Stealth +11, Survival +12
Languages Aquan, Common
SQ snow move, snow vision

Environment any (Plane of Water)
Organization solitary, pair, gang (3–5)
Treasure standard (spear, other treasure)

Bitter Cold (Ex) All creatures within 10 feet of an ice salamander take 1d6 points of cold damage each round on the ice salamander's turn. Additionally, creatures that takes cold damage from the salamander's aura must succeed on a DC 16 Fortitude save or be staggered for 1 round. The save DC is Constitution-based.
Snow Move (Ex) An ice salamander suffers no penalties for moving through snow-covered terrain.
Snow Vision (Ex) An ice salamander can see perfectly well in snowy conditions and does not take any penalties on Perception checks while in snow.

Ice salamanders are malign creatures that dwell on the elemental planes where Water meets Air. Scholars speculate an entire plane (a para-elemental plane of cold or ice) exists where the Plane of Air and Plane of Water meet. There, the great ice salamanders make their homes carved into great icebergs or upon vast sheets of ice. Upon their home plane, the ice salamanders gather in large, loose tribes, led by the strongest member of the group. Infighting is common among tribal members and should a dispute escalate, it is usually settled in a makeshift arena where all participants fight to the death.

When summoned to the Material Plane ice salamanders can be found in arctic regions where the temperatures are constantly freezing or lower (which to an ice salamander is still too warm). On the Material Plane, ice salamanders are often found acting as guards for high-level wizards or temple guardians for clerics of the frost gods. Some ice salamanders find their way to the Material Plane on their own, in areas where the elemental planes have spilled over to the Material Plane.

An ice salamander stands about 6 feet tall with a serpentine head and the lower torso of a salamander. Its scales are blue mottled white, and its underbelly is stark white. Its eyes are ice blue and its pupils are dark. Cold seems to emanate from the creature at all times.

Ice salamanders jump headlong into melee, slashing their opponents with their wicked spears or claws. Prisoners are rarely taken, unless the ice salamanders are instructed to do so. Most of the time, prey is devoured as soon as it's killed.

Sciurian

This halfling-sized creature is covered in gray fur. She has rounded ears, large black eyes, and a long bushy tail that reaches up to the back of her head before curling away.

SCIURIAN	CR 1/2

XP 200
Sciurian ranger 1
NG Small humanoid (sciurian)
Init +3; **Senses** low-light vision; **Perception** +7

AC 17, touch 15, flat-footed 13 (+2 armor, +3 Dex, +1 dodge, +1 size)
hp 12 (1d10+1 plus 1)
Fort +3; **Ref** +5; **Will** +3

Speed 30 ft., climb 20 ft.; scamper
Melee shortspear +2 (1d4)
Ranged short bow +5 (1d4/x3)
Special Attacks favored enemy (+2 magical beasts)

Str 10, **Dex** 17, **Con** 13, **Int** 10, **Wis** 16, **Cha** 8
Base Atk +1; **CMB** +0; **CMD** 14
Feats Dodge
Skills Acrobatics +5, Climb +14, Heal +7, Knowledge (nature) +4, Perception +7, Stealth +11, Survival +7;
Racial Modifiers +2 Acrobatics, +2 Climb
Languages Common, Sciurian
SQ nature's acrobat, scamper, track, wild empathy

Environment temperate forests
Organization solitary, foraging party (2–4), tribe (4–24 non-combatants plus 2d6 1st level warriors, 1d4 1st level aristocrats and one 5th level aristocrat chief)
Treasure standard (leather armor, shortspear, short bow, 20 arrows, other treasure)

Nature's Acrobat (Ex): All sciurians have a +2 racial bonus on Climb and Acrobatics checks. Climb is always class skill for a Sciurian. Once per day, when a sciurian makes a Reflex saving throw, she can roll the saving throw and take the better result. The sciurian must decide to use this ability before the saving throw is attempted.
Scamper (Ex): A sciurian adds +10 ft. to its ground speed when charging, running, or withdrawing.

Sciurians resemble humanoid squirrels. They are a diminutive, furry folk who dwell deep in the forests far from the intrusions of other races. A typical sciurian is curious, but also somewhat skittish. They are prone to nervous twitching of their tails, and often pause to scan the surrounding area for danger. In a comfortable environment, sciurians are amiable creatures and enjoy music and celebration.

Sciurian fur ranges from gray to brown to orange-red, and fades to white on their bellies. They have bushy, s-shaped tails. Their eyes are large and dark, and their rounded ears are situated on the tops of their heads. Sciurians have long fingers and toes tipped with claws which enable them to climb with startling speed. Sciurians use the claws on their hands and feet to climb, so they do not wear any sort of footwear. Magical footwear worn by a sciurian becomes open-toed and thus does not hinder her climbing ability.

Sciurian Society

Sciurians live in small tribal communities in huts built high in the tops of tall trees. The huts are connected by a complex network of narrow walkways, rope bridges, and swing-lines. Aside from allowing the sciurians to take advantage of their natural abilities as agile climbers, these connections also act as defensive barriers for the community, allowing the sciurians to freely move about while hampering the movements of invaders. Sciurians are territorial, and attempt to drive off any interlopers that stray too close to their communities. Sciurian tribes are led by a shaman-chief, elected from among the tribe's spell casters. Most shaman-chiefs are divine spellcasters, but occasionally an arcane spellcaster or even a rogue with magical abilities can be found in the position. Sciurian tribes farm nut-producing trees to provide food for their members, augmented by ground-level foraging. They store away the excess to provide food through harsh winters.

Sciurians relate most easily to elves and gnomes, the former because of the elves' love of the natural world, and the latter because of the gnomes' fey nature. Humans and dwarves tend to think of sciurians as silly and annoying, often overlooking the quiet forest dwellers to their detriment. On those occasions when halflings and sciurians meet, there is a mutual respect between them due in part to their similarities in size and nature. Half-orcs often need to be reminded that sciurians are not food.

Sciurians are fun-loving creatures who enjoy the sights and sounds of the forest. Tall trees are near and dear to the hearts of all sciurians. They revere the Great Oak, an immense, neutral, treant-like goddess who is all things: provider, teacher, protector, creator, and destroyer. Young sciurians bored with the day-to-day routines of tree farming and foraging often seek adventure in the lands beyond their community. Sciurian adventurers tend to be eager to please, hoping to overcome their reputation as being flighty tree-hoppers. Unfortunately, their eagerness often leads to reinforcing those stereotypes instead. Sciurians are not strong in combat, and thus avoid the more combative classes such as barbarian and fighter. Most sciurian adventurers are divine spellcasters, rangers, and rogues.

Sciurian Racial Traits

Sciurians are defined by their class levels—they do not possess racial Hit Dice. Sciurian clerics of the Great Oak can choose from among the following domains: Community, Knowledge, Plant, and Protection. All sciurians have the following racial traits.

–2 Str, +2 Dex, +2 Wis: Sciurians are not physically powerful, but are extremely agile and shrewd.
Small: Sciurians are Small creatures and gain a +1 size bonus to their AC, a +1 size bonus on attack rolls, a –1 penalty to their Combat Maneuver Bonus and Combat Maneuver Defense, and a +4 size bonus on Stealth checks.
Speed: Sciurians have a base speed of 30 ft. and a climb speed 20 ft..
Nature's Acrobat: All sciurians have a +2 racial bonus on Climb and Acrobatics checks. Climb is always class skill for a Sciurian. Once per day, when a sciurian makes a Reflex saving throw, she can roll the saving throw twice and take the better result. The sciurian must decide to use this ability before the saving throw is attempted.
Scamper: A sciurian adds +10 ft. to its ground speed when charging, running, or withdrawing.
Languages: Sciurians begin play speaking Common and Sciurian. Sciurians with high Intelligence scores can choose from the following bonus languages: Elf, Gnome, Sylvan, Halfling, and Terran.

Scorpionfolk

This creature has the upper torso of a muscular bronze-skinned humanoid and the lower torso of a giant sand-colored scorpion.

SCORPIONFOLK	CR 5

XP 1,600
LE Large monstrous humanoid
Init +1; **Senses** darkvision 60 ft., tremorsense 60 ft.;
Perception +14

AC 16, touch 10, flat-footed 15 (+1 Dex, +6 natural, −1 size)
hp 59 (7d10+21)
Fort +5; **Ref** +6; **Will** +9
Defensive Abilities poison resistance; **SR** 16

Speed 40 ft.
Melee mwk falchion +11/+6 (2d6+6), sting +5 (1d6+2 plus poison) or 2 claws +10 (1d6+4), sting +10 (1d6+2 plus poison)
Ranged mwk composite shortbow +8/+3 (1d8+4)
Space 10 ft.; **Reach** 5 ft.

Str 19, **Dex** 12, **Con** 16, **Int** 8, **Wis** 14, **Cha** 15
Base Atk +7; **CMB** +12; **CMD** 23 (35 vs. trip)
Feats Alertness, Cleave, Iron Will, Power Attack
Skills Climb +8, Diplomacy +6, Intimidate +9, Perception +14, Sense Motive +6, Stealth +4, Survival +9; **Racial Modifiers** +4 Climb, +4 Perception
Languages Sadara

Environment warm deserts
Organization solitary, gang (2–5), band (6–10 plus 1–4 medium scorpions), troop (11–20 plus 2–8 medium scorpions and 1 giant scorpion), or tribe (20–40 plus 8–16 medium scorpions and 2–4 giant scorpions)
Treasure standard (masterwork falchion, masterwork composite shortbow, 30 arrows, other treasure)

Poison (Ex) Sting—injury; *save* DC 16 Fort; *frequency* 1/round; *effect* 1d2 Strength damage; *cure* 1 save. The save DC is Constitution-based.
Poison Resistance (Ex) Scorpionfolk gain a +4 racial bonus on all saving throws against poison.

both nomadic and settled, often have a shaman (a cleric or sorcerer of 5th–8th level) in their midst. These shamans tend to the sick and injured and sometimes take part in raids or excursions by the scorpionfolk. Tribal leaders are fighters or barbarians of 6th–9th level.

Scorpionfolk stand just over 6 feet tall and are over 10 feet long from head to the base of the tail. Tails range from 8 to 10 feet long. Scorpionfolk, on average, weigh around 2,000 pounds. Their skin is usually bronze, brown, or black, and the lower scorpion torso dark tan or the color of dark sand. Hair color varies, with most males shaving their heads and females wearing their hair long in tightly knotted ponytails.

Scorpionfolk prefer to attack with weapons and a tail sting, only resorting to their clawed hands if necessary. Favored weapons of these creatures include falchions, spears, scimitars, and shortbows.

The people known as scorpionfolk (known as sadara among their own kind) are a race of nomadic desert-dwellers known for their cruelty and combat prowess. Believed to have once been a just and kind race that became corrupted by magic, scorpionfolk are feared and avoided by most intelligent desert-traveling races.

Most scorpionfolk tribes tend to be nomadic and move around frequently, only settling in one place until the food source runs out. These tribes use tents for shelter and care little for any belongings other than what they can carry. Some few tribes settle in an area and construct small towns and villages of hardened mud, rock, and occasionally limestone. These tribes tend to be slightly more civilized than the nomadic scorpionfolk, and are often looked upon with disdain by their nomadic brothers. Larger tribes,

Screamer

Racing toward you is a ghostly form like the tattered shreds of a translucent pennant. It retains a vaguely humanoid form trailing behind its forward-facing head. Hollows mark its eyes above its most distinguishing feature, a gaping mouth locked in a perpetual scream—like a maw opening into eternal darkness.

SCREAMER	CR 4

XP 1,200
CE Medium undead (incorporeal)
Init +7; **Senses** darkvision 60 ft.; **Perception** +6

AC 17, touch 17, flat-footed 14 (+4 deflection, +3 Dex)
hp 34 (4d8+16)
Fort +5; **Ref** +4; **Will** +4
Defensive Abilities channel resistance +2, incorporeal, rejuvenation; **Immune** undead traits

---

Speed fly 80 ft. (perfect)
Melee incorporeal touch +6 (1d4 Charisma drain)
Special Attacks Charisma drain, malevolence, scream of hopelessness, suicidal frenzy

---

Str —, **Dex** 16, **Con** —, **Int** 6, **Wis** 11, **Cha** 18
Base Atk +3; **CMB** +6; **CMD** 23
Feats Flyby Attack, Improved Initiative
Skills Fly +16, Perception +6, Stealth +9

Environment any
Organization solitary, gang (2–4), or swarm (6–11)
Treasure none

Charisma Drain (Su)
A screamer causes 1d4 points of Charisma drain each time it hits with its incorporeal touch attack. On each successful attack, it gains 5 temporary hit points.

Malevolence (Su) Once per round, a screamer can merge its body with a creature on the Material Plane. This ability is similar to a *magic jar* spell (caster level 10th or the screamer's Hit Dice, whichever is higher), except that it does not require a receptacle. To use this ability the screamer must try to move into the target's space; moving into the target's space to use the malevolence ability does not provoke attacks of opportunity. The target can resist the attack with a successful DC 16 Will save, but the target adds (or subtracts) its Charisma modifier to this saving throw roll. A creature that successfully saves is immune to that same screamer's malevolence for 24 hours, and the screamer cannot enter the target's space. If the save fails, the screamer vanishes into the target's body. Screamers prefer to use this attack after having made several Charisma drain attacks to weaken a target's resistance. The save DC is Charisma-based.

Rejuvenation (Su) A screamer cannot be killed through simple combat. If reduced to 0 hit points it disappears only to reform 24 hours later. The only way for a screamer to be truly laid to rest is for it to die while possessing a host body with its malevolence ability. When the body dies, the screamer spirit ceases to exist.

Scream of Hopelessness (Su) Once every hour, a screamer can loose a horrific, mournful scream. Any living creature within hearing distance of this scream (it can carry up to a mile outdoors) must succeed on a DC 16 Will save or become shaken for 2d4 rounds. This is a sonic, mind-affecting fear attack. Creatures that successfully save cannot be affected by the same screamer's scream of hopelessness for 24 hours. The effects of multiple screamers' screams cannot stack. The save DC is Charisma-based.

Suicidal Frenzy (Su) If a screamer succeeds in possessing a target with its malevolence ability, it immediately begins to make suicidal attacks on the possessed body with the body's own weaponry. Each round, the screamer uses the body's full attacks to direct its weaponry against itself. It uses the possessed victim's attack and damage modifiers and must only succeed on an attack against the body's flat-footed armor class. Damage, including the possibility of critical hits, is rolled normally. Due to the inhabiting spirit, the possessed body continues its attacks even between –1 and –9 hit points, though only single attacks can be made at this point. If the possessed body is made helpless the screamer departs to find another target. If the possessed body dies, the screamer's spirit is destroyed as it goes to its final rest.

These terrible undead are the remnant of soldiers who have fallen to the horrors of mass conflict and warfare. Whether each of these creatures is the remains of a single fallen soldier or a conglomerate of the scarred psyches of several such casualties remains up for debate, however what is known as that all of these creatures harbor an unending hatred of the living and an unceasing quest for the release of death. These mutual drives combine to create a horrifying fate for all those unfortunate enough to encounter a screamer.

A screamer retains no language.

In combat a screamer emits a continual piercing keen which rises in volume and pitch to become its scream attack. It uses this in conjunction with its charisma-draining touch to wear down its victim and make them susceptible to its malevolence attack. A screamer attack that is completely successful always ends in the creature's own destruction.

Credit
Original author Greg A. Vaughan
Originally appearing in *Slumbering Tsar* (© Frog God Games/ Greg A. Vaughan, 2012)

Sea Serpent, Finback

This enormous creature is mottled green and has a dark green dorsal fin that runs the length of its body. Its mouth opens to reveal hundreds of razor-sharp teeth.

FINBACK SEA SERPENT	CR 15

XP 51,200
CE Gargantuan magical beast (aquatic)
Init +7; **Senses** darkvision 60 ft., low-light vision;
Perception +10

AC 30, touch 9, flat-footed 27 (+3 Dex, +21 natural, −4 size)
hp 250 (20d10+140)
Fort +21; **Ref** +15; **Will** +6
Immune cold; **Resist** fire 30

Speed swim 60 ft., surge 500 ft.
Melee bite +28 (4d8+11/19–20 plus grab),
tail slap +22 (3d8+5 plus grab)
Space 20 ft.; **Reach** 15 ft.
Special Attacks breath weapon (60-ft. cone, 8d12 fire damage; DC 27 Ref half, usable every 1d4 rounds), capsize, constrict (3d8+11), swallow whole (4d8+16 bludgeoning damage plus 2d8 fire damage, AC 20, hp 25)

Str 32, **Dex** 16, **Con** 24, **Int** 4, **Wis** 11, **Cha** 11
Base Atk +20; **CMB** +35 (+39 grapple); **CMD** 48 (can't be tripped)
Feats Awesome Blow, Great Fortitude, Improved Bull Rush, Improved Critical (bite), Improved Initiative, Power Attack, Skill Focus (Stealth), Swim-By Attack, Vital Strike, Weapon Focus (bite)
Skills Perception +10, Stealth +5, Swim +27
Languages Aquan (can't speak)

Environment any oceans
Organization solitary
Treasure none

Breath Weapon (Su) The finback sea serpent's breath weapon is a cone of superheated steam and water.
Capsize (Ex) A finback sea serpent can attempt to capsize a boat or ship of its size or smaller by ramming it as a charge attack and making a combat maneuver check. The DC of this check is 25 or the result of the boat captain's Profession (sailor) check, whichever is higher.
Surge (Ex) A finback sea serpent can surge forward as a full-round action at a speed of 500 feet. It must move in a straight line, but does not provoke attacks of opportunity while surging.

Finback sea serpents make their lairs deep beneath the ocean's waves in undersea caverns, often killing the former owner to claim such a lair. Finbacks are malevolent creatures and take great pride in causing death and destruction. These legendary creatures are both feared and respected by sailors and seafarers.

Finbacks spend much of their time dormant in their watery lair. When roused to action, it is most often to feed or to ward off trespassers that have unknowingly entered its domain. Finbacks dine on large aquatic animals such as octopi, giant fish, and even krakens. Aquatic humanoids are a delicacy as are land-based humanoids that sail their ships too close to a finback's lair.

Finback sea serpents reach lengths of up to 60 feet and weigh close to 5,000 pounds. Larger specimens are rumored to exist, but thankfully none have been encountered thus far. Finback sea serpents are long, sleek creatures, usually grayish-green in color, with a large sail-like dorsal fin spanning the length of its body.

Finback sea serpents attack with a powerful breath weapon and ferocious bite. When confronted by ship-sailing creatures, finbacks attack the ship, attempting to capsize it and dump the crew into the water where they are quickly disposed of.

Sealwere

This humanoid has the head of a seal with deep blue eyes. Its mouth is lined with sharpened teeth.

SEALWERE	CR 2

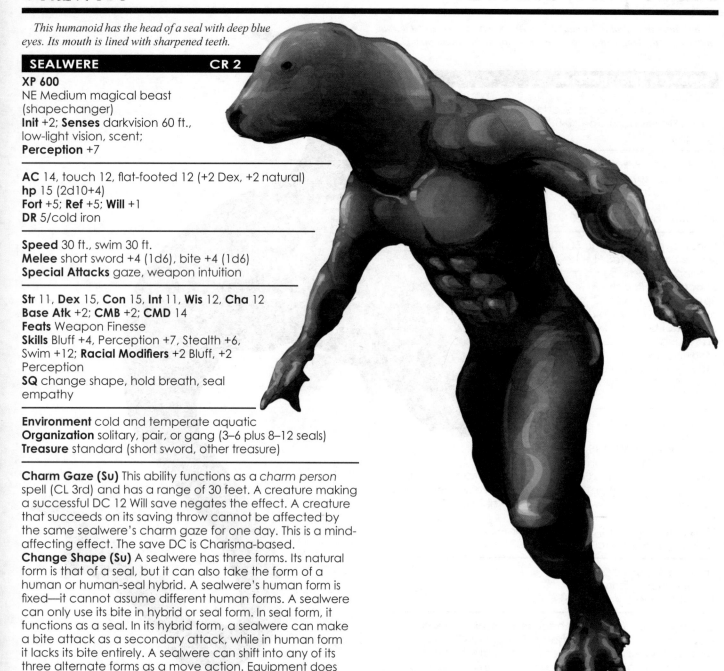

XP 600
NE Medium magical beast (shapechanger)
Init +2; **Senses** darkvision 60 ft., low-light vision, scent;
Perception +7

AC 14, touch 12, flat-footed 12 (+2 Dex, +2 natural)
hp 15 (2d10+4)
Fort +5; **Ref** +5; **Will** +1
DR 5/cold iron

Speed 30 ft., swim 30 ft.
Melee short sword +4 (1d6), bite +4 (1d6)
Special Attacks gaze, weapon intuition

Str 11, **Dex** 15, **Con** 15, **Int** 11, **Wis** 12, **Cha** 12
Base Atk +2; **CMB** +2; **CMD** 14
Feats Weapon Finesse
Skills Bluff +4, Perception +7, Stealth +6, Swim +12; **Racial Modifiers** +2 Bluff, +2 Perception
SQ change shape, hold breath, seal empathy

Environment cold and temperate aquatic
Organization solitary, pair, or gang (3–6 plus 8–12 seals)
Treasure standard (short sword, other treasure)

Charm Gaze (Su) This ability functions as a *charm person* spell (CL 3rd) and has a range of 30 feet. A creature making a successful DC 12 Will save negates the effect. A creature that succeeds on its saving throw cannot be affected by the same sealwere's charm gaze for one day. This is a mind-affecting effect. The save DC is Charisma-based.
Change Shape (Su) A sealwere has three forms. Its natural form is that of a seal, but it can also take the form of a human or human-seal hybrid. A sealwere's human form is fixed—it cannot assume different human forms. A sealwere can only use its bite in hybrid or seal form. In seal form, it functions as a seal. In its hybrid form, a sealwere can make a bite attack as a secondary attack, while in human form it lacks its bite entirely. A sealwere can shift into any of its three alternate forms as a move action. Equipment does not meld with the new form between human and hybrid forms but does between those forms and its seal form.
Hold Breath (Ex) A sealwere in hybrid form can hold its breath for a number of minutes equal to 4 × its Constitution score before it risks drowning.
Seal Empathy (Ex) A sealwere can communicate and empathize with seals, and can use Bluff as if it were Diplomacy to change a seal's attitude, receiving a +4 racial bonus to do so.
Weapon Intuition (Ex) A sealwere is proficient with simple and martial melee weapons.

Sealweres are anthropomorphs: animals that can take human or hybrid form. These creatures spend most of their time in seal form moving among normal animals of their kind. When hungry and on the hunt however, a sealwere assumes human or hybrid form and stalks its prey, preferring to attack from the shadows when possible.

A sealwere stands about 6 feet tall and weighs 150 pounds. Hair and eye color vary among individuals, but eyes are almost always a shade of blue.

Seal

This sleek, aquatic mammal has a pair of flippered limbs, a powerful tail, and a muzzle full of small sharp teeth.

SEAL	CR 1/3

XP 135
N Small animal
Init +1; **Senses** low-light vision; **Perception** +12

AC 13, touch 12, flat-footed 12 (+1 Dex, +1 natural, +1 size)
hp 4 (1d8)
Fort +2; **Ref** +3; **Will** +1

Speed 10 ft., swim 60 ft.
Melee bite +2 (1d4)

Str 10, **Dex** 13, **Con** 11, **Int** 2, **Wis** 13, **Cha** 6
Base Atk +0; **CMB** −1; **CMD** 10 (can't be tripped)
Feats Skill Focus (Perception)
Skills Perception +12, Swim +8; **Racial Modifiers** +4 Perception
SQ hold breath
Languages none

Environment any oceans
Organization solitary, pair, rookery (3–24)
Treasure none

Hold Breath (Ex) A seal can hold its breath for a number of minutes equal to 6 × its Constitution score before it risks drowning.

Sleek-bodied aquatic mammals, seals spend the majority of their lives in the water, whether in the harbors of tropical ports or amid wandering icebergs. They prefer rocky beaches, upon which they rest, raise their young, and dive to hunt fish, squid, sea birds, and other small aquatic creatures. They are well known for their vocal communications consisting of barks, grunts, and flipper slaps, traits that cause many humanoids to remark on their intelligence and the ease with which they can be trained.

Serpent Creeper

This large vine springs to life revealing a serpentine head with fanged mouth.

SERPENT CREEPER	CR 4

XP 1,200
N Large plant
Init +3; **Senses** low-light vision, tremorsense 60 ft.; **Perception** +11

AC 18, touch 12, flat-footed 15 (+3 Dex, +6 natural, –1 size)
hp 51 (6d8+18 plus 6)
Fort +8; **Ref** +5; **Will** +3
Immune plant traits

Speed 30 ft., climb 30 ft.
Melee bite +8 (1d8+7 plus acidic poison and grab)
Space 10 ft.; **Reach** 5 ft.
Special Attacks acidic poison, constrict (1d8+7)

Str 21, **Dex** 17, **Con** 16, **Int** 1, **Wis** 12, **Cha** 2
Base Atk +4; **CMB** +10 (+14 grapple); **CMD** 23 (can't be tripped)
Feats Power Attack, Stealthy, Toughness
Skills Climb +13, Disguise –2 (+10 as vine), Escape Artist +5, Perception +11, Stealth +11;
Racial Modifiers +12 Disguise (as vine), +4 Perception, +4 Stealth
SQ lure

Environment temperate and warm forests
Organization solitary or grove (2–6)
Treasure incidental

Acidic Poison (Ex) The bite of a serpent creeper deals 1d6 points of acid damage initially and 1d2 points of acid damage each round thereafter. A DC 16 Fortitude saving throw or a DC 16 Heal check ends the ongoing acid damage. Multiple bites are cumulative. The save DC and check DC are both Constitution-based.
Lure (Ex) A serpent creeper has a special air sac in its throat that it can turn inside out. By doing so, the air sac appears to be a piece of low-hanging fruit. A serpent creeper uses this ruse to draw its prey in closer. When a serpent creeper does this, it gains a +8 bonus on Disguise checks beyond its normal racial bonus.

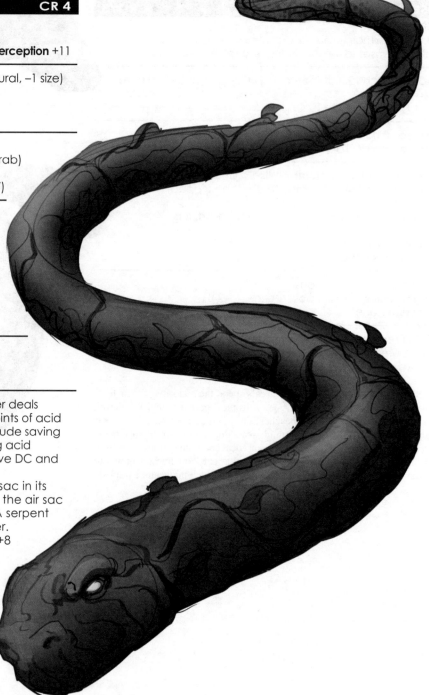

Serpent creepers are dangerous carnivorous plants that resemble 12-foot long pythons. When at rest, their green and brown coloration and the leafy patterns on their scales make them hard to distinguish from ordinary vines. Whether these creatures are naturally occurring or some weird magical cross of serpent and plant is unknown.

Serpent creepers are typically 12–15 feet long. Their bodies are green and brown scales covered with various leaf-like patterns to aid them in their camouflage. Some serpent creepers can change the color of their scales slightly to better match their surroundings, adding to the ruse. Young serpent creepers are rarely encountered, but have been spotted. They appear as smaller versions of the adults, about 3 feet long. Reproduction and life cycles of serpent creepers are unknown.

Serpent creepers are quintessential ambush hunters. When hunting, a

serpent creeper hangs from a tree and puffs out its air sac, disguising it as a fruit indigenous to the local area. When prey moves in to examine or pluck the fruit, the serpent creeper springs to life and quickly coils around the target while biting it. Slain prey is dragged to a safe place and devoured over the course of several hours. An unfinished meal is left to forest scavengers. Serpent creepers have a particular like for the flesh of goblins and halflings.

Sewer Sludge (Spawn of Dungie)

Suddenly, the pile of sewage rises up and extends a long brown pseudopod dripping with vulgar fluids.

SEWER SLUDGE	CR 3

XP 800
N Medium ooze (aquatic)
Init +0; **Senses** blindsight 30 ft.; **Perception** –5
Aura stench (10 ft., DC 17)

AC 14, touch 10, flat-footed 14 (+4 natural)
hp 38 (4d8+20)
Fort +6; **Ref** +1; **Will** -4
Immune cold, electricity, ooze traits

Speed 20 ft., climb 20 ft., swim 20 ft.
Melee slam +6 (1d8+4 plus disease and grab)
Special Attacks constrict (1d8+4)

Str 16, **Dex** 10, **Con** 20, **Int** —, **Wis** 1, **Cha** 1
Base Atk +3; **CMB** +6 (+10 grapple); **CMD** 16 (can't be tripped)
Skills Climb +11, Swim +11
SQ amphibious, camouflage

Environment any
Organization solitary or smattering (2–5)
Treasure none

Camouflage (Ex) Since a sewer sludge looks like normal sludge when at rest, a DC 20 Perception check is required to notice it before it attacks for the first time. Anyone with ranks in Survival or Knowledge (dungeoneering) can use either of those skills instead of Perception to notice the ooze.
Cold Immunity (Ex) A sewer sludge hit by a cold-based attack takes no damage. However, if the amount of damage it would have otherwise taken exceeds its Constitution score, the sewer sludge is slowed (as the *slow* spell) for 1d6 rounds.
Disease (Ex) *Filth fever*: Slam—contact; *save* DC 17 Fort; *onset* 1d3 days; *frequency* 1/day; *effect* 1d3 Dex damage and 1d3 Con damage; *cure* 2 consecutive saves. The save DC is Constitution-based.
Stench Aura (Ex) Creatures entering the area must succeed on a DC 17 Fortitude save or be sickened for as long as they remain in the area and for 1d4 rounds after leaving it. The save DC is Constitution-based.

A sewer sludge is a disgusting ooze that resembles nothing more than a filthy pile of sewage. They lurk in the sewer and waste-water systems of large cities, usually content to feed on rats and refuse that filters down from the streets overhead

A sewer sludge is a globular mass about 4 feet across, and weighing 100 pounds.

Sewer sludges are almost always hungry, and do not hesitate to attack prey larger than themselves. A sewer sludge's usual method of attack is to glom onto the body of a creature struck by its pseudopod, grip it tightly, and liquefy its flesh by releasing acidic digestive enzymes.

Spawn of Dungie

The origin of sewer sludges was unknown until recently. Diligent research by a curious adventurer named Bilark Weterson finally tracked down where these creatures came from, and the news was not good at all. Weterson realized that sewer sludges first appeared in cities often frequented by travelers returning from a certain famous dungeon. Following a hunch, he investigated and was never heard from again. Weterson's diary was recently uncovered in a used book store in Bard's Gate, and in it were discovered his theories about sewer sludges.

It is known that in the upper levels of the dungeon known as Rappan Athuk there exists a creature called the Dung Monster. The good news is that the Dung Monster, nicknamed 'Dungie' by those few who have survived an encounter with that it, is content to remain in Rappan Athuk and not venture into the outside world. The bad news is that Dungie has begun to reproduce.

Once every few years, Dungie grows odd nodules on its surface. These nodules continue to bud until they fall away and take on a life of their own. Sometimes, a bud finds its way outside of Rappan Athuk, either on its own or hidden in the packs and clothing of weary adventurers as they exit the dungeon. If undetected, these buds drop out into the sewers of the great cities of the world and grow into sewer sludges. Fortunately, sewer sludges remain mindless oozes as they age. Were they to mature into adhesive, shape-changing, immortal monsters like their progenitor, the world might surely be doomed!

Shadow Hunter

The shadow hunter is a great, dark serpent that dwells in deep caverns beneath the earth, where it hunts dark elves and other Medium to Large sized creatures. An adult specimen is over 40 ft. long and nearly 5 ft. thick in its midsection. In bright light it can be seen to be covered with non-reflective black scales, and its underbelly is the dark red of clotted blood. Shadow hunters have the supernatural ability to blend in with shadows, both to protect themselves and to stalk and ambush prey. Unlike normal snakes, shadow hunters often work in groups of two or three to corner prey in passages.

SHADOW HUNTER   CR 8

XP 4,800
N Huge magical beast
Init +2; **Senses** darkvision 60 ft., low-light vision, scent, tremorsense 60 ft.; **Perception** +12

AC 18, touch 10, flat-footed 16 (+2 Dex, +8 natural, −2 size)
hp 76 (8d10+32)
Fort +10; **Ref** +8; **Will** +4
Defensive Abilities shadowblend

Speed 30 ft., climb 20 ft., swim 30 ft.
Melee bite +14 (1d8+10 plus poison plus grab)
Space 15 ft.; **Reach** 10 ft.

Str 24, **Dex** 15, **Con** 19, **Int** 5, **Wis** 14, **Cha** 3
Base Atk +8; **CMB** +17 (+21 grapple); **CMD** 29 (can't be tripped)
Feats Ability Focus (poison), Skill Focus (Perception), Skill Focus (Stealth), Weapon Focus (bite)
Skills Climb +15, Perception +12, Stealth +4 (+14 in dimly lit & unlit areas), Swim +15; **Racial Modifiers** +10 racial bonus on Stealth checks in areas of dim or no light.
SQ hunt by scent

Environment underground
Organization solitary, pair, trio, or nest (1–3 adults and 5–8 hatchlings)
Treasure standard

Shadowblend (Su) In areas of dim and no light, shadow hunters gain improved concealment; there is a 40% miss chance when attacking one in such conditions.
Poison (Ex) Bite—injury; *save* DC 20 Fort; *frequency* 1/round for 6 rounds; *effect* 1d4 Constitution damage; *cure* 2 consecutive saves. The save DC is Constitution-based.
Hunt by Scent (Ex) Shadow hunters are expert at tracking prey through the dim warrens where they dwell. They can track using their Perception skill in place of Survival.

Shadow hunters generally prefer to hunt in networks of twisting passages that allow them to move around their intended prey, or even approach it from multiple directions. They are particularly fond of elf flesh, but eats any Small to Large creature as long as it is living, organic, and animal-based (i.e., not a plant or fungus). When they attack, they prefer to strike and envenom their prey, holding on and chewing the poison into their opponent until it stops struggling. If there is more than one foe present, they do not try to grab their prey, preferring to strike at those that threaten it, retreating if need be to return later to consume their hopefully dead prey.

SHADOW HUNTER HATCHLINGS   CR 2

XP 600
N Medium magical beast
Init +1; **Senses** darkvision 30 ft., low-light vision, scent, tremorsense 30 ft.; **Perception** +9

AC 13, touch 11, flat-footed 12 (+1 Dex, +2 natural)
hp 22 (3d10+3)
Fort +4; **Ref** +4; **Will** +1
Defensive Abilities shadowblend

Speed 20 ft., climb 10 ft., swim 20 ft.
Melee bite +6 (1d4+4 plus poison plus grab)

Str 16, **Dex** 13, **Con** 12, **Int** 5, **Wis** 10, **Cha** 3
Base Atk +3; **CMB** +6 (+10 to grapple); **CMD** 17 (can't be tripped)
Feats Ability Focus (poison), Skill Focus (Perception)
Skills Climb +11, Perception +7, Stealth +6 (+16 in dimly lit & unlit areas), Swim +11; **Racial Modifiers** +10 racial bonus on Stealth checks in areas of dim or no light.
SQ hunt by scent

Environment underground
Organization solitary, or nest (5–8 hatchlings)
Treasure standard

Poison (Ex) Bite—injury; *save* DC 14 Fort; *frequency* 1/round for 6 rounds; *effect* 1d4 Constitution damage; *cure* 2 consecutive saves. The save DC is Constitution-based.
Hunt by Scent (Ex) Shadow hunters are expert at tracking prey through the dim warrens where they dwell. They can track using their Perception skill in place of Survival.
Shadowblend (Su) In areas of dim and no light, shadow hunters gain improved concealment; there is a 40% miss chance when attacking one in such conditions.

Credit
Originally appearing in *Rappan Athuk Reloaded* (© Necromancer Games, 2006)

Shadow Wing

This giant creature seemingly composed of the night itself resembles a mix of hawk and manta ray.

SHADOW WING	CR 8

XP 4,800
N Large magical beast
Init +5; **Senses** darkvision 60 ft., superior low-light vision;
Perception +18

AC 23, touch 14, flat-footed 18 (+5 Dex, +9 natural, −1 size)
hp 95 (10d10+40)
Fort +11; **Ref** +12; **Will** +4

Speed 20 ft., fly 80 ft. (average)
Melee bite +13 (2d6+4), 2 wings +8 (1d8+2 plus poison)
Space 10 ft.; **Reach** 5 ft.
Special Attacks shadow blend

Str 19, **Dex** 21, **Con** 18, **Int** 8, **Wis** 12, **Cha** 11
Base Atk +10; **CMB** +15; **CMD** 30
Feats Alertness, Greater Flyby Attack, Flyby Attack, Power Attack, Skill Focus (Stealth)
Skills Fly +8, Perception +18, Sense Motive +3, Stealth +11 (+19 in darkness); **Racial Modifiers** +8 Perception, +8 Stealth in darkness
Languages Auran, Common

Environment temperate mountains
Organization solitary, flock (2–5), or roost (3–6)
Treasure none

Poison (Ex) Wing—injury; *save* DC 19 Fort; *frequency* 1/ round for 6 rounds; *effect* 1d6 Strength damage; *cure* 2 consecutive saves. The save DC is Constitution-based.
Shadow Blend (Su) During any conditions other than bright light, a shadow wing can disappear into the shadows as a move-equivalent action, effectively becoming invisible. Artificial illumination or light spells of 2nd level or lower do not negate this ability.
Superior Low-Light Vision (Ex) A shadow wing can see five times as far as a human in dim light.

Shadow wings are nocturnal predators formed of inky blackness that resemble a cross between a giant hawk and giant tailless manta ray. They are fierce hunters, and once prey is sighted, shadow wings are relentless in their pursuit. A typical shadow wing hunter claims a territory in a 5 mile radius around its lair. To the shadow wing, any living creature entering this area is fair game.

The common shadow wing makes its lair within a secluded and hard to reach cave high in mountainous regions. A typical nest contains 2 adults and 1d4 newborns or 2d4 eggs. Shadow wing eggs are blackish-blue in color and soft and leathery to the touch.

Shadow wings prefer to scout for food under the cover of darkness when their shadow blend ability is the most useful. Using its superior vision it almost always sights its target before they ever know the shadow wing is there. Prey is killed and either devoured on the spot or carried back to the lair.

A shadow wing measures 9 feet long and has a wingspan of 20 feet. Its body is composed of darkness and shadowstuff and it resembles a manta ray with a hawk's head. Its beak is formed of the same inky blackness as the rest of its form. Other than two piercing red eyes no other discernible features can be made out in its form. Shadow wings speak with a low, raspy voice.

A shadow wing attacks by swooping low at an opponent and slashing it with its wings or stabbing with its beak. Since most attacks instigated by shadow wings occur under the cover of darkness, they use their shadow blend ability to conceal themselves from their foes.

Shark, Swordtooth

This giant gray shark opens its great mouth to reveal multiple rows of dagger-like teeth.

SWORDTOOTH SHARK	CR 3

XP 800
N Large animal (aquatic)
Init +5; **Senses** blindsense 60 ft., keen scent, low-light vision; **Perception** +10

AC 16, touch 10, flat-footed 15 (+1 Dex, +6 natural,–1 size)
hp 39 (6d8+12)
Fort +9; **Ref** +6; **Will** +3

Speed swim 60 ft.
Melee bite +8 (2d6+8/18–20 plus bleed)
Space 10 ft.; **Reach** 5 ft.
Special Attacks bleed (1d6, DC 15)

Str 19, **Dex** 12, **Con** 15, **Int** 1, **Wis** 12, **Cha** 2
Base Atk +4; **CMB** +9; **CMD** 20
Feats Great Fortitude, Improved Initiative, Weapon Focus (bite)
Skills Perception +10, Swim +12

Environment any oceans and underground
Organization solitary, school (2–5), or pack (6–9)
Treasure incidental

Keen Scent (Ex) A swordtooth shark can notice creatures by scent in a 180-foot radius underwater and can detect blood in the water at ranges of up to a mile.
Savage Bite (Ex) A swordtooth shark applies twice its Strength bonus to damage dealt with its bite attack, and it threatens a critical hit on an 18–20.

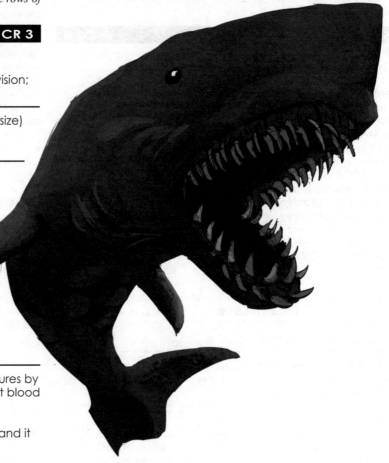

Swordtooth sharks are highly aggressive carnivores that spend most of their time hunting and killing. Swordtooth sharks are found in both freshwater and saltwater, and while most dwell in the large expanse of the world's oceans, some take to underground rivers and lakes where the fish are plentiful and other predators are rare. Swordtooth sharks, like their brethren, are pure killing machines, highly aggressive when hungry, and extremely territorial. A typical swordtooth's territory can cover several square miles.

Swordtooths, like some other sharks, are not required to be in perpetual motion. They often rest on the bottom of the ocean's floors staying motionless for up to 24 hours. When resting, a swordtooth is highly attuned to its surroundings and always has its eyes open and focused on anything moving near it. Because of their resting habits, some swordtooths have developed ambush tactics, lying in wait on the ocean floor for prey to swim nearby before striking with blinding speed.

The average swordtooth shark is 10 feet long and weighs 350 pounds, but can grow to lengths of up to 20 feet and weigh over 500 pounds. A swordtooth shark has three rows of razor-sharp teeth, pointed lower teeth for gripping its prey and serrated upper teeth for tearing flesh and muscle. Smaller prey is usually swallowed whole, while large prey is torn into large chunks before being eaten. Occasionally a swordtooth is cut open and a small amount of treasure spills out; remnants of a previously digested meal. A swordtooth has an average lifespan of 20–30 years while those that have migrated underground have an average lifespan of roughly 20–25 years.

Shattered Soul, Impaled Spirit

This ghostly spirit's face is twisted in eternal torment. The creature clutches a translucent spear-like pole.

IMPALED SPIRIT	CR 10

XP 9,600
CE Medium undead (incorporeal)
Init +7; **Senses** darkvision 60 ft., lifesense 60 ft.;
Perception +17
Aura unnatural aura (30 ft.)

AC 19, touch 19, flat-footed 15 (+5 deflection, +1 dodge, +3 Dex)
hp 126 (12d8+60 plus 12)
Fort +9; **Ref** +7; **Will** +12
Defensive Abilities channel resistance +4, incorporeal;
Immune undead traits

Speed fly 60 ft. (good)
Melee incorporeal spike +12 (1d8 plus impale soul) or incorporeal touch +12 (1d8 plus sickened)
Reach 5 ft. (10 ft. with incorporeal spike)
Special Attacks impale soul

Str —, **Dex** 16, **Con** —, **Int** 15, **Wis** 15, **Cha** 21
Base Atk +9; **CMB** +12; **CMD** 31
Feats Blind-Fight, Combat Reflexes, Dodge, Improved Initiative, Iron Will, Toughness
Skills Fly +22, Intimidate +20, Knowledge (religion) +17, Perception +17, Sense Motive +17, Stealth +18
Languages Common

Environment any
Organization solitary
Treasure standard

Impale Soul (Su): An impaled spirit carries an incorporeal version of the spike that caused its death, a 10-foot long spear-like instrument. On a successful melee attack with this spike, the target must succeed on a DC 21 Will save or have its soul impaled on the ghostly implement. A ghostly duplicate of the impaling instrument and its victim now impaled on the spike appear planted in the ground within 5 feet of the target. A thin silvery cord connects the translucent, impaled creature with its corporeal self. Another thin silvery cord connects the ghostly impalement back to the impaled spirit.

This attack deals 1d6 points of Constitution drain initially and 1 point of Constitution drain each round thereafter until the creature dies or is freed. Each round an impaled victim takes Constitution drain, the impaled spirit connected to it gains 5 temporary hit points. An impaled creature cannot move more than 10 feet from the spot where its soul is impaled, and takes a –2 penalty on all attack rolls, checks, and saves from the pain until freed.

An impaled creature can be freed if the ghostly spike holding the victim is destroyed or pulled from the ground. The ghostly spike is AC 20, hp 20, hardness 10. Corporeal creatures cannot pull the spike from the ground but can attack it with magic weapons. Normal weapons have no effect. Ethereal creatures can attack the spike with normal weapons or remove it from the ground with a successful DC 21 Strength check. A *heal, holy word, wish,* or *miracle* spell destroys the ghostly spike instantly. The save DC is Charisma-based.

Lifesense (Su) An impaled spirit notices and locates living creatures within 60 feet, just as if it possessed the blindsight ability.

Unnatural Aura (Su) Animals do not willingly approach within 30 feet of an impaled spirit, unless a master makes a DC 25 Handle Animal, Ride, or wild empathy check.

Shattered souls are the ghostly spirits of living beings executed through brutal torture: impalement, disembowelment, or worse. Their souls having not entirely departed the Material Plane, they have risen to seek vengeance on the living, particularly clerics or other divine spellcasters whom they blame for having forsaken them and allowed them to die in such a ghastly manner.

Impaled spirits are the ghostly remains of living beings executed through impalement; a brutally slow and extremely painful form of execution.

Impaled spirits are most often encountered above ground in or near the place of their execution; rarely are they found anywhere else. They are completely oblivious to everything but pain, and seek to inflict as much on a living creature as is inhumanly possible. They hold no memories of their former life, save the pain and suffering they endured at their time of execution.

Am impaled spirit appears as a translucent humanoid floating a few feet above the ground carrying a 10-foot long ghostly spike or spear. It makes no noise, though it almost seems to be trying to cry out in agony; a silent reminder of the pain endured as the impalement spike pierced its internal organs while it was dying. Its eyes are glossy white.

An impaled spirit hates all living creatures and attacks any it encounters. Though it can use its incorporeal touch attack, it prefers to attack with its incorporeal spike, attempting to impale its foes. An impaled creature is left to die an agonizing death. The impaled spirit turns its attention to another foe, attempting to repeat the process. Much like other shattered souls, an impaled spirit hates clerics and attacks them first.

Silverfish, Giant

This giant insect is about 6 feet long with silver scales.

GIANT SILVERFISH	CR 2

XP 600
N Medium vermin
Init +3; **Senses** darkvision 60 ft., scent; **Perception** +0

AC 15, touch 13, flat-footed 12 (+3 Dex, +2 natural)
hp 22 (3d8+9)
Fort +6; **Ref** +4; **Will** +1
Immune mind-affecting effects

Speed 30 ft.
Melee bite +3 (1d6+1 plus 1d6 acid)

Str 13, **Dex** 16, **Con** 16, **Int** —, **Wis** 10, **Cha** 2
Base Atk +2; **CMB** +3; **CMD** 16 (20 vs. trip)

Environment temperate and warm forests, underground, and urban
Organization solitary, gang (2–5), or infestation (6–15)
Treasure none

Acid (Ex) A giant silverfish's acid does not harm metal or stone.

These creatures are thought to be one of the oldest insects in the world. Silverfish live in and around dark, damp places replete with moisture but can wander into any environment when hunting. These nocturnal hunters consume just about anything they come across, including using their acid to break down bits of paper and small wooden objects to extract what nutrients they can from the material.

Giant silverfish appear as almost flattened insects tapered at one end, giving them a fish-like appearance. Their scales are grayish-silver in color and their tails are composed of equal-length bristles that trail behind them as they move. They use their long antennae to sense their environment. Giant silverfish can grow to lengths of 8 feet or so, though most are around 6 feet long. Their typical lifespan is up to 8 years.

Giant silverfish avoid combat most of the time unless they are hunting. When attacking, they prefer to attack from ambush, either springing from a secluded location to attack or dropping on unsuspecting prey from above.

Silverfish Swarm

This mass of flattened, silver insects moves forward in a wriggling, fish-like motion.

SILVERFISH SWARM	CR 8

XP 4,800
N Fine vermin (swarm)
Init +3; **Senses** darkvision 60 ft., scent; **Perception** +0

AC 24, touch 21, flat-footed 21 (+3 Dex, +3 natural, +8 size)
hp 105 (14d8+42)
Fort +12; **Ref** +7; **Will** +4
Defensive Abilities swarm traits, vermin traits; **Immune** mind-affecting effects, weapon damage

---

Speed 30 ft.
Melee swarm (3d6 plus distraction and 3d6 acid)
Space 10 ft.; **Reach** 0 ft.
Special Attacks distraction (DC 20)

Str 1, **Dex** 16, **Con** 16, **Int** —, **Wis** 10, **Cha** 2
Base Atk +10; **CMB** —; **CMD** —

Environment temperate and warm forests, underground, and urban
Organization solitary, pair, or infestation (3–6)
Treasure none

Silverfish swarms are highly destructive creatures, consuming anything and everything they encounter.

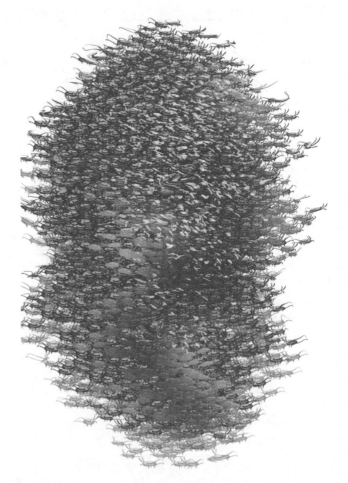

Sirene Flower

This creature appears as an animated plant with a flowering base and several writhing stalks each topped with flowers of red, amber, gold, silver, bronze, and purple.

SIRINE FLOWER	CR 3

XP 800
N Medium plant
Init +4; **Senses** blindsight 60 ft., low-light vision; **Perception** +9

AC 15, touch 10, flat-footed 15 (+5 natural)
hp 32 (5d8+10)
Fort +8; **Ref** +1; **Will** +2
Immune plant traits; **Resist** fire 5

Speed 10 ft.
Melee 4 tendrils +6 (1d4+2 plus grab)
Special Attacks charming song, essence drain

Str 14, **Dex** 10, **Con** 14, **Int** 10, **Wis** 12, **Cha** 14
Base Atk +3; **CMB** +5 (+9 grapple); **CMD** 15
Feats Great Fortitude, Improved Initiative, Weapon Focus (tendril)
Skills Perception +9, Stealth +8 (+18 in undergrowth); **Racial Modifiers** +10 Stealth (in undergrowth)
Languages Common (cannot speak)

Environment temperate forests or marshes
Organization solitary, pair, or grove (3–5)
Treasure incidental

Charming Song (Su) Sirine flowers emit a soothing and tranquil humming in a 60-foot radius that resembles music or birds singing. Those hearing the song must succeed on a DC 16 Will save or become captivated by the sound. A creature that successfully saves is not subject to the same sirine flower's song for one day. A victim under the effects of this ability moves toward the sirine flower using the most direct means available. If the path leads them into a dangerous area such as through fire or off a cliff, that creature receives a second saving throw to end the effect before moving into peril. Captivated creatures can take no actions other than to defend themselves. A victim within 5 feet of the sirine flower simply stands and offers no resistance to the sirine flower's attacks. This effect continues for as long as the sirine flower sings and for 1 round thereafter. This is a sonic mind-affecting charm effect. The save DC is Charisma-based and includes a +2 bonus.

Essence Drain (Su) A grabbed creature takes normal damage plus 1d2 points of Intelligence damage each round until it escapes.

Sirine flowers are sentient, slow-moving, flesh-eating, 5-foot tall flowers with many thick stalks and leaves. The

flower emits a pleasant odor noticeable to a range of 30 feet. They are most often found in dense forests near other plants where they sit waiting for prey to move within range. Typical prey for a sirine flower includes small birds, rodents, and other such creatures. Such creatures supply the sirine flower with sustenance for a time, but in order to gain the nutrients it needs to sustain it, the sirine flower must kill an intelligent creature and feed on its essence.

The sirine flower typically stands about 5 feet tall from base to the tip of its stalks. They can grow to a height of nearly 10 feet, though flowers this large are uncommon at best. The base of a sirine flower is a thick, leathery, brown-colored sac about 2 feet in diameter, located just beneath the surface of the ground. Strong, thick roots grow in all directions from the base, reaching lengths of 5 to 6 feet. Above ground, a thick clump of leaves grows from the base of the plant. From these leaves a series of 6 to 10 stalks reach upward. Each stalk is thick, slightly coarse and leathery to the touch with many small leaves and flowers growing from it. Flowers are red, amber, gold, silver, bronze, purple, or gray. Hidden among the base leaves and stalks are the creature's four tendrils which it uses to ensnare its prey. The tendrils, like the stalks, are grayish-brown in color.

The sirine flower begins combat using its charm ability to lure its prey in where it can attack with its tendrils. Once an opponent is within range, it lashes out, attempting to grab the foe with its tendrils. A grabbed opponent is held and drained of its Intelligence until it escapes, is slain, or rendered unconscious (and helpless). Unconscious foes are slain and devoured by the sirine flower's roots but only if all other attackers have been slain, rendered unconscious, or fled. If the sirine flower still faces aggressors, it turns its attention to them. Only when all are defeated or fled, does the sirine flower digest its meal.

Skin Feaster

This hideous creature is almost completely skinless. Its rotting muscles and sinew are clearly visible as it moves. Its hands end in filthy claws and its eyes are hollow sockets.

SKIN FEASTER	CR 2

XP 600
CE Medium undead
Init +3; **Senses** darkvision 60 ft.; **Perception** +7

AC 16, touch 13, flat-footed 13 (+3 Dex, +3 natural)
hp 26 (4d8+8)
Fort +3; **Ref** +4; **Will** +6
Immune undead traits
Weaknesses flesh consumption

Speed 30 ft.
Melee 2 claws +7 (1d6+1 plus necrotic touch)

Str 12, **Dex** 16, **Con** —, **Int** 6, **Wis** 15, **Cha** 15
Base Atk +3; **CMB** +4; **CMD** 17
Feats Weapon Finesse, Weapon Focus (claw)
Skills Acrobatics +5, Climb +6, Perception +7, Stealth +8
Languages Common
SQ skin regrowth

Environment any
Organization solitary or gang (2–7)
Treasure incidental

Flesh Consumption (Ex) A skin feaster that successfully deals Constitution damage to a living humanoid creature must succeed on a DC 15 Will save or spend its next turn devouring the flesh that has fallen from that opponent. It takes no other actions during this time but can defend itself normally. It consumes an amount of flesh equal to 3 points of Constitution damage (or drain) each round.
Necrotic Touch (Su) The touch of a skin feaster deals 1d3 points of Constitution damage if the target fails a DC 14 Fortitude save. If the save fails by 5 or more, 1 point is actually Constitution drain instead. The save DC is Charisma-based.
Skin Regrowth (Su) If a skin feaster manages to consume an amount of flesh equal to 6 points of Constitution damage in any 24-hour period, it begins to regrow its skin. The process requires 1d6 hours and for the next 1d3 days thereafter, the skin feaster appears just as it did before its death. During this time, the skin feaster loses its flesh consumption weakness and appears human (though it is still undead). Once this period ends, the skin feaster's skin sloughs off, restoring it to its original appearance.

When a humanoid dies as a result of being skinned alive, it often returns to the land of the living as a skin feaster; an undead creature driven by an insatiable hunger for the skin and flesh of living creatures. Only by consuming living flesh can a skin feaster relieve itself of the burning pain of its raw muscles and nerves.

Skin feasters often make their lairs near populated areas where meals are plentiful. The lair itself is usually a nearby cave complex or ruined and abandoned buildings; places that allow the skin feaster to remain hidden, yet keep it close enough to feed when hungry. Skin feaster raids into towns and villages almost always occur at night. While they occasionally consume the flesh of cattle and other small game, they prefer the flesh of humanoids above all others; it's also the only way a skin feaster can regrow its flesh. During times when a skin feaster has regrown its skin, it moves around villages and towns, mingling among living creatures,

planning its next meal.

Skin feasters stand about 6 feet tall and generally weigh 150–180 pounds.

A skin feaster slashes at its opponents with its razor-sharp fingernails, flaying off chunks of flesh with each strike. Skin feasters are so overcome with agony that they often stop in the middle of combat to devour any flesh they manage to tear away from their victims.

Skull Child

This small child's head is a pathetic skinless skull with gnashing teeth and blazing red eyes.

SKULL CHILD	CR 4

XP 1,200
NE Small undead
Init +2; **Senses** darkvision 60 ft.; **Perception** +7

AC 15, touch 14, flat-footed 12 (+2 Dex, +1 dodge, +1 natural, +1 size)
hp 26 (4d8+8)
Fort +3; **Ref** +3; **Will** +4
Immune undead traits

Speed 20 ft.
Melee 2 claws +6 (1d4/19–20 plus energy drain), bite +6 (1d6 plus weakness)
Special Attacks create spawn, energy drain (1 level, DC 14), terrifying gaze, vicious claws, weakness

Str 10, **Dex** 15, **Con** —, **Int** 8, **Wis** 11, **Cha** 15
Base Atk +3; **CMB** +2; **CMD** 15
Feats Dodge, Weapon Finesse
Skills Bluff +13, Climb +5, Perception +7, Stealth +11; **Racial Modifiers** +4 Bluff (Bluff is always a class skill)
Languages Common
SQ daylight powerlessness, masquerade

Environment any land
Organization solitary or gang (2–7)
Treasure none

Create Spawn (Su) A juvenile humanoid slain by a skull child rises the following night as a free-willed skull child. A *bless* spell cast on the body before that time ceases the transformation. Adults and non-humanoids killed by a skull child do not rise as undead.
Daylight Powerlessness (Su) A skull child's energy drain, create spawn, terrifying gaze, and weakness abilities only function after sunset.
Masquerade (Su) Between the hours of dawn and dusk, it is impossible to tell a skull child from another, normal, child of the race it is posing as. Any form of detection, such as *detect undead* reveals nothing. *True seeing* or similar spells show a dark haze around a skull child during the day but nothing else. Additionally, Bluff is always a class skill for a skull child.
Terrifying Gaze (Su) Any living creature that meets the gaze of a skull child must succeed on a DC 14 Will save or be shaken for 1d4 rounds. Creatures with more than 5 HD are immune to this effect. The save DC is Charisma-based.
Vicious Claws (Su) The claws of a skull child are supernaturally sharp. A skull child threatens a critical on a 19–20 with its claw attack.
Weakness (Su) The bite of a skull child deals 1d4 points of Constitution damage on a successful hit unless the target succeeds on a DC 14 Fortitude save. A creature dies if this Constitution damage equals or exceeds its actual Constitution score. The save DC is Charisma-based.

Skull children are small and pathetic but sadistic undead creatures, often spoken of in folklore and myth, though few actually believe in their existence. By day, a skull child is virtually indiscernible from any humanoid child of its size and apparent age. It appears as a happy, playful youngster who mixes with other, more normal children. At night however, its true demeanor becomes all too apparent. As the sun sinks below the horizon, the flesh retreats from the head of a skull child, revealing a bare skull with blazing eye sockets and sharp, needle-like teeth. The rest of the creature's body becomes putrid and rotten. A skull child feeds on the life force of other living creatures, draining the essence of its victims, though only at night. A skull child often poses as an orphan in order to be taken in by a well-meaning and unsuspecting family, while other skull children operate in gangs as destitute children in larger cities.

A skull child seeks to insinuate itself into groups of children, camouflaging itself among the living and slowing preying upon them, one by one. It is not known whether a skull child prefers to stalk children in order to create more of its own kind or simply because children are far easier targets than adults.

Skull children stand between 2 and 4 feet tall, and weigh about 30 to 60 pounds.

Skull children prefer to avoid combat if possible, all too aware that their small forms are unsuited to melee. When forced to fight, however, they attack with their bony claws and a vicious bite.

Slitherrat

These rodents have a long three to four foot long snakelike body covered in fur, with four almost vestigial legs on each side. The long body tapers into a rat-like tail at the end, adding another foot to the creature's overall length. The head, although large, is clearly that of a giant rat; but the long front teeth glitter, for they are made of thin, sharp diamond.

SLITHERRAT	CR 3

XP 800
N Medium animal
Init +3; **Senses** low-light vision, scent; **Perception** +4

AC 14, touch 13, flat-footed 11 (+3 Dex, +1 natural)
hp 25 (4d8+4)
Fort +5; **Ref** +7; **Will** +2

Speed 30 ft., burrow 30 ft.
Melee bite +6 (1d6+1)
Special Attacks diamond teeth

Str 10, **Dex** 17, **Con** 13, **Int** 2, **Wis** 13, **Cha** 4
Base Atk +3; **CMB** +3; **CMD** 16 (20 against trip)
Feats Skill Focus (Perception), Weapon Finesse
Skills Climb +8, Perception +4, Stealth +8; **Racial Modifiers** uses Dex to modify Climb
SQ pass through crystal

Environment any underground
Organization solitary or cache (2–12)
Treasure none

Diamond Teeth (Ex) Because the teeth are so hard and sharp, a slitherrat's bite attack bypasses all hardness and deals 1d6+1 damage
Pass Through Crystal (Ex) Slitherrats may pass through crystal and similar gemstone-like materials as if they were not even present, leaving no trace of their passage.

Slitherrats are a bizarre variant of the giant rat, sometimes found in places with heavy crystalline mineral deposits. These strange creatures use their teeth to dig through earth and solid rock when they encounter such obstacles.

Credit
Original author Matthew J. Finch
Originally appearing in *The Spire of Iron and Crystal* (© Frog God Games/Matthew J. Finch, 2011)

Slug, Dimensional

This gigantic brownish-gray slug drips acid from its shimmering form.

DIMENSIONAL SLUG	CR 10

XP 9,600
N Huge magical beast
Init +2; **Senses** blindsight 60 ft.; **Perception** +10

AC 25, touch 7, flat-footed 24 (–2 Dex, +1 dodge, +18 natural, –2 size)
hp 126 (12d10+60)
Fort +15; **Ref** +6; **Will** +7
Defensive Abilities ethereal jaunt; **DR** 10/slashing or piercing; **Immune** acid
Weaknesses vulnerability to salt

Speed 20 ft.
Melee tongue +20 (2d10+10 plus 2d8 acid)
Ranged spit +8 (12d6 acid)
Space 15 ft.; **Reach** 15 ft.
Special Attacks crush, ethereal ambush

Str 31, **Dex** 6, **Con** 20, **Int** 4, **Wis** 12, **Cha** 10
Base Atk +12; **CMB** +24; **CMD** 33 (can't be tripped)
Feats Dodge[B], Endurance, Great Fortitude, Improved Initiative, Iron Will, Power Attack, Skill Focus (Stealth)
Skills Climb +14, Perception +10, Stealth +1
SQ malleable

Environment any underground
Organization solitary
Treasure none

Crush (Ex) A dimensional slug can rear up and fall on its opponents, affecting as many Medium or smaller size opponents as it can cover. Opponents in the affected area must succeed on a DC 26 Reflex save or be pinned, automatically taking 2d8+15 points of bludgeoning damage during the next round unless the creature moves off them. If the creature chooses to maintain the pin, it must succeed at a combat maneuver check as normal. Pinned foes take damage from the crush each round if they don't escape. The save DC is Strength-based.

Ethereal Ambush (Ex) A dimensional slug that attacks foes on the Material Plane in a surprise round can take a full round of actions if it begins the combat by phasing into the Material Plane from the Ethereal Plane.

Ethereal Jaunt (Su) A dimensional slug can shift from the Ethereal Plane to the Material Plane as a free action, and shift back again as a move action (or as part of a move action). The ability is otherwise identical to *ethereal jaunt* (CL 15th).

Spit Acid (Ex) A dimensional slug can spit acid at an opponent within 60 feet (no range increment). With a successful ranged touch attack, the target takes 12d6 points of acid damage (no save).

Malleable (Ex) A dimensional slug's body is very malleable, allowing it to fit into narrow areas with ease. A dimensional slug takes no penalty to its speed or checks when squeezing in an area that is one size category smaller than its actual size (10 feet wide for most dimensional slugs). A dimensional slug can squeeze normally through an area two size categories smaller than its actual size (5 feet wide for most dimensional slugs).

Vulnerability to Salt (Ex) A handful of salt burns a dimensional slug as if the salt were a flask of acid, causing 1d6 points of damage per use.

Dimensional slugs are offshoots of giant slugs that now dwell in the Ethereal Plane. They feed upon the detritus, which is sometimes drawn into the ether, and occasionally shift themselves into the Material Plane to feed. These creatures detest phase spiders and attack them on sight.

A dimensional slug commonly attacks by spraying acid and crushing its opponents. If combat is going poorly for a dimensional slug, it shifts back to the Ethereal Plane.

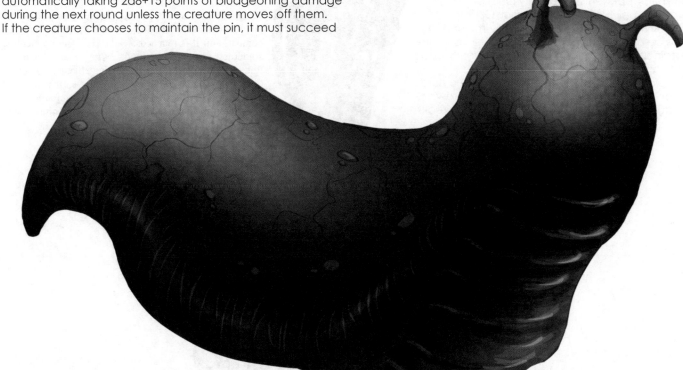

Sojourner of the Sea

This metallic construct appears as a crudely rendered statue of a human male, with fully articulated joints. Though its facial features are nothing more than vague shapes with little definition, its torso is carved with an intricate pattern of runes. Along the area of its left "thigh" is a long silvery abrasion, perhaps the result of some ancient battle.

SOJOURNER OF THE SEA	CR 15

XP 51,200
N Medium construct
Init +0; **Senses** darkvision 60 ft., low-light vision;
Perception +0

AC 30, touch 10, flat-footed 30 (+20 natural)
hp 150 (20d10+40)
Fort +6; **Ref** +6; **Will** +6
DR 20/—; **Immune** construct traits (+40 hp), magic

Speed 20 ft., burrow 20 ft., climb 20 ft.
Melee 2 slams +28 (2d8+12/19–20)
Special Attacks aquatic combat, aquatic entangle

Str 27, **Dex** 11, **Con** —, **Int** —, **Wis** 11, **Cha** 10
Base Atk +20; **CMB** +28; **CMD** 38
Skills Climb +16
SQ resilient

Environment any oceans
Organization solitary
Treasure none

Aquatic Combat (Ex) A sojourner suffers no penalties when fighting underwater.
Aquatic Entangle (Su) Once every four rounds, a sojourner can animate the local sea flora to entrap its opponents. This ability functions as an *entangle* spell (Reflex DC 20 partial; CL 20th).
Immunity to Magic (Ex) A sojourner is immune to spells or spell-like abilities that allow spell resistance. Certain spells and effects function differently against it, as noted below.
A *magic missile* paralyzes a sojourner (as the *hold person* spell) for 1 minute, with no saving throw.
A magical attack that deals cold damage breaks

any *hold* effect on the sojourner and heals 1 point of damage for each 3 points of damage the attack would otherwise deal. If the amount of healing would cause the sojourner to exceed its full normal hit points, it gains any excess as temporary hit points. A sojourner gets no saving throw against cold effects.
A sojourner is unaffected by rust attacks, such as those of a rust monster or a *rusting grasp* spell.
Powerful Blows (Ex) A sojourner deals one and a half times its Strength modifier and threatens a critical hit on a 19–20 with its slam attacks.
Resilient (Ex) A sojourner gains bonus hit points as a construct as if it were two sizes larger.

This metal construct, known as the sojourner of the sea, is believed to be one of a kind, and for that the civilized world is thankful. The sojourner is a man-shaped machine that constantly walks the ocean floor on an unknown quest, destroying anything that attempts to sway it from its inexorable path.

The sojourner was given its name by a maritime explorer who encountered it, fought it, and retreated with his life to tell the tale. No one knows the sojourner's real name, or even if it has one. The sojourner is fashioned from a special, highly resilient metal of unknown origin, its power source hidden somewhere deep inside its nearly impregnable frame. It continuously and unstoppably walks the lightless ocean floor, having traversed thousands of miles since it was first spotted years ago. So far it has proven indestructible. Its purpose remains a mystery. The symbols on its torso are as inscrutable as the sojourner itself.

During its endless trek along the sea bed, if the sojourner encounters an obstacle it cannot pass through or climb over, it walks around the obstacle's perimeter or burrows beneath it, regardless of the distance required. It descends into the deepest ocean trenches and slowly advances up the far side. If a living being attempts to impede its progress, the sojourner attacks without hesitation, though it never initiates combat until it is touched or attacked. The unrelenting sojourner of the sea cannot swim. The creature is immune to the corroding and rusting effects of water.

In combat the sojourner is mindless, fearless, and unremitting. Once battle commences, the sojourner does not relent until all opponents are eliminated or have fled.

Soul Knight

A suit of blackened ornamental armor houses two red orbs where eyes should be, and a cold malignance emanates from the creature like an evil cloud.

SOUL KNIGHT	CR 6

XP 2,400
NE medium undead
Init +6; **Senses** darkvision 60 ft.; **Perception** +12
Aura fear (30 ft., DC 17)

AC 21, touch 11, flat-footed 19 (+9 armor, +2 Dex, +1 Dodge)
hp 68 (9d8+27)
Fort +6; **Ref** +5; **Will** +6
DR 5/bludgeoning; **Immune** undead traits

Speed 30 ft.
Melee mwk greatsword +12/+7 (2d6+6/19–20)

Str 18, **Dex** 14, **Con** —, **Int** 10, **Wis** 10, **Cha** 17
Base Atk +6; **CMB** +10; **CMD** 21
Feats Dodge, Power Attack, Weapon Focus (greatsword), Improved Initiative, Combat Reflexes
Skills Climb +10, Intimidate +15, Perception +12, Knowledge (religion) +12
SQ animated dead
Gear masterwork plate armor, masterwork greatsword

Environment any
Organization solitary
Treasure (masterwork full plate, masterwork weapon, other treasure)

Fear Aura (Su) The soul knight projects a fear aura that functions like the *fear* spell within a 30 ft. radius. Affected creatures must make a DC 17 Will save to resist the effect. Use of this ability is a free action. This save is Charisma-based.

A soul knight is a suit of armor animated by the lingering soul of an evil knight, cursed to undeath as punishment for having committed betrayal, murder or other crimes. The evil spirit continues to inhabit its old armor, repeating the deeds that brought about the living knight's ruin.

Soul knights seek out those that remind them of their past station (good clerics, paladins, etc.) and attack those foes first in combat.

Credit

Original author Mark R. Shipley
Originally appearing in *The Black Monastery* (© Frog God Games/ Mark R. Shipley, 2011)

Sphinx, Dromosphinx

This creature has the black wings of a bird, the body of a lion, and the long neck and head of a camel.

DROMOSPHINX	CR 8

XP 4,800
NE Large magical beast
Init +0; **Senses** darkvision 60 ft., low-light vision; **Perception** +20

AC 19, touch 9, flat-footed 19 (+10 natural, −1 size)
hp 93 (11d10+33)
Fort +10; **Ref** +7; **Will** +5

Speed 30 ft., fly 60 ft. (poor)
Melee 2 claws +17 (1d6+7), bite +17 (1d8+7/19–20 plus 1d6 acid)
Space 10 ft.; **Reach** 5 ft.
Special Attacks pounce, spit acid (+10 ranged touch)

Str 25, **Dex** 10, **Con** 17, **Int** 14, **Wis** 14, **Cha** 14
Base Atk +11; **CMB** +19; **CMD** 29 (33 vs. trip)
Feats Alertness, Flyby Attack, Hover, Improved Critical (bite), Power Attack, Skill Focus (Intimidate)
Skills Bluff +13, Fly +2, Intimidate +19, Knowledge (any one) +8, Perception +20, Sense Motive +4
Languages Common, Sphinx

Environment warm deserts and hills
Organization solitary, pair, or flock (3–6)
Treasure standard

Spit Acid (Ex) Once every 1d4 rounds, a dromosphinx can spit a line of highly caustic saliva at a single target within 20 feet. The target takes 6d6 points of acid damage. A successful DC 18 Reflex save reduces the damage by half. The save DC is Constitution-based.

Some of the strongest and smartest of the sphinxes, dromosphinxes are treacherous and merciless, caring little for anything and anyone. All dromosphinxes are male. Dromosphinxes detest androsphinxes and attack them on sight. Unlike the smaller and weaker hieracosphinxes, dromosphinxes can generally hold their own against androsphinxes. They are indifferent against the other sphinxes and often bully the smaller hieracosphinxes into serving them for a period of time.

Dromosphinxes are highly territorial and do not take intrusions lightly. Trespassers are quickly disposed of when encountered. Since dromosphinxes love riddles, when intelligent creatures are encountered, they often present them with a riddle. If the targets answer incorrectly or cannot answer, dromosphinxes attack and attempt to devour the victims. Those answering the riddle correctly are allowed to continue on their way, much to the dromosphinx's dismay.

When combat begins, a dromosphinx spits its acid at the closest foe. It next pounces on the next closest foe, and disperses its opponents with a combination of claws, bites, and acid. During combat, it often takes to the air and uses a series of diving attacks to rid itself of its opponents while keeping them off balance.

Spider, Albino Cave

This tiny hunting spider is about the size of a man's fist. It is pallid white, often with irregular light brown blotches on its abdomen, which helps it blend in with the toadstools and fungus which is its home. The albino cave spider normally feeds on normal and dire rats, but it attacks anything that comes within range.

ALBINO CAVE SPIDER	CR 1/2

XP 200
N Tiny vermin
Init +4; **Senses** darkvision 60 ft., tremorsense 60 ft.; **Perception** +4

AC 17, touch 16, flat-footed 13 (+4 Dex, +1 natural, +2 size)
hp 4 (1d8)
Fort +2; **Ref** +4; **Will** +0
Immune vermin traits

Speed 20 ft., climb 10 ft.
Melee bite +6 (1d3–3 plus poison)
Space 2 1/2 ft.; **Reach** 2 1/2 ft.

Str 4, **Dex** 18, **Con** 10, **Int** —, **Wis** 10, **Cha** 3
Base Atk +0; **CMB** +2; **CMD** 9
Feats Weapon Finesse [B]
Skills Acrobatics +4 (+12 jump), Climb +12, Stealth +16;

Racial Modifiers +8 to Acrobatics when jumping, +4 Perception, +4 Stealth; use Dex to modify Climb

Environment underground
Organization solitary or nest (2–20)
Treasure standard

Poison (Ex) Bite—injury; *save* DC 14 Fort; *frequency* 1/round for 4 rounds; *effect* 1d2 Constitution damage; *cure* 1 save. The save DC is Constitution-based and includes a +4 racial bonus.

Albino cave spiders hunt rats in caves or in deep underground regions where the sun never reaches. These tiny killers are extremely sensitive to movement, and despite their unique coloring, are highly adept at hiding and stealthy stalking.

The albino cave spider is mildly toxic, as some of the other Under Realm predators have discovered. They use their poisonous bite to sicken prey and follow until they can feast on the remains.

Male and female cave spiders are roughly the same size, with females being slightly larger. The females are the predominant hunters, with the males tending to the web-nest when an eggsack is present. Both sexes are extremely protective of the eggsack, and attack larger foes when it is threatened.

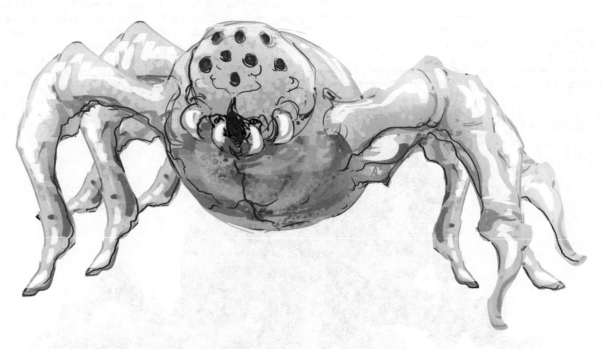

Spider, Giant Funnel-Web

This gigantic spider is glossy bluish-black and hairless. It rears on its back legs and reveals long fangs dripping with venom.

GIANT FUNNEL-WEB SPIDER   CR 6

XP 2,400
N Large vermin
Init +3; **Senses** darkvision 60 ft., tremorsense 60 ft.; **Perception** +4

AC 16, touch 12, flat-footed 13 (+3 Dex, +4 natural, –1 size)
hp 68 (8d8+32)
Fort +10; **Ref** +5; **Will** +2
Immune mind-affecting effects

Speed 30 ft., burrow 10 ft., climb 30 ft.
Melee bite +12 (2d6+14 plus grab and poison)
Space 10 ft.; **Reach** 10 ft.
Special Attacks web (+8 ranged, DC 22, 8 hp)

Str 25, **Dex** 17, **Con** 18, **Int** —, **Wis** 10, **Cha** 2
Base Atk +6; **CMB** +14 (+18 grapple); **CMD** 27 (39 vs. trip)
Feats Lunge[B], Virulent Poison[B]
Skills Climb +23, Perception +4, Stealth +3 (+7 in webs);
Racial Modifiers +8 Climb, +4 Perception, +4 Stealth (+8 in webs)
SQ hold breath

Environment any temperate and warm
Organization solitary or burrow (2–5)
Treasure incidental

Ambush Strike (Ex) A giant funnel-web spider is particularly adept at moving quickly when its foes are surprised. During a surprise round, a giant funnel-web spider gains a +4 racial bonus on its attack roll.

Hold Breath (Ex) By trapping air bubbles on tiny hairs around its abdomen, a funnel-web spider can hold its breath for a number of hours equal to its Constitution score before it risks drowning.

Poison (Ex) Bite—injury; *save* DC 22 Fort; *frequency* 1/round for 8 rounds; *effect* 1d4 Constitution and sickened; *cure* 3 saves. The save DC is Constitution-based and includes a +4 racial bonus.

Powerful Bite (Ex) A giant funnel-web spider applies twice its Strength modifier to bite damage.

Strong Webs (Ex) A giant funnel-web spider's webs gain a +4 bonus to the DC to break or escape.

Giant funnel-web spiders are deadly, nocturnal predators that dine on living creatures. Most of their time is spent inside their tube-like lair where they simply wait for prey to pass by. Once prey is detected, they rush to the attack, quickly poisoning their target, and dragging it back into their lair.

Giant funnel-web lairs are large spiraling tubes with open funnel-like mouths, typically built under large rocks, fallen trees, or straight into the ground. The entirely of the tube is covered with thick spider webs. Trip lines radiate outward from the mouth of the lair, up to 100 feet away. These trip lines signal to the spider that prey is near.

Female funnel-web spiders are generally larger than males, with shorter legs and thicker abdomens. Females lay several egg sacs a few times each year which quickly hatch. The young rapidly develop and reach maturity within 2 years generally, and leave the lair to go out on their own. Giant funnel-web spiders can live up to 20 years.

A giant funnel-web spider is highly aggressive. If threatened or provoked, unlike other spiders, it rears on its back legs and displays its fangs. This warning position signifies the spider is about to strike. When a funnel-web attacks, its grabs its prey and repeatedly injects it with its deadly poison.

Spider, Shard

This large hairy spider has a dull black body shot through with dull red streaks.

SHARD SPIDER	CR 9

XP 6,400
N Large magical beast
Init +8; **Senses** darkvision 60 ft., low-light vision; **Perception** +11

AC 23, touch 13, flat-footed 19 (+4 Dex, +10 natural, −1 size)
hp 114 (12d10+48)
Fort +14; **Ref** +12; **Will** +5
Defensive Abilities split (critical hit, 20 hp)

Speed 40 ft., climb 20 ft.
Melee bite +17 (2d6+9 plus poison and grab)
Space 10 ft.; **Reach** 5 ft.

Str 22, **Dex** 19, **Con** 18, **Int** 7, **Wis** 13, **Cha** 10
Base Atk +12; **CMB** +19 (+23 grapple); **CMD** 33 (45 vs. trip)
Feats Ability Focus (poison), Great Fortitude, Improved Initiative, Power Attack, Skill Focus (Perception, Stealth)
Skills Climb +21, Perception +11, Stealth +10

Environment temperate forests

Organization solitary
Treasure none

Poison (Ex) Bite—injury; *save* DC 22 Fort; *frequency* 1/round for 8 rounds; *effect* 1d6 Strength damage; *cure* 2 saves. The save DC is Constitution-based and includes a +2 racial bonus from the shard spider's Ability Focus feat.

Shard spiders are giant, black, nocturnal hunting spiders that dwell in dark forests and feed upon those creatures unlucky enough to stumble into their lair. Shard spiders live under fallen trees or in tunnels in the ground. A nest typically contains a single shard spider and up to 10 noncombatant young. Shard spiders usually hunt denizens of the forests and drag their prey back to their lair to be divided among the young.

Shard spiders stand 8 feet tall. Their bodies are covered in short, thick black fur. Though intelligent, shard spiders seem unable to converse with any but their own kind. Communication among shard spiders takes the form of body language and hissing sounds. Shard spiders have an average lifespan of 30 years.

A shard spider attacks from ambush, seeking to neutralize its prey as quickly as possible with its poisonous bite. Due to its magical ability to split, a shard spider welcomes melee and engages its foes as quickly as possible.

Spider Lich

This chill of death emanates from this giant skeletal spider. Its blackened eyes show a remarkable intelligence.

SPIDER LICH	**CR 10**

XP 9,600
CE Large undead
Init +3; **Senses** darkvision 60 ft., tremorsense 60 ft.;
Perception +21
Aura fear (60 ft. radius, DC 19)

AC 19, touch 12, flat-footed 16 (+3 Dex, +7 natural, –1 size)
hp 102 (12d8+48)
Fort +7; **Ref** +7; **Will** +10
Defensive Abilities channel resistance +4;
DR 15/bludgeoning and magic; **Immune** cold, electricity, undead traits

Speed 40 ft., climb 40 ft.
Melee bite +11 (2d8+3 plus paralysis and poison)
Space 10 ft.; **Reach** 10 ft.
Special Attacks web (+11 ranged, DC 19, 12 hp)
Spells Known (CL 12th; melee touch +10, ranged touch +11):
6th (3/day)—*chain lightning* (DC 19)
5th (5/day)—*cloudkill* (DC 18), *dominate person* (DC 18)
4th (6/day)—*bestow curse* (DC 17), *crushing despair* (DC 17), *enervation*
3rd (7/day)—*fireball* (DC 16), *haste* (DC 16), *rage*, *slow* (DC 16)
2nd (7/day)—*alter self*, *blur* (DC 15), *darkness*, *see invisibility*, *web* (DC 15)
1st (7/day)—*burning hands* (DC 14), *jump* (DC 14), *ray of enfeeblement* (DC 14), *shield*, *true strike*
0 (at will)—*acid splash*, *bleed* (DC 13), *daze* (DC 13), *detect magic*, *ghost sound* (DC 13), *light*, *mage hand*, *ray of frost*, *touch of fatigue* (DC 13)

Str 15, **Dex** 17, **Con** —, **Int** 16, **Wis** 14, **Cha** 16
Base Atk +9; **CMB** +12; **CMD** 28 (36 vs. trip)
Feats Blind-Fight, Combat Casting, Defensive Combat Training, Empower Spell, Toughness, Weapon Focus (bite)
Skills Acrobatics +11, Climb +25, Intimidate +18, Knowledge (arcana) +18, Knowledge (planes) +9, Perception +21, Sense Motive +11, Spellcraft +18, Stealth +18; **Racial Modifiers** +8 Acrobatics, +4 Perception, +4 Stealth
Languages Common, Undercommon, plus two others
SQ rejuvenation

Environment any
Organization solitary or troop (1 spider lich plus 2–4 wraiths or spectres)
Treasure standard

Fear Aura (Su) Creatures of less than 5 HD in a 60-foot radius that look at the spider lich must succeed on a DC 19 Will save or become frightened. Creatures with 5 HD or more must succeed at a Will save or be shaken for 1d6+6 rounds. A creature that successfully saves cannot be affected again by the same spider lich's aura for one day. This is a mind-affecting fear effect.

Paralyzing Bite (Su) Any living creature a spider lich hits with its bite attack must succeed on a DC 19 Fortitude save or be paralyzed for 1d6+12 minutes. *Remove paralysis* or any spell that can remove a curse can free the victim (see the *bestow curse* spell description). The effect cannot be dispelled. Anyone paralyzed by a spider lich seems dead, though a DC 20 Perception check or a DC 15 Heal check reveals that the victim is still alive.

Poison (Ex) Bite—injury; save DC 21 Fort; *frequency* 1/round for 6/rounds; *effect* 1d4 Strength damage; *cure* 1 save. The save is Charisma-based and includes a +2 racial bonus.

Rejuvenation (Su) When a spider lich is destroyed, its phylactery (which is generally hidden by the spider lich in a safe place far from where it chooses to dwell) immediately begins to rebuild the undead spider lich's body nearby. This process takes 1d10 days—if the body is destroyed before that time passes, the phylactery merely starts the process anew.

Spells A spider lich does not require any verbal, somatic, or material components to cast its spells.

The true origin of the spider lich is shrouded in mystery. Scholars argue constantly about its origins and how it came into existence. Some stand by the theory that intelligent giant spiders, perhaps phase spiders or some offshoot race of that dreaded creature, discovered the path to lichdom. Others contend a spider lich is the byproduct of a failed sorcerer's attempt at lichdom. Still others argue that the spider lich is simply a spellcaster's chosen form once it achieved lichhood. Whatever its true origins, the spider lich is truly a dreaded creature that many adventurers hope they never run across.

Spider liches are most often encountered underground in dungeons, caves, and crypts or in ruined temples and shrines, leading to further speculation among scholars as to the creature's origins. They do not associate with true spiders but are often encountered with other undead, particularly wraiths and spectres.

Spider liches have an insatiable thirst for knowledge. Countless days, months, years are spent pouring over ancient texts and tomes. Though evil by nature, spider liches often work with other creatures, particularly evil spellcasters to quench their thirst for this knowledge.

Spider liches stand over 8 feet tall and resemble skeletal spiders. Their eight eyes are deep black in color. Other than the sound of their bony legs clattering across stone floors, these creatures make no sound. They can speak a variety of languages but rarely do so.

The Spider Lich's Phylactery

An integral part of becoming a spider lich is the creation of the phylactery in which the creature stores its spirit. The only way to get rid of a spider lich for sure is to destroy its phylactery. Unless its phylactery is located and destroyed, a spider lich can rejuvenate after it is killed.

The typical spider lich phylactery is a gemstone of not less than 1,000 gp value. The spider lich hides the gemstone in a safe place and wraps it securely in a complex mesh of super strong webbing (DR 10/—, 24 hp).

Stone Idol

Stone idols are automatons constructed to guard and watch over temples, religious quarters, holy (or unholy) grounds, and often times tombs of now-deceased high priests or other important religious figures. Until disturbed, a stone idol sits or stands unmoving, appearing as nothing more than a stone statue.

Once triggered, a stone idol follows its creator's orders until the condition(s) that triggered it have been removed, destroyed, or otherwise eliminated.

Stone idols vary in shape and size, some appearing as animals or magical creatures, others appearing as humanoids. All are carved of fine and smooth stone, though many may appear aged and weathered. Stone idols often have holy or unholy symbols (representative of the creator's god) carved into their forms upon creation.

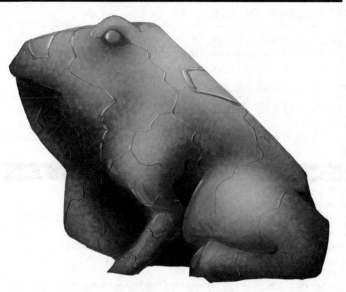

Environment any
Organization solitary or pair
Treasure none

Immunity to Magic (Ex) A stone idol is immune to any spell or spell-like ability that allows spell resistance. In addition, certain spells and effects function differently against the creature, as noted below.

A *transmute rock to mud* spell slows a stone idol (as the *slow* spell) for 2d6 rounds, with no saving throw, while *transmute mud to rock* heals all of its lost hit points.

A *stone to flesh* spell does not actually change the stone idol's structure but negates its damage reduction and immunity to magic for 1 full round.

A *disintegrate* spell deals +50% damage to a stone idol.

A *chaos hammer, holy smite, order's wrath,* or *unholy blight* spell deals 1d4 points of damage per two caster levels to a stone idol if the creator's alignment matches one of the aforementioned spells.

Rejuvenation (Su) Unless a stone idol's main body is shattered into small fragments and scattered to the winds, the creature reforms itself at full strength in 1d4+2 days.

Site Bound (Ex) A stone idol cannot travel more than 200 feet from a central point designated by its creator. Once this point is selected, it can never be changed. A stone idol taken outside the area ceases functioning until it is brought back into the area.

Frog Stone Idol

This giant frog statue has intricate markings and symbols carved into its stony construction.

FROG STONE IDOL	CR 6

XP 2,400
N Large construct
Init +0; **Senses** darkvision 60 ft., low-light vision; **Perception** +0

AC 20, touch 9, flat-footed 20 (+11 natural, −1 size)
hp 79 (9d10+30)
Fort +3; **Ref** +3; **Will** +3
Defensive Abilities rejuvenation; **DR** 10/adamantine;
Immune construct traits (+30 hp), magic

Speed 20 ft.
Melee bite +13 (2d6+7)
Space 10 ft.; **Reach** 5 ft.
Special Attacks crush (4d6+7; DC 16 Ref half)

Str 21, **Dex** 10, **Con** —, **Int** —, **Wis** 11, **Cha** 1

Base Atk +9; **CMB** +15; **CMD** 25 (29 vs. trip)
Skills Acrobatics +0 (+8 jumping); **Racial Modifiers** +8 Acrobatics when jumping
SQ powerful leaper, site bound

Crush (Ex) A frog stone idol can land on foes as a standard action, using its whole body to crush them. Crush attacks are effective only against opponents one or more size categories smaller than the frog stone idol. A crush attack affects as many creatures as fit in the stone idol's space. Creatures in the affected area must succeed on a DC 16 Reflex save or be pinned, automatically taking bludgeoning damage during the next round unless the stone idol moves off them. If the stone idol chooses to maintain the pin, it must succeed at a combat maneuver check as normal. Pinned foes take damage from the crush each round if they don't escape. The save DC is Constitution-based and includes a +2 racial bonus.

Powerful Leaper (Ex) A frog stone idol uses its Strength to modify Acrobatics checks made to jump, and it has a +8 racial bonus on Acrobatics checks made to jump.

A stone idol frog is about 10 feet long and weighs 10,000 pounds. It leaps at its foes attempting to crush as many as it can before resorting to its powerful bite attack.

Variant Frog Stone Idol

The stone idol frog detailed above is not the only known to exist. One such variant is detailed below.

Tsathogga Frog Stone Idol: This creature is identical to the standard stone idol frog. It also gains the following special attack.

Vile Croak (Su) Once every 1d4 rounds as a standard action, a Tsathogga idol can unleash a croak that affects all that hear it within 60 feet. Affected creatures take 5d6 points of negative energy damage. A DC 16 Will save reduces the damage by half. The save DC is Constitution-based and includes a +2 racial bonus.

Construction

A stone idol frog is chiseled from a block of smooth stone that weighs at least 3,000 pounds. It must be of exceptional quality and have a value of not less than 5,000 gp.

FROG STONE IDOL
CL 10th; **Price** 69,000 gp

Requirements Craft Construct, *animate objects, geas/quest, wall of stone,* creator must be caster level 10th; **Skill** Craft (sculpting) or Craft (stonemasonry) DC 16; **Cost** 37,000 gp.

Gargoyle Stone Idol

This crouching horned and winged automaton appears to be carved from stone.

GARGOYLE STONE IDOL	CR 5

XP 1,600
N Medium construct
Init +2; **Senses** darkvision 60 ft., low-light vision; **Perception** +0

AC 20, touch 12, flat-footed 18 (+2 Dex, +8 natural)
hp 47 (5d10+20)
Fort +1; **Ref** +3; **Will** +1
Defensive Abilities rejuvenation; **DR** 10/adamantine;
Immune construct traits (+20 hp), magic

Speed 30 ft.
Melee 2 claws +9 (1d8+4), bite +9 (1d6+4), gore +9 (1d6+4)
Special Attacks breath weapon (30-ft. cone, 4d6 fire damage and see below, Reflex DC 14 half, usable every 1d4 rounds)

Str 19, **Dex** 14, **Con** —, **Int** —, **Wis** 11, **Cha** 7
Base Atk +5; **CMB** +9; **CMD** 21
Skills Acrobatics +2 (+12 jumping); **Racial Modifiers** +10 Acrobatics when jumping
SQ site bound

Breath Weapon (Su) The stone gargoyle's breath weapon is

a cone of superheated steam and water. Creatures of an alignment opposite that of the cleric that created the stone gargoyle are also sickened 1d4+3 rounds if they fail their save. The save DC is Constitution-based and includes a +2 racial bonus.

Stone gargoyles stand 7 feet tall and weigh about 600 pounds. Though they have wings, they cannot fly. They can give the appearance of flight by leaping from high places and flapping their stone wings.

Construction

A stone gargoyle's body is chiseled from a single block of hard stone, such as granite, weighing at least 2,000 pounds. The stone must be of exceptional quality, and costs 3,000 gp.

STONE GARGOYLE
CL 12th; **Price** 39,000 gp

Requirements Craft Construct, *antimagic field, geas/quest, limited wish, bless water* or *curse water,* creator must be caster level 12th; **Skill** Craft (sculpting) or Craft (stonemasonry) DC 17; **Cost** 21,000 gp

Shedu Stone Idol

This gigantic statue has the body of a powerful bull and the head of a bearded human.

SHEDU STONE IDOL	CR11

XP 12,800
N Huge construct
Init -1; **Senses** darkvision 60 ft., low-light vision, *true seeing;*
Perception +0
Aura fear aura (20 ft., DC 13)

AC 27, touch 7, flat-footed 27 (−1 Dex, +20 natural, −2 size)
hp 128 (16d10+40)
Fort +5; **Ref** +4; **Will** +5
Defensive Abilities rejuvenation; **DR** 20/adamantine;
Immune construct traits (+40 hp), magic

Speed 30 ft., fly 60 ft. (average)
Melee gore +23 (2d8+9), 2 hoofs +23 (1d8+9)
Space 15 ft.; **Reach** 10 ft.
Special Attacks trample (4d6+13, DC 27)

Spell-Like Abilities (CL 16th):
Constant—*true seeing*

Str 28, **Dex** 9, **Con** —, **Int** —, **Wis** 11, **Cha** 1
Base Atk +16; **CMB** +27; **CMD** 36 (40 vs. trip)
Skills Fly –5
SQ site bound

Smite (Su) As a free action, every 1d4+1 rounds, a shedu stone idol can unleash a burst of holy energy from its body in a 20-foot-radius burst. All creatures caught within the area take damage as follows: evil-aligned outsiders, 10d6 points of damage; evil-aligned non-outsiders, 6d6 points of damage; good- and neutral-aligned creatures, 6d6 points of damage. A DC 20 Reflex save reduces the damage by half. A creature that fails its save is blinded for 1d4 rounds as well. The save DC is Constitution-based and includes a +2 racial bonus.

A stone idol shedu stands almost 9 feet tall and can reach lengths of 15 feet. It typically weighs about 25,000 pounds. A stone idol shedu when disturbed opens combat with its smite attack before attempting to trample its foes.

Construction

A stone idol shedu is chiseled from a block of smooth stone that weighs at least 6,000 pounds. It must be of exceptional quality and have a value of not less than 10,000 gp.

SHEDU STONE IDOL
CL 12th; **Price** 124,000 gp

Requirements Craft Construct, *animate objects*, *geas/quest*, *holy smite*, *dispel evil*, creator must be caster level 12th; **Skill** Craft (sculpting) or Craft (stonemasonry) DC 20; **Cost** 67,000 gp.

Sphinx Stone Idol

This statue is constructed of smooth stone and has a leonine body with the head of a jackal. Two large stony dragon-like wings protrude from its back. Ruby red gemstones seem to function as eyes.

SPHINX STONE IDOL	CR 10

XP 9,600
N Huge construct
Init +1; **Senses** darkvision 60 ft., low-light vision; **Perception** +0

AC 29, touch 9, flat-footed 28 (+1 Dex, +20 natural, –2 size)
hp 117 (14d10+40)
Fort +4; **Ref** +5; **Will** +4
Defensive Abilities rejuvenation, **DR** 10/adamantine; **Immune** construct traits (+40 hp), magic

---

Speed 30 ft., fly 50 ft. (average)
Melee bite +20 (4d6+8), 2 claws +20 (2d6+8)
Space 15 ft.; **Reach** 10 ft.
Special Attacks breath weapon (30 ft cone, 12d6 acid; DC 17 Ref half, usable every 1d4 rounds), roar

---

Str 27, **Dex** 12, **Con** —, **Int** —, **Wis** 11, **Cha** 10
Base Atk +14; **CMB** +24; **CMD** 35 (39 vs. trip)

Skills Fly +1; **Racial Modifiers** +4 Fly

Environment any
Organization solitary or pair
Treasure none
SQ site bound

Roar (Su) A sphinx stone idol can roar up to three times per day as a standard action. Affected creatures become frightened for 2d6 rounds. A DC 17 Will save negates the effect. The roar is a mind-affecting fear effect and a sonic effect that fills a 100-foot-radius burst, centered on the stone idol sphinx. A creature that successfully saves cannot be affected again by the same sphinx stone idol's roar for one day. The save DC is Charisma-based.

A stone idol sphinx is about 15 feet long and weighs around 29,000 pounds. A sphinx stone idol often has the head of an animal considered sacred by the religion: jackal-headed, goat-headed, vulture-headed, and so on.

A stone idol sphinx attacks first using its roar and then using its vicious bite and slashing with its stony paws. It often takes to the air where it can gain an advantage on its foes.

Construction

A stone idol sphinx is chiseled from a block of smooth stone that weighs at least 6,000 pounds. It must be of exceptional quality and have a value of not less than 10,000 gp.

SPHINX STONE IDOL
CL 14th; **Price** 110,000 gp

Requirements Craft Construct, *acid fog*, *fear*, *shout*, creator must be caster level 14th; **Skill** Craft (sculpting) or Craft (stonemasonry) DC 19; **Cost** 65,000 gp.

Stygian Spawn

This creature resembles a monstrous amphibian, with equal parts toad, newt, and salamander. Its smooth skin erupts here and there with hideous lesions, each one leaking a viscous ichor the color of mucus.

STYGIAN SPAWN — CR 13

XP 25,600
NE Huge outsider (aquatic, evil, extraplanar)
Init +6; **Senses** darkvision 60 ft.; **Perception** +18

AC 24, touch 10, flat-footed 22 (+2 Dex, +14 natural, –2 size)
hp 162 (13d10+91)
Fort +18; **Ref** +10; **Will** +8
DR 10/good; **Resist** acid 10, cold 10, fire 10; **SR** 24

Speed 40 ft., swim 30 ft.
Melee bite +21 (2d6+10), 2 claws +21 (1d8+10), tail slap +19 (1d8+5 plus grab) or tongue +22 touch (1d8+10 plus grab)
Space 15 ft.; **Reach** 15 ft. (30 ft. with tongue)
Special Attacks breath weapon (60 ft. line, 10d6 sonic, DC 23 half, usable every 1d4 rounds), swallow whole (6d6 acid damage, AC 17, 16 hp), tongue
Spell-Like Abilities (CL 9th):
At will—*detect good, detect magic*
3/day—*magic circle against good, unholy blight* (DC 17)

Str 31, **Dex** 15, **Con** 24, **Int** 6, **Wis** 14, **Cha** 16
Base Atk +13; **CMB** +25 (+29 grapple); **CMD** 37 (41 vs. trip)
Feats Critical Focus, Great Fortitude, Improved Initiative, Iron Will, Multiattack, Power Attack, Weapon Focus (tongue)
Skills Acrobatics +9, Intimidate +19, Knowledge (planes) +14, Perception +18, Stealth +16, Swim +18
Languages Abyssal, Common, Infernal
SQ amphibious

Environment any (River Styx)
Organization solitary or pack (2–6)
Treasure standard

Tongue (Ex) A Stygian spawn's tongue is a primary attack with a reach equal to twice the spawn's normal reach. A Stygian spawn's tongue is covered in sharpened barbs and any attempt to break free of a grapple with it, whether successful or not, deals an extra 1d6 points of piercing damage to the target. A Stygian spawn does not gain the grappled condition while using its tongue in this manner.

A Stygian spawn is a creature that lurks along the banks of the River Styx. Unlike amphibians on the Material Plane, Stygian spawn spend very little time in the water. Most of the time, these vile creatures reside deep in the mud in a self-induced state of hibernation. Stygian spawns only eat creatures not native to the lower planes; such creatures are the spawns' only source of food. Travelers in the realms of the lower planes quickly learn to fear the horrid Stygian spawn, which awaken from their hibernation and erupt from the mud of the River Styx with surprising speed. A Stygian spawn summoned to another plane is dangerous to all life there, since it can eat any organic substance that fits in its mouth.

Occasionally, Stygian spawn are awakened on purpose by bored charonadaemons who hunt the creatures for sport. Stygian spawn tadpoles are harmless, and resemble pale, boneless fish that swim mindlessly in the River Styx. These tadpoles are a frequent source of food for hungry hydrodaemons.

A fully-grown Stygian spawn is 20 feet long and weigh 3,000 pounds.

Since their only source of food—extraplanar travelers—are so rare, Stygian spawn attack with their barbed tongue, trying to grapple and swallow their opponents as quickly as possible. In extended combats, however, a Stygian spawn blasts at opponents with its breath weapon.

Swarm, Bladecoin

What appeared at first to be a pile of copper, gold, and platinum coins suddenly takes life and whirls into an amorphous cyclone of coins that jingle, hum, and clank together as the creature moves forward.

BLADECOIN SWARM	CR 6

XP 2,400
N Fine construct (swarm)
Init +1; **Senses** darkvision 60 ft., low-light vision; **Perception** +0

AC 19, touch 19, flat-footed 18 (+1 Dex, +8 size)
hp 66 (12d10)
Fort +4; **Ref** +5; **Will** +4
Defensive Abilities swarm traits; **DR** 5/adamantine; **Immune** construct traits, magic, weapon damage

Speed fly 30 ft. (good)
Melee swarm (3d6 slashing plus distraction and bleed)
Space 10 ft.; **Reach** 0 ft.
Special Attacks bleed (1d6), distraction (DC 16)

Str 1, **Dex** 13, **Con** —, **Int** —, **Wis** 11, **Cha** 1
Base Atk +12; **CMB** —; **CMD** —
Skills Fly +13
SQ swarm traits

Environment any
Organization solitary, bankroll (2–3), or jackpot (4–6)
Treasure none

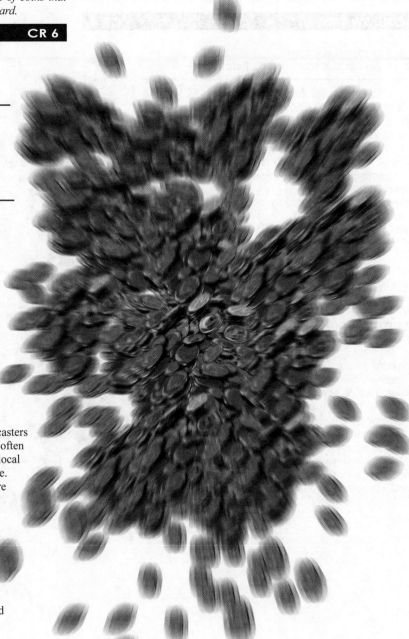

Bladecoins are tiny constructs fashioned by tricky spellcasters hoping to fool and detour would-be thieves. They are often constructed by spellcasters for others, such as merchants, local rulers, and sold to the client at a somewhat reasonable price.

At rest, a bladecoin swarm appears to be nothing more than a pile of brass or copper coins. When it senses intruders entering the area it is tasked with guarding, it swirls into a cyclone form and moves to the attack, slashing its opponents with its razor-sharp edges.

Construction

A bladecoin's body is constructed from melted brass and copper coins with a total value of at least 1,000 gp.

BLADECOIN
CL 9th; **Price** 30,000 gp

Requirements Craft Construct, *alarm, animate objects, bleed, geas/quest, limited wish,* creator must be caster level 9th; **Skill** Craft (sculpting) DC 15; **Cost** 15,500 gp

Swarm, Bone

Swarm, Bladecoil

Tumbling across the floor are the shattered remains of dozens of skeletons: a mass of bone fragments, shards, teeth, and broken skulls.

BONE SWARM	CR 4

XP 1,200
NE Tiny undead (swarm)
Init +6; **Senses** darkvision 60 ft.; **Perception** +0

AC 14, touch 14, flat-footed 12 (+2 Dex, +2 size)
hp 27 (6d8)
Fort +2; **Ref** +4; **Will** +5
Defensive Abilities channel resistance +2, swarm traits; **DR** 5/bludgeoning; **Immune** cold, undead traits, weapon damage

Speed 30 ft.
Melee swarm (2d6 slashing and piercing)
Space 10 ft.; **Reach** 0 ft.
Special Attacks distraction (DC 13)

Str 15, **Dex** 14, **Con** —, **Int** —, **Wis** 10, **Cha** 10
Base Atk +4; **CMB** —; **CMD** —
Feats Improved Initiative[B]

Environment any
Organization any
Treasure none

A bone swarm is created when multiple animated skeletons are destroyed more or less simultaneously, either through a single powerful area attack or by simply being smashed to pieces in melee. The bones of the skeletons are scattered and smashed, but the necromantic magic that animated them lingers on, pulling the bones back together in a mass of clattering fragments.

A bone swarm is ten feet across and is comprised of hundreds of bones and bone shards. When it forms to attack, it appears as a roiling mass of bone shards.

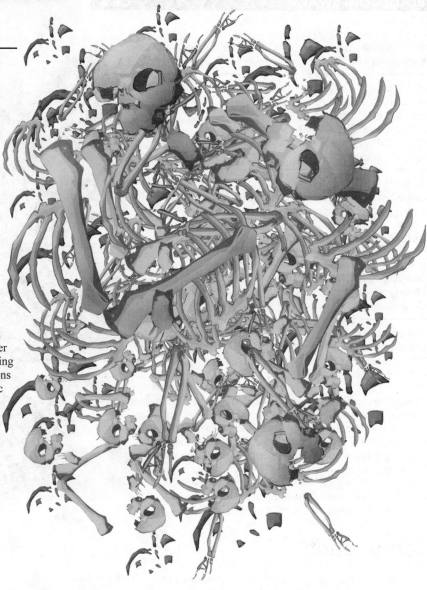

Swarm, Lamprey

A black cloud of eel-like fish swims rapidly forward.

LAMPREY SWARM	CR 5

XP 1,600
N Tiny animal (aquatic, swarm)
Init +6; **Senses** low-light vision; **Perception** +8

AC 14, touch 14, flat-footed 12 (+2 Dex, +2 size)
hp 52 (8d8+16)
Fort +8; **Ref** +10; **Will** +5
Defensive Abilities swarm traits;
Immune weapon damage

Speed 5 ft., swim 30 ft.
Melee swarm (2d6 plus distraction and blood drain)
Space 10 ft.; **Reach** 0 ft.
Special Attacks distraction (DC 16)

Str 5, **Dex** 15, **Con** 14, **Int** 1, **Wis** 12, **Cha** 2
Base Atk +6; **CMB** —; **CMD** —
Feats Improved Initiative, Iron Will, Lightning Reflexes, Skill Focus (Swim)
Skills Escape Artist +10, Perception +8, Swim +15; **Racial Modifiers** +8 Escape Artist
SQ amphibious, swarm traits

Environment temperate and warm aquatic
Organization solitary, pair, cluster (3–6 swarms)
Treasure none

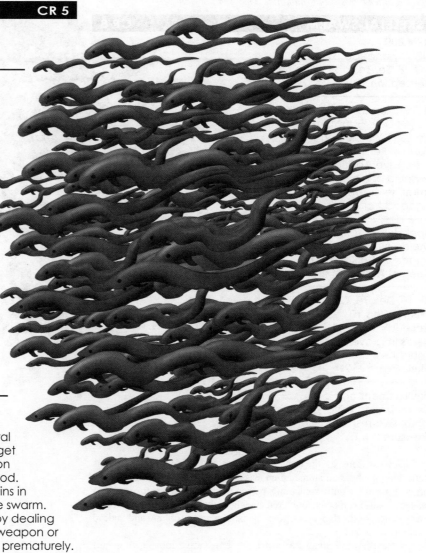

Blood Drain (Ex) Any living creature that takes damage from a lamprey swarm must succeed on a DC 16 Reflex save. On a failed save, several lampreys have attached themselves to the target and the creature takes 1d3 points of Constitution damage each round as the lampreys drain blood. This effect continues as long as the victim remains in the swarm and for 1d6 rounds after it leaves the swarm. The attached lampreys can be killed instantly by dealing at least 6 points of damage to the victim (any weapon or energy-based attacks work), ending the effect prematurely. A successful DC 16 Heal check reduces the duration by 1d6 rounds, ending the effect prematurely. The save DC and check DC are both Constitution-based.

A lamprey swarm is a mass of lampreys numbering in the hundreds, possibly thousands. These creatures are attracted to living creatures in the water and quickly attach themselves to their targeted prey.

Lamprey swarms attack any living prey encountered in their paths, swimming over the creature and draining as much blood as possible. When their prey is dead, they move on, seeking out a new source of nourishment.

Swarm, Skeletal

A clattering mass of dismembered skeletal hands, claws and assorted limbs scuttles across the ground like a moving bony carpet.

SKELETAL SWARM	CR 8

XP 4,800
NE Tiny undead (swarm)
Init +8; **Senses** darkvision 60 ft.;
Perception +0

AC 17, touch 16, flat-footed
13 (+4 Dex, +1 natural, +2 size)
hp 66 (12d8 plus 12)
Fort +4; **Ref** +4; **Will** +8
Defensive Abilities half damage
slashing or piercing;
Immune cold, swarm traits,
undead traits

Speed 20 ft., climb 20 ft.
Melee swarm (3d6)
Space 10 ft.; **Reach** 0 ft.
Special Attacks distraction (DC 16)

Str 18, **Dex** 18, **Con** —, **Int** —,
Wis 10, **Cha** 10
Base Atk +9; **CMB** —; **CMD** —
Feats Improved Initiative[B],
Toughness[B]
Skills Climb +12

Environment any
Organization solitary or pack
(2–14 swarms)
Treasure none

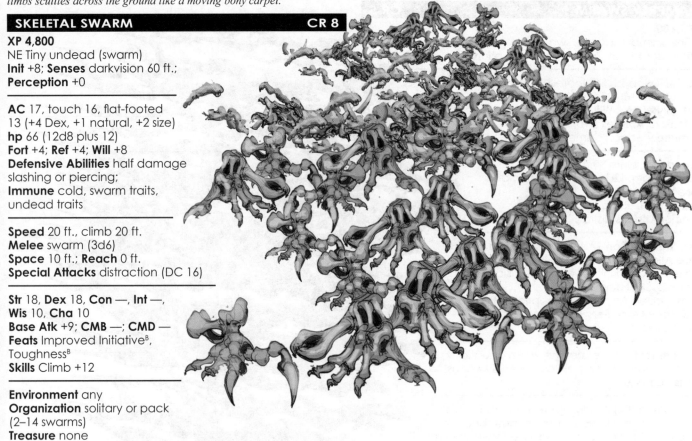

Skeletal swarms are the remains of pieces cast off of whole skeletons collected together and animated en mass. They scuttle about mindlessly, often lying inert until something passes nearby for them to attack. A skeletal swarm can be encountered anywhere that necromancers or other practitioners of the dark arts who participate in grave robbing and undead creation are found.

A skeletal swarm attacks as a massive bony wave moving to engulf whatever living creatures are closest and not moving on until they have been reduced to bloody shreds. Due to its unique composition of animated hand and claw bones, the swarm gets its strength bonus added to its swarm attacks.

Credit

Original author Greg A. Vaughan
Originally appearing in *Slumbering Tsar* (© Frog God Games/
Greg A. Vaughan, 2012)

Swarm, Sparksting

A cloud of two inch blobs resembling airborne jellyfish hover in the air. Sparks of electricity snap and dance from creature to creature, and the swarm produces a noticeable hum.

SPARKSTING SWARM	CR 4

XP 1,200
N Diminutive magical beast (swarm)
Init +8; **Senses** darkvision 60 ft., low-light vision, synapse sense 60 ft.; **Perception** +1

AC 18, touch 18, flat-footed 14 (+4 Dex, +4 size)
hp 44 (8d10)
Fort +6; **Ref** +12; **Will** +5
Defensive Abilities swarm traits; **Immune** electricity, weapon damage

Speed 10 ft., fly 40 ft. (average); speed burst
Melee swarm (2d6 electricity plus distraction)
Space 10 ft.; **Reach** 0 ft.
Special Attacks distraction (DC 14)

Str 3, **Dex** 18, **Con** 11, **Int** 1, **Wis** 12, **Cha** 9
Base Atk +8; **CMB** —; **CMD** —
Feats Improved Initiative, Improved Lightning Reflexes, Iron Will, Lightning Reflexes
Skills Fly +21, Perception +1

Environment warm marshes
Organization solitary, flight (2–5), or cloud (6–12)
Treasure none

Synapse Sense (Ex) A sparksting swarm can detect the tiny charges caused by electrical impulses of brain activity in living creatures within 60 feet. Creatures without an Intelligence score or creatures immune to mind-affecting effects cannot be detected using this ability.
Speed Burst (Ex) A sparksting swarm can increase its speed by 10 feet for 1d6 rounds. After using this ability, it must wait 1 minute before it can use it again.

Sparkstings are found in remote swamps and marshes and from a distance, when the electricity in a swarm flashes, are often mistaken for will-o-wisps. These electrical flashes are used not only for attracting a mate, but also for luring in prey. Sparkstings are insectivores, and hunt by flying into a swarm of insects and flailing about with their tentacles. Electrocuted insects adhere to the tentacles, which the sparksting then draws into its mouth, located under its body.

Sparkstings are asexual and reproduce by budding. Mating season for these creatures is every few months, and the number of spawn is controlled by the amount of readily available light. Newborn sparkstings have tiny tentacles and do not generate the electrical discharge adults do. The tentacles grow rapidly however, and within three months, the creature reaches adulthood. The typical lifespan of a sparksting is roughly 1 year. The sparksting has few natural predators: other sparkstings and a few larger insects seem to enjoy dining on these creatures.

A sparksting is a tiny creature about 2 inches across. It consists of a membranous, fleshy bag with the consistency of egg yolk. Beneath the main body of a sparksting hang its tentacles, a fibrous mass that flickers with electrical arcs.

Sparksting swarms cloud the air around any creature that disturbs them, attacking like angry bees.

Some spellcasters have begun experimenting with using sparkstings as alternate spell components for *lightning bolt* spells and in the construction of *shock*-based magic weapons.

Swarm, Stirge

Even an animal-level of intelligence is enough for a creature to know there is safety in numbers!

STIRGE SWARM	CR 6

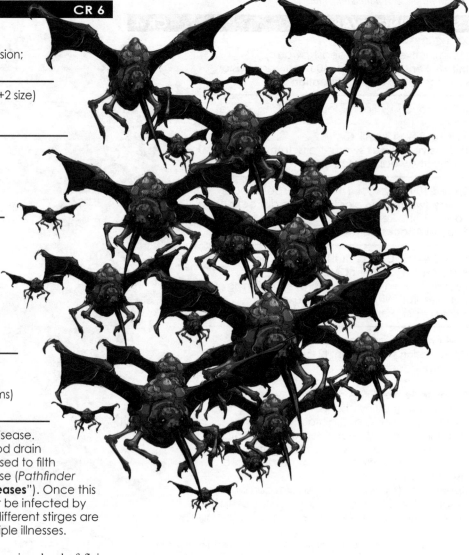

XP 2,400
N Tiny magical beast (swarm)
Init +8; **Senses** darkvision 60 ft., low-light vision;
Perception +11

AC 16, touch 16, flat-footed 12 (+4 Dex, +2 size)
hp 78 (12d10 plus 12)
Fort +8; **Ref** +14; **Will** +5

Speed 10 ft., fly 40 ft. (average)
Melee swarm (3d6 plus blood drain)
Space 10 ft.; **Reach** 0 ft.
Special Attacks blood drain (1d6
Constitution), distraction (DC 16)

Str 3, **Dex** 19, **Con** 10, **Int** 1, **Wis** 12, **Cha** 6
Base Atk +12; **CMB** —; **CMD** —
Feats Improved Initiative, Improved
Lightning Reflexes, Lightning Reflexes,
Skill Focus (Perception), Skill Focus
(Stealth), Toughness
Skills Fly +17, Perception +11,
Stealth +20
SQ diseased

Environment underground or temperate
and warm swamps
Organization solitary, or a pall (2–4 swarms)
Treasure none

Diseased (Ex) Stirges are harbingers of disease.
Any creature subjected to a stirge's blood drain
attack has a 10% chance of being exposed to filth
fever, blinding sickness, or a similar disease (*Pathfinder
Roleplaying Game Core Rulebook*, "**Diseases**"). Once this
check is made, the victim can no longer be infected by
this particular stirge, though attacks by different stirges are
resolved normally and may result in multiple illnesses.

A massive cluster of stirges, the stirge swarm is a band of flying
bloodsuckers combining their relatively small personal power to bring
down larger foes (and for self-preservation). Stirge swarms are found in
the same types of locals as normal stirges; however, they band together
when other predators are too powerful or too numerous for the singular
stirges to survive.

Credit
Originally appearing in *Rappan Athuk* (© Frog God Games,
2012)

Sword Spider

This enormous spider is constructed from steel and its eight legs end in large sharpened blades.

SWORD SPIDER	CR 10

XP 9,600
N Large construct
Init +1; **Senses** darkvision 60 ft., low-light vision; **Perception** +0

AC 25, touch 10, flat-footed 24 (+1 Dex, +15 natural, −1 size)
hp 112 (15d10+30)
Fort +5; **Ref** +6; **Will** +5
DR 10/adamantine; **Immune** construct traits (+30 hp), magic

Speed 20 ft., climb 20 ft.
Melee sword-leg +16/+11/+6 (2d6+2/19–20), 3 sword-legs +16 (2d6+2/19–20), bite +16 (1d8+2 plus poison)
Space 10 ft.; **Reach** 10 ft.
Special Attacks sword-legs

Str 14, **Dex** 12, **Con** —, **Int** —, **Wis** 11, **Cha** 1
Base Atk +15; **CMB** +18; **CMD** 29 (41 vs. trip)
Skills Climb +10

Environment any
Organization solitary or pair
Treasure none

Immunity to Magic (Ex) A sword spider is immune to any spell or spell-like ability that allows spell resistance, except as noted: A *keen edge* spell affects all of a sword spider's sword-leg attacks as if they were slashing weapons.

Transmute metal to wood slows a sword spider for 1d4 rounds (as the *slow* spell), during which time its damage reduction is negated (no save). A magical attack that deals fire damage ends any *slow* effect on the sword spider and heals 1 point of damage for each 3 points of damage the attack would otherwise deal. If the amount of healing would cause the sword spider to exceed its full normal hit points, it gains any excess as temporary hit points. A sword spider gets no saving throw against fire effects. A sword spider is affected normally by rusting attacks, such as those of a rust monster or a *rusting grasp* spell.

Poison (Ex) A sword spider's bite injects poison from a hidden reservoir within its metal body. Because it is a construct, the sword spider does not naturally produce this poison, and its creator must manually refill this reservoir. The reservoir holds enough poison for 5 successful bite attacks, after which the sword spider deals only bite damage. Refilling the reservoir takes 1 minute and provokes attacks of opportunity. The creator can fill the reservoir with any injury poison (typically spider venom), though acid, alchemical substances, and even stranger liquids have been used.

Giant Spider Venom: Bite—injury; *save* DC 14 Fort; *frequency* 1/round for 4 rounds; *effect* 1d2 Strength damage; *cure* 1 save.

Sword-Legs (Ex) A sword spider's legs act as longswords, granting it iterative attacks just as if it wielded multiple weapons. It cannot be disarmed and a sword spider never takes penalties to its attack rolls (for multiweapon fighting) when fighting with its sword-legs.

A sword spider resembles a giant-sized arachnid constructed of steel. Its eight spidery legs end in large sharpened blades resembles longswords or greatswords. A typical sword spider stands 10 feet tall and weighs 3,000 pounds.

When activated, a sword spider fights relentlessly and tirelessly to vanquish its foes, slashing them with up to four of its sword-like legs.

Construction

A sword spider's body is constructed from at least 3,000 pounds of smelted steel. The metal must be of exceptional quality, and costs at least 5,000 gp.

SWORD SPIDER
CL 14th; **Price** 122,000 gp

Requirements Craft Construct, *antimagic field*, *geas/quest*, *keen edge*, *poison*, creator must be caster level 14th; **Skill** Craft (sculpting) or Craft (metalworking) DC 19; **Cost** 63,500 gp

Talorani

This completely hairless humanoid creature has oversized hands and feet which are webbed with thin membranes of flesh. Each finger and toe has an extra joint. It has large, apparently pupil-less eyes and a small nose. Two small gills line each side of its neck, and four larger ones open and close rhythmically on each side of its chest.

TALORANI	CR 1/2

XP 200
Talorani warrior 1
CN Medium humanoid (aquatic, talorani)
Init +0; **Senses** darkvision 120 ft., low-light vision;
Perception +0

AC 11, touch 10, flat-footed 11 (+1 natural)
hp 7 (1d10+2)
Fort +4; **Ref** +0; **Will** +0

Speed 20 ft., swim 30 ft.
Melee longspear +2 (1d8+1)

Str 13, **Dex** 11, **Con** 14, **Int** 9, **Wis** 10, **Cha** 8
Base Atk +1; **CMB** +2; **CMD** 12
Feats Endurance
Skills Swim +13
Languages Talorani; empathic communication
SQ amphibious

Environment any aquatic
Organization solitary, band (2–5), or tribe (6–11)
Treasure standard (longspear, other treasure)

Empathic Communication (Su)
Talorani have the ability to empathically communicate basic ideas (little more than emotion and direction) to any others of their kind within 20 feet. Other creatures must succeed on a DC 20 Sense Motive check to receive empathic imagery from a talorani.

The talorani, more commonly called underdwellers, are an aquatic humanoid race thought to be the descendants of merfolk and elves. They dwell in shallow coastal waters, having carved out a niche for themselves between their aquatic elven ancestors close to shore and their merfolk relatives in deeper waters. Their webbed hands and feet have an extra joint in each finger and toe, allowing them to move through the water with a speed and agility. On land, however, they are slow and ungainly.

Talorani are about 5 feet tall and weigh 125 pounds.

Talorani Society

Underdwellers live in a clan-based social system comprising, in order of increasing size: families – clans – houses – guilds – community. An underdweller known as a Father leads a family, a Grand-Father leads a clan, a Great-Father leads a house, a High-Father leads a guild, and an All-Father leads the community.

There is no true religion amongst the underdwellers as most other races understand it, but the sea, called the Mother, is highly revered within the community as a living entity that controls all within it. It is not worshipped as a god but there are taboos and requirements in place that are observed to avoid retribution from the Mother. A common reprimand from the matriarchs to warn

riotous youngsters is that 'the Mother will see you' if they misbehave. One major taboo that jeopardizes one's relation to the Mother is an unnecessary death. All creatures of the sea are considered an inherent part of it, and a creature's death may mean that somewhere else, something will not come into being because the creature was no longer present. To an underdweller, all creatures need all other creatures, if not now, then in the future to survive. Of course, preventing one's own death is desirable for the same reason.

Death is looked upon as a sad event and underdweller funerals do not differ much from human ritual. The dead are interned within caves near the shore, along with their most prized possessions. The entrance is sealed with rock, and the place is marked. Even enemies are buried this way, though are placed far from the cemeteries of the community.

Humans and all other land-based races are looked on with a mixture of awe, fear, suspicion, and fascination. For centuries untold, the underdwellers have kept to themselves and avoided the petty attentions of the land races. Although there have been no major altercations between the land races and the underdwellers, complete avoidance of all surface-dwelling races is usually the law in underdweller communities.

A normal underdweller mating ritual allows for the complete polygamy of both sexes. Any underdweller may have as many mates as they desire. Children born of such unions are taken to the community nursery to be raised by the matriarchs — rearing children is the responsibility of the entire community rather than just the child's parents. Female underdwellers have the ability to control their own fertility, so the choice to bear a child is a mother's alone, though it is the law for them to inform prospective paramours of her intention to bear children. Other than that, sex is common, often experienced, and willingly shared without many of the taboos and discretion known by other races. A marriage ritual known as life-binding occurs when two underdwellers agree to swear lifelong loyalty to one another in the presence of the community All-Father and the Mother. No other may mate with one who has been life-bound.

Names amongst the underdwellers are descriptive of an individual's appearance, traits or some event in their life. Houses are constructed of worked coral and shipwreck debris, shaped like upturned boats facing into the current with entrances as round holes in the top of the dome. These homes are often decorated with brightly colored rocks, coral, anemones, and ship figureheads or name plates.

Talorani Characters

Talorani are defined by their class levels — they do not possess racial hit dice. Talorani clerics revere "The Mother," and have access to the Animal, Travel, and Water domains. All Talorani have the following racial traits.

+2 Constitution, +2 Wisdom, −2 Charisma: Talorani are hardy and wise but introverted.

Slow: Speed 20 ft. A talorani is slower on land than in the water.

Aquatic: Talorani are aquatic and amphibious. They and can breathe both air and water, and have a swim speed of 30 ft.

Natural Armor Bonus: Talorani have a +1 natural armor bonus.

Deep-Dweller: All talorani have darkvision out to 120 ft. and low-light vision.

Empathic Communication: Talorani have the ability to empathically communicate basic ideas (little more than emotion and direction) to any others of their kind within 20 feet. Other creatures must succeed on a DC 20 Sense Motive check to receive empathic imagery from an underdweller.

Languages: Talorani begin play speaking Talorani. Talorani with high Intelligence scores can choose any of the following bonus languages: Aquan, Common, Draconic, and Sahuagin.

Thought Eater

This bizarre creature is about three feet long with a feline-like hairless body. Its sickly gray and translucent flesh allows its skeletal and muscular systems to be easily seen. The creature's head seems to be a weird mix of feline and avian.

THOUGHT EATER	CR 2

XP 600
N Small aberration
Init +8; **Senses** darkvision 60 ft.; **Perception** +11

AC 17, touch 15, flat-footed 13 (+4 Dex, +2 natural, +1 size)
hp 13 (3d8)
Fort +1; **Ref** +5; **Will** +4
Defensive Abilities ethereal jaunt, spell absorption; **SR** 13

Speed 40 ft.
Melee touch +7 (1d2+1 plus eat thoughts)
Spell-Like Abilities (CL 3rd):
At will—*daze* (DC 12), *detect magic*

Str 12, **Dex** 18, **Con** 11, **Int** 7, **Wis** 12, **Cha** 14
Base Atk +2; **CMB** +2; **CMD** 16
Feats Improved Initiative, Weapon Finesse
Skills Perception +11, Stealth +14; **Racial Modifiers** +4 Perception
SQ precognition

Environment any (Ethereal Plane)
Organization solitary
Treasure none

Detect Magic (Sp) A thought eater can use its *detect magic* spell-like ability to detect magic-using creatures. Magic-using creatures are defined as creatures with levels in a spellcasting class or creatures with spell-like abilities or the ability to cast spells.
Eat Thoughts (Su) The touch of a thought eater deals 1d2 points of Intelligence damage. A thought eater is sated when it has consumed at least 12 points of Intelligence in a given 24-hour period.
Ethereal Jaunt (Su) A thought eater can shift from the Ethereal Plane to the Material Plane as part of any move action, and then shift back again as a free action. This ability is otherwise identical to the *ethereal jaunt* spell (CL 10th).
Precognition (Su) As a standard action, a thought eater can concentrate and glimpse fragments of potential future events—what it sees probably happens if no action is taken to change it. The vision, however, is incomplete, and makes no sense until the events begin to unfold. On its next action, a thought eater gains a +2 insight bonus on a single attack roll, damage roll, saving throw, or skill check. The bonus can be applied to the roll after the results of the dice are known.
Spell Absorption (Su) If a thought eater's spell resistance protects it form a magical effect, the creature absorbs that magical energy into its body. Absorbing a spells heals a thought eater a number of hit points equal to the absorbed spell's level. This cannot increase a thought eater's hit points above its normal maximum hit points.

Thought eaters are bizarre creatures that spend their time swimming the Ethereal Plane feeding on the thoughts and intelligence of living creatures. What little is known of these strange creatures has only recently been discovered. Thought eaters, on average, live about 15 years in the Ethereal Plane. Whether this low life expectancy is the result of predation, natural selection, or the result of some anomaly is unknown. Their diet consists of only the thoughts, intelligence, and mental powers of other creatures. They need not eat or drink anything else to survive. No juvenile or young thought eaters have ever been seen, but it is hypothesized that young are born live and mature very quickly.

When a thought eater detects an intelligent creature, it manifests on the Material Plane and attacks from ambush, seeking to feed its insatiable appetite. A thought eater can spend a maximum of 1 minute (10 rounds) on the Material Plane before its wispy flesh disintegrates and the creature falls dead. If badly wounded, a thought eater seeks escape to the Ethereal Plane rather than continuing the fight.

Tombotu

This creature vaguely resembles a gorilla. It is gray in color, however, and much more powerfully muscled than any natural ape. From its lower jaw sprout two vicious upward-thrusting tusks.

TOMBOTU	CR 4

XP 1,200
N Large monstrous humanoid
Init +2; **Senses** darkvision 60 ft., scent;
Perception +11

AC 15, touch 11, flat-footed 13 (+2 Dex, +4
natural, −1 size)
hp 42 (5d10+15)
Fort +4; **Ref** +6; **Will** +5

Speed 30 ft., climb 30 ft.
Melee 2 claws +9 (1d6+5 plus grab), bite +9 (1d8+5)
Space 10 ft.; **Reach** 10 ft.
Special Attacks rend (2 claws, 1d6+7)

Str 21, **Dex** 15, **Con** 16, **Int** 11, **Wis** 12, **Cha** 11
Base Atk +5; **CMB** +11 (+15 grapple); **CMD** 23
Feats Alertness, Endurance, Power Attack
Skills Acrobatics +6, Climb +19, Diplomacy +3, Perception
+11, Sense Motive +3, Stealth +6
Languages Common, Tombotu

Environment warm forests, hills, mountains, and plains
Organization solitary, pair, or gang (3–6)
Treasure incidental

Tombotu are believed to be the foul offspring of a quasi-deity ape god (believed to be Bonjo Tombo or his twin brother Ponjo Tombo). These gray, apelike humanoids are bred from human or apelike mothers, although the resulting progeny often kills the mother. Tombotu may mate with other tombotu. The tombotu are fairly intelligent aggressors and are often found leading dire apes, girallons, and other ape-like creatures, communicating with them through grunts and body language. Some humanoid cultures journey to the tombotu homelands where they conduct raids, capturing as many tombotu as they can. Captured tombotu are sold as slaves and used as opponents in gladiatorial contests where their ferocious skills are put to the test. Some few tribes of tombotu have actually made truces with other humanoid races, agreeing to sell off their children in exchange for food and other things the tribe may need. Such things are frowned upon by most other tombotu tribes, viewing those who engage in such practices as savages and traitors to their own race.

Tombotu are fond of human flesh and often organized massive hunts where humans are the prey. Some tombotu tribes disdain this practice, feeling it makes them little better than the animals they ascended from. Others however, relish in the hunts, which can lasts for days at a time. Humans are also kept as slaves by many tombotu tribes. Even those tribes that look down upon the hunts keep human slaves. Most human slaves are house slaves, tending to the needs of the family, such as cooking and cleaning.

In combat, a tombotu likes to attack using surprise, often hiding and dangling from jungle trees as its prey pass beneath, snatching up the unsuspecting prey and strangling it to death or breaking the neck of its quarry while it is held immobile by the tombotu's great strength. If threatened with death, a tombotu attempts to flee rather than face certain destruction.

Treant, Razor

This thin and gnarled black tree grows wickedly sharp razors instead of leaves. The razors ring like a thousand tiny bells with every wind gust.

RAZOR TREANT	CR 11

XP 12,800
CE Huge plant
Init +4; **Senses** darkvision 60 ft., low-light vision; **Perception** +25

AC 22, touch 8, flat-footed 22 (+14 natural, −2 size)
hp 171 (18d8+90)
Fort +18; **Ref** +6; **Will** +11
DR 10/slashing; **Immune** plant traits
Weakness vulnerability to fire

Speed 10 ft.
Melee 2 slams +22 (2d6+11 plus 1d4 slashing plus 1 bleed)
Space 15 ft.; **Reach** 10 ft.
Special Attacks bloody autumn (10d4 slashing plus 1d4 bleed; DC 20 Ref for half and no bleed), razor leaves

Str 32, **Dex** 11, **Con** 21, **Int** 15, **Wis** 16, **Cha** 12
Base Atk +13; **CMB** +26; **CMD** 36
Feats Awesome Blow[B], Cleave, Combat Reflexes, Great Cleave, Great Fortitude, Improved Initiative, Improved Sunder, Iron Will, Power Attack, Skill Focus (Perception)
Skills Bluff +15, Intimidate +18, Knowledge (nature) +16, Perception +25, Sense Motive +17
Languages Infernal, Razor Treant, Sylvan

Environment forests or jungle
Organization solitary, pair, or grove (3–6)
Treasure incidental

Bloody Autumn (Ex) In this awesome attack the razor treant violently shakes itself as a full-round action, letting all of its leaves fall off to the ground. All creatures within 30 feet of the razor treant suffer 10d4 slashing damage and 1d4 bleed damage (DC 20 Reflex save for half and no bleed damage). Those who fail the Reflex save must succeed on an additional DC 20 Will save or be staggered for 1 round from the terrible pain of the hundreds of small wounds inflicted on them.

Using this attack leaves the razor treant without its razor leaves for 2–6 days so it only resorts to this tactic in desperate situations.

Razor Leaves (Ex) Razor treants grow razors instead of leaves, hence the name. These extremely keen steel blades range from one to three inches in length and can easily cut through flesh. Any physical attack made by a razor treant is counted as being *keen* and *wounding* (already incorporated into the statistics above). Even merely touching a razor treant (including unarmed melee attacks) inflicts 1d4 points of slashing damage plus wounding on the victim.

When a razor treant is struck for more than 20 points of damage in a single blow, it loses some of its poorly connected leaves. Everyone within 30 feet of the razor treant suffers 1d4 points of wounding slashing damage (DC 20 Reflex negates).

The razor leaves break down quickly after the treant's

death, remaining for only 1d2 rounds. The area around the treant is considered difficult terrain during that time.

Razor treants are the evil and hateful cousins of the treants, often combating with treants over rulership of vast primordial forest in distant and exotic lands. However, unlike their kind cousins, they hate all non-plant creatures with passion and enjoy nothing more than torturing a hapless traveler for hours by inflicting on him hundreds of small wounds, until he finally dies from pain, exhaustion or loss of blood.

Animals know better than to come anywhere near the murderous trees, making the area around the razor treant deathly still when there is no wind.

Because of their slow movement rate, razor treants prefer to trick their opponents into coming within its reach and then attacking with its slam attack if there are few victims or with bloody autumn attack if it is surrounded by a large group. Groups of razor treants enjoy "playing" with their victims by hurling them at each other. Few are the heroes who suffered these sadistic games and lived to tell the tale. Razor treants often let wounded opponents flee on purpose, knowing they will die of loss of blood within minutes anyway.

Credit

Original author Uri Kurlianchik
Originally appearing in *The Hollow Mountain* (© Frog God Games, 2011)

Treant, Stone

This creature looks much like an animated sculpture of a tree. It has a thick, corrugated hide of bark like stone, with many thick branches. It travels along on clusters of humping and twining stone roots. It possesses no discernible face.

STONE TREANT	CR 16

XP 76,800
N Huge outsider (earth, elemental, native)
Init −1; **Senses** darkvision 60 ft., tremorsense 120 ft.; **Perception** +27

AC 22, touch 7, flat-footed 22 (−1 Dex, +15 natural, −2 size)
hp 346 (21d10+210 plus 21)
Fort +17; **Ref** +13; **Will** +17
DR 10/slashing and adamantine; **Immune** elemental traits; **SR** 31

Speed 30 ft., burrow 5 ft.
Melee 6 slams +32 (3d8+12)
Space 15 ft.; **Reach** 15 ft.
Special Attacks acidic blood (5d4 acid, DC 20 Reflex half), trample (3d8+18, DC 32)

Str 35, **Dex** 8, **Con** 30, **Int** 10, **Wis** 16, **Cha** 12
Base Atk +21; **CMB** +35 (+39 bull rush and sunder); **CMD** 44
Feats Awesome Blow, Cleave, Greater Sunder, Improved Bull Rush, Improved Sunder, Iron Will, Lightning Reflexes, Power Attack, Toughness, Vital Strike, Weapon Focus (slam)
Skills Intimidate +25, Knowledge (history) +24, Knowledge (planes) +24, Perception +27, Sense Motive +27, Stealth +15 (+21 in stony underground areas); **Racial Modifiers** +6 Stealth in stony underground areas
Languages Sylvan, Terran
SQ radial symmetry

Environment underground
Organization solitary, or grove (2–16)
Treasure standard

Acidic Blood (Ex) Anyone striking the stone treant with a piercing or slashing attack and inflicting damage releases a gout of acidic blood, which causes 5d4 points of acid damage to the person who struck it. A DC 20 Reflex save reduces this damage by half. The blood becomes inert one round after leaving the elemental's body.
Radial Symmetry (Ex) Because of its shape, the stone treant can bring no more than four of its slam attacks to bear on any one target. However, it also perceives the area around it equally well, and thus it cannot be flanked.

The stone treant is a variant of the treant native to the Plane of Earth. They are very rare even there, located in isolated pockets in the plane where they tend groves of crystals and natural gem outcroppings. Knowledge of their existence has been all but lost, as has the ritual of summoning and binding them into service.

A stone treant stands 20–30 ft. tall, with a trunk about 4 ft. in diameter. It weighs close to 10,000 pounds.

Stone treants are intelligent, and speak Terran. They generally do not bother to communicate with non-earth elemental beings, however.

Credit
Originally appearing in *Rappan Athuk Reloaded* (© Necromancer Games, 2006)

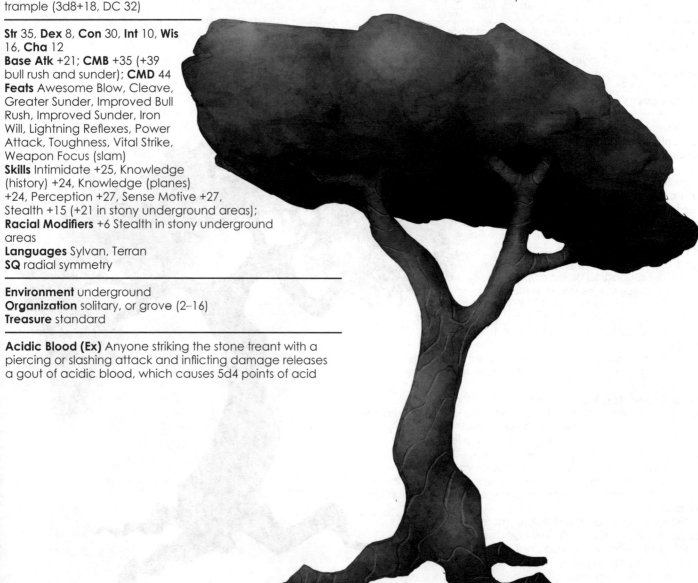

Troll, Black

This tall, grotesque creature has a shiny black hide and hands that end in wicked claws. Two large tusks protrude from its fang-filled mouth.

BLACK TROLL	CR 7

XP 3,200
CE Large humanoid (giant)
Init +1; **Senses** darkvision 60 ft., low-light vision, scent; **Perception** +8

AC 18, touch 10, flat-footed 17 (+1 Dex, +8 natural, –1 size)
hp 84 (8d8+48); regeneration 5 (acid or cold)
Fort +12; **Ref** +3; **Will** +3

Speed 30 ft.
Melee bite +12 (1d8+7), 2 claws +13 (1d6+7)
Space 10 ft.; **Reach** 10 ft.
Special Attacks rend (2 claws, 1d6+9)

Str 24, **Dex** 12, **Con** 23, **Int** 5, **Wis** 9, **Cha** 6
Base Atk +6; **CMB** +14; **CMD** 25
Feats Intimidating Prowess, Iron Will, Skill Focus (Perception), Weapon Focus (claw)
Skills Climb +12, Intimidate +11, Perception +8
Languages Giant

Environment cold mountains
Organization solitary or gang (1–2 plus 2–5 trolls)
Treasure standard

Fire Absorption (Su) Any fire effect that would deal 20 or more points of damage to a fire troll causes the creature to grow to Huge size. A black troll can induce this effect itself by stepping into a large source of fire that deals 20 or more points of damage in a single round. It must spend one full round in the flames for this method to work. This size change lasts 1 hour before the black troll reverts to its normal size.

BLACK TROLL (HUGE SIZE)	CR 7

XP 3,200
CE Huge humanoid (giant)
Init +0; **Senses** darkvision 60 ft., low-light vision, scent; **Perception** +8

AC 18, touch 8, flat-footed 18 (+10 natural, –2 size)
hp 100 (8d8+64); regeneration 5 (acid or cold)
Fort +14; **Ref** +2; **Will** +3

Speed 40 ft.
Melee bite +15 (2d6+11), 2 claws +16 (1d8+11)
Space 15 ft.; **Reach** 15 ft.
Special Attacks rend (2 claws, 1d8+16)

Str 32, **Dex** 10, **Con** 27, **Int** 5, **Wis** 9, **Cha** 6
Base Atk +6; **CMB** +19; **CMD** 29
Feats Intimidating Prowess, Iron Will, Skill Focus (Perception), Weapon Focus (claw)
Skills Climb +16, Intimidate +15, Perception +8
Languages Giant

Black trolls are an offshoot of standard trolls, believed to be supernaturally altered by magic. They dwell in the same climate as their normal brethren and often associate with them as well. Their appetites are no less impressive than other trolls, and some would argue theirs is even greater. Black trolls dine on anything they catch and kill, including scavenging and dining on the leftovers of other animals' meals. Black trolls do not eat other trolls, regardless of the food situation.

Black trolls stand 14 feet tall and weigh around 1,000 pounds. When they swell to Huge size, they reach heights of 21 feet or more and weigh over 3,000 pounds. Black trolls flesh is rubbery to the touch and always shiny black in color. Eyes are almost always dull gray, though a few black trolls have bright blue eyes. Young are born live and reach maturity relatively quickly. Black trolls can mate with other trolls, but the offspring is always the same type as the other parent. Only black trolls mating with their own spawn another black troll.

A black troll attacks by slashing and biting its foes. Its ability to deal horrendous amounts of damage is cause for concern among many that have faced a black troll. Often when in combat, a black troll shuns fire, hoping its opponent senses a weakness and decides to unleash a fire attack at the troll. Many adventurers have met their untimely demise this way. If the ruse doesn't appear to work, and there is a large source of fire nearby, a black troll subjects itself to the fire in order to grow to Huge size.

Troll, River

Similar in many respects to their swamp-loving kin, river trolls prefer a less slimy existence, and prefer to live in forested regions near rivers and streams, or under bridges.

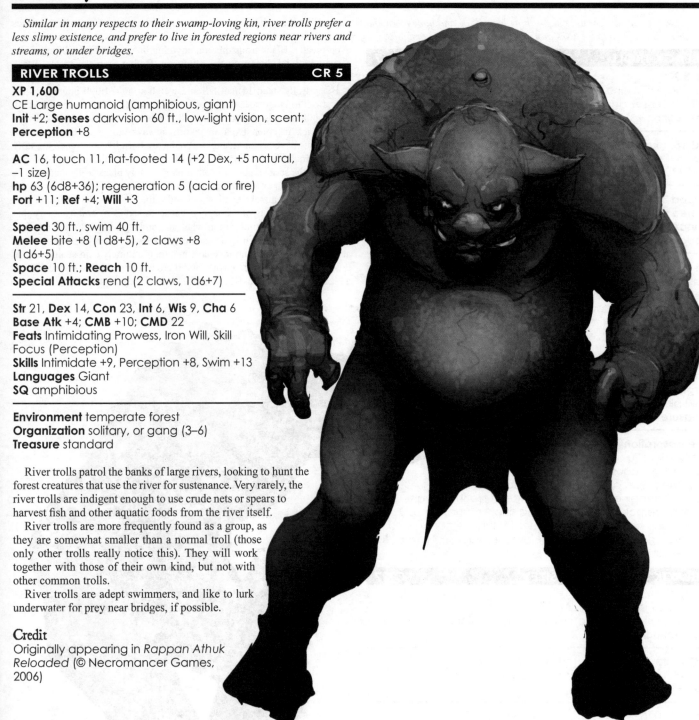

RIVER TROLLS   CR 5

XP 1,600
CE Large humanoid (amphibious, giant)
Init +2; **Senses** darkvision 60 ft., low-light vision, scent; **Perception** +8

AC 16, touch 11, flat-footed 14 (+2 Dex, +5 natural, −1 size)
hp 63 (6d8+36); regeneration 5 (acid or fire)
Fort +11; **Ref** +4; **Will** +3

Speed 30 ft., swim 40 ft.
Melee bite +8 (1d8+5), 2 claws +8 (1d6+5)
Space 10 ft.; **Reach** 10 ft.
Special Attacks rend (2 claws, 1d6+7)

Str 21, **Dex** 14, **Con** 23, **Int** 6, **Wis** 9, **Cha** 6
Base Atk +4; **CMB** +10; **CMD** 22
Feats Intimidating Prowess, Iron Will, Skill Focus (Perception)
Skills Intimidate +9, Perception +8, Swim +13
Languages Giant
SQ amphibious

Environment temperate forest
Organization solitary, or gang (3–6)
Treasure standard

River trolls patrol the banks of large rivers, looking to hunt the forest creatures that use the river for sustenance. Very rarely, the river trolls are indigent enough to use crude nets or spears to harvest fish and other aquatic foods from the river itself.

River trolls are more frequently found as a group, as they are somewhat smaller than a normal troll (those only other trolls really notice this). They will work together with those of their own kind, but not with other common trolls.

River trolls are adept swimmers, and like to lurk underwater for prey near bridges, if possible.

Credit

Originally appearing in *Rappan Athuk Reloaded* (© Necromancer Games, 2006)

Troll, Undead

tThis tall and hideous humanoid has sickly green, rotting flesh and hands that end in filthy claws.

UNDEAD TROLL	CR 6

XP 2,400
CE Large undead
Init +2; **Senses** darkvision 60 ft., darkvision 60 ft., scent;
Perception +10

AC 19, touch 11, flat-footed 17 (+2 Dex, +8 natural, −1 size)
hp 68 (8d8+24 plus 8); fast healing 5
Fort +5; **Ref** +4; **Will** +7
DR 5/magic; **Immune** undead traits; **Resist** cold 10, fire 10

Speed 40 ft.
Melee bite +12 (1d8+7), 2 claws +12 (1d6+7 plus bleed)
Space 10 ft.; **Reach** 10 ft.
Special Attacks bleed (1d6), rend (2 claws, 1d6+10)

Str 24, **Dex** 14, **Con** —, **Int** 6, **Wis** 9, **Cha** 16
Base Atk +6; **CMB** +14; **CMD** 26
Feats Intimidating Prowess, Iron Will, Skill Focus
(Perception), Toughness
Skills Climb +11, Intimidate +18, Perception +10,
Stealth +6
Languages Giant

Environment cold mountains or any
Organization solitary or pair
Treasure standard

Sometimes when a troll dies, the evilness within the creature raises it as an undead troll; a mockery of life and even more evil than it was before (if such is possible). Undead trolls despise all living creatures, especially other trolls. Their sole purpose now seems to be to kill and devour every living thing they encounter. Undeath seems to have cursed them with an eternal hunger, and undead trolls are forever seeking to satiate their appetite. Undead trolls do not eat other undead trolls however. Though they tend to inhabit the same cold mountains they did in life, undead trolls can be found anywhere.

Undead trolls generally resemble normal trolls in stature. Their flesh has taken on a sickly green appearance and is rotting in various places. Their teeth and nails are filthy and these creatures are almost always caked in dried blood.

Undead trolls are relentless in combat, always fighting to the death. They attack as do standard trolls, using wicked claws and bites. While they lack the true regenerative powers of a standard troll, their ability to quickly heal still complicates combat for a lot of would-be troll slayers.

Uggoth

This hideous humanoid creature has the lower torso of an octopus and the upper torso of a human. Two long tentacles protrude from each side of the creature's body, just beneath its arms. Its head, while vaguely human, is hairless and features an elongated skull.

UGGOTH	CR 8

XP 4,800
CE Medium aberration
Init +6; **Senses** darkvision 60 ft., *detect thoughts*; **Perception** +16

AC 22, touch 13, flat-footed 19 (+2 Dex, +1 dodge, +9 natural)
hp 67 (9d8+27)
Fort +6; **Ref** +7; **Will** +12
Defensive Abilities spell reflection; **DR** 10/cold iron; **SR** 19

Speed 30 ft., swim 30 ft.
Melee 2 claws +10 (1d4+4), 4 tentacles +10 (1d6+4 plus grab)
Special Attacks mind thrust
Spell-Like Abilities (CL 12th):
Constant—*detect magic*
At will—*charm person* (DC 16), *detect thoughts* (DC 17), *hypnotic pattern* (DC 17), *suggestion* (DC 18)
1/day—*charm monster* (DC 20), *mass suggestion* (DC 21), *plane shift* (DC 22)

Str 19, **Dex** 15, **Con** 17, **Int** 19, **Wis** 19, **Cha** 21
Base Atk +6; **CMB** +10 (+14 grapple); **CMD** 23
Feats Combat Casting, Dodge, Improved Initiative, Iron Will, Lightning Reflexes
Skills Bluff +14, Diplomacy +14, Intimidate +17, Knowledge (any one) +13, Knowledge (arcana) +16, Perception +16, Sense Motive +13, Spellcraft +12, Swim +12, Use Magical Device +9
Languages Aquan, Common, Draconic, Undercommon
SQ water breathing

Environment any underground
Organization solitary or gang (2–4)
Treasure standard

Mind Thrust (Su) Three times per day, a uggoth can unleash a blast of mental energy at a single target within 40 feet. The blast deals 8d6 points of damage to a single target if it fails a DC 24 Will save. This is a mind-affecting effect. The save DC is Charisma-based.

Spell Reflection (Su) Any spell that fails to overcome a uggoth's spell resistance is reflected back on the caster who becomes the target of the spell. Area spells still affect the area around the uggoth, but the portion that would affect it is reflected back on the caster.

Tentacles (Ex) A uggoth's tentacles are always primary attacks for the creature.

Uggoths are subterranean creatures once bent on destruction and expanding their own realm from the underworld to the surface world. Legends say the uggoth race was formed when a band of ancient humans offended their gods and were forever cursed. Scholars cannot verify or disprove this origin myth.

Uggoths dwell in great underground cities, most of which are built and maintained by slave labor. Once an ambitious race with desires to rule both underground and aboveground, uggoths now spend most of their time lounging in their homes or in public places within the uggoth cities partaking of various dream-inducing narcotics. They are still very active in trade, usually trading with other evil-aligned subterranean races. In exchange for various foods, manufactured weapons, and spices, the uggoth receive slaves, exotic herbs, and the like.

Uggoths stand between 6 and 7 feet tall and weigh 160 to 180 pounds. Their humanoid flesh is dark amber and leathery to the touch. Their lower torsos are even darker amber fading to black near the tips of the tentacles. Uggoths live for 150 years typically.

A uggoth attack with its mind thrust attack in an effort to dispatch its enemies as quickly and efficiently as possible. Creatures that survive are attacked with various spell-like abilities and slashed or grabbed by the creature's tentacles. Opponents that are killed are usually devoured on the spot or carried back to the uggoth's dwelling and eaten later or fed to the young. Opponents that show promise as slaves are captured instead of killed. Potential slaves are carted back to the uggoth's city and placed in a public slave pen where they are eventually sold to the highest bidder. Occasionally the city's overseer allows the uggoth to keep captured slaves.

Undead Elemental, Fire

A pillar of black flame glowing with a bluish nimbus seems to contain a humanoid shape at its heart. The crackling flames give off an intense chill that drains the heat from the surrounding air.

UNDEAD FIRE ELEMENTAL	CR 8

XP 4,800
NE Medium undead (cold)
Init +8; **Senses** darkvision 60 ft.; **Perception** +15

AC 20, touch 15, flat-footed 15 (+4 Dex, +1 dodge, +5 natural)
hp 102 (12d8+36 plus 12)
Fort +7; **Ref** +8; **Will** +8
Defensive Abilities chill shield; **Immune** cold, fire, undead traits

Speed 50 ft.
Melee slam +13 (1d6+4 plus 1d6 cold and coldfire)

Str 16, **Dex** 19, **Con** —, **Int** 4, **Wis** 11, **Cha** 16
Base Atk +9; **CMB** +12; **CMD** 27
Feats Dodge, Improved Initiative, Mobility, Spring Attack, Toughness, Weapon Finesse
Skills Perception +15
Languages Ignan
SQ snuff

Environment any
Organization solitary
Treasure none

Chill Shield (Su) In addition to being immune to cold and fire, the flames that wreath an undead fire elemental also act as a *fire shield* spell. Any creature striking the undead fire elemental with a natural or handheld weapon takes 1d6+12 points of cold damage. This effect cannot be dispelled.

Coldfire (Su) Each time an undead fire elemental successfully hits a living creature, that creature must make a DC 19 Fortitude save or catch on fire from the elemental's cold flames. These flames deal 1d6 Strength damage per round as the life-giving heat is snuffed from its body. The afflicted creature is entitled to a new saving throw each round. This coldfire burns for 1d6 rounds or until a successful save is made. Resistance to cold or fire does not prevent this damage, though *death ward* does. The save is Charisma based.

Snuff (Ex) As a standard action (that does not provoke an attack of opportunity), an undead fire elemental can extinguish itself, thereby reducing itself to the form of its base component — a small pile of cold ashes. The undead fire elemental will rarely do this while in the presence of other creatures because of the inherent vulnerability involved. If the cold ash can be scooped up and placed in a stoppered container, the undead fire elemental is trapped until released. Likewise if the ash pile is exposed to winds of 50 mph or greater, the undead fire elemental's material form is dispersed, and it is unable to manifest its burning form again until it is able to reform its ash pile — a process usually taking several years. While in its ash pile form, an undead fire elemental can burst into its burning form as a free action without provoking an attack of opportunity.

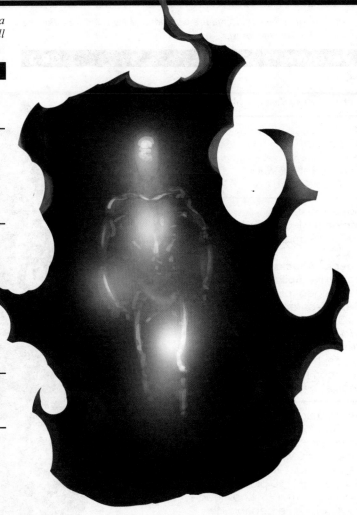

Occasionally a horrible tragedy befalls a summoned fire elemental such that it is destroyed but is not permitted to return to its plane of origin. When this happens, what can eventually form is a horrendous creature composed of its original element infused with raw negative energy. The resulting undead creature is an abomination to its element, seeking nothing more than to snuff out all heat it encounters. Divorced of its natural element, undead fire elementals are no longer hindered by water or bodies of nonflammable liquids.

An undead fire elemental stands 7 feet tall but weighs only 75 pounds due to its ephemeral nature.

Undead fire elementals retain the ability to speak Ignan but rarely deign to speak to those they are about to consume in their cold fury.

Undead fire elementals usually remain in their lairs, morosely remembering their prior warm existence. However, when anything living comes within range, they quickly resume their burning form and surprise attack with glee to forever destroy the heat that they sense in their prey.

Credit
Original author Greg A. Vaughan
Originally appearing in *Slumbering Tsar* (© Frog God Games/ Greg A. Vaughan, 2012)

Valeany

An exquisitely beautiful creature with pointed ears and long flowing hair emerges from the forest.

VALEANY	**CR 3**

XP 800
CN Medium fey
Init +4; **Senses** low-light vision; **Perception** +9

AC 18, touch 15, flat-footed 13 (+4 Dex, +1 dodge, +3 natural)
hp 22 (4d6+8)
Fort +3; **Ref** +8; **Will** +6
DR 5/cold iron

Speed 30 ft.
Melee mwk dagger +7 (1d4/19–20) or touch +6 (mark) or unarmed +6 (1d3 plus grab)
Special Attacks embrace
Spell-Like Abilities (CL 6th; melee touch +2, ranged touch +6)
3/day—*entangle* (DC 15), *hypnotism* (DC 15), *suggestion* (DC 17)
1/day—*call lightning* (DC 17), *dimension door* (DC 18), *flame blade, hold person* (DC 17), *summon nature's ally III, tree shape*

Str 10, **Dex** 19, **Con** 15, **Int** 15, **Wis** 15, **Cha** 19
Base Atk +2; **CMB** +2 (+6 grapple); **CMD** 17
Feats Dodge, Weapon Finesse
Skills Bluff +11, Diplomacy +11, Handle Animal +8, Knowledge (nature) +9, Perception +9, Sense Motive +9, Stealth +11, Survival +6
Languages Common, Sylvan
SQ nature's empathy

Environment temperate forests
Organization
Treasure standard (masterwork dagger, other treasure)

Embrace (Su) A valeany that grapples and pins a foe deals 1d4 points of Strength damage to the target each round the pin is maintained.

Mark (Su) A valeany can "mark" an opponent that instills distrust in all animals. No animal, wild or domesticated, approaches within 30 feet of a marked foe; if forced to do so, the creature panics and remains so as long as it's within 30 feet of the target. The mark can be removed by a *break enchantment* or *dispel magic* (the latter of which must be cast by a spellcaster whose caster level is equal to or higher than the valeany's Hit Dice). Dryads, druids, and valeanys can sense a marked creature within 60 feet.

Nature's Empathy (Su) This ability functions as a druid's wild empathy class feature, except the valeany has a +4 racial bonus on the check. The valeany's effective druid level is equal to her Hit Dice for determining her total modifier to the check.

The valeany or "forest girl" is thought to be distantly related to the dryad and nymph. She makes her home deep in a secluded area of a forest, not far from civilized areas perhaps but secluded enough that it is away from prying eyes. Valeanys are free-spirited creatures that enjoy games, frivolity, and nature. They are often found in the company of dryads, nymphs, sirines, and elves.

A valeany appears as a comely human female with long flowing golden hair that nearly reaches the ground. The eyes of a valeany are a deep golden blue or brown. Skin color ranges from light golden to dark tan. The valeany wears either lightly colored and lightweight gowns or nothing at all.

Valeany, like their cousins the dryad and nymph, are not combatants. They seek to avoid combat when possible, unless they themselves, their homes, or their allies are threatened or harmed. Most often, a valeany uses its spell-like abilities to slip away from battle as soon as possible, marking its enemies as it does so.

If forced into combat, a valeany fights using its spell-like abilities and embrace. Incapacitated or weakened foes are left where they fall.

Vampire Spawn, Feral

This brutish monstrosity appears to have once been a human, though its formerly fine grave clothes are tattered and smeared with the filth of a boneyard. Massive muscles ripple beneath its cold, hard flesh contributing to its hunched posture, and jagged, broken fangs extend from between its bloodless lips.

FERAL VAMPIRE SPAWN	CR 6

XP 2,400
CE Medium undead (augmented human)
Init +6; **Senses** darkvision 60 ft., scent; **Perception** +8

AC 18, touch 12, flat-footed 16 (+2 Dex, +6 natural)
hp 68 (8d8+24 plus 8); fast healing 2
Fort +7; **Ref** +6; **Will** +4
Defensive Abilities channel resistance +4; **DR** 5/silver;
Immune undead traits; **Resist** cold 10, electricity 10
Weaknesses vampire weaknesses

Speed 30 ft.
Melee slam +13 (1d6+10 plus energy drain)
Special Attacks blood drain, energy drain (1 level, DC 10)

Str 25, **Dex** 14, **Con** —, **Int** 2, **Wis** 6, **Cha** 16
Base Atk +6; **CMB** +13; **CMD** 25
Feats Great Fortitude, Improved Initiative, Lightning Reflexes, Toughness
Skills Climb +15, Perception +8, Stealth +13; **Racial Modifiers** +4 Climb, +4 Perception, +4 Stealth
Languages Common (cannot speak)
SQ gaseous form, shadowless, spider climb

Environment any
Organization solitary or pack (2–5)
Treasure none

Blood Drain (Su) A feral vampire spawn can suck blood from a grappled opponent; if the feral vampire spawn establishes or maintains a pin, it drains blood, dealing 1d4 points of Constitution damage. The feral vampire spawn heals 5 hit points or gains 5 temporary hit points for 1 hour (up to a maximum number of temporary hit points equal to its full normal hit points) each round it drains blood.
Energy Drain (Su) A creature hit by a feral vampire spawn's slam gains one negative level. This ability only triggers once per round, regardless of the number of attacks the feral vampire spawn makes.
Fast Healing (Su) A feral vampire spawn has fast healing 2. If reduced to 0 hit points in combat, it assumes gaseous form and attempts to escape. It must reach its coffin home within 2 hours or be utterly destroyed. (It can travel up to 9 miles in 2 hours.) Additional damage dealt to a feral vampire spawn forced into gaseous form has no effect. Once at rest, it is helpless. It regains 1 hit point after 1 hour, then is no longer helpless and resumes healing at the rate of 2 hit points per round.
Gaseous Form (Su) A feral vampire spawn can only assume gaseous form when it has been reduced to 0 hit points in combat. It then assumes *gaseous form* as the spell (caster level 5th) and returns to its coffin. While gaseous it has a fly speed of 20 feet with perfect maneuverability.
Shadowless (Ex) A feral vampire spawn casts no shadows and shows no reflection in a mirror.
Spider Climb (Ex) A feral vampire spawn can climb sheer surfaces as though with a *spider climb* spell.

Sometimes when vampires create minions something horrible happens

to the creature causing a fate worse than even that of a typical vampire spawn. On these occasions whether by accident or design, upon waking to its new undead existence the newly created spawn finds itself trapped within its coffin or tomb and unable to free itself even in gaseous form. In these instances the spawn rages and struggles to escape as it slowly goes insane, a victim of its all-consuming hunger. When the master vampire finally deigns to release its new spawn or it finally manages to break free — sometimes years after its creation — the spawn is feral and nearly mindless, though with a much greater strength due to its incessant rage. Vampire masters often find such spawn less of a threat and easier to dispose of when their usefulness has ended.

Unlike typical vampire spawn, feral vampire spawn resemble primitive or Neanderthal-like versions of their former selves with heavy frames supporting a massive musculature and a face twisted by rage and hate into an almost animal-like mask. They are usually hunched over from long confinement and weigh up to 200 pounds more than typical for a member of their species of their relative size.

Feral vampire spawn have lost the ability to speak beyond inarticulate roars, though they can understand and obey verbal commands from their master.

Feral vampire spawn attack without thought or tactics using their tremendous brute strength to smash their foes and feed. Though it is presumed that they should still be capable of assuming gaseous form at will or using their domination gaze like standard vampire spawn, feral vampire spawn seem to have forgotten how to use these abilities.

Credit
Original author Greg A. Vaughan
Originally appearing in *Slumbering Tsar* (© Frog God Games/ Greg A. Vaughan, 2012)

Voltar

A man-sized humanoid whose body is covered with crackling and arcing blue and white electricity stands before you. Its eyes are oversized empty white sockets. Small sparks of electricity seem to dance inside the empty sockets.

VOLTAR	CR 4

XP 1,200
N Medium outsider (electricity, extraplanar)
Init +2; **Senses** darkvision 60 ft.; **Perception** +8

AC 16, touch 12, flat-footed 14 (+2 Dex, +4 natural)
hp 37 (5d10+10)
Fort +6; **Ref** +6; **Will** +3
DR 5/magic; **Immune** cold, electricity, poison
Weaknesses vulnerability to water

Speed 30 ft.
Melee longsword +9 (1d8+3 plus 1d6 electricity), 2 slams +3 (1d4+3 plus 1d6 electricity)
Ranged lightning bolt +7 (2d6 electricity)
Special Attacks death throes, lightning bolt

Str 17, **Dex** 15, **Con** 15, **Int** 10, **Wis** 11, **Cha** 10
Base Atk +5; **CMB** +8; **CMD** 20
Feats Ability Focus (death throes), Iron Will, Weapon Focus (longsword)
Skills Diplomacy +5, Escape Artist +7, Knowledge (planes) +8, Perception +8, Stealth +10, Survival +5
Languages Common (can't speak), Voltar

Environment any (Quasi-Elemental Plane of Lightning)
Organization solitary or pair
Treasure incidental (longsword, other treasure)

Death Throes (Su) When reduced to 0 hit points or less, a voltar explodes in a blinding flash of electricity that radiates outward and deals 5d6 points of electricity damage to everything within 30 feet. A DC 16 Reflex save reduces the damage by half. The save DC is Constitution-based.
Lightning Bolt (Su) A voltar's lightning bolt has a range of 100 feet.
Vulnerable to Water (Ex) A voltar submerged in enough water to cover its entire body is immediately reduced to 0 hit points and explodes just as if it had used its death throes ability.

Voltars are organic creatures semi-composed of lightning that hail from the Quasi-Elemental Plane of Lightning. Though rarely encountered on other planes, they do enjoy traveling to the Material Plane from time to time, journeying to the plane via lightning storms and riding the lightning bolts to the ground.

On the Material Plane, voltars make their lairs near civilized areas, but not close enough to draw attention to them. Most such lairs consist of well-hidden and camouflaged caves or caverns in dense forests or hilly areas. They enjoy watching natives of the Material Plane and often make forays into nearby civilized areas to observe the locals.

Voltars are nocturnal hunters, preferring to hunt during thunderstorms, rainstorms, and especially lightning storms. A voltar's diet consists primarily of whatever it can catch and kill supplemented with a mix of berries, nuts, and fruits.

A voltar appears as a milky-white slender and lithe humanoid standing about 6-1/2 feet tall. Its body, armor, and weapon is covered in dancing and arcing crackling electricity of blue and white. Its eyes are white and empty (save for the small sparks of electricity that seem to play in them). Its head is long and rectangular and its mouth

long and wide. No teeth seem to be present in its mouth.

A voltar speaks its own tongue consisting of clicks and guttural sounds. It seems to understand Common, but does not appear to be able to speak it.

A lone voltar does not attack if outnumbered (unless it is cornered and cannot escape). When more than one voltar is present, however, they often attack creatures that wander too close to their lair. In combat, a voltar attacks with its electrically-charged fists, weapon, or by hurling a bolt of lightning at an opponent.

War Flower

This beautiful and yet disturbing flower resembles a man-sized sunflower that grows daggers instead of petals and has a great, round eye in its center. From its thin stem a small iron shield and a needle thin rapier sprout. Suddenly, the thing stirs.

WAR FLOWER	CR 4

XP 1,200
N Medium plant
Init +9; **Senses** low-light vision; **Perception** +9

AC 20, touch 15, flat-footed 15 (+5 Dex, +5 natural)
hp 33 (6d8+6)
Fort +6; **Ref** +9; **Will** +2
Immune plant traits
Weakness thin stem

Speed 40 ft.
Melee mwk rapier +10 (1d6+2/18–20), or dagger +9 (1d4+2/19–20)
Special Attacks dagger wind (1d4 daggers; DC 18 Ref avoids)
Spell-like Abilities (CL 6th):
1/day—*haste* (self only)

Str 14, **Dex** 21, **Con** 12, **Int** 1, **Wis** 10, **Cha** 6
Base Atk +4; **CMB** +6; **CMD** 21
Feats Lightning Reflexes, Improved Initiative, Weapon Finesse
Skills Perception +9

Environment temperate forests (The Hollow Mountain)
Organization garden (3–12)
Treasure (masterwork rapier, dagger, other treasure)

Dagger Wind (Ex) A war flower can lunch all its dagger-petals in all directions at once. Every creature in a 30 ft. radius must succeed a DC 18 Reflex save or be hit by 1d4 daggers for 1d4+2 damage each. This attack is usually performed when the flower is mortally wounded or hopelessly outnumbered. The save DC is Dexterity-based.
Thin Stem (Ex) A war flower has a thin and fragile stem. The thin stem makes it extremely vulnerable to slashing weapons. A war flower that suffers a critical hit from a slashing weapon must make a Fortitude save equal to DC 10 + the damage dealt or die as result of its stem being chopped in two.

War flowers were among of the first of the Tree That Sees creations (see *The Hollow Mountain* from **Frog God Games** for more information on the Tree That Sees), a union of the gentleness and beauty of the flower with the grace and deadliness of a rapier. Although only slightly smarter than normal flowers they nevertheless can follow one-word orders, tell the difference between friends and foes and fight with unpredictable style and elegance.

War flowers usually wait until an enemy comes close enough to rain a hail of daggers on him before charging with their rapiers. Since they are nearly mindless they fight until either they or their designated target are dead.

The group stumbles upon a group of warflowers lying in ambush for any trespassers into the Tree That Sees' realm. There is a 20% chance for a dead adventurer along with his treasure to lie in the area.

Credit
Original author Uri Kurlianchik
Originally appearing in *The Hollow Mountain* (© Frog God Games, 2011)

Wasp, Elven

This large wasp has a sapphire blue body and jet black wings.

ELVEN WASP	CR 4

XP 1,200
N Medium vermin
Init +2; **Senses** darkvision 60 ft.; **Perception** +9

AC 17, touch 12, flat-footed 15 (+2 Dex, +5 natural)
hp 58 (9d8+18)
Fort +8; **Ref** +5; **Will** +4
Immune mind-affecting effects

Speed 20 ft., fly 60 ft. (good)
Melee sting +9 (1d6+4 plus poison)

Str 16, **Dex** 15, **Con** 14, **Int** —, **Wis** 12, **Cha** 10
Base Atk +6; **CMB** +9; **CMD** 21
Skills Fly +6, Perception +9, Stealth +6; **Racial Modifiers** +8 Perception, +4 Stealth

Environment temperate forests
Organization solitary, group (2–5), or nest (6–12)
Treasure incidental

Poison (Ex) Sting—injury; *save* Fortitude DC 18; *frequency* 1/round for 6 rounds; *effect* 1d4 Dexterity damage; *cure* 1 save. The save DC is Constitution-based and includes a +2 racial bonus. Non-elves gain a +2 bonus on their Fortitude saves against an elven wasp's poisonous sting.

Elven wasps build their lairs deep within the ground in temperate forests, plains, and hills. A rare species is believed to inhabit warm and tropical forests and hills as well. A typical lair is a spiraling tunnel that empties into a large open chamber. The entrance to the lair is usually well-hidden and difficult to locate (Search DC 20). The wasps also build a special incubating nest nearby (usually within 500 feet of the main nest); another large spiraling tunnel that empties into a large main chamber. It is in this incubating nest where they store their victims and the female lays her eggs.

Elven wasps are hunters; their favorite food being elves. Though not particularly picky with their elven diet, they prefer surface elves to drow or aquatic elves.

Elves that fall prey to these wasps are used not only as food, but also as "incubators" for the young. A paralyzed elf is dragged back to the wasp's incubating lair and dropped into the main chamber. While still alive and paralyzed, the elf's abdomen is slit open and the female elven wasp lays a single large egg in the wound. The female then leaves the chamber and seals the entrance. In a short time the egg hatches and the elven wasp larvae begin devouring the still living elf. After devouring the majority of the elf, the larvae spin cocoons and pupate, hatching several months later as elven wasps—they then dig their way out of the lair and fly off on their own into the world.

Elven wasps are large 6-foot long wasps, though they can grow to be up to 10 feet in length. Females tend to be slightly larger and more aggressive than males.

An elven wasp attacks with a vicious stinger that can paralyze its victim. A paralyzed victim, if it's an elf, is dragged back to the wasp's lair where it is used as food and an incubator for the queen's eggs. Non-elf victims are stung to death or left to other predators and scavengers. Some elven wasps, seemingly aware that their paralyzed victims occasionally shake off the effects of their venom, break an elven victim's legs to prevent or hamper any chance a recovered victim has of escaping the lair.

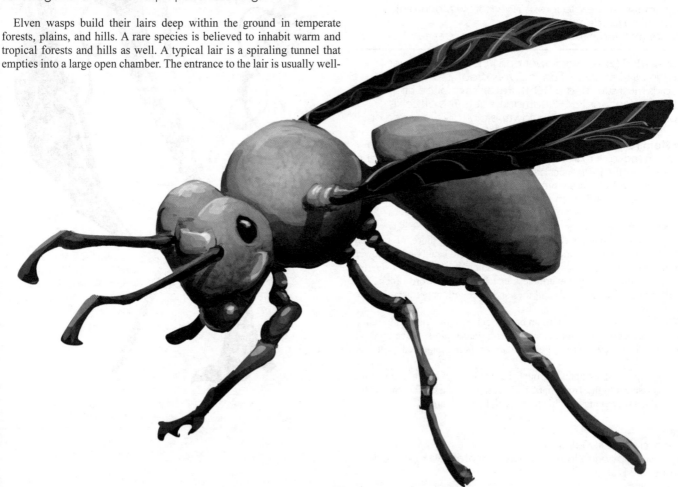

Water Leaper

This creature resembles a dog-sized legless toad with large bat-like wings and a tail. It is a rotund, slimy beast with bulging eyes and a massive mouth filled with dagger-like teeth.

WATER LEAPER	CR 2

XP 600
N Medium magical beast (aquatic)
Init +2; **Senses** darkvision 60 ft., low-light vision; **Perception** +8

AC 17, touch 12, flat-footed 15 (+2 Dex, +5 natural)
hp 22 (3d10+6)
Fort +5; **Ref** +5; **Will** +4

Speed 20 ft., fly 10 ft. (clumsy), swim 30 ft.
Melee bite +5 (1d8+3/19–20), tail barb +5 (1d4+2)
Special Attacks powerful bite

Str 15, **Dex** 15, **Con** 14, **Int** 5, **Wis** 12, **Cha** 16
Base Atk +3; **CMB** +5; **CMD** 17 (21 vs. trip)
Feats Iron Will, Skill Focus (Perception)
Skills Fly –1, Perception +8, Stealth +6 (+14 in water), Swim +10; **Racial Modifiers** +4 Stealth (+12 in water)
SQ amphibious

Environment any aquatic
Organization solitary or brood (2–6)
Treasure none

Powerful Bite (Ex) A water leaper's bite attack always applies 1–1/2 times its Strength modifier on damage rolls and threatens a critical hit on a roll of 19–20.
Wail (Su) As a standard action, a water leaper can unleash a high-pitched wail that causes living creatures within 60 feet that hear it to make a DC 14 Will save or be paralyzed for 1d4 rounds. Whether or not the save succeeds, that creature cannot be affected again by that water leaper's wail for one day. This is a sonic, mind-affecting effect. The save DC is Charisma-based.

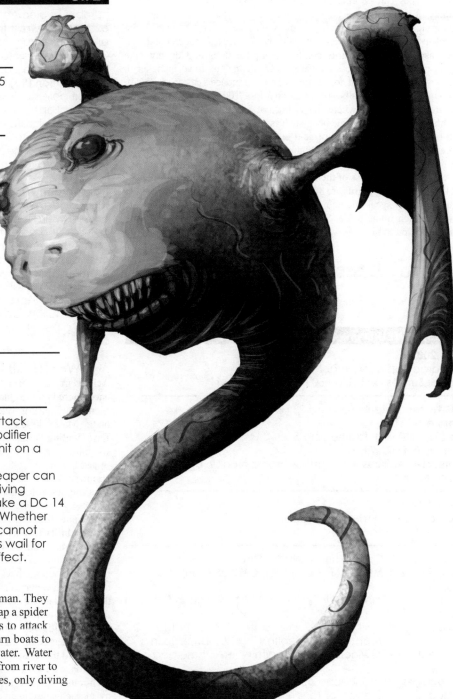

Water leapers are the bane of fresh water fisherman. They snap angling lines and nets as easily one would snap a spider web. They lie in ambush in the shallows of lakes to attack anything that comes down for a drink, and overturn boats to feast on the fishermen as they struggle in the water. Water leapers inhabit nearly any source of fresh water, from river to lakes. They remain in the shallow parts of the lakes, only diving to deeper waters to avoid capture.

A water leaper lair is underwater and usually close to the shoreline. Here the female deposits up to 30 eggs, most of which hatch within two to three weeks. Young water leapers resemble adults save their wings and tail. The wings are almost non-existent, consisting of two small ridges on the water leaper's back. The tail of a young water leaper is short and round, and lacks the barbed stinger of the adult. Both are fully developed by the time the young reaches maturity (in about 5 months). A water leaper has a lifespan of roughly 20 years.

Water leapers are about 6 feet long and weigh 300 pounds. Coloration varies depending on the creature's surroundings and environment (water leapers gradually change colors over time to blend more with their surroundings), but usually consists of gray or brownish-green. Eyes are always dull brown.

Water leapers hide in the water, waiting for prey to move close so they can spring to attack. They wail to immobilize their opponents then leap from their hiding places and attack, biting and stinging their prey.

Weirds

Weirds are creatures from the elemental planes. Lesser weirds are made up of elements from the demi-, para-, and quasi-elemental planes, while greater weirds are composed of elements from the pure elemental planes (air, earth, fire, and water).

Both types can be encountered on the Material Plane, often in the employ of a powerful spellcaster. Bribery is the usual means of gaining the services of a weird, though some spellcasters resort to even more deceitful practices or trickery to gain the services of these creatures. Spellcasters beware! Weirds are intelligent creatures and do not take kindly to deception (unless they are the ones engaging in such trickery). Many weirds are bound to an area when summoned (caster's choice). If bound, the area usually covers an area in a 100-foot radius (or less) centered on the point where the weird first appears. Most casters bind weirds into pools of their element, such as an acid weird being summoned and bound into a large pool of acid or a mud weird being bound into a large mud pool. A weird that is bound to an area can move freely within the area but cannot leave it.

All weirds, regardless of their makeup, are serpent-like creatures about 10 feet long (lesser weirds are 8 feet long), and being of an evil and malign nature. Weirds speak the common language of weirds and the language native to their home plane. Some speak more languages, and still some can speak Common.

Weird, Lesser

This creature resembles an 8-foot long serpent formed of elemental material.

LESSER WEIRD	CR 4

XP 1,200
CE Large outsider (extraplanar, varies)
Init +6; **Senses** darkvision 60 ft.; **Perception** +11

AC 16, touch 12, flat-footed 13 (+2 Dex, +1 dodge, +4 natural, −1 size)
hp 51 (6d10+18); fast healing 5
Fort +8; **Ref** +7; **Will** +4
Defensive Abilities rejuvenation, transparency; **DR** 5/ bludgeoning

Speed 40 ft.
Melee bite +11 (1d8+7 plus grab)
Space 10 ft.; **Reach** 5 ft.

Str 21, **Dex** 15, **Con** 16, **Int** 11, **Wis** 14, **Cha** 11
Base Atk +6; **CMB** +12 (+16 grapple); **CMD** 25 (can't be tripped)
Feats Dodge, Improved Initiative[B], Mobility, Weapon Focus (bite)
Skills Acrobatics +11, Bluff +9, Intimidate +9, Knowledge (planes) +9, Perception +11, Stealth +7 (+19 submergd in element); **Racial Modifiers** +12 Stealth when submerged in element
Languages Weirdling, one appropriate elemental language (Aquan, Auran, Ignan, or Terran)

Environment any (elemental planes, quasi-elemental planes, para-elemental planes)
Organization solitary or pack (2–4)
Treasure standard

Command Elemental (Su) As a standard action, a lesser weird can attempt to enslave elementals of the same type within 30 feet. Elementals receive a DC 15 Will save to negate the effect. Elementals that fail their saves fall under the lesser weird's control, obeying its commands to the best of their ability as if under the effects of a *dominate monster* spell. Intelligent elementals receive a new save once each week to resist command. A lesser weird can command any number of elementals, so long as their total Hit Dice do not exceed its own. If the elemental is under the command of another creature, the lesser weird must make an opposed Charisma check to gain control of the elemental. The save DC is Charisma-based and includes a +2 racial bonus.

Rejuvenation (Su) When reduced to 0 hit points or less, a lesser weird collapses. If contacting its element, it reforms 1 minute later with 5 hit points, allowing its fast healing thereafter to resume healing it.

Transparency (Ex) When submerged in its element, a lesser weird is effectively invisible and gains total concealment (50% miss chance). Additionally, a submerged lesser weird gains a +12 racial bonus on Stealth checks and can move at full speed without taking a penalty on Stealth checks.

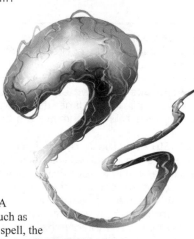

Acid Weird (Acid)

Acid weirds are normally encountered on the Quasi-Elemental Plane of Acid or on the Material Plane.
Fast Healing Works only when in contact with acid.
Speed Swim 40 ft.
Immune Acid
Weaknesses Vulnerability to water
Melee plus 1d8 acid
Vulnerability to Water (Ex) A significant amount of water, such as that created by a *create water* spell, the contents of a large bucket, or a blow from a water elemental, that strikes an acid weird forces the creature to make a DC 20 Fortitude save to avoid being staggered for 2d4 rounds. An acid weird that is immersed in water must make a DC 20 Fortitude save each round (this DC increases by +1 each subsequent round) or take 1d6 points of damage each round until the water is gone.

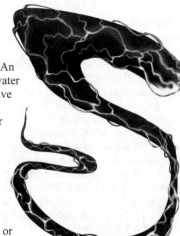

Frost Weird (Cold)

Frost weirds are normally encountered on the Para-Elemental Plane of Ice, the Plane of Water, the Plane of Air, or on the Material Plane.

Fast Healing Works only when in contact with ice or snow.
Immune Cold
Weaknesses Vulnerability to fire
Melee plus 1d6 cold

Magma Weird (Fire)

Magma weirds are normally encountered on the Para-Elemental Plane of Magma, the Plane of Fire, the Plane of Earth, or on the Material Plane.
Fast Healing Works only when in contact with magma or lava.
Speed Burrow 20 ft.; magma glide
Immune Fire
Weaknesses Vulnerability to cold
Melee plus 1d6 fire
Magma Glide (Ex) This ability functions as an earth elemental's earth glide, but allows the magma weird to pass through lava as well.

Mud Weird (Earth)

Mud weirds are normally encountered on the Plane of Earth or on the Material Plane.
Fast Healing Works only when in contact with mud.
Speed Burrow 20 ft.; earth glide
Immune Acid
Melee bite +11 (2d6+7 plus grab) (replaces the line in the stat block)

Ooze Weird (Water)

Ooze weirds are normally encountered on the Para-Elemental Plane of Ooze, the Plane of Water, the Plane of Earth, or on the Material Plane.
Fast Healing Works only in wet or muddy environments.
Speed Swim 30 ft.
Melee plus sickened
Sickened (Ex) Anyone bitten by an ooze weird must succeed on a DC 16 Fortitude save or be sickened for 1d6 rounds.

Smoke Weird (Air)

Smoke weirds are normally encountered on the Para-Elemental Plane of Smoke, the Plane of Air, the Plane of Fire, or on the Material Plane.
Fast Healing Works only in smoky environments.
Immune Fire
Weaknesses Vulnerability to cold, vulnerability to wind
Melee bite +11 (2d6+7 plus grab) (replaces the line in the stat block)
Vulnerability to Wind (Ex) A smoke weird is treated as two sizes smaller for purposes of determining the effects high wind has upon it.

Weird, Greater

This creature resembles a 10-foot long serpent formed of elemental material.

GREATER WEIRD	CR 8

XP 4,800
N Large outsider (elemental, extraplanar, varies)
Init +6; **Senses** darkvision 60 ft.; **Perception** +25

AC 20, touch 12, flat-footed 17 (+2 Dex, +1 dodge, +8 natural, −1 size)
hp 95 (10d10+40); fast healing 5
Fort +11; **Ref** +9; **Will** +5
Defensive Abilities rejuvenation, transparency; **DR** 10/bludgeoning

Speed 40 ft.
Melee bite +15 (1d8+7 plus grab)
Space 10 ft.; **Reach** 5 ft.
Special Attacks command elemental, constrict (1d8+7)

Str 21, **Dex** 15, **Con** 18, **Int** 11, **Wis** 14, **Cha** 14
Base Atk +10; **CMB** +16 (+20 grapple); **CMD** 29 (can't be tripped)
Feats Dodge, Improved Initiative, Mobility, Skill Focus (Perception), Weapon Focus (bite)
Skills Acrobatics +15, Bluff +10, Climb +15, Intimidate +10, Knowledge (planes) +13, Perception +25, Stealth +15 (+27 submerged in element); **Racial Modifiers** +4 Perception, +4 Stealth (+16 when submerged in element)
Languages Weirdling, one appropriate elemental language (Aquan, Auran, Ignan, or Terran)

Environment any (elemental planes, quasi-elemental planes, para-elemental planes)
Organization solitary or pack (1 greater weird plus 2–4 lesser weirds of the same element)
Treasure standard

Command Elemental (Su) As a standard action, a greater weird can attempt to enslave elementals of the same subtype within 30 feet. Elementals receive a DC 19 Will save to negate the effect. Elementals that fail their saves fall under the greater weird's control, obeying its commands to the best of their ability as if under the effects of a *dominate monster* spell. Intelligent elementals receive a new save once each week to resist command. A greater weird can command any number of elementals, so long as their total Hit Dice do not exceed its own. If the elemental is under the command of another creature, the greater weird must make an opposed Charisma check to gain control of the elemental. The save DC is Charisma-based and includes a +2 racial bonus.
Rejuvenation (Su) When reduced to 0 hit points or less, a greater weird collapses. If contacting its element, it reforms 1 minute later with 5 hit points, allowing its fast healing thereafter to resume healing it.
Transparency (Ex) When submerged in its element, a greater weird is effectively invisible and gains total concealment (50% miss chance). Additionally, a submerged greater weird gains a +12 racial bonus on Stealth checks and can move at full speed without taking a penalty on Stealth checks.

Air Weird (Air)

Air weirds are normally encountered on the Plane of Air or on the Material Plane.
Fast Healing Works only in airy environments.

Weaknesses Vulnerability to wind
Speed Fly 60 ft. (good)
Melee bite +15 (2d6+7 plus grab) (replaces the line in the stat block)
Skills Fly +0
Vulnerability to Wind (Ex) An air weird is treated as two sizes smaller for purposes of determining the effects high wind has upon it.

Earth Weird (Earth)

Earth weirds are normally encountered on the Plane of Earth or on the Material Plane.
Fast Healing Works only when in contact with earth.
Immune Acid
Speed Burrow 20 ft.; earth glide
Melee bite +15 (2d6+7 plus grab) (replaces the line in the stat block)

Fire Weird (Fire)

Fire weirds are normally encountered on the Plane of Fire or on the Material Plane.
Fast Healing Works only when in contact with fire.
Immune Fire
Weaknesses Vulnerability to cold
Speed 60 ft. (replaces the line in the stat block)
Melee bite +15 (1d8+7 plus grab and burn) (replaces the line in the stat block)
Burn (Ex) A fire weird deals fire damage in addition to damage dealt on a successful hit in melee. Those affected by its burn ability must also succeed on a DC 19 Reflex save or catch fire, taking 1d8 points of fire damage for an additional 1d4 rounds at the start of its turn. A burning creature can attempt a new save as a full-round action. Dropping and rolling on the ground grants a +4 bonus on this save. Creatures that hit a burning creature with natural weapons or unarmed attacks take fire damage as though hit by the burning creature and must make a DC 19 Reflex save to avoid catching on fire. The save DC is Constitution-based.

Water Weird (Water)

Water weirds are normally encountered on the Plane of Water or on the Material Plane.
Fast Healing Works only in water.
Defensive Abilities Resistance to fire 10
Speed Swim 60 ft.
Special Attacks Drench, water mastery
Skills Swim +13

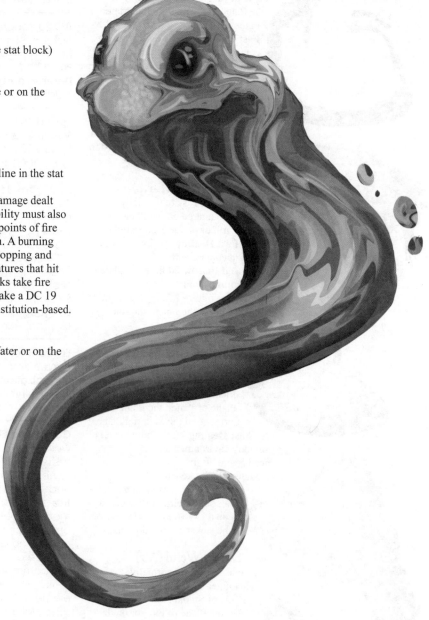

Wichtlein

The creature sliding out of the stone appears to be a tiny man with ugly, bulbous features, dull gray skin, and gemstone teeth. It is clad in dirty overalls and wears a floppy cap on its head.

WICHTLEIN	CR 3

XP 800
NG Tiny fey
Init +3; **Senses** darkvision 60 ft., low-light vision; **Perception** +10

AC 17, touch 15, flat-footed 14 (+3 Dex, +2 natural, +2 size)
hp 19 (3d6+9)
Fort +4; **Ref** +6; **Will** +5
DR 5/cold iron; **SR** 15

Speed 20 ft., earth glide
Melee pickaxe +6 (1d3) or touch +6 (slow)
Space 2 1/2 ft.; **Reach** 0 ft.
Special Attacks fear, slowing touch (as the *slow* spell, CL 5th; DC 13 Will)

Str 10, **Dex** 16, **Con** 17, **Int** 9, **Wis** 14, **Cha** 8
Base Atk +1; **CMB** +2; **CMD** 15
Feats Alertness, Weapon Finesse
Skills Knowledge (dungeoneering) +3, Perception +10, Profession (miner) +5, Stealth +17 (+25 underground), Survival +5; **Racial Modifiers** +8 Stealth while underground
Languages Sylvan
SQ limited precognition, stonecunning

Environment any underground
Organization solitary, gang (2–4), or team (5–25)
Treasure standard

Fear (Su) By scrunching up its face, a wichtlein causes *fear* in those within 30 feet that look upon it. Creatures affected must succeed on a DC 10 Will save or be affected by *fear* (CL 5th). Creatures that save are unaffected by the same wichtlein's fear for one day. Creatures with 6 or more HD are not affected by this fear. The save is Charisma-based.
Limited Precognition (Su) Wichtlein are immediately aware of upcoming danger, so long as the hazard is not deliberately created by an intelligent creature. Thus, a wichtlein could sense a coming cave-in, or the approach of a bestial monster, but not a raiding party of drow or a miner planning a murder. A wichtlein can sense this danger 3d10 minutes before it occurs, and always attempts to warn any other intelligent creatures within the area.
Earth Glide (Ex) A wichtlein can move through any sort of natural earth or stone as easily as a fish swims through water. It leaves no sign of its passage or hint at its presence to creatures that don't possess tremorsense. A *move earth* spell cast on an area containing a wichtlein moves the witchlein back 30 feet, stunning the creature for 1 round unless it succeeds on a DC 15 Fortitude save. A wichtlein moving through stone cannot pick up or carry anything it finds within the stone; thus, they still spend a great deal of their time mining.

Wichtlein are a race of shy yet helpful fey who primarily dwell in mines, caves, and other underground locations. Although they prefer not to be seen, they are well known for warning miners and explorers of coming dangers, such as cave-ins or approaching monsters. Some communities believe the wichtlein are bad omens, actually causing the disasters about which they warn others, but this is just a myth.

Wichtlein are about the size of small halflings, and are occasionally

mistaken for such until the viewer draws near enough to recognize how truly ugly the wichtlein is.

Unfortunately while helpful, wichtlein are not especially bright, and usually fail to accurately convey the sort of danger approaching. Most of the time, wichtlein simply pound on nearby rock and stone to indicate danger, a sign that miners are wise to heed.

Individual wichtlein occasionally leave their mines to dwell in and under the homes of humans or other humanoids. This happens when a wichtlein becomes smitten with a human of the opposite gender, something which occurs rather more frequently than might be expected. These "house wichtlein" maintain the home, cleaning and repairing to the best of their ability while their beloved is away. Such "relationships" most frequently end when the wichtlein finally reveals itself to the object of its affections, and is usually rejected. Some wichtlein, despite their generally good alignment, wreak havoc on the home of the one who rejected it before returning, dejected, to its mine.

Wichtlein dislike confrontation, and prefer to flee when possible. If they have no opportunity to run, and cannot create such an opportunity with their slow and fear abilities, they try to bribe their attackers with knowledge of the local mines and caves. (Wichtlein almost always know where to find gems and valuable metals.) Only if all else fails do they engage in combat.

Wight, Sword

These wicked and depraved creatures lived and died by the sword, and now, their dark taint passes through their weapons to tear at your soul.

SWORD WIGHT	CR 6

XP 2,400
LE Medium undead
Init +1; **Senses** darkvision 60 ft.; **Perception** +15

AC 21, touch 11, flat-footed 20 (+6 armor, +1 Dex, +4 natural)
hp 60 (8d8+16 plus 8)
Fort +4; **Ref** +3; **Will** +7
Defensive Abilities channel resistance +4, undead traits

Speed 20 ft. (base 30 ft.)
Melee greatsword +8/+3 (2d6+1 plus energy drain/19–20), or slam +7 (1d4+1 plus energy drain)

Str 12, **Dex** 12, **Con** —, **Int** 11, **Wis** 13, **Cha** 15
Base Atk +6; **CMB** +7; **CMD** 18
Feats Blind-Fight, Skill Focus (Perception), Toughness, Weapon Focus (greatsword)
Skills Acrobatics +4, Climb +7, Perception +15, Stealth +12
SQ sword channel
Gear chainmail, greatsword, gold circlet set with a sapphire (worth 800 gp for the gem, or 1,000 gp for the entire circlet)

Environment any
Organization solitary, or garrison (2–20)
Treasure standard

Sword Channel (Ex) A sword wight's energy drain ability functions through melee weapon attacks it makes, in addition to its slam attacks.

Much like the standard wight, these undead abominations are warped and twisted caricatures of their former selves. The sword wight bears a massive greatsword, and the cold touch of the grave courses through the creature, through the weapon, into the hapless target.

Credit
Originally appearing in *Rappan Athuk Reloaded* (© Necromancer Games, 2006)

Witchlights

These fey, when young, resemble caterpillars or worms 1/2 in. long with miniscule elven faces. Once they mature they resemble tiny elves no larger than a fat housefly, with moth-like wings on their backs. They emit a beautiful pastel glow, and when doing so at night they appear to be no more than bobbing globes of soft light.

WITCHLIGHTS   CR —

XP 0
N Fine fey
hp 1 (common witchlights have no combat capabilities; see the stats below for elder witchlights and the side bar for further details).

Witchlights are a race of diminutive fey that are bred by pixies and other sylvan creatures to provide illumination and atmosphere to their events. They are born on midsummer in their larval state. In the autumn they spin cocoons for themselves in which they ride out the winter, hatching in early spring in their adult form. As adults, their beating wings release thousands of spores which, when it comes in contact with flower pollen and moonlight, germinate into eggs.

Adult witchlights are vulnerable to cold temperatures, and in all but the warmest climates they die in the fall when the weather turns chilly.

However, favored witchlights may be cared for through the harsh winter months; those that survive become elder witchlights. They increase to 1 HD fey, and gain +1 hit point per year of life until they have reached the maximum possible for their hit dice. Elder witchlights have an Intelligence score of 2, which increases to 3 when they reach maximum hit points. The most intelligent witchlights have limited sentience, capable of understanding the sylvan language to a degree and even speaking a few words of it.

For every point of intelligence an elder witchlight possesses, it gains one of the following spell-like abilities usable at will: *stabilize, dancing lights, daze, flare, ghost sound, light, prestidigitation, purify food and drink* (1/hour only), or *virtue*.

Larval and normal witchlights have no combat abilities, and are worth no XP. Elder witchlights may be worth ad-hoc experience (no more than CR 1/4) if they have spell-like abilities usable in combat.

ELDER WITCHLIGHTS   CR 1/4

XP 100
N Fine fey
Init +4; **Senses** low-light vision; **Perception** +4

AC 21, touch 21, flat-footed 18 (+3 Dex, +8 size)
hp 4 (1d6–2)
Fort –2; **Ref** +5; **Will** +3

Speed fly 30 ft. (perfect)
Melee none
Spell-Like Abilities (CL 1st)
At will—*daze* (DC 11), *ghost sound* (DC 11), *virtue* (elder #1)
dancing lights, flare (DC 11), *purify food and drink* (1/hour) (elder #2)
daze (DC 11), *light, prestidigitation* (elder #3)

Str 1, **Dex** 16, **Con** 6, **Int** 3, **Wis** 13, **Cha** 12
Base Atk +0; **CMB** –5; **CMD** 0

Feats Skill Focus (Perception)
Skills Acrobatics +7, Fly +19, Perception +8, Stealth +19
Languages Sylvan (limited)

Environment temperate forest
Organization solitary, pair or cloud (4–20), summer swarm (20–100)
Treasure standard

Glimmer (Su) Witchlights produce a luminance in their larval stage equal to a candle in brightness. In their adult and elder stage the light is up to half torchlight intensity (bright light in a 10 ft. radius). They can change the intensity or extinguish this light as a free action. The glimmer is a steady, soft glow, and may be silvery-white or just about any color, though the fey that raise them favor pastel shades. Each witchlight has its own unique color which it cannot change.

Witchlight Familiars

A witchlight may be taken as a familiar through the Improved Familiar feat. The minimum level to acquire such a familiar is caster level 3. Elder witchlights do not gain additional spell-like abilities for having their intelligence raised due to being a familiar.

Credit

Originally appearing in *Rappan Athuk Reloaded* (© Necromancer Games, 2006)

Worg, Dire

A black-furred wolf the size of a horse, this beast has eyes that seem to glow with a sinister intelligence.

DIRE WORG	CR 6

XP 2,400
NE Large magical beast
Init +2; **Senses** darkvision 60 ft., low-light vision, scent; **Perception** +12

AC 18, touch 11, flat-footed 16 (+2 Dex, +7 natural, −1 size)
hp 68 (8d10+24)
Fort +9; **Ref** +8; **Will** +4

Speed 50 ft.
Melee bite +17 (2d6+13 plus trip)
Space 10 ft.; **Reach** 5 ft.

Str 29, **Dex** 15, **Con** 17, **Int** 6, **Wis** 14, **Cha** 14
Base Atk +8; **CMB** +18; **CMD** 31 (34 vs. trip)
Feats Improved Natural Attack (bite), Run, Skill Focus (Perception), Weapon Focus (bite)
Skills Acrobatics +7, Perception +12, Stealth +5, Survival +6;
Racial Modifiers +2 Perception, +2 Stealth, +2 Survival
Languages Common, Giant

Environment temperate forests and plains
Organization solitary, pair, or pack (6–11)
Treasure 1/10 coins; 50% goods; 50% items

These creatures are to worgs what dire wolves are to their more ordinary kin. They still tend to associate with evil creatures but rarely anything as mundane or insignificant as a goblinoid. Occasionally they serve as mounts for ogres or hill giants. Like their lesser kin, dire worgs typically hunt in packs, though they don't limit their fare to herbivores or the sick and infirm.

Dire worgs often challenge the most powerful member of an animal pack knowing that if the leader is killed, the rest are usually easy pickings. They have also been known to seek out isolated humanoid settlements and leave them as little more than smashed buildings and a few well-chewed and bloody bones.

A dire worg has black fur, sometimes with reddish highlights, giving it an almost demonic appearance, and grows to be 10 feet long and 7 feet high at the shoulder. It weighs 1,200 pounds.

Dire worgs typically attack in packs holding particularly powerful prey at bay until their giant allies or additional worgs arrive. A mated pair of dire worgs often has a pack of normal worgs serving them as bush beaters to chase prey into the dire worgs' clutches. Like their lesser cousins, they prefer to harry and exhaust tougher prey before moving in with flanking and trip attacks.

Xacon

This creature resembles a mottled-green humanoid, about 6 feet tall, composed of bark, vines, leaves, and other plant material. Its hand end in wicked claws and a gaping maw dominates its head. No eyes appear to be present.

XACON	CR 2

XP 600
N Medium plant
Init +2; **Senses** blindsight 60 ft., low-light vision; **Perception** +3

AC 14, touch 12, flat-footed 12 (+2 Dex, +2 natural)
hp 22 (4d8+4)
Fort +5; **Ref** +3; **Will** +2
Immune plant traits

Speed 30 ft., climb 30 ft.
Melee 2 claws +5 (1d4+2), bite +5 (1d6+2)

Str 15, **Dex** 15, **Con** 12, **Int** 6, **Wis** 12, **Cha** 8
Base Atk +3; **CMB** +5; **CMD** 17
Feats Alertness, Stealthy
Skills Climb +10, Escape Artist +4, Perception +7, Sense Motive +3, Stealth +10 (+18 in undergrowth); **Racial Modifiers** +8 Stealth in undergrowth
SQ adaptation, tree meld
Languages Sylvan (can't speak)

Environment temperate forests
Organization solitary, pair, or pack (3–6)
Treasure standard

Adaptation (Su) A xacon can, by touching an earthen, metal, stone, or wooden item of Small or larger size, can absorb a portion of the item's properties. A xacon that touches a wooden or earthen item (including the ground), increases its natural armor bonus to +5 (granting the xacon AC 17, touch 12, flat-footed 15). If the xacon touches a metal or stone item, its natural armor bonus increases to +8 (granting the xacon AC 20, touch 12, flat-footed 18). This bonus to its natural armor lasts for 1 minute. After using this ability, the xacon must wait 1d4 rounds before it uses it again.

Tree Meld (Su) Once per day, a xacon can meld its body and possessions into a tree. This ability functions similar to a *meld into stone* spell with no duration.

Xacons are plant creatures that inhabit thickly wooded forests and forested hills and mountains. They act as protectors of nature, often times working with good- or neutral-aligned druids and other forest denizens when the area comes under attack or defilement by evil-aligned druids, foresters, and others who destroy the trees and surroundings without care or recourse.

Xacons make their homes in treetops, using the largest and sturdiest of the trees to hold their dwellings (small wooden huts). A typical dwelling holds up to four of these creatures (who may or may not be an interrelated family). All inhabitants of a single dwelling are adults. No young xacons have ever been seen. Xacon reproduction methods are unknown but sages believe they procreate through some form of budding.

Xacons stand 6 feet tall and weigh around 160 pounds. They seem to converse with others of their own kind through a series of hand signals and other gestures. They understand Sylvan but cannot speak.

A xacon attacks by slashing and tearing at its foes with its thorny claws. During battle (or before battle if it is aware of its foes), a xacon contacts a natural object (such as a large stone or tree) in order to fortify its natural armor against its foes.

Xothotak

This primitive humanoid clutches a spear in its hand. Its skin tone seems to change colors shifting to match its surroundings.

XOTHOTAK	CR 1/2

XP 200
Xothotak warrior 1
N Medium humanoid (xothotak)
Init +1; **Senses** low-light vision; **Perception** +2

AC 12, touch 11, flat-footed 11 (+1 Dex, +1 natural)
hp 7 (1d10+2 plus 1)
Fort +4; **Ref** +1; **Will** +0

Speed 30 ft.
Melee spear +3 (1d8+3)

Str 14, **Dex** 13, **Con** 14, **Int** 8, **Wis** 11, **Cha** 9
Base Atk +1; **CMB** +3; **CMD** 14
Feats Alertness
Skills Perception +2, Sense Motive +2, Stealth +9 (+13 when not moving); **Racial Modifiers** +4 Stealth (+8 when not moving)
Languages Xothotak

Environment warm jungles and forests
Organization solitary, gang (2–4), hunting band (5–12 plus 1 leader of 3rd–6th level), or tribe (30–100 plus 150% noncombatants, 1 tribal warrior of 3rd level per 10 adults, 1–3 shamans of 3rd–6th level, 1 veteran warrior of 5th level per 20 adults, plus 1 leader of 8th level)
Treasure standard (leather armor, spear, other treasure)

The xothotak are a savage race of cannibals that make their homes deep in the jungles and forests, far away from civilized lands. Bands of xothotak conduct raids into civilized settlements when food, women, and sacrifices are scarce. Captured men, women, and children are beaten, bound, and forced into slavery for a period of time, before being sacrificed to one of the xothotak's dark gods or served as a meal at a xothotak banquet. Xothotak bands also conduct raids on other xothotak tribes, often traveling many miles to attack a tribe. Many tribes form loose alliances with each other, trading food and women when needed or in abundance; but even that doesn't protect one from the other when food is scarce or when the gods demand a sacrifice. Tribes also form alliances when the son or daughter of the tribal leader marries into another tribe. Such an alliance is considered sacred, and breaking it is believed to bring the wrath of the gods down on one that betrays such an allegiance.

Xothotak culture and civilization varies from tribe to tribe, with some living in mud or wooden huts hidden among the trees, and larger more advanced tribes building clearing great expanses of trees and undergrowth to build elaborate cities of stone.

Smaller xothotak tribes dwell in crude huts fashioned of timber and other resources found in the jungles or forests. Such huts are usually built in a circular formation around a great tree or sacred spring. One hut, larger than the others, houses the tribal leader and his family. A sacred hut where the xothotak shaman lives often adjoins or sits nearby. This temple is considered sacred by all in the tribe. To desecrate it is to bring death upon oneself.

Larger and more advanced xothotak tribes live in what could only be called small cities or towns. Such locations tend to integrate the surrounding land and natural resources into their construction, such as houses or temples built into the sides of rock formations. These cities seem to have a haphazard and scattered design about them, the only organized and planned area being the plazas, temples, and shrines usually found at the center of a xothotak city. Large open plazas are where the xothotak gather to communicate, trade, buy, worship, or sell whatever they can find and whatever they can afford. These plazas are surrounded by temples, great pyramids dedicated to a plethora of gods, shrines, and the palace of the xothotak leader. As one leaves the plaza's center, smaller temples and shrines, as well as noble houses can be found encircling those closest to the plaza. Poor and common houses are found at the outer band of such a layout.

Xothotaks standing still are extremely hard to detect as they can alter their skin coloration to blend with their surroundings just as a chameleon can. Thus, these humanoids prefer to attack from ambush whenever possible. Traps are sometimes set to injure, maim or capture their prey. Xothotak warriors rely on primitive weapons in battle, and rarely if ever wear armor. Xothotak shamans rarely enter battle, preferring to use their magic to aid those going into battle or tend to those returning from battle. Xothotaks fear arcane magic and do not associate with arcane spellcasters (except to sacrifice such a caster to one of their gods or to serve the caster as food at an elaborate xothotak feast).

Xothotaks tend to be warriors, fighters, or barbarians. Xothotaks never take levels in any arcane spellcasting class. Xothotak shamans are always clerics.

Xothotak Characters

Xothotaks are defined by their class levels—they do not possess racial Hit Dice. All xothotaks have the following racial traits.

+2 Strength, +2 Dexterity, +2 Constitution, –2 Intelligence, –2 Charisma.

Sneaky: Xothotaks have a +4 racial bonus on Stealth checks. This bonus increases to +8 when the xothotak isn't moving. Stealth is always a class skill for a xothotak.

Languages: All xothotaks begin play speaking their own native language. Xothotaks with high Intelligence scores can choose any of the following bonus languages: Common, Goblinoid, Sylvan, and Orc.

> **Below is a listing of some of the Xothotak gods and goddesses:**
> **Itlatl** — The Creator
> **Xolaca** — The Lord of the Sky
> **Quentzalma** — Lord of the Underworld
> **Atzin** — God of Rain and Storms
> **Ochactl** — The Lord of Thunder and Lightning
> **Ahuaxpin** — God of the Hunt
> **Malacihe** — Goddess of Marriage and Sexuality
> **Cahitli** — Goddess of Midwives and Fertility

Yhakkor

This slavering humanoid has feral eyes and elongated claws. Its tattered clothes hang loosely on its emaciated frame.

YHAKKOR	CR 2

XP 600
CE Medium monstrous humanoid
Init +1; **Senses** darkvision 60 ft., scent; **Perception** +6
Aura putrid stench (10 ft., DC 15)

AC 14, touch 11, flat-footed 13 (+1 Dex, +3 natural)
hp 28 (3d10+12)
Fort +5; **Ref** +4; **Will** +3
Immune undead immunities

Speed 40 ft.
Melee 2 claws +8 (1d4+4 plus disease)
Special Attacks rend (2 claws, 1d4+6)

Str 19, **Dex** 13, **Con** 18, **Int** 6, **Wis** 10, **Cha** 9
Base Atk +3; **CMB** +7; **CMD** 18
Feats Stealthy, Weapon Focus (claw)
Skills Escape Artist +3, Perception +6, Stealth +9
Languages Common

Environment any land and underground
Organization gang (2–5) or pack (6–20)
Treasure standard

Disease (Ex) *Filth Fever:* Claw—injury; *save* DC 15 Fort; *onset* 1d3 days; *frequency* 1/day; *effect* 1d3 Dex damage and 1d3 Con damage; *cure* 2 consecutive saves. The save DC is Constitution-based.
Putrid Stench Aura (Ex) Yhakkor emanate the stench of death in a 10-foot radius. Those within 10 feet must succeed on a DC 15 Fortitude save or be nauseated for as long as they remain in the area and sickened for 1d4+1 minutes after leaving the area. A creature that makes its save cannot be affected again by the same yhakkor's putrid stench for one day. The save DC is Constitution-based.
Undead Immunities (Ex) Immunity to all mind-affecting effects (charms, compulsions, morale effects, patterns, and phantasms); immunity to bleed, death effects, disease, paralysis, poison, sleep effects, and stunning; not subject to nonlethal damage, ability drain, or energy drain. Immune to damage to its physical ability scores (Constitution, Dexterity, and Strength), as well as to exhaustion and fatigue effects.

Yhakkor are half-bestial, stunted creatures; the result of foul necromantic rites merging the essences of ghouls with human slaves. According to lore, these creatures are named for their creators, dark and foul necromancers from an ancient civilization. Yhakkor are usually found in the employ of powerful wizards and necromancers, while others are found prowling ruins, and other such places.

Yhakkor are slavering humanoid things, with feral eyes and elongated nail-claws. The rituals used in their creation have drained them of much intelligence, but greatly increased their strength. Yhakkor might easily be mistaken for ghouls, but they are not undead and have none of their weaknesses. They remember little of their former human lives. These unsavoury creatures prefer a diet of human flesh above all else.

Due to their low intelligence, yhakkor are usually assigned to simple guard duty or other menial tasks. A strong-minded individual, such as a wizard, is required to control their chaotic nature. Yhakkor seem to understand Common; it is unknown if they can actually speak it.

In melee, yhakkor gang up on a single opponent and attempt to tear it to pieces with their knife-like claws. Yhakkor tactics consist of attacking a foe until it is dead. Combat with yhakkor is always a savage and bloody affair.

Zombie, Pyre

A rotting corpse walks forward, without the usual hesitation and stuttering steps. After a few steps, it bursts into flames that lick its entire body, although it does not seem harmed in the slightest bit.

PYRE ZOMBIE	CR 1

XP 200
NE Medium undead
Init +0; **Senses** darkvision 60 ft.; **Perception** +0

AC 12, touch 10, flat-footed 12 (+2 natural)
hp 12 (2d8 plus 3)
Fort +0; **Ref** +0; **Will** +3
DR 5/slashing; **Immune** fire, undead traits

Speed 30 ft.
Melee slam +4 (1d6+4)
Special Attacks immolation

Str 17, **Dex** 10, **Con** —, **Int** —, **Wis** 10, **Cha** 10
Base Atk +1; **CMB** +4; **CMD** 14
Feats Toughness[B]
Special Qualities non-staggered

Immolation (Ex) The pyre zombie may immolate itself 1/day to cause 2d6 fire damage to all creatures in a 5 ft. radius for 2 rounds. If a pyre zombie is reduced to 0 hot points, it immediately explodes for 1d6 points of fire damage in a 10 ft. radius.
Non-Staggered (Ex) Pyre zombies do not gain the staggered condition as normal zombies.

Pyre zombies are the sad, tortured remains of those who were killed just before being burned alive. When the soul departed, their body was taken over by some malignant spirit. The spirit fortified the body from destruction by the fire, and the undead form escape the pyre to wreak its vengeance on the living.

Pyre zombies are not harmed by fire, but neither do they seek it out.

Credit

Original author James C. Boney
Originally appearing in *Dread Saecaroth* (© Frog God Games, 2011)

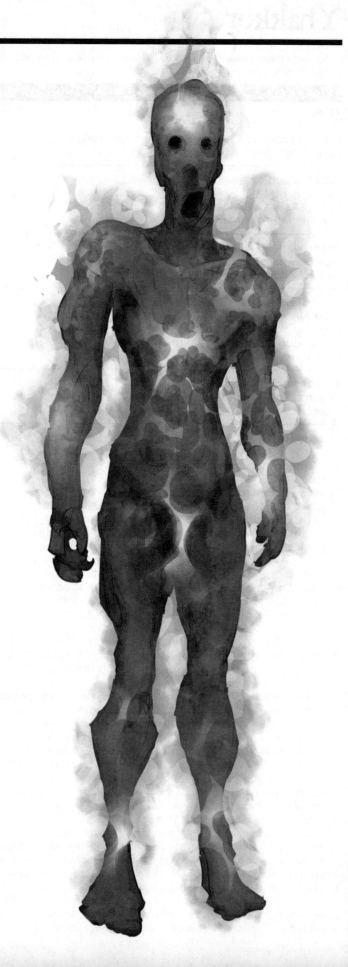

Zombyre

This creature appears to be a rotting corpse, dressed in tattered and torn clothing. Its form is bloated and drips a constant stream of foul, dark water.

ZOMBYRE	CR 3

XP 800
NE Medium undead (aquatic, extraplanar)
Init −1; **Senses** darkvision 60 ft.; **Perception** +7
Aura nausea (10 ft., DC 14)

AC 15, touch 9, flat-footed 15 (−1 Dex, +6 natural)
hp 37 (5d8+10 plus 5)
Fort +3; **Ref** +0; **Will** +7
Immune undead traits, effects of the River Styx; **Resist** fire 20
Weaknesses vulnerability to electricity

Speed 20 ft., swim 60 ft.
Melee slam +6 (1d8+3 plus grab), bite +6 (1d6+3 plus disease)

Str 17, **Dex** 8, **Con** —, **Int** 4, **Wis** 12, **Cha** 14
Base Atk +3; **CMB** +6 (+10 grapple); **CMD** 15
Feats Iron Will, Power Attack, Toughness
Skills Perception +4, Swim +16
SQ staggered, Stygian healing
Languages Common (can't speak)

Environment any (River Styx)
Organization solitary, pair, or pack (3–8)
Treasure none

Aura of Nausea (Ex) A zombyre exudes a sickly stench of death and decay in a 10-foot radius. Creatures entering or within the area must succeed on a DC 14 Fortitude save or become nauseated for as long as they remain in the area plus 1d4 rounds after. Creatures succeeding on their save are immune to the effects of the aura for one day. The save DC is Charisma-based.
Disease (Ex) *Stygian Sickness:* Bite; *save* DC 14 Fort; *onset* 1 day; *frequency* 1/day; *effect* 1d4 Intelligence and 1d2 Constitution damage; *cure* 2 consecutive saves. Anyone who dies while infected rises as a zombyre in 2d6 hours. The save is Charisma-based.
Staggered (Ex) Zombyres have poor reflexes and can only perform a single move action or standard action each round. A zombyre can move up to its speed and attack in the same round as a charge action. This flaw only affects zombyres when on land; while underwater, in combat, a zombyre loses this flaw.
Stygian Healing (Su) A zombyre regains 1 hit point each hour when fully submerged in the River Styx. This healing cannot restore more hit points than the maximum the zombyre possesses and it does not restore any lost limbs.

A zombyre is a living creature that drowned in the River Styx, reanimated by the magic of the Stygian waters for some unknown purpose. It is a free-willed, semi-intelligent creature appearing much as a normal zombie, though bloated from its time spent underwater.

Zombyres tend to dwell in packs, loosely organized but seemingly bound together by some unknown force. Some sages speculate this happens when a group of individuals all drown together, such as a group of sailors who perish when their ship sinks. Zombyres tend to stay within the area where they drowned; sometimes making their lair in the very ship that sank beneath the waves and cost them their life. They do not appear to be bound to the area as some undead are to the place where they died. Zombyres are most active at night, rarely venturing onto land during the day. Even nighttime excursions rarely see a zombyre travel more than several hundred feet from the water's edge. Creatures that venture too close to a zombyre pack are attacked and dragged into the water, where the zombyre pack feasts and dines on the remnants of those so foolhardy.

In battle, groups of zombyres are relentless combatants and generally swarm their opponents, attacking with their powerful fists and diseased bite. Large packs of zombyres have been known to climb aboard anchored ships, pull the seamen overboard, and attack them in the Stygian waters where the zombyres are faster and more at home. Such sailors pulled overboard are often times held under the water and drowned.

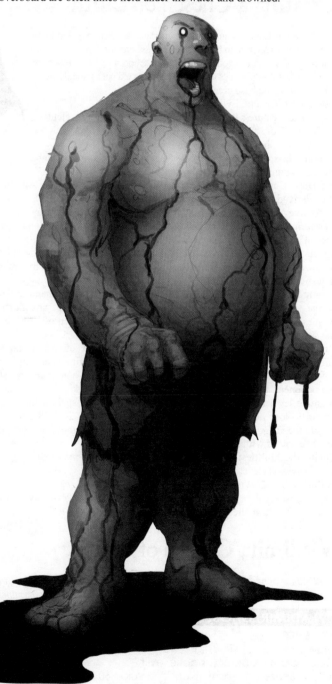

Appendix A: Templates

Chosen of Lilith

The Chosen of Lilith are those fallen elves that have gained the favor of the succubus goddess Lilith. Creatures must be of Chaotic Evil alignment to be a Chosen of Lilith. Apply the following changes to creatures that take on this template. All other entries (those not shown here) remain the same as the base creature.

Creating a Chosen of Lilith

"Chosen of Lilith" is an acquired template that can be added to any living creature (referred to hereafter as the base creature), provided it has gained the favor of the goddess Lilith. The Chosen of Lilith retains all the base creature's statistics and special abilities except as noted here.

CR: Same as the base creature + 2.

Alignment: Chaotic Evil.

Type: The creature's type changes to Outsider. Do not recalculate BAB, saves, or skill ranks.

Senses: The Chosen gain darkvision 60 ft.

Armor Class: The Chosen gain a +5 natural armor bonus or the base creature's natural armor bonus, whichever is better.

Hit Dice: Change all of the creature's racial Hit Dice to d10s. All Hit Dice derived from class levels remain unchanged.

Defensive Abilities: The Chosen of Lilith gain **DR** 10/cold iron and good; **Resistance** to acid 5, cold 5, electricity 10, fire 5; **Immunity** fallen harpy special abilities, poison; **SR** 15.

Special Attacks: The Chosen of Lilith gain the special attacks described below. Save DCs are equal to 10 + 1/2 the Chosen's HD + Cha modifier unless otherwise noted.

Command Fallen Harpies (Su) Chosen of Lilith may command fallen harpies as a free action when within a one-mile radius of any fallen harpies This is a supernatural ability granted to the chosen of Lilith by the succubus goddess.

Energy Drain, kiss (Ex) Any Chosen of Lilith may drain a victim's energy with a single kiss. This is most often done by first charming the victim, but need not be. Otherwise she must succeed in a grapple against the opponent, provoking an attack of opportunity. The kiss bestows one negative level on the victim, and acts as a *suggestion* spell, asking the victim to kiss her again. The victim is allowed a DC 20 Will save to negate the *suggestion*, and a DC 20 Fortitude save to remove a negative level bestowed with a kiss.

Spell-Like Abilities: Constant—*tongues*; 3/day—*suggestion* (DC 16); 1/day—*summon* (level 6, 1 succubus 30%).

Abilities: Int +2, Wis +4, Cha +6.

Feats: Base creature gains the Augment Summoning and Persuasive feats if she did not have them already.

Vladimir, Chosen of Lilith

Vladimer appears as a beautiful man with large bat wings, covered in scars. Whether these are battle scars, or self-inflicted, is difficult to determine.

VLADIMIR, CHOSEN OF LILITH	CR 16

XP 76,800
Male fallen elf cleric 8/fighter 6
CE Medium Outsider (chaotic, evil)
Init +2; **Senses** low-light vision, darkvision 60 ft.; **Perception** +6

AC 26, touch 12, flat-footed 24 (+9 armor, +2 Dex, +5 natural)

hp 121 (8d8+24 plus 6d10+18 plus 6)
Fort +14; **Ref** +6; **Will** +12; +14 vs. fear
Defensive abilities bravery 2; **DR** 10/cold iron and good; **Immunities** fallen harpy special abilities, poison, sleep; **Resist** acid 5, cold 5, electricity 10 fire 5; **SR** 15

Speed 30 ft., fly 50 ft.
Melee +2 *shock greatsword* +19/+14/+9 (2d6+9/17–20)
Special Attacks channel negative energy (4d6, DC 18, 7/day), command fallen harpies, death's embrace, energy drain (kiss), scythe of evil (4 rounds, 1/day), weapon training (heavy blades +1)
Domain Spell-Like Abilities (CL 8th; melee touch +15. ranged touch+14):
7/day—*bleeding touch* (1d6 bleed, 4 rounds), *touch of evil* (sickened, 4 rounds)
Spell-Like Abilities (CL 12th; melee touch +15. ranged touch+14):
Constant—*tongues*
3/day—*suggestion* (DC 17)
1/day—*summon* (level 6, 1 succubus 30%)
Spells Prepared (CL 8th; melee touch +15, ranged touch+14):
4th—*cure critical wounds, dimensional anchor, dismissal* (DC 18), *unholy blight*^D (DC 18)

3rd—*bestow curse* (DC 17), *dispel magic, invisibility purge, magic circle against good*D, *searing light*
2nd—*aid, bear's endurance, bull's strength, desecrate, death knell*D (DC 16)
1st—*command* (DC 15), *detect good, divine favor, doom* (DC 15), *cause fear*D (DC 15), *summon monster I*
0 (at will)—*bleed, detect magic, light, read magic*
D domain spell; **Domains** Death, Evil

Str 17, **Dex** 14, **Con** 16, **Int** 10, **Wis** 18, **Cha** 18
Base Atk +12; **CMB** +15; **CMD** 27
Feats Augment SummoningB, Cleave, Combat Casting, Critical Focus, Dazzling Display, Improved Critical, Improved Vital Strike, PersuasiveB, Power Attack, Skill Focus (Intimidate), Vital Strike, Weapon Focus (greatsword), Weapon Specialization (greatsword)
Skills Diplomacy +14, Fly +7, Intimidate +15, Knowledge (religion) +13, Perception +6, Sense Motive +13
Languages Abyssal, Common, Elven, *tongues*, telepathy 100 ft.
SQ armor training 1
Gear +2 *shock greatsword*, +3 *elven chain*, castle keys

Environment Novgorod (temperate forest)
Organization solitary
Treasure standard (+2 *shock greatsword*, +3 *elven chain*, castle keys, other treasure)

Command Fallen Harpies (Sp) Vladimir may command fallen harpies as a free action when within a one-mile radius of any fallen harpies. This is a supernatural ability granted to the chosen of Lilith by the succubus goddess.
Energy Drain, Kiss (Su) As a chosen of Lilith, Vladimir may drain a victim's energy with a single kiss. This is most often done by first charming the victim, but need not be. Otherwise he must succeed in a grapple against the opponent, provoking an attack of opportunity. The kiss bestows one negative level on the victim, and acts as a *suggestion* spell, asking the victim to kiss him again. The victim is allowed a DC 17 Will save to negate the *suggestion*, and a DC 17 Fortitude save to remove a negative level bestowed with a kiss.
Immune to Effects of Fallen Harpies (Ex) Vladimir is immune to the wail of insanity and captivating song of all fallen harpies

Fallen Harpy

Fallen harpies were once fallen elves that sought power through service to the goddess Lilith. For one reason or another, Lilith spurned the favors of these followers, and transformed them into creatures doomed to serve the other fallen elves as slaves. The creatures still retain the beauty of the fallen elves, and interestingly enough, oftentimes grow more beautiful. Their beauty is no doubt a mask for their inherent evil, and the creatures often tempt victims with their beauty and harmonious songs.

FALLEN HARPY	CR 11

XP 12,800
CE Medium monstrous humanoid
Init +2; **Senses** darkvision 60 ft.; **Perception** +15

AC 18, touch 15, flat-footed 13 (+2 armor, +4 Dex, +1 dodge, +1 natural)
hp 91 (14d10+14)
Fort +7; **Ref** +13; **Will** +10

Speed 20 ft., fly 80 ft. (average)
Melee longsword +14/+9/+4 (1d8) or 2 talons +9/+4 (1d6)
Special Attacks captivating song (DC 23), wail of insanity (DC 21)

Str 10, **Dex** 18, **Con** 12, **Int** 10, **Wis** 12, **Cha** 18
Base Atk +14; **CMB** +14; **CMD** 29
Feats Ability Focus (captivating song), Dodge, Flyby Attack, Great Fortitude, Hover, Skill Focus (bluff), Skill Focus (perform)
Skills Bluff +22, Fly +18, Intimidate +18, Perception +15, Perform (song) +18
SQ commanded by the Chosen of Lilith
Languages common
Gear Longswords

Environment temperate forest
Organization solitary, pair or flight (4–12)
Treasure none

Captivating Song (Su) When fallen harpies sing all within a 300 foot spread must succeed on a DC 19 Will save or become captivated. Those succeeding cannot be affected by the same fallen harpy's song for another 24 hours. Those that become captivated move in the most direct route toward the fallen harpy. If the path leads through a dangerous area the character is allowed a second save.
Wail of Insanity (Su) Fallen harpies can let loose a wail of insanity once per day. All within a 100 foot spread of the fallen harpy must succeed on a DC 21 Will save or become insane, as described under the *insanity* spell.
Commanded by the Chosen of Lilith (Sp) Any chosen of Lilith can command fallen harpies when within a one-mile radius of any such creatures. The fallen harpies are under the complete command of the chosen, and thus implicitly follow all of their orders.

Like standard harpies, the fallen harpy has a captivating song ability that it uses to lure its victims. Unlike standard harpies, fallen harpies have no claw attacks, and so are often equipped with longswords by their fallen elf keepers.

Crazed

Wild-eyed and insane, a crazed creature is slightly more than a wild animal.

Creating a Crazed creature

"Crazed" is an acquired template that can be added to any living, corporeal creature with an Intelligence score of 3 or greater (hereafter referred to as the "base creature." Normally, when a creature is reduced to 0 Wisdom, it falls unconscious; within the confines of levels Rappan Athuk, however, such creatures instead gain this template. A crazed creature retains all the abilities of the base creature, except it cannot cast spells or use spell-like abilities, nor can it make use of ranged weapons of any kind.

A crazed creature cannot easily be cured of its insanity. In order to cure a crazed creature, it must first be targeted with a *heal* spell followed immediately with a *remove curse* spell. At that point, the curse is broken, and creatures loses the crazed template; it has a Wisdom score of 1, making it susceptible to suffering the curse again the next day.

CR: Same as the base creature.

Immune: A crazed creature is immune to all mind-affecting effects— including those that would otherwise be beneficial, such as the spells *aid* and *bless*.

Melee Attacks: A crazed creature gains a bite attack, if it didn't already have one. This attack is a primary natural attack, or can be used as a secondary natural attack if the creature opts to attack with manufactured weapons.

If the base creature gains a bite attack from this template the damage is given on **Table 3–1:** Natural Attacks by Size in the *Pathfinder Roleplaying Game Bestiary* as if the base creature was one size category smaller.

Special Attacks: A crazed creature gains the following special attack.

Disease (Ex) Filth fever: Bite—injury; *save* Fortitude DC 12; *onset* 1d3 days; *frequency* 1/day; *effect* 1d3 Dex damage and 1d3 Con damage; *cure* 2 consecutive saves.

Abilities: A crazed creature has a –2 racial modifier to Charisma and a Wisdom score of 0. Treat the creature's Wisdom as being 1 (–5 modifier) for all abilities and effects, such as Will save and skill modifiers.

SQ: Add the following special quality to the base creature:

Insane (Ex) A crazed creature's mind is shattered. A crazed creature no longer desires magical trinkets such as weapons, armor, or wondrous items. Instead, it seeks only to take trophies from those it kills, such as teeth or ears. It leaves behind anything of actual value. Typically a crazed creature possesses one weapon and ratty leather or hide armor.

Crazed Goblin Scout

A wild-eyed goblin rushes out from the darkness, drooling and gibbering the entire time!

CRAZED GOBLIN SCOUT	CR 3

XP 800
Male or female crazed goblin rogue 4 (*Pathfinder Roleplaying Game Bestiary,* "Goblin")
NE Small humanoid (goblinoid)
Init +5; **Senses** darkvision 60 ft.; **Perception** –5

AC 19, touch 17, flat-footed 13 (+2 armor, +5 Dex, +1 dodge, +1 size)
hp 29 (4d8+4 plus 4)
Fort +2; **Ref** +9; **Will** –4
Defensive Abilities evasion, trap sense +1, uncanny dodge; **Immune** mind-affecting effects

Speed 30 ft.

Melee handaxe +5 (1d4+1/x3) and bite +0 (1d3 plus disease)
Special Attacks disease, rogue talent (surprise attack), sneak attack +2d6

Str 12, **Dex** 20, **Con** 13, **Int** 10, **Wis** 0, **Cha** 4
Base Atk +3; **CMB** +7; **CMD** 19
Feats Agile Maneuvers, Dodge
Skills Acrobatics +12, Climb +10, Disable Device +10, Escape Artist +12, Ride +13, Sleight of Hand +12, Stealth +20, Swim +8; **Racial Modifiers** +4 Ride, +4 Stealth
Languages Goblin
SQ insane, rogue talent (ledge walker), trapfinding (+2)
Gear leather armor, handaxe, ear trophies

Environment Rappan Athuk (level 9B and 9C)
Organization solitary or gaggle (2–20)
Treasure none

Disease (Ex) *Filth Fever:* Bite—Injury; *save* DC 12 Fort; *onset* 1d3 days; *frequency* 1/day; *effect* 1d3 Dex damage and 1d3 Con damage; *cure* 2 consecutive saves.

Insane (Ex) A crazed creature's mind is shattered. A crazed creature no longer desires magical trinkets such as weapons, armor, or wondrous items. Instead, it seeks only to take trophies from those it kills, such as teeth or ears. It leaves behind anything of actual value. Typically, a crazed creature possesses one weapon and ratty leather or hide armor.

Crystalline Creature

Crystalline creatures are those that have been exposed to the petrifying effects of the Demiplane of Crystal, and rather than petrify and be absorbed by the plane, actually survive the process and changed form.

Creating a Crystalline Creature

"Crystalline Creature" is an acquired template that can be added to any corporeal living creature. A crystalline creature retains all the base creature's statistics and special abilities except as noted here.

Challenge Rating: Same as the base creature +1.

Type: The creature's type changes to outsider. It gains the earth, elemental and extraplanar subtypes if it did not already have them. Do not recalculate HD, BAB, saves, or skill ranks.

Senses: A crystalline creature has darkvision 60 ft.

Armor Class: A crystalline creature gains a +4 natural armor bonus. This stacks with any existing natural armor bonus the base creature possesses.

Immune blindness, light-based attacks, and polymorph; **Resist** cold 10, electricity 10; DR 5/magic (if HD 11 or less) or DR 10/magic (if HD 12 or more).

Weakness: A crystalline creature gains the following weakness.

Vulnerable to Sonic (Ex) A crystalline creature takes half again as much damage (+50%) from sonic-based attacks, regardless of whether a saving throw is allowed or if the save is a success or failure.

Speed: A crystalline creature's base speed (all forms of movement) is reduced by 10 ft. (to a minimum of 20 ft.). A creature whose speed is already 20 ft. or less does not further reduce its speed.

Special Attacks: A crystalline creature gains the following special attacks.

Spell-Like Abilities (Su) A crystalline creature with a Charisma score of 8 or higher has a cumulative number of spell-like abilities set by its Hit Dice. Unless otherwise noted, each is usable 1/day. CL equals the creature's Hit Dice (or the CL of the base creature's spell-like abilities, whichever is higher).

Crystalline Creature Special Attacks

HD	Spell-Like Abilities
1–4	*color spray*
5–8	*rainbow pattern*
9–12	*prismatic spray*
13+	*scintillating pattern*

Ability Scores: A crystalline creature gains a +2 bonus to Strength and a +2 bonus to Constitution. A crystalline creature receives a –4 penalty to Dexterity (to a minimum of 8).

Crystalline Scorpion

This massive scorpion appears to be constructed from opaque crystal.

CRYSTALLINE SCORPION	CR 4

XP 1,200
N Large outsider (earth, elemental, extraplanar)
Init –1; **Senses** darkvision 60 ft., tremorsense 60 ft.; **Perception** +4

AC 19, touch 8, flat-footed 19 (–1 Dex, +11 natural, –1 size)
hp 42 (5d8+20)
Fort +8; **Ref** +0; **Will** +1
DR 5/magic; **Immune** blindness, light-based effects, polymorph; **Resist** cold 10, electricity 10
Weaknesses vulnerable to sonic

Speed 40 ft.
Melee 2 claws +7 (1d6+5 plus grab), sting +7 (1d6+5 plus poison)
Space 10 ft.; **Reach** 10 ft.
Special Attacks constrict (1d6+5)

Str 21, **Dex** 8, **Con** 18, **Int** —, **Wis** 10, **Cha** 2
Base Atk +3; **CMB** +9 (+13 grapple); **CMD** 18 (30 vs. trip)
Skills Climb +9, Perception +4, Stealth –1; **Racial Modifiers** +4 Climb, +4 Perception, +4 Stealth

Environment any (Elemental Plane of Earth)
Organization solitary
Treasure none

Poison (Ex) Sting—injury; *save* DC 18 Fort; *frequency* 1/round for 6 rounds; *effect* 1d2 Strength damage; *cure* 1 save. The save DC is Constitution-based and includes a +2 racial bonus.

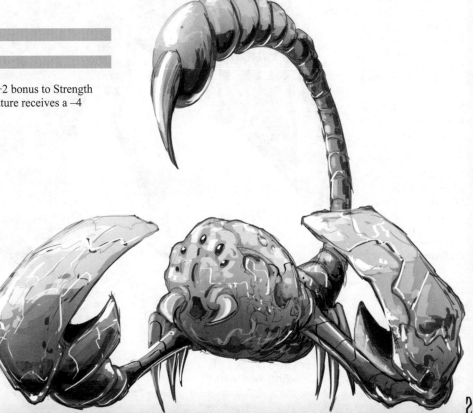

Crystalline Succubus

Tiny horns, bat-like wings, and a sinuous tail betray the demonic nature of this alluring woman who appears to be made of finely polished and translucent crystal.

CRYSTALLINE SUCCUBUS	CR 8

XP 4,800
CE Medium outsider (chaotic, demon, earth, elemental, evil, extraplanar)
Init +1; **Senses** darkvision 60 ft., detect good; **Perception** +21

AC 23, touch 12, flat-footed 21 (+2 Dex, +11 natural)
hp 92 (8d10+48)
Fort +8; **Ref** +7; **Will** +10
DR 10/cold iron or good, 5/magic; **Immune** blindness, electricity, fire, light-based effects, poison, polymorph; **Resist** acid 10, cold 10; **SR** 18
Weaknesses vulnerable to sonic

Speed 20 ft., fly 40 ft.
Melee 2 claws +10 (1d6+2)
Special Attacks energy drain, profane gift
Spell-Like Abilities (CL 12th; melee touch +10, ranged touch +10):
Constant—*detect good, tongues*
At will—*charm monster* (DC 22), *detect thoughts* (DC 20), *ethereal jaunt* (self plus 50 lbs. of objects only), *suggestion* (DC 21), *greater teleport* (self plus 50 lbs. of objects only), *vampiric touch*
1/day— *color spray* (DC 19), *dominate person* (DC 23), *rainbow pattern* (DC 22), summon (level 3, babau 50%)

Str 15, **Dex** 13, **Con** 22, **Int** 18, **Wis** 14, **Cha** 27
Base Atk +8; **CMB** +10; **CMD** 22
Feats Agile Maneuvers, Combat Reflexes, Iron Will, Weapon Finesse
Skills Bluff +27, Diplomacy +19, Disguise +19, Escape Artist +9, Fly +12, Intimidate +16, Knowledge (local) +15, Perception +21, Sense Motive +13, Stealth +12; **Racial Modifiers** +8 Bluff, +8 Perception
Languages Abyssal, Celestial, Common, Draconic; *tongues*, telepathy 100 ft.
SQ change shape (*alter* self, *Small* or Medium humanoid)

Environment any (Elemental Plane of Earth)
Organization solitary, pair, or harem (3–12)
Treasure double standard

Energy Drain (Su) A crystalline succubus drains energy from a mortal she lures into an act of passion, such as a kiss. An unwilling victim must be grappled before the crystalline succubus can use this ability. The crystalline succubus's kiss bestows one negative level. The kiss also has the effect of a *suggestion* spell, asking the victim to accept another act of passion from the crystalline succubus. The victim must succeed on a DC 22 Will save to negate the suggestion. The DC is 22 for the Fortitude save to remove a negative level. These save DCs are Charisma-based.

Profane Gift (Su) Once per day as a full-round action, a crystalline succubus may grant a profane gift to a willing humanoid creature by touching it for 1 full round. The target gains a +2 profane bonus to an ability score of his choice. A single creature may have no more than one profane gift from a crystalline succubus at a time. As long as the profane gift persists, the crystalline succubus can communicate telepathically with the target across any distance (and may use her suggestion spell-like ability through it). A profane gift is removed by *dispel evil* or *dispel chaos*. The crystalline succubus can remove it as well as a free action (causing 2d6 Charisma drain to the victim, no save).

Death Knight

Creating a Death Knight

"Death knight" is an acquired template that can be applied to any lawful humanoid or monstrous humanoid with 5 or more Hit Dice (referred to hereafter as the base creature). A death knight retains all the base creature's statistics and special abilities except as noted here.

Special Note: A paladin that rises as a death knight trades its paladin class levels for anti-paladin class levels on a one-for-one basis (see the *Pathfinder Roleplaying Games Advanced Player's Guide, "Antipaladin"*).

Challenge Rating: Same as base creature +2

Alignment: A death knight is always lawful evil, unless it was a paladin before its transformation. Death knights who were paladins in life return as depraved monsters, and are always chaotic evil.

Type: The creature's type changes to undead, and it gains the augmented subtype. Do not recalculate class Hit Dice, BAB, saves, or skill ranks.

Senses: A death knight gains darkvision 60 ft.

Aura A death night emanates the following aura.

Fear Aura (Su) Creatures of less than 5 HD in a 10-foot radius that look at the death knight must succeed on a Will save or become frightened. Creatures with 5 HD or more must succeed at a Will save or be shaken for a number of rounds equal to the death knight's Hit Dice. A creature that successfully saves cannot be affected again by the same death knight's aura for one day. This is a mind-affecting fear effect and is Charisma-based.

Armor Class: The base creature's natural armor improves by +4.

Hit Dice: Change all racial Hit Dice to d8s. Class Hit Dice are unaffected. As undead, a death knight uses its Charisma modifier to determine bonus hit points (instead of Constitution).

Defensive Abilities: A death knight gains channel resistance +4, damage resistance 15/bludgeoning and magic, spell resistance equal to 15 + the death knight's adjusted CR, and immunity to cold and electricity (in addition to those granted by its undead traits).

Special Attacks: A death knight gains the special attacks described below. Save DCs are Charisma-based unless otherwise noted.

Command Undead (Su) A death knight can, as a standard action, attempt to control an undead creature within 60 feet. The undead must succeed on a Will save or fall under command of the death knight. For unintelligent undead, this command is permanent. Intelligent undead can make a new save once a week to break the control. A creature that successfully saves cannot be affected again by the same death knight's command undead for one day. A death knight may control a number of undead whose Hit Dice total no more than twice the death knight's own Hit Dice. It can release commanded undead at any time in order to command another undead. A death knight cannot command an undead that's Hit Dice is higher than its own.

Infuse Weapon (Su) A death knight can channel negative energy through its weapon. A number of times per day equal to 3 + its Charisma modifier, a death knight can deal extra damage on a successful weapon attack. This damage is negative energy damage and is equal to 1d6 points of damage plus 1d6 points of damage for every two Hit Dice the death knight has beyond the first (2d6 at 3rd, 3d6 at 5th, and so on). A successful Will save reduces the damage by half.

Spell-Like Abilities At will—*darkness, desecrate, detect good, detect magic,* and *see invisibility*; 1/day—*animate dead, blasphemy, protection from good,* plus the death knight's choice of *symbol of pain* or *symbol of fear*, to be selected when the template is applied. The death knight's caster level is equal to its total Hit Dice.

Special Qualities: A death knight gains the following special quality.

Undead Mount (Su) A death knight loses the base creature's special mount (if it had one) and gains the service of an undead mount (see below for statistics). A death knight of 10th level or higher gains the service of a grave mount (see the **grave mount** entry) instead. If a death knight's mount is destroyed, it can summon a new one after one week.

Ability Scores: A death knight gains +4 Strength, +2 Wisdom, and +4 Charisma. As an undead creature, a death knight has no Constitution score.

Skills: Death knights gain a +8 racial bonus to Intimidate and Perception checks. A death knight always treats Intimidate and Perception as class skills. Otherwise, skills are the same as the base creature.

Feats: Death knights gain Toughness as a bonus feat.

Death Knight

This knight, dressed in cold black armor and wielding a shining silver sword, stands silent and motionless.

DEATH KNIGHT	CR 10

XP 12,800
Human death knight cavalier 9 (*Pathfinder Roleplaying Game Advanced Player's Guide*, "Cavalier")
LE Medium undead (augmented human)
Init +2; **Senses** darkvision 60 ft.; **Perception** +16
Aura fear (10 ft., DC 18)

AC 28, touch 11, flat-footed 27 (+10 armor, +1 Dex, +4 natural, +3 shield)
hp 99 (9d10+36 plus 9)
Fort +10; **Ref** +5; **Will** +5
Defensive Abilities channel resistance +4; **DR** 15/ bludgeoning and magic; **Immune** cold, electricity, undead traits; **SR** 26

Speed 20 ft. (30 ft. unarmored)
Melee *+1 longsword* +16/+11 (1d8+6/19–20)
Special Attacks cavalier's charge, challenge 3/day, command undead, infuse weapon (7/day, 5d6 negative energy; DC 18 Will half), steal glory
Spell-Like Abilities (CL 9th):
At will—*darkness, desecrate, detect good, detect magic, see invisibility*
1/day—*animate dead, blasphemy* (DC 21), *protection from good* (DC 15), *symbol of pain* (DC 19)

Str 20, **Dex** 14, **Con**—, **Int** 11, **Wis** 10, **Cha** 18
Base Atk +9; **CMB** +14; **CMD** 25
Feats Cleave, Dazzling Display[B], Great Cleave, Iron Will, Mounted Combat, Power Attack, Quick Draw, Shatter Defenses[B], Toughness[B], Vital Strike, Weapon Focus (longsword)
Skills Diplomacy +12, Handle Animal +16, Intimidate +19, Knowledge (local) +9, Knowledge (nobility) +4, Knowledge (religion) +9, Perception +16, Ride +8 (+14 own mount);
Racial Modifiers +8 Intimidate, +8 Perception
Languages Common
SQ banner, braggart (order of the cockatrice), greater tactician, expert trainer

Environment any
Organization solitary
Treasure standard (*+1 full plate armor, +1 heavy steel shield, +1 longsword*, other treasure)

Doomed to devastate the world they once cherished and sought to protect, death knights are the result of damning curses visited upon once noble knights who fell from grace at the moment of death. A lifetime of duty and loyalty becomes forfeit as the undead creature, rising from its grave within days of being laid to rest, is driven by an intense desire to annihilate all life and bring as much harm as it can muster to any within reach. It is the tragedy of the death knight that most remain conscious and aware of their actions within unlife, forever grieving for their actions, past and present, yet unable to withstand the compulsion to destroy.

They retain all the fighting skills they learned in their former life and, melded with the powers of the undead, a death knight can prove to be a fearsome foe as it swings its weapon with consummate ease, ignoring the puny strikes of its enemies whilst staring into their eyes with orbs of dull crimson that betray nothing but pure evil.

UNDEAD HORSE MOUNT	CR 2

XP 600
N Large undead
Init +8; **Senses** low-light vision, scent; **Perception** +9

AC 19, touch 13, flat-footed 15 (+2 armor, +4 Dex, +4 natural, –1 size)
hp 27 (5d8+5)
Fort +9; **Ref** +8; **Will** +4
Defensive Abilities evasion; **Immune** undead traits

Speed 50 ft.
Melee bite +7 (1d4+5), 2 hooves +2 (1d6+2)
Space 10 ft.; **Reach** 5 ft.

Str 21, **Dex** 19, **Con** —, **Int** 2, **Wis** 17, **Cha** 13
Base Atk +3; **CMB** +9; **CMD** 23 (27 vs. trip)
Feats Armor Proficiency (Light), Endurance, Improved Initiative, Run[B]
Skills Intimidate +5, Perception +9
SQ link, tricks (combat trained; attack, come, defend, down, guard, heel, stay, seek)

Environment any
Organization solitary
Treasure none (leather barding)

Fallen Elf

Fallen elves have elven features, and generally have black or dark hair and blue or green eyes. The fallen elves have an unearthly beauty and glow about them, and many have small horns protruding from their heads due to their many dealings with the succubus goddess and her demonic forces.

The fallen elves are the ancestors of Vargoth and the faction of elves that were driven from Caer Myrridon long ago. For millennia they have dwelled within Harwood Forest, where they have built a thriving metropolis (Novgorod) and several smaller surrounding settlements, all in relative seclusion to the outside world.

Creating a Fallen Elf

"Fallen Elf" is an acquired template that can be added to any living creature with the elf subtype (referred to hereafter as the base creature), provided it is native to the Novgorod area. A Fallen Elf retains all the base creature's statistics and special abilities except as noted here.

CR: Same as the base creature.
Alignment: Chaotic Evil.
Abilities: Dex +2, Con −2, Cha +2.
Languages: Abyssal, Common, Elven. **Bonus Languages:** Draconic, Gnoll, Gnome, Goblin, Infernal, Orc, and Sylvan.

Ivan the Warmaster

With a body forged on the anvil of war and tempered with pure evil, Ivan is an impressive sight. Highly toned and fluid of movement, not a single wasted motion is detected in his arrogant stride.

IVAN THE WARMASTER	CR 16

XP 102,400
Male fallen elf fighter 17
CN Medium humanoid elf)
Init +4; **Senses** low-light vision; **Perception** +9

AC 24, touch 15, flat-footed 19 (+9 armor, +4 Dex, +1 dodge)
hp 183 (17d10+68 plus 17)
Fort +16; **Ref** +11; **Will** +7; +9 vs. enchantment, +11 vs. fear
Defensive Abilities bravery +4; **Immunities** sleep

Speed 30 ft.
Melee +2 longsword +27/+22/+17/+12 (1d8+14/19–20) and +2 light mace +26/+21/+16 (1d6+13)
Special Attacks two weapon rend (1d10+6) , weapon training (heavy blades +4, hammers +3, crossbows +2, close +1)

Str 18, **Dex** 19, **Con** 18, **Int** 10, **Wis** 10, **Cha** 12
Base Atk +17; **CMB** +21; **CMD** 36
Feats Critical Focus, Dodge, Double Slice, Greater Two Weapon Fighting, Greater Weapon Focus (longsword), Greater Weapon Focus (light mace), Greater Weapon Specialization (longsword), Greater Weapon Specialization (light mace), Improved Two Weapon Fighting, Mobility, Spring Attack, Two-Weapon Fighting, Two-Weapon Rend, Vital Strike, Weapon Focus (light mace), Weapon Focus (longsword), Weapon Specialization (light mace), Weapon Specialization (longsword)
Skills Acrobatics +15, Climb +15, Intimidate +12, Perception +9
Languages Common, Elven
SQ armor training 4
Gear +3 elven chain, +2 longsword, +2 light mace, belt of mighty constitution +2, cloak of resistance +2

Environment Novgorod (temperate forest)
Organization solitary
Treasure standard (+3 elven chain, +2 longsword, +2 light mace, amulet of health +2, cloak of resistance +2, other treasure)

Fleshewn

A fleshewn is a macabre construct made from corpses. Virtually any corporeal living creature can be fashioned into whatever the creator desires. Normally, these constructs are built to guard treasure or act as servants. Fleshewns retain a semblance of their former self, but other creatures' features may be grafted to their new form.

The creator of a fleshewn must be evil and able to cast 8th-level spells. A fleshewn costs 10,000 gp per HD and a *manual of the golems (flesh)* is required. While several creatures may be used to fashion a fleshewn, only the base creature retains its abilities. Additional parts are simply grotesque additions. Fleshewns cannot speak but obey their creator to the best of their ability. They can be given fairly complex instructions, up to 4 or 5 sentences.

Creating a Fleshewn

"Fleshewn" is an acquired template that can be added to any corporeal once-living creature (referred to hereafter as the base creatureA fleshewn has the base creature's statistics and special abilities except as noted:

Challenge Rating: Same as the base creature –1.
Alignment: Always Neutral.
Size: Usually the same as the base creature, but can be up to one size category larger depending on how it was constructed.
Type: The creature's type changes to It retains any subtype except for alignment subtypes (such as good) and subtypes that indicate kind. It does not gain the augmented subtype. It uses all the base creature's statistics and special abilities except as noted here.
Armor Class: A fleshewn retains the base creature's natural armor bonus only.
Hit Dice: All Hit Dice change to d10s. A fleshewn gains bonus hit points based on size as other constructs.
Defensive Abilities: A fleshewn gains DR 5/adamantine and gains all of a constructs immunities and the following.
Immunity to Magic (Ex) Certain spells and effects function differently against a fleshewn. An attack that deals electricity damage heals 1 point of damage for every 3 points of damage the attack would otherwise deal. If the amount of healing would cause the fleshewn to exceed its full normal hit points, it gains any excess as temporary hit points. For example, a fleshewn hit by a *lightning bolt* heals 3 points of damage if the attack would have dealt 11 points of damage. A fleshewn gets no saving throw against attacks that deal electricity damage, but is otherwise immune to electricity damage.
Speed: The fleshewn is similar to an animated object of the appropriate size. Fleshewns move at a base of 30 ft. Fleshewns with two legs (or a similar means of movement) have a +10 ft. speed bonus. Multiple legs (tables, chairs) have a +20 foot bonus. Wheeled fleshewns have a +40 foot bonus. Other fleshewns can float, climb or fly (clumsy maneuverability) at half their normal land speed.
Melee: A flehewn retains all natural weapons. If the base creature had no natural weapons, it gains a slam attack. A fleshewn cannot use weapons or items. A fleshewn maintains the base creature's natural attacks but all its natural attacks are considered magical for the purpose of overcoming damage reduction.
Abilities: A fleshewn's Dex and Wis become 11 and its Cha becomes 1. A fleshewn has no Int or Con score.
Skills: A fleshewn loses all skills.
Feats: A fleshewn loses all feats.

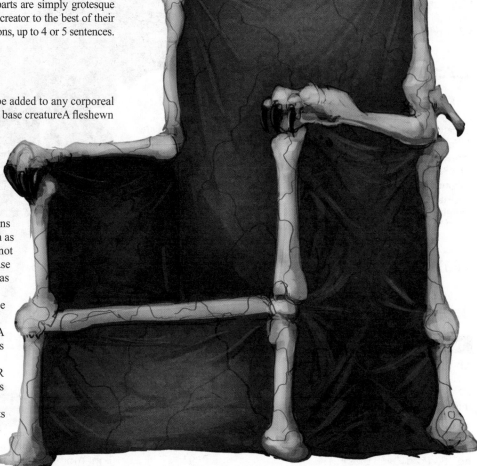

Environment: Any
Organization: Solitary
Treasure: None.

Construction

The largest portion of a fleshewn must come from the base creature. The corpses used must be recently deceased. Assembly requires anatomy tomes worth 5,000 gp are required to complete the task. Skill checks (DC 20 + fleshewn HD) from Craft (leatherworking), Knowledge (alchemy), and the appropriate Knowledge skill for the base creature type (arcana for dragons and magical beasts, dungeoneering for aberrations and ooes, etc.) are required when constructing a fleshewn.

FLESHEWN
CL 18th; **Price** 20,000 gp

CONSTRUCTION
Requirements Craft Construct, Craft Wondrous Item, *animate dead, gentle repose, mending, major item, geas/quest, limited wish,* caster must be at least 18th level; **Cost** 10,000 gp.

Fleshewn Troll Throne

Fleshewn troll thrones are large bone chairs covered in the taut flesh of a troll. The chairs "arms" can attack, and the chair can move to carry anyone sitting on it. A tooth-filled maw is hidden under a cushion.

FLESHEWN (TROLL THRONE)	CR 5

N Large construct
Init +0; **Senses** darkvision 60 ft., low-light vision, scent; **Perception** +0

AC 14, touch 9, flat-footed 14 (+5 natural, −1 size)
hp 63 (6d10+30); regeneration 5 (acid or fire)
Fort +2; **Ref** +2; **Will** +2
DR 5/adamantine; **Immune** construct immunities (+30 hp), magic

Speed 40 ft.
Melee bite +6 (1d8+6), 2 claws +6 (1d6+6)
Space 10 ft.; **Reach** 10 ft.

Special Attacks rend (2 claws, 1d6+9)

Str 23, **Dex** 11, **Con** —, **Int** —, **Wis** 11, **Cha** 1
Base Atk +6; **CMB** +13; **CMD** 23

Environment Any
Organization solitary
Treasure none

Regeneration (Ex) Fire and acid deal normal damage to a troll throne. If the throne loses a feature, it regrows in 3d6 minutes. The construct can reattach the severed member instantly by holding it to the stump.

A troll throne fleshewn is a large throne made of stretched and taut troll skin covering a bone structure. The legs (or arms at the creator's discretion) have the claw attacks of the base troll creature. The troll throne can carry a seated individual by following simple commands.

Guardian Beast Template

Elves of the thick forests have been in the world for longer than even they can recall. Their long-time presence, stewardship of the land and druidic connections have brought them into close contact with the animals of the forest — so close in fact, that many of the animals now serve the elves as a free-willed act. These creatures are bound to elven communities by mystic energies generated by the living forest, and can communicate telepathically with elves and fey creatures. This makes them ideal sentries and messengers, and they help secure the elven forest nation against outside threats.

Creating a Guardian Beast

"Guardian Beast" is an acquired template that can be added to any animal (referred to hereafter as the "base animal"). A guardian beast uses the base animal's statistics and special abilities, except as noted here.
Alignment: Usually neutral.
Challenge Rating: Same as base animal +1.
Type: Animals with this template have their type changed to magical beast and gain the augmented subtype. Do not recalculate base attack, saves, or skill points.
Hit Dice: Increase all Hit Dice to d10.
Saves: Guardian beasts get a +2 racial saving throw bonus against enchantment spells and effects.
Defensive Abilities: A guardian beast gains immunity to magic sleep effects and SR equal to the base animal's HD + 5. It also gains DR; the amount and type depends on its Hit Dice.

HD	DR
1–5	5/cold iron
6–10	5/cold iron, magic
11+	10/cold iron

Special Qualities: A guardian beast retains all the special qualities of the base animal and also gains the following.
Telepathy (Su) A guardian beast can communicate telepathically with any humanoid with the elf subtype and creatures of the fey type at will within 100 ft. Full-blooded elves as well as fey creatures, can understand the creature to the full extent of its intelligence. Half-elves can only receive empathic sensations (fear, hunger, curiosity, etc.) regardless of the creature's intellect.
Abilities: Intelligence +1 per Hit Die.
Environment: Same as base animal or as proscribed by the community or

race the guardian beast serves.
Organization: Same as base animal or as proscribed by the community or race the guardian beast serves.
Treasure: Usually none; animals rarely have treasures as it is, and guardian beasts have priorities other than hoarding goods.

Guardian Bear

Watching from the deep shadows of the dense forest is a large brown bear. Its eyes have a spark of intelligence.

GUARDIAN BEAR	CR 5

XP 1,600
N Large magical beast (augmented animal)
Init +1; **Senses** low-light vision, scent; **Perception** +6

AC 16, touch 10, flat-footed 15 (+1 Dex, +6 natural, −1 size)
hp 47 (5d10+20)
Fort +8; **Ref** +5; **Will** +2; +4 vs. enchantment spells and effects
DR 5/cold iron, magic; **Immune** magic sleep effects; **SR** 10

Speed 40 ft.
Melee 2 claws +7 (1d6+5 plus grab), bite +7 (1d6+5)
Space 10 ft.; **Reach** 5 ft.

Str 21, **Dex** 13, **Con** 19, **Int** 6, **Wis** 12, **Cha** 6
Base Atk +3; **CMB** +9 (+13 grapple); **CMD** 20 (24 vs. trip)
Feats Endurance, Run, Skill Focus (Survival)
Skills Perception +6, Survival +5, Swim +14; **Racial Modifiers** +4 Swim
Languages telepathy 100 ft. (elves and fey only); empathy 100 ft. (half-elves)

Environment cold forests
Organization solitary or pair
Treasure none

The strength, speed and guile of the brown bear are traits that elf barbarians admire and emulate. Thus the bear is often an important for them, and elven druids favor its form when altering their own shape for meditation, travel or battle. Many brown bears manifest the telepathic link and become guardian creatures after witnessing the ferocity of elven berserkers in battle. An interloper venturing into the elven forest nation is likely to be met by a guardian bear whose task is to assess the vitality of the foreigner and report the worth of their opponent to elven scouts nearby. On the rare occasions that raiders appear in groups, the guardian bear is favored as combat support of the elves, accompanying their berserkers into confrontation. Guardian bears look no different than regular brown bears, except that the look of bemused curiosity that so many bears have is replaced by one of keen intelligence. When encountered, they merely watch until the outsider moves on or the bear grows bored.

Corrupted Guardian Beast

If an elven enclave falls to evil forces, corrupting the lands the elves once kept pure, so too are the guardian beasts corrupted. Just as loyal guardian beasts may communicate at will with the elves and their fey allies, the corrupted guardians may hide from elves and fey at will, making them brutally effective hunters and turning the elves' forest home into a killing ground.

Creating a Corrupted Guardian Beast

"Corrupted Guardian Beast" is an acquired template that can be added to any guardian beast (referred to hereafter as the "base creature"). A corrupted guardian beast uses the base creature's statistics and special abilities, except as noted here.

Channelege Rating: Same as base creature +2

Defensives Abilities: As the base guardian beast, except that its SR increases by +5, and it gains the following.

Hide from Elves and Fey (Su) Elves and fey cannot easily see, hear, or smell a corrupted guardian beast. Even extraordinary or supernatural sensory capabilities, such as blindsense, blindsight, scent, and tremorsense, cannot detect or locate the corrupted guardian beast. Elves receive a DC 20 Will save to see, hear or sense the creatures. On a failed save, the elf or fey cannot sense the corrupted guardian beast. The elf or fey can attempt Perception checks to locate the corrupted guardian beast, and may make attacks against it in accordance with the rules for invisibility (50% miss chance). Due to their mixed blood, half-elves must only pass a DC 15 Will save to see, hear or sense the creatures. Even if this save is passed, the creature appears insubstantial or is only visible intermittently, and is treated as having concealment (20% miss chance). This ability is compromised by direct sunlight (not magical or otherwise synthesized light). In sunlight, a corrupted guardian beats is wholly visible to all viewers, elven or otherwise.

Sunlight Vulnerability (Ex) In natural sunlight, but not a daylight spell, a corrupted guardian beast loses its DR and its hide from elves and fey ability. A corrupted guardian beast has a –2 penalty to skill checks, saves, and attack rolls while in natural sunlight.

Skills: Corrupted guardian beasts have a +8 racial bonus on Stealth checks.

Meat Puppet

Meat puppets are boneless, skinless corpses reanimated after being exposed to necromantic energies.

Creating a Meat Puppet

"Meat puppet" is an acquired template that can be added to any corporeal creature (other than an undead) that had a skeletal system at one point, but had its bones extracted or completely crushed (referred to hereafter as the base creature).

Challenge Rating: This depends on the creature's new total number of Hit Dice, as follows:

HD	CR	HD	CR
4 or less	4	18–20	12
6–7	5	21–24	14
8–11	6	25–27	16
12–14	8	28 or higher	18
15–17	10		

Alignment: Always neutral evil.

Type: The creature's type changes to undead. It retains any subtype except for alignment subtypes (such as good) and subtypes that indicate kind. It does not gain the augmented subtype. It uses all the base creature's statistics and special abilities except as noted here.

Senses: Meat puppets have darkvision out to 60 ft.

Armor Class: A meat puppet has no bones to reinforce its body, and has only half the base creature's natural armor bonus (round down). It tends to shed any possessions it had in life, and so is only 5% likely to be encountered wearing any armor it once had.

Hit Dice: Drop HD gained from class levels (minimum of 1) and change racial HD to d8s. Meat Puppets gain a number of additional HD as noted on the following table.

MEAT PUPPET SIZE	BONUS HIT DICE
Tiny or smaller	+1 HD
Small or Medium	+3 HD
Large	+5 HD
Huge	+7 HD
Gargantuan	+11 HD
Colossal	+15 HD

Meat Puppets use their Charisma modifiers to determine bonus hit points (instead of Constitution).

Defensive Abilities: Meat puppets lose their defensive abilities and gain all of the qualities and immunities granted by the undead type. Meat puppets gain channel resistance +4, DR 5/slashing or piercing, and regeneration (cold iron or good) which heals 1 hp per round per Hit Die.

Speed: The base creature loses fly and burrow speeds, but retains land, swim, and climb speeds, if any.

Attacks: A meat puppet loses all of the base creature's natural attacks and gains 2 slam attacks, or one slam attack for every natural attack it lost (whichever is greater). It retains all weapon proficiencies of the base

creature, but as with armor is only 5% likely to be encountered with a weapon in hand. Its slam attacks deal damage based on the meat puppet's size, but as if it were one size category larger than its actual size (see **Table 3-1: Natural Attacks by Size** in the *Pathfinder Roleplaying Game Bestiary*). It retains any extraordinary special abilities that improve its melee or ranged attacks.

Special Attacks: A meat puppet retains none of the base creature's special attacks. However, it gains the grab and constrict special attacks.

Special Qualities: A meat puppet loses most special qualities of the base creature.

Abilities: Str +6, Dex +4. A meat puppet has no Constitution score, its Intelligence changes to 3, its Wisdom and Charisma change to 14.

Skills: A meat puppet does not retain the skills of the base creature, but it has 1 skill rank per Hit Die. The following are class skills for a meat puppet: Climb, Disguise, Fly, Intimidate, Knowledge (arcana), Knowledge (religion), Perception, Sense Motive, Spellcraft, and Stealth.

Feats: A meat puppet gains feats normally based on its Hit Dice, but loses all feats possessed by the base creature. A meat puppet also gains Toughness as a bonus feat.

Environment: Any land and underground.

Organization: Any.

Treasure: 5% chance of standard goods.

HUMAN MEAT PUPPET — CR 4

XP 1,200
NE Medium undead
Init +6; **Senses** darkvision 60 ft.; **Perception** +9

AC 13, touch 13, flat-footed 10 (+2 Dex, +1 dodge)
hp 30 (4d8+8 plus 4); regeneration 4 (cold iron or good)
Fort +3; **Ref** +3; **Will** +6
Defensive Abilities channel resistance +4; **DR** 5/slashing or piercing; **Immune** undead traits

---

Speed 30 ft.
Melee 2 slams +6 (1d6+3 plus grab)
Special Attacks constrict (1d6+3)

Str 17, **Dex** 14, **Con** —, **Int** 3, **Wis** 14, **Cha** 14
Base Atk +3; **CMB** +6 (+10 to grapple); **CMD** 19
Feats Dodge, Improved Initiative, Toughness[B]
Skills Perception +9

Environment any
Organization solitary or abattoir (2–8)
Treasure none

OTYUGH MEAT PUPPET — CR 8

XP 4,800
NE Large undead
Init +5; **Senses** darkvision 60 ft.; **Perception** +17

AC 10, touch 10, flat-footed 9 (+1 Dex, −1 size)

hp 82 (11d8+22 plus 11); regeneration 12 (cold iron or good)
Fort +5; **Ref** +7; **Will** +9
Defensive Abilities channel resistance +4; **DR** 5/slashing or piercing; **Immune** undead traits

Speed 30 ft.
Melee 3 slams +15 (2d6+7/19–20 plus grab)
Special Attacks constrict (1d8+7)

Str 24, **Dex** 14, **Con** —, **Int** 3, **Wis** 14, **Cha** 14

Base Atk +8; **CMB** +16 (+20 to grapple); **CMD** 29 (31 vs. trip)
Feats Dodge, Improved Critical (slam), Improved Initiative, Improved Natural Attack (slam), Lightning Reflexes, Toughness[B], Weapon Focus (slam)
Skills Perception +16

Environment any
Organization solitary or abattoir (2–8)
Treasure none

Minikin (Miniature Creature)

Minikins are smaller versions of normal creatures, made so through experimental magic. They are always smaller than their true counterparts and rarely associate with them. Minikins tend to congregate and associate with others of their own kind.

Creating a Minikin

"Minikin" is an acquired or inherited template that can be added to any corporeal living animal or vermin of Diminutive size or larger (referred to hereafter as the base creature). A minikin retains all the base creature's statistics and special abilities except as noted here.

Challenge Rating Decrease the base creature's CR by 2, plus an additional –1 for every 3 HD it loses when applying this template.

Size Decrease the base creature's size by one category.

Hit Dice Reduce the base creature's Hit Dice by one-half (minimum 1).

Armor Class Reduce the creature's natural armor bonus by –2 (minimum +0).

Hit Points Recalculate the creature's hit points based on its decreased Hit Dice.

Saves Recalculate the creature's saving throws based on its decreased Hit Dice. A minikin gains a +1 racial bonus on all saves.

Speed Reduce the creature's speed (all forms of movement) by 10 ft. (to a minimum of 10 ft.)

Attacks A minikin retains all the attacks of the base creature. Recalculate its attack bonus based on its new BAB and size.

Space/Reach Recalculate the creature's space and reach based on its new size.

Damage Decrease damage for all attacks by 1 step.

Ability Scores –4 Strength, –4 Constitution, +2 Dexterity

Base Attack/CMB/CMD Recalculate the creature's BAB based on its decreased Hit Dice. Recalculate its CMB and CMD based on its new BAB and size.

Feats Feats remain unchanged. Feats above what a creature would normally have based on the minikin's reduced Hit Dice are treated as bonus feats. A minikin gains Toughness as a bonus feat (if it doesn't already possess it). If the creature's new Dexterity score exceeds its new Strength score, it also gains Weapon Finesse as a bonus feat (if it doesn't already possess it).

Skills Recalculate the creature's skills (if it had any) based on its reduced Hit Dice.

Organization solitary, pair, and double any other listed.

MINIKIN GRIZZLY BEAR	CR 1

XP 600
N Medium animal
Init +2; **Senses** low-light vision, scent; **Perception** +5

AC 16, touch 12, flat-footed 14 (+2 Dex, +4 natural)
hp 16 (2d8+4 plus 3)
Fort +6; **Ref** +6; **Will** +2

Speed 30 ft.
Melee 2 claws +4 (1d4+3 plus grab), bite +4 (1d4+3)

Str 17, **Dex** 15, **Con** 14, **Int** 2, **Wis** 12, **Cha** 6

Base Atk +1; **CMB** +4 (+8 grapple); **CMD** 16
Feats Endurance, Run[B], Skill Focus (Survival)[B], Toughness[B]
Skills Perception +5, Survival +5, Swim +7; **Racial Modifiers** +4 Swim

Environment cold forests
Organization solitary or pair
Treasure none

MINIKIN MASTODON	CR 5

XP 1,600
N Large animal
Init +2; **Senses** low-light vision, scent; **Perception** +17

AC 21, touch 11, flat-footed 19 (+2 Dex, +10 natural, –1 size)
hp 59 (7d8+21 plus 7)
Fort +9; **Ref** +8; **Will** +6

Speed 30 ft.
Melee gore +15 (2d6+10), slam +14 (1d10+10)
Space 10 ft.; **Reach** 5 ft.
Special Attacks trample (2d6+15, DC 23)

Str 30, **Dex** 14, **Con** 17, **Int** 2, **Wis** 13, **Cha** 7
Base Atk +5; **CMB** +16; **CMD** 28 (32 vs. trip)
Feats Endurance, Improved Bull Rush, Improved Iron Will, Iron Will, Power Attack[B], Skill Focus (Perception)[B], Toughness[B], Weapon Focus (gore)[B]
Skills Perception +17

Environment cold or temperate forests and plains
Organization solitary, pair, or herd (12–60)
Treasure none

Reborn

The creature looks like a twisted humanoid with features from everything natural—a bit of shaggy fur, some scales, fingers that resemble gnarled roots and the cold and viscous eyes of a snake. It moves like a reasonable being however and wields its weapons with confidence and proficiency.

The reborn are the most devoted servants of the Tree That Sees who have been given the gift of transformation. To become a reborn one must spend three days buried by the Tree That Sees' roots. There he dies and then is reborn in the likeness of the Twisted Deity.

The reborn fight like normal members of their race except that they are utterly fearless and far more savage.

Creating a Reborn

"Reborn" is an acquired template that can be added to any humanoid creature (referred to hereafter as the base creature). A reborn uses all the base creature's statistics and special abilities except as noted here.

Challenge Rating: Same as base creature +1.

Alignment: The base creature's alignment changes to chaotic, retaining its good/neutral/evil axis.

Size and Type: The base creature's size changes according to its total HD: 1–4 Medium or as base creature, whichever is larger, 5–8 Large or as base creature, whichever is larger, 9+ Huge or as base creature, whichever is larger.

Armor Class: The base creature's natural armor class, if any, increases by +2.

Defensive Abilities: The base creature gains fast healing 5 if it didn't already have it.

Abilities: Str +4, Dex +4, Con +4

Feats: The reborn gain Alertness, Athletic, Power Attack, and Weapon Finesse even if the base creature doesn't have the base perquisites for these feats.

Skills: The reborn gain a +4 racial bonus on Perception checks and a racial bonus equal to their HD in Knowledge (history). Reborn always treat Climb, Knowledge (history), Perception, and Swim as class skills.

Special Qualities: Random feature. Every reborn gains a random feature of an animal, a reptile or a plant when it is created and another every 4 levels after that. Most reborn have feature of only one type and stick to their kind but powerful or lucky reborn often have features of various types. Roll on the table below for every reborn encountered. Any natural attack gained by the reborn inflicts damage as specified in **Table 3-1: Natural Attacks by Size** in the *Pathfinder Roleplaying Game Bestiary* unless otherwise noted.

TYPE (1D3):

Roll	Type
1	Animal
2	Reptile
3	Plant

ANIMALISTIC FEATURES (1D10):

Roll	Feature	Effect
1	Wings	Fly 30 ft. (poor)
2	Muzzle/Beak	Bite attack. Treat reborn as one size category larger for purposes of damage.
3	Claws/Talons	2 claw attacks
4	Tough Hide	+4 natural armor
5	Horns	Gore 1d6 points of damage
6	Hooves	Gain Endurance and Run as bonus feats, speed 40 ft.
7	Ape Nimbleness	+8 to Acrobatics and Climb checks
8	Tiger Feet	Pounce and rake attack. Rake damage as a claw attack, but at one size category higher.
9	Sharp Senses	+4 to Perception checks
10	Reroll Twice	—

REPTILIAN FEATURES (1D10):

Roll	Reptile	Effect
1	Tongue	Acts as a whip that cannot be dropped
2	Turtle Shell	+8 armor bonus, base speed 10 ft.
3	Hypnotic Eyes	Can cast *hypnotism* 3/day like a sorcerer of the reborn's level
4	Poisonous Bite	Bite plus poison, (Bite–injury; save Fortitude , frequency 1/round for 6 rounds, effect 1d6 Str, cure 1 save) Poison DCi s Constitution-based. Treat bite as two size categories smaller for purposes of damage.
5	Snake tail	Amphibious, speed 20 ft., swim speed 20 ft. constrict medium or smaller creatures for 1d6 point of damage
6	Frog Eyes	+4 to Perception checks
7	Salamander Skin	Fire resistance 15
8	Crocodile Bite	Bite attack. Treat as one size category larger for purposes of damage.
9	Spit Acid	10-foot line of acid once per 1d4 rounds for 2d4 points of damage, Reflex DC 13 half
10	Reroll twice	—

PLANT FEATURES (1D10):

Roll	Feature	Effect
1	Vines	Gain slam attack with the grab special ability
2	Barkskin	+4 natural armor
3	Sticky Sap	**Sticky Sap (Ex)** Anyone who makes a melee attack against the reborn must succeed on a DC 15 Reflex save or the attacker's weapon sticks to the reborn and is yanked out of the wielder's grasp. The weapon can be retrieved with a successful touch attack (provoking an attack of opportunity) followed by a DC 15 Strength check as a free action.
4	Poisonous Spores	**Poisonous Spores (Ex)** When damaged for the first time all non-plants within 15-foot radius must succeed on a DC 15 fort save or be nauseated for 1d6 rounds.
5	Roots	Speed is 10 ft. lower, can cast *entangle* 3/day as a druid of the reborn's level
6	Leaves	+8 to Stealth checks in forested areas
7	Barbs	Unarmed attacks against the reborn inflict 1d4 points of damage on the attacker

8	Plant Anatomy	Plant traits as if the reborn was of the plant type
9	Flowers	Can cast *color spray* 3/day as a sorcerer of the reborn's level
10	Reroll twice	—

Environment: any forest (Hollow Mountain)
Organization: any
Treasure: none

Plant Reborn

These elves look like topiary versions of normal demi-humans; leaves and twigs jut from their armor, and the creaking of their clubs is mimicked by the straining of their roots to gain stability.

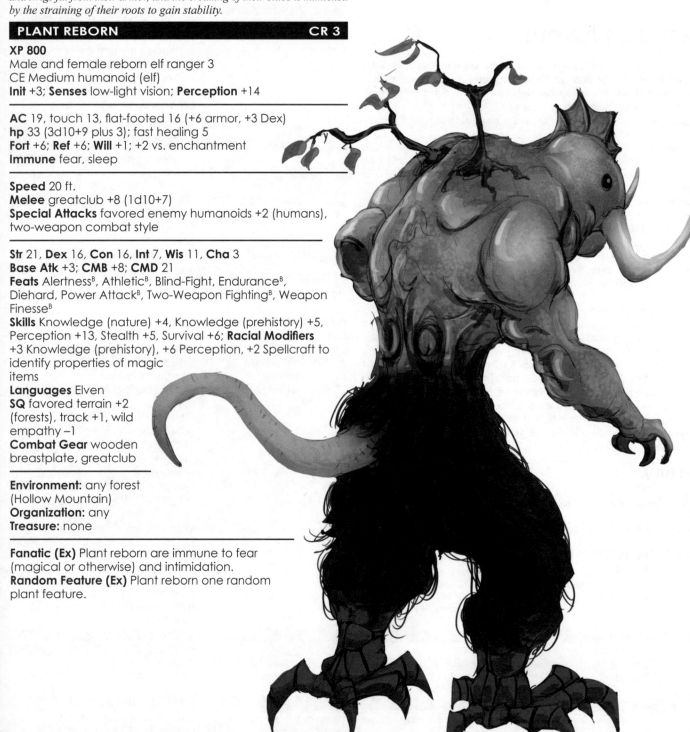

PLANT REBORN	CR 3

XP 800
Male and female reborn elf ranger 3
CE Medium humanoid (elf)
Init +3; **Senses** low-light vision; **Perception** +14

AC 19, touch 13, flat-footed 16 (+6 armor, +3 Dex)
hp 33 (3d10+9 plus 3); fast healing 5
Fort +6; **Ref** +6; **Will** +1; +2 vs. enchantment
Immune fear, sleep

Speed 20 ft.
Melee greatclub +8 (1d10+7)
Special Attacks favored enemy humanoids +2 (humans), two-weapon combat style

Str 21, **Dex** 16, **Con** 16, **Int** 7, **Wis** 11, **Cha** 3
Base Atk +3; **CMB** +8; **CMD** 21
Feats Alertness[B], Athletic[B], Blind-Fight, Endurance[B], Diehard, Power Attack[B], Two-Weapon Fighting[B], Weapon Finesse[B]
Skills Knowledge (nature) +4, Knowledge (prehistory) +5, Perception +13, Stealth +5, Survival +6; **Racial Modifiers** +3 Knowledge (prehistory), +6 Perception, +2 Spellcraft to identify properties of magic items
Languages Elven
SQ favored terrain +2 (forests), track +1, wild empathy –1
Combat Gear wooden breastplate, greatclub

Environment: any forest (Hollow Mountain)
Organization: any
Treasure: none

Fanatic (Ex) Plant reborn are immune to fear (magical or otherwise) and intimidation.
Random Feature (Ex) Plant reborn one random plant feature.

Refracted Creature

Refracted creatures are native to a strange demiplane that is a bizarre reflection of the Material Plane. They resemble their normal counterparts whose form seems to ripple and bend making their location difficult to discern. Refracted creatures often find their way onto the Material Plane as a result of a failed *teleport* spell, but occasionally they slip through natural rifts between dimensions.

Creating a Refracted Creature

"Refracted Creature" is an inherited template that can be added to any animal, referred to hereafter as the base creature. A refracted creature retains all the base creature's statistics and abilities except as noted here.

Challenge Rating: As base creature +2.

Alignment: The base creature's alignment shifts one step towards evil on the good/evil alignment axis.

Type: The base creature's type changes to magical beast. It gains the augmented subtype. Do not recalculate BAB, saves, or skill ranks. Refracted creatures on the Material Plane have the extraplanar subtype.

Senses: As the base creature, plus darkvision 60 feet.

Armor Class: A refracted creature's natural armor bonus increases by +2.

Hit Dice: The base creature's racial Hit Dice change to d10s.

Defensive Abilities: A refracted creature retains all of the base creature's defensive abilities and special qualities. It also gains the following.

Displacement (Su) Even when visible, the refracted creature appears to be about 2 feet away from its true location. The creature benefits from a 50% miss chance as if it had total concealment. Unlike actual total concealment, displacement does not prevent enemies from targeting the creature normally. *True seeing* reveals its true location and negates the miss chance.

Evasion (Ex) A refracted creature can avoid even magical and unusual attacks with great agility. If it makes a successful Reflex save against an attack that normally deals half damage on a successful save, it instead takes no damage. A helpless refracted creature does not gain the benefit of evasion.

Special Attacks: A refracted creature retains the special attacks of the base creature, and gains the following.

Refraction (Su) At will, a refracted creature can cause any of its attacks to emanate from a point a short distance from its body, effectively increasing its reach by 10 ft. A refracted creature capable of making ranged attacks can effectively reduce the overall range to its target by 10 ft. as well.

Ability Scores: +4 Int

Feats: A refracted creature gains Dodge and Mobility as bonus feats.

Skills: A refracted creature gains a +8 racial bonus on Stealth checks. This bonus does not stack with any other racial bonus to Stealth.

Languages: All refracted creatures speak Common.

Treasure: As the base creature or standard, whichever is better.

Refracted Dire Shark

This giant shark's form appears to shimmer and ripple just as the water surrounding it, making it difficult to discern its true location.

REFRACTED DIRE SHARK	CR 11

XP 12,800
N Gargantuan magical beast (augmented animal, extraplanar)
Init +6; **Senses** darkvision 60 ft., keen scent, low-light vision; **Perception** +25

AC 26, touch 9, flat-footed 23 (+2 Dex, +1 dodge, +17 natural, −4 size)
hp 127 (15d10+45)
Fort +14; **Ref** +13; **Will** +8
Defensive Abilities displacement, evasion

Speed swim 60 ft.
Melee bite +17 (4d10+15/19–20 plus grab)
Space 20 ft.; **Reach** 20 ft.
Special Attacks refraction, swallow whole (2d6+15 damage, AC 18, 12 hp)

Str 30, **Dex** 15, **Con** 17, **Int** 5, **Wis** 12, **Cha** 10
Base Atk +11; **CMB** +25 (+29 grapple); **CMD** 38
Feats Bleeding Critical, Critical Focus, Dodge[B], Great Fortitude, Improved Critical (bite), Improved Initiative, Iron Will, Lightning Reflexes, Mobility[B], Skill Focus (Perception)
Skills Perception +25, Stealth −2, Swim +18; **Racial Modifiers** +8 Stealth
Languages Common

Environment any oceans
Organization solitary
Treasure standard

Refracted Tiger

This tiger resembles a normal tiger as if viewed through a mirror. Its form seems slightly disjointed and its location is hard to pinpoint.

REFREACTED TIGER	CR 6

XP 2,400
NE Large magical beast (augmented animal, extraplanar)
Init +6; **Senses** darkvision 60 ft., low-light vision, scent; **Perception** +8

AC 17, touch 12, flat-footed 14 (+2 Dex, +1 dodge, +5 natural, −1 size)
hp 51 (6d10+18)
Fort +8; **Ref** +7; **Will** +3
Defensive Abilities displacement, evasion

Speed 40 ft.
Melee 2 claws +10 (1d8+6 plus grab), bite +9 (2d6+6 plus grab)

Space 10 ft.; **Reach** 5 ft.
Special Attacks pounce, rake (2 claws +10, 1d8+6), refraction

Str 23, **Dex** 15, **Con** 17, **Int** 6, **Wis** 12, **Cha** 6
Base Atk +4; **CMB** +11 (+15 grapple); **CMD** 24 (28 vs. trip)
Feats Dodge[B], Improved Initiative, Mobility[B], Skill Focus (Perception), Weapon Focus (claw)
Skills Acrobatics +10, Perception +8, Stealth +11 (+15 in tall grass), Swim +11; **Racial Modifiers** +4 Acrobatics, +8 Stealth (+12 in tall grass)
Languages Common

Environment any forests
Organization solitary or pair
Treasure standard

Shade

Shades are creatures of shadowstuff. A mortal either chooses to infuse its body with the essence of shadows or it is cursed by some powerful entity for a slight against it. On the Plane of Molten Skies and within the City of Brass, shades are known as afya.

Creating a Shade

"Shade" is an inherited template that can be added to any living corporeal humanoid that has at least 5 HD, referred to hereafter as the base creature. A shade retains all the base creature's statistics and abilities except as noted here.

Challenge Rating Same as the base creature +1
Alignment Any non-good
Type The creature's type changes to outsider. It gains the augmented and extraplanar subtypes. Do not recalculate base attack bonus, saves, or skill ranks.
Senses A shade gains darkvision 60 ft, if the base creature doesn't already have it. A shade also gains the ability to see in darkness. It can see perfectly in darkness of any kind, including that created by *deeper darkness.*
Armor Class A shade gains a +2 deflection bonus to its AC. It loses this bonus in areas of bright light or normal light.
Hit Dice The base creature's racial Hit Dice change to d10s.
Defensive Abilities A shade retains all of the base creature's defensive abilities and special qualities. It also gains the following:
Fast Healing (Su) A shade gains fast healing 5. It loses its fast healing in areas of bright light or normal light.
Spell Resistance (Ex) A shade gains SR equal to the creature's CR + 11. It loses its spell resistance in areas of bright light or normal light.
Shadowy Resolve (Ex) A shade gains a +2 bonus on all saving throws. It loses these bonuses in areas of bright light or normal light.
Weakness A shade gains light blindness. If exposed to bright light, it is blinded for 1 round, and dazzled as long as it remains in areas of bright light or normal light.
Speed All forms of movement the base creature possesses increases by +20 feet. It loses this bonus in areas of bright light or normal light.
Attacks A shade gains a +2 racial bonus on attack rolls and damage rolls. It loses these bonuses in areas of bright light or normal light.
Special Abilities A shade retains all of the base creature's special attacks and special abilities. It also gains the following.
Shadow Images (Sp) A number of times per day equal to the shade's Charisma modifier, it can create an effect identical to a *mirror image* spell (CL equals the shade's Hit Dice). This ability can only be used in areas of dim light or darkness.
Shadow Stride (Sp) Once per day, a shade of 9 Hit Dice or more can use *teleport without error* to reach any shadowy area on the same plane. Alternately, it can use *plane shift* once per day to reach the Plane of Shadow.
Shadow Walk (Sp) Once per day, a shade of 9 Hit Dice or more can create an effect identical to a *shadow walk* spell (CL equals the shade's Hit Dice). This ability transports only the shade and non-living objects it is carrying.
Abilities +2 Strength, +2 Constitution, +2 Charisma. It loses these bonuses in areas of bright light or normal light.
Skills A shade gains a +8 racial bonus to Stealth checks in areas of dim light or darkness. This bonus increases to +12 in areas of total darkness. Stealth and Knowledge (the planes) are always class skills for a shade.

Shade

The dusky figure almost melds into the gloom of the room.

SHADE SORCERER	CR 11

XP 12,800
Human shade sorcerer 11
CE Medium outsider (augmented human)
Init +2; **Senses** darkvision 60 ft., see in darkness; **Perception** +5

AC 15, touch 15, flat-footed 12 (+2 Dex, +1 dodge, +2 deflection)
hp 74 (11d6+22 plus 11); fast healing 5
Fort +7; **Ref** +9; **Will** +11; +4 on saves vs. poison
Resist electricity 10; **SR** 22
Weakness light blindness

Speed 50 ft.
Melee shortspear +6 (1d6+3)
Ranged light crossbow +7 (1d8+2/19–20)
Special Attacks abyssal claws (2 claws +8, 1d6+2 plus 1d6 fire, usable 6 rounds per day), shadow images
Spells Known (CL 11th; melee touch +6, ranged touch+7):
5th (4/day)—*cone of cold* (DC 19), *dismissal* (DC 19), *dominate person* (DC 19)
4th (6/day)—*bestow curse* (DC 18), *crushing despair* (DC 18), *ice storm, stoneskin*
3rd (7/day)—*deep slumber* (DC 17), *dispel magic, lightning bolt* (DC 17), *protection from energy* (DC 17), *rage*
2nd (7/day)—*blur* (DC 16), *bull's strength, darkness, detect thoughts* (DC 16), *shatter* (DC 16), *web* (DC 16)
1st (7/day)—*burning hands* (DC 15), *cause fear* (DC 15), *charm person* (DC 15), *chill touch* (DC 15), *feather fall* (DC 15), *hypnotism* (DC 15)
0 (at will)—*arcane mark, bleed* (DC 14), *daze* (DC 14), *detect magic, flare* (DC 14), *mage hand, open/close* (DC 14), *read magic, resistance* (DC 14)
Bloodline Abyssal

Str 12, **Dex** 14, **Con** 14, **Int** 13, **Wis** 11, **Cha** 19
Base Atk +5; **CMB** +6; **CMD** 19
Feats Arcane Strike, Combat Casting, Dodge, Empower Spell, Eschew Materials[B], Iron Will, Lightning Reflexes, Maximize Spell, Toughness
Skills Bluff +18, Intimidate +13, Knowledge (arcana) +15, Knowledge (planes) +10, Perception +5, Spellcraft +15, Stealth +2 (+10 in dim light, +14 in darkness), Use Magical Device +12; **Racial Modifiers** +8 Stealth in dim light (+12 in darkness)
SQ shadowy resolve, shadow stride, shadow walk
Languages Common

Environment any
Organization solitary
Treasure standard (shortspear, light crossbow, 30 bolts, other treasure)

Soulless

In his eternal war against the gods, Orcus, the Prince of Demons, discovered a way to sever the connection between living beings and their divine creators. He learned that by stripping the soul of a humanoid while leaving the body alive and intact, he could create a soulless creature beholden only to him and outside the influence of the divine.

A soulless creature becomes a being without connection to the divine or living creatures. Flensed of all distinctions of alignment, the soulless embrace true amorality, characterized by acts of depravity and destruction. The soulless creature takes no pleasure in this behavior, they are disturbingly without expression or emotion, but engage in it as an automaton.

Though a soulless shares some characteristics with the undead, they remain alive and fully sentient creatures. They eat, breathe, and sleep. The absence of an animating spark means a soulless lacks the natural fears and desires of normal humanoids and some of their vulnerabilities, but they also have no final energy to cling to when the body is severely damaged.

The stripped soul ends up in an Abyssal prison where Orcus can subject it to further experiments or employ it in some other hideous plan.

Creating a Soulless

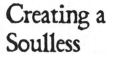

"Soulless" is an acquired template that can be added to any living corporeal humanoid, magical beast, or monstrous humanoid (referred to hereafter as the base creature), provided it possesses a soul separate from its physical body. A soulless retains all the base creature's statistics and special abilities except as noted here.

CR: Same as base creature +1.

Alignment: Neutral

Senses: A soulless gains darkvision 60 ft.

Armor Class: A soulless has a +2 natural armor bonus or the base creature's natural armor bonus, whichever is better.

Defensive Abilities: A soulless possesses no connection to the divine and also lacks the vulnerabilities of other corporeal creatures. As such it is gains the following immunities:

Immune to Critical Hits (Ex) The disconnection between a soulless creature's physical and immaterial forms turns it into a semi-automaton and immune to precision damage.

Immune to Fear (Ex) A soulless creature has already confronted the black infinity that lies beyond the mortal coil. It does not fear anything.

Immune to Positive and Negative Energy (Ex) This includes effects linked to positive and negative energy such *cure* and *inflict* spells, ability and level damage and drain and abilities that modify or alter a cleric's channel energy ability.

Immune to Soul Magic (Ex) The soulless creature is immune to all types of magic that manipulate or affect the soul such as *magic jar* or *soul bind*.

Weaknesses: The soulless gain the following weakness:

Soulless (Ex) The soulless have no innate desire to remain alive. A soulless creature reduced to 0 or fewer hit points is destroyed in the way of an undead creature.

Special Attacks: The soulless retains all of the base creature's special attacks and gains those described here.

Abyssal Stare (Su) As a standard action a soulless creature can stare into the eyes of another living being within 30 feet and force it to confront the infinite, empty void beyond death. Targets who fail a Will save (DC 10 +1/2 soulless HD + Charisma modifier) waver in their will to survive and take a –4 penalty to all saves and skill and ability checks for 1d4 rounds. Divine casters are particularly disturbed. They must succeed on a caster level check (20 + spell level) to cast a divine spell while under the effect of abyssal stare or the spell is lost. Creatures affected by the abyssal stare gaze are immune to other uses of the stare for 24 hours. This is a mind-affecting, fear effect.

Abilities: +2 Con, –2 Wis, +4 Cha.

Feats: A soulless gains Ability Focus (abyssal stare) as a bonus feat.

Skills: A soulless gains a +4 racial bonus on Intimidate. All other skills are the same as the base creature.

Special Qualities: The soulless creature gains the following special quality:

Bound Soul (Ex) The soul of a soulless creature resides in a special prison in the Abyss. This soul cannot return to the base creature without the permission of Orcus. A soulless creature cannot be raised or resurrected, nor do these spells have any effect on a soulless creature.

Divine Exclusion (Ex) The soulless creature has no connection to the divine. A soulless creature cannot take levels in any divine class, cast divine spells, or use magic items constructed with spells found only on a divine caster's spell list. Previous levels in a divine class are not lost, however any abilities associated with those levels are lost.

Vessel of Orcus (Su) By manipulating an imprisoned soul Orcus can possess a soulless creature, enabling the demon lord to see and hear through the soulless creature's body.

SOULLESS HILL GIANT   **CR 8**

XP 4,800

N Large humanoid (giant)

Init –1; **Senses** darkvision 60 ft., low-light vision; **Perception** +5

AC 21, touch 8, flat-footed 21 (+4 armor, –1 Dex, +9 natural, –1 size)

hp 95 (10d8+50)

Fort +12; **Ref** +2; **Will** +2

Defensive Abilities rock catching; **Immune** critical hits, fear, positive and negative energy, soul-affecting magic

Weaknesses soulless

Speed 40 ft. (30 ft. in armor)

Melee greatclub +14/+9 (2d8+10) or 2 slams +13 (1d8+7)

Ranged rock +6 (1d8+10)

Space 10 ft.; **Reach** 10 ft.

Special Attacks abyssal stare (DC 17), rock throwing (120 ft.)

Str 25, **Dex** 8, **Con** 21, **Int** 6, **Wis** 8, **Cha** 11

Base Atk +7; **CMB** +15; **CMD** 24

Feats Ability Focus (abyssal stare)[B], Cleave, Intimidating Prowess, Martial Weapon Proficiency (greatclub), Power Attack, Weapon Focus (greatclub)

Skills Climb +10, Intimidate +18, Perception +5; **Racial Modifiers** +4 Intimidate

Languages Giant

SQ bound soul, divine exclusion, vessel of Orcus

Ecology any land

Organization solitary, gang (2–5), band (6–8), raiding party (9–12 plus 1d4 zombie dire wolves)

Treasure standard (hide armor, greatclub, other treasure)

Vapor Creature

Along the border between the Planes of Water and Air lies a chill realm of rain and mist. Legends speak widely of the creatures of this plane, wispy, grey-blue versions of worldly beasts that slip in from the fog to prey on the weak and unwary, then fade back into the mists without a trace. The monsters that these myths refer to are the vapor creatures, inhabitants of the foggy planar fringe and regular visitors to any land plagued by mist and rain.

These creatures have adapted to reap the greatest benefit from the heavy precipitation that always shrouds their forested home. Vapor creatures are indiscernible from their normal counterparts and are often mistaken for such creatures. These creatures are highly intelligent (compared to the normal creatures they resemble) and their cunning and wits often show themselves in battle or interaction with other creatures. Vapor creatures are no more or less aggressive than the creatures they resemble.

Creating a Vapor Creature

"Vapor Creature" is an inherited template that can be applied to any corporeal animal, fey, humanoid (giant), magical beast or vermin (hereafter referred to as the "base creature"). It retains any elemental type modifiers except "cold" A vapor creature uses the base creature's statistics and special abilities except as noted below.

CR: Same as the base creature's +1.

Alignment: Same as base creature; through their ties to the ebb and flow of weather patterns and the shapelessness of the vapors that comprise them, enigmatic vapor creatures tend towards neutrality, asceticism and abstention from the affairs of their fellows.

Size and Type: Animals and vermin become magical beasts, but otherwise the creature's type is unchanged. Animals and vermin gain the augmented subtype because their type changes.

Defensive Abilities: A vapor creature loses any resistances to cold but otherwise retains all the defensive abilities of the base creature and also gains the following.

Fast Healing (Ex) As they are composed in part of water vapor, vapor creatures may use it to knit their wounds and gain fast healing 2. They heal only if in a body of mist or fog large enough to completely engulf their body, or if touching a body of water. If the base creature already has fast healing, they do not stack — they overlap. For example, a base creature with fast healing 5 that takes this template now has fast healing 5 and fast healing 2. It follows the normal rules for its fast healing 5 ability and follows the rules above for fast healing gained from this template (that is, it would still only heal 2 points of damage when touching fog or water, not 7 points of damage).

Fire Resistance (Ex) Due to their watery nature and the thin layer of vapor that shrouds them at all times, vapor creatures have fire resistance 5. If the base creature already has fire resistance, use its original value or this one, whichever is higher.

Weaknesses: A vapor creature gains the following weakness:

Cold Susceptibility (Ex) A vapor creature in vaporous form is sensitive to low temperatures that affect the evaporated state of vapor in the air around them. A cold-based effect or attack freezes the vapor creature's form causing it to function as if affected by a *slow* spell for 3 rounds.

Special Attacks: A vapor creature retains all the special attacks of the base creature and also gains the special attack listed below.

Death Throes (Ex) When a vapor creature is slain, its body bursts and releases a nauseating cloud of grayish-green vapor that fills a 10-foot radius. This cloud acts as a *stinking cloud* spell (caster level 5th). Affected creatures must make a successful Fortitude save (DC 10 + 1/2 the vaporous creature's HD + the vapor creature's Constitution modifier) or be nauseated as long as they remain within the cloud and for 1d4+1 rounds after they leave. A creature that makes its save but remains in the cloud must continue to save each round.

Special Qualities: A vapor creature retains all the special qualities of the base creature and also gains the following. If the base creature already has one or more of these special qualities, use the better value.

Vaporous Form (Su) As a standard action, once per day, a vapor creature can assume a grayish, misty form. Its general body shape and size remains the same and it takes on a wispy, translucent appearance. It can spend up to 1 hour per day in vaporous form, spent in 1-minute increments. In smoke form, the vapor creature acts as if under the effects of a *gaseous form* spell.

Abilities: Same as base creature. Vapor creatures have a +1 per Hit Die bonus to Intelligence due to their planar origins and superior learning ability, and a +1 bonus to Charisma due to their stoic self-sufficiency.

Skills: Same as the base creature. Vapor creatures have a +8 racial bonus on Stealth checks in areas of smoke, fog, mist, or vapor.

Environment: Same as the base creature.

Organization: Same as the base creature. Vapor creatures are frequently encountered singly, due to their frosty personalities and preference for inhospitable lair locations. A vapor creature may also be found leading a group of its base creature.

Treasure: Same as base creature.

Fomor-Kin (Vapor-Ogre)

Stomping out of the mist is a warty, blue-skinned ogre with shaggy white hair.

FOMOR-KIN (VAPOR OGRE)	CR 4

XP 1,200
CE Large humanoid (giant)
Init –1; **Senses** darkvision 60 ft., low-light vision; **Perception** +7

AC 17, touch 8, flat-footed 17 (+4 armor, –1 Dex, +5 natural, –1 size)
hp 30 (4d8+8 plus 4); fast healing 2 (mist or fog)
Fort +6; **Ref** +0; **Will** +3
Resist fire 5
Weakness cold susceptibility

Speed 30 ft. (40 ft. base)
Melee greatclub +7 (2d8+7)

277

Ranged javelin +1 (1d8+5)
Space 10 ft.; **Reach** 10 ft.
Special Attacks death throes (DC 14)

Str 21, **Dex** 8, **Con** 15, **Int** 10, **Wis** 10, **Cha** 8
Base Atk +3; **CMB** +9; **CMD** 18
Feats Iron Will, Toughness
Skills Climb +10, Intimidate +4, Perception +7, Stealth –5 (+3 in fog or mist); **Racial Modifiers** +8 Stealth in areas of fog or mist
Languages Giant
SQ vaporous form

Environment temperate hills
Organization solitary, pair, gang (3–4), or family (5–16)
Treasure standard (hide armor, greatclub, 4 javelins, other treasure)

The fomor-kin are oversized humanoid marauders of windswept moors and boggy highlands. Their reign over extensive and inhospitable terrain is often uncontested by other creatures due to the limited visibility. They raid for food along the edges of the moors, striking out at humanoid settlements and disappearing back into the drifting mist and rain. Fomor-kin can be sighted loping along through the fog with a long, uneven gait, providing ample bed-time story material for willful children.

Winged Creature

A winged creature is one that is nearly identical to its land-bound counterpart but which possesses wings capable of flight. The type of wings that a winged creature has is generally based on its alignment, the usual being that good creatures have feathered wings, neutral creatures have insect-like wings, and evil creatures have bat-like wings. This is not a strict rule, however, especially as regards insect wings; some can be like those of a butterfly, others like those of a dragonfly.

Winged creatures bear a strong resemblance to other creatures and are often mistaken as such. A winged horse is likely to be called a pegasus, although it possesses none of the magical abilities or intelligence of a pegasus. Winged elves or humans might be mistaken for celestials.

Creating a Winged Creature

"Winged" is an inherited template that can be added to any corporeal creature that is not an elemental or an ooze and that does not already have a fly speed (referred to hereafter as the "base creature"). It uses all the special abilities and ability scores of the base creature, except as noted here.

Challenge Rating: Same as base creature +1
Type: An animal with this template changes to a magical beast. Do not recalculate Hit Dice, BAB, saves, or skill ranks. An animal that changes to a magical beast gains the augmented subtype.
Armor Class: Flying creatures are more lightly-built than their normal counterparts. Decrease the base creature's natural armor bonus (if any) by 2.
Speed: A winged creature gains a fly speed equal to its land speed + 10 feet per size category larger or smaller than Medium. A winged creature's maneuverability is based on its Dexterity and size.

DEXTERITY SCORE	MANEUVERABILITY
5 or lower	clumsy
6–8	poor
9–12	average
13–16	good
17 or higher	perfect

Modify the winged creature's maneuverability based on its size. Use the table below. Adjusting by "+1 step" moves the winged creature's maneuverability one step up the chart (average to good, for example). Adjusting by "–1 step" moves the creature's maneuverability one step down the chart (average to poor, for example).

SIZE	MANEUVERABILITY
Tiny or smaller	+2 steps
Small	+1 step
Medium	+0
Large/Huge	–1 step
Gargantuan	–2 steps
Colossal	–4 steps

Attacks: Creatures of Large size or larger gain a wing attack as a secondary attack. Use the table below to determine the damage of that attack.

SIZE	DAMAGE
Large	1d4
Huge	1d6
Gargantuan	1d8
Colossal	2d6

Abilities: +2 Dexterity, –2 Strength. Winged creatures have lighter, more nimble frames, and most of their body strength is in their wings rather than sheer physical power.
Feats: A winged creature gains Weapon Finesse as a bonus feat.
Skills: Fly is always a class skill for a winged creature. It can reassign some of its skill ranks to the Fly skill when this template is applied.

Winged Ape

A large pair of brown feathered wings grows from this great ape's back.

WINGED APE	CR 3

XP 800
N Large magical beast (augmented animal)
Init +3; **Senses** low-light vision, scent; **Perception** +8

AC 13, touch 12, flat-footed 10 (+3 Dex, +1 natural, –1 size)
hp 19 (3d8+6)
Fort +7; **Ref** +6; **Will** +2

Speed 30 ft., climb 30 ft., fly 40 ft. (good)
Melee 2 slams +4 (1d6+1), wings –1 (1d4)
Space 10 ft.; **Reach** 10 ft.

Str 13, **Dex** 17, **Con** 14, **Int** 2, **Wis** 12, **Cha** 7
Base Atk +2; **CMB** +4; **CMD** 17
Feats Great Fortitude, Skill Focus (Perception), Weapon Finesse[B]
Skills Acrobatics +7, Climb +13, Fly +5, Perception +8

Environment warm forests

Organization solitary, pair, or wing (3–12)
Treasure none

Winged Ogre

Large, bat-like wings flap on this lean ogre's back, carrying it through the air with surprising speed.

WINGED OGRE	CR 4

XP 1,200
CE Large humanoid (giant)
Init +0; **Senses** darkvision 60 ft., low-light vision; **Perception** +4

AC 15, touch 9, flat-footed 15
(+4 armor, +2 natural, −1 size)
hp 30 (4d8+8 plus 4)
Fort +6; **Ref** +1; **Will** +3

Speed 30 ft. (40 ft. base), fly 40 ft.
(50 ft. base) (poor)
Melee greatclub +6 (2d8+6), wings +1
(1d4+2)
Ranged javelin +2 (1d8+4)
Space 10 ft.; **Reach** 10 ft.

Str 19, **Dex** 10, **Con** 15, **Int** 6, **Wis** 10, **Cha** 7
Base Atk +3; **CMB** +8; **CMD** 18
Feats Iron Will, Toughness, Weapon Finesse[B]
Skills Climb +5, Fly −4, Perception +4
Languages Giant

Environment temperate or cold hills
Organization solitary, pair, wing (3–4), or family (5–16)
Treasure standard (hide armor, greatclub, 4 javelins, other treasure)

Zombie, Hungry

Hungry zombies are variants of standard zombies as found in the *Pathfinder Roleplaying Game Bestiary*.

In most respects hungry zombies appear to be otherwise normal zombies, however they have a spark of savage intelligence. Adventurers who mistake hungry zombies for normal zombies are in for a horrifying surprise: the hungry zombies are undead creatures that crave the flesh of the living. They rise from the grave and hunt day and night, ever seeking victims to satiate their eternal hunger. Hungry zombies do not eat other undead, only freshly-slain corpses.

Creating a Hungry Zombie

Hungry zombies have all the qualities and abilities of a standard zombie except as noted here.

Challenge Rating: Increase the zombie's CR by +1.

Defensive Abilities: A hungry zombie does not gain DR 5/slashing. Instead it gains DR 10/— (if HD 3 or less) or DR 20/— (if HD 4 or more).

Weaknesses: The hungry zombie gains the following weakness.

Head Shot (Ex) Any attack that targets a hungry zombie's head bypasses its damage reduction entirely. See the sidebar for rules on called shots.

Attacks: A hungry zombie gains a bite attack that deals damage based on the zombie's size if it didn't already have one.

ZOMBIE SIZE	BITE
Fine	1
Diminutive	1d2
Tiny	1d3
Small	1d4
Medium	1d6
Large	1d8
Huge	2d6
Gargantuan	2d8
Colossal	4d6

Special Attacks: A hungry zombie gains the grab special attack with its slam attack. It also gains the following special attack.

Grab and Bite (Ex): A hungry zombie that succeeds on a grapple check automatically bites its opponent as an immediate action in the round it establishes the grapple.

Ability Scores: As a standard zombie, except its Strength is increased by +2.

Hungry Human Zombie

This rotting humanoid is dressed in tattered and ragged clothing. It shambles forward with an uneven gait.

HUMAN ZOMBIE	CR 1

XP 200
NE Medium undead
Init +0; **Senses** darkvision 60 ft.; **Perception** +0

AC 12, touch 10, flat-footed 12 (+2 natural)
hp 12 (2d8+3)
Fort +0; **Ref** +0; **Will** +3
DR 10/—; **Immune** undead traits
Weaknesses head shot

Speed 30 ft.

Melee slam +5 (1d6+6 plus grab)
Special Attacks grab and bite

Str 19, **Dex** 10, **Con** —, **Int** —, **Wis** 10, **Cha** 10
Base Atk +1; **CMB** +5 (+9 grapple); **CMD** 15
Feats Toughness[B]
SQ staggered

Environment any
Organization any
Treasure none

Zombies are the animated corpses of dead creatures, forced into foul unlife via necromantic magic like *animate dead*. While the most commonly encountered zombies are slow and tough, others possess a variety of traits, allowing them to spread disease or move with increased speed.

Zombies are unthinking automatons, and can do little more than follow orders. When left unattended, zombies tend to mill about in search of living creatures to slaughter and devour. Zombies attack until destroyed, having no regard for their own safety.

Making Called Shots

A called shot is an attack aimed at a particular part of the body, in the hope of gaining some extra effect from the attack. The smaller or better guarded the area, the more difficult the called shot. A called shot is a single attack made as a full-round action, and thus can't be combined with a charge, feats like Vital Strike, or multiple attacks with a full-attack action. A called shot to the head is a tricky shot and takes a –5 penalty on the attack roll.

Range and Reach: Called shots work best at close range. Melee called shots are at a –2 penalty if the target isn't adjacent to its attacker. For called shots made at range, all range penalties due to range increment are doubled, with a minimum penalty of –2 for any called shot against a target that's not within 30 feet.

Critical Hits and Critical Threats: A called shot has the normal chance for a critical hit, and inflicts an extra effect if one is confirmed. A critical hit to the head deals 1d6 points of Intelligence, Wisdom, or Charisma damage (randomly determine which).

Appendix B: Universal Monster Rules

The following rules are standard and are referenced (but not repeated) in monster stat blocks. Each rule includes a format guide for how it appears in a monster's listing and its location in the stat block.

Ability Damage and Drain (Ex or Su) Some attacks or special abilities cause ability damage or drain, reducing the designated ability score by the listed amount. Ability damage can be healed naturally. Ability drain is permanent and can only be restored through magic. *Format*: 1d4 Str drain; *Location*: Special Attacks or individual attacks.

All-Around Vision (Ex) The creature sees in all directions at once. It cannot be flanked. *Format*: all-around vision; *Location*: Defensive Abilities.

Amorphous (Ex) The creature's body is malleable and shapeless. It is immune to precision damage (like sneak attacks) and critical hits. *Format*: amorphous; *Location*: Defensive Abilities.

Amphibious (Ex) Creatures with this special quality have the aquatic subtype, but they can survive indefinitely on land. *Format*: amphibious; *Location*: SQ.

Attach (Ex) The creature automatically latches onto its target when it successfully makes the listed attack. The creature is considered grappling, but the target is not. The target can attack or grapple the creature as normal, or break the attach with a successful grapple or Escape Artist check. Most creatures with this ability have a racial bonus to maintain a grapple (listed in its CMB entry). *Format*: attach; *Location*: individual attacks.

Bleed (Ex) A creature with this ability causes wounds that continue to bleed, dealing the listed damage each round at the start of the affected creature's turn. This bleeding can be stopped by a successful DC 15 Heal skill check or through the application of any magical healing. The amount of damage each round is determined in the creature's entry. *Format*: bleed (2d6); *Location*: Special Attacks and individual attacks.

Blindsense (Ex) Using nonvisual senses, such as acute smell or hearing, a creature with blindsense notices things it cannot see. The creature usually does not need to make Perception checks to pinpoint the location of a creature within range of its blindsense ability, provided that it has line of effect to that creature. Any opponent the creature cannot see still has total concealment from the creature with blindsense, and the creature still has the normal miss chance when attacking foes that have concealment. Visibility still affects the movement of a creature with blindsense. A creature with blindsense is still denied its Dexterity bonus to Armor Class against attacks from creatures it cannot see. *Format*: blindsense 60 ft.; *Location*: Senses.

Blindsight (Ex) This ability is similar to blindsense, but is far more discerning. Using nonvisual senses, such as sensitivity to vibrations, keen smell, acute hearing, or echolocation, a creature with blindsight maneuvers and fights as well as a sighted creature. Invisibility, darkness, and most kinds of concealment are irrelevant, though the creature must have line of effect to a creature or object to discern that creature or object. The ability's range is specified in the creature's descriptive text. The creature usually does not need to make Perception checks to notice creatures within this range. Unless noted otherwise, blindsight is continuous, and the creature need do nothing to use it. Some forms of blindsight, however, must be triggered as a free action. If so, this is noted in the creature's description. If a creature must trigger its blindsight ability, the creature gains the benefits of blindsight only during its turn. *Format*: blindsight 60 ft.; *Location*: Senses.

Blood Drain (Ex) The creature drains blood at the end of its turn if it grapples a foe, inflicting Constitution damage. *Format*: blood drain (1d2 Constitution); *Location*: Special Attacks.

Breath Weapon (Su) Some creatures can exhale a cone, line, or cloud of energy or other magical effects. A breath weapon attack usually deals damage and is often based on some type of energy. Breath weapons allow a Reflex save for half damage (DC 10 + 1/2 the breathing creature's racial HD + the breathing creature's Con modifier; the exact DC is given in the creature's descriptive text). A creature is immune to its own breath weapon unless otherwise noted. Some breath weapons allow a Fortitude save or a Will save instead of a Reflex save. Each breath weapon also includes notes on how often it can be used, even if this number is limited in times per day. *Format*: breath weapon (60-ft. cone, 8d6 fire damage, Reflex DC 20 for half, usable every 1d4 rounds); *Location*: Special Attacks; if the breath is more complicated than damage, it also appears under Special Abilities with its own entry.

Burn (Ex) A creature with the burn special attack deals fire damage in addition to damage dealt on a successful hit in melee. A creature affected by the burn ability must also succeed at a Reflex save or catch fire, taking the listed damage at the start of its turn for an additional 1d4 rounds (DC 10 + 1/2 the attacking creature's racial HD + the attacking creature's Con modifier). A burning creature can attempt a new save as a full-round action. Dropping and rolling on the ground grants a +4 bonus on this save. Creatures that hit the monster with natural weapons or unarmed attacks take fire damage as though hit by the monster's burn attack and must make a Reflex save to avoid catching on fire (see page 444 of the Pathfinder RPG Core Rulebook). *Format*: burn (2d6, DC 15); *Location*: Special Attacks and individual attacks.

Capsize (Ex) A creature with this special quality can attempt to capsize a boat or a ship by ramming it as a charge attack and making a combat maneuver check. The DC of this check is 25, or the result of the captain's Profession (sailor) check, whichever is higher. For each size category the ship is larger than the creature attempting to capsize it, the creature attempting to capsize the ship takes a cumulative –10 penalty on its combat maneuver check. *Format*: capsize; *Location*: special attacks.

Change Shape (Su) A creature with this special quality has the ability to assume the appearance of a specific creature or type of creature (usually a humanoid), but retains most of its own physical qualities. The creature cannot change shape to a form more than one size category smaller or larger than its original form. This ability functions as a polymorph spell, the type of which is listed in the creature's description, but the creature does not adjust its ability scores (although it gains any other abilities of the creature it mimics). Unless otherwise stated, it can remain in an alternate form indefinitely. Some creatures, such as lycanthropes, can transform into unique forms with special modifiers and abilities. These creatures do adjust their ability scores, as noted in their descriptions. *Format*: change shape (wolf; beast form I); *Location*: SQ, and in Special Abilities for creatures with a unique listing.

Channel Resistance (Ex) A creature with this special quality (usually an undead) is less easily affected by channeled negative or positive energy. The creature adds the listed bonus on saves made to resist the effects of channel energy, including effects that rely on the use of channel energy (such as the Command Undead feat). *Format*: channel resistance +4; *Location*: Defensive Abilities.

Compression (Ex) The creature can move through an area as small as one-quarter its space without squeezing or one-eighth its space when squeezing. *Format*: compression; *Location*: SQ.

Constrict (Ex) A creature with this special attack can crush an opponent, dealing bludgeoning damage, when it makes a successful grapple check (in addition to any other effects caused by a successful check, including additional damage). The amount of damage is given in the creature's entry and is typically equal to the amount of damage caused by the creature's melee attack. *Format*: constrict (1d8+6); *Location*: Special Attacks.

Appendix B: Universal Monster Rules

Construct Traits (Ex) Constructs are immune to death effects, disease, mind-affecting effects (charms, compulsions, phantasms, patterns, and morale effects), necromancy effects, paralysis, poison, sleep, stun, and any effect that requires a Fortitude save (unless the effect also works on objects, or is harmless). Constructs are not subject to nonlethal damage, ability damage, ability drain, fatigue, exhaustion, or energy drain. Constructs are not at risk of death from massive damage. *Format:* construct traits; *Location:* Immune.

Curse (Su) A creature with this ability bestows a curse upon its enemies. The effects of the curse, including its save, frequency, and cure, are included in the creature's description. If a curse allows a saving throw, it is usually a Will save (DC 10 + 1/2 the cursing creature's racial HD + the creature's Cha modifier; the exact DC is given in the creature's descriptive text). Curses can be removed through remove curse and similar effects. *Format:* Curse Name (Su) Slam—contact; *save* DC 14 Will, *frequency* 1 day, *effect* 1d4 Str drain; *Location:* Special Attacks and individual attacks.

Damage Reduction (Ex or Su) A creature with this special quality ignores damage from most weapons and natural attacks. Wounds heal immediately, or the weapon bounces off harmlessly (in either case, the opponent knows the attack was ineffective). The creature takes normal damage from energy attacks (even nonmagical ones), spells, spell-like abilities, and supernatural abilities. A certain kind of weapon can sometimes damage the creature normally, as noted below.

The entry indicates the amount of damage ignored (usually 5 to 15 points) and the type of weapon that negates the ability.

Some monsters are vulnerable to piercing, bludgeoning, or slashing damage. Others are vulnerable to certain materials, such as adamantine, alchemical silver, or cold-forged iron. Attacks from weapons that are not of the correct type or made of the correct material have their damage reduced, although a high enhancement bonus can overcome some forms of damage reduction.

Some monsters are vulnerable to magic weapons. Any weapon with at least a +1 magical enhancement bonus on attack and damage rolls overcomes the damage reduction of these monsters. Such creatures' natural weapons (but not their attacks with weapons) are treated as magic weapons for the purpose of overcoming damage reduction.

A few very powerful monsters are vulnerable only to epic weapons—that is, magic weapons with at least a +6 enhancement bonus. Such creatures' natural weapons are also treated as epic weapons for the purpose of overcoming damage reduction.

Some monsters are vulnerable to good-, evil-, chaotic-, or lawful-aligned weapons, such as from an align weapon spell or the holy magical weapon property. A creature with an alignment subtype (chaotic, evil, good, or lawful) can overcome this type of damage reduction with its natural weapons and weapons it wields as if the weapons or natural weapons had an alignment (or alignments) that matched the subtype(s) of the creature.

When a damage reduction entry has a dash (—) after the slash, no weapon negates the damage reduction.

A few creatures are harmed by more than one kind of weapon, such as "cold iron or magic." A weapon that deals damage of either of these types overcomes this damage reduction.

A few other creatures require combinations of different types of attacks to overcome their damage reduction (such as "magic and silver"), and a weapon must be both types to overcome this type of damage reduction. A weapon that is only one type is still subject to damage reduction. *Format:* DR 5/silver; *Location:* Defensive Abilities.

Disease (Ex or Su) A creature with this ability causes disease in those it contacts. The effects of the disease, including its save, frequency, and cure, are included in the creature's description. The saving throw to negate the disease is usually a Fort save (DC 10 + 1/2 the infecting creature's racial HD + the creature's Con modifier; the exact DC is given in the creature's descriptive text). Disease can be removed through remove disease and similar effects. *Format:* Disease Name (Ex) Bite—injury; *save* DC 15 Fort, onset 1d3 days, frequency 1 day, effect 1 Con damage, cure 2 consecutive saves; *Location:* Special Attacks and individual attacks.

Distraction (Ex) A creature with this ability can nauseate the creatures that it damages. Any living creature that takes damage from a creature with the distraction ability is nauseated for 1 round; a Fortitude save (DC 10 + the 1/2 creature's HD + the creature's Con modifier) negates the effect. *Format:* distraction (DC 14); *Location:* Special Attacks.

Earth Glide (Ex) When the creature burrows, it can pass through stone, dirt, or almost any other sort of earth except metal as easily as a fish swims through water. If protected against fire damage, it can even glide through lava. Its burrowing leaves behind no tunnel or hole, nor does it create any ripple or other sign of its presence. A move earth spell cast on an area containing the burrowing creature flings it back 30 feet, stunning it for 1 round unless it succeeds at a DC 15 Fortitude save. *Format:* earth glide; *Location:* Speed.

Energy Drain (Su) This attack saps a living opponent's vital energy and happens automatically when a melee or ranged attack hits. Each successful energy drain bestows one or more negative levels (the creature's description specifies how many). If an attack that includes an energy drain scores a critical hit, it bestows twice the listed number of negative levels. Unless otherwise specified in the creature's description, a draining creature gains 5 temporary hit points for each negative level it bestows on an opponent. These temporary hit points last for a maximum of 1 hour. Negative levels remain until 24 hours have passed or until they are removed with a spell such as restoration. If a negative level is not removed before 24 hours have passed, the affected creature must attempt a Fortitude save (DC 10 + 1/2 the draining creature's racial HD + the draining creature's Cha modifier; the exact DC is given in the creature's descriptive text). On a success, the negative level goes away with no harm to the creature. On a failure, the negative level becomes permanent. A separate saving throw is required for each negative level. *Format:* energy drain (2 levels, DC 18); *Location:* Special Attacks and individual attacks.

Engulf (Ex) The creature can engulf creatures in its path as part of a standard action. It cannot make other attacks during a round in which it engulfs. The creature merely has to move over its opponents, affecting as many as it can cover. Targeted creatures can make attacks of opportunity against the creature, but if they do so, they are not entitled to a saving throw against the engulf attack. Those who do not attempt attacks of opportunity can attempt a Reflex save to avoid being engulfed—on a success, they are pushed back or aside (target's choice) as the creature moves forward. Engulfed opponents gain the pinned condition, are in danger of suffocating, are trapped within the creature's body until they are no longer pinned, and may be subject to other special attacks from the creature. The save DC is Strength-based. *Format:* engulf (DC 12, 1d6 acid and paralysis); *Location:* Special Attacks.

Entrap (Ex or Su) The creature has an ability that restricts another creature's movement, usually with a physical attack such as ice, mud, lava, or webs. The target of an entrap attack must make a Fortitude save or become entangled for the listed duration. If a target is already entangled by this ability, a second entrap attack means the target must make a Fortitude save or become helpless for the listed duration. The save DCs are Constitution-based. A target made helpless by this ability is conscious but can take no physical actions (except attempting to break free) until the entrapping material is removed. The target can use spells with only verbal components or spell-like abilities if it can make a DC 20 concentration check. An entangled creature can make a Strength check (at the same DC as the entrap saving throw DC) as a full-round action to break free; the DC for a helpless creature is +5 greater than the saving throw DC. Destroying the entrapping material frees the creature. *Format:* entrap (DC 13, 1d10 minutes, hardness 5, hp 10); *Location:* special attacks and individual attacks.

Fast Healing (Ex) A creature with fast healing regains hit points at an exceptional rate, usually 1 or more hit points per round, as given in the creature's entry. Except where noted here, fast healing is just like natural healing. Fast healing does not restore hit points lost from starvation, thirst, or suffocation, nor does it allow a creature to regrow lost body parts. Unless otherwise stated, it does not allow lost body parts to be reattached. Fast healing continues to function (even at negative hit points) until a creature dies, at which point the effects of fast healing end immediately. *Format:* fast healing 5; *Location:* hp.

Fast Swallow (Ex) The creature can use its swallow whole ability as a free action at any time during its turn, not just at the start of its turn. *Format*: fast swallow; *Location*: Special Attacks.

Fear (Su or Sp) Fear attacks can have various effects.

Fear Aura (Su) The use of this ability is a free action. The aura can freeze an opponent (as in the case of a mummy's despair) or function like the fear spell. Other effects are possible. A fear aura is an area effect. The descriptive text gives the size and kind of the area.

Fear Cone (Sp) and Ray (Su) These effects usually work like the fear spell. If a fear effect allows a saving throw, it is a Will save (DC 10 + 1/2 the fearsome creature's racial HD + the creature's Cha modifier; the exact DC is given in the creature's descriptive text). All fear attacks are mind-affecting fear effects.

Format: fear aura (30 ft., DC 17); *Location*: Aura.
Format: fear cone (50 ft., DC 19); *Location*: Special Attacks.

Ferocity (Ex) A creature with ferocity remains conscious and can continue fighting even if its hit point total is below 0. The creature is still staggered and loses 1 hit point each round. The creature still dies when its hit point total reaches a negative amount equal to its Constitution score. *Format*: ferocity; *Location*: Defensive Abilities.

Flight (Ex, Sp, or Su) A creature with this ability can cease or resume flight as a free action. If the creature has wings, flight is an extraordinary ability. Otherwise, it is spell-like or supernatural, and it is ineffective in an antimagic field; the creature loses its ability to fly for as long as the antimagic effect persists. *Format*: fly 30 ft. (average); *Location*: Speed.

Freeze (Ex) The creature can hold itself so still it appears to be an inanimate object of the appropriate shape (a statue, patch of fungus, and so on). The creature can take 20 on its Stealth check to hide in plain sight as this kind of inanimate object. *Format*: freeze; *Location*: SQ.

Frightful Presence (Ex) This special quality makes a creature's very presence unsettling to foes. Activating this ability is a free action that is usually part of an attack or charge. Opponents within range who witness the action may become frightened or shaken. The range is usually 30 feet, and the duration is usually 5d6 rounds. This ability affects only opponents with fewer Hit Dice than the creature has. An opponent can resist the effects with a successful Will save (DC 10 + 1/2 the frightful creature's racial HD + the frightful creature's Cha modifier; the exact DC is given in the creature's descriptive text). On a failed save, the opponent is shaken, or panicked if it has 4 Hit Dice or fewer. An opponent that succeeds at the saving throw is immune to that same creature's frightful presence for 24 hours. Frightful presence is a mind-affecting fear effect. *Format*: frightful presence (60 ft., DC 21); *Location*: Aura.

Gaze (Su) A gaze attack takes effect when foes look at the attacking creature's eyes. The attack can have any sort of effect; petrification, death, and charm are common. The typical range is 30 feet. The type of saving throw for a gaze attack is usually a Will or Fortitude save (DC 10 + the 1/2 gazing creature's racial HD + the gazing creature's Cha modifier; the exact DC is given in the creature's text). A successful saving throw negates the effect. A monster's gaze attack is described in abbreviated form in its description. Each opponent within range of a gaze attack must attempt a saving throw each round at the beginning of his or her turn in the initiative order. Opponents can avoid the need to make the saving throw by not looking at the creature, in one of two ways.

Averting Eyes: The opponent avoids looking at the creature's face, instead looking at its body, watching its shadow, tracking it in a reflective surface, etc. Each round, the opponent has a 50% chance to avoid having to make a saving throw against the gaze attack. The creature with the gaze attack, however, gains concealment from that opponent.

Wearing a Blindfold: The foe cannot see the creature at all (also possible to achieve by turning one's back on the creature or shutting one's eyes) and does not have to make saving throws against the gaze. However, the creature with the gaze attack gains total concealment from the opponent.

A creature with a gaze attack can actively gaze as an attack action by choosing a target within range. That opponent must attempt a saving throw but can try to avoid this as described above. Thus, it is possible for an opponent to save against a creature's gaze twice during the same round, once before the opponent's action and once during the creature's turn.

Gaze attacks can affect ethereal opponents. A creature is immune to the gaze attacks of others of its kind unless otherwise noted. Allies of a creature with a gaze attack might be affected; these allies are considered to be averting their eyes from the creature with the gaze attack, and have a 50% chance to not need to make a saving throw against the gaze attack each round. The creature can also veil its eyes, thus negating its gaze ability.

Format: gaze; *Location*: Special Attacks.

Grab (Ex) If a creature with this special attack hits with the indicated attack (usually a claw or bite attack), it deals normal damage and attempts to start a grapple as a free action without provoking an attack of opportunity. The creature has the option to conduct the grapple normally, or simply to use the part of its body it used in the grab to hold the opponent. If it chooses to do the latter, it takes a –20 penalty on its combat maneuver check to make and maintain the grapple, but does not gain the grappled condition itself. A successful hold does not deal any extra damage unless the creature also has the constrict special attack. If the creature does not constrict, each successful grapple check it makes during successive rounds automatically deals the damage indicated for the attack that established the hold. Otherwise, it deals constriction damage as well (the amount is given in the creature's descriptive text).

Creatures with grab receive a +4 bonus on combat maneuver checks made to start and maintain a grapple.

Unless otherwise noted, grab works only against opponents no larger than the same size category as the creature. If the creature can use grab on sizes other than the default, this is noted in the creature's Special Attacks line.

Format: grab; *Location*: individual attacks.
Format: grab (Colossal); *Location*: Special Attacks.

Heat (Ex) The creature generates so much heat that its mere touch deals additional fire damage. The creature's metallic melee weapons also conduct this heat. *Format*: heat (1d6 fire); *Location*: Special Attacks.

Hold Breath (Ex) The creature can hold its breath for a number of minutes equal to 6 times its Constitution score before it risks drowning. *Format*: hold breath; *Location*: SQ.

Immunity (Ex or Su) A creature with immunities takes no damage from listed sources. Immunities can also apply to afflictions, conditions, spells (based on school, level, or save type), and other effects. A creature that is immune does not suffer from these effects, or any secondary effects that are triggered due to an immune effect. *Format*: Immune acid, fire, paralysis; *Location*: Defensive Abilities.

Incorporeal (Ex) An incorporeal creature has no physical body. It can be harmed only by other incorporeal creatures, magic weapons or creatures that strike as magic weapons, and spells, spell-like abilities, or supernatural abilities. It is immune to all nonmagical attack forms. Even when hit by spells or magic weapons, it takes only half damage from a corporeal source. Although it is not a magical attack, holy water affects incorporeal undead. Corporeal spells and effects that do not cause damage only have a 50% chance of affecting an incorporeal creature (except for channel energy). Force spells and effects, such as from a magic missile, affect an incorporeal creature normally.

An incorporeal creature has no natural armor bonus but has a deflection bonus equal to its Charisma bonus (minimum +1, even if the creature's Charisma score does not normally provide a bonus).

An incorporeal creature can enter or pass through solid objects, but must remain adjacent to the object's exterior, and so cannot pass entirely through an object whose space is larger than its own. It can sense the presence of creatures or objects within a square adjacent to its current location, but enemies have total concealment (50% miss chance) from an incorporeal creature that is inside an object. In order to see beyond the object it is in and attack normally, the incorporeal creature must emerge. An incorporeal creature inside an object has total cover, but when it attacks a creature outside the object it only has cover, so a creature outside with a readied action could strike at it as it attacks. An incorporeal creature cannot pass through a force effect.

An incorporeal creature's attacks pass through (ignore) natural armor, armor, and shields, although deflection bonuses and force effects (such as mage armor) work normally against it. Incorporeal creatures pass through and operate in water as easily as they do in air. Incorporeal creatures cannot fall or take falling damage. Incorporeal creatures cannot make trip or grapple attacks, nor can they be tripped or grappled. In fact, they cannot take any physical action that would move or manipulate an opponent or its equipment, nor are they subject to such actions. Incorporeal creatures have no weight and do not set off traps that are triggered by weight.

An incorporeal creature moves silently and cannot be heard with Perception checks if it doesn't wish to be. It has no Strength score, so its Dexterity modifier applies to its melee attacks, ranged attacks, and CMB. Nonvisual senses, such as scent and blindsight, are either ineffective or only partly effective with regard to incorporeal creatures. Incorporeal creatures have an innate sense of direction and can move at full speed even when they cannot see. *Format*: incorporeal; *Location*: Defensive Abilities.

Jet (Ex) The creature can swim backward as a full-round action at the listed speed. It must move in a straight line while jetting, and does not provoke attacks of opportunity when it does so. *Format*: jet (200 ft.); *Location*: Speed.

Keen Scent (Ex) The creature can notice other creatures by scent in a 180-foot radius underwater and can detect blood in the water at ranges of up to a mile. *Format*: keen senses; *Location*: Senses.

Lifesense (Su) The creature notices and locates living creatures within 60 feet, just as if it possessed the blindsight ability. *Format*: lifesense; *Location*: Senses.

Light Blindness (Ex) Creatures with light blindness are blinded for 1 round if exposed to bright light, such as sunlight or the daylight spell. Such creatures are dazzled as long as they remain in areas of bright light. *Format*: light blindness; *Location*: Weaknesses.

Light Sensitivity (Ex) Creatures with light sensitivity are dazzled in areas of bright sunlight or within the radius of a daylight spell. *Format*: Weaknesses light sensitivity; *Location*: Weaknesses.

Multiweapon Mastery (Ex) The creature never takes penalties on its attack rolls when fighting with multiple weapons. *Format*: multiweapon mastery; *Location*: Special Attacks.

Natural Attacks Most creatures possess one or more natural attacks (attacks made without a weapon). These attacks fall into one of two categories: primary or secondary attacks. Primary attacks are made using the creature's full base attack bonus and add the creature's full Strength bonus on damage rolls. Secondary attacks are made using the creature's base attack bonus –5 and add only 1/2 the creature's Strength bonus on damage rolls. If a creature has only one natural attack, it is always made using the creature's full base attack bonus and adds 1-1/2 times the creature's Strength bonus on damage rolls. This increase does not apply if the creature has multiple attacks but only takes one. If a creature has only one type of attack, but has multiple attacks per round, that attack is treated as a primary attack, regardless of its type.

Some creatures treat one or more of their attacks differently, such as dragons, which always receive 1-1/2 times their Strength bonus on damage rolls with their bite attack. These exceptions are noted in the creature's description.

Creatures with natural attacks and attacks made with weapons can use both as part of a full-attack action (although often a creature must forgo one natural attack for each weapon clutched in that limb, be it a claw, tentacle, or slam). Such creatures attack with their weapons normally but treat all of their available natural attacks as secondary attacks during that attack, regardless of the attack's original type.

Some creatures do not have natural attacks. These creatures can make unarmed strikes just like humans do. *Format*: bite +5 (1d6+1), 2 claws +5 (1d4+2), 4 tentacles +0 (1d4+1); *Location*: Melee and Ranged.

Negative Energy Affinity (Ex) The creature is alive, but is treated as undead for all effects that affect undead differently than living creatures, such as cure spells and channeled energy. *Format:* negative energy affinity; *Location:* Defensive Abilities.

No Breath (Ex) The monster does not breathe, and is immune to effects that require breathing (such as inhaled poison). This does not give immunity to cloud or gas attacks that do not require breathing. *Format*: no breath; *Location*: SQ.

Paralysis (Ex or Su) This special attack renders the victim immobile. Paralyzed creatures cannot move, speak, or take any physical actions. The creature is rooted to the spot, frozen and helpless. Paralysis works on the body, and a character can usually resist it with a Fortitude saving throw (DC 10 + 1/2 the paralyzing creature's racial HD + the paralyzing creature's Con modifier; the DC is given in the creature's description). Unlike hold person and similar effects, a paralysis effect does not allow a new save each round. A winged creature flying in the air at the time that it is paralyzed cannot flap its wings and falls. A swimmer can't swim and may drown. The duration of the paralysis varies and is included in the creature's description. *Format*: paralysis (1d4 rounds, DC 18); *Location*: Special Attacks and individual attacks.

Plant Traits (Ex) Plants are immune to all mind-affecting effects (charms, compulsions, morale effects, patterns, and phantasms), paralysis, poison, polymorph, sleep, and stun. *Format*: plant traits; *Location*: Immune.

Poison (Ex or Su) A creature with this ability can poison those it attacks. The effects of the poison, including its save, frequency, and cure, are included in the creature's description. The saving throw to resist a poison is usually a Fort save (DC 10 + 1/2 the poisoning creature's racial HD + the creature's Con modifier; the exact DC is given in the creature's descriptive text). Poisons can be removed through neutralize poison and similar effects. *Format*: Poison Name (Ex) Sting—injury; *save* DC 22 Fort, *frequency* 1/round for 6 rounds, *effect* 1d4 Con, *cure* 2 consecutive saves; *Location*: Special Attacks and individual attacks.

Pounce (Ex) When a creature with this special attack makes a charge, it can make a full attack (including rake attacks if the creature also has the rake ability). *Format*: pounce; *Location*: Special Attacks.

Powerful Charge (Ex) When a creature with this special attack makes a charge, its attack deals extra damage in addition to the normal benefits and hazards of a charge. The attack and amount of damage from the attack is given in the creature's description. *Format*: powerful charge (gore, 4d8+24); *Location*: Special Attacks.

Pull (Ex) A creature with this ability can choose to make a free combat maneuver check with a successful attack. If successful, this check pulls an opponent closer. The distance pulled is set by this ability. The type of attack that causes the pull and the distance pulled are included in the creature's description. This ability only works on creatures of a size equal to or smaller than the pulling creature. Creatures pulled in this way do not provoke attacks of opportunity and stop if the pull would move them into a solid object or creature. *Format*: pull (tentacle, 5 ft.); *Location*: Special Attacks and individual attacks.

Push (Ex) A creature with the push ability can choose to make a free combat maneuver check with a particular successful attack (often a slam attack). If successful, this check pushes an opponent directly away as with a bull rush, but the distance moved is set by this ability. The type of attack that causes the push and the distance pushed are included in the creature's description. This ability only works on creatures of a size equal to or smaller than the pushing creature. Creatures pushed in this way do not provoke attacks of opportunity and stop if the push would move them into a solid object or creature. *Format*: push (slam, 10 ft.); *Location*: Special Attacks and individual attacks.

Rake (Ex) A creature with this special attack gains extra natural attacks under certain conditions, typically when it grapples its foe. In addition to the options available to all grapplers, a monster with the rake ability gains two free claw attacks that it can use only against a grappled foe. The bonus and damage caused by these attacks is included in the creature's description. A monster with the rake ability must begin its turn already grappling to use its rake—it can't begin a grapple and rake in the same turn. *Format*: rake (2 claws +8, 1d4+2); *Location*: Special Attacks.

Regeneration (Ex) A creature with this ability is difficult to kill. Creatures with regeneration heal damage at a fixed rate, as with fast healing, but they cannot die as long as their regeneration is still functioning (although creatures with regeneration still fall unconscious when their hit points are below 0). Certain attack forms, typically fire and acid, cause a creature's regeneration to stop functioning on the round following the attack. During this round, the creature does not heal any damage and can die normally. The creature's descriptive text describes the types of damage that cause the regeneration to cease functioning.

Attack forms that don't deal hit point damage are not healed by regeneration. Regeneration also does not restore hit points lost from starvation, thirst, or suffocation. Regenerating creatures can regrow lost portions of their bodies and can reattach severed limbs or body parts if they are brought together within 1 hour of severing. Severed parts that are not reattached wither and die normally.

A creature must have a Constitution score to have the regeneration ability.
Format: regeneration 5 (fire, acid); *Location*: hp.

Rend (Ex) If it hits with two or more natural attacks in 1 round, a creature with the rend special attack can cause tremendous damage by latching onto the opponent's body and tearing flesh. This attack deals an additional amount of damage, but no more than once per round. The type of attacks that must hit and the additional damage are included in the creature's description. The additional damage is usually equal to the damage caused by one of the attacks plus 1-1/2 times the creature's Strength bonus. *Format*: rend (2 claws, 1d8+9); *Location*: Special Attacks.

Resistance (Ex) A creature with this special quality ignores some damage of the indicated type each time it takes damage of that kind (commonly acid, cold, electricity, or fire). The entry indicates the amount and type of damage ignored. *Format*: Resist acid 10; *Location*: Defensive Abilities.

Rock Catching (Ex) The creature (which must be of at least Large size) can catch Small, Medium, or Large rocks (or projectiles of similar shape). Once per round, a creature that would normally be hit by a rock can make a Reflex save to catch it as a free action. The DC is 15 for a Small rock, 20 for a Medium one, and 25 for a Large one. (If the projectile provides a magical bonus on attack rolls, the DC increases by that amount.) The creature must be aware of the attack in order to make a rock catching attempt. *Format*: rock catching; *Location*: Defensive Abilities.

Rock Throwing (Ex) This creature is an accomplished rock thrower and has a +1 racial bonus on attack rolls with thrown rocks. The creature can hurl rocks up to two categories smaller than its size; for example, a Large hill giant can hurl Small rocks. A "rock" is any large, bulky, and relatively regularly shaped object made of any material with a hardness of at least 5. The creature can hurl the rock up to five range increments. The size of the range increment varies with the creature. Damage from a thrown rock is generally twice the creature's base slam damage plus 1-1/2 times its Strength bonus. *Format*: rock throwing (120 ft.); *Location*: Special Attacks (damage is listed in Ranged attack).

Scent (Ex) This special quality allows a creature to detect approaching enemies, sniff out hidden foes, and track by sense of smell. Creatures with the scent ability can identify familiar odors just as humans do familiar sights.

The creature can detect opponents within 30 feet by sense of smell. If the opponent is upwind, the range increases to 60 feet; if downwind, it drops to 15 feet. Strong scents, such as smoke or rotting garbage, can be detected at twice the ranges noted above. Overpowering scents, such as skunk musk or troglodyte stench, can be detected at triple normal range.

When a creature detects a scent, the exact location of the source is not revealed—only its presence somewhere within range. The creature can take a move action to note the direction of the scent. When the creature is within 5 feet of the source, it pinpoints the source's location.

A creature with the scent ability can follow tracks by smell, making a Wisdom (or Survival) check to find or follow a track. The typical DC for a fresh trail is 10 (no matter what kind of surface holds the scent). This DC increases or decreases depending on how strong the quarry's odor is, the number of creatures, and the age of the trail. For each hour that the trail is cold, the DC increases by 2. The ability otherwise follows the rules for the Survival skill. Creatures tracking by scent ignore the effects of surface conditions and poor visibility.
Format: scent; *Location*: Senses.

See in Darkness (Su) The creature can see perfectly in darkness of any kind, including that created by deeper darkness. *Format*: see in darkness; *Location*: Senses.

Sound Mimicry (Ex) The creature perfectly imitates certain sounds or even specific voices. The creature makes a Bluff check opposed by the listener's Sense Motive check to recognize the mimicry, although if the listener isn't familiar with the person or type of creatures mimicked, it takes a –8 penalty on its Sense Motive check. The creature has a +8 racial bonus on its Bluff check to mimic sounds (including accents and speech patterns, if a voice mimic) it has listened to for at least 10 minutes. The creature cannot duplicate the effects of magical abilities (such as bardic performance or a harpy's captivating song), though it may be able to mimic the sound of those abilities. This ability does not allow the creature to speak or understand languages it doesn't know. *Format*: sound mimicry (voices); *Location*: SQ.

Spell-Like Abilities (Sp) Spell-like abilities are magical and work just like spells (though they are not spells and so have no verbal, somatic, focus, or material components). They go away in an antimagic field and are subject to spell resistance if the spell the ability is based on would be subject to spell resistance.

A spell-like ability usually has a limit on how often it can be used. A constant spell-like ability or one that can be used at will has no use limit; unless otherwise stated, a creature can only use a constant spell-like ability on itself. Reactivating a constant spell-like ability is a swift action. Using all other spell-like abilities is a standard action unless noted otherwise, and doing so provokes attacks of opportunity. It is possible to make a concentration check to use a spell-like ability defensively and avoid provoking an attack of opportunity, just as when casting a spell. A spell-like ability can be disrupted just as a spell can be. Spell-like abilities cannot be used to counterspell, nor can they be counterspelled.

For creatures with spell-like abilities, a designated caster level defines how difficult it is to dispel their spell-like effects and to define any level-dependent variables (such as range and duration) the abilities might have. The creature's caster level never affects which spell-like abilities the creature has; sometimes the given caster level is lower than the level a spellcasting character would need to cast the spell of the same name. If no caster level is specified, the caster level is equal to the creature's Hit Dice. The saving throw (if any) against a spell-like ability is 10 + the level of the spell the ability resembles or duplicates + the creature's Charisma modifier.

Some spell-like abilities duplicate spells that work differently when cast by characters of different classes. A monster's spell-like abilities are presumed to be the sorcerer/wizard versions. If the spell in question is not a sorcerer/wizard spell, then default to cleric, druid, bard, paladin, and ranger, in that order.
Format: At will—*burning hands* (DC 13); *Location*: Spell-Like Abilities.

Spell Resistance (Ex) A creature with spell resistance can avoid the effects of spells and spell-like abilities that directly affect it. To determine whether a spell or spell-like ability works against a creature with spell resistance, the caster must make a caster level check (1d20 + caster level).

If the result equals or exceeds the creature's spell resistance, the spell works normally, although the creature is still allowed a saving throw if the spell would normally permit one. *Format*: SR 18; *Location*: Defensive Abilities.

Split (Ex) The creature splits into two identical copies of itself if subject to certain attacks or effects. Each copy has half the original's current hit points (rounded down). A creature reduced below the listed hit points cannot be further split and can be killed normally. *Format*: split (piercing and slashing, 10 hp); *Location*: Defensive Abilities.

Stench (Ex) A creature with the stench special ability secretes an oily chemical that nearly every other creature finds offensive. All living creatures (except those with this ability) within 30 feet must succeed at a Fortitude save (DC 10 + 1/2 the stench creature's racial HD + the stench creature's Con modifier; the exact DC is given in the creature's descriptive text) or be sickened. The duration of the sickened condition is given in the creature's descriptive text. Creatures that successfully save cannot be affected by the same creature's stench for 24 hours. A delay poison or neutralize poison spell removes the effect from the sickened creature. Creatures with immunity to poison are unaffected, and creatures resistant to poison receive their normal bonus on their saving throws. *Format*: stench (DC 15, 10 rounds); *Location*: Aura.

Summon (Sp) A creature with the summon ability can summon other specific creatures of its kind much as though casting a summon monster spell, but it usually has only a limited chance of success (as specified in the creature's entry). Roll d%: On a failure, no creature answers the summons. Summoned creatures automatically return from whence they came after 1 hour. A creature that is summoned in this way cannot use any spells or spell-like abilities that require material components costing more than 1 gp unless those components are supplied, nor can it use its own summon ability for 1 hour. An appropriate spell level is given for each summoning ability for the purposes of Will saves, caster level checks, and concentration checks. No experience points are awarded for defeating summoned monsters. *Format*: 1/day—summon (level 6, 1 pairaka 60%); *Location*: Spell-Like Abilities.

Sunlight Powerlessness (Ex) If the creature is in sunlight (but not in an area of daylight or similar spells), it cannot attack and is staggered. *Format*: sunlight powerlessness; *Location*: Weaknesses.

Swallow Whole (Ex) If a creature with this special attack begins its turn with an opponent grappled in its mouth (see Grab), it can attempt a new combat maneuver check (as though attempting to pin the opponent). If it succeeds, it swallows its prey, and the opponent takes bite damage. Unless otherwise noted, the opponent can be up to one size category smaller than the swallowing creature. Being swallowed causes the target to take damage each round. The amount and type of damage varies and is given in the swallowing creature's statistics. A swallowed creature keeps the grappled condition, while the creature that did the swallowing does not. A swallowed creature can try to cut its way free with any light slashing or piercing weapon (the amount of cutting damage required to get free is equal to 1/10 the creature's total hit points), or it can just try to escape the grapple. The Armor Class of the interior of a creature that swallows whole is normally 10 + 1/2 its natural armor bonus, with no modifiers for size or Dexterity. If a swallowed creature cuts its way out, the swallowing creature cannot use swallow whole again until the damage is healed. If the swallowed creature escapes the grapple, success puts it back in the attacker's mouth, where it may be bitten or swallowed again. *Format*: swallow whole (5d6 acid damage, AC 15, 18 hp); *Location*: Special Attacks.

Telepathy (Su) The creature can mentally communicate with any other creature within a certain range (specified in the creature's entry, usually 100 feet) that has a language. It is possible to address multiple creatures at once telepathically, although maintaining a telepathic conversation with more than one creature at a time is just as difficult as simultaneously speaking and listening to multiple people at the same time. *Format*: telepathy 100 ft.; *Location*: Languages.

Trample (Ex) As a full-round action, a creature with the trample ability can attempt to overrun any creature that is at least one size category smaller than itself. This works just like the overrun combat maneuver, but the trampling creature does not need to make a check—it merely has to move over opponents in its path. Targets of a trample take an amount of damage equal to the trampling creature's slam damage + 1-1/2 times its Strength modifier. Targets of a trample can make an attack of opportunity, but at a –4 penalty. If targets forgo an attack of opportunity, they can attempt to avoid the trampling creature and receive a Reflex save to take half damage. The save DC against a creature's trample attack is 10 + 1/2 the creature's HD + the creature's Strength modifier (the exact DC is given in the creature's descriptive text). A trampling creature can only deal trampling damage to each target once per round, no matter how many times its movement takes it over a target creature. *Format*: trample (2d6+9, DC 20); *Location*: Special Attacks.

Tremorsense (Ex) A creature with tremorsense is sensitive to vibrations in the ground and can automatically pinpoint the location of anything that is in contact with the ground. Aquatic creatures with tremorsense can also sense the location of creatures moving through water. The ability's range is specified in the creature's descriptive text. *Format*: tremorsense 60 ft.; *Location*: Senses.

Trip (Ex) A creature with the trip special attack can attempt to trip its opponent as a free action without provoking an attack of opportunity if it hits with the specified attack. If the attempt fails, the creature is not tripped in return. Format: trip; Location: individual attacks.

Undead Traits (Ex) Undead are immune to death effects, disease, mind-affecting effects (charms, compulsions, morale effects, phantasms, and patterns), paralysis, poison, sleep, stun, and any effect that requires a Fortitude save (unless the effect also works on objects or is harmless). Undead are not subject to ability drain, energy drain, or nonlethal damage. Undead are immune to damage or penalties to their physical ability scores (Strength, Dexterity, and Constitution), as well as to fatigue and exhaustion effects. Undead are not at risk of death from massive damage. *Format*: undead traits; *Location*: Immune.

Undersized Weapons (Ex) The creature uses manufactured weapons as if it were one size category smaller than the creature's actual size. *Format*: undersized weapons; *Location*: SQ.

Vulnerabilities (Ex or Su) A creature with vulnerabilities takes half again as much damage (+50%) from a specific energy type, regardless of whether a saving throw is allowed or whether the save is a success or failure. Creatures with a vulnerability that is not an energy type instead take a –4 penalty on saves against spells and effects that cause or use the listed vulnerability (such as spells with the light descriptor). Some creatures might suffer additional effects, as noted in their descriptions. *Format*: vulnerability to fire; *Location*: Weaknesses.

Water Breathing (Ex) A creature with this special ability can breathe underwater indefinitely. It can freely use any breath weapon, spells, or other abilities while submerged. *Format*: water breathing; *Location*: SQ.

Water Dependency (Ex) A creature with this special ability can survive out of water for 1 minute per point of Constitution. Beyond this limit, this creature runs the risk of suffocation, as if it were drowning. *Format*: water dependency; *Location*: SQ.

Web (Ex) Creatures with the web ability can use webs to support themselves and up to one additional creature of the same size. In addition, such creatures can throw a web up to eight times per day. This is similar to an attack with a net but has a maximum range of 50 feet, with a range increment of 10 feet, and is effective against targets up to one size category larger than the web spinner. An entangled target can escape with a successful Escape Artist check or burst the web with a Strength check. Both are standard actions with a DC equal to 10 + 1/2 the creature's Hit Dice + the creature's Constitution modifier. Attempts to burst a web by those caught in it take a –4 penalty.

Web spinners can create sheets of sticky webbing up to three times their size. They usually position these sheets to snare flying creatures but can also try to trap prey on the ground. Approaching creatures must succeed at a DC 20 Perception check to notice a web; otherwise they stumble into it and become trapped as though by a successful web attack. Attempts to escape or burst the webbing gain a +5 bonus if the trapped creature has something to walk on or grab while pulling free. Each 5-foot-square section of web has a number of hit points equal to the Hit Dice of the creature that created it and DR 5/—. A creature can move across its own web at its climb speed and can pinpoint the location of any creatures touching its web. *Format*: web (+8 ranged, DC 16, 5 hp); *Location*: Special Attacks.

Whirlwind (Su) Some creatures can transform themselves into whirlwinds and remain in that form for up to 1 round for every 2 HD they have. If the creature has a fly speed, it can continue to fly at that same speed while in whirlwind form; otherwise it gains a fly speed equal to its base land speed (average maneuverability) while in whirlwind form.

The whirlwind is always 5 feet wide at its base, but its height and width at the top vary from creature to creature (minimum 10 feet high). A whirlwind's width at its peak is always equal to half its height. The creature controls the exact height, but it must be at least 10 feet high.

The whirlwind form does not provoke attacks of opportunity, even if the creature enters the space another creature occupies. Another creature might be caught in the whirlwind if it touches or enters the whirlwind, or if the whirlwind moves into or through the creature's space. A creature in whirlwind form cannot make its normal attacks and does not threaten the area around it.

A creature that comes in contact with the whirlwind must succeed at a Reflex save (DC 10 + 1/2 the monster's HD + the monster's Strength modifier) or take damage as if it were hit by the whirlwind creature's slam attack. It must also succeed at a second Reflex save or be picked up bodily and held suspended in the powerful winds, automatically taking the indicated damage each round. A creature that can fly is allowed a Reflex save each round on its turn to escape the whirlwind. The creature still takes damage that round but can leave if the save is successful.

Creatures trapped in the whirlwind cannot move except to go where the whirlwind carries them or to escape the whirlwind. Trapped creatures can otherwise act normally, but must succeed at a concentration check (DC 15 + spell level) to cast a spell. Creatures caught in the whirlwind take a –4 penalty to Dexterity and a –2 penalty on attack rolls. The whirlwind can have only as many creatures trapped inside at one time as will fit inside the whirlwind's volume. As a free action, the whirlwind can eject any carried creatures whenever it wishes, depositing them in its space.

If the whirlwind's base touches the ground, it creates a swirling cloud of debris. This cloud is centered on the creature and has a diameter equal to half the whirlwind's height. The cloud obscures all vision, including darkvision, beyond 5 feet. Creatures 5 feet away have concealment, while those farther away have total concealment. Those caught in the cloud of debris must succeed at a concentration check (DC 15 + spell level) to cast a spell.

Format: whirlwind (3/day, 10–30 ft. high, 1d6+6 damage, DC 15); *Location*: Special Attacks.

Appendix C: New Monster Feats

This appendix details new feats available and typically used by monsters. Several monsters detailed within this book make use of these feats.

Crush (Combat)
The creature can deal damage by jumping, falling, or landing on its foes.
Prerequisites: Huge or larger size
Benefit: The creature can fly, jump, or fall on foes as a standard action, using its whole body to crush them. Crush attacks are effective only against opponents three or more size categories smaller than the creature. A crush attack affects as many opponents as fit in the creature's space. Opponents in the affected area must succeed on a Reflex save (DC 10 + 1/2 creature's Hit Dice + Str modifier) or be pinned, automatically taking bludgeoning damage during the next round unless the creature moves off them. If the creature chooses to maintain the pin, it must succeed at a combat maneuver check as normal. Pinned foes take damage from the crush each round if they don't escape. A crush attack deals the indicated damage plus 1-1/2 times the creature's Strength bonus.

SIZE	CRUSH DAMAGE
Huge	2d8
Gargantuan	4d6
Colossal	4d8

Greater Flyby Attack (Combat)
The creature can make an attack against each opponent before and after it moves while flying.
Prerequisites: Dex 13, Fly speed, Flyby Attack, base attack bonus +8
Benefit: When making a flyby attack and flying in a straight line, the creature can make a single attack at its highest attack bonus against each opponent within reach at any point during the move. The creature makes a separate attack roll against each opponent, and does not provoke attacks of opportunity from a targeted opponent.
Normal: Without this feat, the creature makes a single attack during a flyby attack.

Improved Multiattack (Combat)
This creature is particularly skilled at making attacks with its natural weapons.
Prerequisites: Three or more natural attacks, Multiattack, base attack bonus +8
Benefit: The creature's secondary attacks with natural weapons do not take a penalty.
Normal: Without this feat, the creature's secondary attacks with natural weapons take a –5 penalty (or a –2 penalty with the Multiattack feat).

Maximize Spell-Like Ability
One of the creature's spell-like abilities has the maximum possible effect.
Prerequisites: Spell-like ability at caster level 6th or higher.
Benefit: Choose one of the creature's spell-like abilities, subject to the restrictions below. The creature can use that ability as a maximized spell-like ability three times per day (or less, if the ability is normally usable only once or twice per day). When a creature uses a maximized spell-like ability all variable, numeric effects of a spell-like ability modified by this feat are maximized. Saving throws and opposed rolls are not affected. Spell-like abilities without random variables are not affected.
The creature can only select a spell-like ability duplicating a spell with a level less than or equal to 1/2 its caster level (round down) – 3.
Special: This feat can be taken multiple times. Each time it is taken, the creature can apply it to a different spell-like ability.

Quicken Breath Weapon (Combat)
The creature's breath weapon recharges quicker.
Prerequisites: Con 15, breath weapon attack
Benefit: The creature can reduce the amount of time required to recharge its breath weapon. This feat reduces the time by 1 round if the recharge time is in rounds, such as a dragon's breath. This cannot reduce the recharge time below 1 round. If the recharge time is in hours, minutes, days, etc., the recharge time is halved. (Thus, a creature that can use its breath weapon once per day can now use it twice a day.) If the creature has multiple breath weapons, it affects them all.

Swim-By Attack (Combat)
The creature can move before and after it makes an attack while swimming.
Prerequisites: Swim speed
Benefit: When swimming, the creature can take a move action and another standard action at any point during the move. The creature cannot take a second move action during a round it makes a swim-by attack.
Normal: Without this feat, the creature takes a standard action either before or after its move.

Uncontrolled Rage (Combat)
The creature flies into a rage when struck for damage.
Prerequisites: Con 17
Benefit: When the creature is struck by a single attack that deals an amount of damage equal to half of its hit points (minimum 20 points of damage) or more and it doesn't kill it outright, it must make a DC 15 Fortitude save. If the saving throw succeeds, the creature flies into an uncontrolled rage and gains the following: +2 morale bonus on all Strength and Constitution checks, and on all attack rolls, damage rolls, and Will saves, a –2 penalty to AC, and bonus hit points equal to 2 hit points per Hit Dice. These bonus hit points disappear when the rage ends. While in a rage, the creature cannot use any Charisma-, Dexterity-, or Intelligence-based skills (except Acrobatics, Fly, Intimidate, and Ride) or any ability that requires patience and concentration. This rage lasts until the end of the encounter at which point the creature is fatigued for 10 minutes.

Virulent Poison
The creature's poison is harder to overcome.
Prerequisites: Poison attack
Benefit: Increase the number of saves required to overcome the creature's poison by one. Thus, a creature whose poison requires two saves to end the effects now requires three saves.

Appendix D: Creature Types

Each creature has a single type. Some creatures also have one or more subtypes. Types and subtypes are explained below.

Aberration

An aberration has a bizarre anatomy, strange abilities, an alien mindset, or any combination of the three. An aberration has the following features.
- d8 Hit Die
- Base attack bonus equal to 3/4 total Hit Dice (medium progression)
- Good Will Saves
- Skill points equal to 4 + Int modifier (minimum 1) per Hit Die. The following are class skills for aberrations: Acrobatics, Climb, Escape Artist, Fly, Intimidate, Knowledge (pick one), Perception, Spellcraft, Stealth, Survival, and Swim.

Traits: An aberration possesses the following traits (unless otherwise noted in a creature's entry).t
- Darkvision 60 feet
- Proficient with its natural weapons. If generally humanoid in form, proficient with all simple weapons and any weapon it is described as using.
- Proficient with whatever type of armor (light, medium, or heavy) it is described as wearing, as well as all lighter types. Aberrations not indicated as wearing armor are not proficient with armor. Aberrations are proficient with shields if they are proficient with any form of armor.
- Aberrations breathe, eat, and sleep.

Animal

An animal is a living, nonhuman creature, usually a vertebrate with no magical abilities and no innate capacity for language or culture. Animals usually have additional information on how they can serve as companions. An animal has the following features (unless otherwise noted).
- d8 Hit Die
- Base attack bonus equal to 3/4 total Hit Dice (medium progression)
- Good Fortitude and Reflex saves
- Skill points equal to 2 + Int modifier (minimum 1) per Hit Die. The following are class skills for animals: Acrobatics, Climb, Fly, Perception, Stealth, and Swim.

Traits: An animal possesses the following traits (unless otherwise noted in a creature's entry).
- Intelligence score of 1 or 2 (no creature with an Intelligence score of 3 or higher can be an animal)
- Low-light vision
- **Alignment:** Always neutral
- **Treasure:** None
- Proficient with its natural weapons only. A noncombative herbivore treats its natural weapons as secondary attacks. Such attacks are made with a –5 penalty on the creature's attack rolls, and the animal receives only 1/2 its Strength modifier as a damage adjustment.
- Proficient with no armor unless trained for war.
- Animals breathe, eat, and sleep.

Construct

A construct is an animated object or artificially created creature. A construct has the following features.
- d10 Hit Die
- Base attack bonus equal to total Hit Dice (fast progression)
- No good saving throws
- Skill points equal to 2 + Int modifier (minimum 1) per Hit Die. However, most constructs are mindless and gain no skill points or

feats. Constructs do not have any class skills, regardless of their Intelligence scores.

Traits: A construct possesses the following traits (unless otherwise noted in a creature's entry).
- No Constitution score. Any DCs or other Statistics that rely on a Constitution score treat a construct as having a score of 10 (no bonus or penalty).
- Low-light vision
- Darkvision 60 feet
- Immunity to all mind-affecting effects (charms, compulsions, morale effects, patterns, and phantasms).
- Immunity to bleed, disease, death effects, necromancy effects, paralysis, poison, sleep effects, and stunning.
- Cannot heal damage on its own, but often can be repaired via exposure to a certain kind of effect (see the creature's description for details) or through the use of the Craft Construct feat. Constructs can also be healed through spells such as make whole. A construct with the fast healing special quality still benefits from that quality.
- Not subject to ability damage, ability drain, fatigue, exhaustion, energy drain, or nonlethal damage.
- Immunity to any effect that requires a Fortitude save (unless the effect also works on objects, or is harmless).
- Not at risk of death from massive damage. Immediately destroyed when reduced to 0 hit points or less.
- A construct cannot be raised or resurrected.
- A construct is hard to destroy, and gains bonus hit points based on size, as shown on the following table.
- Proficient with its natural weapons only, unless generally humanoid in form, in which case proficient with any weapon mentioned in its entry.
- Proficient with no armor.
- Constructs do not breathe, eat, or sleep.

Dragon

A dragon is a reptile-like creature, usually winged, with magical or unusual abilities. A dragon has the following features.
- d12 Hit Die
- Base attack bonus equal to total Hit Dice (fast progression).
- Good Fortitude, Reflex, and Will Saves.
- Skill points equal to 6 + Int modifier (minimum 1) per Hit Die. The following are class skills for dragons: Appraise, Bluff, Climb, Craft, Diplomacy, Fly, Heal, Intimidate, Knowledge (all), Linguistics, Perception, Sense Motive, Spellcraft, Stealth, Survival, Swim, and Use Magic Device.

Traits: A dragon possesses the following traits (unless otherwise noted in a creature's entry).
- Darkvision 60 feet and low-light vision
- Immunity to magic sleep effects and paralysis effects
- Proficient with its natural weapons only unless humanoid in form (or capable of assuming humanoid form), in which case proficient with all simple weapons and any weapons mentioned in its entry.
- Proficient with no armor.
- Dragons breathe, eat, and sleep.

Fey

A fey is a creature with supernatural abilities and connections to nature or to some other force or place. Fey are usually human-shaped. A fey has the following features.
- d6 Hit Die
- Base attack bonus equal to 1/2 total Hit Dice (slow progression)
- Good Reflex and Will Saves
- Skill points equal to 6 + Int modifier (minimum 1) per Hit Die. The

following are class skills for fey: Acrobatics, Bluff, Climb, Craft, Diplomacy, Disguise, Escape Artist, Fly, Knowledge (geography), Knowledge (local), Knowledge (nature), Perception, Perform, Sense Motive, Sleight of Hand, Stealth, Swim, Use Magic Device.

Traits: A fey possesses the following traits (unless otherwise noted in a creature's entry).

- Low-light vision
- Proficient with all simple weapons and any weapons mentioned in its entry.
- Proficient with whatever type of armor (light, medium, or heavy) it is described as wearing, as well as all lighter types. Fey not indicated as wearing armor are not proficient with armor. Fey are proficient with shields if they are proficient with any form of armor.
- Fey breathe, eat, and sleep.

Humanoid

A humanoid usually has two arms, two legs, and one head, or a human-like torso, arms, and a head. Humanoids have few or no supernatural or extraordinary abilities, but most can speak and usually have well-developed societies. They are usually Small or Medium (with the exception of giants). Every humanoid creature also has a specific subtype to match its race, such as human, dark folk, or goblinoid.

Humanoids with 1 Hit Die exchange the features of their humanoid Hit Die for the class features of a PC or NPC class. Humanoids of this sort are typically presented as 1st-level warriors, which mean they have average combat ability and poor saving throws. Humanoids with more than 1 Hit Die (such as giants) are the only humanoids that make use of the features of the humanoid type. A humanoid has the following features (unless otherwise noted in a creature's entry).

- d8 Hit Die, or by character class
- Base attack bonus equal to 3/4 total Hit Dice (medium progression)
- One good save, usually Reflex
- Skill points equal to 2 + Int modifier (minimum 1) per Hit Die or by character class. The following are class skills for humanoids without a character class: Climb, Craft, Handle Animal, Heal, Profession, Ride, and Survival. Humanoids with both a character class and racial HD add these skills to their list of class skills.

Traits: A humanoid possesses the following traits (unless otherwise noted in a creature's entry).

- Proficient with all simple weapons, or by character class.
- Proficient with whatever type of armor (light, medium, or heavy) it is described as wearing, or by character class. If a humanoid does not have a class and wears armor, it is proficient with that type of armor and all lighter types. Humanoids not indicated as wearing armor are not proficient with armor. Humanoids are proficient with shields if they are proficient with any form of armor.
- Humanoids breathe, eat, and sleep.

Magical Beast

Magical Beasts are similar to animals but can have Intelligence scores higher than 2 (in which case the creature knows at least one language, but can't necessarily speak). Magical Beasts usually have supernatural or extraordinary abilities, but are sometimes merely bizarre in appearance or habits. A magical beast has the following features.

- d10 Hit Die
- Base attack bonus equal to total Hit Dice (fast progression)
- Good Fortitude and Reflex saves
- Skill points equal to 2 + Int modifier (minimum 1) per Hit Die. The following are class skills for magical beasts: Acrobatics, Climb, Fly, Perception, Stealth, Swim.

Traits: A magical beast possesses the following traits (unless otherwise noted in a creature's entry).

- Darkvision 60 feet
- Low-light vision
- Proficient with its natural weapons only.
- Proficient with no armor.
- Magical beasts breathe, eat, and sleep.

Monstrous Humanoid

Monstrous humanoids are similar to humanoids, but with monstrous or animalistic features. They often have magical abilities as well. A monstrous humanoid has the following features.

- d10 Hit Die
- Base attack bonus equal to total Hit Dice (fast progression)
- Good Reflex and Will Saves
- Skill points equal to 4 + Int modifier (minimum 1) per Hit Die. The following are class skills for monstrous humanoids: Climb, Craft, Fly, Intimidate, Perception, Ride, Stealth, Survival, and Swim.

Traits: A monstrous humanoid possesses the following traits (unless otherwise noted in a creature's entry).

- Darkvision 60 feet
- Proficient with all simple weapons and any weapons mentioned in its entry.
- Proficient with whatever type of armor (light, medium, or heavy) it is described as wearing, as well as all lighter types. Monstrous humanoids not indicated as wearing armor are not proficient with armor. Monstrous humanoids are proficient with shields if they are proficient with any form of armor.
- Monstrous humanoids breathe, eat, and sleep.

Ooze

An ooze is an amorphous or mutable creature, usually mindless. An ooze has the following features.

- d8 Hit Die
- Base attack bonus equal to 3/4 total Hit Dice (medium progression)
- No good saving throws.
- Skill points equal to 2 + Int modifier (minimum 1) per Hit Die. However, most oozes are mindless and gain no skill points or feats. Oozes do not have any class skills.

Traits: An ooze possesses the following traits (unless otherwise noted in a creature's entry).

- **Mindless:** No Intelligence score, and immunity to all mind-affecting effects (charms, compulsions, phantasms, patterns, and morale effects). An ooze with an Intelligence score loses this trait.
- Blind (but have the blindsight special quality), with immunity to gaze attacks, visual effects, illusions, and other attack forms that rely on sight.
- Immunity to poison, sleep effects, paralysis, polymorph, and stunning.
- Some oozes have the ability to deal acid damage to objects.
- Not subject to critical hits or flanking. Does not take additional damage from precision-based attacks, such as sneak attack.
- Proficient with its natural weapons only.
- Proficient with no armor.
- Oozes eat and breathe, but do not sleep.

Outsider

An outsider is at least partially composed of the essence (but not necessarily the material) of some plane other than the Material Plane. Some creatures start out as some other type and become outsiders when they attain a higher (or lower) state of spiritual existence. An outsider has the following features.

- d10 Hit Dice
- Base attack bonus equal to total Hit Dice (fast progression)
- Two good saving throws, usually Reflex and Will.
- Skill points equal to 6 + Int modifier (minimum 1) per Hit Die. The following are class skills for outsiders: Bluff, Craft, Knowledge (planes), Perception, Sense Motive, and Stealth. Due to their varied nature, outsiders also receive 4 additional class skills determined by the creature's theme.

Traits: An outsider possesses the following traits (unless otherwise noted in a creature's entry).

- Darkvision 60 feet
- Unlike most living creatures, an outsider does not have a dual nature—its soul and body form one unit. When an outsider is slain,

no soul is set loose. Spells that restore souls to their bodies, such as raise dead, reincarnate, and resurrection, don't work on an outsider. It takes a different magical effect, such as limited wish, wish, miracle, or true resurrection to restore it to life. An outsider with the native subtype can be raised, reincarnated, or resurrected just as other living creatures can be.
- Proficient with all simple and martial weapons and any weapons mentioned in its entry.
- Proficient with whatever type of armor (light, medium, or heavy) it is described as wearing, as well as all lighter types. Outsiders not indicated as wearing armor are not proficient with armor. Outsiders are proficient with shields if they are proficient with any form of armor.
- Outsiders breathe, but do not need to eat or sleep (although they can do so if they wish). Native outsiders breathe, eat, and sleep.

Plant

This type comprises vegetable creatures. Note that regular plants, such as one finds growing in gardens and fields, lack Intelligence, Wisdom, and Charisma scores; even though plants are alive, they are objects, not creatures. A plant creature has the following features.
- d8 Hit Die
- Base attack bonus equal to 3/4 total Hit Dice (medium progression)
- Good Fortitude saves
- Skill points equal to 2 + Int modifier (minimum 1) per Hit Die. Some plant creatures, however, are mindless and gain no skill points or feats. The following are class skills for plants: Perception and Stealth.

Traits: A plant creature possesses the following traits (unless noted in a creature's entry).
- Low-light vision
- Immunity to all mind-affecting effects (charms, compulsions, morale effects, patterns, and phantasms).
- Immunity to paralysis, poison, polymorph, sleep effects, and stunning.
- Proficient with its natural weapons only.
- Not proficient with armor.
- Plants breathe and eat, but do not sleep.

Undead

Undead are once-living creatures animated by spiritual or supernatural forces. An undead creature has the following features.
- d8 Hit Die
- Base attack bonus equal to 3/4 total Hit Dice (medium progression)
- Good Will Saves
- Skill points equal to 4 + Int modifier (minimum 1) per Hit Die. Many undead, however, are mindless and gain no skill points or feats. The following are class skills for undead: Climb, Disguise, Fly, Intimidate, Knowledge (arcana), Knowledge (religion), Perception, Sense Motive, Spellcraft, and Stealth.

Traits: An undead creature possesses the following traits (unless otherwise noted in a creature's entry).
- No Constitution score. Undead use their Charisma score in place of their Constitution score when calculating hit points, Fortitude saves, and any special ability that relies on Constitution (such as when calculating a breath weapon's DC).
- Darkvision 60 feet.
- Immunity to all mind-affecting effects (charms, compulsions, morale effects, patterns, and phantasms).
- Immunity to bleed, death effects, disease, paralysis, poison, sleep effects, and stunning.
- Not subject to nonlethal damage, ability drain, or energy drain. Immune to damage to its physical ability scores (Constitution, Dexterity, and Strength), as well as to exhaustion and fatigue effects.
- Cannot heal damage on its own if it has no Intelligence score, although it can be healed. Negative energy (such as an inflict spell) can heal undead creatures. The fast healing special quality works

regardless of the creature's Intelligence score.
- Immunity to any effect that requires a Fortitude save (unless the effect also works on objects or is harmless).
- Not at risk of death from massive damage, but is immediately destroyed when reduced to 0 hit points.
- Not affected by raise dead and reincarnate spells or abilities. Resurrection and true resurrection can affect undead creatures. These spells turn undead creatures back into the living creatures they were before becoming undead.
- Proficient with its natural weapons, all simple weapons, and any weapons mentioned in its entry.
- Proficient with whatever type of armor (light, medium, or heavy) it is described as wearing, as well as all lighter types. Undead not indicated as wearing armor are not proficient with armor. Undead are proficient with shields if they are proficient with any form of armor.
- Undead do not breathe, eat, or sleep.

Vermin

This type includes insects, arachnids, other arthropods, worms, and similar invertebrates. Vermin have the following features.
- d8 Hit Die
- Base attack bonus equal to 3/4 total Hit Dice (medium progression)
- Good Fortitude saves
- Skill points equal to 2 + Int modifier (minimum 1) per Hit Die. Most vermin, however, are mindless and gain no skill points or feats. Vermin have no class skills.

Traits: Vermin possess the following traits (unless otherwise noted in a creature's entry).
- **Mindless:** No Intelligence score, and immunity to all mind-affecting effects (charms, compulsions, morale effects, patterns, and phantasms). Mindless creatures have no feats or skills. A vermin-like creature with an Intelligence score is usually either an animal or a magical beast, depending on its other abilities.
- Darkvision 60 feet.
- Proficient with its natural weapons only.
- Proficient with no armor.
- Vermin breathe, eat, and sleep.

Creature Subtypes

Some creatures have one or more subtypes. Subtypes add additional abilities and qualities to a creature. These are detailed below.

Acid Subtype

This subtype is usually used for outsiders with a connection to the Quasi-Elemental Plane of Acid. Acid creatures always have swim speeds and treat Swim as a class skill. An acid creature possesses the following traits (unless otherwise noted in the creature's entry).
- Immunity to acid
- Vulnerability to Water (Ex) A significant amount of water, such as that created by a create water spell, the contents of a large bucket, or a blow from a water elemental, that strikes an acid creature forces the creature to make a DC 20 Fortitude save to avoid being staggered for 2d4 rounds. An acid creature that is immersed in water must make a DC 20 Fortitude save each round (this DC increases by +1 each subsequent round) or take 1d6 points of damage each round until the water is gone.

Air Subtype

This subtype is usually used for outsiders with a connection to the Elemental Planes of Air. Air creatures always have fly speeds and usually have perfect maneuverability. Air creatures treat Fly as a class skill.

Angel Subtype

Angels are a race of celestials, or good outsiders, native to the good-aligned outer planes. An angel possesses the following traits (unless otherwise noted in a creature's entry).

- Darkvision 60 feet and low-light vision.
- Immunity to acid, cold, and petrification.
- Resistance to electricity 10 and fire 10.
- +4 racial bonus on saves against poison.
- *Protective Aura (Su)* Against attacks made or effects created by evil creatures, this ability provides a +4 deflection bonus to AC and a +4 resistance bonus on saving throws to anyone within 20 feet of the angel. Otherwise, it functions as a magic circle against evil effect and a lesser globe of invulnerability, both with a radius of 20 feet (caster level equals angel's HD). The defensive benefits from the circle are not included in an angel's statistics block.
- *Truespeech (Su)* All angels can speak with any creature that has a language, as though using a *tongues* spell (caster level equal to angel's Hit Dice). This ability is always active.

Aquatic Subtype

These creatures always have swim speeds and can move in water without making Swim checks. An aquatic creature can breathe water. It cannot breathe air unless it has the amphibious special quality. Aquatic creatures always treat Swim as a class skill.

Archon Subtype

Archons are a race of celestials, or good outsiders, native to lawful good-aligned outer planes. An archon possesses the following traits (unless otherwise noted in a creature's entry).

- Darkvision 60 feet and low-light vision.
- *Aura of Menace (Su)* A righteous aura surrounds archons that fight or get angry. Any hostile creature within a 20-foot radius of an archon must succeed on a Will save to resist its effects. The save DC varies with the type of archon, is Charisma-based, and includes a +2 racial bonus. Those who fail take a –2 penalty on attacks, AC, and saves for 24 hours or until they successfully hit the archon that generated the aura. A creature that has resisted or broken the effect cannot be affected again by the same archon's aura for 24 hours.
- Immunity to electricity and petrification.
- +4 racial bonus on saves against poison.
- *Teleport (Sp)* Archons can use greater teleport at will, as the spell (caster level 14th), except that the creature can transport only itself and up to 50 pounds of carried objects.
- *Truespeech (Su)* All archons can speak with any creature that has a language, as though using a *tongues* spell (caster level 14th). This ability is always active.

Augmented Subtype

A creature receives this subtype when something (usually a template) changes its original type. Some creatures (those with an inherited template) are born with this subtype; others acquire it when they take on an acquired template. The augmented subtype is always paired with the creature's original type.

Chaotic Subtype

This subtype is usually applied to outsiders native to the chaotic-aligned Outer Planes. Most creatures that have this subtype also have chaotic alignments; however, if their alignments change, they still retain the subtype. Any effect that depends on alignment affects a creature with this subtype as if the creature had a chaotic alignment, no matter what its alignment actually is. The creature also suffers effects according to its actual alignment. A creature with the chaotic subtype overcomes damage reduction as if its natural weapons and any weapons it wields are chaotically aligned.

Clockwork Subtype

Clockworks are constructs created through a fusion of magic and technology. They have the following traits unless otherwise noted.

- *Winding (Ex)* Clockwork constructs must be wound with special keys in order to function. As a general rule, a fully wound clockwork can remain active for 1 day per Hit Die, but shorter or longer durations are possible.
- *Vulnerable to Electricity (Ex)* Clockwork constructs take 150% as

much damage as normal from electricity attacks.
- *Swift Reactions (Ex)* Clockwork constructs generally react much more swiftly than other constructs. They gain Improved Initiative and Lightning Reflexes as bonus feats, and gain a +2 dodge bonus to AC.
- *Difficult to Create (Ex)* The time and gp cost required to create a clockwork is 150% of normal. Construction requirements in individual clockwork monster entries are already increased.

Cold Subtype

A creature with the cold subtype has immunity to cold and vulnerability to fire.

Daemon Subtype

Daemons are neutral evil outsiders that eat souls and thrive on disaster and ruin. Daemons inhabit the planes of Gehenna and Hades. Daemons have the following traits (unless otherwise noted)

- Immunity to acid, death effects, disease, and poison.
- Resistance to cold 10, electricity 10, and fire 10.
- *Summon (Sp)* Daemons share the ability to summon others of their kind, typically another of their type or a small number of less powerful daemons.
- Telepathy.
- Except where otherwise noted, daemons speak Abyssal, Draconic, and Infernal.

Demodand Subtype

Demodands are chaotic evil outsiders who stalk the Abyss. Unless otherwise noted in a creature's entry, demodands possess the following traits.

- Immunity to acid and poison.
- Resistance to fire 10 and cold 10.
- *Summon (Sp)* Demodands share the ability to summon others of their kind, typically another of their type or a small number of less powerful demodands.
- *Faith-Stealing Strike (Su)* When a demodand's natural attack or melee weapon damages a creature capable of casting divine spells, that creature must make a Will saving throw or be unable to cast any divine spells for 1 round. Once a creature makes this save, it is immune to further faith-stealing strikes from that particular demodand for 24 hours. The save DC is Charisma-based.
- *Heretical Soul (Ex)* All demodands gain a +4 bonus on saving throws against divine spells. In addition, any attempts to scry on a demodand using divine magic automatically fail. The caster can see the scryed area normally, but the demodand simply does not appear.
- Except when otherwise noted, demodands speak Abyssal, Celestial, and Common.
- A demodand's natural weapons, as well as any weapons it wields, are treated as chaotic and evil for the purpose of resolving damage reduction.

Demon Subtype

Demons are chaotic evil outsiders that call the Abyss their home. Demons possess a particular suite of traits (unless otherwise noted in a creature's entry) as summarized here.

- Immunity to electricity and poison.
- Resistance to acid 10, cold 10, and fire 10.
- *Summon (Sp)* Demons share the ability to summon others of their kind, typically another of their type or a small number of less powerful demons.
- Telepathy.
- Except where otherwise noted, demons speak Abyssal, Celestial, and Draconic.
- A demon's natural weapons, as well as any weapon it wields, is treated as chaotic and evil for the purpose of resolving damage reduction

Devil Subtype

Devils are lawful evil outsiders that hail from the plane of Hell. Devils possess a particular suite of traits (unless otherwise noted in a creature's entry).

- Immunity to fire and poison.
- Resistance to acid 10 and cold 10.
- *See in Darkness (Su)* Some devils can see perfectly in darkness of any kind, even that created by a deeper darkness spell.
- *Summon (Sp)* Devils share the ability to summon others of their kind, typically another of their type or a small number of less-powerful devils.
- Telepathy.
- Except when otherwise noted, devils speak Celestial, Draconic, and Infernal.
- A devil's natural weapons, as well as any weapons it wields, are treated as lawful and evil for the purpose of resolving damage reduction.

Dwarf Subtype

This subtype is applied to dwarves and creatures related to dwarves. Creatures with the dwarf subtype have darkvision 60 feet.

Earth Subtype

This subtype is usually used for outsiders with a connection to the Elemental Planes of Earth. Earth creatures usually have burrow speeds, and most earth creatures can burrow through solid rock. Earth creatures with a burrow speed possess tremorsense.

Elemental Subtype

An elemental is a being composed entirely from one of the four classical elements: air, earth, fire, or water. An elemental has the following features.

- Immunity to bleed, paralysis, poison, sleep effects, and stunning.
- Not subject to critical hits or flanking. Does not take additional damage from precision-based attacks, such as sneak attack.
- Proficient with natural weapons only, unless generally humanoid in form, in which case proficient with all simple weapons and any weapons mentioned in its entry.
- Proficient with whatever type of armor (light, medium, or heavy) it is described as wearing, as well as all lighter types. Elementals not indicated as wearing armor are not proficient with armor. Elementals are proficient with shields if they are proficient with any form of armor.
- Elementals do not breathe, eat, or sleep.

Electricity Subtype

This subtype is usually used for outsiders with a connection to the Quasi-Elemental Plane of Lightning. They have the following traits unless otherwise noted.

- Electricity creatures always have fly speeds and usually have perfect maneuverability. Electricity creatures treat the Fly skill as a class skill.
- Immunity to electricity.
- *Vulnerability to water (Ex)* Unless otherwise noted in the creature's description, a water-based effect or spell deals 1d4 points of damage per spell level to a creature with this subtype. The creature usually receives a save (Fortitude or Reflex) for half damage.

Elf Subtype

This subtype is applied to elves and creatures related to elves. Creatures with the elf subtype have low-light vision.

Evil Subtype

This subtype is usually applied to Outsiders native to the evil-aligned Outer Planes. Evil Outsiders are also called fiends. Most creatures that have this subtype also have evil alignments; however, if their alignments change, they still retain the subtype. Any effect that depends on alignment affects a creature with this subtype as if the creature has an evil alignment, no matter what its alignment actually is. The creature also suffers effects according to its actual alignment. A creature with the evil subtype overcomes damage reduction as if its natural weapons and any weapons it wields are evil-aligned.

Extraplanar Subtype

This subtype is applied to any creature when it is on a plane other than its native plane. A creature that travels the planes can gain or lose this subtype as it goes from plane to plane. Monster entries assume that encounters with creatures take place on the Material Plane, and every creature whose native plane is not the Material Plane has the extraplanar subtype (but would not have it when on its home plane). Every extraplanar creature in this book has a home plane mentioned in its description. creatures not labeled as extraplanar are natives of the Material Plane, and they gain the extraplanar subtype if they leave the Material Plane. No creature has the extraplanar subtype when it is on a transitive plane, such as the Astral Plane, the Ethereal Plane, or the Plane of Shadow.

Fire Subtype

A creature with the fire subtype has immunity to fire and vulnerability to cold.

Fungus Subtype

This subtype is applied to plant creatures that are primary composed of fungi. It distinguishes common plant creatures like treants from other plant creatures such as shriekers and ascomoids.

Giant Subtype

A giant is a humanoid creature of great strength, usually of at least Large size. Giants have a number of racial Hit Dice and never substitute such Hit Dice for class levels like some humanoids. Giants have low-light vision, and treat Intimidate and Perception as class skills.

Gnome Subtype

This subtype is applied to gnomes and creatures related to gnomes. Creatures with the gnome subtype have low-light vision.

Goblinoid Subtype

Goblinoids are stealthy humanoids who live by hunting and raiding and who all speak Goblin. Goblinoids treat Stealth as a class skill.

Good Subtype

This subtype is usually applied to outsiders native to the good-aligned Outer Planes. Most creatures that have this subtype also have good alignments; however, if their alignments change, they still retain the subtype. Any effect that depends on alignment affects a creature with this subtype as if the creature has a good alignment, no matter what its alignment actually is. The creature also suffers effects according to its actual alignment. A creature with the good subtype overcomes damage reduction as if its natural weapons and any weapons it wields are good-aligned.

Halfling Subtype

This subtype is applied to halflings and creatures related to halflings.

Human Subtype

This subtype is applied to humans and creatures related to humans.

Incorporeal Subtype

An incorporeal creature has no physical body. An incorporeal creature is immune to critical hits and precision-based damage (such as sneak attack damage) unless the attacks are made using a weapon with the ghost touch special weapon quality. In addition, creatures with the incorporeal subtype gain the incorporeal special quality.

Lawful Subtype

This subtype is usually applied to outsiders native to the lawful-aligned Outer Planes. Most creatures that have this subtype also have lawful alignments; however, if their alignments change, they still retain the subtype. Any effect that depends on alignment affects a creature with this subtype as if the creature had a lawful alignment, no matter what its alignment actually is. The creature also suffers effects according to its actual alignment. A creature with the lawful subtype overcomes damage reduction as if its natural weapons and any weapons it wields are lawful-aligned.

Native Subtype

This subtype is applied only to outsiders. These creatures have mortal ancestors or a strong connection to the Material Plane and can be raised, reincarnated, or resurrected just as other living creatures can be. Creatures with this subtype are native to the Material Plane. Unlike true outsiders, native outsiders need to eat and sleep.

Orc Subtype

This subtype is applied to orcs and creatures related to orcs, such as half-orcs. creatures with the orc subtype have darkvision 60 feet and light sensitivity (half-orcs do not have light sensitivity).

Reptilian Subtype

These creatures are scaly and usually cold-blooded. The reptilian subtype is only used to describe a set of humanoid races, not all animals and monsters that are true reptiles.

Shapechanger Subtype

A shapechanger has the supernatural ability to assume one or more alternate forms. Many magical effects allow some kind of shapeshifting, and not every creature that can change shape has the shapechanger subtype. A shapechanger possesses the following traits (unless otherwise noted in a creature's entry).

- Proficient with its natural weapons, with simple weapons, and with any weapons mentioned in the creature's description.
- Proficient with any armor mentioned in the creature's description, as well as all lighter forms. If no form of armor is mentioned, the shapechanger is not proficient with armor. A shapechanger is proficient with shields if it is proficient with any type of armor.

Swarm Subtype

A swarm is a collection of Fine, Diminutive, or Tiny creatures that acts as a single creature. A swarm has the characteristics of its type, except as noted here. A swarm has a single pool of Hit Dice and hit points, a single initiative modifier, a single speed, and a single Armor Class. A swarm makes saving throws as a single creature. A single swarm occupies a square (if it is made up of nonflying creatures) or a cube (of flying creatures) 10 feet on a side, but its reach is 0 feet, like its component creatures. In order to attack, it moves into an opponent's space, which provokes an attack of opportunity. A swarm can occupy the same space as a creature of any size, since it crawls all over its prey. A swarm can move through squares occupied by enemies and vice versa without impediment, although the swarm provokes an attack of opportunity if it does so. A swarm can move through cracks or holes large enough for its component creatures.

- A swarm of Tiny creatures consists of 300 nonflying creatures or 1,000 flying creatures. A swarm of Diminutive creatures consists of 1,500 nonflying creatures or 5,000 flying creatures. A swarm of Fine creatures consists of 10,000 creatures, whether they are flying or not. Swarms of nonflying creatures include many more creatures than could normally fit in a 10-foot square based on their normal space, because creatures in a swarm are packed tightly together and generally crawl over each other and their prey when moving or attacking. Larger swarms are represented by multiples of single swarms. The area occupied by a large swarm is completely shapeable, though the swarm usually remains in contiguous squares.
- *Swarm Traits:* A swarm has no clear front or back and no discernible anatomy, so it is not subject to critical hits or flanking. A swarm made up of Tiny creatures takes half damage from slashing and piercing weapons. A swarm composed of Fine or Diminutive creatures is immune to all weapon damage. Reducing a swarm to 0 hit points or less causes it to break up, though damage taken until that point does not degrade its ability to attack or resist attack. Swarms are never staggered or reduced to a dying state by damage. Also, they cannot be tripped, grappled, or bull rushed, and they cannot grapple an opponent.
- A swarm is immune to any spell or effect that targets a specific

number of creatures (including single-target spells such as disintegrate), with the exception of mind-affecting effects (charms, compulsions, morale effects, patterns, and phantasms) if the swarm has an Intelligence score and a hive mind. A swarm takes half again as much damage (+50%) from spells or effects that affect an area, such as splash weapons and many evocation spells.

- Swarms made up of Diminutive or Fine creatures are susceptible to high winds, such as those created by a gust of wind spell. For purposes of determining the effects of wind on a swarm, treat the swarm as a creature of the same size as its constituent creatures. A swarm rendered unconscious by means of nonlethal damage becomes disorganized and dispersed, and does not reform until its hit points exceed its nonlethal damage.
- *Swarm Attacks:* creatures with the swarm subtype don't make standard melee attacks. Instead, they deal automatic damage to any creature whose space they occupy at the end of their move, with no attack roll needed. Swarm attacks are not subject to a miss chance for concealment or cover. A swarm's stat block has "swarm" in the Melee entries, with no attack bonus given.
- The amount of damage a swarm deals is based on its Hit Dice, as shown on Table: Swarm Damage by Size.
- A swarm's attacks are nonmagical, unless the swarm's description states otherwise. Damage reduction sufficient to reduce a swarm attack's damage to 0, being incorporeal, or other Special Abilities usually give a creature immunity (or at least resistance) to damage from a swarm. Some swarms also have acid, blood drain, poison, or other special attacks in addition to normal damage.
- Swarms do not threaten creatures, and do not make attacks of opportunity with their swarm attack. However, they distract foes whose squares they occupy, as described below.
- Swarms possess the distraction ability. Spellcasting or concentrating on spells within the area of a swarm requires a caster level check (DC 20 + spell level). Using skills that involve patience and concentration requires a DC 20 Will save.

Time Subtype

This subtype is applied to creatures (usually outsiders) with a connection to the Plane of Time. These creatures often exist outside the normal flow of time and sometimes age differently, sometimes not aging at all and other times actually aging backwards. They possess the following traits unless otherwise noted.

- Immunity to time-related spells and effects (such as *time stop* or those that affect aging).
- *Foresight (Su)* Time creatures can see a few seconds into the future. This ability prevents a creature from being surprised, caught flat-footed, or flanked. It also grants the creature an insight bonus to AC equal to its Wisdom bonus. This ability can be negated, but can be restarted as a free action on the creature's next turn.

Water Subtype

This subtype is usually used for Outsiders with a connection to the Elemental Planes of Water. Creatures with the water subtype always have swim speeds and can move in water without making Swim checks. A water creature can breathe underwater and can usually breathe air as well. Water creatures treat the Swim skill as a class skill.

Appendix D: Monsters by Type

Listed below are all of the monsters in **Tome of Horrors 4**, sorted by type.

Aberration addath, blood orchid, bone crawler, chuul-ttaen, crawling offspring, crimson death, ghaggurath, gibbering abomination, gibbering orb, lesser gibbering orb, ha-naga, kulgreer, neomimic, nithu, thought eater, uddoth

(Air) smoke elemental, storm drake

Animal dinosaurs, dire fox, dire mastiff, dire stag, fire fish, giant flying piranha, giant forest lizard, Rhianna horse, lamprey swarm, minikins, northlands aurochs, piranha swarm, slitherrat, spire monkey, spirit toad, swordtooth shark

(Aquatic) argos, boobrie, brine drake, burrowing lamprey, chuul-ttaen, fire fish, finback sea serpent, fire eel, fisherman, giant flying piranha, kulgreer, lamprey swarm, peg powler, piranha swarm, sewer sludge, Stygian spawn, swordtooth shark, talorani, water leaper, zombyre

(Augmented) feral vampire spawn, refracted dire shark, shade, refracted tiger, winged ape

(Chaotic) gelatinous emperor

(Cold) algidarch, frost drakeling, frost dwarf, glacial haunt, jotun

Construct amalgamation, amber skeleton, battlehulk, bladecoin swarm, bronze minotaur, crystalline golem, necromantic golem, ossuary golem, pestilential cadaver, petrified horror, philosopher golem, skiff golem, sojourner of the sea, stone idols, sword spider

(Demon) ciratto demon, kytha demon, tatarux demon

(Devil) Dantalion (Duke of Hell)

Dragon brine drake, flame drakeling, frost drakeling, gray dragon, storm drake, vile drake

(Dwarf) frost dwarf

(Earth) spitting gargoyle

(Elemental) cinder knight, crysolax, crystalline scorpion, crystalline succubus, elemental lords, greater weird, salt elemental, smoke elemental, stone treant, wood elemental

(Evil) gelatinous emperor

(Extraplanar) bloodsoaker vine, cinder knight, ciratto demon, cobalt viper, crystalline scorpion, crystalline succubus, daochyn, Dantalion (Duke of Hell), demonic mist, ebony horse, elemental lords, flayed angel, gelatinous emperor, ghirru, greater weird, grimshrike, hellwidow, ice salamander, kytha demon, plantoid, refracted dire shark, refracted tiger, salt elemental, seraph genie, skiff golem, smoke elemental, spawn of Jubilex, Stygian spawn, tatarux demon, voltar, zombyre

Fey conshee, dobie, domovoi, elder witchlights, hag nymph, hedon, jynx, kapre, niserie, wichtlein, valeany

(Fire) burning ghat, char shambler, fire crab (small and medium), fire fish, flame drakeling, ghirru

(Giant) algidarch, black troll, coral giant, crag giant, fachan, jotun, river troll, winged ogre

(Good) battlehulk

Humanoid algidarch, black troll, chike, crag giant, fachan, frost dwarf, coral giant, jotun, korog technician, korog scientist, lupin, river troll, sciruian, talorani, winged ogre, xothotak

(Incorporeal) lesser banshee, shadow dire bear, dark custodian, ekimmu, galley beggar, gloom haunt, grey spirit, impaled spirit (shattered soul), kamarupa, screamer,

(Korog) korog technician, korog scientist

(Lupin) lupin

Magical Beast baboonwere, blaze boa, boarfolk, boobrie, burrowing lamprey, carrion claw, cavern crawler, char shambler, cobalt viper, deathstroke serpent, dimensional slug, dracohydra, dromosphinx, dune horror, edon, finback sea serpent, fire eel, firebird, hellwidow, lava lizard, lightning lamprey, malkeen, narwhal, noble steed, ommoth, refracted dire shark, ravager, ravager spawn, refracted tiger, sealwere, shadow hunter, shadow wing, shard spider, sparksting swarm, stirge swarm, water leaper, winged ape

Monstrous Humanoid argos, baba yaga, borsin, bucentaur, death's head inphidian, spitting gargoyle, gray scale inphidian, gribbon, grimlock, leonine, peg powler, proto-creature, scorpionfolk, tombotu, yhakkor

Ooze ebon ooze, gelatinous emperor, jolly jelly, lightning bladder, living monolith, sewer sludge, spawn of Jubilex

Outsider astral spider, daochyn, ebony horse, fisherman, seraph genie, shade, Stygian spawn, voltar

Outsider (Acid) acid weird

Outsider (Air) greater weird, ice salamander, smoke elemental, smoke weird, Susir (elemental lord)

Outsider (chaotic) ciratto demon, crystalline succubus, demonic mist, kytha demon, pestilenzi demon, tatarux demon

Outsider (cold) frost weird, ice salamander

Outsider (demon) crystalline succubus, kytha demon, pestilenzi demon

Outsider (devil) Dantalion (Duke of Hell)

Outsider (earth) crysolax, crystalline scorpion, crystalline succubus, greater weird, mud weird, Onyst (elemental lord), salt elemental, stone treant

Outsider (electricity) voltar

Outsider (evil) ciratto demon, crystalline succubus, Dantalion (Duke of Hell), demonic mist, fisherman, kytha demon, pestilenzi demon, Stygian spawn, tatarux demon

Outsider (fire) cinder knight, greater weird, Inder (elemental lord), magma weird, seraph genie, smoke elemental

Outsider (lawful) Dantalion (Duke of Hell), fisherman

Outsider (native) defender globe, ebony horse, fisherman, stone treant, wood elemental

Outsider (water) daochyn, greater weird, ice salamander, Lypso (elemental lord), ooze weird

Plant algant (plant guardian), banyant (plant guardian), bloodsoaker vine, cactant (plant guardian), deadly mandrake, dreadweed, emberleaf, fountain fungus, fungus man, plantoid, plantoid servitor, rakewood, razor treant, serpent creeper, sirine flower, war flower, xacon

(Reptilian) chike, death's head inphidian, gray scale inphidian

(Sciurian) sciruian

(Shapechanger) baboonwere, sealwere, werewolverine (lycanthrope), undead mimic

(Swarm) black rot (living disease), bladecoin swarm, bone swarm, devouring mist, festering lung (living disease), lamprey swarm, piranha swarm, silverfish swarm, skeletal swarm, sparksting swarm, stirge swarm

(Talorani) talorani

Template crystalline creature, death knight, hungry zombie, miniature creature, refracted creature, shade, winged creature

Undead aswang, asp mummy, lesser banshee, bone delver, bone swarm, burning ghat, cimota, dark custodian, death knight, death naga, devouring mist, ekimmu, feral vampire spawn, flayed angel, galley beggar, ghirru, ghoul monkey, glacial haunt, gloom haunt, grave mount, grey spirit, grimshrike, zombie horde, hooded horror, hungry zombie, kamarupa, knight gaunt, lurker wraith, impaled spirit (shattered soul), mordnaissant, necro-phantom, oozeanderthal, rat-ghoul, screamer, shadow dire bear, skeletal swarm, skin feaster, skull child, soul knight, spider lich, sword wight, undead mimic, undead mount, undead troll, zombyre

Vermin albino cave spider, bloodworm, elven wasp, festering lung (living disease), fire crab (small and medium), giant funnel-web spider, giant silverfish, ravager beetle, silverfish swarm, stench beetle

(Water) daochyn, gray dragon, niserie, vile drake

(Xothotak) xothotak

Appendix E: Monsters by Challenge Rating

Listed below are all of the monsters in *Tome of Horrors 4*, sorted by CR.

CR 1/4 elder witchlights, spire monkey

CR 1/3 conshee, podokesaurus

CR 1/2 albino cave spider, euparkeria, small fire crab, gribbon, small salt elemental, oozeanderthal, sciruian, stench beetle, talorani, xothotak

CR 1 edon, fire fish, frost dwarf, grimlock, ghoul monkey, hungry zombie, Rhianna horse, rat-ghoul, small smoke elemental

CR 2 baboonwere, bone delver, burrowing lamprey, chike, deadly mandrake, dire fox, medium fire crab, flame drakeling, fungus man, giant flying piranha, giant silverfish, glacial haunt, gray dragon, jynx, kapre, lightning lamprey, lupin, medium salt elemental, minikin grizzly bear, plantoid servitor, ravager beetle, sealwere, shadow hunter hatchling, skin feaster, thought eater, undead horse mount, water leaper, xacon, yhakkor

CR 3 argos, borsin, burning ghat, defender globe, pestilenzi demon, dire mastiff, dire stag, frost drakeling, hedon, knight gaunt, medium smoke elemental, necro-phantom, peg powler, sewer sludge, sirine flower, slitherrat, swordtooth shark, wichtlein, valeany, werewolverine (lycanthrope), winged ape, zombyre

CR 4 bloodworm, bone swarm, cavern crawler, cimota, cobalt viper, crystalline scorpion, dobie, domovoi, emberleaf, elven wasp, fungus man king, grave mount, gray dragon, grimshrike, large salt elemental, korog technician, leonine, narwhal, noble steed, piranha swarm, plantoid, screamer, serpent creeper, skull child, sparksting swarm, voltar, war flower, weirds, winged ogre

CR 5 algidarch, blood orchid, boobrie, crawling offspring, daochyn, death's head inphidian, demonic mist, fire eel, spitting gargoyle, giant forest lizard, gloom haunt, crystalline golem, grey spirit, ice salamander, jolly jelly, lamprey swarm, large smoke elemental, lightning bladder, minikin mastodon, neomimic, ommoth, river troll, scorpionfolk, stone idol gargoyle, tombotu

CR 6 amber skeleton, asp mummy, aswang, bladecoin swarm, blaze boa, blood orchid savant, bucentaur, cactant (plant guardian), carrion claw, guardian cimota, cobalt viper, ebon ooze, ebony horse, fachan, feral vampire spawn, giant funnel web spider, gray dragon, gray scale inphidian, huge salt elemental, malkeen, nithu, nothosaurus, refracted tiger, soul knight, spawn of Jubilex, stirge swarm, stone idol frog, sword wight, undead mimic, undead troll

CR 7 algant (plant guardian), black troll, giant cobalt viper, ekimmu, gorgosaurus, gray dragon, huge smoke elemental, kamarupa, mordnaissant, niserie, northlands aurochs, pestilential cadaver, storm drake

CR 8 astral spider, crystalline succubus, dreadweed, dromosphinx, firebird, fountain fungus, galley beggar, greater salt elemental, greater weird, hellwidow, hooded horror, lava lizard, necromantic golem, proto-creature, seraph genie, shadow hunter, shadow wing, silverfish swarm, skeletal swarm, uddoth, vile drake

CR 9 banyant (plant guardian), blood orchid grand savant, bloodsoaker vine, brine drake, chuul-ttaen, high cimota, coral giant, dark custodian, ghirru, gray dragon, greater smoke elemental, kytha demon, philosopher golem, rakewood, shard spider

CR 10 baba yaga, boarfolk, crimson death, devouring mist, dimensional slug, dracohydra, elder salt elemental, festering lung (living disease), gray dragon, hag nymph, lurker wraith, impaled spider lich, shadow dire bear, spirit (shattered soul), stone idol sphinx, sword spider

CR 11 bronze minotaur, char shambler, cinder knight, crag giant, death knight, elder smoke elemental, lesser gibbering orb, ossuary golem, gray dragon, jotun, razor treant, refracted dire shark, skiff golem, stone idol shedu

CR 12 bone crawler, death naga, deathstroke serpent, giant proto-creature, korog scientist, shade sorcerer

CR 13 lesser banshee, battlehulk, dune horror, gibbering abomination, gray dragon, living monolith, Stygian spawn, tatarux demon

CR 14 gray dragon, zombie horde

CR 15 crysolax, finback sea serpent, fisherman, gray dragon, petrified horror, sojourner of the sea, spirit toad

CR 16 addath, black rot (living disease), ciratto demon, flayed angel, gray dragon, ha-naga, kulgreer, stone treant, wood elemental

CR 17 gelatinous emperor

CR 18 ghaggurath, gray dragon

CR 19 leviathan

CR 20 amalgamtion, ravager spawn

CR 23 elemental lords

CR 24 Dantalion (Duke of Hell), elemental lords

CR 27 gibbering orb

CR 30 ravager

Tome of Horrors 4

This printing of ***Tome of Horrors 4*** is done under version 1.0a of the Open Game License, below, and the Paizo Publishing, LLC Pathfinder® Roleplaying Game Compatibility License.

Notice of Open Game Content: This product contains Open Game Content, as defined in the Open Game License, below. Open Game Content may only be Used under and in terms of the Open Game License.

Designation of Open Game Content: All text contained within this product (including monster names, stats, and descriptions) is hereby designated as Open Game Content, with the following exceptions:

1. Any text on the inside or outside of the front or back cover or on the Credits or Preface pages is not Open Game Content;

2. Any advertising material — including the text of any advertising material — is not Open Game Content;

Designation of Product Identity: The following items are hereby designated as Product Identity as provided in section 1(e) of the Open Game License: Any and all material or content that could be claimed as Product Identity pursuant to section 1(e), below, is hereby claimed as product identity, including but not limited to:

1. The name "Necromancer Games" and "Frog God Games" as well as all logos and identifying marks of Necromancer Games, Inc. and Frog God Games, including but not limited to the Orcus logo and the phrase "Third Edition Rules, First Edition Feel" as well as the trade dress of Necromancer Games products and similar logos, identifying phrases and trade dress of Frog God Games;

2. The product name *Tome of Horrors, Tome of Horrors Revised*, *Tome of Horrors II*, *Tome of Horrors III* and *Tome of Horrors Complete* by Necromancer Games, Inc. as well as any and all Necromancer Games Inc. and/or Frog God Games product names referenced in the work;

3. All artwork, illustration, graphic design, maps, and cartography, including any text contained within such artwork, illustration, maps or cartography;

4. The proper names, personality, descriptions and/or motivations of all artifacts, characters, races, countries, geographic locations, plane or planes of existence, gods, deities, events, magic items, organizations and/ or groups unique to this book, but not their stat blocks or other game mechanic descriptions (if any), and also excluding any such names when they are included in monster, spell or feat names;

5. Any other content previously designated as Product Identity is hereby designated as Product Identity and is used with permission and/or pursuant to license.

OPEN GAME LICENSE

Version 1.0a

The following text is the property of Wizards of the Coast, Inc. and is Copyright 2000 Wizards of the Coast, Inc ("Wizards"). All Rights Reserved.

1. Definitions: (a)"Contributors" means the copyright and/or trademark owners who have contributed Open Game Content; (b)"Derivative Material" means copyrighted material including derivative works and translations (including into other computer languages), potation, modification, correction, addition, extension, upgrade, improvement, compilation, abridgment or other form in which an existing work may be recast, transformed or adapted; (c) "Distribute" means to reproduce, license, rent, lease, sell, broadcast, publicly display, transmit or otherwise distribute; (d)"Open Game Content" means the game mechanic and includes the methods, procedures, processes and routines to the extent such content does not embody the Product Identity and is an enhancement over the prior art and any additional content clearly identified as Open Game Content by the Contributor, and means any work covered by this License, including translations and derivative works under copyright law, but specifically excludes Product Identity. (e) "Product Identity" means product and product line names, logos and identifying marks including trade dress; artifacts; creatures characters; stories, storylines, plots, thematic elements, dialogue, incidents, language, artwork, symbols, designs, depictions, likenesses, formats, poses, concepts, themes and graphic, photographic and other visual or audio representations; names and descriptions of characters, spells, enchantments, personalities, teams, personas, likenesses and special abilities; places, locations, environments, creatures, equipment, magical or supernatural abilities or effects, logos, symbols, or graphic designs; and any other trademark or registered trademark clearly identified as Product identity by the owner of the Product Identity, and which specifically excludes the Open Game Content; (f) "Trademark" means the logos, names, mark, sign, motto, designs that are used by a Contributor to identify itself or its products or the associated products contributed to the Open Game License by the Contributor (g) "Use", "Used" or "Using" means to use, Distribute, copy, edit, format, modify, translate and otherwise create Derivative Material of Open Game Content. (h) "You" or "Your" means the licensee in terms of this agreement.

2. The License: This License applies to any Open Game Content that contains a notice indicating that the Open Game Content may only be Used under and in terms of this License. You must affix such a notice to any Open Game Content that you Use. No terms may be added to or subtracted from this License except as described by the License itself. No other terms or conditions may be applied to any Open Game Content distributed using this License.

3. Offer and Acceptance: By Using the Open Game Content You indicate Your acceptance of the terms of this License.

4. Grant and Consideration: In consideration for agreeing to use this License, the Contributors grant You a perpetual, worldwide, royalty-free, non-exclusive license with the exact terms of this License to Use, the Open Game Content.

5. Representation of Authority to Contribute: If You are contributing original material as Open Game Content, You represent that Your Contributions are Your original creation and/or You have sufficient rights to grant the rights conveyed by this License.

6. Notice of License Copyright: You must update the COPYRIGHT NOTICE portion of this License to include the exact text of the COPYRIGHT NOTICE of any Open Game Content You are copying, modifying or distributing, and You must add the title, the copyright date, and the copyright holder's name to the COPYRIGHT NOTICE of any original Open Game Content you Distribute.

7. Use of Product Identity: You agree not to Use any Product Identity, including as an indication as to compatibility, except as expressly licensed in another, independent Agreement with the owner of each element of that Product Identity. You agree not to indicate compatibility or co-adaptability with any Trademark or Registered Trademark in conjunction with a work containing Open Game Content except as expressly licensed in another, independent Agreement with the owner of such Trademark or Registered Trademark. The use of any Product Identity in Open Game Content does not constitute a challenge to the ownership of that Product Identity. The owner of any Product Identity used in Open Game Content shall retain all rights, title and interest in and to that Product Identity.

8. Identification: If you distribute Open Game Content You must clearly indicate which portions of the work that you are distributing are Open Game Content.

9. Updating the License: Wizards or its designated Agents may publish updated versions of this License. You may use any authorized version of this License to copy, modify and distribute any Open Game Content originally distributed under any version of this License.

10. Copy of this License: You MUST include a copy of this License with every copy of the Open Game Content You Distribute.

11. Use of Contributor Credits: You may not market or advertise the Open Game Content using the name of any Contributor unless You have written permission from the Contributor to do so.

12. Inability to Comply: If it is impossible for You to comply with any of the terms of this License with respect to some or all of the Open Game Content due to statute, judicial order, or governmental regulation then You may not Use any Open Game Material so affected.

13. Termination: This License will terminate automatically if You fail to comply with all terms herein and fail to cure such breach within 30 days of becoming aware of the breach. All sublicenses shall survive the termination of this License.

14. Reformation: If any provision of this License is held to be unenforceable, such provision shall be reformed only to the extent necessary to make it enforceable.

15. COPYRIGHT NOTICE

Open Game License v 1.0a © 2000, Wizards of the Coast, Inc.

System Reference Document, © 2000, Wizards of the Coast, Inc.; Authors Jonathan Tweet, Monte Cook, Skip Williams, based on material by E. Gary Gygax and Dave Arneson.

Modern System Reference Document, © 2002–2004, Wizards of the Coast, Inc.; Authors Bill Slavicsek, Jeff Grubb, Rich Redman, Charles Ryan, Eric Cagle, David Noonan, Stan!, Christopher Perkins, Rodney Thompson, and JD Wiker, based on material by Jonathan Tweet, Monte Cook, Skip Williams, Richard Baker, Peter Adkison, Bruce R. Cordell, John Tynes, Andy Collins, and JD Wiker.

Pathfinder RPG Core Rulebook, © 2009, Paizo Publishing, LLC; Author: Jason Bulmahn, based on material by Jonathan Tweet, Monte Cook, and Skip Williams.

Pathfinder Advanced Player's Guide, © 2010, Paizo Publishing, LLC; Author Jason Bulmahn.

Pathfinder RPG Bestiary, © 2009, Paizo Publishing, LLC; Author: Jason Bulmahn, based on material by Jonathan Tweet, Monte Cook, and Skip Williams.

Pathfinder Roleplaying Game: Bonus Bestiary, © 2009, Paizo Publishing, LLC; Author: Jason Bulmahn.

Pathfinder Roleplaying Game Bestiary 2, © 2010, Paizo Publishing, LLC; Authors Wolfgang Baur, Jason Bulmahn, Adam Daigle, Graeme Davis, Crystal Frasier, Joshua J. Frost, Tim Hitchcock, Brandon Hodge, James Jacobs, Steve Kenson, Hal MacLean, Martin Mason, Rob McCreary, Erik Mona, Jason Nelson, Patrick Renie, Sean K Reynolds, F. Wesley Schneider, Owen K.C. Stephens, James L. Sutter, Russ Taylor, and Greg A. Vaughan, based on material by Jonathan Tweet, Monte Cook, and Skip Williams.

Pathfinder Roleplaying Game Bestiary 3, © 2011, Paizo Publishing, LLC; Authors Jesse Benner, Jason Bulmahn, Adam Daigle, James Jacobs, Michael Kenway, Rob McCreary, Patrick Renie, Chris Sims, F. Wesley Schneider, James L. Sutter, and Russ Taylor, based on material by Jonathan Tweet, Monte Cook, and Skip Williams.

Pathfinder RPG GameMastery Guide, © 2010 Paizo Publishing, LLC; Authors Cam Banks, Wolfgang Baur, Jason Buhlman, Jim Butler, Eric Cagle, Graeme Davis, Adam Daigle, Jashua J. Frost, James Jacobs, Kenneth Hite, Steven Kenson, Robin Laws, Tito Leati, Rob McCreart, Hal Maclean, Colin McComb, Jason Nelson, David Noonan, Richard Pett, Rich Redman, Sean K Reynolds, F. Wesley Schneider, Amber Scott, Doug Seacat, Mike Selinker, Lisa Stevens, James L Sutter, Russ Taylor, Penny Williams, Teeuwynn Woodruff.

Pathfi nder Chronicles: Classic Treasures Revisited. Copyright 2010, Paizo Publishing, LLC; Authors: Jacob Burgess, Brian Cortijo, Jonathan H. Keith, Michael Kortes, Jeff Quick, Amber Scott, Todd Stewart, and Russ Taylor.

Pathfi nder Companion: Adventurer's Armory. Copyright 2010, Paizo Publishing, LLC; Authors: Jonathan Keith, Hal Maclean, Jeff Quick, Christopher Self, JD Wiker, and Keri Wiker.

Advanced Player's Guide. Copyright 2010, Paizo Publishing, LLC; Author: Jason Bulmahn.

Pathfi nder Roleplaying Game Ultimate Combat. © 2011, Paizo Publishing, LLC; Authors: Jason Bulmahn, Tim Hitchcock, Colin McComb, Rob McCreary, Jason Nelson, Stephen Radney-MacFarland, Sean K Reynolds, Owen K.C. Stephens, and Russ Taylor.

Pathfi nder Adventure Path #43: The Haunting of Harrowstone. © 2011, Paizo Publishing,LLC; Author: Michael Kortes.

Pathfinder Adventure Path #55: The Wormwood Mutiny, © 2012, Paizo Publishing, LLC; Author Richard Pett.

Aberrations, © 2003, Necromancer Games, Inc; Author Casey Christofferson.

Asgard Magazine #2, © 2001, ENWorld.

Chaos Rising, © 2003, Necromancer Games, Inc; Author James Collura.

City of Brass, © 2007, Necromancer Games, Inc.; Authors Casey Christofferson and Scott Greene, with Clark Peterson.

Encyclopaedia Arcane: Necromancy Beyond the Grave, © 2001, Mongoose Publishing; Authors Matthew Sprange, Teresa Capsey, William J. Pennington, Erica Balsley, Scott Greene.

The Genius Guide To: Ice Magic, © 2010, Super Genius Games. Author Owen K.C. Stephens.

The Lost City of Barakus, © 2003 Necromancer Games, Inc; Authors W.D.B. Kenower, Bill Webb.

Seas of Blood: Fantasy on the High Seas, © 2001, Mongoose Publishing; Authors Matthew Sprange, Theresa Capsey, Ian Barstow, Scott Greene (uncredited), Erica Balsley (uncredited).

The Eamonvale Incursion Copyright 2007 Necromancer Games, Inc.; Author Nathan Douglas Paul, with Jack Barger.

The Grey Citadel Copyright 2003, Necromancer Games, Inc.; Author Nathan Douglas Paul.

Original Spell Name Compendium Copyright 2002 Clark Peterson; based on NPC-named spells from the Player's Handbook that were renamed in the System Reference Document. The Compendium can be found on the legal page of www.necromancergames.com.

Tome of Horrors Copyright 2002, Necromancer Games, Inc.; Authors: Scott Greene, with Clark Peterson, Erica Balsley, Kevin Baase, Casey Christofferson, Lance Hawvermale, Travis

CHARACTER MANAGEMENT SOFTWARE FOR PLAYERS AND GMS

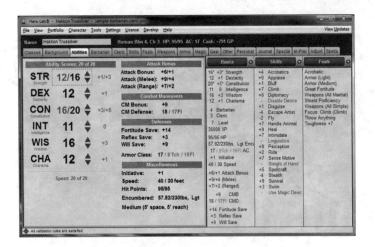

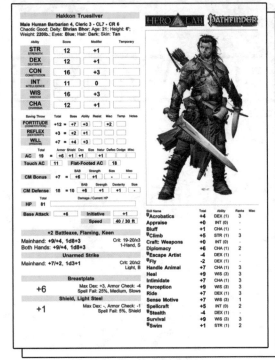

FIGHT THE MONSTERS... NOT THE TOOLS!

- Winner of 2011 Gold ENnie Award for Best RPG Aid or Accessory.

- Intuitive interface guides you through all the stages of character creation and points out details that still need to be completed.

- View a complete list of all available options for easy review and selection.

- Cascading effects are instantly calculated and applied, while summary panels keep details clearly in view.

- Real-time validation alerts you to rule violations, while still readily enabling house rule exceptions.

- Produce easy-to-read printouts and statblocks, or save to PDF.

- Extensive In-Play support tracks in-game effects and conditions with just a few clicks of the mouse.

- Dashboard and Tactical Console make it easy to manage entire encounters.

- Document your hero's backstory, attach character portraits, and journal your hero's exploits.

- Integrated Editor allows you to add custom content unique to your game.

Games supported include:

3.5
d20 OGL

TRY IT FOR FREE AT WWW.WOLFLAIR.COM

Now available at
www.talesofthefroggod.com